Sweet Exile

SWEET EXILE

Alison McLeay

CENTURY

LONDON SYDNEY AUCKLAND JOHANNESBURG

The right of Alison McLeay to be identified as the author of this
work has been asserted by her in accordance with the Copyright,
Designs and Patents Act 1988.

First published in Great Britain in 1991 by
Random Century Group
20 Vauxhall Bridge Road, London SW1V 2SA

Century Hutchinson South Africa (Pty) Ltd
PO Box 337, Bergvlei 2012, South Africa

Random Century Australia Pty Ltd
20 Alfred Street, Milsons Point, Sydney, NSW 2061
Australia

Random Century New Zealand Ltd
PO Box 40–086, Glenfield, Auckland 10
New Zealand

British Library Cataloguing in Publication Data

McLeay, Alison
Sweet exile.
I. Title
823 [F]

ISBN 0–7126–4616–7

Photoset by Deltatype Ltd, Ellesmere Port, Cheshire
Printed and bound in Great Britain by
Mackays of Chatham plc, Kent

To Adam, and the rest.

Chapter One

1

For a man who'd regularly beaten his wife, my father had very fixed ideas on what was decent and what was not. It wasn't decent to wash my petticoats and drawers on the lower deck of the *Bellflower* where Sam and Luke could see. Smoking cigars wasn't decent in a woman, though sometimes I did it anyhow. And what happened between Matthew Oliver and me on the night of the cotton-burning certainly wasn't decent – not by a long, long way, it wasn't.

By chance, it was the eve of my seventeenth birthday, which in New Orleans in 1862 made me damn near an old maid and getting so's a man might think I had something against the opposite sex. That was a good enough reason to be restless, and maybe, like Pa said later, the Devil did see a chance of entering into my obstinate soul and firing me up with lewd notions. If I'd been black, no doubt Sam Duck would have blamed it all on a voodoo *gris-gris*; and certainly, the way we all went crazy on the levee that night, dancing and laughing among the blazing cotton, you'd have thought the whole city had been possessed by demons bent on making master out of slave and slave out of master – which was near enough what we expected, when the Federal warships came up the river next day.

Not that Pa reckoned the problems of the city folk were any of our business. As far as Ben Summerbee was concerned, the war raging between the states, tearing families apart and scarring a whole generation, was none of his concern. Our battle was with the river which gave us our living – and with the railroads which seemed to snatch away more of it every year. At least the war had stopped the march of the iron tracks, which in Pa's book was a fine thing. The time to start worrying about the war was when it reached our river, and not before.

Yet now when I look at the yellowing photographs of dead, twisted horses and broken young men in blue and grey, old before their time, I wonder how we could have known so little of it then. For a whole year it hardly touched us – river vagabonds as we were, Pa and I. Then in the spring of 1862 things began to change. The war was in everyone's mouth – on the plantations, at the river landings, in the woodyards – and even Pa could no longer suck at his pipe and ignore it.

There'd been a terrible battle at Shiloh: we'd tied up at New Orleans in time to watch the body of Albert Sidney Johnston borne in sorrow up St Charles Street, bright hope slaughtered along with innumerable husbands, fathers, sons and brothers. Yet the muffled drums had no sooner died away when a long, drawn-out quiet seemed to fall over the city – an incongruous quiet, a holding of breath, a hush so profound that it was possible, in the midst of a war which was rending a nation in two, to be wakened by no more than the faint, persistent scratch of a penknife on wood . . .

To this day I can remember lying, suddenly alert, in my narrow berth aboard the *Bellflower*, staring up at the shimmering golden net cast by the river on the smoke-blackened roof of the cabin, my ears straining once more for the soft *scrape-scrape* which had roused me.

In normal times, no one could have slept late at the New Orleans levee. At the crack of dawn, the steamboats moored flank to flank along the embankment from Jackson Square almost to the foot of Poydras Street came alive with pounding feet and a ringing chorus of blasphemies; tugs churned and hooted in the river, flocks of fat casks rumbled over the hard shell pavement like broken bunches of grapes, and dray-mules and windlasses squealed in hideous concert.

I never minded the din. I'd been raised to it. By the time I was three years old I could tell the whistle of the *Hattie Morgan* from the double whoop of the *Discus*, and pretty much know who was in each pilot house. Silence – now, that was another matter. Silence meant hard times.

By the middle of April 1862 the war had finally tightened its grip on the Mississippi, shrinking the river traffic until the great steamers huddled in a forlorn, silent pack on the far shore, and the New Orleans levee lay deserted, as if under some sleep-inducing spell. Clumps of weed sprouted where a thousand feet had daily pressed the white pavement; the dry-docks across the river had been empty for weeks, and the long curve of ship-hungry wharves on the city side rotted in mossy neglect. Only the river was never still, sucking at its banks, jostling the idle shipping, tugging the rickety paddle-wheel at the *Bellflower*'s stern as if pleading with us to forget the war on the city's doorstep and come out once more to play upon its waters.

The hush along the levee only added to the dreamlike quality of days in which the impossible unfolded, slowly and irresistibly, before our disbelieving eyes. For no one expected New Orleans to fall to the bully-boys of the North. If it took a miracle to save it, then a miracle there'd be, since God was surely honour-bound to keep the Yankees from strutting up Canal Street and grinning down from the windows of the City Hall. Let North and South tear at one another's throats if they must – languorous, elegant New Orleans, the greatest port of the Confederacy, was secure within her impenetrable swamps, guarded from the sea by unassailable forts.

Yet the Yankees persisted, and suddenly, against all the odds, it seemed that Farragut's Federal warships were waiting at the entrance to the Mississippi . . . and no one was quite so confident any more. Twice, I caught my father sucking at an empty pipe-stem without even realising the fire in the bowl had gone out. And I – waking late on the 17th of April in an unnatural silence – had the hairs on my neck set on end by the faint scrape of a penknife on wood.

2

It was no more than a picking, rasping, scratch of a sound, but it stood out clearly from the sighing of the river and the creak of the *Bellflower*'s mooring ropes.

At the after end of the *Bellflower*'s cabin, my father was giving out almighty snores, great gusty exhalations of breath strong enough to stir the calico curtain which hung in front of his berth, and in my first waking seconds I imagined the rasping sound had been part of his private concerto. And then I heard it once more, quite clearly –*scrape-scrape* – from somewhere outside, beyond the peeling pine boards of the cabin.

If I'd heard footsteps on the lower deck to indicate that Luke or Sam Duck were up and about, I'd never have given the sound a second thought. But the silence was otherwise so complete that I guessed the *Bellflower*'s crew were still rolled in their blankets between the engines in the stern of the boat, dead to the world.

A rat.

We often carried rats, bright-eyed devils that crept up our cables from the wharf or from pig-infested woodyards where melon rinds and corn cobs studded the muddy foreshore like cherries in a cake. Pa and the other two dealt with any rat they could corner by stamping on it with their heavy boots, but I'd an enduring horror of sharp little claws making a dash for safety up my cotton skirts, and I preferred to keep my distance and sweep the filthy creatures into the river with a broom. At that particular moment I could just imagine Mister Rat smugly combing his whiskers and imagining himself safe in the peace of the morning, and my fingers fairly itched to have a chance at him.

There was no doubt that my father was asleep. This was important: if

3

I waited to put on a skirt and print shirt over my shift, I'd surely lose my rat, but nakedness, to my father's way of thinking, was one of the biggest indecencies of all. Apart from the nights he roared back to the *Bellflower* hopelessly drunk, he slept in flannel vest and drawers, no matter how hot the weather. Drunk, he slept in all he had, including his hat, and on the rare occasions when he changed vest and drawers for others, the operation was performed stealthily behind a blanket curtain, though the writhings and oaths which went with it indicated all too graphically what was afoot. Which isn't to say we talked about *gentleman cows* and the *limbs of the table* like fancy Richmond ladies, but until . . . well, until the night of the cotton-fires I'd never seen a man entirely naked – nor a white man even half-way in the raw. Still, right at that moment I was sure I could deal with the rat and be back in the cabin to dress before my father even knew I'd sneaked outside.

Clutching my thin blanket around me, I swung my feet cautiously to the boarded floor and pattered towards the door at the after end of the cabin where a heavy deck-broom swung from its hook on the wall.

The door opened on to a small area of open deck – part of the "boiler deck" as Pa insisted on calling it, as if it were the first storey of some white-painted side-wheeler racing up to St Louis, instead of an old, stern-wheeled vagrant stained by rust and weather. Our whole upper deck was hardly sixty feet long by twenty wide with a ramshackle cabin set down amidships, but to my father it signified the all-important gulf between master and crew. Ben Summerbee owned his vessel – let no one forget it – and so he and I were deemed to live in state on the "boiler deck" while the other two scrambled among the piled freight on the deck below, tending the fireboxes and the engines and the thrashing paddle-wheel at our stern which was the slow-beating heart of the *Bellflower*.

But on that day at least – since the sun was already so high – the boiler deck lived up to its name. I hadn't realised the hour was so late, and the heat of the deck planking took me by surprise, forcing me to hop, stork-like, across the baking wood until my bare feet could wriggle into a patch of cool shade behind our upturned yawl. From there, clinging to my broom and the blanket which was all that protected my precious decency, I peered round my oddly silent world.

That's when I saw him first, standing cool as you please half-way up the stage-plank of the *Bellflower*, in the act of stabbing the battered timbers of our guard with one of those little knives gentlemen used to keep for sharpening pens. So much for my rat, I thought – unless rats in New Orleans had taken to wearing battered pilot-coats and broad-brimmed hats and stealing gold-handled pocket knives for a living.

4

In my indignation I let the broom clatter to the deck, and the man drew back, shading his eyes and squinting up towards the source of the sound. He was quite young, now that I could see his face – by which I mean he could have given my father thirty years, Pa being a little over fifty by then, and somewhat coarsened by drink. You may say I took a good deal of notice of an unknown drifter for a young woman whose father was master of his own vessel – but being that the vessel in question was only the old *Bellflower*, and that I was almost seventeen and not even spoken for yet, I'd fallen into the habit of taking notice of male persons in general, and privately examining the curious geometry of man which could produce such variations on the theme as a low-slung rear or the long red wrists of the share-croppers' sons.

I remember regretting that this one was obviously a no-account. He was tall – taller than Pa maybe by a couple of inches, even with Pa standing straight – and perched there on our stage-plank he looked spring-loaded, watchful as a white-tailed buck caught out on the open riverbank, ready to run or to fight, whichever came first. But there was no deer-like softness in his glance, only shrewdness . . . and then, as he caught sight of me in my holey blanket with the broom at my feet, a sly amusement which tightened the corners of his mouth into an insolent smile.

I'd never seen such a creature before. Oh, I'd seen plenty of loafers and shirkers and wharf rats on my travels, but not one of them had stood so defiantly or had stared at me with quite the same calculated assurance. In fact, nothing about this man seemed quite as it should be, from the rather too clean state of his workaday clothes to the elegance of the narrow hand which shaded his eyes. For a start, at that stage in the war he was too young to be decently out of uniform, yet he'd no crutches and no eye-patch to show why he'd been sent home from army lines. And there was more – his hair was too light for a Creole and his glance too sharp and pale, though I was sure he was no planter's son, dispossessed by the war. Even down on their luck there was an indolence to those upriver gentry which I missed in this keen-eyed stranger.

For a few heart-stopping moments I concluded he must be a Union agent, sent ahead to spy on Confederate vessels on the direct orders of Abe Lincoln. . . . Then common sense prevailed. No one in his right mind would take the *Bellflower* for an enemy warship, not even some ignorant city fellow from the North.

I saw him relax and drop his shading hand, content that I was only a girl with a broom and not a riverman with a shotgun. His self-possession annoyed me all over again.

"Are you thinking of buying the boat, mister, or just looking to carve your name on her?"

For a moment the stranger continued to regard me in silence, sizing me up as if I were part of the old *Bellflower*, like a spar or a hatch-cover he'd be happy to test with his little gilt knife if I'd only stand still long enough.

"Is she for sale?" he enquired at last.

"Don't reckon so. Leastways, Pa'd want more than you could raise, by the look of you."

"I wouldn't give you ten dollars for her as she stands now." The stranger pointed to a patch of spongy woodwork just above the waterline. "See that rot? I bet I could put my fist through the hull down there." He kicked idly at the butter-soft planking.

"Best clear off, mister, before Pa throws you off or turns you in for a deserter. Is that what you are? An army deserter?"

The stranger stepped down from the stage-plank at that, and I thought maybe I'd put my finger on the truth. But as soon as he was ashore he turned back, put his hands in his pockets, and surveyed the *Bellflower* slowly from stem to stern like a man with something important on his mind. Then he squinted up at me again.

"Where does she trade?"

"All over," I said quickly. "Not right now, of course, with the river being closed by the war, but she's been all the way up to Fort Benton. Anywhere you can float a turtle, Pa says."

The stranger seemed unimpressed. But then, he didn't sound like a Westerner: perhaps he didn't know where Fort Benton was, or how the little *Bellflower* had struggled through sandbars and rapids to get there. "You ain't a New Orleans man, I guess."

"*Nawlins*." He seemed amused by my pronunciation. "No, I'm not from these parts."

"A New Englander? From Boston, maybe?" A further thought struck me. "Say – are you English, or something?"

"Does it matter?"

"I just wondered."

"All right, then. I'm English."

Here was something new – a right-down Englishman, no less, standing at the foot of our stage-plank dressed up like a steamboat mud clerk but carrying a gold-handled knife as if such gewgaws were ten cents a dozen. All my earlier suspicions returned.

"Are you a spy of some kind, mister?"

"Do you always ask so many questions?"

"Do you mind my askin'?"

"Have you nothing to wear besides a blanket?" he snapped back, quick as a flash, like a man bent on getting the upper hand.

"I've got clothes," I said, my pride stung. "But I don't sleep in them. I just got out of bed to see who was pickin' at the boat."

He was grinning at me now, his eyes crinkled up with amusement, and I had to admit he looked better when he smiled – considerably better, in fact. And to tell the truth, in that instant I'd have given a great deal to know exactly what he saw there on the deck above him. I was just at that awkward age which puts a value only on what others admire and wishes everything else transformed.

Unfortunately it was all too easy to guess the picture I presented at that moment: a long-legged, half-ripe young woman – an explosion of auburn curls round a face lamentably brown from too much sun, with tilted bones which hinted at something exotic . . . and wide, unexpected eyes the colour of lilac-blue water orchids, or of *maraises* under a blue sky, those sudden, clear, circular ponds in the short-turfed flatlands of the Louisiana prairie.

"How old are you?"

Caught on the point of a lie, I settled for the truth.

"Seventeen. Well – seventeen in eight days' time."

"Hard to tell, under all that hair."

"Well, if that ain't the rudest thing! Is that how you Englishmen speak to a lady when you meet one?"

I thought he was going to choke. Instead, he swept off the broad-brimmed hat and made an extravagant bow.

"I beg your pardon, ma'am, to be sure." He was making fun of me again, but I liked the sound of that *ma'am*. Being English he said it to rhyme with *harm*, and I could almost hear trumpets blow as he spoke.

"And now I'd better get back." He folded the knife and slipped it into his waistcoat pocket. "My friends will be wondering what's become of me." He crammed the hat firmly over hair the colour of dry prairie grass, and began to turn away.

"Don't go." I saw his head lift in surprise. "I mean – you haven't told me what you want with the *Bellflower* yet."

"I had an idea, that was all. But it was probably a bad one."

"Something I should tell Pa?"

"No need, Miss – "

"Summerbee. Katherine Summerbee."

"Well then, Miss Summerbee, I won't interrupt your sweeping any longer." He indicated the broom at my feet. "Good day to you."

7

"Wait a bit! What's your name, mister?"

"Goodbye, Miss Summerbee." With a wave which was no more than a brief twist of the fingers, he set off unhurriedly across the levee, his hands thrust once more into his pockets and his shoulders squared, the whole set of his back indicating a man thoroughly pleased with whatever he'd just discovered.

3

I watched the Englishman till he was out of sight. I knew his kind, all right: he was a sharp – a swindler – the sort of man who posed as a rich English fool on the big river steamers to lure others into a game of cards which the "mark" would inexplicably win, cleaning out the poor saps who'd thought him a pigeon ripe for the plucking. His breed had fallen on hard times since the war had swept the steamers from the Mississippi, and now here, clearly, was one pigeon who'd taken to pecking among the deserted vessels at the levee for any crumbs he could carry off. I remember thinking how lucky it was Pa hadn't come out and caught me.

Yet if the voices of angels couldn't have roused him, the sound of a steam-engine a mile away was enough to bring Pa leaping from his bed to see who was passing, and I swear he heard the frantic huffing of the tug *Benjamin Franklin* a good five minutes before I saw her swing round Slaughterhouse Point, smoke blotching the sky above and spume flying from her paddles as she shouldered her way pell-mell up the river towards us.

Before I could duck back into the cabin, my father had sprung out on deck, buttoning his trousers and peering downriver, his short-cropped head thrown back and his mouth open as he tried to make out the cause of all the commotion.

As the *Franklin* drew abreast of the revenue cutter *Washington*, I saw her master lean out of his wheelhouse and make a trumpet of his hands to pass on some momentous piece of news.

"How's that, Silas?" my father bawled across the water as the big tug thundered towards us.

"The Yankees! They're movin' up to the forts!" The tugmaster veered his vessel as near to us as he dared, sending a wash of foam over our lower deck. "*Pensacola* got over the bar days ago," he yelled, "and all the rest of 'em too."

"Silas Webster, you're a bigger fool than any Yankee!" roared my father. "Just keep that damned, coal-eatin' pickle-barrel off my side!" He clutched the rail wildly as the *Bellflower* bucked and wrenched at her moorings.

"I said the Yankee mortar-boats are comin' up to the forts!" howled the tugmaster. "D'you hear me, Ben? There's goin' to be a big ole battle any day now – "

The tug was drawing away from us, the gap between the two vessels widening and the tugmaster's voice becoming fainter.

"I guarantee they won't get past the forts," my father shouted confidently. "Gen'ral Duncan'll soon see them off."

"Do-o-on't be too sure, Ben!" Silas Webster's voice drifted back to us. "Better lock up that girl of yours – the Yankees are comin' this time, for sure!" I heard him cackle with laughter, but anything more he tried to say was lost in the thrashing of the tug's huge paddles.

"Katherine, you get yourself back in the cabin this minute, 'fore I raise my hand to you." My father had suddenly noticed me standing there with nothing but a blanket clinging to my almost naked shoulders. "Look at you! Showin' me up in front of a sorry feller like Silas Webster! Get some clothes on, an' don't you come back out here till you're decent."

4

When I came out on the upper deck again, Pa was still brooding about the news from the "lower coast" as the downriver Mississippi was called. For a long time no one had believed the Federals could drag their big ships over the river bar and into the Passes – the long channels through the delta mud which connected the lower Mississippi with the clear waters of the Gulf. Yet one way or another, by pushing and pulling and taking off stores, it seemed that even the hulking *Pensacola* had eventually been hauled awkwardly over the barrier of silt to join her slighter sisters, the *Hartford*, the *Brooklyn* and the rest, in the deeper waters of the channel. Any day now they'd come upriver to challenge the two forts and the line of chained hulks which barred the river highway to New Orleans.

My father watched sourly as I emerged from the cabin, a flour-sack apron tied over my cotton skirt.

"What've you got there, girl?"

"Nothing." Quickly, I thrust my hand deeper into my pocket.

"Don't seem like nothing."

I shrugged in elaborate unconcern, but my silence only confirmed his suspicions.

"Give it here."

"Aw, Pa – "

"Give it here, I said!"

9

Reluctantly, I pulled my hand from my pocket and he grabbed my wrist at once, prising my fingers painfully apart.

"Nothing, is it?" Wrathfully, he held up the crushed remains of a black cheroot. "Where'd you get this, girl? For weeks I've been filling my pipe with any old thing because there ain't no proper tobacco, an' now I catch you walking round with a ceegar in your pocket! Where'd you get it, I said?"

"Jeannot gave it to me in the market."

"Well then, he'd no business to do any such thing – and you'd no business to take it. I've told you before – " Pa's hand flashed out and caught me a heavy blow on the shoulder. "No daughter of mine's going to soil her lips with tobacco. Understand me?"

Nursing my bruised shoulder, I watched him turn to knock the ashes of his first morning pipe into the waterlogged trash which eddied along our sides, before turning to pack the bowl with the crumbled cheroot. The sweet, dark, almost forgotten fragrance of real tobacco tickled the back of my throat.

"D'you think they'll get past the forts, Pa? The Federals, I mean?"

"Not a chance of it. The guns'll make short work of them if they try. I reckon they'll get so sick of bangin' their heads against a wall, they'll just give up an' leave us in peace."

"But if they do get past," I persisted, enviously watching him suck a match flame into the scented mass in the pipe-bowl. "If they do get past, will they do anything to us on the *Bellflower*? It ain't as if we're Confederate soldiers, or anything."

"Ten to one, they won't bother us." Pa puffed complacently at his stolen tobacco while I rubbed my still-aching shoulder. "What in the world would they want with a girl and a defenceless old man?"

5

All along the levee, word passed from craft to craft: *the Yankees are coming! They're almost at the forts.* . . . Small boys yelled it along the silent wharf where Morgan's big Texas steamers had tied up in better times, and flung it at the watchmen aboard the huge white side-wheelers laid up cold-boilered at their moorings. *Now we're for it – the Yankees are coming* . . .

With its faith shaken, New Orleans began to edge towards hysteria. So many of its gilded young men – confident, laughing, gallant young men – had marched away to the shrilling of fife and drum, only to perish with Johnston on the bloody field of Shiloh or be carried back, broken and fevered, their laughter silenced for good. The same sun shone

10

down, white and unforgiving, but now their grey-headed fathers and uncles drilled in Coliseum Place or on the levee, grimly waiting their call to the barricades of the Old South.

I watched them next day, on my way back to the *Bellflower* with Luke at my heels, clutching a handful of okra and the few purplish, shrivelled sweet potatoes I'd been able to buy in the French market. There'd been no real money for months – at least, not what Pa called money, which was negotiable gold and silver; instead, we used streetcar tickets or filthy scraps of paper, greasy and stinking of a thousand hands, issued by all and sundry and worth almost nothing. Not much of it ever came our way, in any case: towards the end, the four of us on the *Bellflower* were living on molasses and blackcurrants and whatever Sam Duck could hook out of the dun-coloured river – may I never see another slab of mud-tasting catfish as long as I live.

Aboard the *Bellflower* we were in the city but not *of* it, in spite of the fact that we'd been tied up near the foot of Canal Street for so long we'd almost taken root amongst the rotting rubbish along the *batture*, the skins and peelings, the slaughterhouse refuse, the boiled bones and worse which the citizens of New Orleans flung into their all-devouring river.

We'd been among the last to tie up there. While the Mississippi had remained open beyond Memphis we'd stubbornly ranged the "coast" like a mongrel sniffing for scraps, smuggling a little contraband, dodging behind islands, scuttling through backwaters and chutes, somehow managing to scrape a living from the river as we'd always done.

While it was still possible to make ends meet on that toiling flood, Pa had persevered. For whatever else he might be or do, my father knew the river – I was going to say *like the back of his hand*, but the truth was that he knew it even better than one of his own blunt, mottled paws. My father lived and breathed the river: he dreamed the river; when he wasn't awash with liquor he drank the river; and on the odd occasions when he soaped himself down, it was the yellow water of the Mississippi which rinsed the suds from his stringy hide.

No doubt the pilots of the big steamers knew its waters well enough from their lordly pilot-houses, but my father knew as much and more. He'd long since hunted out the secret, sluggish nooks and crannies where the side-wheelers never came; he knew the backwoods landings and the canebrakes, the stump-fields and the haunts of the juiciest canvasback ducks; he seemed to sense each new bend and wriggle of the river almost before it came about, as if the Mississippi ate up and spat out its muddy banks according to some logic he understood.

11

He always claimed he could grope his way in pitch darkness from the Head of the Passes to St Paul at any stage of the river without ever scraping a bar – and what was more, he'd a working knowledge of the Cumberland River too, and the Arkansas, and the Missouri and the Monongahela, the Ohio and the Illinois – anywhere the little *Bellflower* might scratch up a freight to pay for her fuel.

All the same, in that year of 1862 the *Bellflower* was nineteen years old, on a river where steamboats were veterans at five. She was a wooden raft barely eighty feet long, a two-storey, stern-wheeled warehouse loading less than 100 tons and drawing a mere two and a half feet even then, a canvas and twine wonder of a boat with two rusty black smokestacks, bulging boiler-plates and safety valves wired shut in lunatic bravado. Summerbee's *Bellflower* – Pa's pride and joy, and the only home I'd ever known.

There were times, when the river was high and slopping over the levee, that we swept down into New Orleans at rooftop level, peering in at the windows of the houses. . . . And at such moments I wondered what it must be like to live inside four solid walls with grass and trees round about and the smell of orange blossom instead of the fetid stink of the *batture*, and a white-painted fence with creeper thick on the rails . . . and a real family at a lamplit table, faces drawn together round the green paper shade . . .

But, mostly, for a river child the *Bellflower* was home enough – tied up in sprawling St Louis, or in sleepy Hannibal or Napoleon. The boat and the river were all I knew, and New Orleans wasn't my city, any more than Helena or St Paul, or any of the hundred wood-stops where the *Bellflower* put in for fuel.

Besides, the whole atmosphere of New Orleans had changed since our last visit. Martial law had been declared some time before, and now grey-uniformed Confederate Guards patrolled the city, or the green-clad ranks scratched up from all the foreigners willing to bear arms. I was glad of their presence; I didn't like the mood of the crowds in the city streets, or the sudden surliness of the shopkeepers. The news of Farragut's arrival at the forts had spread like wildfire, and New Orleans was jittery and snappish, ready to break out into quarrels at the slightest thing in order to hide its gnawing fear.

That's where I found him again – my English swindler – loitering on the fringe of a small crowd gathered on a corner of Canal Street, not far from the Customs House. He was listening to the talk but somehow apart from it, tall enough to see over most heads but standing a pace or two back from the rest, every line of his body suggesting detachment

12

from these excited, gesticulating people so near to being overwhelmed by their enemies.

The surprising thing is that I noticed him at all: remember, I'm talking about a city where Spanish and French blood-lines mixed freely with a dozen varieties of American, and – a little less freely, of course – with every shade of "colour" from ebony black to high yellow. But I noticed my stranger at once, perhaps because he was different from the rest in the way I, too, was different – out of place – odd – far from home.

I must have stared too long, my gaze like a touch on his shoulder, because he turned and stared squarely back at me on the hot street corner as I clutched my shrunken vegetables to my chest and shamelessly craned my neck for a better view.

He recognised me, too, touching his hat and giving me a little half-smile. But that was all the attention he would spare. After a moment he turned back to his public meeting, and though I waited on the spot for as long as I decently could, he never gave me a second glance.

6

I'd have stood there longer if I'd dared, but Luke, who'd no inkling of why I'd suddenly halted on our way back to the *Bellflower*, was becoming restless, kicking at the edge of the gutter and looking longingly at each passing streetcar. Luke, at eighteen, had the understanding of a baby and the strength of a titan. Shortly after our German fireman deserted us in St Louis for better things, Pa discovered Luke chained in an iron cage, bare-knuckling all comers for the profit of a Memphis showman, and with the aid of a shotgun had carried him off on the *Bellflower* to work honestly for his keep. Whenever I went ashore, Luke was sent along as escort, and lately there had been moments when I was grateful for the reassurance of his shambling step a pace or two behind my own.

On this particular day we'd hardly gone thirty yards from the street-corner meeting when I heard a sudden commotion behind me as if the discussion had abruptly ended in blows. I turned to see what was afoot, just in time to be almost run down by the flying figure of my Englishman, hatless and moving faster than I would have believed possible, with the whole mob howling at his heels.

It seemed I wasn't the only one to suspect him of being a spy: the city was fidgety enough to hoist any loitering stranger to the top of the nearest lamppost, and now they were stampeding in the wake of this one with rage in their faces, sticks and pistols in their hands and a bloodcurdling whooping in their throats.

The Englishman didn't know Canal Street well enough, that was clear. I saw him dart across towards the American side, dodge round a streetcar and then slacken pace and hesitate, scanning the dark shade under the verandahs for a possible hiding place.

"Down here – "

I was pretty fleet myself once I'd kicked off my shoes, and since he'd almost come to a standstill I was able to catch his arm and drag him towards the mouth of an alley which I knew led down the side of a store towards Common Street.

There were boxes and casks stacked in the lane and plenty of rubbish underfoot to hinder our flight, but we skipped through it like running deer, the Englishman and I, with Luke crashing in our wake, petulantly hurling the crates over his shoulder as he lumbered along. Far behind, a stream of oaths from the shadows indicated that the spy-hunters were falling foul of Luke's handiwork.

"When we get to the end – " I managed to blurt out, "turn left. Head for the river. Lose yourself among the side-wheelers. Understand?"

"I know where the river is, thank you." He was breathing heavily just behind me, but he managed to be sassy all the same. I'd never seen such a man for ingratitude.

The sunlit rectangle of the end of the alley was before us as we ran, and at last we poured out into Common Street – right into the arms of a green-uniformed squad of "Foreign Legion", dressed up with guns and plumes and gold lace.

Being French and Spanish for the most part, they immediately took the part of a young lady escaping from a rabble of shouting layabouts who found it hard to account for their actions – hard in French and Spanish, at any rate – and once I'd smiled a good deal at the lieutenant and thanked him excessively in my own halting French, he muttered *charmante, charmante* several times and the crowd were soon sent about their business.

And then, darn it if I didn't look round for my Englishman, only to discover he'd disappeared again. He wasn't anywhere to be seen in Common Street; he wasn't in the alley; he'd simply vanished once more into thin air, without so much as a word of thanks for my having saved his ungrateful hide.

Chapter Two

1

All through next day, the 19th of April, New Orleans held its breath. Sixty miles downriver, Farragut's mortar-ships were shelling Fort Jackson and Fort St Philip, doggedly trying to open a path to the city which had imagined itself safe behind them. The truth was that the forts must hold out, for there was little else. New Orleans had pinned its faith on General Lovell to show the Federal fleet what the South was made of (such a gallant figure, with his moustaches and his beautiful horse); but so many of Lovell's men had been sent away to make up the numbers of battle-weary Confederate battalions elsewhere that he had precious little left beyond gallantry.

In the leafy walks of the garden district and the hidden courtyards of the old quarter, the citizens speculated on their future. Surely the ram *Manassas* would see the Federals off, and the ironclad *Louisiana*, and, if a driveshaft could only be found for her in time, the armoured dreadnought *Mississippi*, named to find favour with the river itself.

Nevertheless, the people became more anxious still. Silver spoons were hidden in cellars, the best brandy under the cisterns. Women sewed their jewellery into the mattresses of their children's cots, and then, fearful for their children's safety (for didn't Federal troops eat innocent babes?), they began to pack their boxes and trunks for flight.

I heard all this from Louis Boudreaux when he strolled down to the levee that morning and tossed me a crimson silk scarf he claimed he'd been given by a Virginia lady, clearing her house before running off to her sister in Richmond. Louis was a "cub" pilot, training to take the big steamboats up and down the river, and would one day be a person of consequence on the levee, but my father grumbled whenever he appeared and hardly returned Louis's greeting. It outraged him to see Louis, the son of a French share-cropper from Bayou La Fourche, sitting in the shade on the *Bellflower*'s guard with his feet dangling over the water, passing the time of day with us as if he owned the vessel – and staring at any likely-looking female who might be promenading along the shore. But whiskey had been scarce in the city for months: sober and judicious for once, my father kept his outrage to himself and allowed Louis to flash his dark smile and give us the news of the city.

15

I worshipped at Louis's shrine like the rest, but he only ever treated me as a younger sister, laughing at me and teasing me, and calling me *Tite-chaouache* – Cajun French for "little savage". I was doomed to admire from a decent distance. Mine weren't the eager fingers which ran through his black, shining curls on hot nights behind the marble ovens of the cemetery. I'd heard what went on there, though not from Louis, who for all his swagger was a little afraid of my father's unpredictable rages and the cut-down 10-gauge shotgun which hung over his bunk on the *Bellflower*.

It was all so unfair. As far as I could see, Pa's temper and his shotgun were quite likely to turn me into an old maid, if I didn't die of humiliation first. Here I was, seventeen in less than a week's time, and the best-looking man for a mile in any direction laughed at me for a savage and treated me like a babe in arms!

Except that on this particular day for once I found my attention straying from Louis's smooth, olive-tinted skin with its fascinating bluish shadows to the recollection of another face, narrower and fairer altogether, and of another, tauter, longer-limbed frame, quite different from Louis Boudreaux's dark opulence.

2

I was still dreaming of a pair of shrewd, mocking grey eyes when I went ashore next morning. There was hardly any point in visiting the cool tunnels of the market now: the rich tapestry of scents had all but faded from its lanes, and those traders who still had something to sell wanted solid coin, not illegible paper about to become worthless at any moment. But I continued to go there just the same, with Luke at my heels, walking slowly – very slowly – by way of the foot of Canal Street, just in case my stranger had decided to risk his life once more to loiter on a corner, observing the growing despair of the South with that curious sharp stare of his.

At two o'clock – two hours past midnight – on the 24th of April Farragut's fleet finally ran under the guns of the forts, divided the chain which closed off the river, stormed through the rams and steamers and fire-rafts sent against them, and gained the open water above.

By daylight the unthinkable had come to pass. A formidable body of Federal ships lay at anchor a mere twenty miles downriver from New Orleans, and unless the Chalmette batteries could stop them – and no one now held out much hope of that – the Crescent City lay helpless before her Northern enemies.

The first I knew of all this was when a frantic clanging of alarm bells broke out within the city. The old revenue cutter *Washington* had made a sortie downriver to ascertain the true state of affairs, and returned, furling her sails in flustered disbelief, to report that within a day, but for the long-awaited miracle, Farragut's warships would be upon us and the Union flag would fly over New Orleans.

All over the city, those who had somewhere to go to finally fled, leaving their homes to the mercy of looters and General Butler's troops. Precious objects were dropped from balconies into the arms of those below; carriages jammed the narrow streets of the old quarter, their horses kicking and plunging as those ready to leave tried to force a way through the rest.

Lovell was gone or going, and other officers with him – some said in panic, others in drink, but most reckoned he'd simply run out of ideas. A whole regiment had surrendered downstream – if you could imagine such a thing – crowding the riverbank, begging to give up their arms to a paltry gunboat. Nervously, citizens eyed their house slaves: would they rise in a body against their masters, as the Northern abolitionists had urged? As rumours and counter-rumours flew from street to street, those with no refuge surged up and down in a mass, searching for news, hunting for family and friends, clinging to one another in their frenzy.

By noon, the panic had turned to fury. The city was enraged. There had been no miracle after all: New Orleans would fall, and no one could save it, but by Heaven, someone would suffer for the betrayal!

Close by us on the levee, the multitude fell on an old wooden shed containing provisions laid by for transport upriver. Within minutes a fog of flour enveloped the doorway as casks were dragged out and broken open on the paving and sexless forms scrabbled and fought on hands and knees for handfuls of cornmeal and the tobacco spilling from stove-in hogsheads.

I watched enviously from the deck of the *Bellflower*, wondering if I dare race ashore with a tin bowl to see what I could salvage myself, but I was too afraid of Pa's thick leather belt to risk it. Poor whites we might be, but no daughter of Ben Summerbee's went squabbling in the dust for a few ounces of corn. Let us eat molasses and catfish, if that was all we had, but let us starve decently.

In the afternoon Louis Boudreaux came by clutching a brass clock thrown to him by a man in the Vieux Carré who'd overloaded his carriage for flight. Shops had been set on fire, Louis reported, and a foreigner beaten half to death on Race Street. Down near the market, a couple of moored hulks had been pushed out into mid-river, consumed by flames, to drift down as a present for the Yankees.

17

"*Bellflower* could be next," he warned with a grin, before setting off to see what favours his clock might extract from a woman friend in Girod Street.

I wasn't concerned for the *Bellflower*: Pa's shotgun would soon take care of anyone thinking of turning us into a fireship. But the news of the beating on Race Street was alarming. My Englishman was out there – no doubt blundering into all sorts of trouble in his pig-headed, know-all sort of way. It was only by sheer luck I'd been on hand to rescue him from the mob in Canal Street, and though his vanishing act afterwards had been downright uncivil by any standard, the image of sharp grey eyes glazed in choking death kept returning to torment me, until I finally decided to go ashore. Fortunately, it was Sam Duck who caught me stuffing my flour-sack apron under the stairway and draping Louis's crimson silk scarf over my calico shirt.

"Best stay on the boat, Miss Kate, and wait till he com' to you." Sam's dark eyes gleamed in the shadow of the upper deck. "Monsieur Agasu will see that pretty red scarf of yours and bring him runnin', don't you fret."

I knew about Agasu – more than I should have done, I dare say, for a white woman; but my mother had borne me a year after losing stillborn twin boys, and to Sam that circumstance made me more than a little interesting, in spite of my white skin and blue eyes. For Sam was an *oungan*, an important man among the practitioners of voodoo. I'd often seen the *ason*, the gourd rattle which was his symbol of office, folded among his blankets at night: when I was small, he'd let me play with the net of snake vertebrae which covered it, watching me all the time with brooding eyes which proclaimed more loudly than words, *if you were only black, little one . . . what powers you might have . . .*

Sam himself wasn't properly black, for all he was a slave. Technically he was a mulatto, with the sculpted features of a Spanish don and skin the colour of Mississippi water where it swirls like pale chocolate round the cypress knees. We didn't own Sam – oh, dear me no, he'd have cost more than a thousand dollars – but for as long as I could remember Pa had hired him from his owner as a bondman because Sam was the only one who understood the secret language of bangs and hisses in which the *Bellflower*'s engines made their desires known.

He applied the same logic to the management of the world around him, a world rich in spirits and omens and herbal remedies; and partly because of the circumstances of my birth, and also, perhaps, because no one else bothered to offer me any solutions to the mysteries of life, Sam contributed a great deal to my education which would have been frowned upon in a more formal academy. There was too much blood in it all for me – I couldn't even sit through a cock fight after the first stained feathers had started to fly – yet, paradoxically, Sam taught me a reverence for living things which to my awakening child's mind seemed as rational as breathing.

Pa must have known I was growing up on nodding terms with Agué, the *loa* of water, who by some miracle kept the *Bellflower* afloat, with Damballah, the snake spirit, with Papa Legba, the opener of doors, and a hundred other hovering presences. But if he ever noticed me pour a spoonful of beer sweetened with molasses on our stage-plank to ensure a safe passage for any suitors who might call, out of respect for his engineer he kept his objections to himself.

I swear it was pure vanity that made me tie crimson silk about my neck before venturing ashore – the same vanity which inspired me to stuff my rough apron under the lowest step of the stairway. Monsieur Agasu, I knew, liked the colour red and was inclined to interest himself in affairs of the heart, but I'd no notion of his views on the subject of flour-sack aprons, and in that department I'd followed a line of my own.

"I reckon he'll come back, Miss Kate. You don't need to go huntin' for him."

"Oh yes? And who do you see with your *quatre yeux*, Sam? Louis Boudreaux, by any chance?"

"Maybe." Sam regarded me from under half-shut lids.

"Well that just shows how little you know. Louis has gone off to visit some woman in Girod Street, and he's welcome to her, for all I care."

"I didn't say Louis. That was the name you gave."

"Hah!"

Unfortunately, the sound of voices had brought my father to the top of the stairs; as soon as he saw me by the stage-plank, about to leave, he came crashing down, two steps at a time.

"Where in tarnation d'you think you're going?"

"To the market, I guess." The words came out with less assurance than I'd intended.

"You sure as Hell are not!"

"We have to get something to eat, Pa."

"Sam'll fish something up for us." My father swung round to glare at Sam, who'd left his fishing line tied off to the grasshopper spar. "So you can just stay on the boat." All at once, he caught sight of the silk scarf draped round my neck. "Is that what you got from the Boudreaux boy?"

"What if it is?"

"Give it here."

"Why should I?"

"Because I don't like that good-for-nothing givin' you presents, an' hanging round all day, callin' you *Kate* as if he didn't know any better. Your name's Katherine – d'you hear me? And from now on I don't want to see you danglin' over the deck rail up there, showin' off your body to trash like Louis Boudreaux. I've got the honour of my name to think of, an' don't you forget it." He pronounced it *on-ah*, for all the world like some old plantation owner demanding pistols at dawn.

"*On-ah*," repeated my father severely, "is what marks out the gentleman from the scoundrel. It raises shipowners like myself above big-talkin' rogues like Louis Boudreaux."

I could hardly believe my ears. All this from a man so often outrageously, publicly drunk – a man who cheated on freight charges and thought nothing of dumping his cargo at some backwoods landing where fancy had led him – a man suddenly trying to set himself up as a fine Southern gentleman.

"Either you give me that scarf right now – or so help me, I'll take it from you."

"I won't let you take it!" I spread my hands over my prize. "Why shouldn't I have something pretty to wear for a change?"

"Something one of Boudreaux's lady friends has no more use for? Not my daughter! Not Ben Summerbee's daughter." My father held out a hand, his expression ominous. "Give it here."

"What are you going to do?"

"I'm going to put it in the firebox and burn it, that's what."

"I won't give it to you! It was my present, and I won't let you have it!"

Pa seized my arm and twisted it painfully, wrestling with the knot of the scarf. "By Heaven, I'll see you set a light to it yourself."

"I won't!" The pain in my arm was so bad I had to bite my lip to prevent myself crying out, but I was determined not to give in without a fight. In the end, no doubt, he'd force me to do as he wanted by sheer brute strength, but I'd inherited a fair measure of Pa's obstinate wilfulness, and besides on that day I was infected to the core with the reckless, dangerous mood of the city.

I swung my free arm as hard as I could, and by good luck my elbow caught Pa full in the stomach. Before he could recover, I'd squirmed from his grasp and taken refuge behind the derrick.

"So much for your famous *honour*!" I yelled at him. "Bullying women – that's all you're good for, *Captain* Summerbee!"

"Why, you little baggage – " Colour suffusing his face, he turned towards me, half disbelieving what he'd heard. His hands flew to his belt buckle, but I'd already begun to move swiftly back along the deck. These days he had to catch me unawares to give me a beating.

"Come back here!" Stripping the belt from his trousers, he set off after me past the fireboxes and the boiler, dodging piled cordwood as he came.

I was skipping in and out of the posts supporting the upper deck now; hoping to delay him, I scrambled over the main steam line which ran back towards the engines in the stern.

"A beating's your answer for everything, isn't it? Just like you thrashed my mother if she ever stood up to you!" I'd already said too much – oh, far too much – but I was determined to get full value of the welts that sooner or later would stripe my shoulders.

"You wash out that mouth of yours! Your ma may have been a cripple, but she knew her duty. She was a good woman, God rest her!"

"It was the first rest she ever got, married to you, Ben Summerbee. Everybody knows you worked her to death!"

I'd passed the engines now; I was standing by the tiller arms, right next to the big paddle-wheel in the stern of the boat, and I didn't want my father to corner me there. I waited until he was almost upon me, squeezed out on to the narrow guard and scuttled back along it towards the open space of the main deck, heading for the bow again, my skirt scooped up in both hands to clear my knees. Behind me, breathing heavily, my father ploughed in my wake, the heavy belt looped ready to strike as soon as he could pin me down.

"Come here, damn you!"

"Come and catch me, you old devil!" From the *Bellflower*'s bow the narrow stage-plank stretched out to the levee, where a crowd still lingered round the plundered warehouse. Here was a chance to hide until the worst of my father's rage had passed off; sooner or later he'd punish me for my rebellion – either with his belt or simply with his bony fist – but those heavy, deliberate blows never hurt so much as a thrashing delivered in the white heat of fury.

I flew to the top of the plank, glancing back to see how near my father might be. He was alarmingly close; without any hesitation I plunged towards the shore, taking the plank in a couple of bounds and crashing at full tilt into someone standing just beyond the far end of it.

I must have knocked all the wind out of him. As it was, I almost felled him in my haste, and had he not thrown both arms around me to preserve his balance, no doubt we'd both have rolled in the drifts of

cornmeal and dirty flour which covered the levee. There we stood –
clinging together like a couple of shinplasters, his shirt-stud in my nose,
a strand of my hair between his teeth . . . wedged closer than seeds in a
watermelon – me and my English swindler from the corner of Canal
Street.

3

"That's the man."

McCartney the banker was standing at the stranger's shoulder,
pointing towards the *Bellflower*, where my father stood, transfixed at
the top of the makeshift gangway, belt in hand, trousers sagging, his
mouth open, and his face – still crimson with rage – contrasting
unpleasantly with the faded red-gold of his hair.

"That," McCartney repeated acidly, "is Captain Summerbee. What
you have there, Mr Oliver, is his daughter."

Hastily, I peeled myself from the stranger's chest and smoothed
down my skirts. This was no sightseeing visit, I was sure: for one thing,
Mr McCartney was immaculate in the grey uniform of a Confederate
Guard officer and another figure in grey sat on the carriage box with a
sergeant's stripes on his arm and a rifle pushed down beside the seat
cushion.

I noticed that my Englishman still wore the same nondescript coat
and trousers I'd seen a few days earlier. No doubt he'd chosen the
clothes to make himself invisible in the crowded city streets, but that
mysterious quality of "otherness" singled him out in spite of them. No
matter how hard he tried, he just didn't belong.

"You can't say I didn't warn you, Mr Oliver." The banker yanked at
his tight grey tunic and brushed some imaginary dust from his sleeve.
"That's the *Bellflower*, all right, but she's hardly a showpiece, I think
you'll agree."

"I don't see why that should make any difference." The Englishman
stood his ground. "In fact, perhaps it's all to the good. Who'd ever
suspect a boat like this?"

"You don't seriously mean to go ahead with the scheme?"
McCartney had turned away towards his carriage, but now walked back
incredulously to stand at the stranger's side. "It's your choice, of
course, but I can't say I'd advise it." For a few seconds the two men
scrutinised the ramshackle length of our vessel while I hovered nearby,
staring just as intently at the man Oliver, wondering what crazy
deception he could have dreamed up to suck in a man like McCartney.

"What d'you mean, mister – *a boat like this?*" His daughter

22

forgotten, Pa had discovered a new source of offence. "What's the matter with my boat, I'd like to know?"

"Nothing at all, from where I stand." Mr Oliver turned to inspect my father. "If you're Ben Summerbee, then I may have a business proposition for you."

"I'm Summerbee, all right." Mollified, but still suspicious, my father waited at the top of the plank, stuffing his shirt back into the waistband of his trousers. "What sort of business d'you have in mind, mister?"

"They tell me you know the river between here and the Passes, Captain Summerbee."

My father thrust out his chin. "They told you right."

"Better than anyone, they said."

"I reckon that's true."

"Could you make it to South-West Pass in this vessel?"

"If I wanted to – and if half the United States navy warn't squatting in the way."

"How about at night, then?"

"At night's no problem." A thought struck him. "Do you mean past Farragut's ships?"

"That's what I had in mind." Mr Oliver held my father in his level stare.

"Well then, mister, you'd better find someone else for your business proposition. I'm in no hurry to get blowed out of the water."

"Captain! Think of your duty to the Confederacy!" The grey-clad banker could hardly contain his indignation.

"*Duty* ain't a word I've much time for, Mr McCartney. But if the Confederacy was to start talkin' about paying me . . ." My father looked wolfish. "And in gold, mind. None of these car-tickets of yours."

"Well, Mr Oliver – you've heard it from his own lips. I told you that's what he'd say," McCartney remarked dismissively. "I reckon you're wasting your time here."

"Maybe." I thought I saw the ghost of a smile in those pale eyes. "Can I come aboard and talk to you, Captain Summerbee?"

"I guess you can, if there's something you think I'll want to hear. Come aboard then, Mr Oliver. And you too, girl." My father's glare indicated that the banker wasn't included in the invitation.

"You're crazy even to consider it, in my opinion," McCartney called after the Englishman's departing back. "Still – it's your funeral. I'll come back for you in half an hour, as we agreed."

The carriage rocked as he climbed aboard, and my father watched sourly while it pulled away across the levee.

4

"So you're Adam Gaunt's boy. Well, I'm damned." From the far side of the cabin table, Pa treated the Englishman to a searching stare. "I can see a likeness, sure enough, now you mention it. Same hair. Same eyes."

Lurking behind the iron stove, I considered the startling possibility of there being two such singular creatures, father and son, and of my own father's being acquainted with Mr Oliver's. Pa hardly ever spoke of his early years on the headwaters of the Missouri in the heyday of the fur trade, when beaver pelts were still so much brown gold. But the name "Gaunt" had evidently stirred memories, and I wondered what tales I might hear now.

"So your pa told you to come looking for me, did he?"

"Not exactly. But I've heard him speak of you, and I recognised the name when I came across it."

"And what did Adam Gaunt have to say about me, then? Nothing favourable, I reckon." My father leaned forward suddenly, his eyes alight. "Did he tell you how we once fought off near two dozen Injuns from a raft of beaver plews on the Yellowstone? Never thought I'd see nightfall that day, an' that's the truth. There I was, trapped on a snag with no more'n an Englishman for company. . . . Yet he got his share of Injuns, your pa, an' I realised then he warn't quite what I'd thought."

My father grinned as a new thought struck him. "Did he ever tell you how he stole the *bourgeois*'s daughter from under my nose at Fort Union? No? Oh, he'd a way with women, had Adam Gaunt. Not that he ever put himself out for 'em, mind. Not a bit of it. But they still hung round him like bees round a honey pot."

"I wouldn't know about that." Mr Oliver's eyes briefly met mine over my father's shoulder.

"Never met your ma," continued my father, unabashed. "Though I did hear your pa had got himself married and settled down some." A sudden suspicion flickered over Pa's face. "But how come you call yourself Matthew *Oliver* if you're Adam Gaunt's son?"

"My stepfather was a man called Jonas Oliver."

"Your stepfather?" My father looked puzzled.

"My parents were separated for a time. My mother believed my father was dead, and went back to England."

24

"And married this feller Oliver?"

"Something like that." Matthew Oliver seemed unwilling to satisfy my father's curiosity.

"Then how is it you're here in New Orleans, Mr Oliver, if your family's all settled in England? This is a fine time to pay us a visit, in the middle of a war."

"It's the war that brought me." Matthew Oliver smiled fleetingly at my father's heavy-handed humour. "I had business with the cotton-brokers on behalf of some people at home."

"There's an awful lot of cotton here, going nowhere," my father remarked sagely.

"A good part of it bought and paid for by Lancashire mill-owners, who can't lay their hands on it unless someone's willing to run the blockade to fetch their property out."

"Such as you, maybe?"

Matthew Oliver shrugged. "I know of a ship that's done business of that kind," he said evasively. "But I'm no sea-captain, myself."

"Just a man durned anxious to get down to Pilot Town, it seems to me. This ship you mentioned – is she coming in to pick you up?"

"She'll send a boat ashore for the next few nights."

My father shook his head. "Too risky," he said finally. "I'd be a fool to try it. And so would you, young feller."

"I'd pay you. Passenger and freight."

"Freight?" Mr father's thick brows rose in amazement. "*Cotton?*"

"No – just a few small boxes."

"It's still too risky, I reckon."

"Too risky for a man who stood off a couple of dozen Indians on the Yellowstone? That doesn't sound like the Ben Summerbee I was told about."

"Times have changed since those days. And I have a daughter to think of now," my father added self-righteously. "What's in these boxes of yours anyway, that's so all-fired important?"

"Nothing in particular." Matthew Oliver challenged my father's stare until Pa looked away.

"I've no interest in your business," he said thickly.

"I don't mean to be rude, Captain Summerbee, but the less anyone knows about it the better. All I can tell you is that I've undertaken to carry these boxes out of New Orleans – tonight, if possible. I'm not over-keen on the idea myself, but when I heard that Ben Summerbee – *the* Ben Summerbee – was the owner of this vessel . . . well, I thought my problems were solved."

25

"As simple as that?"

"I never imagined you'd be scared off by a handful of Federal ships. Not a man of your reputation."

My father leaned across the table, and fixed Matthew Oliver with a resentful glare.

"You're Adam Gaunt's son, all right. Nothin' stops you, does it, mister?"

"Will you take me down to Pilot Town?"

My father considered the possibility in silence for a few moments, torn between the hazards of the journey and the large price he could ask for it.

"I won't do it for old times' sake, Mr Oliver," he warned at last. "I don't owe your pa any favours, whatever you may think. If I do take you, it'll only be because I've named my price, and you've agreed to pay it."

"That's fair. You'll get your money at Pilot Town."

"If we get there," conceded Pa morosely.

"When we get there, surely, Captain Summerbee."

5

The banker's carriage was drawn up again on the levee when we walked out on deck, with McCartney standing truculently beside it. Pa and the Englishman went ashore, and I could soon tell by the banker's scowl and his uplifted palms that he wanted nothing at all to do with the business. Mr Oliver's scheme was entirely his own affair.

I was still brooding about what I'd overheard in the cabin, and wondering how much of it was true. It was easy for an Englishman to claim an interest in cotton: everyone knew what a long-drawn-out war in America would mean to the British mills. And this mysterious ship which might or might not be waiting at Pilot Town. . . . That tale seemed highly unlikely, too, with Federal warships buzzing thick as mosquitoes in a saltmarsh round every mouth of the delta. Besides, everyone knew that blockade runners were dashing, resourceful buccaneers – not fools who got themselves chased down side alleys and had to be rescued by sixteen-year-old girls. Seventeen tomorrow, I reminded myself automatically.

Still – Pa had smelt money, and after a lifetime's exercise his nose was more often right than wrong. And I was the last one to object to my Englishman coming aboard. Swindler or smuggler, Mr Matthew Oliver was by far the most interesting thing to have happened to me for weeks, and I waited aboard the *Bellflower*, almost holding my breath with anticipation, while the other three conferred ashore. After a moment or two I found Sam Duck at my shoulder, wiping his hands on an oily rag and watching the proceedings with equal curiosity.

"You watch your pa there, Miss Kate. Whenever I see him scratch his ear like that an' put the other hand deep in his pocket, I know there's real money in the deal, whatever it is." Sam Duck tugged his cap over his eyes, and tilted his head back. "An' I reckon it's something dangerous, but he's goin' to do it anyway."

"How can you tell all that, Sam?"

The engineer shook his head.

"I just know it. I guess I've been with your pa so long I can pretty well read his mind."

"Sam – " I struggled to put an awkward thought into words. "Will you take the chance of running off when the Yankees get here? You could earn a good wage as a free man, working as an engineer on one of the big steamers."

Sam's eyes remained fixed on my father's broad back while he considered the question.

"I won't tell him, Sam – I promise."

"Nothin' to tell, anyhow. Reckon I'll stay till I see how things work out. Maybe these Federal fellers'll make us all free, an' maybe they won't. No sense in making myself a runaway ahead of time. 'Sides – who'd keep the *Bellflower* sweet if I went off?"

"Sam!" My father's voice rang out from the wharf.

"Yes, Cap'n?" Effortlessly, Sam slipped back into the role of deferential Negro.

"Come ashore here, will you?"

"Right away, Cap'n." As Sam swung himself ashore from the derrick I had to hide a smile. Orders aboard the *Bellflower* were seldom so polite.

"You and the sergeant stow those boxes in the cabin."

Whatever had been discussed ashore, an agreement had been reached and hands shaken upon it. *Revolvers or ammunition*, I decided as I watched Sam and the Confederate sergeant stagger aboard with five small, heavy wooden chests. So that was Matthew Oliver's game – we were to be gun-runners for the Confederacy, slipping downriver with arms for the Confederate sharpshooters on the riverbanks.

But I said nothing as the last of the boxes was carried aboard and stowed safely at the forward end of the cabin. "On the boiler deck," my father repeated pompously, as if he were talking about the *Atlantic* or one of her mighty sisters.

In the wake of the five wooden boxes came the Englishman, his hand shaken by banker McCartney in a way which implied *Good luck, my friend – you'll need it.*

On deck, my father swelled with the importance of command, sweeping an arm in a gesture which embraced the whole of Louisiana.

"Mr Oliver, that's my crew there, and you've already met my daughter, Katherine. She helps out aboard, doin' – well – anything that needs doin'. I'm a widower, as you may have heard, with no sons to follow me, but Katherine is near as useful as a boy, allowin' she's only female."

Matthew Oliver's eyes swept over me as if he'd have liked to check this last point for himself, and for an awful moment I thought he was going to say something about our early morning conversation a few days earlier, when my gender had been hidden by no more than a thin blanket. Fortunately, he had the sense to keep quiet.

"Miss Summerbee," he said, and nodded.

"I guess you heard, Katherine, that we're taking this gentleman down to the Passes tonight." My father simpered horribly, as if it was normal practice to discuss his plans with me, but his eyes remained narrow with warning. I might have escaped a beating earlier, but I could count on catching one as soon as we were alone together if I spoke out of turn.

"And now, my dear, why don't you go and fix us all some food?"

"Yes, Pa."

The man Oliver's eyes lingered on me as we spoke. He'd had a front-row view of the quarrel earlier in the afternoon, and I sensed he understood what that *Yes, Pa* signified.

"If you'd be so kind, Miss Summerbee," he said . . . and smiled.

Chapter Three

1

Fortunately, Sam had caught a catfish – small by Mississippi standards, but enough to provide a fried meal for us all. The Englishman appeared just as I was laying its blunt-skulled grey bulk on the deck rail and tweezing out the big nail I kept stuck there for the purpose of fixing catfish for skinning. I noticed he had his hands in his pockets again as if he continually expected us to rifle them, but he watched gravely enough while I banged my nail through the creature's head and began to pull off its skin with Pa's engine pliers. Then, for some unknown reason – maybe Mr Oliver didn't like the way the fish was scowling at him – he reached out a tentative finger towards the spines standing proud on its back.

"Don't touch those, 'less you want to get stung. Why d'you think I'm using these pliers?"

He withdrew his hand at once, absently rubbing together finger and thumb.

"Are the spines very poisonous?"

"This feller ain't so bad, but his kin down near the Gulf – whoo-ee! One touch, an' you'd swell up like a dead hog in the sun."

"Is he worth all the trouble?"

"Depends on what he's been eating, down in the mud." I saw the Englishman's eyes flick to the filthy flotsam eddying round our hull. "Don't worry, I'll cook him so's you can't tell."

"I'll look forward to that."

His sarcasm hurt me: I'd meant to make a special effort with that fish.

"Go ashore to Antoine's, why don't you?" I snapped at him. "See if you can do better there."

I didn't expect him to apologise for his rudeness – and sure enough, he didn't. Instead, he put his head on one side and considered me solemnly with those careful grey eyes of his, for all the world as if he were trying to assess the precise degree of my annoyance, and what exactly he might lose by it. I went on ripping off catfish skin, beginning to wish it was his.

"You don't seem to like me much, Miss Summerbee."

"I might like you better if you learned some manners." I put down the pliers and turned to face him squarely. "What did you mean by running off without a word, when I'd just saved you from a hanging, that day in Canal Street? Didn't anyone ever teach you to say *thank you*?"

"It's possible you saved me from a beating, certainly."

"Possible? Another minute and they'd have strung you up, for sure. You'd have been dead as this feller here – " I indicated the catfish, monstrously naked except for his scowling head. "And you didn't even stay long enough to say a word of thanks!"

"Thank you."

"Huh?"

"I said *thank you*. Isn't that what you wanted?" He was leaning on the rail now, half twisted towards me, turning the pliers between his long fingers, absently drawing the handles apart in what was as near to a caress as I'd seen.

I was unnerved enough to give ground.

"I guess that's better. But I'd still like to know why you disappeared so fast."

"I had to leave in a hurry, that's all."

"I'm not a fool, Mr Oliver."

"I never thought you were, Miss Summerbee."

We were still standing there, staring at one another, when I heard Pa's voice bawling from the cabin, demanding to know what in blue blazes was keeping his fish.

In all honesty, it doesn't take much skill to fix catfish. First, you steal an egg from somewhere, beat it well, and dip in the cut-up pieces. Next, you roll them in cornmeal (if you happen to have a dusty scraping left at the bottom of the tub), heat the fat in the pan until a floating match catches light by itself, and fry your fish.

I could tell our passenger didn't care for the result. No doubt he was accustomed to more elegant company, too, on his big river steamers, though my father – who normally stowed his food away in absolute silence – for once made an effort to keep up something passing for conversation.

" 'Course," he announced through a mouthful of catfish, "you ain't seein' the *Bellflower* at her best right now. I've known us loaded down with steel rails – oh, as far as the boiler deck. Stoker couldn't move from the firebox for three days, he was so jammed in. Had to toss cordwood to him over the cargo."

This was an outrageous lie. Steel rails were carried by the big, fast steamers which arrived and left to a strict schedule. Pa had been known to burn rags in the *Bellflower*'s smokestacks to make shippers think we were getting up steam to leave, and then sit tight for eight days until he'd scratched up enough cargo to make his trip worth while.

"Now, you take these danged railroads – " This was one of Pa's favourite themes, and I waited for him to develop it along the usual lines. But he stopped, and frowned, and closed his mouth abruptly as if it had dawned on him at last that Matthew Oliver had said nothing beyond *ah* and *oh* at appropriate moments, leaving the burden of conversation to his host.

"And what's your own line, Mr Oliver? Are you in shipping yourself – or in munitions, maybe?" Pa's eyes wandered to the five wooden boxes, stacked against the forward bulkhead of the cabin.

"A bit of this and a bit of that, Captain. You could say I have an interest in one or two vessels."

St Louis steam packets, I thought to myself, *and jackass passengers with their pockets full of city money and their brains full of whiskey.*

But my father, steaming ahead on a course of his own, imagined he'd detected a kindred spirit.

"Ah . . ." He paused, his knife half-way to his mouth. "An *owner*! Well then, I'm even more pleased to have you aboard the *Bellflower*, young man. Of course, as soon as I heard you speak back there, I said to myself 'That feller has more sense in his little finger than Clem McCartney and his partners have between 'em.' Because once you have a ship of your own – well, then you know a thing or two." He indicated the narrow space of the cabin with his laden knife. "Like I said, business is slow right now – which is why I'm able to accommodate your little proposition – but if these were normal times. . . . Well . . . Adam Gaunt's boy or not, I reckon I'd have had to tell you to go elsewhere. Pressure of trade, you understand. Isn't that so, Katherine?"

"If you say so, Pa." I didn't raise my eyes from my plate. I hated to be dragged into his extravagant lies.

"Yes, pressure of trade . . ."

But the lie was too enormous even for my father to maintain in the face of our present troubles, and after a few seconds' silence he shook his head sombrely, as if the whole weight of the annual Mississippi freight was pressing down on his shoulders.

"And look at us now! All thanks to those damned Yankees, bringin' their ships an' their soldiers down here where folks were just goin' about their business, makin' a living the only way they know how."

He leaned forward, his eyes suddenly bright with resentment. "They

31

closed off my river, Mr Oliver, like putting a cork in a bottle! Choked off the Mississippi, God's own waterway, as if they owned it all an' could say who had a right to go up and down! I've never counted myself North or South – neither for nor against. I'd no quarrel with the Union, Lord knows, but now here's the *Bellflower*, tied up and useless along with the rest."

This was the first time I'd heard my father speak about the war at such length, or with such passion. All he'd ever said in the past was that we were too poor to afford high-falutin' principles, and the rich folks with land and slaves to think of should keep their war to themselves. Even the loss of thousands of young lives hadn't moved him an inch from this position. But now that the war had reached the river – his river – and was no longer something which could be put off until the next bend, Ben Summerbee had begun to question where his loyalties lay.

"When I think of those danged Yankees – closin' up my river, takin' it upon themselves to chase me down here till they're pleased to say I can go. . . . It's like being in jail, Mr Oliver, I can tell you. An' now they've got past the forts, though I never thought I'd live to see it. Not for a moment! There was trickery there, so I've heard: mastheads covered in brushwood so's no one could see 'em against the trees, and I don't know all what." My father sucked his teeth in disgust at this new evidence of Yankee duplicity.

"Still – I reckon the forts have something to answer for, letting the Federals sneak through like that." He rapped the handle of his knife a couple of times on the table, like the gunshots which should have dispatched the Union warships. "An' now we've got them at both ends of the river, above us an' below us, squeezing us all to blazes. So I guess I'm good an' ready to take you down to the Passes tonight, young man, if only to show those Yankees they can't keep Ben Summerbee shut up in New Orleans if he don't want to be!"

"For the glory of the Confederacy." The Englishman had kept silent for so long that I was startled by the sound of his voice, quietly ironic in the stillness of the cabin.

My father leaned forward again. "For the satisfaction of Ben Summerbee," he said with finality.

"And a considerable sum of money, of course."

"I didn't hear that, Mr Oliver." My father dug in his pocket for his pipe. "That money is for runnin' expenses, as you should know, being an owner yourself. Repairs contingent on being fired upon by a bunch of blue-bellies." He sucked experimentally at the empty pipe. "Katherine – clear the plates."

32

I brewed up the last of our coffee – not parched rye for once, but the fragrant handful I'd been saving for a birthday treat next day. By the time I returned to the table with the pot, the discussion had moved on to the details of the journey.

"We don't want to get past English Turn till it's full dark," my father declared as I set the coffee down before him. "Then all the way to Poverty Point we'll shave the shore so close you could climb the trees, an' keep right under the big bluffs at Johnson's and Grand Prairie. Ten to one those Yankee boys'll never know we're there – and even if they did chance to hear us . . . well, the *Bellflower* couldn't sound like a gunboat if she tried, an' it's dark as a cow's inside under those cypresses. I reckon they'll let us be."

"How long will it take us to reach the Passes?" The Englishman watched my father intently.

"With the river as high as this – oh, maybe nine or ten hours."

"Then we'll be at Pilot Town a little after daylight."

"I reckon so. We've wood enough to make it."

"What do we do in the meantime?"

My father shrugged, tipped back his chair, and scraped out the bowl of his blackened pipe before he spoke. "I guess we wait for it to get dark – that's about all."

"Oh." I sensed Matthew Oliver would have liked to set off at that very moment, as if waiting for anything was a burden to him, something to be avoided at all costs. With a quick sigh of annoyance he pushed both hands deep into the pockets of his coat again, and for the next few moments studied the table-top, then the cabin roof, and finally the small patch of sky visible through the nearest window. All of five minutes passed in this way, while my father, an expert at wasting idle hours, methodically filled his pipe and then noisily lit it.

But if waiting was unavoidable, suffocation was another matter entirely. I guessed Pa was smoking "yarb", a mixture of grasses and leaves he'd learned from the fur trappers in the old tobaccoless days on the upper Missouri. However it tasted through a pipe-stem, it seasoned the air around him with the mellow flavour of roasting feathers, and after a minute or two of Pa's puffing, Mr Oliver suddenly sprang to his feet and stalked out of the cabin to the open deck over the stern of the boat where I discovered him ten minutes later, leaning on the rail and sourly contemplating the iron-bound paddle-wheel below.

"I'm sorry about that pipe. It smokes like Satan's kitchen, but he can't see the harm in it, and it does keep off the mosquitoes."

"I'm not surprised."

An awkward silence descended. Idly, I leaned over to squash a fat bug that had crawled out of a crack in the woodwork, pressing down with my thumb until I heard the faint *plop* of extinction and then flicking the splayed corpse into the river. All of a sudden it didn't seem very ladylike to have bug blood on my thumb, so I wiped it off hastily on my petticoat. I looked up to find the Englishman watching me once more.

"They only come out at this time of year. I guess they're looking for other bugs to have babies with."

Thoughtfully, he traced the damp stain of squashed bug on the sun-faded rail. "And you don't approve of such goings-on?"

"Not when they do it in the cornmeal."

The mocking look had come into his eyes again; irritated, I cast round for a way of cutting him down to size.

"Is it true your father was a fur trapper in the Rockies? Years back, like Pa said?"

"So I believe. He was a hunter for the fur brigades, and other things besides."

Before I could ask any more, the Englishman briskly changed the subject.

"Where's your home when you're not on the river, you and the Captain?"

I was taken aback by his directness. "You're standing on it. The *Bellflower*'s the only home we have."

"Then where were you born?"

"Ma used to say it was round the back of island Hundred-and-Three – the one they call Pawpaw Island, at the foot of Millikin's bend. The river was high, so Pa was running the chute that day and she had to manage pretty much by herself. I always look for the spot when we get past Vicksburg, but the bend's changed a bit since then, and it's hard to tell."

He was staring at me, for once astonished out of his self-assurance.

"Born on the river – and you've never lived ashore at all?"

"Never more'n a day or so at a time."

I'd never thought of myself as being anything much out of the ordinary, but seeing his amazement I began to wonder if things were done differently elsewhere.

"Don't people live on boats in England?"

"There are families who spend most of their lives on narrow-boats on the canals, I suppose."

"Well, then. I wish you'd stop looking at me as if I'd got loose from a freak show. Where do you live, if it's so downright normal?"

"I have a house in Liverpool."

"Oh, I've heard of Liverpool. Before the war began, we used to see Liverpool ships tied up at the wharves here, loading cotton and sugar."

The Englishman's eyes had strayed to the far side of the river, half a mile distant, and he didn't bother to answer, as if he felt my curiosity ought to have been satisfied. But all of a sudden I was insatiable. The more I discovered about Mr Oliver, the more I wanted to know, and I was frustrated by his secretiveness.

"What's it like, this house of yours?"

"Pretty big."

"How many rooms, then?"

"Goodness, what a question. . . . Oh, more than forty rooms, I suppose, if you count all the boxrooms and larders."

"Forty rooms?" Clearly, he was teasing me, trying to punish me for my prying. "I suppose you live there with a wife for each month of the year, not to mention this fur trapper father of yours – "

He laughed at that, and for a moment his face lost its hardness.

"Nothing so interesting. I live there all alone, except for the servants."

"Oh, sure! Servants, of course." I wriggled my shoulders, just to let him know how little I was impressed by his nonsense. "Listen, my friend – you might cut a shine on the *John Roe* with tall tales like that, but after years of living with Ben Summerbee I've heard more lies than I'd care to count. Believe me, I know horseshit when I smell it."

"I'm sure you do. Tell me what you've smelt out about me, then."

"You're a small-time swindler, I'd say. A riverboat gambling man, down on your luck now the river's closed, and turned errand boy for McCartney and his Confederate friends. Isn't that so?"

"There's some truth in it, certainly."

"I'll bet it's nearer the truth than a forty-room palace and a crowd of servants."

As if he'd suddenly tired of the game, the Englishman fished in his waistcoat pocket, drew out a watch and casually flipped it open in the palm of his hand. I was surprised to see that not only was it a gold watch, but the dial was inlaid with fancy enamel and other gimcracks. I was still staring when he put the watch away.

"Ten minutes past seven," he volunteered.

"That's a pretty fine watch."

"I suppose it is."

"Was it honestly come by?"

For a second, he hesitated. "I borrowed it, as a matter of fact."

"Sure – I know that kind of borrow. Listen – " I added, seeing him frown, "I don't mean any harm by that. You've got a living to make, same as anyone else. We all have our own rocks to jump over. I'm just glad to see you have a talent for your own particular line."

I never heard his answer. At that moment the cabin door opened and my father emerged, wreathed in foul pipe-smoke, distrustful as a farmer round his hen coop.

"You still out here, Katherine? I was beginning to wonder what was keepin' you."

"We were just talkin' steamboats, Pa. You know how time flies."

"I guess that's true." For a moment he inspected us narrowly, and then, satisfied from our positions at the rail that nothing more sinful than steamboat lore was being exchanged, he turned to go back inside. "Don't you stay out here too long now, girl."

I waited until the cabin door had banged shut behind him.

"You won't ever tell Pa, will you, about that day in the city? Or seeing me on the boat in the morning?"

"Why? Would he mind?"

"I'd probably get a beating for bein' forward. Pa don't hold with forwardness."

"Would he really have hit you with that belt today?"

"I reckon so, if you hadn't come by. He'd have got me sooner or later."

"And you're what – seventeen, did you tell me?"

"Seventeen tomorrow."

"Then it's monstrous."

He said it vehemently enough to make me stare in surprise. There was something about the look in his eyes . . . a hollowness, maybe, like the mystery of half-open shutters in a sunlit wall . . . that convinced me he'd meant what he'd said. Suddenly uneasy, I passed off the moment with a swift shrug.

"That's Pa, I guess. Didn't your father ever thrash you when you were young?"

"Most of the time he wasn't there to thrash me."

"Have your parents been divorced, then?" I hesitated to ask: divorce was regarded as a habit of the ungodly North.

"No, they haven't been divorced." In the bright wall of his face, the shutters closed with a snap. "I wish they had."

"Don't you like your father, then?"

36

"I hate him." He glanced up defiantly. "Does that shock you?"

"I guess not." I considered the point. "I'd probably hate Pa, if he wasn't all I'd got." Then with a rush of suspicion it occurred to me I might have fallen for another of his tall stories. "How come you had a stepfather, if your ma and pa are still married?"

"My parents were apart for a long time. Then my stepfather died, and my own father came back. Unfortunately," he added.

"Sounds pretty peculiar to me."

"It was."

"Is it legal in England, to change around like that?"

"No." He leaned both forearms on the rail and gazed out over the river. "But the Gaunts don't feel any need to behave like other people. Fortunately I only ever see my father when I visit my mother in the country. We can't even stay in the same room for long without quarrelling over something."

"What's odd about that? We argue all the time, Pa and me."

The notion of life without squabbling and rows was as foreign to me as the idea of a forty-room house, larders included – though Pa generally put an end to any disagreement by lashing out hard whenever he fancied I was defying him. *Insolence* and *dumb insolence* were the two prime sins in Pa's book. I was guilty of insolence when I dared to answer him back, and of dumb insolence when I said nothing. Either way, I was sure to be in the wrong.

Before I could think of something more to say, Matthew Oliver's attention had been distracted by a commotion which had broken out ashore, and he began to walk along by the rail towards the *Bellflower*'s bow for a better view.

"What in Heaven's name is going on down there?"

Not far off on the levee, a lumbering dray hauled by four horses had forced its way through the throng of idlers spilling out from the foot of Canal Street. As soon as the great, squat wagon came to a halt, four or five Negroes leaped down and began to heave out bales of cotton, rolling them end over end to an empty flatboat moored nearby.

"Who's loading cotton at a time like this?"

I was as puzzled as he was, and even more baffled when a red-faced, white-whiskered man I recognised as one of the leading cotton merchants of the city drove up in his carriage with his wife very straight and grave by his side. Another wagon arrived, and before long, under the solemn eyes of the couple in the carriage, the flatboat was piled high with bales, its sides almost under water.

"They're cutting the bales open! Look – that fellow with the knife, and the other man in the bow."

"I've never seen such a thing before."

A small skiff had taken the flatboat in tow, dragging it awkwardly out into the river. Before long the current had caught the two craft, tugging and straining at the line which linked them, and we watched anxiously as the men left aboard the flatboat scrambled to safety, the last one lingering for a moment to break open a small cask and splash its contents over the piled cotton. Even before he'd leaped into the skiff with his comrades and cut the flatboat free, yellow tongues of flame had begun to lick the sides of the stacked bales, flicking with serpent-like caution at the tightly packed fibres.

In seconds, fanned by the breeze and fed with sprinkled liquor, the fires began to bite into the cotton, each little outburst ripping along the side of the pyre to meet its neighbours and rise with them into the air as a great smoking, slowly revolving torch.

Motionless in his carriage, the merchant watched his cotton burn. Aboard the *Bellflower* I watched too, seized by sudden dread, the desperate straits of the city brought home to me at last.

Even during the past hungry weeks I'd been able to push fear from my mind amid the growing difficulties of life on the river. Sometimes, to my shame, my little part of the war had almost seemed like an adventure – I was hardly seventeen, after all, still young enough to believe myself immortal. It was difficult to remember the awfulness of war when there was excitement, and love, and the new life of each day to be lived. But if they were burning the cotton – the *cotton*, of all things – then this must, truly, be the end of our world. Nothing but the Apocalypse would have made them destroy the cotton crop to keep it from the hands of the demons of the North.

At my side, the Englishman looked on in silence as if the horror of the scene had touched even his astringent soul.

Down at the river's edge, another raft was ready to leave; more drays arrived, and as soon as they were emptied others took their places, until the levee came alive with bales of cotton tumbling towards the river and any available craft. Everywhere was haste and impatience, as if the brokers and merchants were anxious to finish their work and see their year's profit beyond recall before anyone could change his mind.

The biggest rafts had been fired with a kindling of pine knots and tufts of loose cotton. The cremation must be total: the Federals would be forced to watch from their ships as every scrap of the precious fibre turned to ashes before their eyes.

When transport ran out, the bales themselves were launched into the flood, trailing ribbons of smoke as they bobbed and spun in the eddies, for all the world like the raftlets Sam sent off each year in honour of Agué, the water *loa*. From where we stood aboard the *Bellflower* it seemed as if all the presses and yards in New Orleans had been emptied in a frenzied festival of fire, a sacrifice of Southern prosperity in the face of the looming enemy.

From the upper deck we had a perfect view, and I was so absorbed in watching the extraordinary scene below that I actually jumped when the Englishman spoke.

"I've come a long way for a handful of ash."

He'd murmured the words almost to himself, but I turned on him, furious that he should keep up his lies at such a moment.

"I thought we'd agreed you'd drop all that talk! You aren't a blockade runner any more'n you're Jeff Davis, so you needn't bother pretending it's so." I gazed at him in something approaching despair. "I wish for once you'd be honest with me, an' we could be friends."

"Hey there, Katherine!" A voice floated up to us from the smoke and confusion of the levee, and I saw a tall, thin figure in black, arms spread wide like dusky wings, swooping through the crowd, dodging rolling bales as he came.

"Pastor Bonnet!"

"Where's your father, child?" The flying figure came to a sudden halt at the water's edge and squinted up at us with his one good eye, the other rolled disconcertingly at right angles over his unshaven cheek.

"He's in the cabin, Pastor. Hey, Pa! Come out here! You've got a visitor!"

Down on the shore, the Pastor kept glancing nervously over his shoulder at the heavy bales of cotton tumbling everywhere towards the river. It had struck me more than once that for a churchman he'd very little faith in his Maker; moreover, for a pillar of the Rivermen's Bible and Tract Society he drank a surprising amount, most of the time in my father's company, and I often wondered when he found a few moments to save souls.

"Eli!" My father was hanging over the rail, his pipe wagging in the corner of his jaw. "What in Hell's going on down there?"

"They're burning the cotton, Ben!" Pastor Bonnet jigged up and down on the levee, flapping his great wings. "And worse'n that – they're huntin' out all the liquor in the place, and pouring it on the bales!"

"Well, by all the saints!" My father's voice vibrated with outrage. For weeks now, whiskey and brandy had cost far more than he could afford, even when he could find a supply: the prospect of standing by while the last of it went up in smoke was almost more than he could bear.

"But there's liquor in town, all right," the Pastor babbled on. "Someone's broken into a grog shop on Bourbon Street, and a few others too. There's whiskey runnin' in the gutters, Ben – I stuck my fingers in an' tasted it!"

The Pastor's frantic mime was too much for my father, starved for so long of the mainstay of life itself.

"Hold on, Eli – I'm comin'!" In that instant the war was forgotten, the boat was forgotten and his undefended daughter along with it. With nothing more in his head than the need to get his fair share of that criminally wasted drink, my father made a dash for the stairway to the lower deck, only to find his passenger there before him, barring the way below.

"You're taking me downriver tonight, remember?"

"Sure. I remember."

"Then where do you think you're going?"

"I'm goin' ashore for a while with the Pastor there. You got any objection to that?"

"How do I know you'll be back when it's time to leave?"

"Dammit, you're frettin' like an old woman! I'll be back long before I'm needed, an' I've no intention of letting good liquor fall into enemy hands. Say – " My father had a sudden inspiration. "Why don't you come ashore with us? That'd set your mind at rest."

"I doubt it. It isn't safe to leave the boat, with all this burning cotton around. Suppose some of those bales wash up against the *Bellflower*?"

"Sam Duck's here, and the boy. Katherine can look after things."

"Be-en!" The Pastor's voice floated up anxiously once more. "What's keeping you?"

"I'll be right along!" my father shouted back. "Now, are you comin' or not?"

"No. And I'll thank you to remember we had a bargain."

"We made a deal concernin' *tonight*. I don't remember a single word about *this evenin'*! So right now I'm on my own time, an' I'll do what I please – " My father took a breath. "An' no damned Englisher's goin' to tell me different."

"Be-en! Get along there! Liquor's a-wastin'!"

"You'd better be aboard when you're needed, or – "

"Or what? Take your arm away, boy, I'm warnin' you."

They couldn't have looked more different, standing there, confronting one another – my father bulky and muscular, the Englishman lithe

40

and quick, both much of a height and yet apparently so ill matched. But there was a familiar, crazy glint in my father's eye – familiar to me, at any rate, and perhaps familiar to Matthew Oliver too, since he removed his hand from the rail and reluctantly allowed Pa to pass on his way to the lower deck. Pa took the stairs in a couple of leaps, and the last I saw of the two pleasure-seekers was the Pastor's tall black hat weaving away along the levee like a steamer chimney in a crowd of shipping.

Chapter Four

1

"You couldn't have stopped him, truly you couldn't. He hasn't so much as smelled liquor for weeks now, and it would've killed him just to sit tight."

"As long as he's back in time to leave for the Passes." The Englishman glanced across the levee in the direction my father had taken, and I sensed that his recent defeat still rankled.

"If you're paying Pa good money, you can bet he'll be back. And I can take care of the *Bellflower* until then." In the heady freedom of my father's absence, I couldn't resist trying to impress. "I'm pretty much one of the crew these days. I take the wheel while Pa catnaps or eats his meals – sometimes for a goodish way. He won't let me steer the hardest sections yet, but I can do fairly well when I can't get out of the river."

"You can steer this thing?"

"Sure. I'm a pretty good steersman, if I say it myself." Too late, it occurred to me that this might not be a womanly accomplishment in Matthew Oliver's eyes. "Do English ladies steer boats much?"

"Not a great deal, generally."

"Well, if I didn't steer we'd have to pay a man to do it. Though you don't need to be over-strong." I was afraid I'd made myself sound like a fairground Amazon. "The old *Bell* answers the helm real quick. I've no trouble with her on that score."

"Still – I'm sure your father can manage without you tonight."

"I'm darn sure he can't – especially if he's loaded up with forty-rod whiskey."

"Absolutely not." The Englishman shook his head with finality. "Anything might happen to us. It's far too dangerous a trip for a woman."

I felt myself flush with pleasure. A *woman*, he'd said – not a girl: he considered me a full-blown, right-down fragile female, and he was gallantly concerned for my safety. Now I was more determined than ever not to be left behind.

" 'Course I'm coming. I'm not afraid of a parcel of Yankees! Besides – where else would I go, if not on the *Bellflower*?'

He stared at me for a moment, perplexed.

"Is there no one but your father to take charge of you?"

"There's just Pa and me. Ma died when I was eight, when the Yellow Fever came in '53."

Pa always told it like that, as if Ma had been snatched away from us by the impartial epidemic, cut down in the bloom of her young life. But even as a child, I'd divined it wasn't so – that the fever had only been part of her trouble, and she'd simply lain down to die one day, tired of life with Ben Summerbee, of the drinking and beatings and the constant carping she'd had to endure since she'd married him ten years before.

"Ma had a lame foot," I explained. "They called her Cripple Mary on the river, though I've heard people say she was beautiful when she was first married. She was only thirteen then, and halted when she walked." Matthew Oliver's face wore an expression I'd seen before. "And you can take that look off your face, mister. Ma was decently married to my father with a paper to prove it, and she kept that paper folded in an old bible till the day she died."

Pa had come across her at Fort Smith on the Arkansas, one summer when the river was so low that even the *Bellflower* could count on a dollar-a-hundred-pounds for heavy freight. I've no idea why Mary was there, except that her own father was a pedlar, creeping across the West in a shuddering wagon festooned with kettles and skillets, needles and looking-glasses, tin cups and bunches of ribbon – anything a woman in a sod hut might gaze on with a few cents' worth of desire. His limping daughter was no more use to him than a busted johnny-pot, but like everything else on the cart, if someone wanted her, she had her price.

Ben Summerbee paid fifty dollars for the pretty face, and the lame foot was thrown in for nothing. Soon after they were married the river rose again, freight fell to fifteen cents, and my father sold Mary's Shawnee silver brooches to keep himself in forty-rod whiskey and enough tobacco to fill his pipe. I often thought that if tobacco was a truthteller to The Grandmother as the Shawnee people believed, Pa's pipe-smoke must have had a fine old tale to tell when it reached the Other World.

"They married in the summer," I said aloud, "and she was carryin' by fall. Too young, I guess. Twin boys, born dead. And then I came along, and after that she was too wore out to carry another right through. She was only twenty-three when she died."

I glanced up to find the Englishman watching me with that odd, half-shuttered look on his face again.

"How old are you, Mr Oliver?"

"I'm twenty-four. That must seem like old age from where you stand."

43

"From where I stand, twenty-four's pretty young to be a blockade runner and a shipowner and all those other things you hinted at."

He said nothing, as if the point was unanswerable, and I pressed ahead with my peace terms.

"I've told you what I think you're doing aboard the *Bellflower*, and you haven't denied it. I think you're taking guns down to the Confederate sharpshooters in the swamps between here and the Passes, so they can make things hot for the Yankees if they try to land."

Again he said nothing.

"So now you know something about me, an' I know a bit about you, and maybe we can quit playing guessing games for the rest of the night until Pa gets back. It'll be a darn sight more comfortable if we can shake hands an' be friends."

He was leaning on the rail, watching me with lazy eyes.

"That's all I wanted to say," I added needlessly.

"Shake on it, then."

He reached out a hand – long-jointed and brown, near enough to touch my shirt buttons and make me uneasily aware of the faint sheen of his skin and the fair hairs lying over the surface of it like cornstalks in a wind. The last thing I wanted just then was to surrender my own hand to that warm captivity.

"Still don't trust me?" The hand remained, until I had no choice but to give mine up in return.

With a little half-smile he lifted my imprisoned fingers and kissed the soft cushions at their tips.

Immediately, I snatched my hand away.

"Don't! That's the kind of thing Louis does when he wants to tease me."

"Louis?" Now his eyes searched my face, trawling for information.

"Louis Boudreaux. He's a river pilot. Well, nearly a pilot."

"And a friend of yours?"

"I guess so. Pa doesn't like him, because Louis calls me Kate instead of Katherine."

"He must be a very good friend, then, to take liberties with your name."

"Not that good." The Englishman was staring hard enough to make me squirm uncomfortably. "You can call me Katherine, if you like."

"Katherine." He tried it out. "I'm Matthew, as you know."

"Do they call you Matt?"

"No, they don't."

"Oh."

I was conscious of having sinned, but at least we'd abandoned the subject of Louis Boudreaux. Stealthily, I moved further away from him along the rail, and he didn't try to follow. In my heart I knew he didn't care for me at all – not really. He'd condescended to tease me as Louis did, to flirt with me routinely like a man flexing an idle muscle, giving it no more thought than the owner of an old dog reaching out to pat the animal's head. I'd only caught his attention by mentioning another man's name, and as soon as he was satisfied of Louis's essential harmlessness, he'd passed on at once to other matters.

"At least now you understand why we must be under way before dark."

I gazed towards the city, where the sun had already disappeared behind the rooftops. Below us on the levee the cotton-burning was proceeding at a fine pace, although the fires seemed more vivid than before, the flames drawing deeper colour from the fading red-gold of the sky.

"I reckon we'll see Pa back before long." I wished I could say it with more conviction.

"I hope you're right." Pushing himself up from the rail, the Englishman strolled into the cabin and flung himself down on the chair he'd occupied earlier.

"Nothing to do except sit here and wait." He glanced up morosely as I followed him inside. "Wait – and hope all the whiskey in New Orleans runs out in the next hour or so."

If he'd been anyone else, I might have felt sorry for him. But Matthew Oliver wasn't the kind of man who invited sympathy. Quite the reverse. He'd only to speak, and the words *I can make my own way* echoed in the air.

"Will you take some brandy?"

"You have brandy here?"

"Only a little. Pa fell asleep one night with the best part of a pint left in the bottle, so I took it away and hid it. He'd forgotten all about it by next day."

"I dare say a glass of brandy might make things look a little more promising." Matthew Oliver watched with interest as I drew the bottle from its hiding place near the stove and set it down in front of him alongside a battered tin mug.

"There isn't a glass. I'm sorry."

"It'll taste just the same, I've no doubt. Will you join me, Katherine?"

"I don't usually drink." The truth was that I didn't much like the taste of the stuff, but I was conscious of sounding like a priggish child, and so I set down another mug beside the first.

"I'll take a little, just to keep you company. Oh my stars – that's plenty."

"Your health then, Katherine." He raised his mug. "And a safe journey to us both, since you're determined to come."

"Oh . . . yes." The brandy burned my throat, and I was glad I'd only allowed him to pour me a little.

"Are you all right?"

I nodded, my throat too raw for conversation.

"You don't have to drink it on my account."

"I'm not!" I gasped, and took a great gulp of coarse spirit. This time my throat was too numbed to notice the pain. "See?"

"A hardened drinker, obviously."

"Will you stop laughing at me in that condescending manner?" Without thinking, I added, "You're as bad as Louis!"

"Louis again . . ." Once more I became aware of Matthew Oliver's keen, pale stare. "Are you engaged to him?"

"I should think not."

"That's the second time you've mentioned him, all the same. And he calls you Kate."

"Well . . . I'm called a lot of things. *Kate*, or *Katherine* – or *Cripple Mary's girl*, on the river. You're about the only person who's ever called me Miss Summerbee."

"And Louis is. . . ?" He was determined to pursue the question.

"There's nothing between Louis Boudreaux and me, if that's what you're asking." It seemed important to make the situation quite clear. "I've known Louis almost all my life, but he's more like a brother than anything else."

"I'm pleased to hear it."

"Why should that please you?"

"It occurred to me that he mightn't understand why his bride-to-be was sharing a cosy bottle of spirits with a common gun-runner." Matthew Oliver was looking directly into my eyes now, pretending conspiracy, turning two mugs of firewater brandy into a lovers' tryst.

"More brandy?" Deliberately, I pushed the bottle forward. I'd got the measure of his game now, and I wasn't prepared to play it.

"Thank you, but no more brandy. I may need a clear head before tonight's over." He turned away from me, and consulted his elaborate gold watch once more. "It's getting late."

"I'll light the lamp."

46

It was becoming quite gloomy in the little cabin, though the flickering flames of the burning cotton continued to dance and *whoosh* beyond the windows, and the shouts of the crowd and the rumbling of drays and wagons came to us louder than ever.

I fiddled unnecessarily with the lamp, turning its lighting into a drawn-out ritual. I was furious with Pa for delaying so long, though in all honesty it was no more than I'd expected. I knew Pa's priorities of old, and I knew he wouldn't return until either the liquor was exhausted or he was.

And in the meantime I was left to placate Matthew Oliver, who was growing more restless by the moment.

2

People ashore seldom realise how clearly their voices carry to anyone on a moored boat. Matthew and I had long since run out of conversation and were sitting at the table in resentful silence when I heard a murmuring very near at hand, quite distinct from the general hubbub and with that particular nervous tremor which indicates the speakers are up to no good. All of a sudden, Sam Duck's footsteps thudded along the lower deck of the *Bellflower*, followed by a shout of indignation.

"You leave those lines alone, you hear! You leave us be!"

"Come down from there, nigger, or you'll fry with the boat." This produced general laughter. "I'll give you a count of three to jump ashore: one . . . two . . ."

"I reckon he's skeared of us, Charlie!"

". . . Here's your last chance, boy!"

Furious, I rushed outside; from the rail of the upper deck I saw a group of men ranged along the water's edge – perhaps half a dozen grinning, loutish whites, four of them holding smoking torches above their heads while the others wrenched at our mooring lines.

"Never mind the nigger, Ned – he'll jump fast enough with a fire at his tail, I reckon."

"Put a torch to the boat, then, and we'll push her out with some of that lumber back there."

"Miss Kate!"

"I'm here, Sam. Hey – you men down there! Leave those ropes alone! And you – get your dirty foot off my boat!" For one of the men had already begun to push against the *Bellflower*'s guard.

Below me at the water's edge, six faces tilted upwards and six voices fell suddenly silent. Then one of the men let out a loud guffaw.

"Well, if that don't beat all! Look at the little lady up there – all alone on this worm-eaten piece of firewood!"

"That's Summerbee's daughter," added another. "Cripple Mary's girl."

"How about some comp'ny, darlin'? Maybe we'll come up an' visit with you for a while."

"An' fire the boat afterwards, hey boys?"

"You'll do nothing of the sort – you miserable, yellow-faced corpse stealers!" *Corpse stealers* was a particular favourite of my father's. "On your way, jackasses, and leave this boat alone!"

"Oho!" came a shout. "The kitty-cat's got claws!"

"Them's the best kind, Ned!"

A torch flickered as one of the men reached out to swing himself aboard.

"The first one to put his foot on this boat gets both barrels in the face." Matthew Oliver materialised beside me at the rail, tall and dangerous in the darkness, my father's 10-gauge shotgun in his hands.

Below us I saw the boarder hesitate, lose his balance and hop clumsily backwards, cannoning into the rest. The nearest man peered upwards, shading his eyes against the light of the torches.

"That ain't Ben Summerbee."

"You heard me. Get away from the boat."

"Who are you, stranger?"

"That's none of your business."

"Maybe there's more of them up there, Ned." One of the group, at least, was having second thoughts.

"Horseshit! I reckon there's six of us, an' only one of him."

"An' that gun of his."

"Just one man an' one shotgun, all the same."

"Tell you what, boys – " came another, wiser voice from the rear. "While we're wastin' time here, there's Whitney's old lugger tied up further down. That'd burn even better, I guess."

"Well, you could be right."

"We could always come back for this one later."

"We could, at that."

But retreat was awkward for them without loss of face. Stiff-legged and self-conscious, laughing over-loudly, punching one another in rowdy fun, the pack began to drift away towards their new victim. Only one man stood his ground, a smoking torch in his hand, reluctant to be chased off by a girl, a Negro, and a cold-voiced foreigner with a shotgun.

"Your friends are waiting for you." The muzzle of the gun nudged a fraction towards the laggard on the shore. "I'll use this if I have to."

48

Something in Matthew Oliver's tone convinced the man he'd gain nothing by staying, and with an oath he swung away down the levee to join his comrades.

Lowering the butt of the gun to the deck, Matthew leaned on the rail.

"Better check the moorings, Sam."

"Yes, sir. Right away."

"And fill a few buckets, if you can find some – just in case we need to put out a fire. Where's that other fellow – Luke, is it?"

"Gone off down the levee a piece to pick up some wood from a burned-out flatboat. Cap'n Ben 'spects him to collect any driftwood he sees an' dry it out for the firebox."

"He picked a fine time to leave the boat. When he comes back, tell him to stay aboard."

"Yes, sir. Sure will."

"Any orders for me while you're about it?"

The resentment in my voice made him turn at once.

"You'll stay in the cabin from now on, in case those fellows come back."

"How dare you order me about on my own boat!"

"It's your father's boat. Until he comes back, you'll do as I say."

"Go to Hell! There was no need for you to interfere."

"I think there was. Those men were going to fire the boat, whatever fancy names you called them."

"Blast you, I can deal with trash like that any day."

"No, you can't. That's why I told your father he should have stayed aboard, instead of chasing off after free liquor."

"I'm quite capable of looking after the *Bellflower* without any help from you, Mr Matthew Oliver."

"I've no intention of arguing with you."

"*Why not*, dammit?"

"Because I'm right." He turned, picked up the gun, and walked back towards the cabin.

After a moment he reappeared, the gold watch in his hand. He thrust it towards me resentfully.

"See that? It's gone ten o'clock already. Where the devil's your father?"

3

With the final fading of daylight, the scene along the levee became utterly fantastic. As far as the eye could see, the curving shoreline was a ribbon of flame in either direction; blazing flatboats and rafts whirled and collided in the flast-flowing river, shedding gobbets of fire to smoulder in their wake; here and there single bales floated like lamps, bobbing and hissing in ripples unable to drown their oily glow.

There were so many drays and carts drawn up on the shore now that the newest arrivals unloaded and lit their pyres wherever they could. Freakish figures – black and white reduced to the same frantic silhouettes – dashed through alleyways of fire, rolling bales, hurling broached casks of spirit on the flames, calling for more cotton – more cotton. . . . Better than a year's labour in the cotton-fields, snatched by that greedy inferno out of the hands of the approaching Yankees.

Blizzards of sparks drove across the levee. Showered in fiery flakes, the shed smashed open by the mob earlier in the day caught light with a great roar, and was quickly engulfed in a ballooning mass of flame. It was immediately beyond saving; no doubt the volunteer firemen were busy elsewhere or had long since gone over to the side of the arsonists on the shore.

Aboard the *Bellflower* we fended off burning baulks of wood and cotton which dragged along our hull, and drenched the decks with endless buckets of water. Every shift of the breeze brought a cloud of pinpoint fire to glow briefly and fizzle to a damp death on our planking, though no one ashore gave a second's thought to our predicament. One ancient steamer more or less; what did that matter, compared with the urgency of destroying the cotton – no, *saving* the cotton, since that was how they saw it – preventing hundreds of thousands of dollars' worth from fuelling the Union war machine.

Somewhere towards Canal Street ragged singing broke out, "The Bonny Blue Flag" just audible above the shouts of the cotton-burners and the incessant *whumph* of new infernos.

"Someone's having a good time." The expression on Matthew Oliver's face indicated anything but enjoyment. Frustrated, bitter – almost disbelieving of the scene being acted out before his eyes – he stood on the upper deck of the *Bellflower*, his coat thrown off and his hands on his thighs, shoulders squared, glaring out over that raging shore.

"We should have been on our way an hour ago. And where's Ben Summerbee?" He shot me a glance of angry despair. "Well? Where's that father of yours?"

"Somewhere in the city, I expect."

"Anywhere but here, where he should be."

"I guess something's kept him."

With an angry snort, Matthew Oliver turned back to his fierce contemplation of the shore.

"Must you go downriver tonight? Wouldn't tomorrow night do as well?"

"By tomorrow night, Farragut's ships will be anchored off the city. I don't intend to be trapped here with what's in those boxes."

"We could heave them over the side, if there's any chance of being searched."

"We can't risk a search. And we can't drop the boxes in the river – not under any circumstances."

"I just thought – "

"Never. One way or another, we have to get them away from here."

"If it's so important to you."

My concern must have sounded half-hearted, because he turned as I spoke and laid hold of my shoulders, cupping their roundness in his long fingers and staring down into my face.

"Katherine, if the boxes were mine alone, I'd see them go to the devil sooner than risk a life for them." Sculpted in pale fire, his features drew a kind of grandeur from the blaze. "But I've given my word. I've no choice in the matter any more. Now do you understand?"

He was willing me to understand – to take his side against my father's fecklessness. He'd never swallowed his pride so far as to ask me for a single thing before, and I was furious that he'd wasted so much passion on a few old guns.

"Are you telling me you need my help?"

He didn't answer at once; his eyes continued to absorb my face as if he was wondering whether to trust me, his lips pressed into a defensive line.

"Would you help me, if I asked you?"

My head spun. This was no fancy game any more. He was in genuine trouble, and he needed me.

"I'll help. If you want me to."

He nodded, as if that was enough. A moment later, he released my shoulders and stepped back a pace.

"I've put the boxes out of sight under one of the bunks. It isn't much, but it's the best we can do in the meantime."

"They'll be safe enough there, unless someone's mighty determined to find them." I tried desperately to hold out a little hope. "If Pa comes back soon, there'll still be enough time to get past the Federals before it's light. That would do, wouldn't it?"

"It would be better than nothing – but not much better."

He'd taken the hope I'd offered and broken it savagely over his knee; yet already I understood that his anger wasn't directed at me but at life –

at the unfairness of fate, and at my father as its most treacherous instrument.

4

It took Matthew Oliver exactly eight steps to cross the damp and glistening deck – eight stalking, measured paces followed by a sudden turn and another eight paces to return to his starting point. The turn at the rail was swift and violent: anger wrenched him round as if all the furious helplessness within him, piling up with the passing of each empty minute, had to find a release in action.

"More brandy?" Liquor was my father's refuge, and so I offered it now.

"What's the good of that?" And then, more softly, after a pause, "But thank you for the thought, at least."

Down on the levee the wagons were fewer now, though the fires burned on, watched by small knots of onlookers. No doubt when Jericho fell crowds of citizens rushed to gaze on their ruined walls and carry home chips of stone as mementoes of the day.

At least the *Bellflower* was no longer in danger; the wind had finally changed, carrying the whirling sparks towards the city.

"Please . . ."

"What is it?" He stopped pacing to confront me.

"You're driving me crazy, with all this stamping up and down."

"Oh." Sullenly, he sat down next to me on the upturned yawl and drummed his fingers instead. I reached out and gently stilled them with my own, and for a moment he returned the pressure.

"I'm sorry – I can't stand all this waiting."

"We could talk." When he didn't answer I added, "It passes the time."

"You talk then, and I'll listen."

"What do you want me to talk about?"

"Oh . . . tell me about yourself. The future. Are you going to spend the rest of your life slaving for your father on this godforsaken hulk?"

"Well, no . . . I guess not. I expect I'll be married one day, and have children of my own – and a house, maybe," I added as an afterthought.

It was hard to lay bare my secret hopes. How could I be sure that to name them aloud might not prevent them from coming to pass? But I blundered on, giving up my secrets in the hope of distracting him from his pain.

"I'd like to try living in a real house for once, with a white fence and magnolia blossom – and rooms to walk into, and doors to close – and a

52

melon patch, maybe, and trees in the same place every morning when I wake up. . . ." I stopped, overwhelmed by the extravagance of my dream.

"And what else?"

"How do you mean, *what else?*"

"You must want more than that!"

"Isn't it enough?"

He turned to stare at me incredulously, and then looked away with a little snort of astonishment.

"It's hardly anything!"

"It seems like a great deal to me. I can't imagine wanting more than that." I sensed that I'd disappointed him in some way. "Go on, then – if someone gave you a wishing ring, what would you ask for that's so wonderful?"

"Ships."

"*Ships?*"

"Whole fleets of ships. Fifty – sixty – " He was gazing out over the river as if his mind had already choked it with masts and spars, but there was no empty wistfulness in his face; if anything, his expression was more determined than before, as if sheer will-power could conjure iron hulls out of thin air.

"Only sixty ships? Why not seventy, while you're about it?"

Why shouldn't he ask for the moon? In a single leap he'd soared above commonplace lies – left my poor little white-fenced house far behind and entered the realms of pure fantasy. I scurried to catch up, to build crazy dream-ships alongside his own.

"Seventy, then – " Effortlessly, he absorbed my contribution. "Seventy ships, going all over the world – "

"Sail or steam?"

"Oh, steam. Bigger and better engines. Bigger ships – "

"The Matthew Oliver Line!"

"The Oliver Steam Navigation Company."

If it occurred to me that it was a surprisingly explicit madness for a riverboat card-sharp, I pushed the thought aside and clapped my hands in delight.

"Oh yes – a Steam Navigation Company! Far better! And when you've made your fortune you can buy yourself a country estate and become a lord, and retire from business."

"Only when it's big enough." He made the condition in all seriousness. "Only when the company is the biggest shipping line in the world. And then I'd want to hand it over to my sons."

53

"You'd better ask your wishing ring for a wife, then."

"That's true."

We were both light-headed, intoxicated by the frustration of waiting; but I was desperate to keep our fiction afloat, dancing in the air between us – honest fantasy now, not the clever lies that were his stock in trade. He'd allowed me to share the secret, impossible yearning of his soul, to touch it and remain close – and I was afraid of letting silence come between us.

"Do you want me to tell you how long you'll have to wait for a wife?"

He stared at me, only half understanding.

"We can ask the *loa* when you'll be married. It's the voodoo way. Sam showed me how. Though it's pretty much a parlour trick when I do it, of course."

I saw him hesitate, then yield to his curiosity.

"Go on, then. Show me."

He watched me turn away towards the cabin, following my movements as if I was something entirely beyond his experience. He was still watching the door when I emerged again bearing the stub of a candle and a small glass jar, emptied of the fistful of wilted flowers with which I'd tried to prettify the cabin.

"I've found a little cane syrup for the bottom of the jar, but we'd need all sorts of other things if we were going to do it properly. You must give me some money first – a few cents would be enough. Good – now hold the jar in both hands, will you?"

Obediently, Matthew Oliver reached out for the jar, in which a couple of spoonfuls of cane syrup rolled round the last half-inch.

"Sam says there are special candles for each ceremony, but we'll have to make do with the one I use at night after Pa puts the lamps out."

I bent over his cupped hands and placed the candle vertically in the syrup.

"What's the brandy for?"

I'd brought out the bottle tucked under my arm, and now I removed the cork and splashed a little of the strong-smelling spirit on the deck around us.

"That's for the *loa*, to let him see we're grateful."

"You're a proper little heathen, aren't you? I hadn't realised."

For a moment I stood still, facing him.

"The truth is, I'm nothing at all. I don't know what to believe in – North or South, church or voodoo. I don't even have grand dreams like yours, however crazy they may be. Perhaps that's my trouble."

Before he could answer I bent my head over the jar and lit the candle, murmuring the words Sam had taught me.

"You must concentrate, too. Imagine yourself with a wife."

"And how would you like me to do that, exactly?"

I was glad he couldn't see me blush in the dark.

"I'm sure you can think of something. Now, concentrate."

We both bent over the jar, I laid my hands over his, and with our heads almost touching we watched the flame as it grew to a slender spear of gold.

"What's supposed to happen?"

"Shhh. . . . The flame will bend. Watch the wick."

"Of course it'll bend!" he whispered indignantly. "There's a breeze out here tonight."

"Not in the jar. Watch the flame."

Breeze or not, the candle flame burned high and steady between our hands, a wisp of fire like the *feu folie* of the bayou tales. Our fingers, united, glowed like a blood-red lantern; almost at once I saw the flame quiver and begin to incline gradually towards Matthew, curling its wick as it went as if drawn by the restless heat that consumed him.

"I told you. It's the breeze."

"It's blowing the other way."

"Nonsense."

"I've never seen the flame bend so quickly. You'll be married very soon. The *loa* says so."

Matthew stood up suddenly, wrenching his hands free as if they'd been scorched and taking the jar with him. The candle flickered for an instant in the darkness and then dropped, smoking, as he deliberately spilled syrup and all on the deck.

"There's nothing to be afraid of, Matthew. The *loas* won't hurt you."

"I'm not afraid! It's no more than a piece of parlour magic."

"I don't believe this! You held off those men who were going to fire the boat – but you're afraid of knowing what's to come."

"You can't see into the future. No one can. It's just so much superstition."

"No, it isn't!" I protested hotly. "Sam Duck talks to the spirits in their own language, and they give him answers."

"Then you're meddling in something you don't understand. Maybe I am afraid of knowing what's ahead for me – but perhaps it's time you learned to be afraid of it too."

The shuttered windows of his eyes had swung wide again, their swollen pupils discs of blackness which devoured the night and me along with it.

Howls and shouts from the levee turned both our heads towards the shore. The last drays had gone, but the sooty, oily heaps of blazing cotton remained; and now it seemed as if the entire living contents of the Swamp – that shifty, seething, six-block, upriver section of town – had come tumbling out of the shadows to see what was afoot. Black, white and universally three-parts drunk, they stumbled between the fires, some with their arms linked in a ragged chain, men and women together, surging and then falling back, whooping and shrieking with excitement.

A few yards from our stage-plank, a reveller in cap and shirt-sleeves snatched a burning barrel-stave from the flames and hurled it in a brilliant arc towards the river, trailing sparks like a lesser comet. Hooting and waving his arms with delight, he ran off to join a line of men, crazy with whiskey and bravado, competing to leap one of the smaller fires, racing towards it in turn and flinging themselves with wild howls through its shivering heat. The Yankees might be coming, but a little life still remained to be lived. The enemy was at the gate, but there was still a night of delirious freedom to be savoured.

Besides, these were people with nothing to lose and nowhere to flee to. Times would be hard for a while, no doubt, but sooner or later they'd make a niche for themselves in a Yankee city as easily as they had in a Confederate one, burrowing into the roots of the place, scavenging what they could and scuttling back to their holes in the Swamp. Blue or grey, it would make little difference as long as someone's back was turned for a few precious seconds. Now, on this night of nights, they spilled out into the streets in a horde, hooting, yelling, drunk on destruction and bad liquor.

From somewhere nearby came the sudden scrape of a fiddle.

"It's Nonc Albert – there, by the ruins of the shed! *Adjieu, Albert! Adjieu!* Over there, do you see?" Eagerly, I seized Matthew's arm and pointed to where the old Cajun fiddler had perched himself on an empty barrel and struck up a wild reel, his bow arm flying to and fro and his foot twitching with a life of its own.

The tottering human chain had already broken up; now the fire-leapers deserted their sport and ran with the rest towards the source of the music. Someone produced a tin whistle, someone else a second fiddle; the rest paired off and began to skip up and down the paving in a bizarre two-step. The pairs became a ring round the musicians which lurched into haphazard motion and then dissolved into twosomes again, their double shadows vaulting and diving among the twists of flame. All over our part of the levee, people were dancing now – dancing away their fear – beating out their dread under pounding feet – leaping, twirling, losing themselves in the insistent rhythm of the music.

"Come on!" Matthew Oliver grabbed me by the wrist and strode towards the rickety steps leading below, almost pulling me off my feet in his haste.

"Where are we going?"

"Ashore."

"But – "

"Come on! What else is there to do?"

"But the *Bellflower* – and those boxes of yours – "

"They're safe enough for the moment, as you said yourself. Besides – it's too late now. What's done is done. We'll deal with tomorrow when it comes." He glanced at me over his shoulder, the reckless dreamer of dreams once more. "Well? Don't you want to dance?"

"Oh – so much . . ."

Deep inside me, the madness had taken hold. Devils were dancing over the doomed city, bent on turning master into slave and slave into master. I'd be seventeen next day, and the rhythm was in me, too. I wanted to dance – oh, so much . . .

I can hardly remember scrambling ashore – only the frightening, electrifying moment as we were swallowed up in the whirling horde, borne along by a great boiling tide of dancing figures. The faces of the musicians streamed with sweat as they drove on without pause, Nonc Albert's elbow sawing with fanatical speed, one tune rushing headlong into the next. We were submerged in the crowd, nudged, trampled, collided with; no one cared; no one stopped or even slackened pace. Sam Duck careered past, jumping and spinning in some delirium of his own, blind to anything around him. Not far off, a huge whore had trapped a man under each arm, and now she was keening to the fiery sky, her head thrown back, crushing her captives to her ample breasts as they swayed to and fro. Men danced with men, women with women, black with white, old with young. I heard a shout of *Calinda-a-a-a* . . . the ancient dance of the slave-pens and Congo Square: *Dansez! Dansez! Dansez jusqu'à mort!* And in the midst of it all, Matthew and I, body to supple body, limbs tangling, clasped one another as if the end of the world had come.

Someone had discovered the masks from the Mardi Gras parade. A tribe of horrible, swollen-headed demons bobbed and swayed among the dancers – crimson, vermilion, every shade of red – leering faces moulded in wickedness, their long drooping noses wagging suggestively from side to side as they capered past on bodies grown dwarfish in comparison, their shrunken arms held out, fingers splayed, in an attempt to avoid tumbling under the feet of the dancers.

One of the grotesques reared up at my elbow, glowing like a live ember in the light of the cotton-fires. For a moment it stared into my face, lewd and gloating, enamelled lips bulging in sensual encouragement; then with a clumsy bow, hardly more than a tilt of its bizarre head, it rolled away through the crowd, the streamers at its ears flying out on a hundred whispers of parched air.

It had been a devil's blessing: the music was faster now, driving us relentlessly as Matthew and I spun and whirled like crazy things, touching – always touching – shamelessly coupled in the frenzy of that dance.

I can't remember going back aboard the *Bellflower*, except that knives had flashed among the dancers, and those of us with no part in the quarrel quickly moved away to safety. But the musicians played on – *dansez jusqu'à mort* – as content to play for a knife fight as for a dance; and while that glorious, pulsing rhythm possessed my body, I couldn't let Matthew go – no, not for a thousand fathers. He'd no intention of releasing me in any case, and somehow, still clinging together, breathing, whispering, kissing, we fell entwined on my narrow bunk in the cabin.

Dansez . . . dansez. . . . My blood was hot from the dance: I wanted to feel a man's flesh hard and insistent against mine . . . this man – this Matthew Oliver – this man afraid for the dawn but hell-bent on one heedless night.

Katherine – I remember him whispering it – *Katherine* – and his lips on my breasts, and my throat, and in my hair . . . *Katherine*.

I hadn't realised there could be tenderness in it. All I knew I'd learned from the contemplation of bulls in fields and the fumbling, jerking traffic of the corners of moonlit wharves which passed for business, the whore's knees pale beyond the thighs of her standing partner.

It wasn't like that at all: it was flesh, and yet spirit too. And I'd expected it to hurt – everyone knew it should hurt the first time, the price of that irrevocable, delightful, delicious sin – yet for some reason it didn't. *Dansez . . . dansez. . . .* All I feared was that he would stop and leave me with the rhythm of the dance still alive in me and calling . . . *Jusqu'à mort . . .* until with a new, woman's wisdom I watched him die a minor death, and resurrect himself, and hold me in his arms, wonderingly, as if I was part of one of his dreams on that night of madness.

And then the dancing devil let me sleep at last. . . . For too long, too long.

Chapter Five

1

I slept until almost midday, quite oblivious to the tramp of feet on the deck below, the hollow *donk* of cordwood against the fireboxes and the clatter of iron shovels as Sam Duck and Luke got up steam in the boilers of the *Bellflower*. After years of working for my father, Sam knew his habits better than Pa would have liked to allow. He'd guessed Pa would return from his spree in mid-morning, roaring like a madman and demanding to know why the vessel wasn't ready to leave right away. And Sam was right: it was my father's voice, trading insults with the crowd gathering on the levee and flinging orders to his crew as he clambered unsteadily up the stage-plank, which finally roused me to consciousness.

"Oh, by all that's holy!"

At my side, pressed close against me in that narrow bunk, Matthew Oliver lay asleep and strangely boyish, one arm flung across his brow, the other stretched out on the blanket which was all that covered our combined nakedness.

"Wake up! Oh, wake up, for any sake! Pa's back!" Urgently, I shook him by the shoulder. My father's heavy tread – stumbling at every second step – was mounting the stairway to the upper deck.

"Matthew! Wake up!"

At the sound of his name his eyes flew open at last. An instant's bemusement was followed immediately by a rush of comprehension. Somewhere outside, my father kicked another step, and swore. All at once Matthew seemed to hurl himself into movement, bounding from the bed towards the clothes strewn everywhere on the cabin floor.

My father was still considerably drunk. Flinging the door wide, he paused, swaying, in the doorway, breathing loudly through his nose, his cap tipped to the back of his head. The same sight had greeted me at a thousand middays – but never before swathed from chest to knee in the bold red, white and blue of the old Confederate "Stars and Bars" banner. The proud galaxy of stars was crushed under Pa's armpit and the three broad stripes draped his legs like a sagging skirt. Over his shoulder, the single good eye of Pastor Eli Bonnet blinked dimly at us from under the skewed brim of his tall hat.

59

With ponderous ceremony, my father made a grab for the doorpost, missed it, and staggered forward into the cabin – in time to behold his daughter almost naked in her bunk and her recent lover hastily buttoning his trousers in the middle of the floor.

It was almost more than Pa's fuddled brain could absorb. For a long moment he gaped at me in stupefied disbelief, his mouth opening and shutting like a man chewing on rubber. As realisation dawned he swung round to stare at Matthew – and I'll swear the whole of New Orleans heard that roar, a great inarticulate howl of rage almost loud enough to blow the sides out of the *Bellflower*'s flimsy cabin.

"WHAT IN HELL'S BEEN GOIN' ON HERE – as if I didn't know! You an' her together – naked as jay birds in a cottonwood! Mark that, Eli – that's evidence of his black guilt."

Pa made a heroic effort to stand straight. "You connivin', low-down child stealer! Soon's my back's turned, you go defilin' my little daughter – soiling that pure blossom – "

"Pa!"

"You just hush up, Katherine!" My father thrashed an impatient hand. "I'll deal with you when I've finished with that long streak of depravity there! Shame my daughter, would you? Turn her innocent head with your lies? I ought to break you in half for what you've done – "

Making a furious lunge across the cabin, he collided with Pastor Bonnet, who'd edged forward to get a better view, and fell heavily against the table.

"Pa!" I wriggled frantically in my bunk. "Leave him alone! It ain't what you think!"

Matthew had moved swiftly to the far side of the table, out of reach of my father's flailing fists.

"We'll talk about this when you're sober – "

"TALK?" My father pushed himself up off the table-top, shaking with impotent fury. "TALK? It's too late for talking, mister! Any fool can see that!" He made another futile lunge, losing his balance long before his swinging fist could make contact.

Wheeling about, infuriated, he plunged back along the cabin to his curtained bunk. When he spun round to face us a moment later, the 10-gauge shotgun was in his hands.

"No! Pa! You can't!"

He took six unsteady steps forward, loading the gun as he came. I heard the silken double click of its hammers with mounting dread. Drunk or sober, my father could handle that gun. Suddenly he was no longer a tottering fool, but a madman with a lethal weapon in his hands.

"Put the gun away, Summerbee – " Shirtless, barefoot and cornered, Matthew Oliver held out a warning hand. "I told you – we'll talk when you're sober."

"I'm sober as I need to be." My father's voice was dangerously quiet now.

"It wasn't Matthew's fault, Pa. You don't know what it was like here last night."

"If you'd been here when you were wanted – " Matthew, too, was becoming angry, despite the toad-brown muzzle of the gun hovering at his chest.

"I had business ashore." My father's voice was thick with liquor, his knuckles white on the hardwood stock of the gun, yet he no longer swayed. He simply stood there, motionless as a rock, a huge and fantastic figure amid the draggled red, white and blue tails of his slowly unwinding flag.

All at once, like a spring wound past breaking point, Matthew Oliver lost his temper.

"You were ashore all right – swilling like a drunken pig while the rest of us worked to save this floating slop-bucket from the fire-raisers! So much for the fearless Ben Summerbee! So much for the famous *Bellflower*, the boat that'll go anywhere there's water! You're a poor joke, Summerbee, like this wreck of a vessel!"

At my father's side I saw the Pastor shake his head till his face was no more than a blur, his cheeks wobbling in horrified alarm. But Pa's finger was already tightening on the trigger.

"By Heaven, I'm goin' to blow your damned head off for that!"

"Pa! Don't you dare do any such thing!"

I was panic-stricken. With my father in this alcoholic, flag-draped rage I could only see one end to the confrontation: at any moment he'd restore his outraged honour by sending Matthew to join his ancestors. I didn't doubt for a second that he'd do it. Pa was capable of anything when that blind rage was on him – I had plenty of bruises to prove it.

Clutching the patched blanket around me, I slid from the bunk and pattered across the floor to stand between them, the muzzle of the gun falling almost between my breasts.

"Katherine Summerbee, what the devil d'you think you're doin'? Get out of my way, an' let me get a clear shot!"

"I will not! If you want to shoot Matthew, you'll have to shoot me first."

"Get away, Katherine!" Disengaging one hand from the gun barrel, my father groped for me unsuccessfully beyond its muzzle. "Eli – drag her aside."

61

"I'll bite," I warned, as the Pastor edged forward.

"This is fam'ly business, Ben." Pastor Bonnet promptly retreated again. "Nothin' to do with me."

"Hide behind a woman's skirts, would you?" I could hear my father grinding his teeth in frustration as he tried to outflank me for a clear shot at Matthew. "You dirty, yellow-livered coward!"

"Matthew's no coward – or you'd have no boat to come back to, after the fire-raising last night." I'd had enough of being treated like a wayward child, and my temper was rising to match my father's. "And besides – I ain't wearin' skirts, as you can see!" Recklessly, I stuck out a bare leg, and the Pastor shuddered.

"Where's your modesty, child!"

"Where'd you learn behaviour like that, girl?" my father cried wrathfully. "Do you want the Pastor to think you encouraged this scoundrel to lay his lustful hands on you?"

"Of course I encouraged him! Though I dare say if you'd come back when you agreed, most likely it wouldn't have happened. So if you're goin' to start laying blame, then I reckon it was your fault as much as anyone's – you and the Pastor."

For a second my father hesitated, and I took advantage of the distraction to lay hold of the end of the shotgun and turn it firmly aside.

"Maybe it's time you realised I'm a grown woman, Pa, and I want the kind of things most women want in their lives. Perhaps I didn't go about it the right way, but that's for me to decide. Now put the gun away, and take this man downriver like you promised."

For a second or two, my father stared from my face to Matthew's and then back again. My connivance in the staining of the Summerbee honour seemed to have struck him a body-blow. "*Babylon!*" I heard him mutter under his breath. "Thou scarlet woman . . ."

"Are you going to take this boat to Pilot Town, or not?" Behind me, Matthew Oliver's voice was cold. "You demanded a big enough price for it yesterday."

At once, my father drew himself up with a hiss of contempt.

"You dishonour my daughter, an' you have the gall to offer me *money*!"

"Now don't you get on your high horse, Ben," the Pastor put in quickly. "Like Katherine said, there ain't nothin' you can do for her now except hope she repents of her wilfulness. This feller hasn't done any more than another healthy young man would have done in his place – an' money's money, when all's said an' done. Better take his while you still can."

I watched my father consider the sense of this, his eyes narrow and his lips pursed. A calculating look had come into his face, and I wondered uneasily what new scheme had been born among the liquor fumes in his brain.

"Just forgive an' forget, Eli? Is that how you see it?"

"Forgive an' forget, Ben."

"An' there's nothin' more I can do for Katherine?"

"Her flower's been well picked, I reckon."

"Maybe so. Maybe so." My father turned back to his passenger. "You still want to go down to the Passes, mister?"

"I have to go. I've no choice."

"The Yankees will be well on their way here by now."

"That's a risk I'll have to run. Will you take the *Bellflower* downriver?"

"I will – since it's so important to you. But you'll find the price has changed some since yesterday."

"That's blackmail! You've no right to ask for more!"

"And you'd no right to do what you did to a stainless child left in your care!"

"That ain't fair, Pa – I'm seventeen today!"

My father ignored me completely. "You'll take my terms, mister, or you'll stay here in New Orleans for the Yankees to find. Nothin' but warships'll be movin' on the river today."

"I don't seem to have any choice, do I?" Matthew said grimly. "You'd better tell me how much you want."

Carelessly, my father twitched the muzzle of the gun out of my grasp, pushed me aside, and trained the weapon squarely on Matthew Oliver's naked chest.

"The Pastor here says there's nothin' I can do to mend matters between you an' Katherine. But I don't see it that way. I reckon if you expect me to save your worthless hide, mister, you'd better give me good reason to do it. Now, if you were to marry my daughter – make a decent woman of her – we could leave for Pilot Town as soon as you were man an' wife."

All of a sudden there was absolute silence in the narrow cabin, except for the murmur of the restive, excited crowd on the levee, swelling and fading beyond our makeshift shelter.

"*Marry* her?" Matthew murmured at last, glancing quickly in my direction.

"That's what I said, mister. Since you two have gone ahead with the honeymoon, you might as well catch up to the marriage. That way

Katherine ain't shamed after all, an' you get a pretty good wife. You'll find she can stack cordwood an' haul water near as fast as a man."

"But I hardly know her!"

He'd made a bad choice of words, and my father leaped on it with indignation.

"Hardly know'd her? Of course you know'd her! The two of you rollin' naked on the bed, an' you expect me to believe you ain't *know'd* her? Hell – what kind of man are you?"

"*And Adam know'd Eve his wife!*" The Pastor was weaving from side to side with excitement. "*An' she conceived – AN' BARE CAIN!*"

"Besides – I'm engaged to be married to a young lady in England," Matthew said quickly, snatching at straws.

"That don't signify!" snapped my father. "So long's you're still a single feller, there ain't nothin' to prevent you marryin' Katherine."

"Dammit man, the Federal ships are almost off the city! There's no time for this kind of nonsense."

"Sure there is! The Pastor here'll do the needful. You're a man of God, Eli – a prayerful man, ain't you? Well then – "

"Don't I get a say in all this?" I couldn't believe Pa was about to marry me off without even asking me once what I wanted.

"The time for speakin' up was last night, girl. Just you get some clothes on your bare backside, if you can do it decently under that blanket – an' comb your hair an' make yourself respectable for your weddin'."

"But Pa—"

"You're insane!" Matthew Oliver stared hotly at my father over the barrel of the 10-gauge. "You don't seriously expect me to – " For an instant his eyes flicked towards mine, and I saw him falter. "I mean – Katherine's a fine girl – but *marriage* – "

"Yes, *marriage*, Mr Shipowner Oliver – between my daughter and a big-talking rogue who's seen fit to take liberties with her. I don't know what you young fellers get up to back in England, but here in the South we take care of the reputation of our womenfolk. You ain't what I'd have chosen for Katherine – not by a long way – but you've spoiled her chances of anything better, an' I'm damn sure you're goin' to make good the harm you've done. You understand me?"

In mutinous silence, Matthew folded his arms across his chest; but his resistance simply made Pa more determined.

"You're goin' to marry that girl, or you can rot in New Orleans till the Federals come, an' I'll take great pleasure in handin' you over to Admiral Farragut – together with whatever you've got packed in those boxes you're so concerned about. Is that clear to you?"

My father paused and glared savagely from face to face.

"Eli – you come here, an' take the gun. If that feller moves a muscle, just shoot. Don't waste time on a warnin'. Right now there's somethin' I have to do."

Laboriously unwinding the flag from his body, he tramped to the forward cabin door, and for several minutes afterwards we heard footsteps and muffled oaths as he busied himself with some project at the fore end of the boiler deck.

2

It wasn't easy to get dressed under such conditions, but somehow I succeeded.

"You don't mean to go through with this charade, do you?" Matthew hissed at me as I struggled into my skirt one-handed. "This ridiculous marriage, I mean."

"You saw the candle," I reminded him. "Last night. The *loa* said there'd be a marriage."

"Oh, for Heaven's sake!"

"You hush up, young feller," commanded the Pastor, working his jaw and rolling his good eye like a great brown marble. "You can talk all you want once she's yours."

To my horror, I noticed Matthew carefully inspecting Pastor Bonnet, clearly wondering if a one-eyed, half-drunk evangelist was capable of hitting his mark.

"Don't try anything with the Pastor," I whispered quickly. "They say he once shot out a man's cigar that was smoking at a revival meetin'. He can see better'n you'd think."

"An' I can hear good, too," growled the Pastor, twitching the gun.

"Call yourself a churchman?" Matthew glared at the man of God. "Whatever happened to *Thou shalt not kill?*"

The Pastor looked stern. "*Whoso findeth a wife findeth a good thing*, friend. That's what it says in the Holy Book. 'Sides – Katherine's a handsome girl when she's cleaned up, you'll see."

"We can't let this go ahead," Matthew muttered to me under cover of reaching for his discarded shirt. "There's a pistol in my coat pocket, but it's out on deck where I left it last night. Could you manage to sneak out for it?"

"No," I whispered back. "Pa'll see me, for sure."

Matthew gave me a hard look – wondering, I dare say, exactly where my loyalties lay in all this.

"Katherine – " With difficulty, he kept his anxiety to a murmur.

"Last night just . . . happened. You do understand that? I never thought . . . I mean, I don't imagine you want me for a husband any more than I want you for a wife."

"What?" Pride drove me to a furious hiss. "Want a low-down, fly-by-night swindler like you for a husband? I should say not!"

I was deeply hurt by his desperate efforts to avoid matrimony. He could have done a great deal worse than marry me, after all. I wasn't stupid: I was passably pretty (or so he'd seemed to think the previous night), and I'd been a virgin until that moment, as he must have realised. Thanks to seventeen years with my father, I was used to a life of lies and swift disappearances – hadn't I saved Matthew himself from the mob, that day in the city? And I'd been happy to share the risks of his escape from New Orleans. In the dark of the night I'd been certain there was . . . well, some feeling between us – and if he thought I'd done more than a lady should do in sharing her favours, he was surely ill placed to object to it.

Yet now, after all that, he was indecently anxious to be rid of me. No wonder I was hurt.

"Matthew Oliver, I'd marry the Devil himself, sooner than you!"

Even as I spoke the words, I knew it wasn't true: if he'd once suggested marriage himself I'd have said *yes – oh, yes* . . . and forgotten all the mistrust and the prickliness in the memory of a boyish, sleeping face . . . of valiant, impossible dreams . . . and a voice murmuring *Katherine* as if it said *my soul* . . .

Matthew Oliver's wife . . . though I knew nothing of being a wife except the sight of my mother's impassive face, all black and yellow bruises and suffering eyes. But because somehow I sensed that such a thing would never happen with Matthew for a husband, and because I had no idea there could be other kinds of torment between a man and a woman, I said no more, and let my father's wrath run its course.

3

My father returned without the flag but wiping his mouth on the back of his hand, which made me think he'd been taking a gulp from some bottle or other he'd kept hidden in a coat pocket. He stared round the cabin, blinking and licking his lips.

"Give me the gun, Eli. Best get on with this weddin' before the Yankees get here."

"Witnesses, Ben – we need another witness to make it legal."

Without turning his head, my father stamped hard on the rough boards of the cabin floor and roared "Sam! Leave the boy to tend the fires, an' get your idle carcass up here right now!" In a moment Sam Duck's frowning face appeared in the doorway.

"Mast-tops, Cap'n Ben, coming round Slaughterhouse Point. Too late to go anywheres now."

"Get in here, Sam, before I kick your backside downstairs."

"Listen to the man, Summerbee!" On the point of leaping to a window, Matthew was halted by a sudden jab from my father's gun. "Farragut's here already! Our only chance is to go now."

"Then we'd best get on with your marriage vows, hadn't we? C'mon, Eli – we ain't got all day."

"Now see here, Ben – maybe it'd be best – " The Pastor shifted nervously from foot to foot.

"JUST SAY THE WORDS, DAMMIT! Ain't you got a bible somewhere?"

Fumbling and tearing at his coat pockets, the Pastor could discover no more than a sheaf of old tracts, their corners curled and grimy. "Best I can do, Ben," he muttered doubtfully.

"GET ON WITH IT, THEN, MAN!" With a great swipe of his hand, my father knocked Sam Duck's hat into the corner of the cabin. "Don't you know better'n that? This is my daughter's weddin' you're at, not some darky dance hall!"

"Brothers an' sisters, we're gathered here today – " The Pastor held the peeling wad of paper before him like the tablets from Mount Sinai.

"Never mind the fancy stuff!" my father commanded. "Stick to the important bits."

"This is ludicrous!" Matthew was unable to contain himself any longer. "We're wasting time on this travesty when we should be off downriver – "

"You hold your tongue!" My father poked him with the gun once more. "Don't open your mouth except to say *I will*, an' I'll tell you when. Go ahead, Eli."

The Pastor groped for the thread of his discourse. "I'm supposed to explain what matri-mony is for, Ben – " he said plaintively.

"Don't you think they KNOW what it's for, muttonhead! Go on to the next bit."

Flustered, the Pastor hesitated again, mentally editing the marriage service. It was only a moment's silence, but it was significant enough: from beyond the windows came the ominous thunder of many paddles thrashing water and the regular beat of iron screws. Nearer to hand, ragged shouts of defiance rose from the crowded levee.

"I guess I ought to ask if anyone knows why the marriage shouldn't

67

go ahead," Eli Bonnet explained with a rush. "I reckon that's important."

"No one's objectin'." My father shot Matthew a warning glare. "Now, get on."

"What's your name, son?" the Pastor demanded of Matthew in a stage whisper. "I can't rightly marry you without it."

"His name's Matthew Oliver," my father put in. "An' you know her name's Katherine, so there's nothin' to stop you now. Face front, you!" For Matthew had turned to glance out of a window, through which the dark bowsprit of a warship could now be seen in mid-river, followed by a foremast and spars and a black, puffing smokestack.

"I told you the Yankees were here, Cap'n." His back towards us, Sam Duck observed the advance of the war fleet.

"Come on, Eli, for any sake!" My father was becoming agitated.

"What did you say this feller's name was?"

I saw my father's mouth open to reply, but all I heard was a sharp explosion from the direction of the river and the evil whine of a bullet passing close over the canvas-covered roof of our cabin. Almost immediately a second shot tore through the flimsy quarter-inch boards of the wall, missing my father by a hair's breadth and splintering the planking behind his head.

"Down!" Matthew Oliver threw himself flat on the floor, dragging me down at his side. With surprising speed, Pastor Bonnet whipped about and scampered for the door, only to be halted by my father's grip on his coat-tails and jerked face down on the floor with the rest of us.

"What in Hell have you done, Ben?" he wailed. "They're shootin' at us out there!"

"He's tied that durned ol' flag to the jackstaff – that's what he's done!" Sam Duck's voice issued furiously from under the table. "He'll get us all killed, for sure."

A distant hail drifted across the water, no doubt warning the *Bellflower* to lower her colours or take the consequences. The opening shots had merely been a taste of what was to come.

"FINISH THE WEDDIN', ELI!" roared my father in an awful voice.

"Haul your flag down, Summerbee!" Matthew shouted at him. "Or there won't be anyone left to marry."

Stubbornly, my father shook the prostrate Pastor like a puppet.

"Will you . . ." mumbled the writer of tracts, and then stopped again.

"MATTHEW, dammit!"

"Will you – Matthew. . . . Oh, to blazes!" The Pastor gasped convulsively. "For the love of God, will you take Katherine for a wife before we all get blowed to Kingdom Come . . ."

"I'm having nothing to do with this – "

Another shot burst through the cabin wall and whined over our heads to *ping* obliquely off the stove chimney. Someone on a Yankee ship was enjoying a little target practice with his Enfield rifle.

"Get your flag down, you madman!"

"Ben – I'm beggin' you. . . . Haul down the flag – " The Pastor was almost weeping with fright.

"NOT TILL HE SAYS HE'LL HAVE HER!"

"Say it, brother, say it!" begged the Pastor.

Still Matthew hesitated.

The next shot shattered the cracked mirror above my bunk, and as the shards tinkled down over the mattress I heard Matthew mutter something indistinct towards the deck-boards.

"HE SAYS HE'LL TAKE HER – YOU HEARD THAT, SAM!"

"K-k-k-Katherine – " The Pastor was on his knees, his forehead pressed into the floor, my father's hand still fastened to his coat-tails.

"Katherine, honey, are you gonna have this – whatever his name is – "

"SHE'LL HAVE HIM!"

"Oh my God, Ben – there ain't a ring!" The Pastor raised his face from the dusty boards, petrified by calamity. "We forgot the ring!"

This time a whole salvo of shots spattered the superstructure of the *Bellflower*, and I heard poor, half-witted Luke whimpering somewhere on the deck below.

"I guess I don't need a ring, Pa," I conceded hastily.

"You can wear your ma's, if we ever find it."

"*Will you get that flag down now?*"

"Reckon you've said enough, Eli?"

"Oh, that's them wed, Ben." The Pastor had already begun to scuffle away on hands and knees. "Like the Prayer Book says – God's joined 'em together, ain't no one gonna unstick 'em now."

Eli Bonnet had almost reached the door when my father flung himself over his retreating legs and dragged him back into the cabin.

"Where's the certificate?"

"Ben, I gotta get out of here – "

"Write—" My father thrust a stub of crayon and the back of one of the Pastor's own tracts into his hands. "Write how it's all legal."

"Ben—"

"Write!"

Once more the warship hailed us, unheeded, across the water.

For a few desperate seconds the Pastor moaned and scribbled, then thrust the crumpled paper into my father's hands and crawled madly for the cabin door. My father sucked the crayon and solemnly printed his name at the foot of the paper before sliding it under the table to Sam Duck.

"Put your mark, boy." Sam scratched with the crayon. "Here, gal, you keep this. You're a married woman now, but you might need it to keep hold of that slippery customer you've picked."

I thrust the paper, unread, into the pocket of my skirt – with some difficulty, since I was lying as flat as I could on the cabin floor. My father clambered heavily to his feet, dusted himself down and straightened his cap. The peril of the situation seemed to have had a marvellously sobering effect on him.

"Now I'm goin' to settle things with that Yankee gunboat that's makin' matchwood of my vessel." Shotgun in hand, he stalked out of the cabin.

"Pa!" My father gave no sign that he'd heard me, and I clutched Matthew by the arm. "He's going to do something stupid – I know it."

"Stay where you are." Matthew pressed me back to the floor. "I'll go out and take a look."

"I'm coming with you." I could hear my father's heavy tread over our heads now, pacing with remarkable steadiness along the paint-and-canvas roof he insisted on calling the "hurricane deck" towards the rickety wooden hutch which served the *Bellflower* for a wheelhouse.

"I knew this would happen. This time the whiskey's driven him clean off his head," mourned Sam Duck from under the table. "Crazy old man! He's gonna get us blowed right out of the water!"

Matthew was already moving at a crouch towards the aft cabin door. Ignoring his instructions, I set off after him with some vague idea that if we really were going to be blown up, it was my duty as a married woman to be blasted skywards at my husband's side.

4

My hands and knees were a mass of splinters by the time I was able to peer cautiously round the edge of the door.

For the first time, the full horror of the war was brought home to me. Until then it had always been something apart from us – something to deplore at a distance without ever being touched by the stark, awful truth of death and destruction. Now it seemed as if reality had replaced all the alarms and fears with something ten times more terrible.

The river – the broad Mississippi which only the previous day had seemed so peaceful and empty – had suddenly filled with great, grim warships, passing in solemn line astern past the waterfront of the helpless city. These were no graceful, winged merchant vessels, but dark beasts of battle, their squat masts criss-crossed by heavy spars, their black smokestacks surrounded by thick cages of rigging. Ugly gun-mouths gaped from ports in massive black-and-white sides; along the flanks of the larger vessels, the smaller gunships slunk like wolves – it was evidently the first of these which had fired on the Confederate flag flying defiantly over the *Bellflower*.

On they came, black-hulled and ominous, those battered veterans of conflict, the rail of every ship lined with silent men gazing at the city which was their prize of war. All along the levee, the crowd whooped and howled with rage, flinging futile insults across the intervening stretch of water; and between those two opposing forces lay the little *Bellflower*, stubbornly flying her outsize flag to mark my father's drunken transformation into passionate Southern patriot.

By raising myself into a half-crouch I could see him standing at our wheelhouse, shoulders set, his head flung back, loudly defying Farragut, Lincoln and the Union – all the infamous rogues who had dared to keep Ben Summerbee from earning his God-given livelihood. The nearest gunboat had just threatened through its loud-hailer to send a boarding party to haul down our flag, and I heard my father yell back, daring them to try.

Overhead, the sky had darkened significantly and the first heavy drops of rain began to splash down, dark spots on the bleached wood of our deck. For a few minutes there was no response from the gunboat; I guessed the Admiral's orders had been to avoid any provocative incident. But their very silence seemed to spur my father on to greater rashness. Springing forward to the edge of the cabin roof, he pointed to the jackstaff where the great red, white and blue flag stirred gently in the breeze. With his arms wide, he roared out his challenge – let Farragut's boys take the flag by force if they thought they could. . . . Then all at once I heard the greater, sharper roar of Enfield rifles out in the river.

The first shot knocked Pa backwards, lifting him off his feet and wresting the gun from his grasp. Before he could even fall to the deck a second bullet found him, snapping his body like a broken twig as its momentum catapulted him from his perch, limbs outflung, far beyond the boat's side into the rain-pocked river.

Chapter Six

1

A warning to the rest, I suppose the Yankees would have called it: better one madman shot down than half a city in uproar. Everyone on our part of the levee had seen my father fall and knew beyond doubt that the Federal ships meant business. If New Orleans tried to defy the Union, the city would be shelled into submission just as my father's voice had been summarily silenced.

In the first, horrified shock of it all I hadn't even noticed Sam Duck crawl after me to the cabin door. I was still on my knees, staring stupidly at the patch of clear deck where my father had stood only seconds before, when Sam pushed past me and with a great moan of distress hurled himself headlong towards the stairway to the lower deck.

"Crazy ol' man! What've you done now?"

"Are you all right, Kate?" Matthew glanced back from the shelter of *Bellflower*'s yawl. I nodded, too numb with disbelief to take in what had happened. All along the levee the crowd, too, had fallen into sudden, astounded silence.

"Go down and see if anything can be done for your father." Matthew's voice was grim, his eyes fixed on the nearest warships. "I'll go forward and lower the flag. Maybe that'll satisfy them."

Blindly, I stumbled down to the lower deck, where Sam Duck, with Luke's help, was fishing with a boat-hook over the *Bellflower*'s guard; a few feet away I could see my father wallowing on his back among the fetid litter of the river's edge.

Hours later, I learned what had taken place above our heads while we struggled with the wounded man – how Matthew Oliver had slowly and deliberately walked out along the rain-splashed boiler deck in full view of the Yankee marksmen, and calmly unfastened the cords which held the huge flag to our jackstaff. At the time I knew nothing of his courage, entirely absorbed as I was in dragging Pa, white-faced and moaning, alongside the *Bellflower*. I didn't even notice the ragged cheer which went up from the nearest warships as the Confederate flag was finally lowered over our vessel.

By the time Matthew came below with the bedraggled flag over his arm and Pa's 10-gauge in his hand, Sam and Luke had managed to haul my father aboard – with difficulty, since he was a heavy man – and had laid him as gently as they could in a sheltered spot near the fireboxes, out of the rain now sluicing down around the *Bellflower*. He was barely conscious, but clawing feebly at a round wound just below his ribs which was oozing blood into his soaking shirt.

Bullet wounds were beyond my simple medical experience. All I could think of was to stop the flow of blood from his chest and the freely bleeding hole in his thigh, but after pressing as firmly as I dared with the towels Luke brought from the cabin, I'd come to the end of my resources.

Pa had never suffered a day's illness in his life, too vigorous and stubborn to succumb to anything worse than a drunkard's headache. To see him now, lying helpless on the damp boards of our deck, his reddish curls matted to his head and stark fear in his eyes, was enough to rob me of sensible thought. Down in the river, a slimy blue-green spiral of potato skin had become tangled in his hair, and the sight of it outraged me; I flew at it with furious fingers, picking at the jelly-like coil as if its removal would be enough to save his life . . .

"Please allow me . . .". A precise, Germanic voice spoke at my ear. "Please . . . I am a doctor of medicine."

Dark, gentle hands disengaged mine as Sam Duck drew me aside, allowing the bespectacled man who'd materialised from the crowd on the levee to take my place. He'd come aboard with the river pilot Linus Ransome, Louis Boudreaux's superior, who'd watched the drama aboard the *Bellflower* with growing alarm.

"Your father's a brave man, I'll say that for him, Katherine . . .". The stocky pilot shook his head as if adequate words escaped him. "But to try to face down the whole Union fleet – that ain't the act of a sane man."

"He'd been drinking, Mr Ransome. You know how he is. And he was mad as a hornet at being cooped up in New Orleans. He reckoned the Yankees had taken away his living."

"Mine too, until the steamers run again. Hannah says I'm like a bear with a sore head these days."

In anxious silence we watched the bent black back of the doctor as he methodically examined my father's wounds to the accompaniment of tut-tuttings and hissings of breath. After a few minutes, the little doctor straightened up, pushed his spectacles thoughtfully to the bridge of his nose, and stepped across the deck to join us.

"Is Pa going to live, Doctor?"

"The first bullet passed quite cleanly through the flesh of the thigh, which is good." The doctor nodded, and tugged his goatee beard. "Unfortunately the second bullet remains in the chest cavity, and must be removed as soon as possible if your father is to recover." He gazed with some distaste round the soiled deck of the *Bellflower*. "It is impossible for me to do such a thing here – on this dirty boat, you understand. Already, it's my belief the patient is in more danger from that filth – " the doctor pointed towards the offal-strewn water which slopped between the *Bellflower* and the shore "– than from his wounds. Poison to the blood. Most pernicious."

"Then we can move him from here?" Linus Ransome put in.

"Most certainly, with care."

"Well then, he can come home with me, and Hannah can look after him. The house is quite near. A handcart would do it in a few minutes."

"Excellent. I shall need the most strictly clean conditions for the removal of the bullet."

The pilot smiled ruefully. "Dr Heinrich, I guarantee you won't find a single speck of dust in Hannah Ransome's house. Don't let her catch you lookin' for one, either."

"Doctor – " I laid a hand on the physician's sleeve. "I don't have the money to pay you for all this – though I'm sure Pa will find it when he's well again, if you can wait for trade to pick up."

Dr Heinrich stared at me severely through his spectacles. "Young lady, I'm a doctor of medicine, not a boot-maker or a seller of nails. I don't put a price on the saving of human life, especially the life of a brave man. My eldest boy fought at Shiloh – but he did not return."

Silently blessing Providence that a ducking in the river had washed away the rank smell of whiskey which had clung to my father ever since his night ashore, I dispatched Luke to find a handcart, while the doctor returned with fastidious dignity to his patient's side.

2

New wife that I was, I'd completely forgotten about Matthew. I only remembered his existence with a guilty start when I caught sight of him standing a little distance away, still holding the flag and the shotgun, watching the scene stony-faced.

I almost ran towards him. "Pa's going to get well again, the doctor says, once the bullet's out of his chest." Relief had made me thoughtless: I'd put down Matthew's sombre mood solely to concern for my father.

He attempted a fleeting smile.

"Good."

For a moment his continued gloom puzzled me; and then I remembered the five wooden boxes pushed out of sight under my bunk in the cabin.

"Oh, Matthew – you should have been far away from here by now, or at least on your way downriver!"

He shrugged. "It's too late to worry about that."

"But suppose men from those Federal ships decide to search the *Bellflower* after what Pa did? Suppose they find the boxes of guns? Oh, Matthew – maybe you should throw them into the river after all. Anything's better than being put in jail!"

"Something wrong, Katherine?" Frowning, Linus Ransome came across to join us.

"Don't worry," I assured Matthew, "Mr Ransome's an old friend of Pa's. He doesn't have any particular love for the Yankees either." Quickly, I explained to the pilot how Pa had been supposed to take Matthew downriver the previous night.

Linus Ransome grinned. "That's always been Ben's trouble. More grit than most – and a bigger thirst to go along with it. This time it's put him in a hole he can't get out of." He turned to Matthew. "But he's left you in a heap of difficulty, young man. You'd be well advised to heave your Confederate guns over the side, an' lose yourself ashore."

"Maybe so . . . if there were only guns in those boxes." Matthew's eyes met mine in mute apology.

"What's in 'em, then, if it ain't guns?"

Matthew took a breath, hesitated, and then apparently decided he'd no choice but to confide in us. "Come up to the cabin for a moment."

"But Pa could be . . ." I stopped, confused, my loyalties divided. "The handcart could be here in a second."

"Please, Katherine." Matthew glanced bleakly at the line of warships anchoring in the river. "Farragut's making himself at home out there now. Once his men come ashore, it'll be too late for me. I have to get away from here, and find a hiding place for the boxes."

"Go on then, young man." Linus Ransome had been studying Matthew intently. "Let's see whatever it is you're so concerned about. Ben's going nowhere right now, and Sam can tell us when Luke gets back with the cart."

3

The five wooden crates were still under the bunk where we'd slept the previous night. Kneeling, Matthew laid hold of the nearest and heaved it out into the middle of the floor before thrusting a small key into its double padlocks. The lid swung open with a pained squeal, and for the second time that day I gaped like a fool. Four small, pitted yellow ingots filled the wooden rim as perfectly as tiles in a frame. I could almost believe they were tiles, so innocent did they look – almost humdrum, as if their sheer quantity made them commonplace instead of infinitely precious.

"Gold!" Linus Ransome whistled softly in amazement. "Bar bullion."

"Half a million dollars' worth of Confederate funds, between the five boxes. And I wish to Heaven I'd never seen any of it." With a sigh, Matthew slammed the lid and locked the box again.

"Did that come from the New Orleans banks?" The pilot gestured towards the gold. "I thought all their bullion had gone to Richmond."

"The rest of it did. But not this. I've undertaken to carry this half-million to England, to keep the Confederate agents in funds."

"Then you aren't a card-sharp?" I demanded suddenly. "You don't work the riverboats after all?"

"No, Katherine, I'm afraid not."

I stared at him, my wits reeling. All I could think of was that he'd turned out to have no profession at all, this vagabond I'd married.

"How were you going to ship out the gold?" Linus Ransome returned to practicalities.

"There's a steamship – the *Vixen* – waiting for me at the Gulf. We sailed from Havana to look for cotton in New Orleans, since the Federals have got Wilmington and Charleston so well bottled up these days."

Matthew shook his head over the irony of the situation. "No wonder we had such a clear run through the Gulf! Farragut's fleet were all at Ship Island, preparing to cross the Mississippi bar. If we hadn't got wind of them off Pilot Town and ducked into West Bay, things might have turned out badly for the *Vixen*. As it was, I came ashore myself and let the ship go on to Galveston."

"Is there much cotton in Galveston?" the pilot wanted to know.

"It's hard to find a full cargo. That's the only reason I agreed to take this gold when the *Vixen* returned to pick me up." Matthew made a rueful face. "At the time it seemed worth the risk. The *Vixen* can outrun anything the Federal navy might send after her, and I reckoned I could move the gold down to the Gulf overland while Farragut was busy at the mouth of the river. Then all of a sudden the Federals were over the bar and shelling the forts – and the riverbanks were alive with armed men. The best plan seemed to be to smuggle the bullion downriver – the last thing the Federals would expect. The *Bellflower* was just what I needed for the trip. No one would have given her a second glance."

"Except that Ben smelled liquor, and went ashore instead." Linus Ransome shook his head and sighed. "It's too bad he didn't think of going down through the bayous to Barataria Bay. Fort Livingston's still in Confederate hands, I hear – and anyway, no Federal ship drawing more than seven feet could get into the bay from seaward, even supposing she could run past the fort. Once you'd reached Grand Isle, one of the fishermen down there would have taken you out to the *Vixen*."

Without thinking, I remarked, "You must know the bayous pretty well, Mr Ransome."

"I knew them well enough as a boy. I guess I could still find my way to Barataria Bay if I had to."

"What about now – today?" Matthew's voice had come alive with new hope. "Could you find your way through the bayous in the *Bellflower*, do you think?"

"With the river full of Federal ships?" I was appalled at Matthew's recklessness. "You saw what happened to Pa, didn't you?"

"Maybe that's something in our favour, Katherine." Linus Ransome raised his head thoughtfully. "Maybe now your pa's been shot and his flag hauled down, the Yankees will reckon *Bellflower*'s learned her lesson." He paused for a moment to glance out of the nearest window towards the warships taking up station in the river. "Right now, those fellers have got their minds set on seeing the Union flag flying over City Hall. I reckon if we were to go now – if we were to go off slowly *up*river – no one would bother us."

"*Up*river?" Matthew frowned. "What good would that do?"

"We'd go upriver about eight miles, as far as McCarty's Point. Directly opposite is the mouth of the Bayou St James, which leads into Bayou Segnette and on down to Barataria Bay. With the river as high as it is now, the *Bellflower* could slide through the smallest channels with no trouble at all."

"And you're willing to risk it?" Matthew's eyes shone with eagerness.

"I am – but not for your sake, young feller. I'd be doin' it for Ben – and because there's Confederate bullion in those boxes. I'd hate to see that gold turned into Federal guns to shoot down more of our poor boys."

"When do we leave?" Matthew got to his feet.

"Seems to me there's one point you've missed, young man." The pilot's expression remained stern. "The *Bellflower* belongs to Ben Summerbee – not to you, or to me. And while Ben's laid up, it's Katherine here who has to agree to the trip." He turned to me. "It's your decision, Katherine. If you think it's too much of a risk, well then, no one can fault you. But if you'll lend us the boat, I'll do my best to keep her in one piece and bring her back as soon as I can. Hannah will take care of you and your pa while I'm away."

He was waiting for me to speak, to give my blessing to the whole crazy business. Yet I'd already forgotten all about the boxes of gold. All I could think of was that Matthew Oliver – the man I'd married not an hour earlier – was leaving for England, and I wasn't expected to go with him.

"Matthew – "

Linus Ransome glanced between our faces. Without knowing the cause, he'd guessed there was more to the matter than could be discussed in his presence.

"You two talk it through, and let me know what you decide." He turned, dusted off his cap against his thigh, and headed for the door.

Matthew rounded on me as soon as we were alone.

"Kate, if I don't go, the Federals will put me in jail."

"Perhaps we could hide away somewhere, and take the gold with us. . . . Out in the bayous, maybe – there are places out there no one ever goes."

Matthew shook his head.

"The gold is needed in England. I gave my word I'd take it there."

"Then put the boxes aboard your ship, and come back here yourself."

"That's impossible, Kate."

"But how can I go to England with you, Matthew? Oh, I know what I've said about Pa in the past, but I'm all he's got in the world. Someone has to stay here and see he gets well again. I can't just walk out and leave him. I can't, Matthew – not yet."

My eyes were beginning to prick with tears, but I couldn't see any solution to the hideous mess we'd created. Thanks to Pa and the Pastor I'd become Matthew's wife, whether he'd wanted me or not, and I was determined to show him what a good wife I could be. Clearly, it was my duty to go to Havana with him on the *Vixen*, if that was where he was bound, and then on to England . . .

Yet I couldn't leave Pa – not in his present state.

Across the small cabin, I gazed at the man who was my husband . . . one flesh with my own. For all we'd shared the previous night, we were still virtual strangers, united only by the home-made certificate rustling stiffly in my skirt pocket. I didn't want us to be dragged apart so soon – not with Matthew still nursing resentment of a marriage he'd never wanted, a marriage which pinched and flapped like an ill-fitting shoe. If he'd only give me a few weeks – a few days, even, to show him how it could be . . . the two of us, together . . .

All I had to do was say *no*. I had only to insist that Pa would never allow the *Bellflower* to stir from the levee without him, and Matthew would be trapped with me in New Orleans. That way, I'd gain a precious few days for talking and making plans for the future we'd vowed to share. . . .

And then I remembered. If things went wrong, Matthew would spend a good part of that future in a Federal jail.

"Kate – please." Matthew himself broke in on my thoughts. "Last night you promised you'd help me, if I asked."

From the deck below, I heard Sam Duck's voice.

"Miss Ka-a-ate! Luke's back with the cart! You coming to Mr Ransome's house, or what?"

"Kate – "

He'd taken to calling me *Kate*, though if anyone was entitled to do it, I guess he was.

"Kate – " He gathered me into his arms, and held me close. "I don't want to leave you behind, but I've no choice. And you must stay with your father – I understand that."

"You do?"

"Of course. He needs you more than I do."

It occurred to me resentfully that Matthew was being more generous than I'd have liked.

"Maybe if Hannah Ransome was prepared to—"

"No, Kate. Even if you could leave your father, anything might happen on the way back to Havana. The *Vixen* might be fired on, or chased – who knows? You'll have to stay here . . . for now."

"If you say so." I hoped that sounded like wifely devotion.

"And in the meantime – you'll let us take the *Bellflower*?"

I remained silent. I couldn't bring myself to say the words that would send him away.

"Miss Ka-a-ate!"

"Please, Kate . . ." He sounded impatient. "Do you want to see your husband dragged off to a Federal prison?"

"No! Oh Matthew, no! I'd never forgive myself if you were arrested. Of course you must go! Take the *Bellflower*," I said quickly. "If Sam and Luke are willing to go along, take the *Bellflower*, but please – please be careful." I looked up into his face, drawing comfort from the relief in his eyes. "Matthew . . . I love you . . ."

Many times afterwards, I tried to analyse the expression on his face at that moment. Startled – fearful – guilty – bewildered: it was all of those things, and more.

Clasped in his arms, my face tilted up to his, I was taken aback. Whatever I'd expected at that moment, it wasn't the sudden unshuttering, the violent throwing open of darkened windows I'd seen. But before I could speak, he'd bent his head to mine, blotting out the light between us.

The kiss began badly – awkwardly – as if something had made us complete strangers once more. Yet a little of that devilish madness of the previous night must have remained in our veins, since our lips had hardly met, warm and self-conscious, when the sudden, fierce longing which had possessed us then united us once more. It was a yearning of the flesh – we'd never had time to learn the language of affection – and yet with its release came a wholeness, a completeness which seemed to do away with all doubt.

"Come on, Kate! What's keeping you?" Linus Ransome's voice drifted up from below.

"Write to me," I instructed him anxiously. "As soon as you're safe in England, write to me – and when Pa's better I'll come and join you, wherever you are."

"Oh . . . yes."

All of a sudden, I wanted Matthew to have physical proof of the bond between us. The Pastor's certificate was still in the pocket of my skirt, and now I pulled it out.

"You'd better take this."

Without a word, he accepted the paper and folded it away into his coat pocket. For a moment he simply stood there, gazing at me as if trying to fix my image in his mind.

"Kate – " he began softly, and then shook his head. "Not now, it isn't the time. Look – " He dug in a waistcoat pocket. "I want you to have this. As a keepsake."

He thrust an object into my hand – something cold and smooth, with a short length of chain attached to it. When I opened my fingers, his watch lay in my palm, in all its engraved gold magnificence.

"It's yours now," he said.

80

"I'll keep it until I see you again."

"Ka-a-ate! Come on!"

"Goodbye, Matthew. And – oh, please take care." Before he could answer, I sped out of the cabin, the watch in my hand, to follow Pa's handcart to my temporary home.

4

Seven days passed before Linus Ransome brought the *Bellflower* back to New Orleans, and by that time every part of my life had begun to go so disastrously wrong that I was sure, in spite of all Hannah Ransome's reassurances, that neither her husband nor Matthew could have survived the journey to Barataria Bay.

"Never saw a Yankee the whole way," the pilot reported. "Plenty of trigger-happy Southern boys ready to bang a shot through the boat, though, thinking we were part of Farragut's fleet." He nodded at the memory. "And we almost got lost a couple of times. I was quite pleased to see Barataria Bay, I can tell you, and to send that young feller of yours off in a boat to the *Vixen* with his precious boxes. I reckon he'll be safely in Havana by now – or even on his way back to England."

Linus Ransome had said "young feller", not "husband", I realised with a pang of disappointment. I could tell from the pilot's account of his journey through the bayous that Matthew had said no more to Linus than I'd confided to his wife. But perhaps it was just as well. Hannah Ransome's views on decency were even narrower than Pa's, and while we were dependent on the Ransomes for nursing and shelter, I didn't dare scandalise her with the details of my hasty wedding.

In the darkness of the night, I blessed whatever power had led Matthew and his boxes of gold safely clear of the Mississippi. He'd cheated that Federal jail – yet the knowledge that every passing hour put more miles between us only added to my sense of impending disaster and loneliness. I found myself missing him dreadfully – missing his quick, darting glance – the sureness and pride which drove him – the unexpected glory of his secret dreams.

Now that we were apart, I understood the tension that had existed between us from the first moment we'd set eyes on one another. The very air had crackled with the prospect of battle – hard-fought and with no quarter given, Matthew Oliver's armoured arrogance against all the scorn of my seventeen years. And, like perfectly matched foes, we'd found ourselves falling half in love, danger only adding relish to the discovery.

Except that now that Matthew had gone from me I knew I was no longer half in love, but hopelessly lost to my enemy. By chance I'd glimpsed another Matthew – less sure, less proud – a shadow-creature against whom I'd been utterly defenceless. Now I was certain with all the passion of my soul that our marriage had not come about by accident. Monsieur Agasu – or Fate – or the Pastor's inflexible God – had surely intended us for one another, and would bring us together once more.

Through the days that followed, I clung desperately to that belief and to Matthew's gold watch, the token of his own faith in our eventual reunion. But with nothing but his memory to sustain me I felt frighteningly, achingly alone.

For three days after the shooting, my father appeared to recover his strength quickly. As soon as we were installed in the pilot's house, Dr Heinrich removed the second bullet as he'd promised, assisted by Hannah Ransome, whose ideas of cleanliness passed even his own stringent requirements. Next day my father was already well enough to grumble about the *Bellflower*'s being dispatched to Barataria Bay without him, until Hannah lost patience and pointed out tartly that it was his own weakness for liquor which had made the journey necessary at all.

Two days later Pa woke with a sore throat, which made it difficult to swallow the bread cut fresh from Hannah's oven. The Federals had brought in supplies of meat and flour; the loaf was wonderfully soft and doughy, and I was puzzled to find that by three o'clock in the afternoon Pa couldn't even chew it properly. By evening his speech was slurred, and he had difficulty in opening his mouth wide enough to admit a spoonful of broth.

Next morning, when he was unable to turn his head on the pillow, I hurried at once to find Dr Heinrich.

"This is exactly what I feared," he told me. "Poison has entered his body through his wounds. This is tetanus, Miss Summerbee. Do you know what that is? Lockjaw."

Even I, medical innocent that I was, had heard of lockjaw.

My father had received a death sentence, and he knew it. One glance at the strained faces round his bed and a few moments of our forced cheerfulness had been enough to confirm his worst fears. Yet he made no concessions even then. Ben Summerbee had already made up his mind to meet death as he had met every other event in his haphazard life – head-on, and as stubbornly as he knew how.

"Katherine – " he hissed, as soon as the doctor had left and we were alone. "Why the devil didn't you go after that husband of yours?"

I had to put my ear to his lips to understand the distorted syllables, but eventually his meaning was clear.

"I had to stay here to look after you."

"Shhhhoot!" My father hissed his impatience. "You little fool! You should never have let him go without you! A man like that. . . . Don't trust him out of your sight."

"Then why did you make me marry him?" I cried in a passion, outraged by such disloyalty to Matthew.

My father glared at me. "Decently wed!" he gasped indignantly. "My daughter – decently wed!" His hand twitched on the sheet. "Go an' find him. Go to England, soon's you can."

"I won't leave you."

"Soon." The answer was a desperate hiss. "Whatever he calls himself, he's Adam Gaunt's son. He even looks like him, dammit! Don't wait here – go an' find him. Make him . . . Make . . ."

My father's words became unintelligible, no more than a spasm of grating breath through rigid jaws. To my horror, I saw his head draw back as his body stiffened and his spine began to arch convulsively until it seemed that he was supported on the bed only by his head and his heels. His face was chalk white, his eyes almost starting from their sockets with the agony of fighting for breath, but it was the tears that frightened me more than anything – great tears of anguish coursing down the cheeks of a man who'd never given way to anything in his whole, obstinate existence.

In blind panic I shouted for Hannah Ransome to come – to do whatever she could to ease his pain, to dry those obscene tears I couldn't bear to watch. Gradually the convulsion subsided, and Dr Heinrich came with belladonna and quinine, and sulphate of soda – though where he managed to find these things in the drug-starved South was a mystery.

My father should be kept absolutely quiet in a darkened room, the doctor instructed, free from anything that might agitate him. Yet in spite of our precautions, next day he had several more convulsions, and on the day after that the spasms were almost hourly until they began to run into one another in a continuous, drawn-out torment of near-strangulation and agonising cramps which gripped every muscle, twisting and rending his body, sinew by straining sinew.

By the time Linus Ransome brought the *Bellflower* back to New Orleans, my father was very close to the end, his lips drawn back in the rigid, grinning mask which characterised his illness. Next day he died, exhausted but fully aware, killed by a final, throttling convulsion which seemed to last for ever – and, if Dr Heinrich was right, by the foulness of the river which had given him life.

5

"What'll you do now, my dear?"

Hannah Ransome eyed me severely from her rocking chair, though I realised she'd done her best to adopt a tone of kindly enquiry. My feelings still had to be considered: after all, we'd only just seen Pa's body lowered into a damp, brick-lined hole in the swampy cemetery ground, from where it would soon sink away into the underlying marsh – a pauper's burial, but the best I could afford.

"Not that I want to hurry you away," Hannah added carefully. "You know you're welcome to stay here until your mind's made up. I was just wondering if you had family somewhere who would take you."

There was no one, of course: I knew that only too well. My father had long since cut himself off from any family he'd ever had – with bad feeling on both sides, no doubt – and goodness only knew what had become of my mother's father, the wandering pedlar who'd turned his lame daughter into a fifty-dollar sale.

I had no family at all – but what did that matter? I had Matthew, my husband and my future, whose fancy gold watch nestled under my pillow each night just as his beloved image nestled in my heart. Matthew must still be on the high seas, with no notion that Pa had died, and I was alone in the world except for him. It would be at least another two or three weeks before he reached Liverpool and safety, while I . . . would be thousands of miles away, in New Orleans.

I'd urged him to write to me, but letters were hard to come by since the start of the war. Matthew would know where to find me, but his letters might never arrive. If the war dragged on for months – or even years – we mightn't meet again until it was over, or even exchange a word . . . and that was unthinkable.

If Matthew couldn't come to me, I would have to follow him to England.

Yet to set out from New Orleans was no guarantee of finding my way to England. Even if I managed to reach a port such as Wilmington or Charleston on the eastern seaboard of America, the only way of sailing from the Confederate States was aboard a blockade runner like the *Vixen*, if I could find a vessel prepared to carry passengers as it darted through the line of patrolling warships.

And the city of Liverpool sounded very big. Even if I reached that distant seaport, how easy would it be to find one man in its teeming

84

streets? All I knew was the name of Matthew's ship. I'd have to hope that someone in the docks would be able to direct me to his home.

And what if I never reached Liverpool, but became trapped by the war in some beleaguered town on my way across the Confederacy? At least if I remained in New Orleans, Matthew would know where his wife was to be found.

But even while I wrestled with the problem, the time for decision-making was running out. General Benjamin Butler had swiftly taken over command of the city from Admiral Farragut, installing himself in the splendour of the St Charles Hotel and granting women and children a bare two weeks to leave – presuming, of course, they had somewhere to go. If I wanted to follow Matthew to England, I'd have to set out at once or finally be imprisoned in New Orleans for as long as the war might last.

All that night I lay sleepless, hugging Matthew's gold watch to my breasts, my fingers twined round its warm smoothness. If only the enigmatic, enamelled face would offer me an answer . . . tell me what I ought to do.

In the half-light of dawn I wound the watch with careful absorption, fascinated by the inner dial of heavenly constellations, wondering if Sam Duck, with his understanding of the spirits of the night, could read a message for me among those inlaid stars.

At last, for the sake of the Ransomes' feelings, I invented an aunt in Wilmington, and made swift preparations to join her there. With Linus Ransome's help I managed to dispose of the *Bellflower*, though with trade gone from the Mississippi I didn't so much sell the boat as persuade someone to take her off my hands. It seemed a betrayal, after all she'd been to me: I stood desolate on the dockside amid the pathetic clutter of belongings which was all that remained of my life aboard her, hiding the modest roll of dollars I'd received for her against a fold of my skirt. The boat looked suddenly forlorn, like a scruffy old dog unfairly shut out of doors, and I turned on my heel and walked quickly away, not daring to glance back at her.

Feeling desperately guilty, I paid Sam Duck and Luke rather more than I could afford out of the proceeds of the sale, and watched them disappear into the verandah-hung streets of the old quarter, Sam leading the way and Luke shambling happily at his heels. Sam Duck was well known among the free people of colour in the city; with the Federals in charge he was as good as free himself, and I was sure that when river traffic ran once more up and down the Mississippi, Sam would quickly find work as an engineer – a free, well-paid engineer – and I trusted him to take care of Luke as he'd promised.

Carefully, I counted the money I had left. I'd worked out how much I might need for my travel and lodgings on the long trip to England, and now added another fifty dollars for safety's sake. That would be my emergency fund: it left me with very little for unforeseen expenses, but the thought of finding myself penniless in a strange place was too dreadful to contemplate.

Hannah Ransome had pursed her lips over my decision to leave for Wilmington, but she didn't try to talk me out of it. Her own children had long since grown up and left home, and I sensed that the prospect of having a motherless, fatherless and apparently rootless young woman in her home for an indefinite period was the last thing she wanted. With a dry peck on my cheek, she managed to smile as she waved me goodbye.

The railroads were still running – Pa's hated railroads – their much-vaunted schedules now given over to the business of moving troops and supplies across the South. The train which carried me out of the city was crowded with refugees damning the eyes of the blue-bellies and assuring one another they'd return in triumph before long, and as we moved further from New Orleans and Butler's Federal troops, their mood became more belligerent still. Whenever we passed a troop of grey-coated cavalry or an ambling company of volunteers, a cheer went up from the railroad cars for the brave boys who'd soon send the Yankees away with their tails between their legs.

The trains belonged to the soldiery in these days of war; civilians were made courteously aware they'd be accommodated with a place – if one was available – on a train – if one happened to be going in the right direction – whenever it suited the military authorities to let them travel. Beyond that, we should have to shift for ourselves, sitting on our boxes and bags in wayside stations while eager recruits were packed aboard with all their shining, rattling tackle.

They were so often no more than boys, those newborn soldiers; yet a few weeks would weather them to match the straggling lines of veterans I'd seen from railroad windows, shorn of everything but a blanket, a rifle and the most basic of rations, often no more than a lump of fat bacon speared on the end of a bayonet.

Here at last was the war, or its anteroom: a procession of dust-streaked, shuddering ambulances, heavy with their jolting burden of pain and hopelessness; roads deserted but for cart-tracks, a thousand footprints in the dust and blackened circles under the trees where two or three had turned aside to brew coffee; a path beaten along the soft verge where the footsore or bootless had preferred to walk, a discarded cap or a muddied blanket . . . or a grave, with no more than a patch of turned soil to show where some nameless rifleman had lost the ultimate battle.

Blue or Grey. . . . My loyalties should have lain with the Confederacy, considering the manner of my father's death. But I was a river child, neither of North nor South, and though Pa was dead, countless other fathers and brothers and husbands had also died, and would go on dying until the end of that wretched war of pride and principle.

I developed the habit of glancing from face to face in the railroad cars – examining the women, particularly. Wars, it seemed to me, were the projects of men, not of women, who find it hard to die for abstractions. A woman will fight to the death, and with less scruple than a man, but only for what lies under her hand – her children, her home, her mate if she loves him even a little. In this man's war the women waited at home or in endless railroad cars, searching the faces of other mothers' sons and wondering when they, too, would have to tend the broken wreckage that battle had been pleased to return.

And yet the whole business seemed like the falling out of two brothers who'd taken off their coats in order to resolve matters with their fists in the yard.

Travelling from place to place on the *Bellflower* we'd dealt with Louisiana folk one day and Pennsylvanians a couple of months later – and dealt differently with North and South, because we understood that the brothers were different in the way they expected to live their lives and in the things which were important to them. The keeping of slaves, I'd come to realise, was only the most obvious sign of that difference.

Up north, people were quick and dry, always pushing on, doing business, building, making, working, inventing. . . . And it had never been like that in the South, where the summers were mostly too hot for such insect-like busyness. Southern feelings ran slow and deep. What Southern folk prized was the way things had always been done: respect and tradition, and everyone having their place in the scheme of things. The white folks had their place, the quadroons had theirs, and the slaves had another – and it seemed to the Confederates that if they didn't stick to their own way of living, the world as they knew it would come to an end. That was important even to those Southerners who didn't hold with slavery: no one wanted to be told how to run things by a bunch of hardware salesmen from the North.

And so the brothers fought, and everyone in the world, it seemed, rushed to line up behind one or the other.

Everyone, that is, except for me.

"I don't belong, any more'n you do," Sam had reminded me as we said our goodbyes. "My folks came over from Africa, two generations back – and they didn't have any say in the matter, either. But I know who I am, just the same – an' I know better times are comin', if I hold on."

He'd made a protective charm for me – crushed basil leaves, incense, feathers and bones, all wrapped up in a small leather pouch and tied with cord.

"You ain't one of my people, Miss Kate, and you never will be. But you've got powers of your own, just the same." Gravely, Sam slipped the cord of the leather pouch over my head.

"The day you were born, back of Island One-oh-three, I looked at you, an' I knew right away you could put your hand on the world an' feel it turnin'. You've got a secret of livin' that ain't given to just anyone – the same spirit that makes little shoots push up through the earth, an' leaves come on some ol' tree everyone thought was dead. You're the spark that lights the firebox, honey – an' the biggest steamboat in the world's useless without that."

He put a length of red thread into my hand.

"Go an' find that man of yours. Tie this red thread to the watch you're carryin', and you go an' find him. That's your future now."

And so I fixed my mind on Matthew, and on the moment when he might be expected to reach England – first of all when he *might* be home, then when he'd *probably* be home . . . and finally when he must beyond all doubt be at home again, planning how I could best be fetched from America to join him. I pictured him on the deck of his ship, looking back as the last sliver of the New World fell below the horizon, and tried to imagine the expression on his face. In my mind's eye, I carried him off to a dockside in Liverpool – or what I imagined a Liverpool wharf might look like. I tried to place him in a home, among a family – even with the father he resented so much . . . and there my invention failed me, and made me realise how little I really knew of him. I would simply have to wait for whatever might lie ahead.

In fits and starts, it took me the best part of three weeks to make the journey from New Orleans to Birmingham, Alabama, then on to Atlanta, from Atlanta to Columbia in South Carolina and finally to Wilmington, just over its northern border. I'd known it would be hard to arrange a passage out of Wilmington and through the blockade, but I hadn't reckoned on having to wait for weeks for a permit to leave the Confederate States at all. At first I was told there was no question of obtaining one of these magic pieces of paper: didn't I know the South was at war? Then at last, but only after I'd laid endless siege to his office, the Confederate Secretary of War suddenly signed his name on a pass entitling me to depart for a port in the British possessions as soon as I was ready.

Ready? I could pack my single carpet-bag in minutes, even allowing for the few extra items of clothing I'd managed to acquire in Wilmington for the journey to England. The Confederacy was already short of such things. Stockings could be had, but corsets were at a premium, and silks (not that I could ever have aspired to such elegance) were out of the question. Luckily I managed to find a plain calico blouse and a skirt in dark milled cloth which I folded away at the bottom of my bag, ready to present a decent appearance before my new in-laws.

The *Hilda* sailed for Bermuda after dark on the 30th of June, 1862, loaded down with cotton, the cargo larded with oil barrels so the ship could be run aground and set on fire if there was any danger of capture. Fortunately we saw nothing but the sudden flare of signal rockets on the horizon before anchoring in St George's harbour on the island of Bermuda, and ten days later I left for Liverpool aboard the barque *Amethyst* by way of Halifax, Nova Scotia.

Even for a wandering river child, born on broad waters which themselves were never still, the sea was a fearful thing to behold. Wide though it was, the Mississippi had had its banks to confine it. This was the limitless ocean, and as I contemplated the grey expanse of it from the deck of my tossing, slithering ship, I began to feel a very small figure against the greatness of infinity.

How often, on the river, had I dreamed of being free of my father's tyranny? I was as free now as one of the nameless waves which formed and dissolved upon the surface of the sea. Pa was dead; Sam Duck and Luke, Louis Boudreaux, the Ransomes and the rest were far away in New Orleans; even Pastor Bonnet was rumoured to have run off to some bolt-hole of his own. I'd left them all behind – all the witnesses to my past, the small handful capable of testifying to who Kate Summerbee was, or where she'd sprung from. My home – my life – must lie ahead of me now in Liverpool, where Matthew Oliver was waiting.

The *Amethyst* was off Cape Clear when it occurred to me to ask the friendly purser if he'd heard of a ship called the *Vixen* and a man by the name of Oliver.

"Mr Matthew Oliver?" The purser laughed. "Sure – everyone in Liverpool knows Mr Oliver."

"Then . . . the *Vixen* is his own ship?"

"The *Vixen* belongs to his company – and about three dozen others besides. Keep a look-out to port here, and you might see the *Antares* on her way to New York. She's an Oliver ship – and one of the biggest afloat. Do I know Mr Oliver? By crikey, I wish I did!"

Chapter Seven

1

I reached Liverpool at last on the 19th of August.

The *Amethyst*'s purser had assured me that anyone in the city could show me the way to the Oliver offices, but I still had to ask the policeman at the dock gates twice to repeat the directions he gave me. The first time I spoke, he didn't understand me at all; then, after I'd managed to make him aware of what I wanted, he rattled away in an accent so strong I could hardly make out a word of his reply, and it hardly seemed possible we were both using the same language. But even I could follow a pointing finger, and once I'd discovered the foot of Water Street not far from the docks, I reckoned all that remained was to make my way slowly along it examining every brass plate at every door for the name *J. G. Oliver & Company Ltd.*

The Oliver plate, when I reached it, was very large indeed; I could well believe that the masters of three dozen ships might look to it for their orders, and for a moment the panic which had gripped me after the purser's account of the Oliver fleet kept me rooted to the spot. Sternly, I reminded myself that Matthew Oliver was the same man with one ship or thirty-six, and I was his lawful wife. I made a mental note to come back and polish that over-large plate just as soon as I discovered where Matthew kept his brass-cloths.

The doorway next to the plate was outsize too, a great arched and pillared affair of shallow steps and massive, brass-mounted doors with leaping dolphins for handles. The doors stood open, but any hint of invitation was quelled by a stern, uniformed porter standing just inside.

"Yes, miss?" The man pounced on me at once as if pleased to have something to lighten the boredom of his existence. "If you're engaging a passage, miss, it's next door down."

"Thank you kindly, but I don't want a ship."

"Oh-ho? An American person, are we?" The porter pointed to the street. "New York sailings, third desk from the left, next door down, just as I said."

"I told you, I'm not looking for a ship. I've come here to see Mr Matthew Oliver. I dare say you'll know where I can find him."

The door-keeper seemed to swell with indignation until he filled the hallway like a giant mastiff, barring entrance to all comers, and my panic almost got the better of me.

"Do you have an appointment, miss?" The porter laid out the words with slow significance.

"Well . . . no, he isn't expecting me."

"No, I'm sure he ain't. And he ain't here, anyhow. Mr Oliver never sees anyone without an appointment, otherwise he'd get any sort of Tom, Dick or Harry walking in from the street and taking up his valuable time with their worthless chin-wag. That's why I'm here, see? To keep out the chin-wag."

The expression on the porter's face placed me firmly among the time-wasters, and I began to regret the low-crowned straw hat I'd bought in Wilmington specially for the occasion. Perhaps it did look a trifle jaunty with my thick cotton skirt and drab coat, but even that tiny expense had called for a good deal of heart-searching. Unfortunately the short walk from the docks had already shown me that young English ladies – or young women with shoes and gloves to their name, at any rate – didn't wear their hair loose down their backs in the American fashion, and certainly not with an explosion of crimson poppies at their hat-brims.

For a moment I considered announcing myself as Matthew Oliver's wife, there and then – until I realised with dismay that the porter probably wouldn't believe me.

"If Mr Oliver isn't here today, will I find him at home?"

"I don't see as that's any of your business, miss." The porter straightened his back and clasped his hands behind it.

"Then I reckon you don't know where he is." I put infinite scorn into the words. "I don't suppose Mr Oliver tells the fellow who minds his front door where he's going to be all day."

"Oh, doesn't he?" the porter cried wrathfully, his dignity insulted. "Well, that's just where you're wrong, young woman. I happen to know exactly where Mr Oliver is, 'cos he told me himself on Friday night, before he went home."

"I don't believe you!"

"He did, too! 'Hobbs,' he said – standin' just where you are now – 'Hobbs, I shall be in Norfolk next week, so I shan't need a *Post* while I'm gone.' " The porter looked triumphant. " 'Yes, sir,' I said. 'And I'll have it ready for you when you get back, sir. Exactly as usual, sir.' "

The porter bent down, putting his face so close to mine that I could almost feel the prickle of his whiskers. "So there, Miss American Clever. What do you say to that?"

"But why in the world would he want to go to Norfolk?" I persisted. "Are there ships in this Norfolk?"

"He'll be visiting his mother at Hawk's Dyke, I shouldn't wonder." The porter straightened up again and stroked his moustache grandly. "Though as I said, it's no affair of yours what Mr Oliver's doing. He ain't here, and I dare say he wouldn't see you if he was."

2

A few days before, when the purser on the *Amethyst* changed my dollars for less than a quarter as many sovereigns, I was sure the man had robbed me. And though after some frantic calculation it turned out to have been a fair rate of exchange after all, the transaction still left me feeling more of a pauper than ever.

Now the Oliver's porter had sniffed my penury in the magnificence of his burnished hallway, and had promptly chased me out. After the encounter, I examined myself in the plate-glass window of a shop near the Oliver offices and tried to decide what sort of picture I presented. I was certainly beginning to feel uncomfortably like a beggar: for any sake, did I look like one, too?

This was a new and unsettling discovery. In the Confederate States we'd been poor, Pa and I, but never without self-respect. A pale skin had always been enough to keep the most destitute of whites from the bottom of the heap, a guaranteed step or two above the great mass of black or coloured humanity. However prosperous a free Negro grocer or carpenter might be, he was a Negro still, and my father, with the seat worn out of his trousers, condescended to give him trade.

Here in Britain, it seemed, there was nothing to check that downward slide to the gutter. Respectability must be guarded at all costs, and a young woman with loose hair and a poppy-strewn straw hat gave the wrong impression entirely.

But I couldn't bear to part with my bright poppies; instead, I scrabbled most of my wayward curls into the round straw crown, and set the hat square on my head.

I had to decide what to do next. I couldn't afford to wait for long in Liverpool, that was clear: I'd no idea when Matthew would return, or even if he mightn't go off somewhere else when he'd finished his stay in Norfolk. On the other hand, I did know where he was to be found for the next few days – and Heavens above, Britain was such a little island, when I'd already come all the way across an ocean! Surely another few hours would be enough to find a place called Hawk's Dyke in the county of Norfolk.

Except that it turned out to be further off than I'd thought, an apparently endless railroad journey across England by way of places called Crewe and Bletchley and Ely, between one echoing, sooty terminus and another, from one hard wooden seat to the next, squashed between harassed mothers and their squalling children or huge, many-skirted and beshawled women with hampers, or – when the line passed through country districts – whiskery old ladies perching baskets of hens on their knees.

And no one spoke. Even pressed so close in a third-class carriage that to scratch an ear took the co-operation of the travellers on either side, not a word passed between us for mile after mile. I thought of American railroad cars where friends were made and lost in the space of a stop or two, and wondered if it was the chilliness of the climate which made the British so frigidly distant.

It was almost eight in the evening when at last I reached the small town of Downham where the guard had warned me to alight, and found a bed for the night in a posting inn on the main street, curling up between well-used sheets while four other women snored noisily around me. It still wasn't Hawk's Dyke, but at least it seemed to be Norfolk.

Next morning early I enquired for Hawk's Dyke and was directed to the local carrier, who was believed to pass the place on his weekly progress to the village of Stainham St Agnes, ten miles away to the south-east.

"Don't tell me, now," growled the carrier as soon as I was perched up beside him under the hood of his high-wheeled wagon. "Let me guess."

The horse ambled slowly down the road towards Stainham, while the carrier screwed up his eyes. After a few minutes' consideration, he stabbed the air in front of my nose with his pipe-stem.

"Housemaid from somewhere up north – that's you, I'll wager. Sure as eggs is eggs."

"Certainly not." I hugged the carpet-bag containing my few possessions an inch closer to my chest.

"Oh." The man seemed disappointed, but not deterred. "Don't tell me, now. Don't spoil the game. I'll guess you by and by." He clucked to his horse and then turned to look me over again, still perplexed by the conundrum. "You're a hard one, you are. Stowe Hall has a Scotch cook that sounds a bit like you . . . but you're too young and thin for a cook, I'd say. Yet I don't see you as a parlourmaid, though you seem sharp enough."

"I'm not a servant at all." I lifted my chin, and heard the poppies on my hat flutter valiantly in the breeze. "I'm an American citizen."

"Ho!" The carrier digested this information for a long time. Then he removed the pipe from his mouth once more.

"There's nothin' wrong with housemaidin'. My niece is a housemaid at Sourwell Abbey, Lord Wellborough's place. 'Bout three miles from where you're bound."

He flicked his long reins across the horse's rump to encourage it to quicken its pace, but his heart wasn't in the business. "All right, I give up. What are you, then, if you ain't in service?"

"I told you. I'm an American citizen, and nobody's servant. Where I come from, we don't hold with bowing and scraping as if some men were better than their neighbours. Eighty years ago," I informed him severely, "we threw out kings and queens for good."

"Lord love us," muttered the carrier darkly, "one of them foreign anarchists!" And he lapsed into brooding silence for the rest of the morning.

At least the man's taciturnity allowed me to gaze out from my high vantage point above the horse's back and take stock of the countryside through which we were travelling. I was amazed to find it so flat. Somehow I'd thought of Britain as a hilly country, and yet from only a little height I could see for a great distance in either direction, almost as far as across the flat marshlands of the Mississippi delta. The farmhouses of this part of Norfolk, too, weren't so different from the *îles* of the Cajun farmers, those low-roofed houses in their groves of oaks and China trees – though here the roofs were steep enough to look as if they were squashing the dwellings below them deep into the surrounding greenery.

There were even rush-bordered lakes like the *maraises* I knew of old, with mallard and teal and *poules d'eau* dotting their surface. I saw a heron, and a *pique en terre* – and high above, a bird which might almost have been a turkey buzzard, balancing full-span against the breezy sky like a tightrope walker. At once I began to feel better; I think it might only have taken a melon patch or a cluster of orange trees to make me feel truly at home.

It was noon when the carrier left me at the end of a narrow road which, he assured me, led to Hawk's Dyke.

"About quarter of a mile further on," he advised, pointing with his pipe-stem to a distant stand of trees. "If it wasn't for the spinney there, you'd see the house across the fields." He leaned over to hand down my carpet-bag before rumbling off, whistling and flicking his reins, towards the village which was his next port of call.

It was quite warm now that the sun was high, and I was glad of a

94

chance to stretch my legs after the interminable jolting of the cart. Taking a firm grip on my bag I set off up the dusty, hedge-bordered road.

"Good day to you, miss."

At the first bend a very old man in a frayed, mud-stained coat was solemnly scything the verge. As I drew level with him he peered at me with faded eyes and set down his scythe to wipe the sleeve of his coat across his white whiskers.

"Good day to you, too. Am I on the right road for Hawk's Dyke?"

"If you mean the Old Hall, it's up yonder." The old man pointed up the road. "Not much further."

It was just as well he spoke slowly, or the flat vowels and the ups and downs of Norfolk speech would have baffled me as easily as the impenetrable twang of the Liverpool folk. For his own part, the old man continued to stare at me, obviously wondering what business such an exotic creature might have at the Old Hall.

"I'm looking for Mr Matthew Oliver. Will I find him there?"

"Ordinarily you might have done, miss, but there's none of them at home today. Neither Mr and Mrs Gaunt, nor Miss Louise either. They've gone over to the Abbey, so I heard, for some celebration or other. I doubt if they'll be back before dark, now."

"The Abbey?" For a moment I had a vision of a church service.

"Sourwell Abbey, where His Lordship lives. His Lordship's a Gaunt too, you understand."

"Ah – Lord Wells's house." I remembered the carrier's remarks about his niece.

"Lord Wellborough, you mean. That's the new Earl, of course, his father bein' dead a year since." Reluctantly, the man lifted his scythe once more. "But that's where they are, so I'm told. Over at Sourwell, all of 'em."

I stood in the lane, my carpet-bag at my feet, and wondered what to do next. I had no shelter in view for that night. My plans had depended entirely on finding Matthew before evening, and the carrier had long since gone on his way.

"Where is Sourwell Abbey?"

The old man pointed. "About three miles off to the nor'east – less, if you go across the fields." He looked doubtfully at my dilapidated boots. "Though maybe you'd best keep by the hedges where you can."

The choices were hardly attractive. I could either turn myself about and trudge in the wake of the carrier, trusting to find lodgings for the night in the village he'd mentioned, or I could walk to Sourwell Abbey and seek out my husband.

To begin with, I favoured the village. Then the thought of another day's delay became unbearable. I desperately wanted to be with Matthew – to laugh at the fears which had haunted me ever since the discovery of his three dozen ships and the outsize brass plate at his door: I wanted to meet his family, to be among people who knew who I was and would greet me as a friend. If Matthew was at Sourwell Abbey at that moment, then I should go there without delay.

"Exactly how do I get to the Abbey from here?"

"Well, if you mean to walk it, miss, keep the trees of the Hall on your left hand and skirt the farm you'll see about a mile beyond. You'll pick up the Wellborough road a little further on, an' after that there's no difficulty. Just go on till you come to the Abbey gates and the lodge."

I thanked the man, picked up my bag once more and started to trudge towards Sourwell Abbey – surely the last stage of my odyssey.

3

A two-and-a-half-mile walk is no hardship on a good road, but two and a half miles where four-fifths of the way runs along ditches and over stubble fields is a different matter. The tenants of the Hawk's Dyke farms seemed to take scant care of their hedges, and more than once my hat was knocked askew and my hair snagged by stray branches of thorn as I stumbled over tussocky grass or struggled among the weedy clods of the field edges. Hot and cross, I persisted, flushing partridges and rabbits from my path as I tramped along, furiously retrieving my boots from unexpected patches of mud which had tried to swallow them. Before I'd gone very far I was caked to the ankle with filth and sheep droppings, the hem of my skirt was stained brown with mire and my hat clung at a rakish angle to a tangle of hair.

It was a relief at last to reach the tree-lined road and to plod along its coach-ruts as far as the lion-crested stone pillars which guarded the gates of Sourwell Abbey. I'd half-expected to be stopped and questioned at the lodge, but though a dog barked frantically somewhere behind the house, no one came out to ask my business, and not a quarter of a mile further on, where the trees thinned out at the side of the carriage drive, I had my first sight of the Abbey itself.

I noticed the chimneys before the rest, outlined against the sky like knobbed, arthritic fingers, whole fists of them reaching up from the massed grey gables of the roof. Gradually the house detached itself from the surrounding trees, a turret here and a wing there, continually adding to itself until at last it stood in its entirety, a sprawl of stone and dark brick the colour of dried blood, brooding as a distant cliff even on that sunlit afternoon. From every face of it tall, many-paned windows stared out upon the world, yet Sourwell Abbey seemed as empty of life as a quarry face, a chill, morose dwelling amid its encircling trees.

I stared at the house, appalled. It was only to be expected, I suppose, that people who owned three dozen ships and a brass plate the size of a table-top might also live in a sizeable dwelling – but where were all the balconies and the cool, pillared verandahs? Where were the gay shutters and painted dormers and airy gazebos? This house, for all its size, looked like a prison or an asylum for the insane, and my hand flew instinctively to Sam Duck's leather pouch on its cord round my neck.

I promptly scolded myself for my timidity. This wasn't Matthew's house, or even his mother's home. The people who lived here were cousins or such-like – the old man with the scythe had told me so. And wasn't I Matthew's bride, come all the way from America despite the war and the miles between us, to be reunited with my husband? His family would be astonished and relieved to see me; they'd probably insist on hearing the story of my journey over and over again. I hummed a little march under my breath as I set off again up the drive, and tried out *this is Matthew's wife* in various tones of voice. But mud still squelched from the holes in my boots at every step, and it was hard to give myself over entirely to bliss.

How, by all that was holy, had they known I was coming?

However I'd tried to imagine my arrival in the bosom of Matthew's family, the last thing I'd expected was a welcoming committee. Yet as I rounded the final bend of the carriage sweep and trailed wearily on to the great desert of gravel in front of the house, a small crowd of people was drawn up in three solemn rows on the steps at the door, from where three rows of curious eyes swivelled to follow my straggling progress towards them.

It was only when I left the trees behind that I discovered the real reason for that strange, strangled stare. In the space between us a photographer hovered beside his long-legged tripod, his bent back towards me, one hand steadying his camera under its draping of black velvet, the other flourishing the cap of the lens.

This was no welcoming committee after all – just three dull, rigid ranks of English gentry, recording their unsmiling presence at some family event.

Even now, I've only to close my eyes to see them again – the ladies in their lacy, ribboned caps perched on dining chairs brought outside for the purpose, the gentlemen standing gravely behind them or disposed at their feet – every hand still, every face obediently turned to the camera . . . all except one.

I've seen the finished photograph. Where Matthew Oliver's face should be, there's only a white blur of movement, all that was left when he twisted round to gape at the muddy, bedraggled – but still recognisable – figure advancing upon him, carpet-bag in hand, auburn curls trailing from under a straw hat crowned crazily with poppies.

4

Of course, the instant the cap was replaced on the lens they all turned to stare – the three blonde young women like bright silken flowers in the centre of the group, an older woman nearby with dark, compassionate eyes in a pale oval face, the man next to her like a harder, sterner edition of Matthew, who murmured "At last!" as the photographer finished his work. . . . Those are the faces I remember best, though there were many others – inquisitive, hostile, amused – all turned to me as I halted before them and set my carpet-bag down at my feet, shedding clods of earth on their clean-swept gravel.

"Go round to the kitchen yard, girl!" called an imperious voice. "For goodness' sake don't stand there gawping like a half-wit!"

I saw Matthew detach himself from the group and almost sprint towards me, his elegant frock coat flying open, alarm mingling with vexation in his voice.

"Katherine – for heaven's sake, you might have warned me! I'd have met you at the docks, or met your train, or whatever – but to come here like a bolt from the blue. . . . When I've only just come back from—" I saw his eyes slide in alarm towards the dispersing group on the steps. " – from Italy," he finished hastily. "Look here – have you said anything to anyone? About us – in New Orleans, I mean."

"About us being married? No, not at all. There was no one to tell, and besides – I expected you'd want to make a proper announcement. Isn't that the polite way to do it?"

All of a sudden, Matthew became unaccountably angry.

"You must be out of your mind to come here like this."

I gaped at him, thunderstruck.

"I told you I'd come as soon as I could."

"You said you'd *wait*, as I recall. You said you'd wait until I wrote a letter, explaining everything."

"I only had three days to leave New Orleans, Matthew. There was no time to wait for a letter."

"But just to come to the Abbey – "

98

"I went to Hawk's Dyke first, and a man there told me where to find you. Oh, Matthew, I've walked so far, looking for you . . . I reckon my feet must be all over blisters by now."

Matthew ran a hand distractedly through his hair.

"Everyone's watching us. Now do you see what you've done? They'll all want to know who you are and what you're doing here. What am I supposed to tell them?"

"Tell them the truth, why don't you? Introduce me to your folks."

Matthew looked at me as if I'd escaped from an institution for dangerous lunatics.

"*Introduce you?*"

His eyes swept over me, aghast.

"I'm pretty untidy, I guess. Maybe it'd be better if I waited to meet them until I'm cleaned up some. I want to make a good impression, after all." Another thought occurred to me. "I've brought your watch."

"Never mind the damned watch!"

"I thought you'd want it back."

"Oh, give it here!" Abruptly, Matthew snatched the watch with its trailing red thread and thrust it into his coat pocket, glancing towards the steps once more. "Oh Lord, they're all looking this way. We can't stand here talking."

"If we went indoors I could clean up a bit – " I stamped my feet to rid them of some of the mud, and a small moat of water oozed out round the soles of my boots.

"Not here!" Matthew glanced wildly about him. "Somewhere else. Anywhere but here. There's an inn of sorts in Stainham . . ." He frowned over the idea for a moment, and then thought better of it. "No, that's impossible. There'd only be gossip. I'll have to take you back to Hawk's Dyke until we decide what's to be done."

Picking up my bag and gripping my arm like a jailer, Matthew marched me to a wooden bench under a tree at the edge of the gravelled area where he seemed to feel I'd be less conspicuous.

"Wait here while I order the carriage and make some excuse to leave early. Don't move from this spot until I come back. And if anyone speaks to you, or asks who you are, tell them . . . well, tell them you're the daughter of an acquaintance from New Orleans. Tell them you've brought the bloody watch back, if you must, but no more than that. Not a word."

He stared at me, not convinced that his warning had been enough to ensure my silence. "It's very important to me, Katherine."

"You mean I mustn't say anything about our being married?"

"Shhh!" Matthew made frantic signs with his hands. "Especially not about that."

"Sure – if that's what you want. But I still don't see why it has to be such a secret."

"I'll explain it all later," he promised grimly. "Now, stay here for a few minutes, and *please* remember what I said."

With a final, nervous glance towards the door of the Abbey to reassure himself that no one seemed about to approach our sanctuary, Matthew strode briskly away until the top of his head had disappeared among the last few stragglers on the steps.

A significant time seemed to pass with no sign of Matthew's return. Miserable and bewildered, I kept my hands clasped in my lap and my eyes fixed on the muddy toes of my boots, hoping in some vague way to make myself invisible. Yet someone's eyes were upon me; I could feel their scrutiny like the touch of a finger, and when the sensation became absolutely unbearable I was compelled to look up and see whose they were.

In the first confused seconds I thought Matthew had returned and had stopped to examine me from a little way off. The stranger was as tall and spare as Matthew; he'd fixed me with the same sharp glance, and as he lifted his head, allowing the light to fall on his face, I fancied his eyes were exactly the same, moody, shifting grey as Matthew's.

But he wasn't Matthew. What I'd taken in the sunlight to be thick, tawny hair was well streaked with silver and there was a hardness to the angles of his face and a pattern of fine lines round his eyes which indicated that this man was considerably older.

"The carriage will be here in a moment."

Matthew's voice at my elbow startled me out of my reverie, and I realised he must have emerged from a side door while my attention was distracted.

"I'll take you straight to Hawk's Dyke, and then send the carriage back for the others. I've told my mother you've come to England to stay with relatives because of the war in America, and she's agreed to your spending the night at her house. Tomorrow I'll take you back to Liverpool."

"But Matthew – I don't understand – "

"*Later*. I promise I'll explain everything later. Just let's get away from here, that's all."

My eye was caught by the flutter of bright silks in the doorway of the Abbey, and by three blonde heads which drew together and separated again as three young women finished their conference and turned their eyes once more in my direction. A further discussion followed, until the palest blonde of the three parted from the others, attached herself to the arm of a florid, middle-aged man nearby and tripped gracefully at his side down the shallow steps before advancing across the gravel towards us.

The girl was beautiful, there was no doubt of it – possessed of a pure, crystal English loveliness, a brilliance of clear skin and white-blonde hair. She was beautiful, and she was aware of her beauty and its power: I could tell as much by her little surging steps as she walked, by the way she held her elbows and shoulders – a trifle awkwardly, like a child – and by the constant movement of her head this way and that, just as a woman would show off a diamond in the sunlight.

In half a minute she was upon us.

"Why, Matthew – " Disengaging the middle-aged man, she slid a dainty white hand into the crook of Matthew's arm. "Your mother tells me you're leaving us all of a sudden. I do think you might have mentioned it to me first." Her pink fondant lips pushed forward in a pout. "Papa and I – " she indicated the plump, red-faced man at her side, "are really most put out."

"I couldn't find you, Violet, that was all."

"And anyway – what's so important that you have to run off to Hawk's Dyke in such a hurry?" The remark was addressed to Matthew, but her eyes were on me as she spoke, as clear and as cold as perfect aquamarines.

"Do we know this young woman who seems to be taking up so much of your time?" The florid man's voice was a breathy baritone, but there was an imperious note in it which demanded an explanation.

"Ah . . ." Alarm leaped into Matthew's eyes, but he tried gamely to carry off the moment. "Violet – this is Miss Summerbee, from New Orleans. In America," he added needlessly. "Miss Summerbee, may I present Miss Violet Broadney, and her father, Sir George . . ." His voice dwindled to a murmur.

"For God's sake, Matthew!" boomed the red-faced man. "What on earth are you thinking of? What kind of an introduction do you call that? Miss Summerbee – what Mr Oliver meant to say – " He half-turned, and father and daughter exchanged fond smiles. "Is that since the seventeenth of last month, my daughter is no longer Miss Violet Broadney, but *Mrs Matthew Oliver.*"

Chapter Eight

1

Mrs Matthew Oliver. The words repeated themselves over and over again in my head – incredible – outrageous – impossible to believe. *Mrs Matthew Oliver* . . . drumming in the beat of the coach-horses' hooves as we flew down the Abbey drive, murmuring among the landau's wheels with each relentless turn.

Matthew already has a wife! I'd wanted to shout – *a wife of five months' standing – married in good faith, and come four thousand miles to find her husband!* I'd wanted to shout it out there and then – to wipe the smug smiles from their lips and the disdain from their eyes. Let the photographer record them after that, in his round black lens! What a fine picture that would make in the family album, for future generations to stare at!

But at the last minute, even as the words boiled in my throat, I held my peace. There must be some mistake – some explanation . . . I was so awkward and out of place in this world of abbeys and earls: perhaps I'd misunderstood the situation, and would only make a bigger fool of myself by blurting out reckless accusations.

I couldn't believe – couldn't bring myself to believe – that Matthew Oliver, the man whose beloved image I'd followed across half a continent and then an ocean, had deliberately, cold-bloodedly, betrayed the vows we'd made aboard the *Bellflower*. Oh, he was self-serving and stubborn – I'd no illusions about that – but I couldn't believe he was capable of cruelty as well. Not Matthew – surely not Matthew.

Yet I meant to have it out with him, the instant we were alone. *I* was Matthew's wife, for goodness' sake – not that silken, sparkling young woman who called herself *Mrs Matthew Oliver* with such dimpling affectation. I was Matthew's wife, and the sooner that was made clear to one and all, the better.

We arrived back at Hawk's Dyke in what seemed to be seconds. On that warm September afternoon the landau was open and a groom clung to the straps at the rear; I'd never ridden in such an elegant conveyance before, but even so, I knew better than to speak where I could be overheard. And because Matthew and I had nothing else to say to one another, we sat in furious silence until the carriage rolled to a halt in front of the Old Hall and Matthew got down, brusquely offering me his hand to do likewise.

I can't remember seeing anything of the house on that first afternoon. I was too angry to notice more than a rambling old building with the comforting solidity of a tea-chest before we passed inside to a low-ceilinged hallway.

I desperately wanted to be alone with Matthew, but Mrs Finch, the housekeeper, had already taken charge of me. By Heaven, were these people never free of watching eyes and listening ears?

In a moment, Matthew had vanished, and I was ushered upstairs to "Miss Alice's old room" – Alice Oliver, Matthew's seventeen-year-old half-sister having married Charles Gaunt earlier in the year and departed to live at Sourwell Abbey.

"Of course, she's Lady Wellborough now, with her husband being the new Earl," the housekeeper informed me briskly as she made up the bed. "And a fine young Countess she makes, to be sure. Nell! Where have you gone to with those towels?"

With a sharp tug Mrs Finch twitched the counterpane smooth where I'd dropped my straw hat on its snowy perfection.

"With Miss Alice away at the Abbey there's only Miss Louise here, and Mr and Mrs Gaunt. And I dare say we won't have Miss Louise for much longer, with her looks." The housekeeper sniffed her approval. "She's a lovely girl, is Miss Louise. Some young man will sweep her off her feet before long, I reckon. But of course, you'll have met her for yourself this afternoon."

My mind still in turmoil, I wished the woman would stop talking and leave me to think. I confessed that I hadn't met Matthew's sister at the Abbey. I'd only been introduced to – I repeated the words experimentally " – to Mrs Oliver."

"Ah, Mr Matthew's bride." The housekeeper pursed her lips. "We haven't seen much of Mrs Oliver at Hawk's Dyke. She prefers the Abbey, so they say." Mrs Finch's tone indicated exactly what she thought of Violet's taste in houses. "And the Abbey's such a barn of a place, for all it's so grand. Still, maybe she'll call here more often now they're married and back from the honeymoon."

Honeymoon? Married?

What the housekeeper thought of me that first day, I dread to think. My brain could hold nothing but the words *Mrs Matthew Oliver* – and my stomach could hold nothing at all, certainly not the cold roast fowl and apple pudding which Mrs Finch insisted on bringing to me in lonely state in the dining-room. Not two hours earlier I'd been both tired and hungry. Now I was neither, but so dizzy with outrage I could have flown round the ceiling on wings of sheer delirium.

Matthew came in just as I was crumbling a piece of pudding into the magnificent silver rose-bowl to make it seem as if I'd eaten a little, and could decently escape from the table.

"Come out into the Italian garden when you're ready. We won't be overheard there."

"Oh, don't you worry – I'm ready right now."

Out in the passage our footsteps echoed starkly on the bare, polished boards. A few yards further on, Matthew opened the door set deep in the outside wall and ushered me through it into the garden.

As soon as I stepped outside I felt cheated. I was sure Matthew had chosen his ground with deliberate cunning, knowing an argument in such a place would seem like warfare in Paradise.

It isn't right for us to quarrel here: I almost spoke the words aloud, awed by the green abundance which spilled from old stone urns and tumbled over lichen-blotched walls and statuary. All around us the burden of late summer whispered on the trees which shaded the mossy paths, while the fading sunlight filled that sublime acre with a haze charged with the sweetness of lemonade, a veil of soft light through which gilded particles flicked and spiralled as the evening insects gathered in restless clouds.

"This is my mother's garden."

"It's beautiful."

It was, I think, the most beautiful thing I'd ever seen – on that, the ugliest day of my life.

"Katherine – " Matthew's voice was sharp with strain. "I never meant things to turn out like this. It's a mess from beginning to end."

Suddenly, I didn't want to listen. I wanted to walk away – to let my own thoughts speak to me in that amber silence – to explain the inexplicable. I set off down the nearest path, and Matthew followed. Ridiculously in step, we patrolled the edge of a flower bed under the kindly, mottled eyes of a stone faun.

"I was going to write to you, to tell you – well, to try to settle any misunderstanding between us." He sighed. "But it was hard to find the words."

"Because there was no misunderstanding!" The anger which had lain like a knot in my stomach instantly found its way into my voice. "*I'm* Mrs Oliver – not that woman at the Abbey! How could you possibly go through with a marriage to her when you already had a wife? Because that's what you've done, Matthew, isn't it? Tricked that girl into a bigamous marriage – and a honeymoon too, by all accounts! How *could* you, Matthew? If it hadn't been so downright shameful, I'd have had it out with you there and then."

"Katherine – " Matthew made a frustrated gesture with his hands. "There's nothing to be gained by being theatrical. Surely we can discuss this like civilised people?"

"Civilised? Do you call it civilised, what you've done? I suppose you thought I'd never find out – that I was safely in America, caught up in the war."

"I didn't think anything of the kind! You're wrong about all of this, Katherine – completely wrong. If you give me a chance, I'll try to explain – but please remember I was engaged to be married to Violet Broadney long before I came to New Orleans. I told you as much on the *Bellflower*, that morning, when . . . when . . ."

"When we became man and wife."

"When we were forced to go through with a ridiculous charade," Matthew continued heavily. "Let's be quite clear about this: you and I were *not* married that day on the *Bellflower*. We were never man and wife, whatever you may have believed at the time."

"Of course we were!" This was a line I'd never expected: I was stunned by his bare-faced effrontery. "The Pastor married us, fair and square. We said all the words, didn't we? We took the vows."

"Yes – with your father's shotgun at our heads! What kind of a marriage do you call that?"

"It doesn't make any difference *why* we were married! Pa was only trying to do right by me. You married me, all right – the reason doesn't matter a bit."

"I did nothing of the sort! I said whatever I had to say to get that damned boat of yours on its way out of New Orleans, because I didn't want to spend years in a Yankee prison."

"As long as you said *I will* – "

"It takes more than words to make a marriage, Katherine. You must know that!"

"I've every reason to know it! I don't suppose it occurred to you I might be carrying your child."

"What?" He stared at me in alarm. "You aren't . . . are you?"

"No, I'm not, as it happens. But I might have been! Suppose I'd come here with a belly like a brandy keg – would you still have said we were never married?"

"Let's be quite straight about this – "

105

With cruel clarity, Matthew counted off the facts on his fingers.

"First – I don't believe that drunken fool of a pastor was entitled to marry anyone. Second – the marriage was never registered or made official in any way, which makes it invalid. Third – and finally – I didn't want to marry you, I doubt if we could bear one another's company for more than a week at a time, and *we were never man and wife*." He closed his fingers into a hard, obdurate fist, defying disagreement. "Do you understand me, or shall I say it all again?"

I was shaking – literally shaking – with anger and outrage.

"Do you mean to tell me you always meant to go home and marry this – this Violet woman? Even while you were saying *I will* to me?"

"Of course I meant to marry her!" Matthew snapped back.

"Just because she was beautiful, and I wasn't?"

"Oh, don't be so naïve! Do you honestly think men in my position marry for a pretty face?" He stared at me as if I'd taken leave of my senses, and then added anxiously, "You aren't going to start crying, are you?"

"I haven't cried since I was five years old," I snarled at him, sniffing.

Matthew took a deep breath, and made a huge effort to soften his tone.

"Katherine . . . I know you didn't realise it, but I own the best part of a major shipping line in this country – and one day it'll be the biggest in the world. I need a particular kind of woman for my wife. I married Violet Broadney because she's an intelligent, socially accomplished young lady who can entertain anyone from a sultan to the President of the United States without putting a foot wrong. And there are other reasons." He waved a hand dismissively.

"Such as?" I meant to pursue Violet Broadney's virtues to the bitter end.

"Well, for one thing, her father holds a large amount of Oliver stock, which means that with my own shares and with Violet as my wife, I can do virtually what I please with the company. And more than that, Violet knows almost everyone in London. Her uncles are either cabinet ministers or ambassadors. Can't you see how useful that is in opening up new opportunities for business?"

"You don't want a wife – you want a bank draft!" I raved at him. "A bill of exchange! A parcel of shares!"

"Keep your voice down! Everyone in the house will hear you!"

"It's true! You haven't once said you love her – that you couldn't have lived without her – "

"Oh, for goodness' sake, grow up, Katherine!"

"I have grown up! I've grown up about twenty years since this afternoon!"

"I don't see much sign of it, then."

"I'm trying to find excuses for you, Matthew, don't you see? Because I'd have understood if you'd warned me you were in love with a girl in England, and you were only going through with our marriage because Pa was holding a gun on you. Or if you'd said to me later, after he was shot, that you hadn't meant a bit of it – or if you'd even explained to me how things stood before you left New Orleans. But you never said a word. You knew I believed we were lawfully married and you let me go on believing it – just so's I'd help you get your wretched gold bars out of the Confederacy. That makes you the lowest thing out, Matthew! How could you be such a damned snake?"

Matthew shrugged uneasily.

"I didn't realise you'd taken it all so seriously."

"You knew exactly how I'd taken it! I'd just turned seventeen, after all – and you never said a word about shipping lines or entertaining sultans then. All I knew was that Pa had married me off to a riverboat swindler so's I wouldn't disgrace him by being unwed."

I lifted my hands helplessly, trying to convey the crystal innocence of the trust he'd betrayed. "Even if you'd told me the truth, I'd still have helped you anyway, as a friend in trouble. But you didn't ask as a friend. Not after the marriage. *Do you want to see your husband in a Yankee jail?* That's what you said – I remember exactly. Did you have to lie to make sure of me?"

"Katherine, I was desperate. I couldn't think of anything beyond getting away."

"You could have saved your skin by leaving the gold behind, couldn't you? You'd have got out alive. It's more than Pa did."

He swung round to look at me then. "What are you talking about? Has something happened to your father?"

"Pa's dead."

A pigeon soared from a tree, and with a single clap of its wings dived into the next.

"Pa died of lockjaw not long after you left. He was getting better of his wounds, too, until the sickness set in."

"Oh." Matthew digested this information in silence. "Then I'm sorry your father's dead, Katherine, but that doesn't alter the fact that he was no friend to me."

"What did you expect after that night we spent together aboard the

Bellflower? Did you expect him to thank you for forcing yourself on his daughter?"

Matthew halted, and turned, and looked at me with eyes that would have burned every bale of cotton in the Confederacy.

After a few seconds I dropped my gaze. "I shouldn't have said that. I was as much to blame for what happened as you were."

We walked on in chastened silence for another few yards until the chatter of a small fountain took pity on us, cooling our discomfort with its guileless trickle.

"Believe me, Kate – if I'd known your father was dead and you were left on your own, I'd have managed to send money to you somehow through one of our agents, or even through the New York office." Thoughtfully, Matthew reached out to brush some bright flower-spikes of golden rod near the path. "Why didn't you sell that watch I left? You'd have got a fair sum for it, even in the middle of a war."

"Sell your watch?" I couldn't believe my ears. "I'd have starved sooner than sell it."

"But why?"

"Because it was yours."

"You should have sold it. That's what I meant – " He stopped abruptly.

"You *intended* me to sell your watch?" A horrible suspicion had begun to take hold of me. "Do you mean to say you left the watch deliberately – as payment for services rendered? Was that it, Matthew? Did you imagine that watch squared your account?"

Matthew spread his hands, helpless to answer.

"You bastard! What sort of a woman do you take me for? That night on the *Bellflower* was the first time I'd even so much as touched a man – you must have known that! And you thought you could buy me for the price of a fancy watch – "

"It wasn't like that."

"Then tell me how it was, Matthew! I suppose in your world of sultans and shipping lines a night with the captain's daughter comes with the price of a passage, does it?"

"No, of course not! I didn't intend it to happen, any more than you did. And if your father had come back when he was supposed to – "

"Trust you to blame a dead man!"

"I'm not blaming anyone. It just . . . happened. For some reason, you and I . . . well, you know yourself how it was."

"I remember how it was." And I could tell from his face that he remembered, too. "It was because of that night – because of how we felt

108

then – that I thought we might be able to get along together as man and wife. We might have done," I said softly, "if you hadn't gone rushing off so quick."

He shook his head as if ridding himself of a persistent fly.

"Impossible. There was never a chance of that, Kate."

"You could have loved me, if you'd let yourself try."

"Dammit, will you stop harping on about *love*, like some shilling novelette? When you get to be my age – "

"All of twenty-four."

"When you're a bit older, you'll realise how little *love* has to do with anything!"

"Then I never want to be older! And whatever you say, I still reckon we're man and wife, and you ought not to be living with that Violet woman." Before he could object, I repeated my point. "We were married that day on the *Bellflower* – licence or no licence – "

All of a sudden I remembered Pastor Bonnet's certificate, the precious scrap of paper I'd given to Matthew for safe-keeping.

"I guess you tore up the certificate, if you saw no worth in it."

"I wondered when you'd ask about that."

He reached inside his coat and drew out a folded sheet of paper, curled at the corners and stained from the Pastor's pocket, still savoury with the flavour of tobacco, its outer surface marked with the sturdy playbill type of a tract on Intoxication. Without a word, he held it out to me.

"You kept it? Well, I'm surprised, I must say."

In truth, I was downright amazed. If he'd had the sense to throw the certificate into the fire, I'd have had no way of proving we were legally married. My fingers fairly trembled as I unfolded the limp paper.

"April 25, 1862. I, Elias Bonnet, Preacher, hereby certify I have joined in wedlock Ben Summerbee's daughter, Cripple Mary's girl, and an English feller, name of Oliver.

He says he will have her and her pa says she will take him, and God save us all from the Yankees if we last the day, Amen to that.
Elias Bonnet, Preacher."

Underneath was my father's scrawled signature and a ragged black cross where Sam Duck had put his mark.

"Now do you understand?" Matthew's stare was unwavering. "Does that look to you like a legal document?"

"I wouldn't know." Yet even I had begun to doubt the value of the Pastor's certificate.

"My lawyers tell me it's no more a marriage certificate than a steamer ticket. According to Louisiana statute, all marriages must be licensed and registered before they can be legal."

"What would British lawyers know about Louisiana law?" I tried to sound scornful, but my voice was painfully unsteady.

"The truth is that we were never married, Kate, whatever you imagined. Violet's my wife in the eyes of the law."

"And in the sight of God, Matthew? What about that?"

Matthew threw out his arms in a gesture of frustration. "What more do you want from me? If you want me to admit I wasn't straight with you that day in New Orleans – "

"I believed in you, Matthew. Goodness knows why I believed in you, but I did – and what really hurts – even more than not being married after all – is to find out how little you cared about me."

"You shouldn't have believed in me." He avoided my eye. "I'm no better than the rest of humanity. No man's a saint where women are concerned."

"Oh, I've learned my lesson, never fear." I rounded the corner a little ahead of him, only to find a wall of pitted red brick guiding me inexorably back towards the house.

"I'm truly sorry, Katherine. I know I ought to have written to you – or, better still, I should have been straight with you at the time. But you have to remember I was in a pretty desperate fix. I'd have done anything – cheated, lied, bribed – whatever I had to do to keep myself out of a Federal jail."

"And what about *trusting* me, Matthew? Would that have been so hard for you?"

For a moment he didn't answer, his gaze held by the old house lying ahead of us beyond a fuzz of rose-bushes.

"It's true – I prefer to look after myself in this world. Perhaps I've just been unlucky in the people I've tried to trust in the past, but there it is."

And then, as if he thought his answer had been unduly harsh, he added softly, "I know I deceived you, Kate. I let you go on believing something that wasn't true, and that was wrong of me. But I don't want you to think there was any deceit about – about the night we spent together aboard the boat. That was real, all of it. Everything." He glanced away, absorbed in kicking aside a pebble which had strayed on to the path. "I just wanted you to understand that."

This was more than flesh and blood could bear. I knew I must either shout at him or burst into tears. In the end, I shouted.

110

"Do you expect me to believe a heap of humbug like that? When you've made a downright fool out of me – and I let you do it because I was young and silly, and sweet on a good-looking stranger?"

He wouldn't look at me. He was still rolling the pebble with his foot, infuriatingly silent.

"Don't you dare tell me any more of your lies, just to make me feel better about all this! Don't! Because let me tell you – " I took a couple of steps forward and spun round to face him, wagging a finger under his nose. "Let me tell you something, Mister Shipowner Oliver. . . . If it's true what you say about us not being married – and I don't admit to believing it, mind – but if it *is* true, then I reckon I've had a merciful deliverance from a husband that's more of a swindling, black-hearted crook than ever I took him for! Go and tell your lies to dear Violet – and I wish her joy of them."

I wheeled round and began to march towards the house.

"Katherine – wait, please." Matthew came striding after me, and caught me by the arm. "You can't just go off like that. Where will you go when you leave here?"

"How should I know?" Brusquely, I shook off his hand. "I'll go back to America, I suppose. Why? Do you give a damn what becomes of me?"

"I'm concerned about you, whatever you may think. Do you have any family left in America? Any friends you could go to?"

"I dare say I'll find someone."

"Let me send you home in comfort on an Oliver ship, then. The *Alcyon* sails for New York in ten days' time. We can take the train back to Liverpool tomorrow and find a room for you in a good hotel until then. I'll take care of all the bills. And if you need money to keep you for a while – "

"Anything to get me away from your family and your precious wife – is that it, Matthew? Are you afraid I'll tell them the whole rotten story, and let them see what a rat you really are?"

Matthew's temper was rising to match mine.

"No, Kate, I don't think you'd do that. You've too much pride to tell anyone what happened between us in New Orleans. But if you want me to be brutally frank – I'm concerned that you haven't a cent left in the world, or any means of making a living, now your father's dead. If I could think of a way of keeping you in decent comfort for a while without offending your precious feelings, then I'd do it."

"Keep your dirty money!" Even drawn up to my full height I was almost a head shorter than he was, and it annoyed me to have to look up to defy him. "But if you're so determined to help – why don't you give me another watch, Matthew? That's how you paid me off last time!"

He shook his head wearily. "Be sensible, Kate. Let me help you. Take it as payment of a debt, if you like. It's far less than I owe you."

"Oh, far, far less! Let's see – so much for the hire of the *Bellflower* – so much for the catfish you had for dinner – so much for my services – "

"Kate!"

"*Business is business*, Matthew – isn't that what you said? Everything reckoned up in parcels of shares and pounds sterling? Let's not allow our feelings to get in the way!"

"Please, Kate – "

"Except that I don't happen to believe feelings can be paid for – not pain, nor shame, nor disgrace – nor any of it. That's why I won't take a penny from you."

"Think about it. Wait until you've calmed down a bit. I'm sure you'll see the sense of it by morning."

"Never." On the point of sweeping indoors, I added, "Pa would've laid you out with his shotgun for what you've just told me, Matthew. I can't do that – but I won't let you clear your conscience with a few pounds, all the same. I truly believe we're man and wife, and one day you'll be called to account for disbelieving it. I only hope I live to see that day."

Chapter Nine

1

I was too overwrought to sleep that night, but also too exhausted to stay fully awake. Instead, I drifted in a limbo of shadows, weightless and self-absorbed, while my spent strength called out for the relief of an oblivion which wouldn't come.

Tears might have helped – an outpouring of salty misery in honour of the disaster which had overtaken me. But I hadn't shed tears since gashing my leg in a fall from the *Bellflower*'s derrick at the age of five, when Pa had come near to bursting his sides with laughter at the sight of my anguished face. It was Sam Duck who'd dried my tears and staunched the blood running from my knee to the parched decking.

After that I hadn't allowed myself to indulge in tears. I didn't weep when Ma died or after any of Pa's beatings, though sometimes they hurt like Hades. And now I lay dry-eyed, weeping inside for the shock of my lost love and the sharp agony of humiliation.

Sam Duck's charm of leaves and bones lay on the table next to my bed, the bag and its cord like a bloodstain in the moonlight. Was that what had called up the shades of my past, or were they simply the refuge of an exhausted mind?

I had to turn my eyes away from a vision of Ma, all bruised and mutely reproachful. Why hadn't she stayed long enough to explain the conventions of loving, the games by which love is won or lost? Fathers give their girl-children a thousand words for *no*: it takes a mother to teach *perhaps*, and *we'll see*, and the smile under the lashes which turns *never* into *one day, if you are constant*. Woman's wisdom. . . . Though perhaps Ma herself had never had a chance to learn it, sold into wedlock as she was.

A vision of Pa came between us – Pa, planted flat-footed on the *Bellflower*'s deck, his cap pushed back and his unshaven chin thrust forward as he contemplated some outrageous swindle of his own.

I knew only too well what he'd have done in my place.

"Go for the prag-matical," he'd have said for the hundredth time. "If your back's to the wall, go for the prag-matical" – by which he meant "Take as much as you can get, and to Hell with pride".

And goodness knows, I had precious little pride left to lose. By the standards of the American South I was a thoroughly disgraced woman, cast aside for something better by the man I'd taken for a husband.

For someone in my position, there was no doubt that the most "pragmatical" course was to screw every last farthing I could out of Matthew Oliver while he was disposed to give it. My own little store of money had dwindled rapidly, and I hadn't a soul in the world to whom I could turn for help. Yet to take Matthew's money was to let him buy back the pain I'd suffered, to confirm that wretchedness and deceit had a market price, and that betrayal could be wiped out simply by settling the bill.

He'd probably give me whatever I asked – provided the bargain was kept to pounds, shillings and pence. I understood now that he'd never meant to give more: no love, no affection, no trust. The love I believed I'd felt for him was my own affair: Matthew himself had long since ceased looking for any return on an investment of that kind.

In the darkness outside my window, a carriage pulled up on the gravel; doors banged, and a murmur of voices indicated that Matthew's parents and his sister Louise had returned from Sourwell Abbey. The comfortable sounds of a family arriving home drifted up to my window – half-heard asides leading to little bursts of laughter, the swinging open of a stout door, a call of *Mamma!* . . . all the things which Matthew had snatched away from me with such frigid brutality.

Miserably, I considered the beamed ceiling in "Miss Alice's room", wondering why Alice Oliver, who by all accounts was little more than my own age, should be a happily married young woman while everything had gone so horribly wrong for me.

Next to the window, Alice's doll's house reared its dark gables against the wall, left behind at Hawk's Dyke when its mistress abandoned it for another, grander establishment. Despairing of sleep, I lit my lamp, climbed out of bed, and released the catch on the wooden eaves, swinging open the tall brick frontage of the house on a miniature play-world more magnificent than anything I'd dreamed of in my own haphazard childhood.

Alice's house had been furnished to the last detail, from the minute harmonium in the hall to the tiny trunks in the attics. Umbrellas like toothpicks were arranged in a stand, fingertip cups on a tray in the parlour; there were hairbrushes and playing-cards of infinitesimal smallness, and johnny-pots in the bedside cupboards. I even found a faded posy of yarrow and forget-me-nots on the dining-room sideboard, the last evidence of housekeeping before Alice had closed the front door for good.

114

Naturally, a play-family inhabited that play-world – bespectacled Papa in his wing chair surrounded by dutiful Mamma and a brood of wool-headed, beady-eyed children. A nanny with fearsomely stiff skirts presided over the nursery in the garret; a china-faced cook reigned in the kitchen; a maid waited in the parlour, decently apart from the threadbare footman who lay on his back, forgotten, at the foot of the stairs. All was as it should be in a well-regulated home – the curtains neatly tied, the coverlets square, the halfpenny-sized plates ranged on their dresser. . . . If play-tragedies had ever taken place in that doll's house, there was no sign of them now: and here Alice Oliver had rehearsed her future life. Why shouldn't she have gone on to another well-regulated home and a family of her own? God knows, she'd never expected anything else.

And I was of different clay, or so her brother seemed to think: a rattle-brained girl – a trifling inconvenience, to be disposed of with a few pounds and a steamer ticket.

Rattle-brained I might be, and innocent in the ways of English gentry, but I meant to stand on the little dignity that was left to me. I'd go back to America all right, since there was clearly nothing to keep me in England – but I'd travel by the cheapest steerage passage in the oldest sailing ship capable of making the journey. If I had to beg for my bread when I reached New York, I was determined not to touch Matthew's conscience money. Katherine Summerbee might be broken-hearted, but the price of her pride was still more than anything Matthew Oliver could afford.

And having made my decision, I climbed back into bed and fell asleep.

2

I slept later than usual next morning, slaking my exhaustion in the wonder of a deep feather bed spread with the most amazing lavender-scented, daintily embroidered sheets.

"Nell will tell you when to come down to breakfast when she brings the hot water," Mrs Finch had promised the previous night as I fled past her to the sanctuary of my room. Yet the first of the sun had already laid out the squared pattern of the window-panes on the rug next to my bed, and no Nell had appeared.

For a few minutes more I lay under the whitework coverlet, contemplating the blue sky beyond the latticed panes. I hitched my chin above the sheet, already feeling more like the old Katherine of the *Bellflower*. I was almost grateful for Matthew's deceit: if he was bound

115

to reject me, then it was just as well he'd done it in such a low-down, underhand manner, since the memory of it made me furious all over again. And when I was good and mad, there was no room in my head for fear and self-pity. Come what may, I'd never give Matthew the satisfaction of knowing how deep the hurt of his behaviour still ran.

Perhaps English rural gentry were in the habit of lying late in the mornings, but that dawn was the first of a new life for me, and far too precious to waste. Slipping out of bed, I pattered across to the window, hoisted myself on to its deep sill and, pushing open the casement, leaned out as far as I dared.

The day was still fresh and luminous, hardly touched by the heat of the sun. By craning out over the sill, clinging to the window-frame for safety, I could look down into the blue shadows of the Italian garden, where one of the house cats rolled ecstatically on the warming flags of the steps. From my dormer vantage point the animal took on the colour of crusty lichen, a wriggling grey stain on the paving as it curled and uncurled, dragging its claws through the stems of the fading pink blossom which bordered the path.

Still lazy from my feather bed, I put off my troubles in shared contentment, hanging out of the window, the first few buttons of my nightgown undone to let the clean coolness touch my throat and shoulders, wondering why my life could not be as simple and as selfish as a cat's.

All at once the peace of the morning was broken by the barking of a dog in a small coppice beyond the lawn. Down below in the garden, the cat froze, head erect, eyes and ears directed towards the source of the sound; another bark, and it had fled, ferny tail streaming behind, to the safety of the stable yard.

I raised my eyes towards the coppice in time to see a horseman emerge from the trees, a tall figure on a well-muscled bay which ambled towards the house at its own pace, leaving a large black dog rooting joyfully among the bushes. My first panic-stricken thought was that this was Matthew, arriving earlier than he'd arranged to bear me off to Liverpool. Then the rider left the dappled shadow cast by the coppice, and the sun shone on the light-haired stranger I'd seen studying me the previous day at the Abbey.

It was the second time I'd mistaken that older man for Matthew – and once more I was astonished by the resemblance between them. Gone were the formal clothes of the day before, but even a country coat and breeches couldn't disguise the same blend of ease and swift movement I'd noticed in Matthew. Almost alone among a nation wallowing in

116

moustaches and sidewhiskers, they were both clean-shaven, which gave them the sleek sharpness of hawks among ruffled farmyard fowl. They shared the hard stare of the hawk, too – and the same unabashed curiosity. If he was surprised to find a latter-day Rapunzel craning down in her nightgown from an upper window, the rider gave no sign of it, but studied me with undisguised interest as he dawdled towards the house at his leisurely gait, halting a few moments later on the gravel directly below me.

"It's a fine day." I plunged into conversation to ward off that disconcerting stare.

"It is indeed. A very fine day."

The horseman allowed his gaze to wander for a moment over the prospect of lawns and pasture and ancient walls which surrounded us before returning to rest exclusively on me.

"You must be the American visitor my son told me about. The young woman who brought the watch back."

"I guess I am. My name is Katherine Summerbee."

"Welcome to Hawk's Dyke, then, Miss Summerbee. Don't fall out of that window, will you." The horseman continued to gaze upwards towards my perch. "And thank you for returning the watch. I'm very pleased to have it back."

"You are? But I thought it was Matthew's watch."

"No, it's mine. My wife had it made as a present for me, many years ago. Matthew had no right to borrow it for his adventures simply because his own was broken."

I thought guiltily of the nights I'd spent with that watch clasped close against my breasts. No wonder I'd confused Monsieur Agasu with my wishful length of red thread.

"If it's your watch, then I guess you can tell me why all those stars go round and round on the dial."

"That's a long story." The man smiled, the golden light softening the hard angles of his face. "I've always been interested in the stars."

"Are you really . . . Matthew's father?" It hardly seemed possible that this nut-brown stranger regarding me steadily from the back of his horse was the same implacable tyrant Matthew had described to me on the *Bellflower*.

"My name is Adam Gaunt," the rider admitted. "And yes, I'm Matthew's father."

I had a sudden, fleeting image of Pa sitting with Matthew at the cabin table on the *Bellflower*, telling yarns of his youth when he'd roamed the headwaters of the Missouri in company with the fur traders.

"If you're Adam Gaunt – then you must have known my father, a long time back, on the Missouri and the Yellowstone."

"I've spent a good deal of time in that part of the world, certainly."

"My father's name was Ben Summerbee. He was a riverman all his life, but he started out as a boy on the flatboats, and then hauled supplies for the fur traders. You might remember him from Fort Union when he took the German prince upriver with his artist friend. Or at Fort McKenzie, with Mitchell and Berger, when the Bloods killed the Blackfoot boy for his gold-lace hat. He remembered you, all right," I added irrelevantly.

The man continued to gaze up at me in silence, as though searching for another face behind the flesh of my own.

"Well, I'm damned," he said at last. "So you're Ben Summerbee's girl. I never even knew he had family – but then, you must have been born after I left those parts." He nodded, as if the discovery had given him genuine pleasure. "What's the old rogue been up to, since I saw him last?"

"He's dead," I said shortly. "Farragut's men shot him down, back in April on the day they took New Orleans."

"I'm sorry to hear it, though it sounds as if he died a hero."

"It didn't seem so at the time. He made it easy for them."

"Ah." Adam Gaunt's expression indicated that he understood perfectly how my father's end had come about. "Ben was a pretty wild young man, as I remember, always in trouble of some kind. He could drink most of us under the table when the mood took him."

I found myself smiling. "The years didn't change him, Mr Gaunt."

"And why should they, after all? Don't believe what the churchmen tell you. The years don't change us in any way, except to make us more aware of our true natures."

The horse tossed its head impatiently and the rider leaned forward to pat its neck.

"Well, I'm delighted to meet you at last, Katherine Summerbee. How strange that you should arrive at Hawk's Dyke like this, simply because of a lost watch." He was curious; he'd already divined there was more to the tale than the return of a watch, and I found myself plunged back into all the miserable turmoil of the previous night. But Adam Gaunt simply nodded, and raised a hand in dismissal.

"I'll see you at breakfast then, Katherine."

With an easy movement he turned his horse's head towards the stable yard, the black dog trotting at his heels. I lingered at my post until the sound of shod hooves had been swallowed up in the returning peace of the morning, reflecting that Adam Gaunt was not at all the sort of tyrant I'd been led to expect.

3

I hadn't imagined I'd be hungry by breakfast time. Jilted young ladies were supposed to go into a decline and become wan and delicate – and I was as heart-sore as I'd ever been the previous night. But as Matthew had pointed out, I was no lady – and so I found myself unaccountably hungry, and relieved to hear that the maid who came to my room at eight o'clock with a copper pitcher of water had been told to return in half an hour to guide me downstairs for breakfast. In that rambling house it was quite probable I'd never have found the dining-room at all.

Matthew's mother was seated alone at one end of the long table when I arrived, and as soon as I opened the door I realised it had been Rachel Gaunt's dark eyes and pale, oval face which had gazed down at me sympathetically the day before from the photographer's carefully marshalled group.

"I should sit here, if I were you, Katherine." She glanced up and smiled as I entered the room, appraising me with her calm, intelligent gaze and indicating the chair next to her own.

"We're left to introduce ourselves, I'm afraid, since Matthew hasn't arrived from the Abbey yet – but I hope you don't mind my calling you Katherine. You seem much of an age with my daughter Alice, and you'll find we don't stand much on ceremony here at Hawk's Dyke."

A bustling maid pulled the chair clear of the table for me, then picked up a dish and left the room.

"My husband and my younger daughter come to breakfast when it suits them," Rachel Gaunt continued, "but I'm sure we can keep one another company in the meantime."

I slid quickly into my chair, afraid the maid would return to push it back into its place if I was a moment late in occupying it. Keeping my hands in my lap, I gazed round apprehensively at the battery of silverware and porcelain which crowded the cloth. I'd certainly expected these people to live better than we did on the *Bellflower*, where the loss of one of our cross-tined forks meant eating with the fingers or waiting a turn for another, but nothing I'd seen since leaving the Mississippi had prepared me for such a ritual. If this was an English breakfast, whatever must dinner be like?

The table was a sea of white damask, upon which a fleet of slop basins, sugar bowls and jugs circled the pots of tea and coffee like tugboats round a couple of steamers, rigged out with tongs and spoons; there

119

were cellars of salt and mustard, a rack of fresh toast and two separate butter plates, salt and plain, next to a raft of conserve pots and cups and saucers – and marvel of marvels, at Mrs Gaunt's left hand, a fat little silver urn with a spirit-heater, bubbling the water for tea.

"I expect you prefer coffee in the mornings." Rachel Gaunt picked up a little velvet pad in the form of a parrot, wrapped it round the handle of the coffee pot, and began to pour into the nearest of the empty cups. "You'll find boiled eggs in that chafing-dish, and kidneys and kedgeree just beyond it. There's cold veal-and-ham pie on the side table if you're really hungry."

Out of the corner of her eye, she noticed that embarrassment had kept me rooted to my seat.

"You must find us very old-fashioned here in England," she suggested tactfully. "You Americans are so progressive – so modern. You'll have to make allowances for our quaintness, Katherine, and ask for anything you can't find."

Mentally blessing Matthew's mother for her infinite understanding, I spent the next ten minutes investigating the stacked plates and covered dishes at the far end of the table. I'd hardly sat down again with my spoils when the door opened and Adam Gaunt came in.

His wife looked up at once, smiling like a sunrise; she must have heard his step in the hall.

"Katherine – this is Matthew's father. Miss Summerbee is our American guest, my dear."

"We've met."

He lingered for a moment at her chair, and I saw Rachel Gaunt reach up to touch her fingers briefly to her husband's cheek. It was a tiny gesture – just the lightest brush of the fingertips, almost accidental, over in an instant – yet within a single day I noticed them repeat that fleeting caress over and over again, Rachel's fingers gently tracing the curve of his cheekbone, their hands meeting almost by chance, or Adam's teasing an imaginary strand of hair from her eyes. And each time it filled me with an aching envy because of the emptiness of my own life and the obvious fullness of theirs.

Adam Gaunt had just taken his seat when the door opened once more and Matthew's fifteen-year-old half-sister Louise swept in with a great hissing of skirts and a bright clatter of heels on the floor. Alice and Louise, I gathered, were the daughters of Rachel's marriage to Jonas Oliver; together with Violet Broadney, they were the possessors of the three strikingly blonde heads I'd seen at the Abbey. Louise's features, unlike those of her sister-in-law Violet, were too small and fine to give promise of true beauty, but there was determination in the set of her narrow chin, and curiosity in her glance as soon as she saw me. She continued to examine me in the manner of someone inspecting an exotic insect while her stepfather explained my connection with Ben Summerbee and his own distant past.

"Katherine–" he added suddenly, frowning, "didn't you tell me you and your father were in New Orleans when the Federal ships arrived?"

"That's true – or I'd probably never have met Matthew."

"Was it your father's boat, then, that rescued Matthew and his gold bullion from under the noses of the Yankees?"

"Pa agreed to take him downriver, certainly. But after Pa was shot, one of the river pilots took the *Bellflower* through the bayous to the Gulf, so that Matthew could get back to his ship."

Almost at once I suspected I'd said too much.

"Then why on earth didn't Matthew tell us yesterday who you were, instead of rushing you off to Hawk's Dyke like that?"

Louise Oliver had been watching me covertly from under blonde lashes.

"When Matthew told us how he'd escaped from New Orleans, he never mentioned that the captain of the steamboat had a daughter. But perhaps you weren't on board at the time," she suggested innocently.

"Oh, I was there." And I could well imagine, I added silently to myself, why Matthew had said nothing about me. "I was there when the Federals came, but I had to stay in New Orleans to look after Pa when he was shot. Mr Ransome the pilot said he'd take Matthew to Barataria Bay, if I was willing to lend them the boat."

"I don't suppose Matthew was at all grateful," Louise remarked forthrightly. "He never is. He seems to think everyone's obliged to help him out of scrapes without a word of thanks for it."

"Louise!" murmured her mother. "That's hardly fair."

"Isn't it?" Adam Gaunt glanced across at his wife. "I think Louise is quite right. Ben and his daughter obviously risked their necks to get Matthew out of the mess he was in – and while I don't suppose Ben's death was directly Matthew's fault, the fact remains that he owes Katherine a considerable debt. Now the poor girl's come trailing across half England to bring my blessed watch back, and Matthew hasn't even had the decency to introduce her to his family. It isn't good enough, Rachel."

"Matthew didn't know I was coming here. I guess I surprised him." I felt bound to say something in Matthew's defence, if only to prevent any more questions. "We were suddenly given two weeks to leave New Orleans, and I had to make up my mind in a rush."

"There you are, then." Rachel Gaunt reached out to touch her husband's hand. "You condemned Matthew quite unjustly. Though I must tell you, Katherine, that whatever my son may have said, you have his mother's eternal gratitude. When he first mentioned going on this blockade-running venture, the Oliver directors didn't want him to go at all. In the end, they only agreed on the strict understanding that he'd wait in Havana until the *Vixen* came back with her cotton. But of course he didn't, the reckless boy – and I gather he might easily have spent months in jail if you and your father hadn't helped him." She smiled – a mother's smile, which went straight to my heart. "On behalf of the whole family – thank you for sending him back to us."

"It wasn't so much, really." I stirred my coffee to cover my awkwardness.

"These English friends of yours – the people Matthew told us about – do they live far from here?" Adam Gaunt was watching me intently.

"Oh – " Startled, I groped for the name of an English town – any town where my mythical friends might be thought to live. "They're in Liverpool," I assured him, snatching at straws. "Matthew promised to take me back there by train today."

"After all your travelling yesterday?" Rachel Gaunt was dismayed. "Surely you don't have to rush off so quickly! Why don't you stay with us for a few days, and rest after your journey? It's the least we can do after your kindness to Matthew. She must stay, mustn't she, Adam?"

"Certainly – if Katherine wishes it."

"I can't think why Matthew didn't suggest it himself." Rachel frowned in perplexity. "Oh, I suppose his mind is full of Violet these days, the thoughtless creature."

Adam Gaunt's expression betrayed nothing at all of what he was thinking, but when his eyes met mine for an instant I knew for certain he suspected there was more to the story than either Matthew or I had revealed.

I never found out if he meant to question me further. Before either of us could say a word the dining-room door flew open and Matthew himself strode in, briskly businesslike in a Chesterfield overcoat. His tall silk hat still in his hand, he had the air of a man making a brief detour in a long journey. He checked his pace at once when he caught sight of his father, and completed the last few steps to the table with a scowl on his face.

"Ah – Matthew – " Adam Gaunt turned to regard his son with displeasure. "How providential. We were just discussing you."

"Oh?" Matthew pulled out a chair and threw himself down in it. "I don't suppose I've missed anything to my advantage. Good morning, Mother – good morning, Louise – good morning, Katherine, I trust you slept well. Is there still coffee in that pot, do you think?"

His studied nonchalance only provoked his father further.

"Why didn't you tell me yesterday that Katherine was Ben Summerbee's daughter?"

"Didn't I mention it?" Matthew glared at me under cover of reaching to accept a coffee-cup from his mother.

"No, you didn't mention it. If Katherine hadn't told me herself this morning, I'd never have known." Adam Gaunt leaned forward. "It was Katherine and her father who helped you escape from New Orleans, and yet you never said a word to any of us."

"I must have forgotten to tell you." Defiantly, Matthew met his father's eye.

"You forgot? When Ben Summerbee was killed trying to help you?"

"That wasn't exactly how it happened," I put in quickly. Matthew was regarding me with narrowed eyes, no doubt wondering how much I'd said.

"You didn't even tell us Katherine might call here," his father persisted.

"Didn't think of it, I suppose. When I didn't get a letter, I thought Katherine must have changed her mind."

"There is a war in America," his father pointed out coldly.

"I'm aware of that."

"But you didn't expect it to affect the mails, all the same."

"Letters get through, one way or another."

Knowing that I was the cause of their argument, I tried desperately to distract them.

"It really doesn't – "

"Now do you see?" Ignoring the interruption, Matthew turned to his mother. "Only yesterday, you were complaining because Violet and I prefer to stay at the Abbey instead of at Hawk's Dyke. Well, now you know why. Because *he* – " Matthew leaned forward and jabbed the air in front of his father's nose " – never lets me alone. Nothing I do is ever right. Dammit – I don't know how Louise can stand it here, day after day."

"Don't bring me into this," said Louise quickly. "Adam's your father, not mine."

"Louise! Matthew! That's enough!" Rachel Gaunt rapped the sugar-tongs against the edge of the bowl to restore order. "Matthew, I don't care how unfairly you think you've been treated: I won't tolerate smoking-room language at my breakfast table. And while you're under

123

this roof you'll be civil to your father. Adam – I think you've made your point," she added quickly, forestalling whatever he'd been about to say. "What on earth will Katherine think of us?"

"Oh, don't worry about me," I volunteered, "I'm not a bit shocked. Pa and I used to fight like cat and dog, pretty near all the time. I feel quite at home here."

Adam Gaunt leaned back in his chair, his face alive with ironic amusement.

"Matthew tries hard to make our guests feel welcome."

"Adam – " said his wife warningly.

Across the table, Louise caught my eye, and made a face. "It used to be like this all the time, whenever Matthew was in Norfolk. But now he's married to Violet he has to make a special trip to quarrel with his father."

"And that's quite enough from you, young lady." Rachel Gaunt frowned at her daughter. "I hate all this squabbling and backbiting, particularly at mealtimes. Meals are supposed to be family occasions." She paused to allow a wary silence to settle round the table.

"And now, Matthew, I should tell you that Katherine's changed her plans. We're all agreed it's quite absurd for her to rush straight off to Liverpool after her long journey to get here. She must think England consists of nothing but railway trains and station waiting-rooms. At any rate, I've asked her to stay with us here for a while and enjoy a quiet spell in the country before going on to stay with her friends. It seems a very small recompense for all she and her father did for you in New Orleans."

Matthew had been examining the tablecloth. Now he raised angry eyes towards mine, and I knew at once that if it had been left to Matthew I wouldn't have stayed at Hawk's Dyke for an instant longer than it took to gather together my few belongings.

"Aren't your friends expecting you, Katherine?" His voice was chill with disapproval.

How dare he? I thought to myself, and deliberately set out to annex the imaginary friends he'd invented for me.

"Oh, I don't reckon they're looking for me to arrive on any particular day. I'd be happy to stay here for a bit."

"I see."

"You don't mind, do you, Matthew?" I asked innocently.

"Why should I mind? Do whatever you please." He shrugged with elaborate unconcern, but his face remained stony as he drank his coffee and answered his mother's questions on the day's events at the Abbey.

He seemed to have lost interest in me; but my eye was drawn to a slight movement of his right hand – his coffee-spoon turning over and over between his fingers as he spoke.

At last he pushed back his chair and stood up.

"Well, then – I'll ride back to the Abbey and tell Violet she'll have her husband's company for a day or two longer. Good day to you all."

"I guess I'll walk to the stables with you, Matthew." Before he could disagree, I stood up too. "Would you mind, Mrs Gaunt? I've had more than enough breakfast."

"Of course, Katherine. As I told you, we don't stand on ceremony here."

4

I had to run to keep up with Matthew's long stride. He stalked through the hall towards the front door as if he couldn't wait to be clear of the house, and as soon as we were outside he set off at a rapid march.

"Wait, Matthew – please."

"If you say a single word to me, you'll regret it."

"You've no right to be angry with me."

"How do you expect me to feel? You agreed last night to travel to Liverpool with me and wait for a sailing on the *Alcyon*. Now I discover you've broken your word."

"Let's be straight about this, Matthew. *I* never agreed to anything last night. You were the one who wanted me to go back to Liverpool – and I told you then what I thought of your hotel and your steamer ticket. I'll sail back to America when and how I choose, not at your convenience – and you can make up your mind to that."

He was still walking so quickly I was almost breathless with the effort of keeping up, but suddenly he halted and swung round to face me.

"What are you up to, Katherine? What have you been plotting behind my back – soft-soaping my mother into letting you stay here? Because you've a plan of some kind, I'm sure."

"I've no plan at all." I was hurt that he should think me capable of petty revenge. Why did he know so little of me, when I'd learned so much about him?

"Your mother invited me to stay and I accepted – that's all." I struggled to make my purpose clear. "Hawk's Dyke is such a wonderful place . . . I used to dream of having a home like this. What's so wicked about staying here for a while?"

He continued to search my face for evidence of deceit.

125

"If you expect my family to pay you off, you won't get a penny, I promise you. I'll deny the whole business."

"I've told you – I wouldn't touch your money if I was starving in the gutter. I decided that for certain last night. You've made it quite plain that I'm a free woman, Matthew – so I'll do as I please from now on."

This time it was I who led off again towards the stable yard at the rear of the house. "You've caused me a great deal of pain, it's true, but I don't deal in low tricks like blackmail. If your ma and pa find out about that business on the *Bellflower*, it won't be from me. Now, will you stop scowling at me like that?"

"Hah!"

"Please, Matthew."

He hesitated. "You'll promise to keep silent?"

"I swear it. What would I gain by telling anyone? You've made it shamefully clear you want Violet for a wife, and not me. Well, so be it. After the way you've behaved, I wouldn't want *you* under any circumstances."

And yet even as we walked together past the garden wall, part of me whispered *at any price*. I was fascinated by the sheer, headlong rage which drove him – by his uncompromising pride and sure faith in the future. How could he be so certain – so impossibly assured? I found myself longing to touch him as I'd watched Rachel touch Adam – trustfully, as if no one else existed, just as Matthew had once caressed me in the darkness, with the touch that says *my soul* . . .

Without thinking, he'd fallen into step with me, absently holding aside a low branch to let me pass by. He even halted when I did at the corner of the wall and turned to gaze back at his parents' house – perhaps wondering what it was that all of a sudden I found so hard to leave.

I doubt if I could have enlightened him. I'd only spent one night at Hawk's Dyke; but then, I'd only spent one night with Matthew, and that had been enough to reveal hunger and emptiness I hadn't known I possessed. Matthew had denied himself to me – but the house had enfolded me, his family's house with its walls of russet brick flushed emerald with age, swelling out at their base among cushions of moss and creeper. The house was a live thing – lapped to its door-sills in greenness as if it owed nothing to the hand of man, but had suddenly burst up through the mass of vegetation like some woodland toadstool.

I already loved Hawk's Dyke, as I'd loved – and, to my dismay, I found I continued to love – Matthew. I loved its wildness, its passionate abundance, the warmth it contained . . .

126

"Your mother's so fortunate." I think I even sighed as I spoke.

"Fortunate?"

"To have all this." It was as near as I could come to describing the envy which filled me.

"Fortunate? My mother?" With an exclamation of disbelief, Matthew turned his back on the house and headed briskly for the stables. "If you knew how much she gave up for it you wouldn't say that. I'll never understand how she can stand being buried alive down here – with *him*."

"Your father doesn't seem so awful."

"Doesn't he? You'd know all about that, I suppose."

"Do you think it was easy, living with Pa when he let liquor get on his blind side?"

"Maybe not. But I'll bet your mother didn't make the mistake of marrying your father twice."

I missed a step in surprise. "Your parents have been married twice? Oh, but of course – you had a stepfather."

Matthew snorted. "If Jonas Oliver had still been alive, he'd have saved my mother from the biggest mistake she ever made."

"She doesn't seem to think it was a mistake."

"No – but then, my father's only ever had to crook his little finger to make my mother do whatever he wanted. She was just your age, you know, when she ran off with him to America. Her family were furious. He was older, and they reckoned he was a compulsive wanderer. But Mother wouldn't hear a word against him until the day he walked out and left her alone in a frontier town with a baby and no way of supporting herself."

"Surely not!" I had a sudden vision of Adam Gaunt as I'd seen him in the coolness of the early morning, content with his world, with his horse and his dog. "Why would he do such a thing?"

"He didn't want us any more. What other reason did he need? He just disappeared, and let Mother believe she was a widow – and eventually, when she'd struggled back to England, she married Jonas Oliver, the shipowner, and had Alice and Louise.

"And then, just when her life was comfortable at last, my father coolly turned up out of nowhere and wanted her back. Suddenly it suited him to have a family again. There was no end of trouble, and old Jonas Oliver died in the middle of it all, leaving Mother to take charge of the shipping line until I was old enough to inherit his share of the company."

Matthew turned towards me again, lest I should miss the point.

"Mother took charge of everything. After years with Jonas, there was nothing she couldn't do – including building the biggest, fastest steamship in the world. Jonas may have designed it, but my mother saw it launched."

"All by herself?"

"The other shareholders thought she was mad. But she believed in Jonas Oliver's vision of the future, and she was right."

I struggled to imagine Matthew's mother surrounded by shipwrights and the iron ribs of a half-built vessel.

"And then she went back to my father, in spite of all he'd done." Matthew's voice became grim. "As soon as I was old enough to take over the running of Oliver's on my own, she threw it all up and buried herself down here with him. She's still chairman of the company, but one day she'll turn that over to me, too."

Together, we rounded the last corner before the stable yard.

"It was Mother who made me promise not to go further than Havana in the *Vixen*. I had an older brother once – Reuben – but he was drowned at sea, and now Mother always imagines something awful's going to happen to me. She still thinks of me as a child." He smiled indulgently, but a moment later shook his head. "You're a woman, Katherine – tell me how she managed to forgive my father for abandoning us like that."

"Perhaps she loved him more than her ships." I couldn't forget the fleeting touch of Rachel's fingers to her husband's cheek.

"*Love* again, is it? It sounds more like lunacy to me."

"What else but love could make a woman forgive so much?"

"I don't believe it. That's too simple an explanation. It's more like . . . a mesmerism of some kind. The Gaunt men have always been impossible, yet women seem to be drawn to them in spite of it. My father – Henry Gaunt, the Earl who's just died – his father before that, so I'm told."

"But aren't you a Gaunt, Matthew? Whatever you call yourself, you're Adam Gaunt's son, so you must be a Gaunt too."

"Only by chance," Matthew muttered darkly. "I'd far rather have had old Jonas for a father, like Alice and Louise. Heart and soul, I'm an Oliver."

We walked on in brooding silence for a few moments, until the stone arch of the stable yard became visible through the trees. Now I began to slow my steps to gain time for the questions that were filling my mind.

"Matthew. . . . How old is your father?"

"Sixty. Maybe sixty-one."

128

"Oh, fiddlesticks! He can't be as old as that! Pa was fifty-four when he died and your father looks to be younger, even allowing for whiskey levelling the score."

"I think you can trust me to know how old my father is," Matthew remarked stiffly. "In any case – why are you so interested in him all of a sudden?"

We'd halted under the trees. "I don't know. I just wondered, that's all."

"Well, don't wonder, Katherine. Not about my father."

"I've never met anyone quite like him before."

"You shouldn't have met him at all."

"I'm glad I did. I like your father. And your mother too, of course, but . . . there's a sort of wildness about your father that seems to go with this place." I lifted my hands in futility. "I can't describe it any better than that."

"Katherine – forget about staying here. Come back with me today to Liverpool, and I'll take a room for you in the best hotel in the city. I'll even make sure you have the finest stateroom on the *Alcyon* when it sails. You won't regret leaving here, I promise you."

"I've told you, Matthew. I can pay for my own passage back to America, when I'm ready to go. Why are you so anxious to haul me off to Liverpool?"

"I don't want you here, at Hawk's Dyke. That's all."

"Why not? I've promised not to say anything about our marriage, haven't I? And it's so peaceful here. There's no war, and no killing, and no one insisting I have to cheer for one side or the other. I shall stay here for as long as your parents will have me."

"Katherine, please. Just trust my judgement."

"I reckon you can take your judgement right back to the Abbey and sit on it. Try it on Violet, why don't you?"

"I will not leave you here, in my father's house."

"You're just sore because he pitched into you at breakfast. Though he was no harder on you than I was, yesterday in the garden. In fact, that's something we have in common, Mr Gaunt and I – "

"Stop talking about my father, will you!"

"Maybe I ought to ask him – "

"No!"

And Matthew stopped my lips the only way he knew how – by kissing them, then and there under the trees, holding me tightly against him as if he was determined to keep me from uttering any other name but his, or from thinking of any man but himself.

*

I don't know which of us was angrier about that sudden, fierce kiss among the trees by the stable yard. It had been inspired by the basest of feelings, by vexation and resentment – certainly nothing finer – and as soon as we'd come to our separate senses we sprang furiously apart to stand, with a good six feet between us, glaring as if murder had been committed.

For several seconds I was too affronted to move. Matthew, too, seemed paralysed: then, shaking his head in disbelief at what he'd done, he drew the back of his hand swiftly across his lips and turned away determinedly towards the stables.

I didn't follow. I remained under the boughs of the broad oak, leaning on its moss-furred trunk, my cheek against my spread fingers. A few minutes later a horseman burst from the stable yard in a clatter of hooves and disappeared without a backward glance towards the drive. Matthew, it seemed, had urgent reasons for returning to the Abbey.

Chapter Ten

1

Three days later, according to Louise, Matthew went back to Liverpool, leaving Violet at the Abbey in the company of her friend Alice.

If Louise hadn't reported his absence after one of her morning rides to Sourwell I'd never have known of it. Since the moment he'd been forced to leave me a hostage in his father's house, Matthew Oliver had avoided Hawk's Dyke like the plague.

And without his disapproving presence I was free to revel in the glories of the place as I chose. To be able to lean in the mornings out of my little dormer window, watching the rooks circle raucously over the tops of the trees round the steadings of Old Hall Farm filled me with constant delight. Borne on the breeze, the scent of bruised grasses came to me at my window mingled with the warm, sharp tang of the stackyard. Surely nothing but mean-spiritedness could have prompted Matthew to deny me such pleasure?

The Gaunts had put down their roots in that place, his father told me one day in an expansive mood. He might have been speaking of dragons and giants, for all I knew about English history, but the notion of being descended from a family who'd lived in the same place for hundreds of years utterly entranced me, and I plagued him with questions about the Gaunts who'd gone before.

The family fortunes had been founded, he explained, by a Thomas Gaunt who'd built the first house on the site at Hawk's Dyke. Thomas had been shrewd enough to take Henry VIII's side in the matter of his divorce from Queen Catherine, and when the King threw the monks out of their nearby abbey, Thomas was offered the church lands at a bargain price. Almost immediately he moved to Sourwell, leaving Hawk's Dyke as an outpost of the growing family wealth.

Nowadays fifteen hundred acres of land went with the house, including Old Hall Farm and four more – fifteen hundred acres lying across one of those mysterious rhythm changes deep in the earth which alter the nature of the soil and the landscape within the space of a quarter-mile. To the south-west of the house and its home farm lay flat peat fields reclaimed from an old fen, fields which, when the soil was

131

newly turned, were of such dense, absorbent blackness as to suck in the light of day, lying dark and lustreless in the brightest sunshine. Behind the house and to the east of it the ground began to rise gently towards the uplands of the Breckland Heath – sandy, gravelly country where the roads twisted round spinneys and sudden valleys, and where the eye could no longer span two or three miles in a single, level glance.

And somewhere between Hawk's Dyke and the village of Stainham to the east lay two hundred ragged acres which were all that remained of the great Sourwell Fen; defiantly waterlogged in spite of the old Dutch improvers with their drainage dykes and their windmills. There were still some who claimed to have heard the spring boom of the bittern in its distant fastnesses; thatchers still went there to cut sedge and reeds for cottage roofs, startling its flocks of teal and pintail; and overhead the grey-backed harriers, the "blue hawks" of the fens, skimmed the tops of the clustered alders, scanning their private, secret wilderness.

It was the blue hawks, as far as anyone could remember, which had given the great drainage ditch its name – Hawk's Dyke – and because the dyke cut across the land like an arrow-flight, it had bequeathed that name in turn to the charmed circle of pastures and woods and ploughland which lay on either side.

2

For three hundred years, generations of Gaunts had expanded and altered the Old Hall, transforming cow byres into kitchens and kitchens into parlours, turning their labourers out into cottages and filling the garrets with servants as the family rose up in the world. The result was a warren of rooms linked by corridors which tilted and plunged in all directions, and a front door which had been re-sited on at least three occasions in the life of the house. Even by the time I knew it, the hallway had an impermanent air, linked as it was to the next floor by an eccentric, uneven spiral stairway, its treads too broad at the curving wall to be taken in a single step and too narrow at their inner end even for a toehold.

The house was alive as a tree was alive: perhaps it was the very evolving nature of the place which drew me to it, the evidence in plaster and brick that other feet had trod there before mine, that other eyes had gazed from the windows . . . and would gaze, long after I'd left it. I loved the Italian garden – I loved the little old parlour – even the cavernous, lime-washed kitchen enchanted me with its smell of new bread, its family of pantries and larders, and the china-loaded shelves of its great oak dresser.

But more than anything, I loved the library.

Books, to me, had always been more than a little magical. We'd only ever had three of them aboard the *Bellflower* – and for the last few years after Pa threw my mother's bible into the Ohio River at Evansville, only two. They were *Webster's English Grammar* and *A History of Tom Thumb*, both bought for me by a stoker who wrote an unexpectedly elegant hand and was rumoured to have run off after killing a man in Philadelphia. Jack – I don't think I ever knew his second name – used the idle hours at river landings to teach me to read, and for this reason the first words I ever deciphered were in Ma's bible: *In the beginning God created the heaven and the earth* – not a bad choice, you may say, though for a long time I believed it was Tom Thumb who'd languished in the belly of the whale.

Pa was never book-learned, but he read the New Orleans newspapers, the *Delta* and the *Picayune*, whenever he could find them, breathing earnestly through his nose, his lips moving and his thick finger tracing the print while I hovered nearby, ready to snatch the pages away as soon as he'd done with them. If we were somewhere on the Missouri or the Arkansas he'd buy whatever local news-sheet he could find, so that long after my stoker-teacher had gone on his way, I continued to practise what he'd taught me, copying out words with stubs of charcoal on the sun-bleached planks of the deck and rubbing them out almost immediately with my bare toes before Pa discovered my new-found skill. I'd watched him spend hours copying out receipts, and I knew it would only make him sore to know his daughter could have done it for him in a few triumphant minutes.

Three books and every newspaper I could lay my hands on – that was all the reading I'd known until the day I peeped cautiously round the door of the library at Hawk's Dyke to discover a pirates' cave of treasure.

The library was Adam Gaunt's lair, his refuge from the daily routine of the house. If he wasn't riding, he'd retreat there early in the morning and remain until someone disturbed him, sprawled in an armchair with his heels up on the high brass fender and a leather-bound volume in his hands.

It seemed incredible to me that one person should even possess so many books, let alone attempt to read them all in a single lifetime. The library was panelled like the dining-room in ancient honey-coloured wood, silken to the touch, some of it split lengthwise with age, its mouldings pushed askew by the subtle sinking of the house around it. But the true glory of the room – its principal wonder – was case after case of shelving, crammed from one end to the other with books.

Gold leaf glinted amid the ranks of plain, no-nonsense, battered calfskin or cloth bindings. Fat dictionaries stood shoulder to shoulder with slender, mottled-paper pamphlets batched together with twine; pliant volumes of poetry propped up great, unmanageable coloured folios of plants and animals, rustling with interleaved tissue . . .

The printed word was everywhere, squeezed on its side into the gap between a row of books and the shelf above, piled in corners when space had run out, awaiting attention in tottering stacks on the centre table. . . . The printed word – not only in English, but in Greek and Latin and French – filled the place to the ceiling. The room was a Babel in print, a banquet of knowledge where an intemperate reader could die of words.

And while I greedily explored his shelves, Matthew's father – the brooding, selfish monster of Matthew's tale – lay back in his chair, his heels on the fender and the curled fingers of one hand resting lightly against his cheek, watching me and waiting for my verdict on his hoard.

I will not leave you here in my father's house. Before long, no doubt, Matthew would have his way, and I'd be off on my wanderings once more. But I cherished my dreams, just as he did: where was the harm, for a while, in letting me indulge them a little?

3

To my great joy Adam Gaunt gave me the freedom of his library, only stipulating that his books must be returned when I'd finished with them. After that, whenever I could find a quiet corner of the garden or by lamplight in bed at night, I devoured whatever I'd plundered from his shelves that day.

Besides, there was no embarrassment in reading. I could hardly make a mistake in turning a page, whereas mealtimes, especially, were still haunted by the possibility of disaster. The worst occasion was when I drank the contents of a pretty crystal finger-bowl before discovering what it was meant for. On the whole, reading was safer.

"You'll ruin your eyes," Louise remarked one afternoon, discovering me under one of the trees in the garden, frowning over a volume on animal magnetism and wondering if Dr Mesmer's parlour tricks might have some magical effect on Matthew. "You're worse than my stepfather," she added peevishly. "You always seem to have your nose in a book."

"Don't you like books, Louise?"

She gave a little sigh of impatience and reached up to touch her blonde hair, elegantly confined in a grown-up chignon.

"Books are all very well when you're too old for anything else," she pronounced. "There are lots of other things I'd rather do, but the trouble is, I get awfully bored doing them on my own, now that Alice has gone to live at the Abbey."

"I thought you visited her often."

"Quite often – but it isn't the same as when she was living here. So much of her time is taken up now with being a countess – because she's new to it, I suppose, and there's lots to learn. Though they do have awfully amusing people to stay sometimes, otherwise I don't expect I'd meet anyone at all. Freddie Broadney's there just now – Violet's brother, you know." She made the remark quite casually, but with shining eyes and a little smile of satisfaction which belied her indifference. "Freddie has promised to ride with me one afternoon."

"What does your mother think of that?"

Louise arched her back and tilted her chin petulantly. "Oh, I dare say Mamma would be far happier if I stayed in the parlour at Hawk's Dyke and read books, like you. Oh, Katherine, you can't imagine how boring it is down here! If it wasn't for Alice at the Abbey, I think I'd go out of my mind. Mamma takes me to Liverpool sometimes when she has to go there on business, but what I'd really like is to stay in London like Violet does, and go to dances and dinners, and for carriage drives in the park – and live in a proper house with a ballroom, instead of a poky old farmhouse in the country. Do you know," she added, wide-eyed, "Violet knows the Prince of Wales! Quite well, I believe." When I failed to look properly impressed, she went on, "That means she knows everybody who matters."

Then her face fell, a caricature of dismay under her fashionably dressed hair.

"I won't even be presented for another three years."

"Presented?"

"At a 'drawing-room'. You know – kissing the Queen's hand, and so forth."

"Oh." I wasn't sure why this should matter so much. "I dare say your parents will buy you a ticket as soon as you're old enough."

"It isn't like taking a box at the theatre, you know. And please remember – Adam Gaunt's no parent of mine. Just Mamma. My real father would never have dragged us off to the country like a gang of ditch-diggers, you may be sure. I'm sure Violet and Freddie must think we're very peculiar at Hawk's Dyke. In fact, I know Violet does. *Déclassé* – that's the word she uses. She means *in reduced circumstances*."

"That's pretty high-handed of her, isn't it?"

"It isn't even true." Louise pouted. "Papa left Mamma a great deal of money and my stepfather owns property in London. It just suits him to live like a peasant, for some reason."

"I'd be happy to live here, I can tell you."

"Would you?" Louise looked round, mildly surprised. "Well, I happen to know Violet's sworn to Matthew that she won't spend a night at Hawk's Dyke until he's torn down the house and built a proper gentleman's residence. She means after my stepfather dies, of course."

"What a wicked thing to say!"

"But it's true! Nobody amusing ever comes to visit. Except you," she added quickly. "I've never met anyone quite like you before. But we're going to be friends, Katherine, aren't we?"

"Well, of course. Though I shan't be staying very long, you know."

"I'll tell them I want to keep you here for ever and ever." Louise smiled beatifically. "Then you can stay as long as you like."

4

After ten days, Matthew had decided I'd stayed long enough. But by then, at Rachel Gaunt's insistence, I'd promised to write to the mythical friends awaiting my arrival in Liverpool, asking for another three weeks' grace. I even walked two miles to the village of Stainham in order to pretend I'd started my letter on its way.

"I bet Matthew has only come down here to fetch Violet away from the Abbey," Louise confided sagely. "Violet and Alice are as thick as thieves these days. Gossip-gossip, scandal-scandal, all day long. Who's seeing who else's wife in London, who's been caught cheating at whist, who looked a fright at the races – that sort of thing. And it's my opinion Violet loathes Liverpool. She won't stay there for long, even for Matthew."

"That's a fine way for a wife to behave!" I found myself indignant on Matthew's behalf. "How can Matthew run his company, if he doesn't stay in Liverpool?"

Louise raised an admonishing finger. "Commerce is for grocers, my dear. Not for gentlemen."

"What are gentlemen supposed to do, then?"

"Nothing." Louise looked genuinely surprised. "The most *gentlemanly* gentlemen do nothing at all. The less the better."

"And where do they find the money to live on, I'd like to know?"

"Oh Katherine, you do ask such peculiar questions!"

In spite of all Violet could do, Matthew seemed to prefer an existence half-way between commerce and idleness, which made him slightly suspect in the grandest society. Drag him to a ball, Violet had complained, and she'd soon find him in the supper-room, arranging to ship wine for the caterers. Leave him for five minutes with one of her ambassador uncles, and she'd return to find him urging the invasion of some country to whose ports he wanted free access. Everything was bent to the service of J. G. Oliver & Co. as Matthew laboured to build it into the biggest and most powerful shipping line in the world. He wasn't satisfied merely to compete with the best, Violet had wailed to her friend Alice: Matthew wanted to drive his competitors out of business altogether. And all Violet wanted was to have a little fun.

On the tenth day of my stay at Hawk's Dyke, Matthew arrived to collect his mother's signature on a business document.

I'd always found it hard to believe Matthew's tale of his mother defying the Oliver directors to build her great steamship. Try as I might, I couldn't imagine Rachel Gaunt, with her soft dark eyes, enjoying the battles of business as Matthew did; yet the respect in Matthew's voice when he'd spoken of the way she'd pursued Oliver's dominance of the North Atlantic trade had been real enough. Now, sitting after dinner in the drawing-room at Hawk's Dyke, I watched her lean forward intently in her chair, absorbed in the proposition Matthew had laid before her.

Matthew had decided to sell ships – eighteen of them, almost half of the Oliver fleet. He'd drawn up a list of names: the *Mount Lowell*, the *Marpessa*, the *Boreas*, the *Brander* – one of the first ships Jonas Oliver had built – the *Severn Valley*, the *Hestia*. . . . It was a long list, and Matthew watched his mother's frown deepen as she read it through.

"Every one of those vessels is an old, wooden-hulled sailer which has outlived its usefulness," he reminded her. "And steamships will be masters of the sea once de Lesseps has finished this canal of his."

"If he ever does finish it."

"He'll finish it, or someone else will, if only because it'll cut off the long passage round the Cape of Good Hope. We'll be able to go out to India by way of Suez in next to no time – but only by steam. That canal will make the sailing ship a thing of the past."

"In thirty years' time, perhaps."

"In ten or fifteen years, Mother. You built the *Altair* – you should know. The *Altair* succeeded by being a steamer, and by being big. That's another reason why I want to sell off these older vessels. They're mostly barques or small three-masters – not big enough for the kind of cargo we'll be carrying in the future."

Sitting with Louise on the other side of the room, I eavesdropped on

137

Matthew's plans, carried back in spite of myself to the firelit deck of the *Bellflower* when he'd eclipsed even the burning river with the splendour of his dreams. Magnificent, but impossible: that's what I'd believed at the time, and admired him all the more for the valiance of his ambition. But I'd come to understand that Matthew's dreams were no flight from reality, but plans to be followed with grim determination.

Now he was dreaming of cheap grain from America, to be imported in huge quantities as soon as the war was over. And not only grain: Arctic explorers had reported that Eskimo seal-meat kept fresh indefinitely, packed in ice, which meant that as soon as a way was found of keeping meat frozen at sea, there was no reason why tons of mutton shouldn't be shipped from New Zealand or beef from across the Atlantic.

"I wouldn't mention these plans of yours to the people round Hawk's Dyke," his father warned him. "The farmers will think you're bent on stealing their livelihood. Australian wool is bad enough, but if you start importing huge amounts of grain and meat too. . . . Think what you'll do to the farm workers."

Matthew's chin rose in the defiant expression his father's remarks always produced.

"And what about cheap bread to feed the cities? Don't you think that's a good thing? In any case, this is the shipping trade of the future, whether we like it or not. And this is the time to sell, while I can still get a price for those ships. I want to see the Oliver's fleet in good shape before it's needed, not once it's too late."

He turned to his mother. "Will you support me at the next directors' meeting, Mother?"

Rachel Gaunt hesitated, torn between her misgivings and loyalty to her son.

"You're right, Matthew. I'm sure you are."

Carefully, Matthew folded the documents he'd brought.

"Excellent. I'll take this back to Liverpool tomorrow." And in the same brisk tone he added, "You must be ready to come back to Liverpool with me by now, Katherine. I expect you're bored out of your wits by country life."

"No, she isn't," snapped Louise at once. "What a horrid thing to say! Katherine likes it here with us. Don't you, Katherine?"

"You've all been very kind – "

Matthew's eyes were hard.

"Katherine's too polite to say what she really thinks. I'm sure it's time I rescued her from deepest Norfolk before she grows roots."

"Don't bully the girl, Matthew." Adam Gaunt's voice was deceptively lazy. "Let her make up her own mind."

"Excuse me, but it seems sensible, since I'll be travelling to Liverpool tomorrow – "

"I said let Katherine make up her own mind."

Matthew glanced towards his father as if he meant to make an angry retort – and then thought better of it. Instead he turned to me, his face full of bitter resentment.

"Stay then, if you're so happy here."

"Oh, she will," promised Louise. "I'm sure she will."

I can't think why Louise had taken such a shine to me, except that in her eyes I was as exotic as an Amazon parrot, something to be taken out of its cage when she was bored, to be petted or instructed as the mood took her.

I'd turned her interest into a two-way trade, still smarting from Matthew's dismissal of me as some kind of backwoods savage. Louis Boudreaux had actually used the word *sauvage* in his soft Cajun dialect: Matthew had been too polite, but he'd implied it all the same. Now, in Louise, I found a willing teacher. I told her stories of the pirate Lafitte, and she showed me how to eat an orange with a fork and knife, and grapes without spitting the pips; I bartered Sam's prize gumbo recipe for lessons in climbing daintily into and out of a carriage; in return for the tale of Cannon's *Louisiana* exploding in '49 at the Gravier Street wharf – when it had rained arms and legs for a full two minutes, and the shrapnel cut a mule in two – she made me practise *Delightful!* and *How charming!* over and over again with icy insincerity, until I fancied myself ladylike indeed.

And the longer I stayed, the deeper the seductive peace of Hawk's Dyke sank into my soul and the harder it was to think of setting out on my travels once more. It was too easy to accept my role as Louise's parrot – too easy by a long way. Unfortunately, my education had quickly progressed to the point when Louise felt I was ready to be shown off further afield.

"Ah – Katherine!" she called to me one day as I passed her door, my arms full of booty from the library. "Come in here quickly. I've had the most wonderful idea."

"Oh?" I lingered cautiously in the doorway. "What sort of idea?"

"Mamma's talking of driving over to the Abbey this afternoon. A morning call – the usual thing – "

"How can it be a morning call in the afternoon?"

"Oh, I don't know! That's just what they're called," she said impatiently. "What I'm trying to tell you is that Mamma and I are to drive over to the Abbey after lunch, and I've told her you'd like to go too."

"Why in blue blazes did you tell her that?"

The catastrophic episode of the muddy boots and poppy-laden hat was still fresh in my mind. At Hawk's Dyke the state of my few darned and much-travelled clothes didn't seem to matter at all, but I'd no wish to appear once more before the elegant company at the Abbey looking like a charity child at their gates.

"Why on earth should I want to go visiting at Sourwell? I don't even have anything to wear."

"But you must come with us, Katherine! I want you to come most particularly, to tell me what you think of Freddie Broadney. How can you have an opinion, if you've never seen him? And he's just . . . oh . . . he's just too divine for words." Her face shone ecstatically. "And as for having nothing to wear – "

Snatching my arm, she pulled me over to the huge old wardrobe in her room, its double doors yawning open on the mass of clothing inside.

"Look at all this! And there's a good deal more," she confessed, "but I have to keep it stowed away in trunks because there's no room for it anywhere else. Don't ever tell Adam, will you? He calls me 'fashion's slave' as it is, and even Mamma doesn't know how much I actually spend on clothes. Matthew lets me have a little money when my allowance runs out – but then, he knows how important it is for a woman to look well." In the pier-glass, she surveyed her faultless appearance with satisfaction.

"How in the world do you manage to wear all these dresses?"

I'd never seen such extravagance – though I couldn't resist sliding my fingers over a ripple of rich, cherry-coloured moiré trapped in the hinge of the wardrobe door.

"Oh, I don't wear them all! Only the newest." Louise's eyes grew wide with disarming candour. "But you see, down here there's no one to give my old dresses to, and I just seem to collect more and more." She gazed at her crammed wardrobe in genuine dismay. "You can't imagine what a problem it is. So you see, if all you need is something to wear to the Abbey this afternoon – so that you can look Freddie over for me, and tell me what you think – I'm sure we could find an absolutely ravishing dress for you, really I am." She clung to my arm in her eagerness.

"I don't think so, Louise. I don't reckon to be a fashion plate." I

140

laughed as I saw her face fall. "Don't worry – I know you meant it kindly."

"Well, I think it's too bad of you. Especially after what I told Alice and Violet yesterday."

I pricked up my ears at this. "Didn't Violet go back to Liverpool with Matthew?"

"I should say not! I told you, she hates the place. She's off to London with Freddie and Sir George in a few days, and Matthew's arranged to join her there."

"And just what did you tell Alice and Violet, Louise?"

"Nothing awfully bad . . ." All at once Louise discovered something fascinating in the pattern of her bedroom carpet.

"What exactly?"

"I only said it because Violet was being so mean about you." Louise glanced up, and suddenly the words began to tumble out in a flood of guilty explanation. "If she hadn't been so horrid, I'd never have said a thing, truly I wouldn't. She was making Alice laugh about the day you came to the Abbey when we were having that photograph taken, and you came up the drive – "

"Looking a pretty sight, I imagine."

"Well, you'd walked a long way! I'd like to see how Violet would look after walking for miles across the fields."

"Go on. I expect there's more."

"It was all because of that . . . bag thing round your neck. Violet asked me what was in it, and I said – "

"You didn't tell her? Oh, Louise – how could you!"

"And she said normal people didn't walk about with gunpowder and chewed-up leaves round their necks instead of jewellery – and she called you 'the Voodoo Queen', and wanted to know if you'd put us all under a spell yet. And when Alice asked if you were an acquaintance of Matthew's, she said 'Oh, my dear, not a guttersnipe like that!' And I told them – " Louise's voice rose valiantly in my defence. "I told them you were my friend, and an American lady was just as good as an English lady any day of the week, only different. Because it's true, isn't it?"

"Well, of course it is! Every bit as good!"

I was furious, carried away at once on a hot tide of indignation. Guttersnipe be hanged! Let Violet look out – three weeks of Louise's tuition had shown me that being a lady wasn't so hard after all. Even a guttersnipe could master eating an orange with a knife and fork if she practised long enough, and my *How charming!* was already near

141

enough the genuine article to make the butcher's boy gape in astonishment.

"So you'll come to the Abbey this afternoon?" Louise demanded excitedly. "You'll show them you aren't a voodoo queen?"

Startled, from a great distance, I heard myself declare "You bet I will! Find me something smart to wear, and I'll go."

The rich, heady blood of Ben Summerbee was racing in my veins. Hadn't it all been Violet's fault from the very start? If Violet hadn't had ambassadors for uncles, wouldn't I still be Matthew Oliver's wife?

I revelled in the thought of those hard, ice-blue eyes widening in surprise when she saw me in a great show of finery – even borrowed finery – and sitting in a carriage like a proper lady. How dare she call me a guttersnipe! What was there to choose between us at the end of the day but twenty guineas' worth of taffeta and lace? And here was Louise Oliver, anxious to make good the deficiency!

Louise wasted no time. With a delighted cry, she slammed the door to the passage outside and dragged a huge trunk concealed under an India shawl into the middle of the floor. In a second the lid was flung up and Louise knelt before it, her arms buried to the elbow in a froth of silks and velvets, poplins and foulards and lace. For almost ten minutes she burrowed out forgotten glories, tossing each one across the bed with a little squeal of recognition until it lay heaped with mantles and sashes and gloves and fichus, a discarded rainbow of colour.

"Oh Katherine – yes! You'd look quite perfect in this!" Louise held up a dress of rich grey silk braided on the bodice and cuffs with military black.

"And look, this little parasol goes with it." Throwing the dress down on the bed, she struggled with a dainty grey silk parasol on an ebony stem. At last she held it over her head with all the flourish of a *modiste*. "Still very fashionable, Madame, though I think perhaps the fan will be favourite for next season."

"Heaven's sakes, Louise, I can't wear all that!"

"But of course you can! It will look far more dramatic with your dark hair than it ever did when I wore it. And we're almost the same height, so I'm sure it'll fit. Have you brought a cage?"

"A cage?"

"A cage. A crinoline. *Hoops*," she added when I still failed to understand. "To go under the skirt."

"Oh, a hooped petticoat! Bless you, I've never had one of those. Mine's plain calico."

"Well, you'll have to wear hoops with this dress, or it will look most peculiar."

The borrowed crinoline, when I'd stepped into the centre and raised it gingerly round my waist, made me look like the shade of the big oil lamp which hung over the dining-room table. Whenever I took a step the watchspring hoops swung from side to side like a ship in a gale and twanged against the wooden bedposts as I passed.

"How am I ever going to sit down in this?"

"It bends, you goose! Look!" And Louise seized the nearest hoops in her hands, folding them together until they buckled and twisted with the slithering clash of a fencing school. "My ball crinoline has almost thirty hoops. If it didn't bend, how do you imagine a gentleman would ever get near me to waltz? Don't worry, you'll soon forget it's there."

Forget? How could anyone forget an hour of fiddling with inaccessible hooks and tapes, of hair-brushing and stay-tying and twitching and tugging, simply to put on a dress?

At long last, Louise was satisfied with the finished effect.

"There you are – what did I tell you?" Her blonde head hovered next to mine in the looking-glass as she wiggled the black epaulettes into place. "You look just like one of these American heiresses everyone's talking about."

She'd certainly made a different woman of me. The auburn-haired creature who gazed boldly out of Louise's mirror looked so strange . . . not in the least like the tousled, straw-hatted Katherine who'd come ashore in Liverpool a bare three weeks earlier. The grey silk skirt seemed to go on for ever; there was yard upon sumptuous yard of it, gathered to fullness over my backside as if I were heading into a wind. And by the time I joined Louise and her mother in the landau there were kid gloves on the hands which clutched the grey silk parasol, and a little helmet hat trimmed with ostrich feathers on top of my elegant chignon, like the final cherry on the cake.

I looked . . . I looked *foreign*, to be absolutely honest. Even dressed as a fashionable English lady, there was still something exotic about me, as if the wary eyes of a little animal peered out from behind my fancy Mardi Gras mask. Louise was aware of it too: I saw her frown, suspecting that her plans for me had gone astray, but quite unable to identify the flaw.

"You've worked wonders, Louise. I look more than average ladylike," I assured her, and she beamed again, like a little girl who'd discovered an exciting new doll.

5

All the way to the Abbey, Louise harped on the virtues of Freddie Broadney until her mother told her to stop.

143

"Mr Frederick Broadney is an empty-headed young man, Louise, and I won't have you mooning over him like a lovesick calf."

Louise made a face at me as soon as Mrs Gaunt's attention was distracted. "Wait until you see him . . ." she whispered, and cast her eyes up to Heaven.

But to Louise's great disappointment Mr Frederick Broadney was out shooting when we arrived, together with the other gentlemen of the party, and only a row of long-dead Gaunts scowled down from their frames at my bare-faced impudence as I tottered up the great staircase. The Abbey ladies were taking tea in a saloon the size of a furniture warehouse, the dowager Countess Henrietta poker-straight in her chair, Violet Oliver and Alice, Louise's sister, sitting together over a watercolour album on a sofa nearby. Rachel and Louise advanced into an orgy of duty-kissing while I hung back, giving all my attention to managing the wilful grey silk skirt in which Louise had enveloped me.

I'd never before worn anything which *swished* so much. Now I was obliged to advance under full sail across an ocean of carpet, navigating my skirts round footstools and firescreens to a safe haven on a little satinwood chair, where I only just remembered to tuck my boots under my ample hem so that no one should see them. The ladies were too well bred to stare: if they were astonished by my transformation, none of them showed it by so much as the twitch of an elegant eyebrow. Even Violet Oliver graciously inclined her head when I was introduced, for all the world as if I were one of her sultans from beyond the Arabian Sea.

I was offered tea in a tiny, translucent cup with a painted rose-bush at the rim, and asked what I thought of English weather.

"Delightful!"

And the Norfolk countryside?

"Charming!"

I hadn't expected a round of applause, but as I watched Violet covertly examine me I was as gratified as if the room had erupted in a storm of cheering. I only hoped Violet realised what an incomparable treasure she saw before her. I was a woman of the New World: the natural nobility of my soul made me a match for the Queen of England, now it was no longer hidden by mud and wagging poppies. Thank the Lord for grey silk and black braid – for a carriage parasol and kid gloves! Ben Summerbee's girl was a lady at last, in twelve steel hoops and a plume of ostrich feathers. I felt almost sisterly towards Louise.

6

And for a whole hour I behaved impeccably. I sat so straight in my chair that my back hurt like the very devil. Remembering that Louise had warned me on no account to take off my gloves, I kept them on even when a slice of transparently thin bread-and-butter became plastered to the buttons; with truly ladylike presence of mind I made sure that if the maids found it later, stuck under the edge of the sofa table, they could only assume it had somehow flown sideways from an over-full plate.

I even endured tea without sugar so as not to have to juggle the treacherous spring-loaded tongs, which could easily flick a lump the length of the room if they twisted out of control. And I thought I complimented the dowager Henrietta most elegantly on the slick turn-out of her waiters, though I saw Louise's eyes grow round with alarm as I spoke.

"Ah – liveried footmen," the Countess agreed sombrely. "They're a horrid expense, are they not, however handsome they look on the back of a dress coach?" She leaned towards me, a gleam of amusement in her knowing, monkey eyes. "They're a matched set, those fellows. See the calves of their legs? They're never done, gettin' the housemaids into trouble, but Charles refuses to break up the pack. Help yourself."

For an awful moment I thought she was inviting me to choose one of the hovering footmen with their frogged coats and powdered hair – but she was only referring to the tiny honey-cakes held at my elbow by one of those poker-stiff grandees.

"Delightful," I assured her. "How charming!"

Violet Oliver was still watching me from her seat on the nearby sofa.

"You met my husband in America, I believe, Miss Summerbee," she ventured at last.

"In New Orleans, Mrs Oliver." *Mrs Oliver*, forsooth!

"Is that your home, may I ask, or did the war take you there?"

"Oh, I have several homes," I assured her airily. "My father was in shipping, and we travelled a good deal. Here and there, you know. This way and that."

"Indeed?" Violet Oliver's delicate brows rose a fraction.

"He was a shipowner, you might say. And he'd an interest in distilling, too. Our name is well known all over, I can tell you."

Violet's pale eyes scanned my expensive gown and hat. "Do I gather Mr Summerbee is dead now?"

"He gave his life for the Southern cause, Mrs Oliver. It was a hero's death." I dabbed my eye with a gloved finger.

"I take it you must approve of slave-holding, then, if you are a Southerner."

"Bless my soul, I should think not! No, I freed all my slaves at the start of the war – turned them off the plantation, every one, though they begged and begged me to let them stay. Said they hadn't known a kinder mistress in all Louisiana. Why, you could hear them wailing clear down to the river."

I leaned forward to deposit my teacup on the little table at my knee, Violet involuntarily following the movement. When we were almost nose to nose, a further refinement occurred to me.

"Do you know, Mrs Oliver – since they've gone I find it's the hardest thing in the world to peel my own grapes. Isn't that singular?"

It was probably fortunate that Rachel Gaunt chose to leave just then. Alice and Violet insisted on walking out with us to our carriage, but to Louise's chagrin there was no sign at all of the gentlemen of the party; Lord Wellborough, Sir George Broadney and the gorgeous Freddie were apparently still engrossed in their shooting.

Then, just as we reached the foot of the vast staircase, the gentlemen emerged from the gun-room, Sir George and the Earl genial in country tweeds, Freddie plunging forward in over-tight trousers to show foxy teeth among his whiskers and murmur inanely "By Jove!"

They'd lit cigars – oh, fatal moment – but apparently politeness dictated that gentlemen must not puff while conversing with ladies, and gradually the fragrant smoke disappeared as one by one the havanas went out. I could have wept at the waste – I could tell by the smell that cigars such as those had rarely come my way on the *Bellflower*, and I hadn't smoked one at all since arriving in England.

And because I had no part in the conversation, I stood to one side, sniffing the last scented wraiths of Freddie Broadney's enormous and succulent havana while he made eyes at Louise behind her mother's back. Suddenly, consumed with gallantry, he threw down the cold and half-smoked cigar to snatch his sweetheart's hand.

I was appalled at such extravagance: and to prove that American ladies were as rigorous as any in their notions of thrift, I swooped on the half-smoked cigar, turned aside (not to let the likes of Freddie Broadney gape at my knees) and somehow managed to hitch up my skirts enough to tuck the end of the havana into my garter.

I was suddenly conscious of an awful silence falling all around me with the suddenness of a closing door.

Instantly I thrust my hand behind my back as if it had committed the crime all by itself, but the silence persisted – the dreadful, leaden hush of social disaster – until it was suddenly broken by a choking scream of laughter from Violet Oliver, smothered at once by a dainty hand.

There were tears, I swear it, running down her porcelain cheeks as we

146

left. She was leaning on her father's arm, and he was bending over her, muttering something which only increased her mirth. Beside them stood Freddie, murmuring "By Jove!" over and over again, on his face the dazed expression of a broken marionette.

Chapter Eleven

1

So much for dreams! So much for a leopard changing her spots, or a guttersnipe becoming a *grande dame*! All the way back to Hawk's Dyke I sat mutinously in my ridiculous hoops while the groom behind me coughed in my ear and I nurtured thoughts of massacre.

Louise never uttered a word. Instead, she sat in her corner of the landau, her lips pressed tightly together, glaring out at the passing hedgerows like a woman betrayed. I'd shamed her in front of Freddie Broadney, of all people – the very godlike being for whom she wished to be perfect. If Mr Frederick Broadney ever spoke to her again, Louise's impression implied, it would be an act of the greatest charity.

And Louise was at least partly to blame! If she hadn't insisted on dressing me up like an organ-grinder's monkey and showing me off at the Abbey, the catastrophe would never have happened. In an agony of humiliation I wondered how long it would be before Matthew got to hear of my blunder. No doubt Violet would turn the whole episode into one of her highly amusing stories, and the guttersnipe whose father had "an interest in distilling" would keep the dinner tables of London rocking for weeks.

I could have screamed with fury and mortification. I was incensed with myself for having been drawn into the deception in the first place; if I'd stuck to my plain dress and straw hat the worst they could have said of me was *quaint*. But oh no, I'd been determined to show that two weeks of *Delightful!* and *How charming!* could turn a riverboat woman into an English lady – and for whose sake? Not for my own, that was certain. I'd only done it to prove I was good enough – good enough, mark you – to be the wife of that arrogant, swindling ingrate, Matthew Oliver. Dammit, I was far too good for him – and so cross with myself I could've *spit*, I tell you.

This was what came of trying to play the lady in a fine house full of servants where the most pressing problem was to fill the idle hours until the next meal. Had I completely forgotten that on the other side of the sea, men were killing one another over just such an improbable existence? All the way back to Hawk's Dyke I scolded myself silently for my foolishness, and later, having refused dinner, I continued to scold myself in the privacy of my room.

How could I have been so stupid as to imagine myself accepted by Matthew's family? I was no more than a clown – an amusing eccentricity, tolerated as a small relief from the boredom of their empty lives. I didn't belong in their company, any more than I belonged anywhere else. Though it pained me to admit it, Matthew had been right: my time at Hawk's Dyke had been a fantasy from the start.

2

I'd excused myself from dinner by pleading a headache, but when I didn't come down for breakfast next day, Rachel Gaunt sent Nell to my room with a tray.

I was calmer by then. I'd already been at my window for an hour, gazing out over a countryside grown suddenly inhospitable and strange, and wondering why I'd ever found it welcoming.

I was no longer angry with Louise – only with myself. Louise knew nothing of life and death, or of hunger and cold. Her whole existence was bounded by the doors of her bulging wardrobe and Freddie Broadney's smile. I was the one who should have known better.

Looking down from my window, for the first time I noticed that fall had stolen up on Hawk's Dyke. The trees which shaded the Italian garden had been brushed overnight with red and gold, rudely bright against the dense green of the yews, while below them the house cats rolled on soft mats of early fallen leaves.

There was already something gently conclusive in the air – a tranquil acceptance of the season's end, of fruition, and fulfilment, and completeness. The summer, like my time at Hawk's Dyke, was over. Gulping down a little coffee from the tray, I put on my coat and went out into the last of my Arcadia.

I could only think of one person who might understand my mood – Will, the groom who looked after Louise's mare and rode on the back of the landau when her mother was driven out in the afternoons. Will was thin and shock-headed, and nursed a fierce ambition to ride His Lordship's racehorses which he'd confided to me one afternoon in the echoing shadows of the coach-house, while he polished the glossy paintwork of a brougham. I looked for him there now, and then out in the yard, but he was nowhere to be seen.

"Will, miss?" The coachman regarded me doubtfully. "I sent him home last night, after the carriage came back from the Abbey. Coughing something wicked, he was, and white as a sheet."

149

This was a setback; but the urge to talk to someone – someone who wouldn't judge, or criticise, or think me odd – was too strong to be resisted. If Will Eversedge wasn't in the stables, then I'd visit him at home. Rachel Gaunt wouldn't have approved, I knew: it was one of her few rules that servants' privacy should be respected. But if I wasn't to be a lady, then Will and I had more in common than ever, and Mrs Gaunt should be pleased I'd found company of my own kind.

I already knew the cottage that was Will's home. Nell had pointed it out from my bedroom window one morning while she explained his distant relationship to her own rambling family, and it took me no more than a few minutes to walk there now. His mother answered the door, weariness mingling with suspicion in her face.

"He'll be back at work tomorrow, miss." She gripped the door firmly, her outstretched arm barring me from entering. "He's coughing a bit, that's all – he's always had a weak chest."

"Perhaps a visitor would cheer him up."

"No!" The woman's eyes grew round with alarm. "I mean – no, thank you, miss. Mrs Gaunt wouldn't like it, I'm sure. Not a young lady from the Hall, calling here."

"But I'm a friend of Will's."

"I don't think so, miss. Thank you, all the same."

From somewhere behind her, I heard Will's voice demand to know who the visitor might be. Then a chair creaked, and Will himself appeared at his mother's shoulder, horribly pale and bright-eyed.

"Miss Kate!" He seemed unaccountably puzzled by my presence. "I'll be back at the stables tomorrow, if that's why you're here."

"I hope you won't be." I watched, distressed, as a spasm of coughing racked his thin chest. "You mustn't think of working until that cough's better."

"It'll be better." Still barring the doorway, his mother eyed me fiercely. "Get back to the fire, Will, and away from the air." With her free hand she pushed him into the dimness behind her. "And you go back to the Hall, miss, where you belong. I'm obliged to you for your kindness, but now you'd best leave him be."

"I just thought – "

"Good day to you, miss. Thank you for calling."

Almost bowing her obligation, Will's mother shut the door firmly in my face.

I could have howled aloud at the ludicrous unfairness of it all. If the woman had only seen my disastrous début as a lady the previous day! I was a comic guttersnipe at Sourwell Abbey, but "a young lady from the

Hall" as far as a groom's mother was concerned: I was too little of one thing, and too much of another – unwelcome at the Abbey, unwelcome in a labourer's cottage, and, I'd convinced myself, unwelcome at Hawk's Dyke too.

Bitterness – the distillation of soured hopes and self-pity – began to consume me. I set out again towards the house, but long before I reached it, resentment had driven me off on a determined, directionless march. Before long I'd skirted the stables and climbed to the top of the first rise of ground behind the Hall, from where its grey roof reared like a turtle's back amid a lake of trees. Yet there was no solace to be found there; from that vantage point Hawk's Dyke looked so cosy and self-satisfied that I quickly turned my back and tramped on.

I walked as far as the highway which led to the Abbey and to Stainham, but the thought of that row of smug little shops and gossiping villagers sent me doubling back to trudge over stubble and turnip row, and through pastures where sheep lifted their heads in surprise as I passed. I, who'd once had no further to promenade than the length of the *Bellflower*, sped over the land like the homeless wind, walking out the passion of my soul.

I had no means of telling the hour, but the sun had passed its zenith and begun to sink lower in the sky by the time I arrived at what I took to be Mill Farm: the great black drainage mill stood nearby, its neglected sails and slatted scoop-wheel halted by the coming of the steam-pump almost ten years before. This, I knew, was the last dwelling before Hawk's Dyke land became Abbey land somewhere in the lingering wilderness of Sourwell Fen.

It was time to return to the house. The anger which had carried me forward all day had suddenly ebbed away, leaving me desperately weary and anxious that a search party might have been organised to discover where I'd gone. It was time to go back – and to explain that I'd decided to leave for Liverpool as soon as possible. No doubt, I told myself grimly, they'd be relieved to see the last of such an embarrassment.

I turned my back on the farm – and then halted. Subtly, seductively, the breeze had brought me a scent that I knew, like a familiar voice in a strange land. I hesitated, my nose testing the air like a hunting dog, sifting the common flavours of the farmland for the single note which had called me. And there it was . . . a damp, weedy smell of half-drowned plants, an ancient smell of growth and decay which sang to me of backwaters lined with tall, moss-bearded cypresses, of red-tailed hawks and white egrets, of scarlet-fruited vines and fallen boughs where turtles lay like shiny buttons in the sun.

Instantly, I forgot Hawk's Dyke and passing time, and turned eastward again, following the old, grassy drove beyond the cattle yard wherever it might lead.

At the end of a tussocky field the drove began to fade into an overgrown track among clumps of hawthorn and willow which crossed the mill drain and disappeared into the thorn scrub beyond. Dry stems matted the lower branches of the bushes into a short, dense under-growth, but it was only when the drove became marshy underfoot and finally disappeared altogether into the reedy margins of a mere that I came to a standstill and gazed about me.

This was not a landscape I knew, though the haunting scent of still water was an old, familiar friend. Before me lay a half-drowned and mysterious landscape, neither dry ground nor lake, where straggling undergrowth dwindled into reedy pools and swampy beds of sedge, and all was silent except for the sobbing mutter of wings as a flock of wild duck rose in alarm from the water.

Now I knew for certain where I was. I'd crossed between the two worlds of farm and fen, between new and old; I'd found my way to Sourwell Fen, whose green, fishy breath on the wind had sometimes filled even the opulence of the Italian garden with the giant sighing of its marsh. Not yet ready to retrace my steps, I sat down on a marooned hummock of grass to watch the waterfowl circle and dip, and let the loneliness of the place ease the loneliness in my heart.

If ever land lay as God made it, that marsh was the place. *In the beginning God created the heaven and the earth* – and Hawk's Dyke, and Sourwell Abbey, and the Gaunts – and even the old *Bellflower* in a way, I supposed, though I couldn't fathom why He'd bothered to create me. I had less purpose in His world than one of the nodding moorhen in the shallows at my feet.

The rising breeze shivered the nearest willows, ruffling the bright strips of water. I wondered if there were snakes in Sourwell Fen – Christian snakes, no doubt, subject to St Patrick, instead of the flicking, six-foot vipers of the bayous, the servants of his voodoo cousin Damballah.

Nervously, I glanced into the branches of a nearby tree, though Pa had always maintained that the snakes among the leaves were well-nigh harmless: it was the snakes lower down who'd chased them up there which were the ones to avoid.

My hand moved instinctively to my throat, to touch Sam's charm in

152

its leather pouch. I'd taken to wearing it hidden under my blouse now, and I had to undo a button to worm a couple of fingers next to the soft, reassuring warmth of the leather.

How Violet Oliver would have laughed at my childish fears! Normal people, as she'd been quick to point out, didn't wear potions of basil leaves and incense round their necks in place of jewellery. Normal people – by which she meant confident, unimaginative, unspiritual white people – laughed at the power of drums and rituals. Where, under the temperate politeness of an English sun, was there room for an army of hovering spirits?

Yet now, in that wild place, I wasn't so sure. All around me, the feathery tops of the reeds, speckled like a thrush's breast, nodded their wisdom, whispering among their wind-stirred stems. The very air breathed secrets in that ancient wilderness – cool, solitary mysteries, quite different from the hot magic of the narrow streets of old New Orleans, where the tortured stalks of long-dead plants clung to the gates of dark courtyards, and as a child I'd seen demons waiting to reach out and snap bark-crusted fingers into passing human flesh.

The shadows were growing longer now, as I brooded on my island in a watery waste gradually coming alive with rustlings and snufflings and sudden bird calls. Not far off, a faded, pinkish tuft of agrimony reminded me of the wilted blossoms I'd laid on my father's grave, limp in my hand even before being left for the sun to wither. *What would you tell me to do if you were here now, Pa? Where's the prag-matical in all this? God rest your soul*, I added quickly in case his phantom had wandered near enough to hear my question.

I was startled by a slight movement nearby. A long-billed bird with legs like knotted red string was picking its way through the shallows of the marsh, too intent on hunting for food to notice my presence.

I'd left the cemetery with the Ransomes shortly after the first clods rattled down on my father's coffin, but I suspected Sam Duck and his friends had returned later for rituals of their own which would send Pa's soul safely under the waters before a sorcerer could snatch it for himself.

The red-legged bird peered down into the mere as if the drowned faces of the dead floated under the surface, mutely awaiting recall.

And all of a sudden I saw two eyes watching me.

They were black eyes, glistening like ripe berries among the stippled leaves of a nearby alder buckthorn – though they weren't berries, but real eyes which blinked and flicked from side to side as their owner took stock of the intruder in his sodden wilderness.

153

A breath of wind stirred the leaves, and I saw the outline of a round, blackish head ending in a hairless brow. Between the eyes sprouted a stub of a nose and two nostrils which strained as wide as mouse-holes when without any warning the creature yawned, throwing open a cavernous mouth fringed by strings of black hair. I was transfixed by that animal yawn – by the flinging back of the head – by the baring of teeth and red gums. I was transfixed, and utterly terrified.

To my horror, I realised that Sam's charm had become helpless to protect me. This *thing* from the marsh had simply brushed aside the power of bones and herbs, bent as it was on dragging me down into that mere of demons.

Gathering my skirts about my knees, I rose up like a startled bird and darted off down the edge of the marsh, splashing where the mat of vegetation gave way below my frantic steps, expecting at any moment to hear the thud of feet at my back – of feet or paws, hooves or claws, I couldn't tell. I simply stumbled on until my lungs ached with every breath and only fear drove me forward, clawing my way through overhanging shrubs, slipping and slithering on the tussocks of wet grass.

I'd left the end of the drove far behind me, but there must be other ways out of the fen – tracks leading to the farm, comforting lanes barred by stout gates. Yet when did devils care anything for farm gates?

Suddenly a monstrous man-shape materialised in my path, distorted by tree branches. Beside me the undergrowth heaved and rustled: the fiend at my heels had sent his serpents ahead of him from the darkening mere. I turned once more, my legs unsteady and my lungs bursting, and fell, exhausted, against a tree – just as Adam Gaunt's retriever burst from the thicket and bounded joyously towards me. Adam himself was only a step behind, treading steadily through the underbrush, a shotgun over his arm.

He dropped the gun as I flung myself on him, and gripped me tightly to prevent me from sliding in a heap at his feet.

"Katherine! What on earth – "

"There's a devil in the fen! I saw it! All black, with a great, gaping mouth – "

"Never!"

"There was a devil, I tell you!" I pressed myself against him, clinging to the solidity of flesh and blood in that misty place of spirits. "I saw a devil watching me from the bushes – waiting to jump out at me. I ran away from it and got lost. I didn't know how to get back to the farm – "

"You were running deeper into the fen, not out of it."

154

"Oh, Heavens!" I wound my fingers into the fabric of his coat. "Don't leave me here! Please don't leave me . . . I promise to live like a saint in future. I'll do anything – I swear it – "

"Katherine – " He tried to lift my chin, to look into my face, but when I clung all the harder, he gave up and simply held me close. "Something's frightened you out of your wits, that's certain."

"A devil! A black fen spirit with staring eyes!"

"Katherine, listen to me. I know this stretch of country as well as anyone can. I grew up here. There isn't an animal or a bird in the fen that I haven't seen. If there was a devil here, don't you think I'd know about it?"

"It isn't looking for you! I'm the one who doesn't belong here. I'm the outsider." And all at once, great tears of misery began to roll down my cheeks as if a dozen years of hoarded weeping had been waiting for the sanctuary of his arms.

Gently, he pulled away a strand of hair which had tangled in my damp lashes.

"I wish I knew what you'd seen. Or even what you're doing in this out-of-the-way spot."

"I was walking."

"Hiding, more like."

"No," I moaned. "I went for a walk."

"And met a devil." His voice was thoughtful, but his arms were still securely round my shoulders. I buried my face in the soft tweed of his shooting coat, feeling the warmth of his hand against my ear.

"You've seen a bird of some kind, that's all."

"With a mouth? With teeth and whiskers?"

"A cat, then. They run wild round here."

"The eyes were black, I swear it. I saw them blink. Oh, don't let it come near me, please!"

"Nothing can harm you here, with me. Do you believe that, Katherine?"

"Yes – oh, yes." I believed him. He was a sorcerer himself. No demon could have broken the circle of those arms.

"Now, I've an idea I'm personally acquainted with this devil of yours. Was the head almost round, and greyish-black?"

"Yes."

"With a few straggling hairs, and no nose to speak of?"

"Just like that!" I shuddered through my tears. "Have you seen it yourself?"

"Oh, I've seen it often. Or seen *him*, I should say." For a moment he stared silently out over the marsh. Then I felt him take a breath, his chest swelling against my cheek. "Aaron! Aaron Dann, come out here, you old blackguard!" He waited, but only the sighing of the trees answered him. "What do you mean by frightening a helpless girl! Come out where I can see you!"

Once more, silence descended on the fen.

"He's there – I know it." Above my head, Adam Gaunt continued to gaze across the reed-beds and watery pools. "He'll watch us for a bit, then he'll slink off quietly and hope I'll forget. But I'll catch up with him sooner or later."

"Who's Aaron Dann, for Heaven's sake?"

"He's an old man who lives alone in the middle of this fen – and has done for most of his life. He doesn't have much time for people. If he sees a stranger he'll hide and watch, but he won't speak."

"But the thing I saw can't have been human! It was so ugly . . ." I shivered at the memory of that blackened head.

"*Ugly as an eel-pout*. That's what they say of Aaron Dann round here. He's got a head like a catfish and his skin's almost black with smoke and dirt. He never washes unless he falls in the water."

"Are you sure that's what I saw? Just an old man?"

"Just an old man."

"But where can anyone live in all this water?" I peered out of my refuge, relishing the sense of safety after danger – the oily, faintly animal smell of his tweed coat – the closeness of his body against my own.

"There's a small patch of higher ground about quarter of a mile from here. Old Aaron's built a hut there where he keeps his eel-traps and his nets and fishing-lines. He takes birds when he can, and water-rats when there's nothing else. Mrs Finch gives him something for the fish and eels he brings to the house, and he manages to survive somehow."

Adam Gaunt glanced down, frowning.

"But he'd no right to go frightening you."

"It was my own fault, I guess. I was . . . upset. And the sun was beginning to go down. There were shadows in the trees."

"What were you so upset about?"

"Oh . . . it wasn't important."

"I heard what happened at the Abbey yesterday, if that's what was bothering you."

"And I suppose you're going to be polite, and tell me it doesn't matter."

"Neither it does."

156

I glanced up warily. "You're only saying that to make me feel better."

He smiled as if the idea amused him.

"Do you think I give a damn for society manners and the tattlers at the Abbey? Never! Life's far too precious to waste on such things. I thought you understood that."

"Why should you think so?"

"Oh . . . the poppies in your hat, when you arrived at the Abbey that day. The pleasure in your face as you hung out of your window in the morning sun . . ." He smiled again. "Don't stare at me so suspiciously. You're wise enough to know the truth when you hear it."

He paused for the length of a heartbeat.

"And talking of truth. . . . These friends of yours in Liverpool – "

He felt me draw away in alarm and tightened his grip, imprisoning me against him and preventing me from pulling free.

"They don't exist, do they?"

"What a strange idea."

"I'm not a fool, Katherine, whatever Matthew may believe." When I didn't answer, he asked again. "Do you really have friends in Liverpool?" He lifted my chin, tilting my face up towards his own. "Well, do you?"

"No. There's no one in Liverpool."

"Do you have any friends in England at all – apart from us?"

I shook my head – and then realised how pathetic I must appear.

"Not yet, I don't. But I dare say I will before long."

"I suppose Matthew's behind all this nonsense. Which means the real story concerns him in some way. And don't tell me you travelled more than three thousand miles to return a lost watch, because I won't believe you."

I couldn't bear to lie to him, and so I remained silent.

"Why did you come here, Katherine?"

"I can't tell you. I swore I wouldn't."

He considered this for a moment. "Very well, I won't ask you again. I'll get the truth out of Matthew instead."

"Don't – please. For my sake. I'll be gone in a day or two, and you won't ever see me again. Don't say anything to Matthew – or to anyone else, I beg of you."

"If he's harmed you in some way . . ."

"Please. You said you wouldn't ask."

"I still want to know."

"Forgive me – but this has nothing to do with you."

Even then, he was reluctant to give up. Father and son, they were alike in so many ways. I understood that now, as we stood together in the falling dusk, with the fen whispering all around.

"You can't possibly go back to America in the middle of a war. There's a Confederate army almost within sight of Washington."

"I'll get along, don't worry. Now, will you take me back to Hawk's Dyke, please?"

"Go down to the kitchen, and take a look at your devil," Adam Gaunt instructed me later that evening, as I sat beside the parlour fire nursing a sore throat – a legacy, I was sure, of my desperate chase in the fen. "He must be ashamed of having frightened you. He's brought some eels as a peace offering."

I saw the eels first, a knot of dark, dull-eyed bodies in the scullery sink, threaded on a willow wand. Beyond the kitchen door, Aaron Dann crouched by the range, the light from the open fire-door flickering on the bony hollows of his face, a few locks of dank, dark hair trailing over the collar of a ragged coat as grey-black as his skin.

"Go in and see him – what there is to see," Mrs Finch urged dismissively, adding with a shrug, "His mother and father were first cousins," as if such profligacy explained everything.

For all that, with the firelight in his face he could still have passed for the Devil incarnate, and I felt a tingle of foreboding crawl up my spine. I couldn't rid myself of the sense of dread which had been born in me in the solitude of the mere. Too much had been brought to an end all at once: the summer – my idyll at Hawk's Dyke – and now my peace of mind. It was just as if Aaron Dann had placed his thin, blackened finger on my brow, marking the finish of it all with the sudden completeness of a death.

The housekeeper had compelled the old man to leave his boots in the yard, but even without them his bare feet were damp enough to leave a trail across her clean-scrubbed flags. Yet there was no double-sickle print of cloven hooves on the floor – only, wherever Aaron Dann had passed, the splayed track of ten webbed toes.

3

I'd fully intended to make arrangements to leave Hawk's Dyke within twenty-four hours. But next morning my cold was worse; my head ached now as well as my throat, my nose was blocked and sore and I felt ill at the very thought of breakfast. When Nell came in with her jug of hot water at eight, I was still in bed. The maid, her cap askew, took one look and went off to summon her mistress.

"A feverish chill." Rachel Gaunt felt my forehead with cool fingers. "I'm not surprised, after wandering about in that dreadful marsh. If you'd told me where you meant to go, I'd have warned you to stay away. People used to disappear there in the old days, so they say."

"I can believe it."

"And Aaron Dann. . . . He's a dreadful old man – yet I suppose he has a right to a home of some kind. If we turned him out of his hole in the fen, where would he go? He wouldn't last a day in the workhouse, even supposing they were prepared to take him."

"I was stupid to be afraid."

"Nonsense! One look at Aaron Dann's enough to frighten a regiment. I'd hate to meet him on my own in the half-dark." She gazed down sympathetically at my flushed and swollen features. "Poor Katherine – so much goes wrong for you, doesn't it? It's lucky you're such a strong, practical soul. Now, you stay in bed for a day or two and shake off that chill. I won't hear a word about your leaving until you're completely better."

By next day my nose was sore and streaming, and even my lips and mouth ached. I was furious with myself for becoming ill: I should have been far away from Hawk's Dyke by then, instead of being cooped up, feverish, in bed with a book. I was coughing now, too, the chill persisting long after I felt I should have been on the road to recovery.

"If this doesn't clear up soon, I shall call Dr Clement." It was the seventh day of my illness, and Rachel Gaunt had begun to look pale and concerned. "Perhaps it's more serious than we thought." She coughed behind her hand, and then laughed. "Goodness – now I've started too. Whatever it is, it must be catching!"

"Mamma's sick," Louise reported three days later, anxiety driving my great *faux pas* at the Abbey from her mind and making her confide in me once more.

"Mamma's throat's so sore she can hardly turn her head. I took her a little beef tea, but she couldn't swallow it." Louise's eyes grew round with apprehension. "You're better of it, Katherine, aren't you? Mamma wouldn't hear of calling Dr Clement, but my stepfather's sent a man for him all the same." She hesitated for a second. "You became better on your own, so it can't really be serious."

"I'm a great deal better, Louise." I was still a little unsteady on my feet, the legacy of several days in bed, but my head had cleared and my throat was no longer sore. "Don't worry, I'm sure your mother will be fine in a few days."

159

I was downstairs in the parlour when the doctor left. Adam Gaunt came in, lingered absently for a moment in the middle of the floor, his hand to his brow, then spun round and strode swiftly to the door.

"What did the doctor say?"

He stared at me as if noticing me for the first time.

"Diphtheria. I should think you've had it too."

4

Within hours Rachel Gaunt was gravely ill. Alice arrived from Sourwell Abbey, Matthew was summoned by telegraph from Liverpool and Dr Clement sent trained nurses to ease the patient's rasping gasps with chloroform. Louise had been banned from the sickroom as soon as the nature of the disease was known, but Adam Gaunt refused to leave his wife's side, even when, ashen and blotched with bruises, she made feeble signs that he should go out of danger.

I lay awake for hours that night, and my encounter in the fen weighed heavily upon me. It had been a sign of some kind – I'd been sure of that – but what it meant, I didn't understand. If only Sam Duck had been here to make sense of it all. . . . *Don't let her die. . . . Don't. . . . Don't . . .*

Just after midnight I heard a commotion outside my door. Mrs Finch was there in her long nightgown, her grey hair straying from under a cotton cap. Louise, weeping, was clasped in her arms, and there were tears streaming down the housekeeper's face.

"Oh, my poor lamb," she kept repeating. "And Mr Matthew not here yet! Oh, my poor lamb."

A nurse emerged from the sick woman's room, sighed, and disappeared into the shadows of the corridor. There was no longer any urgency in her step. Even before Mrs Finch caught sight of me across Louise's heaving shoulder and silently mouthed the words *heart failure*, I knew for a certainty that Rachel Gaunt was dead.

160

Chapter Twelve

1

Diphtheria – malignant quinsy: that was Dr Clement's opinion. There'd been haemorrhage, the doctor added, and poisoning of the blood, such as he saw in poor families living among bad drains. Mrs Gaunt had been singularly unfortunate to be taken, but the Lord moved in mysterious ways . . . and I should think myself a remarkably lucky young woman to have escaped so easily. Here the doctor turned to stare at me severely over his spectacles before departing in his trap to break the sad news to the village.

Louise's despair was dreadful to see.

"I wasn't even allowed to speak to Mamma before the end," she wailed. "I wanted to tell her how much I needed her and that she mustn't die. And now it's too late! I'm a silly, thoughtless girl, just as Mamma always said, and now I've been punished for it." And Louise burst into a rage of weeping. "Oh, why did she have to die?"

I couldn't rid myself of a sense of unease. I had lived, while Louise's mother had died; it had been the chance of fate, yet in spite of that I felt guilty, and unable to shake off the memory of the dreadful yawning apparition I'd seen in the fen. Impulsively, I put an arm round Louise's heaving shoulder.

"Dr Clement said nothing could have saved your mother."

"B-b-but I should have been *there*! I should have been with her when she died."

"Mr Gaunt was with her. I guess that must have been a comfort." I thought of those two – touching – consoling one another for the last time.

Leaning against me, Louise continued to sob uncontrollably.

"Why don't you go and find your stepfather?" I suggested. "He must be every bit as miserable. Maybe it would help you both to be together."

"No!" Louise raised her tear-stained face from my shoulder, aghast at the idea. "I don't want to see him, Katherine. Please."

"Later, then."

"No!" Her voice rose to a shriek. "I couldn't bear it."

"Don't upset yourself, Louise. If you don't want to speak to your stepfather, then I guess you don't have to."

161

"And you won't go away, Katherine, will you? Away from Hawk's Dyke, I mean. You'll stay with me, now Mamma's gone?"

I was taken aback. I'd stayed too long as it was, feeling more of an intruder with every passing day.

"I'll stay until the funeral's over, if you want me to."

"Much longer than that, surely!" Louise regarded me with red-rimmed eyes. "You aren't properly well yourself yet – Dr Clement said so."

"I can't stay, Louise. I just can't."

"It isn't fair!" Once more, her body was racked by sobs. "Mamma's gone, and you're about to leave me, and there'll be no one here . . ."

"What about Alice? I know she went back to the Abbey today, but that isn't so far away."

"It isn't the same as having Mamma back again," moaned Louise.

"Well, no." Gently, I tried to move my cramped limbs, and at once Louise was all consternation.

"Where are you going?"

"Nowhere. Not while you need me."

"P-p-promise?"

"Of course."

At first I thought Louise was afraid to be alone with her loss: gradually I came to believe she was afraid to be alone with her stepfather. Yet for the next two days it was almost as if Adam Gaunt had disappeared. If he was in the house at all, he shut himself in the library and no one dared go near him. If he ate any meal, I wasn't aware of it. Doors opened and closed in the middle of the night; more than once I was wakened by the shod hooves of a horse on the gravel below my window, as he returned from a tour of the moonlit countryside.

Louise and I passed the hours alone in the little parlour, Louise retrimming with deep black crape the mourning-silk dress she'd had made in honour of the late Earl, hunched red-eyed over its dusky folds, snipping off the bright jet beads and replacing every second one with the brief sparkle of a tear. Vickers, her mother's elderly maid, had begged to do the work, but Louise refused, as if the long, monotonous rows of stitching somehow focused and controlled her grief.

Then all of a sudden on the morning of the third day, Adam Gaunt emerged from the library like Jove from a thundercloud to announce that black – in any form – was to be prohibited at Hawk's Dyke from that moment.

Louise gaped at him, uncomprehending, yards of black crape spread over her knees – just as she'd covered every mirror in the house, draped every picture, and decorated the wreath of black immortelles on the front door.

"*No black?*"

"No black!" he repeated. "I won't allow it."

"But that's indecent! Everyone wears black when they're in mourning!" Louise's voice had risen to a hysterical pitch, as if she'd sooner have gone naked than flout such an inviolable rule. "Black is the only way to show respect."

"Respect be damned! Look at this heap of mawkish, sanctimonious cant – 'Released from toil' – 'Slumbering at last'—"

Furiously, he thrust a sheaf of letters under her nose, every one bordered in a different width of black – some of them leaving space for no more than a few lines of condolence between their broad, funereal margins. There were black-edged envelopes too, sealed with great cobs of sooty wax, and grotesque cards of weeping angels, Gothic mausoleums or martyrs' crowns overgrown with ivy, testaments to the triumph of death.

Louise was given no time to read the printed verses of comfort. With an oath, her stepfather hurled the whole collection into the hearth, kicking towards the flames the few which had fluttered clear.

"*No!*" Horrified, Louise flung aside her sewing and threw herself on her knees before the grate, snatching back as many of the letters as she could before the flames consumed them. "Oh, how could you! Poor Mamma!"

"Leave them!"

"I will not! They're letters about Mamma, and they must all be kept, every one of them." With frantic fingers she brushed charred specks from the pages, now edged with fantastic fringes of black ash.

"And take this abomination off the looking-glasses. Can't you even bear the sight of yourself now she's gone?" Adam Gaunt turned to attack the heavy gilt mirror on a nearby wall, wrenching furiously at the length of black velvet which covered it.

"No – you mustn't!" Dropping the letters, Louise rushed to him and clung to his arm in a desperate attempt to prevent the profaning of her shrine. But it was too late: she was shaken off like a gnat and the mirror was laid bare, its black pall thrown aside.

"You'll oblige me, Louise, by taking all this down. Every bit of it." Adam Gaunt's voice was utterly cold, and I saw Louise back away from him, her eyes wide. "I don't want to see you creeping about the house in black – or in any other dark colour, for that matter. Wear whatever you'd normally wear."

He turned to me. "And you too, Katherine. Remember my wife for what she was, not as a corpse in a grave. I've already told Mrs Finch I don't expect to see the servants in black, or wearing mourning ribbons or armbands or any other such nonsense. Those who'll miss their mistress can shed their tears in private, and the rest are excused the hypocrisy of it.

"And as for tomorrow, I've made sure there'll be no trays of black feathers or false tails for the horses – and none of those undertakers' men who're so damned drunk they have to be propped up on the black poles they carry. I won't have it, Louise," he added warningly as Louise drew breath to protest. "No gloves, no scarves, no rings to throw into the grave, or any of the rest. I've sent a note to tell them at the Abbey."

It was all too much for Louise.

"I can't believe this!" She burst into tears of vexation, appalled at such sacrilege. "Didn't you care *anything* for Mamma? Are you determined to bury her like a pauper, and then go on as if she'd never existed?"

For a sudden, dreadful instant I thought Adam might be about to hit his stepdaughter, there was such desolate fury in his face.

"We're burying your mother, Louise," he said, his voice horribly soft. "Isn't that enough for you? Must you make a circus out of it as well? Do you want them all hovering round her like a flock of crows, croaking over the grave as if they'd like to turn day into night for decency's sake?"

"Don't say that – "

"Because you can't put the whole world into mourning! The sun will shine tomorrow and the day after that, and next year spring will come and new flowers will grow in the garden – and they won't come up black because Rachel's gone, I promise you. And somehow we'll have to find a way of going on without her. That will be hard enough." He turned on his heel and left the room, slamming the door behind him.

As soon as her stepfather had gone, Louise slumped into a chair, tears pouring down her cheeks.

"Oh, Katherine – I can't bear it! He's insane! Imagine what people will say!" She hid her face in her hands as if the shame of it was too great to be endured, and from the well of her fingers, her voice echoed out indistinctly. "It seems so little to do for her. . . . One last kindness, to give Mamma a decent burial. Doesn't he care about her at all?"

"I think he cares more than any of us realised," I said softly, but Louise didn't hear me, absorbed as she was in her own unhappiness.

"I know I'm silly and feather-brained, and I'm only fifteen," she moaned, gulping back tears. "I'm not clever like Matthew, or grand like Alice. All I can do for Mamma is to see that everything's dignified and in good taste, just as it was for Papa. Is that so much to ask? Alice would have insisted on it, but she doesn't live here any more. And I can't stand up to him, Katherine – not when he's in this sort of mood. Oh Heavens –" she cried in sudden passion, "he's no better than a *savage*! How Mamma could have married such a man – "

"Louise," I ventured gently, "I've never even set eyes on black feathers and mourning rings and what-have-you. When Pa died, we just buried him and said a prayer of sorts, and that seemed decent enough. I don't suppose he minded, one way or the other. Are you sure your mother would have wanted such a fuss?"

"She'd have let my stepfather do as he pleased, I expect," Louise hiccuped miserably. "She always let him have his own way."

"Well, then. No one can fault you for doing the same."

"Oh yes, they will! They'll say it was barbaric! Squalid! They'll say we grudged the price of a decent funeral, and never even went into mourning. I promise you, Katherine – you don't know how vicious people can be. Oh, poor Mamma!"

"But it's what you feel inside that matters most." I made a final effort to console her. "Won't you miss your mother as much in blue silk as you would in crape?"

"Oh, but Katherine – " Louise regarded me with brimming eyes. "It's so hard to be sad in blue silk . . ."

2

The silence continued so long after I knocked on the library door that I began to think the room was empty after all. I'd even turned to tiptoe thankfully away when I heard Adam Gaunt's voice quietly instruct me to enter.

He was sitting as usual in the armchair by the fire, but this time there was no book at his elbow and no black-edged letters – nothing to distract him from the contemplation of his loss.

"Ah . . . Katherine." Those strange grey eyes of his swept over me, but he didn't move.

"May I speak to you for a moment?"

"I wish you would. You've hardly said a word to me for days."

"I couldn't think of anything to say that didn't sound worthless. Words make everything commonplace, somehow. And I thought you might want to be alone."

"Alone?" He repeated the word slowly, testing it against the emptiness of the future. "No . . . I don't want to be alone. Oh, there was a time, many years ago, when I wanted nothing more than freedom and my own company. But now I seem to have lost the knack of being at peace with myself. Ironic, isn't it?" He glanced towards me again. "What can I do for you, Katherine?"

"Nothing – for me."

It had taken all my courage to seek him out; now I'd have cut off my hand sooner than give him more pain, but I'd made a promise to Louise, and I was bound to go on with my mission.

"I did think you might do something for Louise."

"Well?"

"She's very unhappy." Even as I spoke, I realised how stupid I must sound. "What I mean is that besides losing her mother, which is so bad anyway, she's almost crazy at not being allowed to wear black as she thinks fitting. She's making herself ill with crying. I thought . . . maybe you didn't understand how she felt, and that if you did . . ."

Adam waited for me to complete the sentence, and then, when I remained awkwardly silent, finished it for me.

"You thought I'd change my mind, is that so?"

"I thought you might go half-way, certainly."

"Half-way? Put on a small show for the gallery – only in the most refined taste, of course. Is that what you mean?"

His savagery left me without an answer; after a moment he turned away with a little hiss of frustration to stare into the heart of the fire. When he spoke again, his voice was so low that it startled me.

"I never imagined Rachel would die before me, do you know that? Not for a second. It didn't seem possible that I should be the one left behind."

His gaze strayed round the shadowy shelves with their burden of books.

"And yet she's dead. Not 'gone', or 'passed away', or 'departed'. *Dead*. I lie awake in the night, and there's no one beside me. I speak, but she doesn't answer. I have to live with the fact that I'll never hold her or touch her again – " His eyes came to rest bleakly upon me. "And I don't need a house filled with black crape to remind me of that."

My own, desolate soul ached for him . . . . But for Louise's sake, I persisted.

"Louise misses her mother just as much as you do, believe me."

"Nonsense! Louise is still a child. She wants a black parasol and black kid gloves, just as last week her life wasn't supportable without some other piece of frippery. She thinks she'll look fetching in crape, that's all. Everything she does is for show."

"But that's her whole world! It's all she knows. Why must you stop her mourning her mother in her own way – just as you do? It means every bit as much to her."

"I can't believe that." He was staring at me now, his eyes alive with anger. "I suppose you think I'm unreasonable."

"I can't understand you, it's true. You were so hard on Matthew when you thought he'd made me unhappy – and yet when you're faced with the misery of your own stepdaughter, you won't offer her any comfort at all. She needs your compassion more than I ever did!"

"For the last time, Katherine – I will not have my wife's funeral turned into a theatrical event for the amusement of the people of Norfolk, simply for the sake of Louise's social standing. It's no one's business but mine. I shall bury Rachel in my own way, and you may tell that to Louise, if you're so concerned about her. Shut the door behind you as you leave."

An hour later, Matthew fared no better – but, being Matthew, had a short, ugly row with his father before withdrawing coldly to the Abbey to await Violet's arrival at lunchtime from London. After that it was too late to alter the arrangements, though the unconventional plans for Mrs Gaunt's burial next day hovered like a thundercloud over the heads of her children when Matthew and Violet arrived in the afternoon with Lord and Lady Wellborough to pay a family call of condolence.

Violet had made her feelings clear by ignoring the ban on black and appearing in immaculate merino, trimmed and tucked with crape, frilled in black *crêpe lisse* and veiled in net, her bonnet bound with exactly the proper amount of crape to indicate mourning for a mother-in-law of comparatively recent acquisition. I'd no doubt that under-neath it all her drawers were threaded with precisely the correct width of black ribbon, and I saw Adam Gaunt regard her with unconcealed loathing as she took silent possession of the largest drawing-room chair, leaving Matthew and the others to bear the burden of the occasion.

Indeed, Violet was the only person in the room who seemed at ease, serenely aware of the striking contrast between her blonde beauty and the dramatic blackness which enveloped her. Alice hadn't shown Violet's defiance, dressing for the occasion in half-hearted mauve, which was as near as she'd dared go to challenging her stepfather's decree.

The whole gathering was bizarre. The widower clearly itched to escape to the sanctuary of his library; Matthew, Alice and Charles looked as uncomfortable as they were unwelcome; I had no business at all in that family group; and Louise . . . Louise had made plans of her own, which she announced later, long after the callers had departed, when our gloomy dinner was mercifully over and we were together in the hall, on the point of going to bed.

"When Katherine leaves here in a few days," she suddenly informed her stepfather, "I shall leave too."

Adam Gaunt glanced at her and frowned.

"Louise, you don't know what you're saying. How could you possibly leave here? Off to bed with you, and we'll talk about it tomorrow." With the strain of the afternoon behind him, he seemed to be trying to make up for his recent harshness.

"Excuse me, but I know exactly what I'm saying. I won't stay at Hawk's Dyke for a minute longer than I must. If you mean to keep me here against my will, you'll have to lock me up."

Adam Gaunt's frown deepened as he realised Louise was in earnest. "And where do you intend to go, may I ask?"

"If you don't mind, I think I'll go upstairs to bed," I interrupted quickly, embarrassed to be part of their argument.

"Please stay, Katherine," said Louise firmly, catching my sleeve. "I want you here as a witness." She turned back to Adam. "I'm going to live at the Abbey in future, with Alice and Charles. I've asked them if I may stay there, and Charles doesn't mind, provided you allow it. I told him you'd be delighted to be rid of me."

"You don't really believe that, do you?" Adam waited, amazed, but Louise only glared at him in silence.

"Of course I don't want you to leave," he assured her. "This is your home, just as it was your mother's home – and I'm still legally responsible for you, don't forget. If I've been hard on you recently . . . well, I beg your pardon for it. This hasn't been an easy time for either of us." He glanced at me helplessly, as if he hoped I'd add my voice to his.

"I'll be sixteen in January," Louise reminded him acidly, "and I have an allowance from the money Papa left me. When I'm twenty-five – or if I marry before then – I inherit the capital. So I'm not dependent on you for anything at all, and I see no reason why I shouldn't live with my sister in future. After all, she's a blood relation – *Stepfather*."

"Louise, can't we discuss this in the morning, when we've all had some sleep?" Adam Gaunt regarded her with weary resignation.

"Wait until you're calmer," I urged her. "Things will look different then."

"No, Katherine, I've made up my mind. I'll take enough clothes to

168

last me for a few days, and I'll send for the rest as soon as I'm settled at the Abbey."

"For Heaven's sake, Louise!" her stepfather burst out suddenly, "I've just lost my wife! Couldn't you have spared me this, too?"

"Your wife, and *my mother*!" Louise's fists were clenched at her sides. "My mother, don't forget! The woman you're going to bury in such a shabby, shameful grave that I'll hardly be able to hold up my head in the village any more. I'd have buried a dog with more respect!"

"Try to understand – "

"But then, you never really cared about her, did you? If you'd loved her at all, you'd never have dragged her down here to the country where she had *nothing* – nothing but empty fields and marshes and rows of horrible trees. You always hated the time she spent on Papa's ships. You took her away from it as soon as you could, to keep all her attention for yourself. Well, you may have made Mamma your prisoner, but you won't do the same to me. Forbid me to leave if you wish, but the moment your back's turned I'll run off. I'm going to live with Alice, and we shall both wear black for Mamma because we loved her, even if you never did. Come on, Katherine – I've said all I meant to say, and I'm glad of it. You're my witness. He might try to keep me here at Hawk's Dyke, but he can't lock up both of us." Gathering her skirts, Louise began to march up the winding stairs.

"I'd never try to keep you here against your will, Louise. You know that."

Louise marched on determinedly until the bend of the stairs hid her from sight.

"At least let's talk about our differences," he called after her. There was no reply. At the foot of the stairs he gazed at me in perplexity, throwing his arms wide. "Speak to her for me, Katherine. Try to explain – "

"I tried to explain Louise's unhappiness to you, once."

He stared at me – puzzled, and hurt.

"I thought you at least might understand."

Slowly, I shook my head.

"I can't see why you're treating Louise so unfairly. I will tell her I think she ought to stay here for a while, or at least listen to what you have to say. But that's as much as I can do, in all honesty."

My fingers had already gripped the banister-rail, and for a moment Adam laid his hand on mind.

"Thank you, Katherine. It's all I ask."

"Why are you taking his side?"

I'd no sooner perched myself on the edge of Louise's bed and launched into my carefully rehearsed arguments, when she interrupted me crossly.

"I thought you were my friend, not his."

"I am your friend, Louise. And I understand why you're so upset. But Hawk's Dyke is your home, and I'd hate to see you do anything hasty. Why not wait and think it over?"

"What else do you imagine I've been doing, ever since Mamma died?"

"At least give your stepfather a chance to explain."

Louise shook her head firmly. "It isn't just the funeral. You don't know what he's like, Katherine. Even Matthew hates him, and Matthew's actually his *son*."

She'd twisted her handkerchief into a rope between her fingers as if her emotions, like the tightly wound cambric, had been strained to breaking point.

"No," she said with sudden decision. "I don't believe Adam Gaunt has ever cared a bit for anyone but himself, and he'll make Mamma a laughing-stock to the very end. Oh, poor Mamma!" Her eyes filled with renewed tears. "I don't believe he loved her at all."

Yet when I woke next morning and gazed as usual out of my dormer window to see what sort of day had dawned, I thought some trick of the light must be deceiving me. Craning in my nightgown as far out over the deep sill as I dared, I stared down into the Italian garden, only to confirm the astonishing truth.

There wasn't a single flower left in it.

Everything had been cut – every late autumn blossom, every half-open bud, every petal – from the trumpet-shaped flowers of the mallow by the far wall to the soft rosy domes of the asters which had glowed like harvest moons near the steps. Every single bloom had vanished; someone had even cut the low-growing cushions of autumn crocuses, which from my high window had looked no more than a lilac blush at the side of the path.

As quickly as I could, I dressed and went out through the little door in the downstairs passage, still half-expecting to find that the devastation had been an illusion caused by shadows or the morning mist, and that once in the garden I'd find the flowers exactly as I'd seen them the night before.

But the garden was as empty of colour at close quarters as it had been from my window. Goodness knows when the work of execution had been done, but it had been thoroughly carried out. Even the lingering pink and crimson blossoms of the china roses in the most distant corner had been taken, as if the whole garden had gone into mourning for its mistress, casting off its colours in a way forbidden to the rest of us.

But it had been no act of wanton destruction. Every one of Rachel's flowers had been sent to the churchyard, I discovered later that day when I visited the newly filled grave with a few wild flowers from the hedgerow, only to find the grass around it carpeted with blooms for yards in every direction. In the Italian garden, where Rachel had tended her flowers, there was nothing but empty branches: now she lay cold under the turf of Stainham churchyard, and the distraught widower had sent those same flowers to wither alongside her in death.

4

Louise and I weren't expected to attend the funeral, and for both our sakes I was glad. It was only five months since I'd seen my father buried, and in spite of the fact that there had been little love lost between us, I could remember what an ordeal I'd found it.

A chilly quiet hung over Hawk's Dyke that day. Louise's breakfast was taken up to her room; after an hour or so it reappeared, untouched, but Louise did not, and I went upstairs to see if she'd begun to regret her decision to leave.

But Louise remained resolute. Adam Gaunt had ensnared her mother, and hadn't even thought enough of his wife to give her a decent burial. So be it. Rachel Gaunt was dead and beyond help, but Louise was determined to escape from his house. Once the proper period of mourning for her mother was ended, her sister Alice had promised to take her to London for the Season and when she was eighteen would present her at a "drawing-room" and do all that a careful Mamma would have done to launch her in society. Henceforth, Louise would live at Sourwell Abbey, and that was that.

The house remained silent all day, the rooms and the twisting corridors apparently deserted. Even the kitchen, usually a scene of such bustle, was no more than an echoing vault, its pots and kettles standing unused upon their shelves. The heart had gone out of Hawk's Dyke; there was no fire in the hearth, and no warmth in its people.

In the early evening I walked out into the plundered garden. Here at least, in that green serenity of Rachel's own creation, life would continue as before; new buds would open and new shoots jostle into the

171

empty spaces, unaware of calamity, driven only by the need to grow and make good their loss. Soon I, too, would be gone, and somewhere in the garden another flower would open to replace me.

It never occurred to me as I walked slowly along the path, hat in hand, that someone else might be there, sitting on the rhododendron-screened seat by the sundial, silently contemplating the ravaged beds. It was almost as if Adam Gaunt had materialised before my eyes – just as he'd done, days before in the fen – and I was startled enough to cry out when I saw him.

"I beg your pardon, Katherine. I didn't mean to frighten you."

"I thought I was alone. If I'd known you were here, I wouldn't have disturbed you."

I bent to retrieve the hat I'd dropped on the path at my feet, and in straightening up, stole a glance at him. He looked haggard, I thought – hollow about the eyes as if sleep had eluded him for many nights – and there was no welcome in his expression. It remained wintry even while the evening sunshine glinted on the silver in his hair, and I wished devoutly that I'd noticed him before coming outside. I'd already turned to go indoors when he spoke again.

"Louise has given instructions for her mare to be taken over to the Abbey stables. That's her way of saying she's leaving for good." He addressed the words to the top of the wall on the opposite side of the garden.

"Maybe she'll think better of it in a day or two."

"Did she suggest that?"

"No, I can't say she did."

Retreat now seemed out of the question. Awkwardly, I sat down on the bench beside him, wishing I had more comfort to offer.

"I imagine Alice will look after her sister well enough," he went on. "Better than I could, no doubt."

"I don't see why that should follow."

"Don't you?" He turned to stare at me then. "Though I'm a heartless, selfish tyrant? Isn't that what you told me two days ago in the library?"

"I never said any such thing."

"Not in so many words, perhaps."

"Not at all! At least – I never meant it to sound like that."

"But it's the truth, isn't it? Matthew avoids me, Alice has made a new life for herself at the Abbey, and now Louise can't wait to be clear of the place. Their mother – my wife – was the heart of this house . . . and now she's gone there's nothing left."

He'd returned to his study of the bland brick wall opposite; suddenly he swung round towards me, his face full of the bitterness of betrayal.

"*Why* – that's what I've asked myself over and over again since it happened. *Why Rachel?* How did the disease come into the house?"

"How?" My voice was no more than a whisper.

"You brought it." The words were as chill as death itself. "I couldn't believe it, when they told me this morning. You were the one, Katherine – you, of all people."

"That day in the fen, when I ran from the old man . . ." I hid my face in my cupped hands. "I knew something dreadful was going to happen – I knew it . . ."

"What on earth are you talking about? Aaron Dann had nothing to do with any of this. I'm talking about Eversedge – the groom."

"Will Eversedge?"

"Who else? His whole family's rotten with diphtheria, so Dr Clement tells me, but the boy never said a word in case he was dismissed. One of his sisters has died now, or we might never have heard at all. But you knew he was ill, didn't you? And in spite of it you went to his home, after the coachman sent him away from Hawk's Dyke."

"How did you find out?"

"You were seen."

"Then . . . I caught Will's sickness – and Mrs Gaunt caught it from me."

"It seems likely. She was doing her best to care for you when she became ill."

"I never realised – "

"No. I don't suppose you did."

"But I never meant to harm her! Not for a moment! She was so kind to me . . . I should have been the one to die – not Mrs Gaunt."

"That's easily said. It won't bring Rachel back."

He couldn't bear to look at me. Instead, his gaze roamed the garden, grim and comfortless, until I felt as if I'd murdered Rachel with my own hand and consigned Adam himself to a wretched eternity.

"Why did you do it, Katherine?" he burst out suddenly. "Why should you want to destroy me? What harm had I ever done you?"

"Don't say that! I'd never do anything to injure you – not willingly. You must know that."

"I don't know anything any more. Only that Rachel's gone – and you were the one who brought death into my house."

How could I dispute it? Hadn't I sensed as much myself as I watched my marsh-devil grinning to himself and hugging his scrawny chest in the light of the kitchen range? My guilt was stained as dark as his skin, too plain to be denied. And when Adam spoke again, his voice was as flat and emotionless as a judge passing sentence.

"I know I should forgive you for what you've done, Katherine – but I can't. I just can't find it in myself to forgive – and I don't expect I ever shall." He paused for a moment, and then continued. "But that doesn't alter the fact that you are presently a guest under my roof. If you're still set on going back to America, I'll ask Matthew to arrange a passage for you as soon as Dr Clement says you're fit to travel, always providing you've somewhere safe to go."

"I'll leave right away. Tomorrow."

"There's no need. The damage is done. What more misery can you possibly bring us?"

Chapter Thirteen

1

By an effort of will I forced myself to wake at five the following morning, anxious to be well clear of Hawk's Dyke before the kitchen-maid came down from her garret to light the fire in the range.

Beyond my window it was still dark. The lawn which Adam Gaunt had ridden over on the first morning of my stay was a soft, blue-grey plain. Far below me and to the side, Rachel's garden spread its jungle of shadows, while the oaks beyond it where Matthew had kissed me rose like piled black cushions, leafy long after lesser trees had become sparse and thin.

I'd packed my bag the previous night, beginning the task as soon as I reached the sanctuary of my bedroom. *Wait*, Adam Gaunt had said: *wait until you're fit to travel*. But how could I spend another day in the place I'd made so desolate? All I wanted was to remove myself as quickly and silently as possible from the sight of these people whose world I'd pulled down about their ears.

Slinging Pa's leather belt round the bulk of my bag, I hauled it tight. In less than a quarter-hour I'd be gone from Hawk's Dyke and the old house would be no more than a memory. The sound of my footsteps would fade from its wooden floors just as all those others had faded over the years, and my tiny, disastrous part in its long story would be over.

And yet for the first time in my life I felt pain – physical pain – at the moment of parting. Never again to curl up, drowsy with warmth, by the stone hearth in the little old parlour – never again to watch starlings swagger across the rain-drenched lawns . . . I'd known heartache before, but never for a *place* . . . never such a bewildering sense of loss for bricks and mortar, windows and doors.

Bag in hand, I crept downstairs. The bright squares and lozenges of the oriental rugs were no more than a paving of grey in the darkness, but I could still smell the dry, sweet scent of burnt wood in the grates and the buttery reek of peat as it dissolved into creamy ashes. . . . It had been a lesser Paradise, and I had destroyed it.

There were still live coals in the bed of the parlour grate as I roused what was left of the evening's fire. I'd thought long and hard about what

I meant to do next, and the thought of it chilled me, even as I knelt before the kindled embers.

There was an ill-wish upon me – a *wanga* – a curse: I no longer had any doubt of that. Even Adam Gaunt had known – and had said as much the previous day, when he accused me of bringing death into his house. I was *gris-gris* – bewitched: had Damballah, Lord of the Serpents, not come to warn me himself in the fen, disguised as the old eel-man?

I was *gris-gris*, and I could only think of one way to be free of it. With sudden decision I tore Sam Duck's charm from my throat and threw it into the heart of the fire. What a fool I'd been, to imagine that the voodoo spirits of the African forests would ever look kindly on a white skin! Far from buying their favour, Sam's crushed herbs and bones had only served to bring Agasu, Dangny, Agué and all the rest down on my head in outrage at my presumption. Their punishment had been misery for me, and the ruin of my friends.

To my horror, the leather pouch continued to lie dark and intact among the embers, hissing faintly. Desperate to be rid of it, I reached out to press it further into the core of the heat, only to snatch back my hand in sudden pain. The spirits had no intention of taking their leave of me easily.

At last the little pouch began to writhe and curl in the grate, releasing an acrid stench of roasting herbs to bite the back of my throat. There was a sudden fizzing flare-up as the gunpowder in the brew caught fire – and then all at once nothing, as if it had never been. I was left to contemplate empty coals, and the throbbing of my scorched fingers.

Almost soundlessly, I let myself out of the front door of Hawk's Dyke and dropped the latch into place behind me.

And it was done. A second earlier I'd been inside the house; now I'd made myself a stranger, staring at unyielding wood and a handle I'd given up any right to turn.

There was nothing for it now but to put as many miles as possible behind me before my disappearance was discovered. I knew where I was bound: to Downham, on the road I'd travelled with the carrier six weeks before. Trains could be boarded there – that much I knew – but this time there could be no more riding on carriers' carts, however cheap. I'd have to fall back on my emergency fund, or what was left of it: there should be enough to pay for a steerage passage to Boston or New York, and a little over for train fares – but if Downham was a matter of ten miles or so by road, well then, I'd have to walk there.

Somehow, I forced myself to trudge through that windy, rustling darkness with the smell of Sam's magical herbs still in my nostrils and no confidence at all that my injured fingers had bought freedom from the furious demons of the voodoo. Keeping my eyes valiantly on the road ahead, I tried to find comfort in whistling under my breath in time to the steady thump of my boots on the hard-beaten ground.

By the time I reached Stoke Ferry the darkness had thinned to a watery dawn, and it had started to rain. Soon my straw hat was limp about my ears, the poppies dripping colour like a bloodstain on the shoulders of my coat.

Then at last I had a stroke of luck. As I splashed my way through the puddles of the highway, a cutler's wagon slowed to a walk at my side, and a gruff voice announced that while the cutler was bound for Downham, he'd gladly set me down along the way if I'd care to squeeze up beside him.

An hour and a half later the cutler left me at the railway station; within ten minutes I'd boarded a Great Eastern passenger train bound for Cambridge, already far beyond the reach of anyone from Hawk's Dyke, even supposing Adam Gaunt had bothered to send a man to see where I'd gone.

For the rest of that day, dazed by the thoroughness of my flight, I made my way by train towards Liverpool, retracing the miles I'd covered only a few weeks earlier with such high hopes. Then I'd travelled with purpose, and the fields and spinneys had bustled past the carriage windows. Now the same journey seemed interminable.

It began to rain once more as we pulled into Crewe with much huffing and snorting and spurting of steam. Rubbing my finger on the grimy carriage window, I peered out to inspect the platform and its signboards: C-R-E-W-E . . . about an hour and a half, I reckoned, from Lime Street station in Liverpool.

Yet for all the world it seemed as if exactly the same crowd of people I'd left at the last station filled these platforms too, still surging up and down as if giant hands were tipping them about like marbles on a tray.

Above their heads, a row of posters advertised patent medicines and local events. Rubbing the glass a little clearer, I struggled to read the largest print: "Cobbold's Music Hall"; " 'Aureoline' for the Fairest Tresses – 10/6d. per bottle": "The New 'Paragon' Sewing Machine"; "Dr Elias Bonnet of New Orleans will speak on Abolition . . ."

I stopped reading at once, and my mouth fell open. Elias Bonnet of New Orleans. . . . Heaven sakes, how many Elias Bonnets could one city hold? There could surely only be one – Eli Bonnet, my father's drinking crony, who'd bolted, it was said, from the path of the war . . . all the way to England.

177

On a sudden impulse I rose from my seat, gripped my leather bag tightly to my chest, and flew at the carriage door, fighting with the mechanism until the man sitting next to it kindly leaned over to open it for me.

"How long till we leave?"

"A minute or two, maybe."

One minute was enough. Clutching my bag – just in case the train moved off without me – I fought my way through the crowd to the poster-covered wall. The lecture bill had been pasted there quite recently, and the bold black print was fresh and easy to read.

Dr Elias Bonnet, the celebrated Southern preacher and Abolitionist currently visiting England, will give a First-hand Account of the Many Miseries of Slavery hitherto endured by Black Persons in the Confederate States of America, the Easing of whose Lot is so Devoutly to be Wished.

Subscriptions Welcomed.

"A veritable saint," declared a sharp voice in my ear. "A saint – nothing less."

"I beg your pardon?"

A hard-eyed woman in the plainest of black stood at my shoulder, both hands clasping the handle of a tightly rolled umbrella. With a brisk nod, she indicated the poster.

"That man Bonnet. I heard him speak in Hull, and I was moved, I can tell you. Those Southerners must be devils, to behave as they do to poor savages that don't know any better."

"This Dr Bonnet . . ." I struggled to disguise my American speech. "I don't suppose he's a tall, ill-favoured man with a blind eye?"

"Sounds like him, certainly. But what of it, young woman? *'Man looketh on the outward appearance, but the Lord looketh on the heart.'* " The woman rapped the poster with the handle of her umbrella. "Why –the doctor even lost his eye, so they say, when one of those wicked planters attacked him over possession of a runaway slave."

"He did?" Behind me, the Liverpool train pulled slowly out of the station, while I tried to reconcile the image of the saintly doctor with the Pastor Bonnet who'd run away from the *Bellflower* as fast as his spindly legs would carry him the moment my father had allowed it. I knew that blind eye too well to be mistaken, yet nothing the woman had told me tallied with the Eli Bonnet I remembered. Why, Pa had always maintained the eye had been blinded in the course of a grog-shop brawl.

But the woman in black had called him a saint; and certainly, if ever anyone stood in need of a good Christian saint, it was I, with the raw brand of the voodoo charm still gnawing at my fingers. Eli Bonnet . . . my father's friend. . . . Who'd have expected it?

For the first time since Rachel Gaunt's death, a small faint hope began to stir in my heart. If I wanted a sign of salvation, surely I need look no further than this?

And perhaps now another matter could be settled. Pastor Bonnet had made my marriage with his own hands: who was in a better position to know whether it had been legal or not? Oh, it wasn't that I wanted Matthew Oliver for a husband – not any more, goodness knows – but to gather up the shreds of my self-respect . . . to be sure I'd been decently wed, even by the haphazard standards of the river . . . that would be something, at least.

I didn't even try to catch the departing train – Liverpool could wait for another day. Eagerly, I scanned the poster once more. Dr Elias Bonnet was to give three lectures in Crewe. Two were already past; the third had started half an hour earlier in a temperance hall in Albert Street.

"Best hurry, if you want to hear him, sister," the woman in black pointed out.

I was already on my way to the turnstile.

2

The lecture had started at five. By the time I found Albert Street and its Temperance Hall it was ten minutes to six and the meeting was well advanced under the flare of two huge gasoliers, whose yellow flames turned the room into a kind of ochreous, fidgeting hell.

To my amazement, the place was packed – not with the moneyed and the well-to-do, but with shopmen in shiny suits and engineers from the locomotive works standing shoulder to shoulder with home-going bakers' boys with flour still under their fingernails. There were women, too – shop-girls and domestic servants by the look of them – and in a bunch at the rear of the hall, a handful of cab drivers who'd given up a few precious minutes of their time to support their distant comrades in oppression.

The room smelled of ripe humanity – of onions, of stablemen's boots, of sweat and cheap cologne, and all the thousand indefinable smells of a roused, excited crowd. In front of me a young clerk in a patent steel shirt-collar bobbed up and down excitedly; his female companion clung to his arm, begging him to be still and not make an exhibition of himself.

179

These people knew all about cuffs and blows and hunger: no effort of imagination was needed to imagine whippings and starvation. I'd heard it said that the cotton-spinners of Lancashire, who stood to lose more than anyone from a long-drawn-out war, shouted loudest in support of the abolition of slavery and the defeat of the South.

And miracle of miracles, there on the platform, windmilling his scrawny arms and glaring out with his single good eye, Eli Bonnet loomed like a monster of more than normal size, every gesture matched by the giant shadow that leaped and capered across the wall behind him.

I watched him, utterly stunned. In all my years on the river, not being inclined to churchgoing, I'd never seen Pastor Bonnet *fetchin' 'em* as Pa would have put it. True enough, I'd heard reports of women fainting in fright at his camp meetings, when the torments of Hell were dangled before their eyes, but until now the notion had seemed inconceivable.

Yet up on that platform, he appeared almost superhuman. "A saint," the woman in black had said, but for the life of me I couldn't see the resemblance. There was no gentleness about him – no compassion. The Pastor was more like. . . . To be honest, the creature he resembled most in the world was Sam Duck as I'd seen him once, returning from one of his voodoo rituals where the drums had drummed and the spirits had ridden their "horses" long into the ecstatic night. Sam's eyes had burned then just as the Pastor's single orb burned now, lit by an exultation beyond common understanding. A kind of holy madness united them both. . . . My lips began to move of their own accord. If wishing hard enough to heave your entire soul up into your throat was praying, then prayer was what it amounted to at that moment. *Oh please let me be free of the ill-wish upon me! I'm sorry I ever meddled in such things, but I didn't understand. Send the spirits back where they belong . . .*

"And when God looked down upon those poor, wretched Israelites working themselves to death for the Egyptians," the Pastor was thundering, whirling his hands above his head as if the Almighty Himself hovered somewhere between the gasoliers, "did He say 'That's too bad, folks – but it's just the way the dice roll for people of your colour'?"

"NO!" bawled the crowd, beside itself with indignation.

"And did He say 'You're no better than simple children, just made to be put-upon by someone – so it might as well be Pharaoh an' his understrappers as anyone else'? Well – did He?"

"NO!" came an answering roar from the floor of the hall.

"I'll say he didn't!" shouted the Pastor, and went off into a new tirade

180

interwoven with references to Moses leading the Israelites out of Egypt, and the plight of slavewomen helpless before the lustful attentions of their white masters.

At last he halted for breath, and mopped his brow with a spotted red handkerchief.

"I say to you, my friends – *Upon the ungodly He shall rain snares, fire an' brimstone, storm and tempest: this shall be their portion to drink!*" He glared round once more, extending a skinny arm in fearful benediction, and at that moment it seemed as if I, Katherine Summerbee, stood directly under his hand.

3

I found him after the lecture was over, holding court in the empty anteroom beyond the platform, his face still radiant with the grandeur of his own rhetoric. Others had come, bringing compliments, and I hung back among the dusty shadows until the last hand had been pressed and the last quilled bonnet had bobbed on its way.

"Pastor – "

The Pastor wheeled round. The radiance fled as his black brows descended in a disbelieving frown.

"Katherine?" he ventured. "Katherine Summerbee of the *Bell-flower*?"

"Well, yes. . . . Don't you recognise me?" For an awful moment I wondered if the voodoo spirits had altered me more than I knew. "I saw your poster at the station, and I came to find you. Pastor – I need your help. It's important."

The Pastor continued to gaze at me mistrustfully, as if trying to guess my business from my anxious face and dishevelled clothes.

"How long have you been in England?" he demanded. "I suppose you came here to escape from the war."

"Partly, I guess. Is that why you came?"

The Pastor glared at me.

"I'm here to do the Lord's work." He glanced up towards the peeling plaster overhead. "I was *called*."

His gaze descended imperiously upon me, and I watched him take a deep breath, swelling the narrow chest beneath his soiled shirt-front.

"Oh, the power was on me tonight, all right. It was beautiful! Beautiful! Some days He just gets inside my head and fires me up – not that I'd expect a godless creature like you to understand such things."

This touched a raw nerve.

"It isn't my fault if I'm godless," I protested. "Nobody ever bothered to teach me otherwise."

"That's true enough." The Pastor seated himself on one of the discarded benches piled against the anteroom wall, and regarded me sternly. "Time and again, I warned Ben he was raisin' you into a little pagan, but he wouldn't listen. I used to see you, when you was no more'n knee-high to a cricket, sitting on the deck while that black feller Sam filled your mind with his mumbo-jumbo and his magic candle-ends until the Devil had you well-nigh in the palm of his hand. For all I know, he still has."

The Pastor scowled at me so fiercely that the terror I'd carried since my vision in the fen stirred again like a great stone in the pit of my stomach. I almost jumped out of my skin when the anteroom door suddenly creaked open half-way to admit a man in a tight suit carrying a large wooden box.

"Excuse me, Doctor . . . I'm just about to close the doors for the night, and I thought I'd better bring this up here for safety's sake. It's a good collection, sir, if I may say so." The hall-keeper jingled the box experimentally. "We don't usually take so much at meetings here-abouts – but then, we don't often have such deserving causes as them poor misused creatures across the ocean." He cleared his voice modestly. "I put in two shillings of my own, on behalf of Mrs Vernon and myself."

"Bless you for that, Hall-keeper," Pastor Bonnet responded gravely. "Your goodness will be recorded in Heaven."

"Thank you, sir. Thank you, I'm sure." The man touched his hat and withdrew.

As soon as he'd gone, the Pastor prised off the lid of the collection box and peered inside. For a moment he stirred the contents with a long finger, and then whistled.

"There's more than five pounds here, I reckon. That's upwards of twenty dollars for the mission, once I've deducted a few humble expenses." Noticing my blank expression, he added, "The Mission for Relieving the Distress of Souls in Bondage, in the city of Memphis."

"Don't you care about the rivermen any more, then?"

The Pastor waved an impatient hand.

"I had no choice in the matter, child! The good Lord Himself told me I should devote my energies to the slave problem, instead of wasting 'em on a lost cause like the rivermen. Take your pa, now – " Eli Bonnet closed the box with a snap. "Men like Ben Summerbee are just natural-born heathens with no intention of mending their ways. They don't see

182

the need for it – until the day they feel the flames of Hell licking their backsides. *Then* they wish they'd listened, all right."

"Do you really believe Pa's in Hell, Pastor?"

"Bound to be! If ever a man had a first-class ticket to the furnace, it was your pa. I tried hard to save his soul, goodness knows, but I reckon he's still set to spend eternity roasting along with all the other sinners."

"But how can you be so sure?"

"It's God's own truth!" The Pastor's face glowed with conviction. "Unless you trust in the Lord, the Bible says you go straight to Hell, sure as anything. The road to Hell is smooth and wide, but the road to Heaven is narrow as a river channel after a dry summer. The trick is, you have to be a Christian to know the difference," he finished triumphantly.

"But what about me?" By now I was becoming thoroughly frightened. "What if I am full of the Devil's candle-ends and so forth, just as you said? Is it too late to change all that now?"

The Pastor drew a long, dismal breath and shook his head.

"If I was you, my girl, I'd get on my knees and start praying right away. After all the truck you've had with feathers an' fortune-telling an' such – you've got a whole heap of mischief to make up." The Pastor began to boom like an Old Testament prophet. "Repent, and save your immortal soul! *A virtuous woman is a crown to her husband–*" He stopped abruptly, his mouth hanging uneasily ajar.

In that instant, exactly the same thought had occurred to us both.

"Pastor – " I began. "About my marriage – "

4

The hall-keeper was waiting for us to leave, and so the Pastor took me to a restaurant he'd found a couple of streets away, absolutely refusing to discuss the matter until we'd sat down at a table – as if he suspected it might be wise to have solid wood between us when we talked.

The restaurant turned out to be a dingy tearoom, empty at that hour except for a couple of commercial travellers in a distant corner, morosely discussing the state of the hardware trade. The listless, gravy-stained waitress soon became bored with us, and there was no danger of our low-voiced discussion being overheard.

To my amazement, it didn't seem to surprise the Pastor at all that his wedding ceremony had been pronounced worthless.

"Marriage is a singular business, you might say." Pastor Bonnet frowned down at the solitary lamb cutlet on his plate. "I've known marriages made in big city cathedrals that didn't last any longer than a

183

ten-cent streetcar ride. And I've knowed folks get together without so much as a prayer, who've stayed that way for their entire lives and a whole parcel of grandchildren. Who's to say which ones were proper marriages and which weren't?"

He jabbed moodily at his plate. "It seems to me that if both parties believe they're married, then that's enough to make it so. But if either one of 'em don't hold with the idea – or both, for that matter – then no amount of official scribbling's going to turn them into husband and wife. Does that answer your question?"

"No, it doesn't."

The Pastor sighed, and gloomily chewed a mouthful of lamb. "So you've gone and lost the husband we fixed up for you?"

"That's about the truth of it."

"It's all your pa's fault. I always reckoned Ben was a good deal too hasty with that gun of his."

"To blazes with Pa! All I really want to know is whether I was properly wed in the eyes of the law – and whether the whole business was ever registered like it should have been."

The Pastor chewed on in silence for a few minutes.

"Not exactly," he mumbled at last.

"Not exactly what?"

"Not any of it, I guess. But Katherine – " he added swiftly, "you have to remember that an untruth told for a good purpose ain't like a common-or-garden lie. Your pa wasn't in any mood to listen to reason that day. If I'd told him we had no licence to conduct a marriage under Louisiana statute, who knows what he might have done? He might've blowed that young feller's head clean off his shoulders for defilin' his daughter! No, sir – I just had to go right ahead and marry you both, an' hope it would stick for the future." The Pastor nodded with satisfaction. "In fact, I reckon I did a good thing that day. I was carrying out a humanitarian act."

"Oh . . ." I flung up my hands in frustration and shame. "How *could* you?"

"I did what was right under the circumstances." The Pastor regarded me sternly across the width of the table. "I don't reckon *I'll* have anything to blush over, come Judgement Day."

"Well, that settles the matter. I'll go back to America as soon as I can find a ship to take me."

I dare say I sounded resolute, but it was empty bravery. Goodness knows what I expected to do when I arrived in an American port – or where I intended to go from there. I was exhausted after my long

184

journey, and still light-headed from my illness. Nothing remained to anchor me to any kind of reality except . . . my father's old friend, sitting opposite me at that moment, picking shreds of lamb from between his yellow teeth.

"Go back to America?" The Pastor stopped picking to stare at me. "While there's fighting going on? Oh, no, Katherine – I wouldn't do that."

"But why? They don't make war on women and children, do they?"

"Who knows what'll happen when the slaves rise? No one at all will be safe then."

"I haven't heard of any rising."

"No?" The Pastor's thick black brows rose into his untidy hair. "The British newspapers have been full of it, ever since Lincoln declared the slaves free from the first day of the coming year."

"I didn't know about any of this." There had been no newspapers in the gloom of Hawk's Dyke for almost a week.

"Lincoln claims the law holds good in the rebel states too, on account of he's really President of the whole caboodle and Jeff Davis don't matter a hoot. The difference is that the Confederate planters won't get paid for the labour they lose like the folks in the North will."

"But no one can be surprised at that, surely! Even in the South, most people believe the slaves will be freed eventually."

"Ah – but the newspapers here say Lincoln's only done it to put a quick end to the war. They reckon that once the slaves find out they'll be free men as soon as the North wins, they'll rise up and cut their masters' throats quick as winking, an' do the Northerners' work for them."

"Lincoln would never be so dishonest!"

"I don't trust any politician," muttered the man of God. "Not where I can't see him, at least."

In their far corner of the room the commercial travellers rose to go, leaving a newspaper folded on the table. The Pastor glanced over his shoulder.

"Pardon me, friend, but could I take your newspaper, if you've no further use for it? Well, that's handsome of you, sir."

He searched through the borrowed pages. "There you are! Read it for yourself, if you don't believe me. Down there, under the corn prices."

With a sinking heart, I began to read where he'd indicated. It seemed true enough: the British press expected a wholesale slave revolt to sweep across the Confederate states, carrying off rich and poor alike in a rising tide of vengeance. In the North there was talk of conscription, and armies digging in for months of stubborn conflict. Guerrilla bands and looters were ranging along the state borders, killing and scavenging in the wake of the troops. The North had declared themselves determined to crush the rebels if it took for ever: the South scorned to consider surrender, in spite of a dearth of food and medicine which could soon reduce life in the Confederacy to a struggle for survival.

As I closed the page, the Pastor reached out and stabbed the newsprint with a long finger.

"The American news is eleven or twelve days old, don't forget. It takes as long as that for a steamer to get here." He shook his head gloomily. "The whole country's probably ablaze with slaughter by now. Blood running in the streets of Richmond and Washington – gangs of desperadoes hiding out in the backwoods . . ."

"But there's nowhere else I can go." Hope had fled, and at last I was near to despair.

"Well . . . I guess I could take care of you, child."

I glanced up. An expression of benevolence had spread itself over the Pastor's face.

"Just for the time being, of course, until it's safe for you to go back to America as you intend. But you'd have to put all this voodoo wickedness out of your head, Katherine – be clear on that point. You'd have to set to and help me with my blessed mission, and in return, I'll see what I can do about saving your strayin' soul. For Ben's sake – " his good eye rolled up towards the smoke-blackened ceiling, "I'd care for you as if you were my own daughter."

His glance fell on me again, and he smiled serenely.

"I've been thinking for a while that with the lectures goin' so well, it was time I took on an assistant. It ain't dignified for a man of my standing to be seen out with a pot of paste, sticking up bills. And it's a well-known fact, the sight of a woman on the platform lends a kind of . . . *rectitude* to the proceeding. Why – I do believe you were sent to me tonight for that very purpose."

"Do you reckon so?"

The Pastor sat back in his chair and regarded me complacently.

"You were sent, child, I've no doubt of it. I take it you've no great objection to working for the welfare of the oppressed black race?"

"Of course not," I agreed, thinking of Sam Duck.

"Well, then."

I recalled the lightness of my purse, where seven pounds, twelve shillings and twopence was all that stood between me and the world.

"Are you paying wages?"

"*Wages*, child? For the Lord's work? Why, in these troubled times I reckon we should both be glad of a place to lay our heads, without askin' for wages into the bargain."

"I guess you're right," I agreed quickly. "I wouldn't want to misuse the money."

"Then we're agreed you should join the mission?"

It was the word *mission* which finally made up my mind. There was something so wholesome and safe about a *mission* – something earnest and clean and bright after the lurking evil which had followed me from New Orleans. Perhaps the Pastor was right, and some benevolent power had guided me to his door that night.

And besides – what was there for me elsewhere? At least the Pastor was someone to call me "Katherine", and to remember old times with Pa and the *Bellflower*. He'd known me as an infant, almost; if he thought hard, he could even summon up a picture of Cripple Mary, my mother – which made him family, as near as dammit.

He'd already taken my silence to signify agreement.

"Welcome to the Mission for Relieving the Distress of Souls in Bondage, my child. Rest assured, you're in safe hands now."

Chapter Fourteen

1

If the Pastor had been reformed by his mission, then, I reckoned, there
was hope for me. And Heaven sakes – the Pastor had been turned into a
regular puritan. During the weeks that followed I never saw him touch
liquor in any form; he'd taken to pronouncing a sonorous grace before
every meal, and I never heard an oath on his lips, even when he was
roundly abused by a railway porter he'd refused to tip. If rigid
steadfastness of purpose was a mark of sainthood, then perhaps Eli
Bonnet had become a saint after all.

Every penny we raised was for the work of the mission. When we
travelled by train we paid third-class fares and congratulated ourselves
on the few shillings we'd saved for the slaves; we took meals wherever
they were cheapest, and hunted out the lowest-priced boarding houses
consistent with respectability. Not a farthing was spent without the
most anguished heart-searching. The Pastor even bullied the printer of
his posters into halving his bill, and then compelled the poor man to
throw in a pot of paste as a contribution to the cause.

Affronted by my curls, he compelled me to scrape my hair flat round
a centre parting, and to hide it under a cotton cap; he made me let down
my skirts until they covered my ankles, and take out even the tiny gold
hoops I'd worn in my ears since childhood.

"The Devil's gee-gaws!" he'd roar whenever I got up enough
courage to protest. "Think of your soul, Katherine, and thank the Lord
I'm here to save you from the folly of pride and superstition!"

2

"It won't do," he announced suddenly on our third morning in
Stafford, while I waited to hear what new sin I'd managed to commit.
"That coat of yours," he added, "is a disgrace to the cause."

I had to admit there was some truth in this. Try as I might, I'd been
unable to scrub the red stains of the melted poppies from the shoulders
of my poor old coat, and even with a shawl thrown over the mess, I still
resembled a woman whose throat had been cut.

The Pastor waited for me to speak; then I saw his black brows rise
slowly towards his hair like a couple of crows in a breeze.

188

"Well? You surely don't expect me to lay out money on such adornment, do you? Katherine, I'm surprised at you! You must have a few shillings of your own, at least."

"I do have a little," I admitted, remembering the few pounds I'd clung to for my fare across the Atlantic.

"Then I expect you to make yourself respectable for the Lord. You know what the Bible says about layin' up treasures upon earth."

"Yes, Pastor."

"Money just leads young women such as yourself into temptation."

"Yes, Pastor."

"I reckon you should seriously contemplate putting the whole of what you've been hoarding into the collection box."

I stared at him aghast. The money in my purse was for my sea passage: without it I'd be trapped and destitute – no better off than one of the slaves we were trying to help. How much more did I have to do to stay out of the furnace?

The Pastor immediately took my hesitation for defiance.

"That wicked pride of yours will be your downfall, Katherine Summerbee! Crush it! Crush it – or there can only be one ending!"

Yet I couldn't give up the handful of sovereigns I'd clung to through thick and thin. I couldn't bear to lose the last of my independence, though the Devil himself should stand at my shoulder.

Instinctively, I glanced round. Perhaps I could find another way of crushing my troublesome pride.

After breakfast, armed with twelve shillings and twopence of loose change from my purse, I set off for the shops. I returned after an hour bearing a second-hand mantle in stout Melton cloth and a gown in brown rep, only a little faded, which I'd discovered in a Clothing Exchange in one of the narrower streets of the town. Dressed in those, I looked quite depressingly plain; if I'd had any pride left at the start of the day, it was surely crushed now, as flat as the Pastor could wish.

It was a frugal existence altogether, and it hardly varied with each passing week. As soon as we arrived in a new town, I went out with posters and paste and an invitation to the editor of the local newspaper to attend the Doctor's next lecture. I called on any ladies' circle or temperance group which might swell our audience, counted the collection at the end of the evening, and polished the Pastor's boots when occasion demanded.

From Stafford we went to Derby, and from Derby on to Nottingham and a whole string of towns differing only in their possession of foundries or mines or grim rows of textile mills. Eventually our tour

189

ended – as I discovered each one of the Pastor's tours was destined to end – in the city of Liverpool.

The mission committee met in Liverpool, so the Pastor told me, but mercifully I wasn't required at its table. To my delight I found myself free for a whole afternoon, and safe from the Pastor's incessant fault-finding. Sometimes his tyranny made me want to scream aloud; surely by now my feet must be set firmly on the narrow path of virtue instead of the wide and glittering road to Hell?

Yet at least I was doing something good and honourable – something which might make up a little for the pain I'd unintentionally brought to Hawk's Dyke. Even now, there were still nights when Adam Gaunt's bitter, comfortless face was the last image to visit me before I fell into a guilty sleep.

In spite of the weeks that had passed, I'd been unable to put either father or son out of my mind. It was fortunate that the Pastor remembered nothing of my long-lost "husband", since Matthew's name in particular was never out of the newspapers. No sooner had he become chairman of J. G. Oliver & Co. following his mother's death than he'd changed the name of the line to the "Oliver Steam Navigation Company" and ordered four new steam cargo vessels to celebrate the fact. A month later, I read that Oliver's had bought out the floundering Atlantic & Peru Shipping Company, adding another twenty vessels to the current Oliver total of twenty-four and the eighteen already owned by their coastal subsidiary, the Drover Line.

Resentfully, I added them all up on my fingers, and realised with a start how near Matthew had already come to owning the glorious and imaginary fleet he'd once launched upon the burning Mississippi. That, I thought grimly, was the vital difference between us. What Matthew dreamed, he made into reality, while my own modest castles in the air seemed further off than ever.

To make matters worse, at every turn I was confronted by the spectacle of Mr and Mrs Matthew Oliver, united in domestic bliss. Mrs Oliver had been seen wearing a huge jonquil diamond on her elegant hand; Mrs Oliver had held yet another glittering reception; and as Christmas approached in that year of 1862, the Liverpool papers were full of the wonderful steam yacht Mr Oliver had built as a belated wedding gift to his wife. Whole columns were devoted to the screw schooner *Harvester*, two hundred feet of ocean-going luxury in which the divinely blessed couple could cruise the Mediterranean at their leisure, or sail to any port where Mr Oliver's business might take him. Mrs Oliver herself, it was reported, had chosen every priceless hanging, every chandelier, every gilt *torchère* – even the deep-pile carpets which kept the rumble of the engines from reaching the ears of the owner and his guests.

So while the Pastor and his committee occupied the lodging-house parlour, I sat on a chilly Liverpool park bench, hunched in my second-hand mantle and reading in a drizzle-dampened newspaper of the pleasures of being Matthew Oliver's wife.

3

The Pastor and I spent Christmas Day 1862 in a small lodging house in Leicester, where we led the carol singing round the parlour piano after a miserly portion of goose and plum pudding. Later, with the Pastor snoring safely by the fire, the rest of us played nursery games with a toy-salesman's samples, "dowsing" for halfpennies under the frayed rug with a pair of miraculous copper rods, and eating elderly oranges boiled to restore their plumpness.

This high point over, my existence dragged on through a dreary procession of boarding houses and halls and suburban trains, until I began to believe that there must be precious little of the soul of Katherine Summerbee left to save.

The boom in abolition, if I may call it that, continued for most of 1863; Britain and America were too bound up in matters of trade –cotton, most of all – for the British people not to take an interest in the outcome of the domestic struggle across the Atlantic. The newspapers were full of it each day, and since the Pastor had condemned the reading of anything except sermons as sinful, my single relief from tedium was to follow the tide of war which surged endlessly to and fro between North and South.

At first it seemed to flow in favour of the North; the Pastor and I were in Coventry, I remember, when the conscripted Federal forces surged through Tennessee, and in the east crossed the Rappahannock just below Fredericksburg. Then, on the 3rd of May 1863, the tide turned when the Confederates won the bloody battle of Chancellorsville – if you can call it victory to leave marginally fewer thousands of mangled young corpses on the battlefield than your enemy has done.

The news reached us almost a fortnight after the event, when we'd just arrived in Northampton. I read the newspaper report of the battle in growing horror and disbelief, suddenly ashamed to sit safely in the faded dining-room of yet another English lodging house, secure in its dingy gentility from the abominations of war. The Pastor, I noticed, had abandoned his dinner of boiled mackerel to pore over a letter he'd just retrieved from the poste restante.

"Is your letter from America, Pastor? Is it from the mission?"

The Pastor's head was still bent over the closely written page – a little askew, so that our landlady wouldn't catch sight of him from her distant end of the long table. Absently, he murmured, "Instructions from Liverpool. A message I've to deliver on Captain Bulloch's behalf when we arrive in Bedford."

"Captain Bulloch?" I'd been travelling with the Pastor for months now, but I couldn't remember that name among the members of the mission committee.

"Captain James Bulloch," repeated the Pastor crossly. "Captain James Bulloch of Liverpool."

I stared at him, puzzled. I could only recall one Captain James Bulloch in Liverpool who might wish to pass messages through American expatriates. I remembered him clearly from New Orleans, where he'd called with the steamer *Bienville* at the very start of the war. It was widely known that he'd later been sent to England to buy and build warships in secret for the Confederacy – hence his residence in Liverpool.

"Pastor – " I ventured. "Surely not Captain Bulloch . . . the Confederate agent?"

Pastor Bonnet lifted his gaze from the letter.

"And who else should I mean?"

"But we support abolition, Pastor! Don't we want the North to win the war?"

The Pastor's face darkened with sudden anger.

"Katherine Summerbee, I'm ashamed of you! Support the Union? Have you forgotten which side shot down your Pa?"

"But how can you stand on a platform and say slavery is an abomination, and then go off running errands for a Confederate agent?" I hastily lowered my voice as the kitchen-maid swept away our mackerel and slapped down plates for the communal rice pudding.

"Don't you preach morality to me, my girl!" The Pastor wagged his pudding-spoon to emphasise the point. "Please God, the South can win this war – but even if they do, slavery won't last. Sooner or later the planters will have to hire their labour like everyone else." The Pastor drew the dish of pudding towards him. "No – slavery ain't the problem any more. The question is – what are we going to do with all these free black fellers that are going to be clutterin' up the country? That's where the mission comes in."

"That's why we're collecting money – to help them get work and find homes of their own."

For a moment I thought the Pastor was about to have a seizure. As it was, he dropped the ladle into the pudding-dish in his outrage.

"We sure as blazes are not!" He glared at me over the splashed cloth. "Foolish talk like that just goes to show what a dangerous hold that Sam Duck had on your young mind. Lay out money to set a crowd of ex-slaves up in comfort, indeed! No, sir – every cent of that cash will be spent on shippin' them home, for their own good."

"*Home?*"

"To Africa!" declared the Pastor triumphantly. "To the jungle, where God intended them to live in the first place."

I couldn't believe he meant it – not seriously.

For several minutes I watched him guzzle his rice pudding, quite oblivious to the effect his words had produced, while I struggled with the fact that banishing hundreds of thousands of people across an ocean against their will was the "blessed mission" for which I'd scrimped and toiled and gone without.

I tried to imagine Sam Duck, that consummate engineer, set down on some barren African shore to make the best of his future – thanks to my dedicated fund-raising. I'd heard such plans put forward before, and often by people far more eminent than the Pastor, but that still didn't make them right! Surely if it had been evil to snatch Sam's grandfather from his African home, it was every bit as bad to send Sam away from the land of his birth to a place of which he had no memories at all? Goodness knows, I'd endured enough of the bewildering pain of statelessness not to wish it on any other human being – especially those who'd suffered such injustice already.

I longed to seize the Pastor by his narrow shoulders and shake the smug smile from his face.

"And what about the people who come to your lectures?" I demanded instead. "They're good, honest folks who simply want to help the slaves! Do you imagine they'd give you a penny-piece, if they knew what you planned to do with it?"

"The money's for the welfare of their black brethren. That's what I say to them."

"But that's no better than a lie!"

"Don't you dare call me a liar!" The Pastor's brows knitted ominously. "And don't meddle in matters you don't understand. I was *called* to work for this cause, I tell you. I just knew inside myself it was the right thing to do. And as for lying about it – I've had occasion to tell you before, Katherine, an untruth told for a good reason ain't the same as a common lie. Sometimes you have to put God's great plan for the world before tryin' to explain morality to ordinary workin' folks."

I sprang to my feet, and every head at the long table turned in our direction.

"I don't believe it! Maybe I am godless and sinful, but I reckon you're a wicked fraud – *Doctor* Bonnet!"

I couldn't say any more. I simply rushed from the room and fled upstairs, where I locked myself in my bare little bedchamber and stayed there until the Pastor's knockings and threats had finally died away.

4

I felt . . . guilty all over again. I felt I'd been part of a squalid deception which would end by making wretched the very people I'd intended to help. So much for saintliness! If Pa was really roasting in Hell as the Pastor had claimed, then I reckoned that sooner or later, if there was any justice to be had in a Christian world, "Doctor" Eli Bonnet and the members of his mission should find a place in the flames alongside him.

"You're a child of the Devil!" the Pastor had hissed through the keyhole before leaving me alone at last. "You are! I guessed it the first minute I set eyes on you! You're a child of the Devil, Katherine Summerbee, and he'll come for his due in the end – you'll see."

In the dark of the night, I turned the possibility over in my mind. I'd tried to do some good in the world – tried as hard as I could – and yet once more it had all gone dreadfully wrong. Was it possible the ill-wish had followed me from Hawk's Dyke?

Quickly, I lit the comforting candle by my bed. What a disaster I was – eighteen years of age, and still a trembling, superstitious fool. Katherine Summerbee – who'd once thought herself smart as paint and a match for anything on two legs – frightened of shadows!

I looked round for something to keep myself busy. Just outside my door stood a box containing several months' supply of lecture posters – hundreds of them. For the rest of the night, the child of the Devil worked hard with pen and ink, adding after "Subscriptions Welcomed" the words "to force the slaves into ships and pack them off to Africa". For once, the Pastor was going to tell the whole truth. Let him explain that away, if he could!

As I worked, I gave myself a good talking to, and by the time the last poster had been altered and the box restored to its place outside my door, I'd reached a decision Matthew Oliver would have been proud of. From that very moment and for the rest of my life, I'd look out for myself. I'd make my own decisions, trusting no one. And if I was really

194

the Devil's child as the Pastor had said, I'd just have to bear the consequences of it alone.

In the morning, when the new, resolute Katherine Summerbee came downstairs, it was to find that Doctor Bonnet had already left for Bedford, taking his posters with him but leaving a small matter of fourteen shillings for my board and lodging still unpaid.

The landlady, who knew only that the Doctor and his assistant had quarrelled and parted company, at once made it plain that if her fourteen shillings weren't forthcoming, I'd leave without bag and baggage, and the Melton mantle into the bargain.

The sight of one of my precious sovereigns mollified her enough to call me *Miss* once more, and to inform me that if I'd no particular preference for religious work, her brother in Watford was looking for an honest and steady young woman to serve in his confectioner's shop.

I was astonished, and grateful – until I reached Watford. I lasted four days with the confectioner – or, more particularly, with his sharp-tongued wife. They'd no need of a shop assistant; what they wanted was a skivvy to clean their house, scrub greasy pots in their kitchen, live in their mouse-infested garret and run after their six wilful, spoiled children from five in the morning until they could be made to stay in their beds at night. And whatever Katherine Summerbee might have become, she was nobody's skivvy – as I told the confectioner's wife before walking out with my nose in the air.

And if I did add a few sound American precepts on the raising of well-mannered children instead of a brood of young ruffians, I'm sure no one in the world could have blamed me.

By now, for a Mississippi river child, I'd begun to acquire a remarkably thorough knowledge of the geography of the English counties. I knew, for example, that less than twenty miles to the south of Watford lay the metropolis of London, from where I could sail to New York as easily as from Liverpool, when the time came. I no longer had enough even to pay for a steerage passage, but there was bound to be work available in London. Heaven sakes, it was said that in the city there were even women letter-carriers, and women clerks in some of the counting houses!

I ended up in a drugget apron, packing books for a publisher in High Holborn who was too mean to pay a man's wages for the job, but wanted a woman capable of lifting his great boxes of bound volumes on to the carrier's cart. For six days' labour I was paid eight shillings a week, two shillings of which was taken back for a box bed in a candle-lit attic under the roof-leads of the building – and I'm ashamed to say I was glad to get it. If I showed promise, I was told, I might graduate one day to folding the printed pages ready for cutting, at the huge sum of fivepence an hour.

But I was free of the Pastor – and it was only now I realised how much of the simple, harmless pleasure of living he'd frightened me into giving up. There were times, and many of them, when I shivered in the darkness of my attic, sensing the sour smell of still water like a warning that evil spirits hovered near . . . but I was past caring. I let my hair curl once more, hitched my skirts up to practical level, and whistled while I worked. If the Devil came for his daughter, I was ready. At least there was no one else to be hurt by my ruin.

I prefer to forget those months in High Holborn. Several times I found myself on the steps of a shipping office, ready to enquire for their cheapest fare to New York; each time, I retreated. While I might manage to scrape up the passage money, I had nothing more to keep me at the end of my journey while I looked for work. And the more straitened my circumstances became in England, the more terrified I was of starvation in New York.

Besides – the war was eating up all the parts of America I knew. At the beginning of August '63, the pages of the old newspapers we wrapped round our books were full of tales that the Confederates had threatened Washington itself. Yet before long they reported that the South had been beaten back by Lincoln's troops at Gettysburg, and at almost the same moment, that Grant had taken Vicksburg for the North.

Gettysburg was little more than a place name to me, but the news of the dreadful bombardment of the river city of Vicksburg was another story. With Vicksburg lost to the South, I knew that the whole of the Mississippi River – Pa's river – was in the hands of the Union navy, from the headwaters to the Gulf. The spinal column of the Confederacy was snapped, the war to the west of it over. Now the British newspapers began to speculate that if the North could only persist for long enough, the South would soon run out of supplies of every kind and be forced to its knees.

Where in such a conflict could Katherine Summerbee scrape a living?

In London, I had a stroke of luck at last. One of my duties at the publisher's was to rush copies of each new book to Mudie's Select Lending Library in Oxford Street, which prided itself on having the volumes on its shelves the instant they returned from the binder – long before any of the other Mudie's branches round the country could stock them. I desperately missed the library at Hawk's Dyke, with its hotchpotch of ancient and new, and I would have loved to be able to pay Mudie's guinea subscription myself, which gave entrée to the great hall with its rows of long counters. But I needed every penny I could save for more down-to-earth purposes, and I had to content myself with "borrowing" the odd volume from my employer's packing room to read by candlelight in my attic – squinting sideways into folded pages which I didn't dare cut apart.

Then one day in April 1864 a clerk at Mudie's happened to mention that a girl was wanted to work in the cellars among the thousands of books kept ready to be summoned by speaking-tube to the counters upstairs. Nimbleness and a quick eye were the principal qualifications in the half-dark of the underground shelving.

"Are you a reader?" demanded the manager suspiciously when I presented myself before him, very nearly nineteen and in my brown rep gown and shawl. "What was the last book you read right through?"

"Tappan's *Doctrine of the Will*," I told him truthfully, recalling Hawk's Dyke.

"Ah." The man gave me a sideways look. "What about novels? Miss Yonge, for instance – *The Heir of Redclyffe* – do you know it?"

"So uplifting," I said automatically. The Pastor's temperance ladies had always praised it to the skies.

"And Mr Anthony Trollope?"

"I like *The Warden* well enough. And *Dr Thorne*." I'd read both at Hawk's Dyke. "But I do not like his mother's book on America. *Domestic Manners of the Americans* contains a good deal of humbug, it seems to me. Mrs Frances Trollope didn't try to understand the Americans at all."

The manager treated me to another sideways glance.

"Very well, you can start tomorrow. But see here – if I once catch you reading the books instead of fetching 'em, you go out on the street straight off. Those are the 'domestic manners' in my cellar, and you'd better remember them."

5

I enjoyed my work at Mudie's, flying to and fro with copies of *Lady Audley's Secret* or *East Lynne*, and gossiping with the other girls when the chief librarian's back was turned. Mudie's wage, though hardly generous, came to more than I'd earned at the publisher's, and I was able to move into respectable, if cheap, lodgings nearby. To earn a little more, I spent my evenings copying out play-parts for actors in a clear, round hand at a guinea a dozen, until by autumn there was almost ten pounds in my purse. The clamour for peace talks on the other side of the Atlantic was growing louder all the time, and I began to believe that my exile in England was almost over.

Saving for my sea passage had made me as mean as ever my father had been. Some of the bolder of Mudie's girls went to a nearby dance room after work was finished for the day, but I always begged off, using my copying work as an excuse. I hardly ever bought clothes, but spent hours darning stockings that were no more than a patchwork of holes, and unpicking and resewing the drab garments I already had.

But we were eager followers of fashion down in our cellar, where the girls were experts on who was who in London society. After all, even Her Majesty had taken out a Mudie's subscription, and the Princess of Wales, too. The Prince, it was whispered with winks and nudges, had more interesting things to occupy his time than novels, for all he'd only been married a year and a half. We'd crowded the doorway once to see him for ourselves, and hear his guttural voice and barking laugh as he drove past in his carriage.

Inevitably, Mr and Mrs Matthew Oliver came in for their share of discussion, though it was chiefly Violet's comings and goings which were of interest to the girls in Mudie's cellars. I learned no more than I already knew – that Mrs Matthew Oliver was generally acknowledged one of the greatest beauties of the age, as her husband was one of its youngest shipping magnates. Mrs Oliver went racing with the Prince of Wales; a variety of rose had been named for her; she had only to appear at a ball in lace or feathers for dressmakers to be plunged into a frenzy of copying, simply to discover that the *nonpareil* herself had moved on to something even more original.

The shocking fashion for short coats such as gentlemen wore was ascribed to her. The new jockey hats were laid at her door. This was fashion at its very fastest, of course, but then, if Mrs Oliver wore it . . . London society had long since flung itself at Mrs Oliver's exquisite feet: soon, the newspapers predicted, she'd be able to test her powers in America too.

Mrs Oliver, naturally, had a Mudie's subscription – a two-guinea subscription, allowing her to take out more than one volume at a time. I'm sure Violet could have bought a score of books for herself every day, had she chosen to – even three-volume novels at one and a half guineas apiece – but a Mudie's subscription guaranteed that the most talked-about books were delivered on the day of publication, which for the fashionable set was reason enough to borrow.

Two-guinea subscribers had no need to come to Oxford Street in person. A letter posted anywhere in London would reach us the same day, and by evening the Mudie's horse-van would have whisked the selected volumes to the subscriber's door. As the nights grew darker and colder, it was a dreary task to accompany the van, which often didn't complete its rounds until long after the library itself was closed. But one afternoon in the middle of rainy March, making up the list of books for delivery, I saw the name *Mrs Matthew Oliver* against an address in Eaton Square – and promptly volunteered to make the trip.

Goodness knows what made me do it. It was more than two years since I'd set eyes on Matthew – or Violet, for that matter – yet the memory of that night of fire in New Orleans, of my quarrel with Matthew in Rachel's garden and our furious kiss near the stable yard, still returned to haunt me when I least expected it, just when I was certain I'd banished him from my life for ever.

I didn't blame Matthew for my present situation; after all, would I have been so much better off in the Confederacy? But as the months passed and I still found myself catching my breath at the sight of a tall shadow in the street or a direct grey stare suddenly meeting mine across the width of an omnibus, I began to blame him for two years wasted in heartache and misery. And like North and South, behind Matthew stood his father, Adam Gaunt, the flint to Matthew's steel – two proud, uncompromising men locked in their endless battle, each one consumed by the loving dread of a creature so like himself.

That was what I resented – that in their own heedless way, Matthew and his father had poisoned my soul for mere mortals. Who could be satisfied with dance-saloon loafers, after flying so close to the sun?

Scolding myself for reading too many novels, I put on my mantle and bonnet to go out with the van. The Eaton Square address was Sir George Broadney's London house: I guess I was just curious to see what kind of mansion Violet and her family called home.

A footman with powdered hair opened the door at Eaton Square – the front door, I may say, since Mudie's books were never left at the kitchen entrance. I explained to the man that I had three books to deliver and two to collect, and was requested to wait in the hall.

Time passed, while I stared at the colossal carved marble fireplace which ran up one wall to the elaborate cornice, and wondered whether someone had to climb it like a rock-face to keep it clean.

Minutes passed before I heard the footman's steps returning from a long way off along the tiled floor.

" 'Scuse me, miss, but Mr Eames says you're to wait upstairs while we find the books, on account of no one's allowed to clutter up the hall for Mrs Oliver's visitor." He grinned a little sheepishly. "Not that he put it like that, of course."

"Mr Eames?"

"The butler."

"I see."

"Ordinarily, I'd let you wait here, but not today. *Very important person*," he mouthed, nodding significantly.

"And where does Mr Eames say I'm to wait, if I'm not good enough for his hallway?"

"You're to cut upstairs to the pugs' hole, so I'm told. The housekeeper's sitting-room," the footman added helpfully. "Where the upper servants takes their puddings of an evening. Look – " He glanced back down the hallway, checking that no one was nearby. "Mr Eames said I was to take you up there myself, but I'll miss a mug of beer in the servants' hall if I'm not down again sharpish. If I give you directions, could you find your own way upstairs, d'you think?"

"I dare say I'll manage." I wasn't going to let a powdered flunkey imagine I was overawed by the size of his employer's house.

"Good girl!" Vastly relieved, the footman turned to point the way. "Just go through the hallway here, up the steps by the marble urns, past the gong, upstairs to the first floor, through the archway to the left and then the door beyond that. If you go down to the end of the corridor, the pugs' hole is the door you're facing when you get there. You can't miss it. Wait inside, and someone'll come for you with the books. Run along, then – " he urged, seeing me hesitate. "It's more than my job's worth, if they come out and find you lurking here."

Satisfied that I'd set off in the proper direction, the footman vanished abruptly in search of his beer.

The hallway was deserted, wrapped in the shadowy hush of late afternoon, but I could see the marble urns the footman had described at the head of the steps beyond it. The floors were marble too; my feet hardly whispered over the huge black and white slabs or the stone treads of the staircase beyond.

The hallway on the floor above was carpeted with a long runner which led on through the archway the footman had mentioned. After that he'd told me to turn . . . right. Or had it been left? No – I was sure he'd said *right*, though the furnishings of the house seemed equally magnificent in either direction; I could see nothing to indicate where a mere housekeeper's room might lie.

I turned right, convinced I'd chosen correctly. Here the walls were hung with gilt-framed landscapes, and I paused to examine one which had something of a look of Sourwell Abbey, its lawns dotted with pairs of tiny strolling stick figures. I peered at it hopefully, only to find that the faces of the walkers were entirely blank, no more than deceitful blobs of pink from the artist's brush.

Beyond the fifth landscape the passage led through another arch, and there at the end of the corridor was the door of the housekeeper's room, just as the footman had told me, a tall door of panelled mahogany, identical to the rest. I grasped the brass handle and turned it, marvelling at the absolute silence and smoothness of the locks and hinges in that sumptuous house.

The door swung open . . . on a larger room than I'd expected, not a sitting-room at all, but a bedroom – if grandeur like that could be given such a commonplace name. In all honesty, it was more like a ballroom with a bed in it than something designed for the purpose of sleeping. The window curtains were swagged and lined in contrasting silks, the dressing-table was veiled in lace and crowned with a bow, there were lace runners on the tables and silver-topped vials. . . . It was like gaping into Alice Oliver's doll's house all over again; if I'd found the little felt-faced maid propped like a broomstick against the wall, I wouldn't have been at all surprised.

Quite forgetting the purpose of my errand, I closed the door and softly opened its nearest neighbour.

I was disappointed to discover that the furniture in this second room was covered in dust-sheets – like everything in the room next door, and the one beyond that. Disappointment brought me back to my senses. What had the footman said? Through a doorway beyond the arch . . .

I returned to the archway, and this time turned left instead of right. Unfortunately there was no sign of the doorway he'd described, but there was a corridor – and there was a door at the end of it. Hopefully, I turned the handle, only to find myself staring into yet another bedroom . . . a bedroom with two people in it, and man and a woman who'd apparently withdrawn there for their own private purposes.

I say there were two of them, but in fact, I could see no more of the man than his stocking soles and his shins and bare knees beyond. The bed was directly in front of me, one of those four-poster affairs hung about with silk damask and bullion and valances and tassels and what-have-you, and this fellow and his lady-love were well dug into the feathery middle of it – though the principal reason I could see so little was that the lady's naked backside obscured the view. She was kneeling astride him in her stays and white stockings, her stays unfastened and the laces dangling, and as I stood there gaping, her pink rear went on rising and falling, rising and falling, as if the two of them were still quite alone in their love-nest, oblivious to the third party wedged in the doorway . . .

Whoever she was, she'd a bottom like a peach, all downy and flushed – quite beautiful from a detached, artistic point of view, except that my vantage point at that moment was neither detached nor artistic.

I'm sure I only lingered for a second, although it seemed like an astonished eternity while that blissful bottom thrust and the stocking soles twitched – long enough to hear a guttural, barking laugh in response to something the lady had whispered – a laugh I seemed to recognise from a month or so earlier . . . in a carriage . . . in Oxford Street . . .

Perhaps I gasped aloud when the reality of the situation struck me. At any rate, I must have made a noise of some sort, because the owner of that exquisite backside suddenly twisted round to look over her shoulder, exposing one white breast amid the disorder. . . . And our eyes met: mine, wide and appalled in the doorway, and the furious, ice-blue glare of Violet Oliver.

Chapter Fifteen

1

I fled back down that long corridor like a mouse with a cat on her tail – and at the top of the stairs I ran slap-bang into the powder-headed footman, coming to look for me with the two Mudie's volumes in his hand.

"Hey – " Indignantly, the footman put a hand to the wall to steady himself. "Hey – what d'you think you're up to, wandering about the house like this? Where've you been? Just a minute, young woman – "

I'd already snatched the books from his grasp and sped off down the enormous staircase. The footman came running behind me, shouting as he came, his hard-heeled shoes making a fearful clatter. But like most of his kind he was more decorative than nimble, and I was sprinting through the hallway towards the front door before he'd even reached the gong.

The Mudie's van was waiting at the bottom of the steps, the driver sucking morosely on his pipe.

"About time too!" He slapped the reins sharply on the horse's rump. "Get on there, blast you! We'll have to look sharp if we want to get the rest done before eight o'clock."

Encouraged by a sting from the driver's whip, the horse plunged off down the street; somewhere behind us, voices called faintly through the night, their meaning lost in the rumble of shod wheels and the drumming of rain on the van roof.

Damn Violet Oliver! I kept repeating the words to myself as we rattled along. Damn Violet, who'd been given so much of what the world had to offer! Why couldn't she rest content with what she had? One thing was certain – if it had turned out that I was truly Matthew Oliver's wife instead of smug Violet, *I* wouldn't have gone bouncing in a four-poster bed with a prince of the Blood Royal, with my stays all undone and the door left unlocked for anyone to come in. I'd have told the wretched man to go back to his palace and his princess, if he shut me up in the Tower of London as a consequence. Damn, damn, damn!

I want to run – to shout – to explode – to do *something*, at least, to release the despair inside me. All at once I was disgusted with the whole glittering, fashionable social pageant which the Mudie's girls followed so avidly. I suppose in my heartbroken way I'd come to believe what I'd read of Matthew and Violet's "perfect" marriage – steam-yachts, jonquil diamonds and all. Now I could see nothing but ugliness and deceit – a glossy charade for which Matthew had rejected my love.

Goodness knows, I should have been delighted! Devil's child that I was, I should have shouted in triumph to see Matthew betrayed by the flawless wife he'd chosen. Instead, my heart ached for his lonely pride. At that moment, all I wanted was to be free of these people, to run off to a place where their over-furnished mansions and their idle, destructive lives would no longer be continually before my eyes.

It was as much as I could do to finish the delivery round, pushing piles of books into the hands of startled servants and snatching back the returns in furious silence.

It would be my last round as a Mudie's employee. I realised as much when the driver left me at the end of my own street, still angry and still clutching two volumes I'd forgotten to replace in their box. The library was bound to dismiss me: at the very least, I'd made a complete muddle of the deliveries, not to mention being caught wandering in the Broadney mansion, presumably with intent to steal. Would they send policemen to question me? And what happened to people who spied on princes? Would I be locked away in the name of decency, to safeguard the all-important respectability of the Crown?

I was sick and tired of it all. If I could have crawled out of my skin like a sloughing snake, I believe I'd have done it, simply to leave the soiled, tarnished memories behind. I found myself hating Violet and her royal lover, hating the splendour of her house – hating the uncanny chance which had led me to discover her mischief. No – it was more than chance: from the first moment I'd noticed *Mrs Matthew Oliver* on the Mudie's list, I'd been bound to make that discovery. I was to have no peace in this world, no happiness, not even the illusion of happiness in the life of others. The ill-wish would haunt me to the last.

Blind instinct drove me to do what the Summerbees had always done for as long as I could remember: I ran. I packed up my few belongings ready to disappear into the rainy night, just as the *Bellflower* had vanished a hundred times into the twists and turns of some Western river when Pa's wanderlust warned him the moment had come to clear out.

Flight had been our answer to everything, the cure for every ill, and now I was desperate to be off. After all, there were twelve sovereigns sewn into the lining of my Melton mantle and another few shillings in my purse – enough, surely, to carry me off to New York as soon as the way was clear. The end of the war must be very close. A wasteland of charred chimney-stacks already marked the path of General Sherman's march across the Confederacy, and it seemed inevitable that within a month or two the South would have surrendered and the Union would be restored as Lincoln had demanded.

But first, I had to leave London behind.

2

Just after four o'clock in the morning I let myself quietly out into the chilly darkness of the city, and set off on foot towards its western edges. I'd made a mental note to drop the two remaining library books into the first letter-box I saw, but long before I found one a friendly carter on his way home from Covent Garden market offered me a ride on his wagon as far as I cared to go, and as we rolled through the dimly lit streets towards the suburbs, Mudie's cellar and Mudie's mislaid books began to fade into the shadows of another existence.

The carter left me near a lock on the Grand Junction canal, where I sat for a while on the grassy bank near the towpath, watching the strange, snake-like narrow-boats glide on their unhurried way. They were nothing like the old *Bellflower*, of course: for one thing, they moved along in ghostly silence, so far behind their patiently tramping horses as to seem unconnected with them, sliding as if by magic along the shiny ribbon of the canal, a line of snails upon a common trail. And yet . . . perhaps it was the smell of smoke from a passing cabin chimney, or the reek of a tobacco pipe, or the stink of wet cordage . . . but I found myself suddenly homesick for the old boat on which I'd been born, and longing to float off on my travels once more.

With the lock-keeper's help I found a boat in the charge of a widow-woman and her young son who thought it "most likely" their business would take them eventually to the wharves of the Mersey, and who, with only a part-load of hides and ginger and barrels of currants for Leicester, were willing to accept a passenger for three-farthings a mile.

In fits and starts it took us the best part of a month to arrive in the Mersey with a mixed load of Derbyshire lead and earthenware from the Potteries. Our wharf was a weedy channel surrounded by the dripping backs of canal-side warehouses, but an extra few shillings allowed me to lodge aboard long enough to investigate the possibility of a steerage passage to New York.

There no longer seemed any reason to wait. For more than two years I'd watched from my distant side of the Atlantic as the war between the states raged to and fro and the rest of the world dithered over the moral issues, holding back from taking one side or the other until a clear winner should emerge. Now that a Union victory seemed inevitable, a procession of eminent Europeans had already begun to rush to Washington in order to assure the President of their unswerving faith in the justice of the Northern cause. Completely forgetting their earlier speeches in favour of secession, sleek statesmen and well-polished princes competed with one another to declare themselves everlasting allies of the Union.

Down with slavery! Three cheers for equality! Long live the partnership of our two great nations!

I bought a copy of *The Times*, and read their words with disbelief. Was the war forgotten already? In this politicians' market-place the price of a soldier's life – of a patriot's honour – was no longer counted in blood: it had a negotiable value in cotton or tobacco; it could be traded overseas in molasses or table-forks, written up on a board like a rate of foreign exchange – so many lives to the franc or the sovereign, so many dead or crippled sons to the florin. Forget the fallen and their mourners, as long as commerce may boom once more! More than ever, I wondered what there had been to die for. Where now was the glory of a roadside grave – six feet of turned soil saved for the Confederacy or the Union?

Naturally, one of the first to set out for Washington had been Matthew Oliver of the mighty Oliver shipping line, looking to his North Atlantic trade, his previous blockade-running activities politely forgotten. On the 20th of April, the day after my arrival in Liverpool, the newspapers reported Mr Oliver's departure in the SS *Antares* accompanied by his wife, his valet, his wife's maid, his wife's lap-dog and his wife's luggage (which was extensive enough to fill two cabins by itself). And with cruel irony, I found myself confronting the spectacle of Matthew and Violet together once more – the gilded couple – fortune's darlings – knowing that their ten-cent streetcar ride together, as the Pastor would have put it, had already gone sadly astray.

There was nothing to keep me a single day longer in England.

3

I'd reckoned without the Liverpool police, who arrived soon after dawn next morning to arrest me.

At least they allowed me to put on my bonnet and mantle before hauling me from the boat under the eyes of a fascinated crowd and bundling me unceremoniously into the back of a square black wagon with barred windows.

I was still protesting loudly when they marched me, with my hands chained, into the station office.

"Tell me what I'm supposed to have done! What law have I broken? You've no right to arrest me – I'm an American citizen!"

"Oh, we know that, all right." They'd searched me with rough haste – fortunately without finding the twelve sovereigns sewn into the thick Melton cloth of my mantle – before thrusting me brusquely into a small office where a crop-headed inspector was waiting. "We know you're American, all right," he assured me. "And you don't deny your name's Katherine Summerbee, I suppose?"

"Of course I don't deny it."

"But you still maintain you don't know why you're here?" The inspector narrowed his eyes and picked at the edge of his black moustache. He seemed so certain of himself I was sure he must be acting on instructions from his colleagues in London. Spying on the Heir to the Throne was evidently a crime in Britain, and this fiend was hoping I'd condemn myself out of my own mouth. Well, he would hope in vain.

"I haven't the slightest notion why I've been arrested," I told him firmly.

The inspector leaned forward.

"Where's your friend the Doctor? That's what I want to know."

I frowned at him, utterly taken aback, and when I didn't answer at once, he added, "You won't do yourself any good by keeping quiet. You'd better tell us where he is – or I'll see it goes hard with you, when you go up before the judge."

"The Doctor? Pastor Bonnet, do you mean?"

"Who else should I mean? Don't play the innocent with me, girl."

"The Doctor's no friend of mine," I told him indignantly, "any more than he's a proper doctor. And if you haven't found him for yourself, then I've certainly no idea where he is. It's almost two years since I saw him last." I was baffled by this new line of questioning: was the man trying to throw me off balance?

"Not a doctor, and not your friend? And you're going to pretend your name's Sally Nobody, I suppose."

"It's Katherine Summerbee, as you well know."

"Oh, I know a lot about you and your accomplices in Liverpool, Miss Summerbee. I dare say you all think you've been very clever in covering up your tracks, but I've always found that catching one member of a gang will lead to catching the rest before long. I promise you, miss, you'll tell me the whole story before I'm finished with you."

He meant to frighten me; and to my dismay, I was unable to keep a tremor out of my voice.

"I haven't the faintest idea what story you're talking about. I don't even know anyone in Liverpool. Not a soul!"

"Your friend the Doctor does, depend upon it."

"He isn't my friend!" I retorted furiously. "D'you think I'd have a miserable fraud like that for a friend?"

"Aha – " The inspector pounced on my words at once, leaning forward over the desk. "So you admit he's a fraud, this Dr Bonnet?"

"Of course he is! He told the people at his lectures their money would go to helping the slaves to a better life – and all the time, he and his mission people meant to send them away to Africa. There was a pretty good row when I found out about it, and after that he went off on his own. I'm pleased to say I haven't seen him since."

"That's a likely tale."

"It's the truth!"

"Well then, if you haven't seen the Doctor, what about Mr Rance Ponytree and his friend John Ebbage?"

"What about them?" I dimly remembered the names; the Pastor had mentioned them in connection with his mission committee.

"When did you see them last?"

"Two years ago, at least. But I had nothing to do with the committee members – the Pastor dealt with that side of things himself."

"A *committee*, were they?" The inspector curled his lip. "A fine bunch of spies, more like! Hiding here in Liverpool, helping Captain Bulloch fit out ships for the Confederacy – persuading British seamen to enlist with a Belligerent Power – buying guns for that Power in a neutral nation, and smuggling them out to sea as engine parts – "

"Surely not! I mean – I knew the Pastor hoped the South would win the war, but – "

The inspector let out a bark of derision.

"Come now, Miss Summerbee, do you really expect me to believe you didn't know exactly what he was up to?" He gazed at me scornfully. "The Pastor, as you call him, was carrying dispatches to Confederate sympathisers all over England, and it's my belief you helped him do it."

"This is crazy!" I could hardly believe my ears: I'd fallen into a nightmare worse than anything I could have imagined.

"Eli Bonnet persuaded me to work for his mission, it's true – and I did, for a while, because I was stupid enough to think he was a good man. But that was all I did. I had nothing to do with spies, or ships, or any of the rest."

"So you say," the inspector remarked sarcastically.

"It's the truth, I swear it!"

"I've had men out making enquiries about you both for a while, but I'd begun to think you'd vanished into thin air. Then two days ago the lock-keeper's wife at Preston Brook spotted you on the barge where you'd been hiding, and laid information you were the same woman she'd seen at one of the Doctor's meetings."

"I wasn't hiding. I came all the way from London aboard that boat."

"Sneaking back along the canals, hoping you wouldn't be recognised, I suppose. Who told you to come back to Liverpool? Was it the Doctor? Was it Ponytree?"

"No one told me! I came here to find a ship to take me back to America."

"Ah – so you were going to skip the country, were you? Lucky for us we found you when we did, then." The inspector picked triumphantly at his moustache. "And better still, this is Friday, and the magistrates don't sit again until Monday morning. That gives me two or three days to think of something to charge you with, so's you can't run off to America until you've told me everything I want to know." He leaned forward once more. "I promise you, miss – I intend to lay this little nest of plotters by the heels before I'm done, and you can make up your mind to that."

A sharp rap sounded at the half-open door of the office, and a constable came in with my open carpet-bag in his arms. Digging among its contents, he triumphantly laid two books on the table – two yellow-label novels bearing the stamp of Mudie's Select Lending Library in Oxford Street, London.

"Found these in her bag, sir."

The inspector examined the books thoughtfully, and then raised his eyes to mine.

"Are you a subscriber?"

"I worked at Mudie's until a month ago."

"And the library gave you these as a parting gift, I suppose?"

"Of course not! I just forgot to take them back, that's all. I meant to post them, but I haven't got round to it yet."

A smile spread over the inspector's face like syrup over a plate.

"You haven't got round to it? Well, we'll see what Mudie's have to say about that, shall we? And in the meantime, Katherine Summerbee, I'm charging you with the theft of two library books, to the value of – " He examined the books again. "Oh, four shillings and sixpence, I dare say. You'll stay in a cell here until you go before the magistrate on Monday. The constable will tell you your rights."

Stunned into silence by the catastrophic speed of events, I was marched off to a brick-walled cell hardly bigger than a broom cupboard, lit by a tiny arched and barred window high above my head. The cell stank of vomit and urine, and of the damp which had long since begun to flake its brickwork, streaking the walls with soft, greenish stains and leaving crevices where many-legged creatures scuttled for shelter.

For a moment I stood, trembling, in the centre of that rancid space like a beast in a trap, walled up alive in its narrow gloom. My head began to swim; I was suffocating in that dank coffin of a cell . . . I ran to the door and beat on it with my fists, shouting something unintelligible.

A tiny window in the door flew open, and two hostile eyes peered in.

"Stop that screaming! I won't have caterwauling of that sort in my cells."

"Then let me speak to someone! Find me an attorney! Give me pen and paper to write a letter!"

I heard a hollow laugh from the far side of the door, and the window slammed shut once more.

I was kept in that dismal cell for the rest of the day, apart from a couple of visits to a water-closet in the station yard, guarded by a female jailer. When evening came, a thin blanket and a chipped enamel bowl of gruel were pushed into the cell beside me along with a mug of stale beer, but not even a spoon to scrape up the food with. I wasn't allowed a candle-stub either, in case I tried to burn the place to the ground.

When the light failed in my tiny window, I curled up on the wooden bench, covered myself as best I could with the blanket, and reflected that I'd never been so utterly alone in my life.

Even if they'd allowed me pen and paper, to whom could I write for help? I doubted if anyone outside the four walls of the police office even knew or cared where I was. In desperation I'd have swallowed my pride and turned to Matthew Oliver for help – but Matthew was on the other side of an ocean, and out of reach.

I'd heard of people transported to Australia for doing nothing worse than stealing a loaf of bread. What could I expect for making off with four shillings and sixpence-worth of yellow-label novels? Oh, the ill-wish had followed me, all right: in my wretchedness I realised I could rot for years in an English jail, and no one would even remember the name of Katherine Summerbee.

I spent the rest of the night scratching my name on the wooden bench with a nail prised from the heel of my shoe, using my fingertips to guide the scores. In the morning, the light shone thinly on my handiwork. *Katherine Summerbee. Friendless.* At least that was something I'd achieved, some small record of my existence.

5

I was hauled before the inspector again at two o'clock the following afternoon, and our previous conversation was repeated almost word for word. At the end of it he called me stubborn and foolish. If I'd told him what he wanted to know . . . well then, things might have been different. But as it was, the summary court would give me a taste of prison I was unlikely to forget.

And the station-office cells were bad enough. I spent all of Sunday lying on my narrow wooden bench, staring at the white-painted ceiling of my cell and wondering if the dripping gutter outside my window could drive me insane. I was too listless even to scratch on the bench with the nail from my shoe. What more remained to be said, in any case?

On the morning of Monday, April 24th, the day before my twentieth birthday and the day that news of Lee's final surrender appeared in *The Times* by way of magnetic telegraph from Crookstown, I was dispatched to the magistrate's court. A burly policeman took me out of my cell and flung me into a horse-van with two others to be carried a short distance to a dismal courtyard with an iron door at its far end. Beyond the door was a dark passage, and off it, an even darker cell than the one I'd left, but damper and smellier, and large enough to accommodate several people at once.

One of my companions was taken out before me: she'd stolen linen from a bleaching green, and expected hard labour. The other woman had blocked the highway with her market cart, and was also resigned to a term in jail. I wasn't to worry, she said: the first week was always the worst. After a while, the rats and lice seemed to lose their taste for your flesh.

The minutes dragged by, until all of a sudden the heavy door of the cell banged open, and a hoarse voice shouted my name. I stumbled upstairs, tripping on the steps as I tried to scrape back my straggling hair with the few pins which still remained.

The room was packed with bodies, and rank with the smell of sweat and jostling humanity. Hungry-eyed wives and sisters in coarse woollen shawls clustered round the small empty space in the centre of the floor; here and there among them, a man clutched a battered hat to the breast of a coat which had seen better days. They crowded to stare into my face

211

as I was hustled past, a press of worn coat-sleeves, stained aprons, and calloused red hands which clasped and unclasped in restless anxiety.

The dock was a small, railed area at the edge of the arena, directly opposite a shabby desk covered in papers and presided over by a ponderous man with florid jowls whom I took to be the magistrate. He'd half-risen to shout at his police sergeant over the bustle of the court, and now stood, his mouth ajar, one hand to his ear to catch the reply, and his bulging, fish-like eyes malevolently sweeping the crowded courtroom.

The magistrate was deaf – quite hopelessly deaf, I realised as he sat down in a heap on his chair and banged his fist on the desk for silence. There followed five minutes of confusion while he mistook me for the woman he'd just sentenced and bawled for the next prisoner to be brought, whom he insisted should be a man called Somerville.

At last the true situation was explained, and my name written down, and that of Mr Reginald Blake of Mudie's Library in Liverpool, entrusted by his Head Office in London with seeing their book thief brought to justice. Mr Blake was sworn in, a tall youth in a very high collar who read out to the court the telegraphic message he'd received from the Oxford Street branch, telling the story of my sudden disappearance in company with two of their most popular novels. Whenever the witness paused for breath, the clerk relayed his evidence to the magistrate at the top of his voice, commenting on the facts of the case as he went.

And to all intents and purposes, the young man's tale was no more than the truth. There wasn't a word I could disagree with, except the assumption that I'd intended to steal the books in the first place.

"Well?" demanded the magistrate as soon as the Mudie's man had finished. "What have you got to say for yourself, young woman? How d'you propose to explain these?" Indignantly, he brandished one of the books, and I heard a great shuffling as the crowd craned forward to watch me answer.

"Excuse me, Your Worship." An elderly man in gold-rimmed spectacles had pushed his way to the front. "Excuse me – but I appear for this young lady."

"Young *lady* is it, Mr Lightbody?" The magistrate frowned at the interruption, while I craned for a better view of my unexpected ally.

"Oh yes, Your Worship – a young lady, definitely so – although after three nights in the cells, perhaps not immediately apparent as such." Mr Lightbody approached the Bench with the deferential tread of decades' acquaintance with the Law.

"Then perhaps you'll explain what a young *lady* is doing in my court, accused of stealing novels of the sort I wouldn't allow my servants to read?"

The shuffling among the onlookers became a murmur of interest, and I noticed the Mudie's man wriggle indignantly in his place.

"If Your Worship will grant me a moment." With unexpected swiftness, Mr Lightbody slid over to my side.

"You did take the books, I suppose?" he whispered.

"I don't understand – who are you? Why are you here? I didn't expect anyone to take my side."

"Later, dear lady." Mr Lightbody half-turned and made a little bow towards the Bench. "The books – " he hissed behind his hand. "Did you take them, Miss Summerbee?"

"I meant to send them back, but I left London in such a hurry that I forgot all about them."

"Ah." The lawyer regarded me mournfully through his round lenses, and then turned once more to the Bench. "Merely an oversight, Your Worship," he pronounced. "You'll notice that the young lady hasn't attempted to sell the books in question, or dispose of them for money. It was simply a youthful oversight – no more."

"Pleads guilty!" shouted the clerk in the magistrate's ear.

"The young lady is an American citizen," Mr Lightbody added helpfully. "Our ways may be a little strange to her."

"Ignorance of the law is no defence," snapped the magistrate sharply. "Three months."

"I beg your pardon?"

"I said *three months*. With hard labour. Next case."

"Excuse me, Your Worship . . ." Mr Lightbody tried once more. "But the young lady has friends who would be prepared to pay her fine – if you saw fit to impose one. It is, after all, a first offence."

"Eh?"

"A fine!" yelled the clerk. "She has a friend who'd pay a fine for her."

"A *friend*, indeed? A respectable friend, I take it?"

"Oh, eminently respectable, Your Worship."

"I see." The magistrate gnawed the end of his pen for a moment. "And I suppose this friend will stand good for the prisoner's conduct in future, if I set her at liberty?"

"Without hesitation."

The magistrate's bulbous eyes roamed suspiciously round the courtroom. "Is this person – this friend of the prisoner – present in court?"

At the back of the room I heard an outbreak of scuffling as someone detached himself from the general huddle and indicated his whereabouts. To my great frustration I could see nothing at all beyond the two front rows of bobbing heads.

"Ah." The magistrate peered into the crowd, and chewed his lip. "Very well, then – fined thirty shillings. Next case," he snarled at the startled clerk. "What are you waiting for?"

"I still don't understand any of this!" I whispered under cover of the general uproar as Mr Lightbody laid thirty shillings on the clerk's table, collected a receipt for it, and began to clear a path for me towards the rear door of the packed courtroom. "Did Matthew Oliver ask you to come?" I was staring about for a glimpse of my deliverer, but the only familiar face I could see was that of the police Inspector, standing resentfully at the door.

"You were lucky," he remarked sourly as we passed. "But you'll be back, depend on it. Subverting Her Majesty's subjects – agitation on behalf of a foreign power – it'll be the Quarter Sessions for you next time, my girl."

"If you had a shred of proof," the lawyer told him sharply, "you'd have preferred charges. As it is, you'd best stand aside, Inspector. Come along, Miss Summerbee."

If it hadn't been for Mr Lightbody's grip on my arm, I think I'd have fled from that place, desperate to exchange its clamorous stench for the free air of the street beyond.

At the kerb, a carriage was waiting for us. And seated in the carriage, a pensive expression on his face, was Adam Gaunt.

Chapter Sixteen

1

Adam Gaunt – the last person I'd have expected to help me. Yet as I emerged from the black maw of the courtroom he glanced up and caught sight of me, touching my soul with the relief in his eyes.

"Katherine. . . . At last."

He spoke the words softly, almost to himself, but I'd have picked out that voice in a thunderstorm, let alone across a few feet of grimy Liverpool street.

"Mr Gaunt."

"Here – let me help you." Misinterpreting my hesitation, the little lawyer gripped my elbow and pushed me bodily into the carriage before hauling himself up beside me.

"I can't tell you how grateful – " I began, but Adam Gaunt held up a warning hand.

His eyes travelled slowly over my untidy head, over my sleepless face and crumpled skirts.

"Don't say anything now, Katherine. Eat – sleep – and then we'll talk."

We drove to the Adelphi Hotel in Ranelagh Place – a fantasy of laundered sheets and airy ceilings, of hot baths attended by a flurry of crisp towels, of mouth-watering dishes under plated covers delivered to my bedside . . . and of sleep – blissful, healing sleep undisturbed by the rattle of the jailers' keys or the moans of the poor wretch in the cell next to mine.

On my breakfast tray I found a note proposing a drive to the Botanic Garden.

"You've gone to a great deal of trouble on my account," I said to him in the carriage.

"It's no trouble."

Across the width of the carriage we stared at one another, reluctant to speak in case the moment should slip away like water through a net of banalities.

"How did you know where to find me?"

"I met George Broadney in London last month. He could hardly wait to tell me that my American protégée – that was his word – had taken to robbing houses on the pretext of delivering library books."

215

"That wasn't true!"

"I didn't think it was. But by then you'd vanished from Mudie's, and no one knew where to find you."

"Until I was charged with stealing those books."

"And the police telegraphed to London."

Adam had fixed his eyes on a point far beyond the confines of the carriage.

"God bless the circulating library."

"I didn't think you'd want anything to do with me, after – well, after what happened." We'd walked in silence almost the whole way along the main terrace before I dared to drop a word into that pool of unspoken thought.

"Katherine . . ." He shook his head in perplexity. "How could you ever believe it?"

"You told me yourself you'd never forgive me for causing Mrs Gaunt's death. That evening in the garden – "

"I didn't know what I was saying. I was angry with myself, not with you – angry with life. Misery makes people say stupid things."

Leaving the formal urns of the terrace behind, we walked on, unspeaking, to where dwarf pines dripped darkly from a rockery over the bare poles of a rustic bridge.

"Not even a letter," he said suddenly. "Not once in almost three years. You must have hated me very much."

"No – never that."

"Louise accused me of sending you away. She's hardly spoken to me since she left Hawk's Dyke."

"You didn't send me away – and even if you had, I couldn't have blamed you. I never meant any harm, but I caused Mrs Gaunt's death, all the same. I thought you'd be glad to be rid of me."

"Rachel's death wasn't your fault, Katherine, and I shouldn't have accused you like that. By next day I'd come to my senses. I wanted to explain – to apologise – but by then you'd gone. I've blamed myself ever since, for turning you out of the house."

He meant every word: I could see it in his face. He truly believed his wife's death had been nothing but simple misfortune. And I wished – oh, how desperately I wished – that I could have believed it too.

We'd reached an artificial lake, spotted with lily-pads and overlooked by a windy gazebo. Side by side, we watched the ragged clouds mirrored in its surface drift to a slow stranding on the reedy shore.

"Am I really free to go wherever I want?"

"Anywhere at all."

"Even though you've guaranteed my good behaviour in future?"

"I owed you that, at the very least."

"No – you didn't owe me anything. I've caused you nothing but unhappiness, and I don't want you to land in court on my account."

"It isn't very likely."

"The police seem to think I'm a dangerous spy. That inspector's convinced of it. I'm sure if he ever gets the chance he'll arrest me again."

"I doubt it. Walter Lightbody assures me that unless this Doctor fellow turns up, they won't have enough evidence to charge you with anything. Even then, they'd be laughed out of court, trying to prove you were a Confederate spy."

He was so confident of my innocence that I almost lost my temper.

"Oh? And why is that, exactly?"

"Because a jury would only have to look at you, to know you were telling the truth. I doubt if you could tell a lie to save your life."

"I'm not a complete fool, Mr Gaunt."

"I didn't say you were."

Resentfully, I dug in the pocket of my mantle, and thrust out a hand towards him.

"What's this?" He frowned at the coins in my palm.

"The thirty shillings I owe you. The fine you paid for me."

"I don't want your money, Katherine!"

"You've done enough for me. I won't put myself in your debt."

"It isn't a question of debt. I'm only concerned for your happiness."

"Don't be concerned. I can look after myself." I glanced up, and met his eyes. "Well, I can now, at any rate. If I'm free to leave the country, then I'll sail for America as soon as possible, and I don't care to leave debt behind."

"If you're determined to go, I'll arrange a passage for you and see about anything else you might need."

"Thank you, but I can pay my own fare. You may have refused my money, but I won't take yours, either."

"Confound the money! Why won't you let me help you?"

"I won't depend on anyone. Not any more."

I heard him sigh. "Katherine, Katherine – you'd better tell me how you got into this mess."

2

I told him . . . most of the story. I told him how the Pastor had been a

217

friend of Pa's – which was true – and how I'd seen his lecture advertised on a railway platform and gone to it out of curiosity, which was partly true, at least. The rest was straightforward – until I came to the part about delivering books to Sir George Broadney's house. Adam Gaunt had been right when he'd said I couldn't lie to him; but I still couldn't bring myself to explain how I'd found Matthew's wife with the Prince of Wales. Instead, I told him I'd become accidentally lost in the corridors of Violet's London home.

"And now, of course, Violet and Matthew have gone off to Washington," Adam reflected. "That was damnable luck. Matthew would have had you free in a moment, if he'd been here – or Violet, if she hadn't been so set on going to Washington with him. She can't bear to be left out of the excitement."

With an effort, I changed the subject.

"It was lucky for me that you were in London at the time."

"Luckier than you know. I was just about to board a steamer for Genoa, when Mudie's sent a message to my club."

"Then you missed your sailing on my account!"

"It doesn't matter. My luggage will enjoy the trip."

"Oh, my stars . . . I've caused you a great deal of trouble."

"It's worth it to know you're safe."

"Don't say that."

"Why not?"

"Because. . . . Just don't say it, that's all."

We were still by the lake, and somehow the reeds and water plants by its edge reminded me of the wild, wet spaces of Sourwell Fen.

"How is everything at Hawk's Dyke?"

"I hardly know, to be honest."

"Haven't you been living there?"

He shook his head. "I couldn't bear to stay in the place with everyone gone. I've spent most of my time abroad since Louise left and you went away. In three years I've only gone back twice, and then just for a few weeks. I have an agent to look after the land and the tenants, so there's no need for me to be there."

He paused for a moment, frowning at a sudden memory.

"They've finally drained Sourwell Fen. Charles wanted to put rye grass and cole-seed on his half of the land, and the agent agreed to the scheme on my behalf. Progressive farming, they call it."

He gazed down into the cloud-filled water of the lake.

"I suppose I should really turn Hawk's Dyke over to Matthew, since that's what he seems to want."

"But he's going to pull the house down! Louise told me so. It was Violet's idea," I added quickly.

"Perhaps that's the best thing that could happen to it. Sweep the house away, and all the memories along with it."

"How can you say that? You love Hawk's Dyke!"

He turned to face me. "What makes you so sure of that, Katherine?"

"Because. . . . Because I could feel it. I used to see it in your face when you looked at the house, and the lawns, and the stables, and the oak trees. . . . And the cats in the Italian garden. . . . And the library. . . . Don't you remember riding over the lawn with your dog, that first morning when I leaned out of the window? And later, sitting at the library table over a map of the Mississippi, trying to find the island where I was born? And the way the fourth step of the stairs always creaked when anyone walked on it – and that little coloured glass window in the hall—"

"You're the one who loves Hawk's Dyke, it seems to me."

"You, too."

"Not any more. Not as it is now."

"How is it now?"

"Empty. Neglected. Just an old house with an overgrown garden."

"Not the Italian garden! Not Mrs Gaunt's – " I stumbled over the name.

"Even Rachel's garden. There didn't seem any reason to take care of it after she died. There was no one to enjoy it any more."

"But it was so peaceful – just like Paradise. I thought you liked to sit there."

"Not alone, I didn't."

"That's what you told me – one day in the library. You said you'd lost the knack of being at peace with yourself."

"It was the truth. It's still true. That's why it's high time I let Matthew have Hawk's Dyke, and spent the rest of my life travelling."

"How can you simply turn your back and walk away from such a place?"

"Why not? You did, even though you'd fallen in love with it – I can see that now."

Adam had set off again down the path, and I followed hastily in his wake.

"But Hawk's Dyke is your home, not mine. I knew it never could be mine, and the longer I stayed, the harder it became to leave. Especially after what happened. I felt as if I'd ruined everyone's life – yours, Louise's – everyone's."

219

"You only believed that because I told you so. And I believed it because I was selfish and blinded by anger. But it wasn't true, Katherine. You *give* – it isn't in your nature to take away." He halted suddenly, and turned to look down into my face. "It's because of that I hope you'll forgive me."

"It makes no difference. I'm going back to America." I was aware that something had changed – something I didn't understand. He was wrong about me – so wrong – and yet there was an excitement inside me, a knot in my stomach as big as a wasp's nest and twice as lively. I was afraid and elated, all at once.

Katherine Summerbee. Friendless.

Suddenly the fear won, and all I wanted was to escape. Yet he wasn't prepared to let me.

"You'd go off to America without ever seeing Hawk's Dyke again?"

"I don't want to go back there."

"Yes, you do. You can't bear the thought of Matthew pulling the house down."

"I can't believe you'd let him do it. You love it so much."

"Convince me, then."

"It's none of my business. I'm going to America."

He nodded. "After you've visited Hawk's Dyke again."

"No. At once. I've waited so long to go back."

"Don't go. Not just yet. Come back to Hawk's Dyke, and show me why I must let the house live."

"I can't!"

"Why not? You've spent two and a half years wandering all over England – yet you won't spend a week or two under my roof? You were happy enough there last time."

"But that was different!"

He didn't ask me why it should be different.

"Adam, I can't . . ." Hastily, I corrected myself. *"Mr Gaunt,* I mean."

"Adam will do."

"No, it won't! None of it will do! I'm going back to America, right away. You said I could."

"Come back to Hawk's Dyke, Katherine. See if you can bring it back to life for me. That's all I ask. Just be there for a while. Run through the rooms and the garden – chatter – laugh – sing, if the mood takes you. Borrow the books – lose them all, I don't care – but just be there. Not for ever. Just for long enough."

I opened my mouth to answer, but he forestalled me.

"Don't say anything now. It's too soon. Think about it tonight, and give me your answer tomorrow."

"I'm going to America," I insisted weakly. "Truly I am. I'm going to America, just as I always meant to. You said yourself that I could. I'm going to America."

3

I travelled back with him to Hawk's Dyke. I had no choice. I owed him my freedom, goodness knows, and in any case I believe that once the idea was fixed in his mind, he'd have followed me to New York if he'd had to. I'd never seen such single-minded determination – except, perhaps, in Matthew. Matthew, about whom I was resolved not to care.

I sensed the sour rankness of neglect as soon as our hired carriage rolled to a halt at the front door of the old house. It wasn't as if any single piece of the picture had gone obviously astray, like a collapsed chimney or a broken window; it was simply that nothing was as bright and trim and welcoming as I remembered it. The Hawk's Dyke I'd treasured in my mind had never worn blackened brasses at its door or a cockade of weed at the edge of its roof. I couldn't recall dull, creeper-shrunk windows, or uneven pasture in place of the clipped lawns. The house looked blowsy and unkempt, like a woman who'd taken to gin and no longer cared who saw her in a torn cap and a dirty muslin dressing-gown.

In spite of the din of our arrival, the front door remained shut until Adam Gaunt himself flung it open, shouting for assistance. A grim-faced woman appeared on the threshold, wiping her hands on her apron and yelling over her shoulder to someone inside.

"But where's Mrs Finch?"

"She left the year before last." Adam reached out to hand me down from the carriage. "She went off to nurse a consumptive daughter whose children were running wild. The bailiff hired this woman while I was abroad. Mrs Rattle – "

Summoned, the woman reluctantly left the doorway and advanced towards the carriage, staring at me from under heavy brows, her lips pressed together as if she grudged the meanest word of greeting.

"I'd no warning, sir," she complained at once. "If there's no food in the house, it's not my fault. How was I to expect you, if you never wrote to say you were coming?"

"I'm sure our guest will make allowances for that. Miss Summerbee will be staying with us for a while."

221

"For how long?" the woman wanted to know.

Adam looked irritated. "For as long as she chooses to stay. It's immaterial, surely."

"I dare say." Mrs Rattle looked me carefully up and down. "Well, you'd better come in, then . . . miss. I'll have a room made up when Mr Gaunt tells me which one you're to have."

I'd have been more than content to have Alice's old room – the one I'd slept in before, and from whose square dormer window I'd first looked out on the lawns and the pastures beyond. I'd loved that room. The clear, fresh morning view from its window had been a wellspring in my mind during the three years which had passed, and for two pins I'd have asked Mrs Rattle to make up a bed for me there instead of in a proper guest room, larger and grander, on the floor below.

At least Nell was still as I remembered her, the cheerful, round-faced young woman who'd brought hot water to my room each morning and guided me to breakfast on my first day at Hawk's Dyke. She was eighteen now – two years younger than I was, the third child of a swarming family in one of the Mill Farm cottages.

"I'm ever so glad you're back, miss." Nell bustled in and out with soap and towels and a lamp for the table beside the half-tester bed. "But what a surprise! Never a word to say Master was coming home, let alone bringing a lady with him. There ain't half a panic below stairs, believe me."

"I'm sorry to give you so much extra work."

"Oh, bless you, miss, it makes no difference to me! It's Mrs Rattle who's running about like a wet hen, trying to hide all her little fiddlings before Master sees 'em. Not that he'll bother to send for her accounts, I expect. That's what's wrong with the place now. No mistress to take charge of it."

"Do you mean to say Mrs Rattle's dishonest?"

"No more dishonest than any other housekeeper who's given the run of the house and never asked where sixpence has gone. No, that isn't so," Nell corrected herself. "Mrs Finch was a decent, religious woman. She'd have been black affronted to see the state of the place now."

She lifted off the lamp-glass and polished it briskly with the tail of her apron.

"See this lamp? And this one's no worse than the rest. They could all do with a good washing. And these bed-curtains haven't been down since Mrs Finch left two years ago. You know me, Miss Kate – I won't dust round what I can dust under, but if no one else does their share, I can hardly clean the whole house myself."

"Mrs Rattle certainly seems to have let things go."

"Oh, that's no lie! Look here – " Nell twitched back the coverlet. "Do you remember the sheets we had before, all fancy stitching at the hems? Well, Eveline Rattle let those go all right. She picked off the big 'Gs' that were worked on them, and sold them to the Rector's wife as her niece's embroidery!"

Seeing my look of disbelief, she added, "It's true as I'm standing here! And she's 'let go' some of Master's port, too. She mixes it with cider and brandy and cochineal, and Sykes takes it down to Stainham on market day to be sold as 'cider port wine' at ninepence a bottle. Sykes has turned out as bad as she is. I reckon he was only waiting for the chance."

"But why on earth haven't you told Mr Gaunt?"

"Tell Mr Gaunt?" This time it was Nell's turn to stare as though I'd taken leave of my senses. "It's not my place to tell him anything! If he can't see for himself – well, then, he'll have to put up with things as they are, poor gentleman." She drew the bedcover back into place, carefully avoiding my eye. "That isn't to say *you* couldn't tell him, of course. Now that you know what's been going on."

The niceties of the distinction escaped me, but I understood I'd been the one chosen to convey the message. Tale-bearing was a sin below stairs, but the longer-serving members of the kitchen community were tired of seeing their employer cheated, nevertheless.

I went to seek out Adam Gaunt, and found him at last in the Italian garden – or what was left of it – standing by the little fountain at its centre, one hand absently smoothing the edge of the lichen-roughened bowl, the other shading his eyes as he surveyed the devastation all round us.

The great glory of the garden had been its abundance – the profusion of greens and golds and silvers which had poured down its walls and trickled over its beds to the edges of the mossy paths, licking at the tree-trunks in its compulsion to spread and blossom. Now the bounty had become a pestilence – a great, coarse plague of vegetation, a rank undergrowth of nettles and bindweed and grasses which had taken possession of that once-charmed acre. The garden was no longer a place of dancing light and shadow – just of dense, defiant green, as opaque as the surface of the sea.

"I never dreamed it was as bad as this." Thigh-deep in the tide, Adam turned at the sound of the garden door. "It's terrible. Beyond repair."

Over our heads, a robin flew back to its half-built nest on a cracked windowsill, its beak fuzzed with cat fur from the steps.

"The birds seem happy, at least."

Adam had followed the robin's flight with his eyes.

"It isn't just the garden. Even the house is – " He shrugged, lost for a word. "The house is broken-down, somehow. Unfamiliar. Not a home any more."

"The house is dirty, I can tell you that. And your housekeeper's robbing you."

"Is she?" He gazed at me uncomprehendingly. "How do you know?"

"One of the maids told me."

"I never suspected. You've only been here an hour or so, yet you knew at once."

"There was no trick to it. Someone would have told you if you'd asked."

For Adam's sake, I wished I could be as all-knowing as he imagined; but my heart sank as I stared round at the overgrown garden, and behind it at the neglected house he expected me magically to resurrect. I had caused that ruin: if Rachel Gaunt had lived, none of it would have happened. And where I'd brought suffering once, I could do so again.

"I should never have agreed to come back here, Adam. You were wrong to put so much faith in me. I can't work miracles."

He reached out to me across the tangle. "But you can, Katherine! All I ask is that you dream . . . and create . . . and cherish. . . . Isn't that what all women do?"

I shook my head sadly, struck by the irony of the situation. "Some women – but not me. You've picked exactly the wrong person to work the miracle you want. I'd only do more harm than good."

"You're a woman, Katherine. You must know how to make a house into a home."

"I've never had a real home. I've never learned about housekeeping. Not in a place like this."

"To hell with housekeeping! Do you think I brought you here to count pickle-jars all day or measure out beer for the stables?" He stared at me incredulously. "I'm talking about living! About life! I don't give a damn if the Rattle woman's feeding the whole of Stainham on our kitchen accounts. What I do care about is this – " His arm swept out to encompass the wilderness around us. "This – the death of a garden. I care about the emptiness of the house – the cold, hollow smell of the rooms, like the halls of a museum. I care about the silence – about a home that's turned into a tomb."

"But I can't – "

"You can! You can save it, Katherine, because you love it, and because you're a woman. Do whatever you please, but do something. I give you absolute charge of Hawk's Dyke for as long as you'll stay. Send Mrs Rattle away tomorrow. Send them all away if it suits you, and we'll eat bread and cheese and drink claret from the cellar. But bring my house back to life again. That's all I ask."

His blind faith was making me light-headed. And as he spoke, I began to believe. He wanted . . . only what I longed so much to give.

"I'll make all sorts of mistakes."

"It doesn't matter! Just be here – just live in the house. There's enough life in you to light up the whole of Hawk's Dyke. And Katherine – " He hesitated for a moment. "If there's anything you need, you only have to ask. Remember that. Clothes, furs, jewellery – whatever you want."

All at once, my light-headedness evaporated; he realised as much from the expression on my face.

"Don't look at me like that. I just want you to be happy here."

"I don't expect wages from you." My voice was even stiffer and colder than I'd intended.

"It wasn't meant as payment. I was trying to *give* you something – clumsily, I admit. And not for your sake, but for mine. I know I've asked a great deal of you: I'd feel better about it if you'd let me give you something in return."

"There's nothing I need."

"Think. There must be something. Something you've always wanted, and never had."

I want a home. I want a house like yours – like the house you expect me to love and bring alive for you . . . and give back to you at the end of the day.

But I could see that my silence made him unhappy. I had no right to give without asking for anything in return, and I took refuge in a rash suggestion.

"You could teach me to ride – side-saddle, like a proper lady. Would that be enough?"

"I'll do better than that! I'll give you a horse of your own – the finest I can find in the county." He flung his arms wide in sheer relief, and I couldn't help laughing.

"Teach me to ride, and that would be more than enough, thank you! How do you expect me to pack a horse into my bag for the trip to America?"

"America," he repeated softly. "Of course. I'd forgotten."

225

Eveline Rattle was sent off next day in the dogcart, clutching a week's wages and whatever she'd managed to filch during her employment at Hawk's Dyke. I'd gone to some trouble to make sure it was Sykes who drove her to Downham; he came back subdued and humbly anxious to please.

By the time Mrs Rattle's spoon bonnet had cleared the stable yard I'd promised Nell an extra ten pounds a year and a free hand in matters of cleaning the house and looking after the linen. She promptly celebrated the housekeeper's disappearance with an orgy of spring cleaning, hurling open the windows and despoiling them of their curtains, filling the washing-lines with rugs to be shaken and beaten by the penitent Sykes, dragging furniture from its place and letting in the fresh, green scent of young barley to chase the mustiness of years from the rooms and passages.

"Here's your cellar keys, ma'am." Nell laid them next to me in the store-room where I was gingerly examining a sack of flour for maggots.

"I don't like the look of this flour at all. And what do you put down for cockroaches, Nell?"

"Ma swears by hellebore root, ma'am, though I believe borax will do."

The word *ma'am* penetrated my consciousness at last.

"I'm hardly a *ma'am*, Nell."

"If you're mistress of the house, it follows you must be *ma'am*. I can hardly call you *Miss Kate* any more."

"I think I liked it better, all the same. I'm not used to having anyone waiting for me to give orders."

"Well, you'd better get used to it quick if Mr Gaunt says so, hadn't you?"

I was dismayed to discover Mr Gaunt was also set on turning me into a *cavalière* – me – Katherine – the river-brat to whom horses were sullen, four-legged monsters which bit at the bow end and kicked at the stern, and were indifferent sea-boats in between.

How long, for any sake, did he imagine I was going to stay at Hawk's Dyke?

And I'd only suggested riding lessons for his sake. I didn't like owing; when the time came to leave, I wanted to be satisfied we were absolutely even, Adam Gaunt and I, and because of that I'd blurted out the first idea to come into my head. Now I felt he was being unfairly hard on me. Nothing would please him but a perfect seat, a straight but relaxed spine, and light, responsive hands on the reins.

Wearing a long-discarded riding habit of Louise's and mounted on the quietest animal in the stable, I rode out for my daily lesson. Hour after aching hour I walked, trotted and finally cantered in a huge circle until I could start, stop, turn, pass the reins and whip to my left hand without dropping them, and even lean back far enough to touch the horse's tail without pitching out of the saddle.

And still he expected more.

"Don't look so nervous, Katherine!" he'd call from the centre of the ring. "You won't fall out of that saddle unless the horse goes down – so trot round once more, and this time take the pained look off your face. It's no compliment to your escort, I assure you."

"I'll smile when I've something to smile about, thank you. Right now I'm just set on keeping out of the dirt."

"You told me you wanted to ride like a lady. Well, so you will, when I'm done with you."

He was absolutely merciless. He made me learn to mount elegantly with my skirt gathered into my left hand, the reins and the crutch of the saddle in my right, and my left foot in his own palm as he helped me into place. I must be able to lean over and shake hands gracefully with an acquaintance; I must rise to the trot without bumping or wobbling; I must learn to stop short from a canter without hauling on the animal's mouth. I'd no choice in the matter – stiff and sore in every joint, if I was to ride beside Adam Gaunt, I must be a credit to his teaching.

And yet . . . it was all quite different in the Italian garden. I was hardly a horticulturalist, goodness knows, but by some unspoken pact the garden was my province, just as the stable yard was his. He'd venture through the low doorway from the house like a stranger investigating a lady's boudoir, sniffing the mingled perfumes in the air, touching a velvet leaf here, a silken petal there. He kept to the middle of the paths, afraid to presume, and ready to approve of everything I showed him – weed and flower alike.

I'd found a copy of *Country Gardening for Ladies* under the cushions of the parlour window-seat, and discovered that although the book was ten years old, it was filled with helpful engravings. Armed with my text, I went out first thing each morning to give an illustrated lecture to the three men I'd been lent from Old Hall Farm: *these* and *these* were to be pulled out on sight, while *those* were on no account to be touched.

It didn't always turn out as I'd hoped. In the stony trough of an ornamental balustrade, silverweed had rooted among the fleshy rosettes of the sempervivums: its delicate, yellow, five-lobed face had charmed my team of gardeners, and when I went out later to inspect their work I

227

found the dull sempervivums no more than a rustling heap in a barrow, and the silverweed shivering its slender stems in undisputed possession of the balustrade.

But when the labourers went home in the evenings, the garden was mine to mould and to shape as I pleased. That was when Adam would come into it, glance round a little diffidently, nod with satisfaction, and leave again as if he knew he had no business to be there. He never suggested any changes, never lingered for more than a few seconds or sat on the stone seat, as if the garden was an intimate green bower where he had no place. It seemed enough for him that something had been done – that the paths were clear again, that little by little the beds were less choked and the plants no longer warred with their neighbours.

In my own mind, I looked to the completion of the garden as the time when I'd leave Hawk's Dyke, the time when I'd be able to write *amen* to my years in England and leave for America . . . which was beginning to seem disconcertingly like a foreign land.

We often talked of it in the evenings after dinner, while the early summer days dissolved into dusk beyond the parlour windows, and the lamps remained unlit till late. Each evening we set out to read, but the books were soon laid aside as we turned to talk of Pa as a young man, before liquor and the railways soured him; of the *Bellflower* and her kind; of rivers and river-towns whose names sounded to my ear like the verses of an old song.

It was the country of my birth, but Adam spoke of it in a way I'd never heard before. He'd wandered the ranges of the Rocky Mountains in the years when only trappers and Indians knew them; he'd seen San Francisco when it was no more than a mud-ridden gold-rush town, and the great plains when herds of buffalo could still darken the land as far as the eye could see. And more – he'd sailed among the icebergs of Cape Horn and the winged feluccas of the Nile; he'd seen the bones of giant lizards who'd roamed the earth millions of years before man, and walked on rivers of solid ice which flowed no more than a yard or two each year . . .

He'd stored it all in his mind – all the sights and sounds, the stories of the people and the wisdom of the books in his library – endlessly turning it over and over, seeking to make sense of what he'd discovered.

Eternal traveller that I was, I sat on the rug before the empty parlour hearth, conscious of how little of the world I'd seen.

"I've spent my whole life travelling, but never to anywhere even a little exotic."

"Ah, but you had no choice in the matter," Adam pointed out. "I'm a wanderer by nature – one of those people who always believe there's something better waiting round the next bend in the road." He smiled philosophically. "There hardly ever is, but it's a hard condition to cure."

"Yet you lived at Hawk's Dyke for years without wanting to leave."

"I was content at Hawk's Dyke, it's true – when Rachel was here. That's what made the difference."

"Adam . . ." There was a question I wanted to ask, but I couldn't think of a way to frame it that didn't seem impertinent. In the end I just plunged ahead, regardless of politeness.

"Adam . . . long ago . . . did you really go off and leave Matthew and his mother to live on their own in the wilderness?"

"Is that what Matthew told you?"

I nodded. "Is it true?"

For a moment he stared into the empty hearth, as if saddened by this new example of Matthew's hostility. When he spoke, his voice was flat and unemotional.

"We were living in Independence at the time. In those days it was the last place of any size before the journey across the prairies, but it was as near to the mountains as a white woman and a baby could stay in safety. I made a living of a kind, hunting for the fur caravans and trading for pelts with the Indians . . . until one day I went off to California to buy horses, and never came back. I reckoned Rachel would think I was dead, and go back to her family in England." He looked up then, directly into my face, defying me to reproach him.

"But . . . why?"

"Impulse. Just as I told you, a belief that something important to me lay round the next bend in the road – an obsession that blotted out any thought of the misery I'd caused Rachel." He sighed, and stared over the top of my head, out of the darkening windows. "I can't defend it, Katherine. It was utter cruelty – the worst thing I've ever done in my life."

"Yet Rachel forgave you for it in the end."

"She did – somehow. But Matthew hasn't forgiven me, and I don't think he ever will. A restless soul is more of a curse than a blessing, I promise you."

The word *curse* fell on my ears with the force of a blow. Once more I could feel the old fears stirring: had I not burned Sam's charm in that very parlour grate?

"So you do think. . . . You do believe it's possible to be ill-wished? To be under a curse, so that you bring all sorts of trouble to innocent people?"

229

"No," he said, so fiercely that I was startled. "No, I don't believe in curses, Katherine – or hexes, or ill-wishes, or any other nonsense of that kind. Curses aren't magic, they're fear – simple human fear of what we don't understand."

He frowned, searching for an example, and then pointed to the window.

"Nowadays even a child can explain how lightning splits an oak tree. Yet forty thousand years ago it was enough to frighten primitive man out of his wits. So what did he do? He invested the lightning with a name like his own, and a bad temper which demanded presents and flattery – and in that way he shrank it to a comprehensible creature like himself, capable of being bribed into a good mood. That's how your curses and evil spirits are born, Katherine. Every last one has been created from our own fear of the unknown."

Adam paused again for a moment, and then added thoughtfully, "No, if magic really exists, then I believe it's inside us all. *We* are magic. Life is magic: the eternal renewal of life is surely the greatest magic there is. Mortal beings though we are, all we have to do is shout *I am not afraid* – and the worst demons vanish with a bang into thin air."

"Are you sure of that?"

"Absolutely certain."

"Completely, totally certain?"

"One hundred per cent."

My face must have betrayed my doubts, because he added, "Don't tell me *you* believe in such things?"

"No . . . not really," I lied. "It's just that – there was a time when all sorts of dreadful things happened – and I began to wonder . . ."

"Katherine, Katherine – don't you understand your own strength?" Adam leaned forward and tilted my face up towards his own, so that he could look directly into my eyes. "My dear – you have enough courage for a regiment. You storm ahead with every banner flying, and when you're knocked down, you just pick yourself up and march on. I told you once before – there's enough sheer, unstoppable life in you to light up the whole of this house. And now you tell me you're afraid of shadows?"

"I've never thought of it like that."

"Then it's time you did." Adam released me, and leaned back in his chair. "You could snap your fingers in the face of the biggest devil that ever lived."

"What rubbish!" But I was almost laughing with relief.

"Decide what you want from the world, Katherine, and don't be afraid to reach for it. As long as you believe in yourself, nothing can touch you."

His faith in me never wavered, and little by little, as his house and garden settled back into the place of peace they had once been, I began to have faith again in myself. It didn't happen overnight: I'd lived too long in the company of my shadow-fears. But as the days passed I found myself humming snatches of songs among the flower beds and making extravagant lists for an autumn planting; I begged Adam to teach me about the wines in his cellar, and how a pony-cart should be driven; and having heard him speak fondly of backgammon, I made him show me how it was played – recklessly doubling my stake in the hope of becoming a matchstick millionaire. And I discovered that Adam had been right: I was happy again – happy because. . . . It never occurred to me to ask myself why.

One evening – the sun must have dipped quite low, because the mossy fuzz along the top of the wall was alight like an endless green wick – Adam came out into the garden as I was cutting back a rose, *Country Gardening* lying open on a stool at my feet. I heard his step on the path behind me; I no longer had to look round to know who was there, but I was seized by an irrational need to speak, to chatter like a woman caught half-naked before her mirror.

"It's far too late in the year for pruning, but I must do something about this rose-bush. It must be better to lose a few blooms this season than to have the whole plant blown down by the wind during the winter, don't you think?"

He'd kept me an hour longer than usual on my horse that day, and now he heard me gasp as I stretched up to reach a top shoot.

"Give me the secateurs. Where do you want it cut? There?" He reached over my head to snip the wayward shoot. "I can see I'm working you too hard, Katherine. Perhaps you should give up your riding lessons for a few days."

"Oh, no – please. I've nothing to complain of. It's worth all the aches and pains."

I'd meant *learning to ride* – but there was more to it than that. Guiltily, I realised how precious my lessons had become, simply because then I was sure of Adam's undivided attention. Never mind my rubbed fingers or the gnawing soreness in my back: I was the sole focus of that intense grey stare, of his concentrated spirit, and I rejoiced in my possession of him, just as the house cats basked in the sun on the garden

231

steps. I'd sooner have put out the sun itself than relinquish that daily treat.

Absently, he handed me back the secateurs.

"There's a cobweb in your hair." He reached out to brush it away, his fingers skimming my temple as lightly as spider silk, the nearness of his palm warming my cheek. I felt a sudden, startling urge to touch him in return, to test the texture of his skin – of his hair, or the curve of an ear – exactly as I'd seen Rachel do, years before.

Just in time I remembered I didn't share Rachel's licence to let my hand stray where I pleased. In my tightening fingers, the blades of the secateurs made a tiny grating noise and the sound brought me to my senses.

I stepped back, just as Nell tripped lightly towards us down the path.

"Is there anything else I can do for you?" Adam's eyes met mine.

"Thank you, but I can reach the rest."

Thoughtfully, Nell watched him stroll back through the garden to the house, reaching out to stir the fragrant, creamy-white petticoats of the philadelphus as he passed.

"It's good to see Mr Gaunt taking an interest in the garden again."

"I was trying to cut back this rose, but I couldn't reach the top stems." For some reason I felt bound to offer an explanation.

"Are you sure you're all right, ma'am?" From a couple of paces away, Nell scanned me shrewdly. "You look as if you'd been upset."

I snapped my secateurs briskly at the arching branches.

"It's just the breeze blowing in my face."

"Ah – of course. That'll be it."

"Did you want something, Nell?" With finality, I changed the subject.

"I just came to tell you dinner's almost on the table, if you mean to change."

"Heaven sakes, is it as late as that already?"

"Later than you think, ma'am, I'd say," remarked Nell enigmatically, glancing back in the direction in which her employer had vanished.

5

Nell was imagining things, of course, and I thought crossly of the rumours she was no doubt spreading in the kitchen. A kind of understanding had grown up between Adam Gaunt and myself, it was true: we were easy in one another's company, often finding ourselves sharing a thought before any words had been uttered, or sensing a mood without explanation. But there was nothing new in that. It had always been so between us, even when Rachel had been alive.

It was absurd to imagine anything more.

Yet with the awkward notion planted in my head, I became uneasy. Good heavens, Adam was Matthew's father – he should have been decently asexual instead of carelessly, vigorously male. It was unfair of him to look, and smell, and feel as he did – to be exactly as he was. I resented the way his physical nearness was enough to call up memories of passionate exploration in the darkness of a New Orleans night. I reminded myself for the thousandth time what an abject fool that night had made of me, and swore to put it out of my mind even if I was unable to purge the knowledge from my body.

Each morning I renewed my vow, henceforth to be solely my own woman. And every day at noon Adam made nonsense of it by reaching up to lift me down from my horse at the end of the lesson, ignoring the hands I held out to him and clasping my waist, suddenly swinging me to the ground at his feet as if it amused him to hold me there, breathless and hat askew, in the hollow of his arms.

Anxiously, I tried to fix my mind on the details of my journey to America – yet with every day that passed I sank further into the gentle embrace of Hawk's Dyke. No one came calling to disturb our solitude: the Gaunts from the Abbey were in London for the summer, and I did no more than ride out with Adam to discuss the roofing of a tenant's cattle court or the ploughing up of pasture for grain. The farmers called me *ma'am* and the cottagers' wives curtseyed as we passed their doors, making me squirm so uncomfortably in my saddle that Adam laughed and told me I was a closet revolutionary.

"Let them do as they want. They're only trying to please, poor creatures, against the day when they can't pay the rent, or their eldest son's caught taking Abbey birds."

"And what do you do then?"

"Oh, speak up for them, generally. Make some arrangement about the rent – promise Charles he won't catch the boy again – and warn the lad to steer clear of Abbey land if he can't stay ahead of the keepers."

"Some round here would call you soft, for that."

"They've called me a good deal worse in the past. I do what seems right to me, and let the magistrates say what they like."

We'd halted at the top of the rising ground behind the house, the same spot from where I'd once gazed down so desolately on its grey turtle-back roof among the trees. Adam had already dismounted, and now he reached up for me, sliding me from the saddle, pulling me against him until I stood on tiptoe between his feet, his hands still firm about my waist.

It was no more than he'd done a dozen times before, holding me there for a second or two in dizzying intimacy as if it was all the most innocent, laughing fun. Yet this time he held me a moment too long – or perhaps I didn't resist as he'd expected – and in an instant the laughter had become a great surge of energy which seemed to bind us where we pressed together, passing easily between us in slow, shocking waves, as if the division of flesh no longer existed. His arms were around me now, my cheek against the breast of his coat, his lips on my brow. Then all of a sudden he released me, and stepped back. Appalled, we stared at one another.

The lightness of the moment was gone, and almost apologetically, he tried to recapture it.

"Come and see the view from the ridge over here. On a clear day you can almost count the tiles on the barn roof."

After that things were different between us: understood, and deliberate – a slow, awkward exploration of the immense space which separated us. I was twenty years old, Adam more than sixty. We were mortally afraid of passing like ships in the night, but we were even more afraid of meeting in a great wreckage of naked emotion, somewhere in the middle of that void of forty unshared years.

Yet neither of us thought of retreat. Now in the evenings he'd watch from the stone seat as I cut and trimmed in the garden; if I looked up I'd see him sprawled against its grey carving, his legs stretched out, one elbow on the stone arm and a knuckle thoughtfully brushing his lips as I arched my spine like a houri before him. He said nothing – just caressed me gently with his eyes, all the time keeping the bent finger before his lips as though stopping up any rash declaration.

On fine days we scrambled up the slope behind the house to picnic – uphill, so that we could legitimately go hand in hand and I could feel the warm, quiet strength of him sustaining my steps. We'd sit there in that peaceful place, his arm round my waist – like the arm of a good friend – and my head laid against his shoulder – the shoulder of a good friend – and talk about obligation, and trust, and loneliness, the softness of summer nights, the taste of tears. . . . We spoke of the hunger of the senses, and the yearnings of the heart . . . trying all the time to pretend it was airy theory instead of the most blatant need.

"I remember thinking when Matthew was born," he murmured once, "how tragic it is that the first breath, the first glimpse, the first sound and texture of the world are wasted on a moment we'll never be able to recall. Or perhaps it's such an explosion of feeling we must forget it, or go mad."

He trailed a languorous finger down my cheek.

"Imagine sweet skin under the palms for the first time – the soft fullness of the breast – the discovery of tenderness, after solitary, floating dark."

A pair of young lovers or old sweethearts would have laughed at our snail's pace; but we were neither one thing nor the other – not even a true pair, if it came to that. We were an illusion created by faith and mirrors, fragile enough to be destroyed by the breaking of a looking-glass, and we dared not tread too heavily.

Chapter Seventeen

1

If the rest of the world had been allowed to intrude on our idyll it would have been destroyed in an instant, smothered in the guilty embarrassment of two strangers who have collided in a doorway and found themselves embracing by accident. But our peace remained undisturbed, there in that country summer of cuckoos and idle sunshine. I can't remember it raining at all during those golden, misted days, though sometimes when I wandered, restless, from my bed in the early dawn I'd find that a heavy dew had slicked each leaf in the Italian garden, jewelling the spiders' webs and filling the air with the clear, lingering sweetness of eglantine.

At that hour the house cats would materialise one by one from the dripping shadows under the rhododendrons to wait until the kitchen door was opened for them, stalking purposefully over the moist paving, their fur printed with broad-arrows of wet where the rhododendron leaves had marked them. They'd turn to stare at me with hard agate eyes, their blunt little heads still full of the business of the night, angry at being observed in the last wild, half-lit minutes before domesticity reclaimed them.

Only the grey female would speak to me at that moment, and even she put on a parade of indifference, strolling crab-wise to my feet as if in two minds about the whole affair. Once there, however, she'd allow me to scratch her small, hard skull all over, gently rubbing the cropped fur on the bridge of her nose and the warm, oily folds behind her ears while she butted against my hand. At the base of the guard hairs along her spine, her fur was the milky blue-white of moonlit camellias and soft under my fingers while she arched her back, offering her wanton rear like a pale flower in the dimness of the dawn.

"Oh, you little libertine – you've no pride at all!"

At the sound of my voice, she'd roll her head and gaze up with reproachful, almost-white eyes: *mrrraouw . . . You, who have learned to touch me so-o-o-o, dare say that?*

We had declared Hawk's Dyke an island: an island of cats and of half-lit dew-dipped gardens filled with the perfume of eglantine, of the patter of great, giddy moths against lamplit windows, and of two people alone, marooned on a blissful shore. We were willing castaways, fearful of rescue; and I at least, beguiled by the gentle sorcery of the moment, saw no reason to look beyond it.

At the end of June, Mr Lightbody wrote to say that the Liverpool police had abandoned any interest in me. "Doctor" Elias Bonnet and his fellow conspirators were safely on the other side of the Atlantic, the war was already a thing of the past, and there would be no prosecution. I could travel wherever I wished without having to look over my shoulder for the Liverpool inspector.

"Perhaps it's time you went back to America after all."

It was nearing noon, and we'd wandered across the lawn to the black shade of the nearest oak to lie like stealthy eels in the depths of its lake of shadow, coil upon dark coil. When Adam spoke I raised my head suddenly from his shoulder, as if his words had dropped like pebbles into our sinuous peace.

"I don't understand. . . . Do you want me to leave here?"

"What I want doesn't matter. I just think it might be best for you to go. Quite soon."

"But why?"

The touch of my breath at his ear seemed to distract him from his purpose, and I saw him frown.

"Do you have any money?"

"A little over twelve pounds. It took me a long time to save it, but I knew I could sail steerage for five guineas."

"I won't let you go steerage."

"I'm not going at all."

He gazed up into the vault of the oak, a wooden saint with carved hair and a face full of painful wisdom.

"I never meant it to turn out like this. Believe me, Katherine."

"It isn't important. I'm not afraid any more."

"But I am." His eyes remained drowned in green-blue shadow. "I'm afraid of clinging to your youth like a senile old man, as if somehow it might infect me, and hold back time. I despise myself for it – and I can't believe you don't despise me, too. If you don't already, then you will come to despise me, some time in the future."

I stared at him, horrified.

"Never. Oh, never."

"That's why I want you to think seriously about going back to America. Now – while there's nothing to regret, nothing but good

237

memories between us. You won't lose by it. I'll see you have the means to live comfortably as long as you need my help."

"But I don't want to go."

He laid a gentle finger on my lips; I took it softly between my teeth, and he withdrew it.

"Little cat, with your strong white teeth – your dreams won't last, you know. They never do – and I'm afraid these will end sooner than most."

"You're no dream." The tight-drawn skin over his cheekbones was cool beneath my fingertips, a quickening pulse near his ear startlingly clear. "Other things in my life have turned out to be dreams. But not you."

His hands slid up to cover mine – lean, strong hands with supple thumbs – and this time his eyes held me in all their drowning shadow.

"Little cat, you're the fantasy of a foolish old man."

"Then I have a right to be a foolish young woman."

The hands which had contained mine opened and fell away in a gesture of helplessness.

"My darling lunatic, I'm trying to save you from the consequences of your own recklessness. Can't you understand that?"

"I don't want to be saved. I don't want to be free. I want to stay with you."

I heard him sigh . . . and yet above all I wanted to please him, not to make him wretched. I laid my head on his shoulder once more.

"Think about it, Katherine – for my sake, if not for your own. I couldn't bear to have you miserable one day because of me. Put the dreams aside, and give some thought to the future: that's all I ask."

2

"I could catch a train at Hilgay, couldn't I?" I asked next day at breakfast.

He glanced up at once, his entire attention suddenly focused upon me.

"They'll stop the train, if you tell them." He paused, unwilling to continue. "Are you planning to go somewhere?"

"I want to go up to Lynn. Just for the day," I added, and saw him relax again. "There are some things I want to buy."

I'd planned my expedition during the night, sitting up in my bed amid the velvet fragrance of double stocks from the Italian garden, hugging my knees through the coverlet and thinking – just as Adam had demanded – and dreaming, in exactly the way he'd forbidden.

I'd dreamed about Matthew, once, and no one had told me then to *think* and *consider*. I'd filled my head with the sweet, singing insanity which comes once in a lifetime and is never recaptured, no matter how many forms love may take thereafter. I could suffer again, it was true, but never so bitterly.

And so I went to Lynn, and set out quite deliberately to dispose of twelve whole pounds – five shillings of which found its way immediately into the hands of an astonished old woman begging near the Guildhall.

I'd gone there to spend away my independence, to give up my precious freedom, coin by coin. I took a deep breath, strode into the nearest shop and before my courage failed me, bought two cambric handkerchiefs at ninepence apiece, and a modestly trimmed net for my hair.

Dangling from my wrist, the two little parcels were more intoxicating than a diamond bracelet. I'd never spent so much as a cent on frivolity before: Pa had never paid for anything he could beg, borrow or steal, and I'd never taken a penny from the Pastor's collection except for food and lodgings. But now, all of a sudden, I was a lady, out shopping. An explosion of bells heralded my entrance to a store; young men and women wearing two-and-sixpenny smiles rushed to serve me. How could Madam be assisted? Madam spoke, and within minutes Pompeian sashes and a blizzard of lace were spread over the counter for me to compare, and I duly bent to examine them as if the difference between moiré and shot silk was the most engrossing matter of my life.

I was dizzy with wickedness, drunk on acquisition; for once in my life I was about to have what I'd set my heart on, instead of eyeing it wistfully through a plate-glass window.

For two guineas I bought a dashing jacket in white piqué and a striped silk skirt to wear with it (just think, *only* two guineas, my dear!). In the hour that followed I laid out twelve shillings on a dress in Mozambique as blue as my eyes, looped over a white embroidered petticoat and tied with a sash, and forty-five shillings on a printed cambric dressing-gown and two pairs of pearl silk stockings which had blushed like a maiden's cheek in the mahogany gloom of the haberdasher's shop.

Delirious with the glory of my purchases, I flew on airy heels from door to door, darting in and out like a bee in a June border. On the purest whim I indulged in a pair of morocco boots, bewitchingly laced with coloured ribbon; and then, flushed with conspiracy and without removing my left glove – though I still saw the assistant search for the tell-tale ridge of a wedding ring – I bought a handsomely tucked nightdress, three yards round the hem and improbably embroidered with virginal lilies.

A final riot of spending (for whom, after all, was the parade intended?) secured a riding habit of black ribbed cloth, miraculously altered within the afternoon to hug my body as if it were tailored *couture* instead of five and a half guineas ready-made. I'd be a lady on a horse, if I could manage it nowhere else.

Adam had ridden over to Mill Farm by the time Sykes retrieved me from the station in late afternoon, but it never occurred to me to wait quietly at Hawk's Dyke for his return. All thumbs with impatience, I struggled into the new riding habit with its unfamiliar hooks and buttons, and rode off alone on my careful mare to intercept him.

I'd almost reached the farm before I caught sight of his familiar figure in the distance and saw him wave and push his horse into a canter towards me.

"Well, well. . . . So it's you, after all! I thought some grand duchess had decided to pay me a visit."

"But do you like it?" I copied an attitude I'd seen struck by stylish lady riders in public parks.

"Oh, certainly, I like it. There's something about the cut of the bodice which makes you look . . . arresting, to say the least. But you'll have to ride like a demon to carry it off. No slouching in your saddle in finery of that sort."

"There's a good deal more of it, too," I warned him happily as our horses fell into step. "Heaps and heaps of new things. I've never spent so much in one day before – or even in a year, come to that."

"Indeed?" He gave me a sideways glance. "I'd no idea you'd become such a wealthy young woman."

"It's the money I'd saved to go back to America." I straightened my back and lifted my chin, all at once unaccountably near to tears.

"I've spent it all, Adam. Everything but a few shillings. There's nothing left to buy a steamer ticket or even to take me as far as Liverpool. I can't go anywhere now, so I shall have to stay with you. On any terms at all, I'll have to stay."

I couldn't bear to look at him; I kept my eyes fixed on the next turn in the road and waited for him to speak. Now, if he wanted me to leave, he'd have to make all the arrangements himself and turn me out of his house in the face of my longing to stay – and I didn't believe he was capable of doing that.

"Oh, Katherine, my dear . . ." he murmured, shaking his head as if I'd thrown away my life along with my twelve pounds.

But he hadn't said *go*. I waited, but there was no more mention of buying my passage or supporting me in America until I could survive on my own. His silence said *stay*, and my heart began to soar again. I'd finished with caution: it was time for instinct, for unconsidered risk – for wild improvidence – and yes, for folly, if that was what it amounted to.

I wanted Adam to share the glorious lunacy of the moment. Urging the mare into a canter which swiftly became a gallop, I set off down the lane for home.

"I'll race you to the house!"

If he called me back I didn't hear, and in any case, I was in no mood for moderation. The little mare seemed to sense my excitement, and abandoned her normal prudence. Seizing the bit firmly between her teeth, she lengthened her stride and bounded forward, the muscles of her shining shoulders driving us rapidly over the hard-packed ground.

A narrow ditch ran parallel with the lane, a ribbon of water frilled with scrubby sallows and bushes of guelder rose. But the mare knew better than to run near its treacherous side, flying instead along the dry crown of the lane where her little hooves bit fiercely into the earth, spitting contemptuous half-moons of dust towards Adam's gelding in pursuit.

Flicking her ears at the distant boom behind us, the mare developed the quickness of a snake. Together we fled along the great hedgerow which curved into the final straight before Hawk's Dyke, the mare plunging deftly into the bend and bearing me with her, horse and rider united in passionate resolve.

The mare's sharp hooves were skidding on half-buried pebbles by the time the lane opened out before us again – just as a pair of pigeons burst up from our path on stuttering wings, beating to and fro in their panic. Startled, the mare flung up her head, skittering and stumbling, her legs suddenly tangled between gallop and halt; fighting the bit, she danced backwards to the very edge of the ditch, tottered for a moment, slipped, scrambled, and suddenly gave way below me.

All at once I found myself flung forwards, head over heels, supported by nothing but air. From the violet sky I heard Adam's voice – "Katherine!" – before the world rose up to hit me very hard on my spine, cold ditch water opened its green arms to engulf my rolling body, and nothing at all mattered except the pain which gripped my chest and made each new breath an agony.

I pressed my eyes tightly shut, wholly occupied with the process of breathing, of filling the clenched, painful hollows of my lungs with sweet air and clearing the humming confusion from my ears. I was hardly aware of Adam leaping from his horse to plunge after me down the bank, sliding over the squealing grass, splashing knee-deep through the water to my side. I heard him murmur "Katherine!" as he pulled me against the slope of the ditch until I was almost clear of the weedy morass, then again as he threw himself down next to me and began distractedly to strip muddy threads of hair from my eyes and cheeks.

"Not you, Katherine – not you, too . . . I couldn't bear it. . . . Stay with me – stay . . ."

When I looked up he was leaning over me, fearful as a lost child, his eyes filled with helpless tenderness and softly indistinct, like a face glimpsed through a lace curtain.

"Thank God you're conscious – " He pulled me into his arms, as if he'd been afraid of holding a corpse. "No, don't try to speak. Here – " With impatient fingers he twisted open the buttons of my bodice. "I suppose you're wearing corsets like all the rest." In another moment he'd released the fastenings of my stays, and my frantic gulps of air became less desperate.

He kept me silent and motionless in his arms until my breathing was almost normal.

"Ridiculous things, corsets. Can you move your toes?"

A faint splashing proved I could dabble my feet in the ditch water.

"Good. Now your arms."

I slid them up towards his face, feeling the muscles along his jaw tense with anxiety. At last he let me speak.

"I'm sore all over. . . . But just winded, I think."

"No broken ribs?" Gently, he encompassed my chest with his hands, and I shook my head.

"Fell on my back. Knocked all the breath out of me. . . . That's all."

"Are you certain?"

"Pretty sure." Suddenly I remembered the mare. "Where's my horse?"

He twisted round to stare over the top of the bank.

"Cropping the grass as if nothing had happened, the wretch."

"It wasn't her fault. Some pigeons startled her."

"I saw you fall. I thought . . . I was certain you'd broken your neck, or your back at least. I'd forgotten that little cats have nine lives."

Even his lopsided smile told me he'd been afraid: I'd heard fear in his

voice when he called my name, and later, as I lay waist-deep in the green
ditch and he plunged towards me through the nebula of slime. I'd never
seriously imagined him fearful of anything, but he'd been afraid for me
then – or afraid for himself without me.

"Take charge of the eight lives I have left, then. Let me stay at
Hawk's Dyke."

"With me, little cat?"

"With you."

He began to comb my damp hair with his fingertips, dividing and
subdividing it, letting it slide over his skin in dark ribbons.

"We should think of getting you home," he said at last.

But he made no move to rise; his fingers continued to whisper
through my hair as we lay together, trailing a little over my temples as
they passed.

The falling dusk shadowed his eyes as he bent to kiss me, there on the
bank of the green ditch among the stiff stems of guelder rose – once –
twice – three times – each time more disturbingly invasive than the last
– not as I'd ever imagined it, but with a cool, deliberate carnality which
left me trembling and achingly hollow as his lips parted from mine.

"Do you still want to stay with me, Kate?"

"Yes. Oh, yes."

Lazily, he hooked a finger over the edge of my chemise, sliding it
down to expose a pale breast laid bare by my unfastened corset, opaline
in the fading light, the tip startlingly dark and swollen. He bent his head
once more and rolled the pinkness gently between his teeth until he saw
my eyelids close, the lashes fluttering.

"Still?"

"Yes."

"Stay then, and let's be damned together."

4

At Hawk's Dyke I was bathed like a Persian princess in the largest
copper tub with its high back and its sides painted to resemble marble. I
was fussed and exclaimed over, and threatened with a doctor's
examination – which I refused, having all the doctor I wanted in Adam.

In the bath I stared at my breasts, now bland as buttermilk and
innocent as a baby's thumbnail. Gravely, I considered my woman's
body where it became soft and unboyish, too delicate in parts and too
lavish in others to be anything but female. I found myself wondering if
it had looked the same when Matthew had seen it – and hoping it had.
Faintly appalled, I scolded myself, blaming my lapse on the shock of

the fall. Yet perversely, Adam's touch had brought Matthew nearer once more.

Adam's touch: veins of the palest jade began to marble my breasts, and astonished, I watched them blush at the recollection.

The bath was filled up again with fragrant steam. *Best stay in it for a while longer, for the sake of your back.* Curtains were drawn across the darkening windows, and another lamp lit.

Idly, I wondered what Adam had done since he'd delivered me, bedraggled and sore, into the hands of the ministering Nell. He'd passed me into a woman's world of ruined stockings and confidences, and with my newly acquired wisdom I knew I wouldn't see him again until I emerged from it into the half-way house of bed.

Yet even then he didn't come, either to enquire or to reassure, as I wallowed painfully in the great nest of feather bed which overlaid my deep hair mattress. The corridor clock struck a tremulous eleven. A little later, distant sounds indicated that the household was closing its doors for the night; I heard an angry yowl from the garden, where the cats had been sent about their nocturnal brigandry.

Now I ached both inside and out. Sleepless, I left the lamp lit by my bed and occupied myself with counting the pleats of the half-tester canopy above my head.

It was almost midnight when a soft tap at my door brought Adam into the room in shirt-sleeves, his open white collar darkening the skin of his throat to the soft brown of a hare's back. Just inside the door he stopped to regard me for a moment as I lay against my pillows, my hair spread out witch-like around me.

"Can't sleep?"

I shook my head, shivering the aureole.

"Your hair's eaten up with flame, little cat. It must be a trick of the lamplight."

He came towards the bed, and set down a small bottle of clear, straw-coloured liquid on the table beside it.

"Stay and talk to me for a while."

He sat down on the side of the bed, and my feather lair made a hollow to receive him. Near at hand, his shirt smelt faintly of the cedar chest in which it had been stored.

"What's in your bottle?"

"Something to help you sleep."

'Laudanum?" I gazed at the bottle, puzzled by its pale colour.

"Sweet almond oil, blended with neroli." He reached out for the

244

flask and let it lie, fascinatingly luminous, between his long fingers. "Oil from the flowers of the bitter orange."

The bottle was palest topaz; within it, a pearl of air rolled lazily from end to end in response to the slightest movement – a molten oval which exploded into a cluster of seed pearls, only to coalesce to a single perfect unity as soon as stillness was restored.

"How much must I take?"

"You don't drink it. It goes . . . all over." His eyes lingered on my face, then travelled down my throat to my breasts, concealed now by virginal whitework lilies.

"*All over?*"

"All over, little cat. From your nose to your aching tail."

"Oh . . . my . . . stars . . ."

"Take off your nightdress and turn on your stomach."

I'd fallen into the hands of a satyr. To go naked in the passionate darkness was one thing, but this lamplit bacchanal . . . oh, I hoped Pa couldn't see . . .

He pushed the pillows aside; I hid my blushes in the softness of the feather bed, reached out above my head to clutch the cold, prosaic bars of the brass bedstead . . . and waited.

The sharp note of citrus invaded the air as soon as the bottle was opened, followed by a spicy, liquorice sweetness, the scent of honeyed earth loaded with the crushed flowers of bitter orange. I felt a touch, soft as a dropping leaf, between my shoulder blades; the touch transformed itself into a warm, insistent pressure which slowly traced a path down my spine before moving out in ever-increasing arcs across my skin. The warmth grew, surging across my shoulders and over my ribs like a hot tide, drawing into itself the fire of each individual ache, smoothing and squeezing it out of existence until I wriggled with the pleasure of that hypnotic, looping passage over my tingling skin.

I'd long since lost my hold on the reality of the bedstead, to float off on a timeless, bitter-orange-scented, feather-bed river. I was painted like a savage in great circles of fantasy – sculpted in smooth clay, imprinted with the sleek whorls of my creator's hand, only dimly aware that the sculptor had moved to the soles of my feet, separating the toes and caressing the cleft between.

I was ready to turn before he asked me – long before. I was a wide, laden river with the power to drown or sustain: I lay, slow like the river between my banks of feathers, and he gazed at me with lazy, opaque eyes.

This time I watched, fascinated, as his hands surged up over my thighs, over my belly to my swollen breasts, trailing after them their flush of warmth, circling like tranquil seabirds, the long fingers squeezing, probing, sliding back down the oily, glassy, glowing length of me, sliding between my thighs, taking their fire with them.

I reached up, trying to pull him down into the urgent current which rushed through me.

"Slowly . . ."

"I'm not a virgin . . ."

At my ear, I heard him smile. "Not quite."

He raised himself on one elbow, looking down into my eyes as he slid off his shirt, and I realised he'd already guessed what I'd tried so hard to keep from him. He'd known all the time what Matthew and I had done, that night on the *Bellflower* – perhaps from the first day he'd set eyes on me.

"Forget him."

It was an instruction, not a request; but in any case I had no choice, already possessed by a desire which rode my belly with spurs of pure light, making demands no less insistent.

"Forgotten . . . long ago. Oh, forgotten . . ."

Of its own accord, my back arched against him as my body devoured his touch.

"Slowly . . ." For a few seconds he made me rest, stroking my cheek. "Slowly, my little cat. Do you want it all over in a matter of moments? Ah, the blind urgency of youth. . . . Step lightly, my darling. We have all night for this."

Chapter Eighteen

1

Adam wakened before me – or perhaps he hadn't slept at all. I knew he sometimes dressed and went out in the middle of the night: the tell-tale creak of the stairs had occasionally disturbed my dreams, or the sound of a horse's hooves on the gravel below my window.

Through my newly opened eyes I saw him propped on one elbow, regarding me with the same expression of profound pleasure with which I'd sometimes seen him contemplate his house.

He continued to study me indulgently as I swam towards him through the shallows of sleep.

"Now I've wakened you, just by watching."

"It was like being stroked with a feather. . . . You have such strange eyes. I always know when you're looking at me."

"I like to look at you, little cat. I watch you, and I wonder what thoughts are going through your head."

"No thoughts at all. Just dreams . . . such dreams . . ." And I wriggled luxuriously in my trough of soft feathers.

"And how is your poor, bruised back today?"

"Oh . . . much better." I wriggled again. "Almost as good as new."

"Sleep is a great healer."

"You're a great healer. And a good deal more."

I stole a glance at him from under lowered lashes, suddenly reluctant to stare. I'd always thought it must be alarming to wake up in bed with a man – a man who was even more of a stranger for having been part of oneself in the darkness.

In the tumult of that New Orleans dawn, years before, I'd never had time to find out; but I'd often wondered how it would be with Adam – waking up to find a deeper-toned, alien arm across the sheet and a solid, quite differently shaped body in disconcerting proximity . . . a body I'd only glimpsed, for all its nearness to mine. In the crazy loving of the previous night I wouldn't have noticed if he'd been crooked as a sickle moon – nor cared either. But this was morning, and I was afraid of the impartial daylight. Suppose I loathed what I saw? And I felt guilty too, because I knew it shouldn't matter.

Perhaps he understood. At any rate, he casually swung himself out of bed and crossed to open the curtains, standing for a few moments silhouetted against the early sun, narrow-hipped and long-legged, outlined by a thin strip of radiance where the light caught fair, curled hair on his skin. There wasn't an ounce of the loose flesh I'd feared, not a shred of wasted muscle – though he gave me ample time to discover that before turning with the sinewy grace of a lifetime's horsemanship to survey me, surveying him.

"Well?" And when I didn't answer at once, he tilted his chin defiantly. "Do you want alterations, or will you take me as I am?"

"I'd take you any way at all. You know I would."

"Even if I ran to fat and grew a pot belly? You wouldn't think so much of me then, I fancy."

"You've too much pride to let it happen."

"Oho! So you do care, after all." He regarded me with amusement for a second or two, then strolled back to sit on the edge of the bed. "Then at least I shan't have to worry about you running off with some raw-boned young colt while the old stallion's still in stud condition."

"Adam! That's the most shocking thing I ever heard!"

But he only laughed, and stretched himself out backwards across the bedcover, those hawk eyes of his full of lazy wickedness. And it was true: I couldn't resist running my fingers lightly down the lean, flat-muscled length of him in the same way I used to stroke the shining flanks of my little mare.

"I'll have you copied in marble and set up in the front hall. That Michelangelo fellow will die of pure envy."

He laughed, deep in his throat. "You're too late to bother Michelangelo, little cat. You'd only end up frightening the servants."

"Then I'll keep you all to myself."

"And I'll keep you." He raised himself on one elbow. "Every beautiful, impatient, ravenous inch of you."

Why did he make me blush so easily?

"I wish I could be beautiful for you."

For the space of a heartbeat he stared at me, and then reached out for the silver mirror on my night table.

"Here, lunacy. Look at yourself in this."

The woman who gazed back at me from the oval glass wore an expression of pure astonishment – beautiful, wide-eyed astonishment. Her skin, her hair, her lips were charged with liquid colour like the brightness of poppies after a sun-shower – loved into radiance. Such was the power of happiness.

By the end of next day, the scent of bitter-orange flowers had carried all the way to Stainham St Agnes. The village shrugged its collective shoulders and observed that it was no more than you'd expect from the Gaunts – but the villagers were country folk, and the rhythms of life were all around them. The conscience of the village was less indulgent. The whispers from Hawk's Dyke gave the Rector's wife – lying primly between her pilfered sheets – a delightful *frisson* of horror, and led the curate to remark to the schoolmaster that if the gentry set such a poor example to the lower orders, well, really . . . what could one do?

I dare say we'd have been thoroughly discussed at Sourwell Abbey too, if there'd been anyone there besides the staff required to maintain that rambling house until the family returned from London at the beginning of August. But it was still July, and we were left to our own devices. We were near Stainham, but not of it: we were near Sourwell Abbey, but not of that either. The village watched and waited – but whether the house was a place of wickedness or of desperate folly no one had yet decided.

Cocooned in my happiness at Hawk's Dyke, I was quite ignorant of the sensation Adam and I had caused. It never occurred to me to try to hide how matters stood between us. We wakened in whichever bed we'd slept in the night before, wandered half-dressed from room to room whenever we felt the need of company, read to one another in the bath, kissed, touched, and made love with the joyful greed of alley-cats.

No one else in the house seemed to grudge us our contentment. On the contrary, Nell and the other servants smiled upon us as if they'd been responsible for bringing us together in the first place, and even the oily Sykes appeared one morning with a bunch of wild, tawny-throated irises for our breakfast table.

I couldn't believe I might ever want more than I had at that moment. Heavens above – by the end of our first night together, our unsanctified union had already lasted longer than the only marriage I'd ever undertaken! Promises were no more than words, made to be forgotten. Better to give honestly, and not look for more.

"I love you dearly, Adam," I told him one evening in the Italian garden, "but I don't think I'm *in* love with you. You mean everything in the world to me, and I can't imagine life without you . . . but I'm not in love with you. Not the mad, spoony, mountain-climbing sort of love, at any rate. Do you mind very much?"

"I don't mind at all." Adam held a half-open rose next to my face and considered us both. "In fact, I'm relieved to hear you aren't in love with me. What you were never *in*, you can't fall out of. If you said you could barely tolerate me, I'd be even happier."

I pushed the rose away. "What a dreadful cynic you are! Don't you believe it's possible to fall truly in love?"

His gaze slid up, over my head, to the green spaces of the garden beyond.

"I only fell in love once in my life. That was with Rachel, and I don't expect it to happen again. In fact, I'd hate it to happen again. It's the most wretched, topsy-turvy, maddening state I can imagine. The difficulty is to go on loving once you come to your senses."

"You did. Both of you."

"We did . . . but we were fortunate. Love and hate are sometimes too close for comfort." For a moment he remained silent, then suddenly looked down at me and smiled. "That's why I say we should settle for simple tolerance. If you can just about bear my company, I'll do my best to suffer yours, and that should keep us together for years to come."

"Idiot!"

"Will you, Kate – " he intoned solemnly, "promise not to fall in love with this man – not to trust him, or agonise over him, or make impossible demands on his honesty – as long as you both shall live?"

"How can I promise such things? Whatever happens, happens. Isn't that so?"

I was laughing, but Adam had already become serious again, sobered by some thought born of his own mockery.

"Kate. . . . We've never discussed this – but do you expect me to marry you?"

"I've never expected it. I know you still think of Rachel as your wife, and I'd never try to take her place. We're much better off as we are."

He fell silent for a moment.

"You're right – in part. I don't believe we ought to be married, though not for the reason you think. If I imagined it would give us an hour's extra happiness, I'd drag you to the altar by force if necessary."

Once more he stared over my head into the darkening garden, his face partly obscured by leafy shadow. I was seized by a sudden urge to walk away from him, afraid of what was to come; but he held me back and turned me squarely towards him.

"One day, Kate, I'll be an old man. Don't shake your head as if you can't believe it'll ever happen, because it will. One day I'll be an old man – possibly a blind, senile, crippled old man. I'll be precious little use to you then, and I want you to be able to turn your back on me before that happens, and go off wherever you please. Do you understand?" The pressure of his fingers on my shoulders increased. "That's why I won't marry you. Not because of memories of Rachel, but because I don't ever want to see pity in your eyes when you look at me. I couldn't bear it, Kate."

"You'll never be like that."

"Of course I will – if I live long enough. If Rachel had still been alive we'd have grown old together, and it wouldn't have mattered. But with you it's different. You have a life ahead of you. You have to be free to go when the time comes."

"I don't want to talk about it." I put my hands over my ears, but he pulled them away.

"Listen to me, and I won't speak of it again. I want everything honest between us, Kate, or it'll end in arguments and tears."

"I'm listening." But I listened under protest, remembering another 'marriage' I loved him too much to speak of.

"Do you understand what I've said?"

I nodded.

"There's only one reason why I'd marry you in spite of everything. If we had a child – then it would be different. A child needs permanence – a home and a family. I've good reason to know that, and I won't compromise. If we have a child, you and I will have to put up with one another for as long as necessary."

"We'll have to *tolerate* one another?" I suggested lightly. "But isn't that exactly what you wanted for us in the first place?"

I desperately wanted to see him smile again. I hated all the talk of death and decay; it was impossible to imagine Adam blind and bent and witless, and his sombre mood frightened me. The future would surely take care of itself, as it always had done – and as for the present, what did I care about wedding rings and respectability? I'd already learned the worthlessness of those. I had Adam, strong and vital still, and nothing else mattered.

3

But the world was determined we should take notice of its opinion.

Dimly, as autumn settled itself around us and the first leaves flushed yellow in the Italian garden, I became aware of comings and goings at Sourwell Abbey which indicated that the Gaunt family had returned to their fiefdom. Then one afternoon at the beginning of September, a gasping groom arrived at the house to report that the dowager Countess of Wellborough's carriage had skidded and overturned on the dusty high road not far from the turning for Hawk's Dyke. Her ladyship was

251

somewhere inside the wreckage but still very much alive, to judge by the muffled torrent of abuse heaped on her coachman's head from the topsy-turvy vehicle.

Adam went to her aid at once, and I followed as quickly as I could in the landau, piled high with rugs, flasks of brandy and anything else Nell and I thought might be useful to an elderly lady in distress.

I hadn't set eyes on Henrietta since that dreadful day at Sourwell Abbey when I'd picked up Freddie Broadney's cigar, and I had no illusions about what she might think of me. But this was no time for social niceties. The landau swept towards the main road down a lane filled with running figures as every groom in the stables and all the available men from Old Hall Farm sped to the rescue, armed with ropes and fence-posts for the righting of the overturned carriage.

By the time I arrived, the Countess was sitting at the roadside, enthroned on a blue silk cushion near the capsized vehicle which lay across the crown of the highway. Adam and the coachman had already cut the horses free of their tangled harness, and were trying to quiet the skittering, frightened animals while the Countess listed her coachman's shortcomings in ringingly acid tones.

"So the off-leader got the rein under his tail and ran away with the carriage?" I heard her call out as the landau pulled up nearby. "Then why the devil didn't you let the near horse catch hold of the pole and straighten us up, instead of hauling on the brake like a confounded novice? Call yourself a coachman? I've seen better men leading a Cheapside milk-cart!" She caught sight of me advancing along the roadway towards her. "Hah – I remember you! You're the young woman who likes footmen."

"Katherine Summerbee, your ladyship."

"*Countess*, my dear, or you'll sound like a pew-opener. Well, Katherine," she continued without stopping for breath, "this is a how-de-do, ain't it? Bowling along, nice as ninepence, then all of a sudden upset in the road like a stove-in tea-chest. It's all that fellow's fault."

The Countess waved a furious hand towards her coachman, but otherwise showed no sign of wishing to move. Plumped down on the roadside verge, her hat tipped over one eye, her feet stuck out before her in tasselled Polish boots with crimson heels, she looked more than usually like a menagerie monkey.

The rescue party were now debating how best to move the overturned carriage, which had already lost one wheel and seemed bound to lose the others before it was righted.

"Leave them to it, Adam!" shouted the Countess. "And if those blasted fellows of mine are here all night, then so much the worse for them. I'll come back to Hawk's Dyke with you, my dear." She reached up and patted my hand. "In fact, I'll stay for dinner. The Abbey's like a crypt after our house in London."

"I don't know what we can offer you for dinner," I ventured cautiously. "Mrs Rawley's what's known as a *plain cook*, I'm afraid."

"All the better! Most of these damned fricassees and pâtés look as if someone's digested them already."

In the event, Mrs Rawley surpassed herself, producing salmon in caper sauce, braised ham and a gooseberry tart sprinkled with fine sugar and accompanied by a large jug of cream. "Proper food," as the Countess observed through a mouthful of cheese. "None of this messed-about rubbish that Alice insists on nowadays."

The young Earl and Countess, I learned, had just returned from London, accompanied by their French chef and the baby girl born to them the previous year. Louise, now eighteen years old, had "come out" that Season in the approved fashion, and would join her sister at the Abbey the following month.

"Alice is with child again," the Countess remarked later from her wing chair in front of the parlour fire. "Let's hope it's a boy this time, to give Charles an heir." Her small, monkey eyes swivelled to regard Adam, lounging in his chair on the other side of the hearth. "Still no grandchildren, then, Adam? What's that boy of yours up to? He ain't a gelding, I suppose?"

"Not as far as I know. Though I'd be the last one to hear if he was." Adam's voice was drowsy with warmth, a good meal, and a glass of brandy which stood at his elbow. I longed to curl up on the rug at his feet and lean against his knees in the firelight, but I suspected it might be regarded as ill-mannered.

"It must be Violet, then," the Countess continued blandly. "Ten to one she's barren. Damned inconvenient – babies might have kept her at home, where she belongs. Twice last winter she visited the Abbey on her own, you know. Oh, I suppose her father was with her, or that popeyed brother of hers, but there was plenty of carrying on, I'm sure of it."

The Countess waved an expansive hand. "A blind donkey would have noticed the way she was making up to young Oswald Concannon during the New Year shoot. He's a personable sort of fellow, I suppose, and he'll be wealthy enough one day when old Sir Vernon dies, but there's nothing at all between his ears. Not a brain in his head! Now, why on earth should a clever little piece like Violet want to waste her time on fools like young Concannon? Anyone can see Matthew's worth a dozen of him – and it isn't as if Violet was forced into her marriage, either. Not the way I was."

"That was a bad business," Adam agreed sagely. "You should have refused outright to marry a swine like Henry."

"It wouldn't have done me any good if I had refused! When my father said *go*, I went. That's the way it was in our house. I was told off to marry Henry and no one thought to ask my opinion, though I was sorry enough later, when it was too late." The Countess suddenly remembered my existence, sitting quiet as a mouse on the sofa, my feet curled up under my skirts, digesting the news of Matthew and Violet. I'd been astonished to find that neither Adam nor the Countess seemed under any illusions about Violet's behaviour.

"D'you like dogs, Katherine?" The Countess interrupted my thoughts.

"Some dogs." I glanced at Adam's faithful Tess, lying in privileged comfort before the fire. "I like black retrievers best."

"The Earl kept dogs," continued the Countess. "He had a whole pack of them – great, slobbering brutes that ran wild through the Abbey and bit anyone they came across. They were never more than half-trained. Made a mess on the carpet whenever it suited them, and frightened the servants into fits. They terrified me, too, but of course that's why he kept them. Henry liked to see people run."

"He was always a bully."

"And he loathed you, Adam. You never gave in to him, and he hated that." Once more, the Countess peered at me round the side of her chair. "Adam and my husband were half-brothers, you see."

"We had different mothers," Adam observed drily. "The difference being that mine wasn't a countess. She wasn't even married, as a matter of fact." He hauled himself to his feet. "I'm going down to the cellar for more brandy. I'll see if anyone knows what's happened to that carriage of yours."

The Countess waited until the door had closed behind him.

"I married the wrong brother, and that's the truth. If I'd had my choice, I'd have taken Adam, for all he was a year or two younger than me and hadn't a penny to his name." She fixed me with her sly, simian stare. "You're a fortunate young woman, my dear. He's an awkward devil, but they don't come any better. See you take good care of him, that's all."

"But – we aren't – I mean – " In my innocence I'd never expected the Countess to know all the details of my life with Adam.

254

She waved an impatient hand. "For Heaven's sake, girl, you don't have to be coy with me! Do you think I care if he keeps a hundred mistresses at Hawk's Dyke?

"Good gracious, no," she continued easily, "we don't keep secrets from one another, Adam and I. We've been friends for a great many years. He'd already quarrelled with his father and run off to the wilds of America by the time I married Henry, but he came home in – oh – '27 or '28, I forget which, wild as a tiger among all those fat Norfolk hens. He'd been shipwrecked off Newfoundland, and all but drowned – and he cut a very romantic figure, I can tell you. He only stayed here for a few months, of course – " Her eyes gleamed in the firelight. "But he was quite irresistible as a lover."

She laughed suddenly, and I caught a glimpse of the dazzling beauty she must have been.

"Have I shocked you, my dear?" The Countess regarded me quizzically. "Well, I had to pay Henry back somehow for all those dogs, didn't I? I gave him an heir and three other children besides, so I did my duty by the wretched man – and more. But he always took his pleasure whenever he fancied, so why shouldn't I?"

Henrietta pursed her lips for a moment, and stared into the fire. "You must remember, I was still a young woman in those days. . . . And I'd had no life at all, shut up in that prison of a house. It's hard when all you can see ahead is to live with a man you hate until death sets you free." She peered round at me once more as if she wanted to be sure of being understood. "And there were times, my dear, when I didn't care whose death came first."

"The Earl died in a hunting accident, I believe."

"The devil he did! Who on earth told you that nonsense?"

"Louise told me, years ago."

"Bosh! Henry died on top of a housemaid. Weak heart. Runs in the family. The poor girl had to call a footman to get herself free." The Countess delivered this information with bland indifference.

"Wasn't there a dreadful scandal?"

She stared at me as I were slow-witted.

"Why should there be any scandal? Earls die sober, religious deaths – everybody knows that – just as they live sober, religious lives. If the family say he fell on his head on the hunting field, I'd like to see the man who'd dare to suggest otherwise. The fact that every housemaid in the house got pregnant is neither here nor there."

She reached out and patted my hand.

"You don't even understand the rules, my dear, do you? And Adam has never admitted the existence of rules, so you make a fine pair of innocents." The Countess looked at me with something approaching pity. "But you'll learn soon enough, I dare say."

I received my first lesson in the village the very next day. Sykes had driven me in the landau to the post office, and the Rector arrived just as I was leaving.

"Ah . . ." His long nose quivered with apprehension. "Good day to you, Miss – ah – Miss Summerbee." He raised his hat the merest half-inch.

"Good day to *you*, Rector."

The postmaster bent over his ledger – but awkwardly, and at the very edge of the counter, where he could overhear every word. I saw the Rector glance quickly in the man's direction and clear his throat with vigour – St Paul girding himself to rebuke a sinner.

"I do not seem to have seen you, or indeed, to have seen Mr Gaunt in church for some time, Miss Summerbee." He fixed me with a stern eye, and then added hastily, "I am presuming, of course, that Mr Gaunt has not been overseas." Adam Gaunt might be wicked, but he was still the present Earl of Wellborough's half-uncle.

"We don't seem to have seen you at Hawk's Dyke either, Dr Peasup. Or Mrs Peasup either, for that matter. Still – now that Mr Gaunt is to be at home for a while, I hope your wife will call one day." This was a downright lie, but I was determined not to allow him his little victory.

"Well now . . ." A shifty, anxious expression spread itself over the Rector's yellow face. "I'll certainly convey your invitation to Mrs Peasup . . ." He shuffled his feet. "Forgive me, Miss Summerbee, but you are Mr Gaunt's ward . . . is that correct?"

"No, I'm not his ward, Rector."

"His – ah – housekeeper, perhaps?"

"Not his housekeeper either."

"A relative, then? A cousin of the late Mrs Gaunt?"

The postmaster almost fell over the front of the counter in his curiosity.

"No, we aren't related in any way."

"Ahhh . . . I see." The Rector hitched his shoulders inside his black frock coat and looked stern once more. "Well then. . . . Though I'll certainly convey your invitation to Mrs Peasup . . . she does have many claims on her time. Charitable claims, you understand. I'm sure you'll forgive her if perhaps . . . she does *not* call." This time his hat barely left his head. "Good day to you, Miss Summerbee. I trust you'll give my kind regards to Mr Gaunt."

4

"What should I have said to him, Adam?" I demanded later. "He knows perfectly well what my position is here! The whole village knows! Was I supposed to say outright *I'm Adam Gaunt's mistress, and proud of it?*"

"I wish you had, you ferocious creature. He'd have run off into the churchyard, screaming."

"And what if I'd told a lie and said I was your second cousin's third daughter, or some other such nonsense? Would that have been so much better?"

"It would have given you a respectable reason for living here, I suppose."

"Even if everyone knew it wasn't the truth?"

"What they *know* is one thing. What you force them to acknowledge is something else again. All the Rector wanted was an excuse for ignoring our bad behaviour. Then he wouldn't need to be offended by it."

"So if I claimed to be your housekeeper we could spend the whole day making love and no one would care? They could all pretend I was only a housekeeper?"

"Instead of a much-loved mistress." Adam put his arms round me and pulled me against him. "I've never been good at lying to save face, Kate, and now we've rubbed their noses in it. I did warn you it wouldn't be easy."

"But what have we done that's so wrong? We haven't hurt anyone else, have we?"

"We've found happiness where we weren't entitled to find it. That's hard for people like the Rector to forgive. They'd prefer to believe that either I've corrupted an innocent young girl, or you've seduced a besotted old man."

"Oh, they'll say I seduced you," I retorted bitterly. "I'm not even British, after all, so I'm obviously a scheming adventuress."

"I hope that isn't what they say." Adam made a face. "After all, I have the bad reputation of the Gaunts to keep up."

5

It was all very well for Adam to joke about our situation, but I hadn't been raised to notoriety of that kind. I might be a river-brat, but that

257

wasn't the same as being a scarlet woman – not by a long way. I needed silence and privacy to come to terms with my new identity, and I went up to Alice's room under the eaves, which had been my sanctuary during my first days at Hawk's Dyke, and sat down on the floor in front of the doll's house to think.

The logic of it all still escaped me. I couldn't imagine what we'd done that was so essentially wrong. I hadn't run off with someone's husband, or set myself up as a courtesan. I hadn't hurt a single soul, yet I was being made to feel like a criminal.

Idly, I unlatched the front of the little mansion and swung it open on the well-regulated household in which Alice had rehearsed her future. Someone had arranged the doll family round the table in the dining-room since I'd last looked inside, bespectacled Papa at the head of the board and comfortable Mamma at the bottom with a row of wool-headed children on either side. A tiny glass cake-stand stood in the centre of the table next to Alice's flowers, and a musty felt cat lay in front of the painted fire; altogether everything looked as proper and unexceptional as it had the first time I set eyes on it. I had the distinct impression I'd interrupted the saying of grace before dinner.

In every way, the little house was a shrine to rectitude. Here was the family ideal held up as an example to the future wives of the nation – Papa, Mamma and the children, all smiling virtuously, rewarded for their purity with plaster blancmange and wooden fishes. Outwardly, the house was without sin. If Papa ever clasped the stiff-skirted parlourmaid in his wire arms or Mamma lay in a lover's embrace on her tiny *chaise-longue*, there was never a sign of it by the time human eyes peered into their life of just-so.

I tried to imagine flannel Papa drinking in secret and lashing out at the wool-headed children. He looked so firmly stitched – and the decanters were always empty, as if even temptation had been denied him. I suspected Mamma of emptying them – smiling her bright, idiotic smile of domestic sainthood, safely above suspicion. Would her smile waver, I wonder, if Papa gasped his last in the housemaid's bed, ejaculated into the hereafter?

No – Papa would certainly have a *mistress*, a word which hadn't even entered my head until the Countess uttered it, and then somehow seemed to attach itself to the end of a long list which included grooms and nursery-maids and under-parlourmaids. . . . Good Heavens, the Rector must keep company with any number of men who maintained mistresses! The word even had a well-worn, settled, slightly tawdry ring to it, like a household institution – no passion, no spirit, just a facility for Papa when Mamma's services had been withdrawn. . . . A soft, convenient body, always available, very properly preventing him from having to trawl the streets . . .

And now Adam and I had betrayed the doll's house. There'd been no place for us in its cosy, perfect world, and we hadn't even pretended to aspire to one. Far worse – we'd had the effrontery to be happy beyond its charmed walls, and to let our happiness show.

With an angry fingertip I pushed grave, bespectacled Papa until his chair tipped up and he sprawled solemnly on the floor like an overturned crab.

6

It seemed to me, by October of that year, 1865, that everyone must know how things stood at Hawk's Dyke. Yet somehow – perhaps because he'd been immersed in the setting up of an Oliver office in Singapore – Matthew was still unaware that I'd returned to Norfolk. Though why should he know? He didn't correspond with his father, Violet had spent the summer in London, and even the Sourwell Gaunts had only recently discovered my presence when they returned to their country home for the opening of the shooting season.

In the event, it was something quite different which caused Matthew to make a detour to Hawk's Dyke on his way from London to an appointment on the Humber. It was only when I was summoned to the drawing-room and found Matthew gaping at me as if he'd seen a ghost that I realised he'd thought me safely in America, two thousand miles away from his father's house. He'd heard nothing of my adventures with the Pastor or my trial as a book thief – not that I'd expected Violet to boast of what had passed between us in her bedroom in Eaton Square.

"Kate! What in the name of Heaven are you doing here?"

"Kate lives here," Adam informed him shortly. "This is her home."

"Here?" Matthew seemed unable to comprehend the word. "Here – with you?"

"Here at Hawk's Dyke." Adam's voice was smooth and cold. "And now that we've renewed old acquaintances – is this to be a social call, Matthew, or have you come for something in particular?"

With an effort, Matthew dragged his eyes away from me.

"Mother's garden," he began flatly. "Louise wrote to me a few months ago before she left for London, and said it was in a bad state. I haven't had time to come down here before now."

"Ah well, your information's out of date, Matthew. The garden was overgrown, it's true, but that was a long time ago, when I'd been abroad for a while. Kate has done wonders for it since then – it's almost as fine as it ever was. Go and look for yourself."

Once more, Matthew's gaze travelled to me.

"You've been taking care of it?"

"I do my best. I don't know a great deal yet, but I'm learning."

It was strange to see Matthew again. He seemed thinner, I thought, and some of his father's angularity had begun to show itself in his face, hardening the expression in his eyes. I wondered how much he knew about Violet's adventures – or if he did know, how much he cared. But I knew that in his father's company he'd give nothing away. He'd long since learned how to make himself unassailable, squarely filling his chair as if establishing a bridgehead in enemy territory, while Adam dominated the hearthrug. It saddened me to see them so. Father and son, they'd both worshipped Rachel – couldn't they even become reconciled in her garden?

"I love being out there in the last of the sunlight." Artlessly, I chattered on, hoping to create a common cause between them. "The trouble is, the more I learn about plants, the more I realise how little I know. And I can't claim all the credit for the transformation. Three men from the farm have done most of the hard work, or it would have taken forever to put everything back as it should be."

Matthew glanced towards his father, but almost immediately his eyes drifted back to me as if drawn by a magnet.

"May I see it?"

"Of course," Adam agreed evenly. "Kate, my dear, why don't you take Matthew out to admire your handiwork? You're far better qualified to show off your flowers than I am."

Adam had remained standing, and as I rose he smiled, and casually reached out to touch my cheek. At any other moment, the gesture would have implied simple affection – but not with Matthew present. I knew Adam too well to be deceived. I might accompany Matthew into the garden, that touch declared, but he must understand that I was his father's property now. Taken – not open to offer.

I was furious: I felt as if I'd been branded like a slave, and my face, when I turned to Adam, must have shown my indignation. But he met my gaze with implacable defiance. The matter was not for discussion.

Matthew had retreated behind the closed, shuttered expression I knew of old, and which I'd sometimes seen on Adam. In absolute silence he followed me out of the room and along the corridor to the garden door, opening it for me without a word to let me pass through before him.

We'd reached the fountain before he burst out, "You're his mistress, dammit! You're my father's mistress!"

"That's what everyone seems to call me."

"You admit it? You can look me in the face, and admit you're sharing my father's bed?"

"I don't have to admit anything to you! In fact, I don't see that it's any of your business, Matthew. You made it perfectly plain to me – years ago, in this very garden – that you'd no interest in anything I might do."

"Oh, but it is my business! *He's* just made sure of that. Didn't you see – in the parlour, when he touched your face? Like that – " And Matthew reached out to lay a finger on my cheek, exactly as Adam had done.

"That was my father telling me, in his own subtle way, that you belong to him now. What else do you imagine he meant by it?"

"I belong where I please." I was still smarting from Adam's sudden possessiveness. "Nobody owns me. I do what I want."

"Oh, it's pretty obvious what you want!" Matthew snapped unpleasantly. "You want to be a rich man's mistress – since you freely admit that's what you are."

He stared at me for a moment in baffled outrage.

"How could you, Kate? That's what I can't understand – when you came all the way to England to search for me – and insisted we were man and wife, no matter what. Those were your last words on the subject – that you still believed we were married that day in New Orleans. Heavens above, I thought you felt something for me, after all we'd been through . . . for *me*, Kate – not for him!"

"I can't believe your arrogance! After the way you treated me – and after three years when I don't suppose you've given me a single thought – how can you possibly imagine you have any claim on me? What on earth did you expect me to do when you abandoned me for dear Violet? Shut myself up like a nun, and spend the rest of my life weeping over a marriage that never happened?"

"But to throw yourself at my father, Kate! For God's sake, it's indecent!" He seemed bewildered by the fact that I didn't share his revulsion. "All this time, I thought I was the one who'd wronged *you*! I imagined you were . . . innocent, somehow . . . honest. . . . But now – to see you living here brazenly, as my father's mistress! Did you have to choose Adam Gaunt as your lover? Couldn't you have found some other man to keep you, if you were determined to live this sort of life?"

"I'm here at Hawk's Dyke because I love him, Matthew. Can't you

261

understand that? I hate the dependence of it – the helplessness – having to rely on him for everything. But I love your father, and he needs me – and because of that I try to swallow my pride and forget the rest."

I was determined to make Matthew understand my feelings for Adam – as determined as Matthew was to make them sound squalid and calculating.

"Matthew, Adam believed in me when I didn't have another soul in the world. He persuaded me to trust him when everyone else had let me down, and he's never betrayed that trust. Never once. Can't you see why I love him?"

"Oh, I see it plainly enough! It's called selling yourself for as much as you can get! Tell me, Kate – if the workhouse had rescued you from the gutter instead of my father, would you have crawled into bed with each of the commissioners in turn – one after the other?"

Without a word, I turned on my heel and walked swiftly back along the path. Behind me, I heard Matthew's voice still raised in bitter accusation.

"Love him? What kind of a fool do you take me for? It's perfectly obvious that when you discovered you couldn't have me, you took up with my father instead! Turn round and face me, Kate – or can't you bear to listen to the truth? Your plans for me came to nothing, so you took my father as a consolation prize! You haven't done so badly – you got second best, at least!"

Almost at the garden door, I spun round to face him.

"Second best? Is that really what you believe? If you want to know the truth, Matthew – " I took a deep breath. "The truth is that you aren't half the man your father is – not a quarter, even – and you never will be. Never, at any time."

"Thank you, Kate. That's all I wanted to know."

I heard Adam's quiet voice in the same instant I saw Matthew's gaze flick to a point behind me. I turned to see Adam filling the doorway, one hand on the latch of the door he'd opened in time to hear my final words.

I was furious with Matthew, but I was angry with Adam, too. I'd have pushed past him into the house if he'd let me.

"Do you understand now, Matthew?" he was saying softly. "Has Kate made the situation quite clear to you?"

"You're every bit as bad as Matthew!" I shouted at Adam. "He's behaving like a spoilt child, but you deliberately started this quarrel, knowing where it would end. How dare you fight over me like dogs squabbling over a bone?"

"Oh, don't worry, Kate – " I heard Matthew's scornful voice behind me. "I've no intention of fighting for your favours. Keep them for your ancient lover, if that's what gives you pleasure."

"Matthew! That's enough!" All I wanted was to put an end to the row, but Matthew would not be silenced.

"No doubt I'll find my mother's grave covered in nettles and weeds, while you two are rolling in her bed! By God, you disgust me!"

"Get out." Adam's voice was lethally calm. "Get out of my sight, Matthew, and don't come back to Hawk's Dyke while it's still mine. You poison the air, just by standing here."

"Adam! For Heaven's sake – you've every right to be angry – but whatever Matthew's said, he's still your son!" I was appalled by the severity of the sentence.

"Don't beg for me, Kate." Matthew strode towards the door from which Adam had moved aside. "I don't need any pardon from dross like him. I wish you joy of one another."

In a second, he was gone.

"Oh please, Adam, don't send him away like that! I can't bear to be the cause of your quarrel. For my sake, go after him – ask him to wait."

"Wait?" Adam stared at me, daring me to plead Matthew's case any further. "Wait?" he demanded again. "Whatever for?"

Chapter Nineteen

1

I knew better than to argue with Adam about his son. On every other conceivable matter he was patient, and reasonable, and generous to a fault, yet when it came to any mention of Matthew he immediately became as stubbornly inflexible as . . . as Matthew was about Adam. At some distant point in the past, life had become a struggle between them which neither would give up. Matthew demanded a supremacy which Adam wasn't ready to yield, and my presence at Hawk's Dyke only made matters worse.

"Forget him," Adam would remark dismissively whenever Matthew's name cropped up in conversation, but I remained haunted by my part in their quarrel. If only Louise Oliver had stayed at Hawk's Dyke, she might have held the balance between them as Rachel had done. But Louise had withdrawn completely to the Abbey. On the rare occasions when she and Adam had met they'd had very little to say to one another of their widely separated worlds – yet I still believed that if I could only speak to Louise . . .

Louise had returned to Sourwell Abbey in the second week of October, and I was puzzled that although she must have discovered I was staying at Hawk's Dyke she'd made no attempt to contact me. After three weeks had gone by with no sign of a note from her, I sat down to compose one of my own, reminding her of our friendship and adding that I hoped to meet her before long.

A liveried footman from the Abbey brought me her reply, a stiff little letter thanking me for my enquiries about her health, and adding that she was well and intended to stay at the Abbey for the rest of the winter. She refused outright to come to Hawk's Dyke, and as for a meeting between us. . . . Since I was living in the neighbourhood, she conceded it was possible we might see one another before long – though where and when she didn't suggest, and I understood that if we did meet it would only be by accident.

It was clear that the new, independent Louise wanted nothing to do with me. I'd gone over to her stepfather's side in the most scandalous fashion and put an end to any friendship between us. But I was determined to see her in spite of that. I needed her help to bring

Matthew and his father together again, and for their sakes I was prepared to swallow my pride and seek her out. If an accidental meeting was all she'd grant me, the most likely place for it to happen was somewhere in the fields and lanes which lay between Hawk's Dyke and the Abbey, where riding was the single ladylike pursuit we shared.

I rode almost every day now – either with Adam, which I adored, or when he was immersed in business with tenants or his bailiff, on my own with a groom for an escort.

"I haven't forgotten your talent for falling into ditches," he reminded me when I protested that I'd be perfectly safe alone. "I'd prefer to know there's someone around to rescue you, next time it happens."

Nothing would budge him: if I wouldn't consent to take a groom with me, then he'd put off his business until the afternoon and escort me himself. And so – secretly enchanted by his concern – I submitted to riding out like a solemn matron with a silk-hatted groom a few paces behind.

I usually set out to the north on these occasions, crossing the highway to the Abbey land beyond, always in the hope of meeting Louise. Her note had made it plain what she thought of me – chiefly by what it hadn't said. I wondered which of my crimes had annoyed her more – my alliance with her stepfather, or the way I'd helped him turn the household at Hawk's Dyke into a continuing embarrassment to the family. Louise would probably never forgive me for spoiling her social credentials; yet I continued to ride – the very picture of respectability, with my groom at my heels – along the lanes of the Sourwell Abbey land.

I no longer stood in awe of the place. Even when the Abbey itself came in sight across the fields, just as I'd first glimpsed it, I thought the house seemed blanker, and more blood-red, and more wrapped in its own affairs than ever. Its gloom was no longer menacing, but sad. King Henry had set the seal on its mood three hundred years earlier when he turned the monks out of their Abbey for the sake of a new, doomed wife: even during the years I knew about, poor Henrietta had been imprisoned there with her bullying husband and his dogs, Louise had fled there from her stepfather, and Violet Oliver had used it for her own clandestine amusements. Sourwell Abbey was a place of quarrels and wretchedness; those blood-red walls seemed to thrive on the wrangling of the Gaunts.

One morning, after several weeks' fruitless patrolling, I came un-expectedly upon two riders – a man and a woman – chatting idly as their horses ambled towards me down a leafy track. At first I thought the woman was Louise, and my hopes rose at the sight of blonde hair netted elegantly under a feathered hat. But as the riders drew nearer and reluctantly dragged their eyes from one another, I saw that while the man was unknown to me, his companion was Violet Oliver.

She'd begun to paint rather obviously, I noticed as she drew near enough for me to see what brunette powder and a pot of carmine had made of her skin. Her pale eyes were now so dark and luminous that I suspected she'd taken to using belladonna to enhance their fascination; she used them now to some purpose, fastening them upon her young escort in a pantomime of dismay.

"Oh, Mr de Santos, if only I'd thought of bringing a veil! It's so dusty here, my eyes are quite aching already! I'd be forever in your debt if you'd only ride back to the Abbey and fetch one."

The dark young man demurred, twisting his whiskers officiously: it was hardly prudent to leave Mrs Oliver alone on horseback in such a place. . . . But Mrs Oliver bathed him in her fascinating gaze. The lady approaching along the lane was an acquaintance – and see, her groom was in attendance. If Mr de Santos would be so kind, she'd wait for him on that very spot . . . and would be eternally grateful for his care of her . . .

The opposition crumbled, Mr de Santos was dispatched, and Violet turned her eyes on me – no longer soft and fascinating, but coolly appraising, as if my horse and I were a circus act offered for her amusement.

It was the first time we'd met since that dreadful afternoon in London; the episode must have been in both our minds as we stared at one another, yet there was no hint of it in the expression on Violet's face. No doubt Matthew had told her all about the situation at Hawk's Dyke, and for a moment she continued to inspect me with something like curiosity. Then, as my horse came to a halt alongside hers, I saw her glance over my shoulder to satisfy herself that my groom had remained far enough off to keep our conversation private.

"Well, your new life seems to suit you, I must say." Once more, she eyed me speculatively. "Miss Summerbee – or do you call yourself Mrs Gaunt these days? Since Alice tells me you're the old man's mistress."

"Don't call him that." My voice was so sharp it startled me.

"Oh, I didn't mean it as a criticism, I assure you. I've often looked at Adam Gaunt and wondered . . . what it would be like . . . with such a man." She considered the idea for a moment, and then smiled suddenly – a bright, brittle, social smile. "Not that I shall ever find out. That would be a little too close to home, don't you think? No – you may have him, my dear, with my blessing. Besides, you look so *well* on it – so much improved since the last time I saw you."

She was goading me, her glance flicking continually to the groom waiting just out of earshot. With an effort, I kept my temper.

"I don't know how you have the gall to mention that day!"

"When you were caught, wandering round our house, looking for something to steal?" Violet's eyes glittered with dislike.

"You know that isn't true!"

"It's what my father believes. He's heard a rumour that you made off with a couple of library books instead. . . . Is it true that you were arrested in Liverpool?"

"There was – a misunderstanding."

"Oh, naturally. . . . But I hope it taught you a lesson, all the same. Nobody likes being spied on, Miss Summerbee, I assure you." She tilted her head elegantly to one side. "I hope they didn't send you to prison for your little . . . misunderstanding. That would be fearfully disagreeable."

"Adam brought a lawyer, and he prevented it."

"Ah . . . Adam Gaunt. Of course. Dashing to the rescue." She smiled maliciously. "And guttersnipe that you are, you were far too clever to let such a stunning piece of luck slip through your fingers. In two shakes of a feather bed you were installed at Hawk's Dyke, riding round the countryside like a perfect lady with your groom behind you – all bought and paid for by your gallant rescuer. My father-in-law's mistress – and thriving on it, apparently. As I say, you look a great deal better than the last time I saw you."

This time my temper snapped.

"And you look quite different from that day in London when I interrupted your little *assignation*. But then," I added sweetly, "I'd never seen you from such an interesting angle before. I swear I'd never have recognised your backside, if you hadn't turned round to look at me."

I saw her mouth open and close again as she thought better of an angry retort. I was near enough to notice that her lips had been tinted a glossy rose-pink.

"That was an unfortunate accident," she said stiffly.

"Unfortunate for you, at any rate. You should have remembered to lock the door."

She didn't answer at first, but I saw her shift slightly in the saddle as if my directness had brought back uncomfortable memories.

267

"Fortunately, the – " she hesitated over the words, "the gentleman who was with me didn't see you. I told him a maid had opened the door for a moment."

"And that made it quite all right?"

"Well, of course! One's maids can be trusted to be discreet."

"When you're caught in bed with some fellow who isn't your husband."

"*Some fellow?*" She glanced at me, startled. "Then you don't know who the gentleman was?"

"I'm pretty sure I do know."

Violet shifted again in her saddle and folded her right hand delicately over her left, which held the reins.

"As I said, it was . . . an unfortunate accident – particularly unfortunate because of the identity of the gentleman concerned." She seemed to be choosing her words carefully. "There was a great hue and cry in the house after you ran off, of course. But when the police went to the library and then to your lodgings, no one seemed to know where you'd gone."

"But you knew I wasn't a thief." I watched her face, fascinated by her discomfort. "Why should you have been so anxious to find me, I wonder?"

"You know perfectly well why!" Violet rapped out the words. "How was I to know you wouldn't go to a newspaper with what you'd seen? *Reynolds' News* has paid plenty for stories like that in the past. You could have made yourself a great deal of money."

"Put a price on someone else's unhappiness? I'd never be so cruel."

"You're very concerned for my happiness all of a sudden." Violet stared at me suspiciously.

"Your happiness? Oh, don't worry, I didn't give *you* a moment's thought. But if the story had got out it would have hurt people who'd done nothing to deserve it. His wife – and your husband. What about Matthew in all this? Or doesn't he matter at all?"

"My husband is none of your business, Miss Summerbee."

"But Matthew wasn't with you in London, I take it. Or had you found a way of getting rid of him for the afternoon, so that you could entertain your royal lover in peace?"

"As it happens, Matthew was also staying at Eaton Square," Violet remarked stiffly.

"But not all the time, it seems."

"If you wish to be vulgar about it – no, not on that particular afternoon." She said nothing more, but simply sat there, hating me with her eyes.

"So he doesn't know what you were up to? You might as well tell me, Violet – " I saw her wince as I used her first name. "I do know that English husbands are expected to cuckold themselves for royalty and consider it an honour, but I don't believe Matthew Oliver would go along with that for a second."

"Of course he doesn't know!" she hissed scornfully. "But even if he did find out, he only has himself to blame. If I were one of his wretched steamships he might pay more attention to me! He's completely obsessed with that shipping line. He lives for nothing but Oliver's – nothing but launching bigger and faster ships than anyone else." Violet's eyes flashed her resentment. "Heaven knows what he's trying to prove – he's already built one of the largest shipping lines in the country, yet he swears he'll go on ordering new vessels, opening up trade routes and buying other men's companies until every second ship under the British flag is one of his. That's what he wants, you know – to be the biggest, and the most powerful. Nothing else will do. Sometimes I think he's quite mad."

She was breathing quickly, her cheeks flushed under their rouge. Then all at once she seemed to think she'd admitted too much – had almost begged for understanding. Immediately, she retreated into her original sullen hostility.

"I assure you, most women in my position have lovers, otherwise we'd die of boredom. Among my friends, it's quite expected."

"And what about Matthew? Does he have other women?"

Violet shrugged her elegant shoulders. "I've no idea. I don't ask."

"It's a pity you've no children, if you find life so boring."

Her eyes widened in astonishment. "Why on earth should I want children? Pregnancy ruins a woman's figure." She ran her hands with satisfaction over her narrow waist. "I watched it happen to my mother, and I don't intend to make the same mistake. After seven children, no man would have looked at her. My father had long since begun to find his pleasures elsewhere. That's the price of babies." She shuddered. "I take great care to prevent that from happening to me."

Now it was my turn to stare, quite taken aback.

"But how . . . I didn't think it was possible to be so sure."

"Oh, what a fool you are!" Violet regarded me with disdain, unable to resist showing off her cleverness. "For someone in your position, you're really remarkably naïve, my dear. Anything's possible if you can pay for it!" She tilted her chin a little. "Naturally, one keeps it *entre*

269

nous. It wouldn't do for ordinary people to stop having families. Think of all the factories! But there are doctors in London who specialise in such things. No doubt your . . . *protector* would arrange for you to see one. They're very discreet."

I hardly noticed her offensive manner in my indignation on Matthew's behalf.

"But Matthew wanted children! He said as much!"

"I dare say he does want children. I've never discussed it with him."

"Do you mean to say he doesn't know what you're doing?"

"It's really none of his business."

"But that's wicked!"

"If Matthew wanted children he should have married some little brood mare, shouldn't he? But he didn't do that. He married me, because of my father's Oliver stock." She waved a hand. "Oh, don't worry – I know exactly why our marriage came about. It was convenient to both of us. And it's still convenient. As Mrs Matthew Oliver I have a steam-yacht of my own, and houses, and carriages, and for most of the time I can amuse myself as I please. My family's Oliver shares give Matthew complete control of his company, which is what he wanted most in the world. That ought to be enough for him."

"And if it isn't?"

"Why should Matthew Oliver have everything he wants from life?"

Violet shrugged elaborately, and rested her hands once more on the pommel of her saddle.

"You're an odd creature, Katherine Summerbee. Do you know, until a few moments ago I thought you were a clever woman? I didn't like you, but I admired the way you'd hauled yourself out of the gutter by making the most of what you had – trading it for a better life as a rich man's mistress."

"You can keep your admiration. I haven't sold myself to anyone."

"But what else does a woman have to sell?" Violet's eyes were wide with candour. "The truth is that rich or poor, men have left us nothing but our bodies, and we have to get the best price we can while they still have some value."

She raised a gloved hand and gently touched her lower lip, inspecting her fingertip for any sign of rouge.

"But I've learned something this morning," she continued thoughtfully "You aren't nearly as clever as I imagined. You've let your emotions run away with your common sense – and that's a fatal weakness in a mistress. You've become fond of Adam Gaunt, haven't you? Yet he's a man like all the rest. . . . And you're even a little in love

270

with Matthew, too, in your own peculiar way. You're wasting your time there – but I'm sure you know that. Matthew's quite incapable of loving anyone but himself. It's too sad for words, really."

Her cool assurance infuriated me.

"And what if I write to Matthew, and tell him everything you've said to me today? Every syllable of it."

"You won't do any such thing, I'm quite sure of that. In fact, I don't believe you'll breathe a word of this to anyone – or you may be sure I wouldn't have told you my little secret."

Violet leaned forward, narrowing the space between our two mounts. For an extraordinary moment I thought she was about to press her glistening pink lips to mine.

"You won't say a word – because if you did, Matthew would find out what a fool I've made of him. And that would destroy him completely – as I'm sure you understand. There are men who'll survive the worst the world can say of them, but Matthew isn't one of those. He has too much pride. It's the pride of the Gaunts – Oliver or no Oliver." Violet's mouth curved in a little smile. "You see, I know you care about him – and I don't think you'd like to see him hurt."

Her confidence left me almost speechless, but at last I managed to gather my scattered wits.

"He'd divorce you at once, if he knew!"

"And lose control of his precious shipping line? Oh no, my dear – my father's Oliver shares are far too important to Matthew's plans. He'd never risk losing my father's support, you may be sure of that." Violet twitched her expensive shoulders. "So it's best for him not to know about my little adventures, don't you think?"

In the distance, I heard the rapid hoofbeats of the returning de Santos.

"What has Matthew ever done to deserve this?"

"He's just been Matthew, I suppose – poring over his cash-books and his maps of the world instead of behaving like a gentleman." Violet wriggled her fingers more firmly into her gloves. "It's his own fault, really. Or his mother's, perhaps. Did you know her father was a Liverpool clockmaker?"

By now Violet's companion had all but reached us in the lane, skidding to a flashy halt which threw the animal back on its haunches, furiously fighting the bit, and made our own horses fidget nervously in the roadway. With a flourish, de Santos held out the veil he'd brought – then seized Violet's hand as soon as she reached for it, whisked off her glove and began to kiss her outstretched fingers.

"Naughty boy!" she murmured, laughing and snatching her hand away from his luxuriant moustaches.

"Surely a man should have a reward for such a long ride, Mrs Oliver!"

"Then a man should not be impatient," Violet retorted, deftly draping the veil round her face and hat-brim and securing it with a long pin. "Don't you agree, Miss Summerbee? A gentleman should learn to make do with the little indulgences his lady allows him. That's the rule." Her eyes flashed with malice behind her veil.

"I'm sure I wouldn't know." With a swift movement, I gathered up my reins and kicked my horse into motion. "I've never had cause to consider the question. But then, I'm not a married lady. Good day to you both."

2

"Was Violet alone?" Adam wanted to know when I told him of our meeting.

"No – there was a man with her. A dark young man called de Santos who seemed all hair and riding breeches."

"Another of Alice's guests at the Abbey." Adam looked down at the carpet for a moment, tracing its pattern with the toe of his boot. "I don't suppose Matthew's staying there with Violet."

"I don't think so."

He gave a little snort of impatience. "Then he's a bigger fool than I thought. Why doesn't he forget his confounded ships for a while and get his marriage in order, if he cares anything for it at all? Though I suppose he married Violet Broadney as much for the shipping line's sake as for his own. I don't remember the word *love* being mentioned."

"Violet said as much today. She knows she means no more to Matthew than a parcel of Oliver shares. He's never pretended anything else."

"That was honest of him, at least," Adam remarked drily.

"It's a poor sort of marriage, it seems to me."

"It's the marriage he wanted. Matthew always gets what he wants – haven't you noticed?"

"Adam, that isn't true."

"Very well, then – tell me something Matthew's set his heart on, but hasn't been able to buy, or steal, or contrive in some way."

I wanted very badly to tell Adam the truth. I'd told him of finding Violet and the Prince of Wales together once I knew it would come as no surprise, but this was different. However much I wanted to lean on his shoulder and repeat all Violet's malicious secrets, I knew with absolute certainty that if there was one creature on God's earth whom Matthew would hate to know the whole squalid truth about his marriage, it was Adam, his father.

"Perhaps you're right," I conceded.

"I know my son pretty well, Kate. Matthew needed George Broadney's shares to keep his grip on Oliver's – but I suspect there was more to his marriage than that. Marriage to Violet was safe. He probably even spelled out the terms of the partnership, in his cold-blooded way. Violet can have anything material she wants – money, jewels, houses – even a steam-yacht. But Matthew won't – and can't – give her anything of himself."

"How can anyone survive on that?"

"Matthew can. And presumably Violet knew what was expected of her. In many ways, if she learned to behave with a bit more discretion, she'd be the perfect wife for Matthew – a wife who makes no emotional demands on him at all."

"I can't believe that's really what he wants."

"He's a coward, Kate. That's Matthew's trouble."

"How can you say that, Adam! After he saved that poor child from the dock in Liverpool – "

Three weeks earlier, the newspapers had been full of the story of how the Chairman of the Oliver Steam Navigation Company, on an official visit to the SS *Antares* with his fellow directors, had thrown aside hat and coat to plunge into the dirty dock water to rescue the seven-year-old son of the ship's master, Captain Travis. I'd been proud of Matthew, and I'd said so to Adam. Matthew had been nearest to hand when the boy fell from the rail, and he hadn't hesitated. Most shipping-line chairmen, I was sure, would have sent their secretaries to fetch an able seaman – and by then the child could have drowned three times over.

"I don't mean physical courage, Kate. Matthew's never lacked that, to the point of foolhardiness. I'm talking about emotional courage – the courage to commit himself, hook, line and sinker, to another person and damn the consequences."

"Just listen to you!" Fondly, I stroked his cheek. "Not three months ago, you told me you'd be happiest if we could barely tolerate one another. And now you're making a case for passion!"

"Perhaps I'm a coward, too."

"Adam . . ." I gazed at him in perplexity. "Why don't you ever say these things to Matthew? It might make all the difference to him."

"Matthew's made it quite plain he doesn't want either my advice or my interference, wouldn't you say? He's created this mess with Violet, and he'll have to sort it out by himself."

"You pretend you don't care, but you do, in spite of all the quarrelling."

"Nonsense."

"And you understand him better than anyone."

He smiled wryly. "If that's so, it's only because I've made all Matthew's mistakes myself in the past. Every one of them. I even remember having appalling rows with my own father, and being ordered out of the Abbey in a rage."

"Write to him, Adam. Ask Matthew to come back here and talk to you."

"Not yet, Kate." He took my hands in his, capturing my entire attention. "And if you've quite finished fretting about Matthew's problems, can we please talk about something else?"

3

I was still desperately sorry for Matthew – Matthew who had everything, and nothing. For the first time in my own life I knew what it was to be loved and to be able to love in return, and all through the winter of 1865–6, while Adam and I wrapped ourselves contentedly in our scandalous seclusion, Matthew's empty existence seemed correspondingly bleak.

It never occurred to me that there were others beyond the frosted lawns round Hawk's Dyke who had far more claim on my concern than Matthew. Then as winter slackened its grip on the countryside and farm work resumed its cycle, I was riding with my groom one cold afternoon among the fields to the south-east when I came upon a tiny, lonely figure plodding to and fro in a desert of turned earth, and halted to watch. For several minutes the child continued to march up and down in his cracked and muddy boots, a piece of frayed sacking tied round his shoulders and over his head as a hood, banging an old tin milk-can with a stick and singing to himself to keep up his spirits. Catching sight of me, he left off banging and ran to the gate.

"Hey, miss, can you tell us what time it is?" His round face was anxious with the responsibility of his job. "I can go home when it's four, so Farmer Drabber says, and my hands is near frozen with banging this 'ere pot."

"How long have you been in this field today?"

"Since sun-up, miss."

"What – all alone?"

"Mostly. Except for the crows."

"What's your name? And how old are you?"

"Johnny Longstock, miss." The boy seemed quite accustomed to answering the questions of adults. "My sixth birthday was just after Christmas."

"Are you one of the Longstocks from Goosefeather Drove, then?" I watched the boy nod. "Your aunt, Nell Deacon, works for us at Hawk's Dyke. I've heard all about you."

It seemed to me that the boy wore the pinched, hollow-eyed look of the chronically hungry.

"Have you had anything to eat, if you've been here all day?"

"Ma give me some bread – and a bit of cheese, seein' I was out working." He spoke the word with pride – a child eager to be grown up before his time. Then he blew on his frost-reddened fingers and stamped his mud-caked feet, a shivering little boy once more.

I consulted my watch. "It's almost half-past three, and the light's failing. I should think you could go home now, Johnny."

He looked doubtful. "Farmer said four o'clock. He'll dock me for sure if he finds I've gone afore then." He squinted across the field, where circling birds were already choosing a place to settle. "I'd best stay, and see off them crows."

"Shouldn't you be in school?"

The child considered this. "I'll be in school next week, I dare say, 'less I'm wanted again."

And wiping his running nose on the sleeve of his coat, Johnny Longstock adjusted his sacking and stumped determinedly back to his task, a small, brave figure under the grey vastness of the Norfolk sky.

It didn't take more than twenty minutes to ride to the Longstocks' home. Everyone seemed to know the tumbledown cottage at the end of a rutted and weed-infested lane off the Wellborough Road which went by the name of Goosefeather Drove. There, under a mangy covering of thatch whose tattered edge dragged almost to the ground, five children, their parents and their aged grandfather were crammed into two tiny attic rooms and an earth-floored kitchen. Behind the house, a circle of slimy boulders defined the well which was their sole source of water; a dunghill of pig manure, potato peel and weeds stood alongside it, resembling nothing so much as the filthy river water which had cost my father his life.

I'd come to ask why Johnny Longstock wasn't at school where he should have been, but as his mother ushered me apologetically into her soot-blackened kitchen it occurred to me that instead I might try to understand the nature of the miracle which brought him, scrubbed and resolute, to the school door on any morning at all.

"But he's only a child!" I protested to Adam over dinner that night. "Six years old, and left alone in that field all day with no more than a piece of bread and cheese! And it was cold enough to freeze the pools in the roadway."

"In one of Drabber's fields, did you say?"

"That was the name the child mentioned."

Adam nodded. "That's one of the Abbey farms. The Hawk's Dyke tenants know better than to employ children under ten years old, except at harvest time. I've made it a condition of their leases, though the farmers curse me for it, and the children's parents too, as often as not. It's a hard fact that many families hereabouts rely on the few shillings their children can bring in."

"Whatever they earn, it can't be enough. Have you seen how the Longstocks live? I've seen Mississippi plantation slaves in better quarters than Johnny's family."

"Nonsense!" Adam dismissed the possibility at once. "You can't possibly compare them. However poor they may be, nobody *owns* the Longstocks. The slaves were no better than livestock, Kate. In most cases they'd be slaves all their lives, and their children born into slavery with them."

"Maybe so – but the children weren't sent out to the fields at six years of age."

"They weren't taught to read and write, though, were they?" Adam reminded me. "The law forbade it, in case education made them realise the inhumanity of their lives."

"And how much do you think Johnny Longstock will learn, wasting his schooldays scaring birds in a field? How will he ever find out there's a better life than that hovel of a house, and scraping by on a few shillings a week?"

Adam didn't answer. Instead, he stared at me thoughtfully.

"This is important to you, Kate, isn't it?"

"Yes, it is. I want to help the Longstocks in some way. When the war ended in America, I thought all the injustice would end with it. But it's here, in England, in another form."

"Well, then – go ahead, do your worst." With a sigh, Adam picked up the corkscrew and reached for a second bottle of claret. "We can hardly be in more trouble at the Abbey than we are already."

Adam had given me his blessing, and that was enough. The best way to find out more, I decided, was to visit Stainham school.

The school had been built forty years earlier, Adam told me, by his father, the eighth Earl of Wellborough, and the florid stonework of the Wellborough arms above its door had ensured that the estate had continued to meet its costs, though the present Earl remained unconvinced that education did any more than turn good farm workers into dangerous Dissenters and Radicals. Yet Mr Blewitt, the schoolmaster, aimed to teach little more than "narrative monosyllables" – the lowest standard admitted by the state; it was a rare child who soared to the dizzy heights of Standard Four, and proved it by reading proudly before the Rector on his monthly governor's visit, and reciting a list of the cocoa-producing countries of the world.

Mr Edmund Blewitt, I discovered next morning, was a pale, earnest man in his mid-thirties whose neat head rose from pronouncedly sloping shoulders like the neck and cork of a hock bottle. By day he exercised a nervous despotism over the rows of benches where the business of the school was carried on, and each evening he retired to the rest of the building, which housed the parlour, kitchen, three bedrooms and various domestic offices appropriate to a schoolmaster of seventy pounds per annum.

He gazed at me with something approaching dismay as I stood at his door, and only reluctantly allowed me inside.

"Longstock?" His eyes roamed the benches, scanning the lines of heads bent industriously over spider-scratched slates. "Longstock doesn't appear to be with us today. Unless he's late, of course, though that would be unusual. He's normally a very punctual child."

"Could he be sick?"

"If he's unwell, I should have expected to be informed of it by his father or mother. Class! Your attention!" Officiously adjusting his stiff collar, Edmund Blewitt turned to face his pupils, now sitting wide-eyed and silent on the ranks of benches. "John Longstock does not seem to have honoured us with his presence today. Does anyone know what has happened to him?"

Blank looks met his gaze.

"He was quite well at school two days ago, was he not?"

"He were, too," came a voice from the back.

"Indeed he *was*," Mr Blewitt corrected automatically. "There is no need to use the subjunctive mood, since I presume we are dealing with fact and not hypothesis. *If only Longstock were well!* Or, let's say, *were* Longstock to be here today, he would learn something about the

277

production and uses of the mineral Coal since that is our first lesson this morning. Afterwards we shall proceed to the Siege of Troy."

Uneasily, he remembered my presence.

"Does that answer your question, Miss Summerbee? Is there any other way in which I can assist you?"

"I believe Johnny Longstock is scaring birds in a barley field not far from this very room."

"Ah, yes, that is perfectly possible. Regrettable, but quite possible."

"But he should be here, in school, with the others!"

"No doubt he should. But there's nothing I can do to compel him to come – or any of the children who go off in May and June to weed the wheat or cut thistles with their mothers." Mr Blewitt gazed morosely along the rows of faces. "How old is the Rudge child there? Five? Six?" He indicated a pale, undersized girl in the front row whose thin white wrists stuck out beyond the cuffs of her woollen frock with all the luminous fragility of peeled willow wands. "I saw her stone-picking last summer in a field far out along the Wellborough Road. Her older brother and sister were there, too – working with a field gang, miles from the village. Do you know what her father said when I asked if it was strictly necessary to take the youngest one away from school? He said *If she starts now it'll build her up. Next year she'll be able to lift bigger stones.* That's what he said, Miss Summerbee – his very words." Edmund Blewitt paused, and shifted his gaze to the grimy window. "And yet what can we do? Are we to fill the children's stomachs or their heads first?"

"I'd like to help in some way."

"*You?*" Edmund Blewitt stared at me in perplexity. "You want to *teach?*"

"Oh, no – I've no qualifications for that. But I thought there might be something I could do, if you'd let me. I thought I might read to the children, or look after the younger ones. I wouldn't expect to be paid for it."

"Ah . . ." Edmund Blewitt attempted to swallow his discomfort. "I'm afraid I really don't see. . . . That is to say, the problem isn't so much what you might do, as – well – you yourself, Miss Summerbee. To put it bluntly, I imagine the Rector would object quite strongly to your being here. With the children, if you catch my meaning. He's very strict on matters of morality."

"And I live openly with a man to whom I'm not married."

"Miss Summerbee! Please!" Mr Blewitt caught me by the elbow and hustled me a few paces back from the ranks of innocence on the benches. "You must understand, the somewhat *bohemian* style of your household arrangements is common knowledge throughout the village. If you were to have some sort of position here in school – well, it would seem as if the authorities were condoning your . . . alliance. Marriage is a sacred institution, Miss Summerbee. It ought not to be sneezed at."

"I'm not sneezing at anything, Mr Blewitt. But you've only just finished telling me how much these children need our help."

"That's quite true, and ordinarily, I'd be grateful. . . . If the help were offered by anyone other than yourself." The schoolmaster ran an anxious finger round the inside of his collar.

"So you're sending me away, simply because I've no ring on my finger?"

"The children's hearts are pure, Miss Summerbee."

"Mrs Longstock didn't seem to care about that. She was more interested in feeding her children than preaching to them."

"With the greatest respect – " Edmund Blewitt eyed me severely. "We can hardly leave the maintenance of the fabric of society to Mrs Longstock and her kind. We must look to men such as the Rector for an example."

"Ask Mrs Peasup where she bought her bed-sheets, then – that's all I have to say."

"I *beg* your pardon, Miss Summerbee?"

Edmund Blewitt was still staring as I banged the schoolroom door behind me.

Chapter Twenty

1

Less than a fortnight later the carrier's cart trundled up to the door of Hawk's Dyke, loaded to the roof with jars and bottles and boxes. Adam rode up just as the entire collection had been unloaded on to the gravel.

"What in Heaven's name is all this?" Swinging down from his horse, he pulled its enquiring nose from a tin-bound chest. "Cod-liver oil? Colonel White's Military Pickle? And what on earth are Woodcock's Pills?"

"I told you all about it, Adam. You agreed I could buy some things for my dispensary."

"I thought you meant a few pill-bottles and potions – not a whole pharmacist's shop, and half a grocery too!" With a sweep of his arm he indicated the whole pungent, clinking, rustling pile lying at our front door. "The smell of some of this is enough to cure anything." He poked among the jars for a moment. "Tincture of Arnica . . . Quinine Wine. . . . Are you sure you know what to do with this witches' brew?"

"Everyone knows what to do with carbolic soap, at least. I just want to help out with a few home remedies and other things these people can't afford for themselves. Have you seen the dreadful sores on the children's faces? The poor little creatures are scarred for life if they don't heal properly. But look, I've bought oxide of zinc, and aconite liniment – and sulphur for scabies baths. . . . And you won't mind if I take them a little brandy, will you, when there's scarlet fever in the house – "

"Not if I thought the patient would see it. And not my best cognac, Kate, please."

Throwing the reins of his horse to the waiting groom, Adam retreated philosophically to the library, while I set about turning an empty larder next to the fish pantry into a store-room for my treasures. Let the schoolmaster and the Rector look after the children's innocent souls, I thought to myself as I arranged my jars on a shelf: I shall care for their sad little bodies, and I doubt very much if their parents will turn me away.

None of them did. I didn't expect to be rejected by the cottagers on Adam's land, of course, though by and large they needed me less: their houses were in better repair than many. It was when I ventured further afield to visit the Longstocks and their neighbours in the Abbey cottages that I knew I was treading on dangerous ground. Strictly speaking, it was none of my business how these people lived. I wasn't appointed by the parish or the Poor Law Commissioners – and I certainly didn't come with the blessing of the Earl of Wellborough. Yet I was determined to do what I could for the children until someone stopped me. I took them turpentine liniment for their chilblains and Peru Balsam for their racking coughs, though they much preferred to find jam and pickles in my basket, or sultanas, or one of Mrs Rawley's plum cakes. My own childhood had hardly been one of plenty, goodness knows, but it tugged at my heartstrings to see the children's eyes grow round at the sight of such simple treats.

"I met Charles today in Stainham," Adam observed casually one evening in May as we sat together on the sofa in front of the parlour fire. I could tell from his very casualness and the way he'd waited until I was curled comfortably in his arms that he had something awkward to tell me.

"Charles asked me what the devil you thought you were up to, wandering around, doctoring his labourers and their children. He can't understand why you don't leave it all to the Poor Law people."

"But the Poor Law doctor knows less than I do!" Indignantly, I raised my head from his shoulder. "*Tonic wine* – that's his remedy for everything from tuberculosis to a sprained ankle." When Adam didn't answer at once, I added more softly, "Am I making a great deal of trouble for you? I don't mean to. It's just that half the children's illnesses are caused by dirt and the wretched food they eat – and for want of little things I can easily give them. And I do buy them new boots occasionally," I finished guiltily.

Adam dismissed my confession with a smile.

"You can buy boots for every soul in the county, as far as I'm concerned. It's how you go about it that worries Charles. He's concerned about some fellow called Slade, a smallholder over Stainham way, who's been stirring up the labourers to demand higher wages for their work. According to Charles, John Slade spends every Sunday telling his flock that Adam and Eve were created to cultivate the earth, not to play croquet and laze about in carriages."

"Well, then – I guess I agree with Mr Slade."

"I thought you might, you horrible republican." Adam flicked the end of my nose with a lazy fingertip. "Even the labourers still regard Slade as a bit of an oddity, though I dare say it wouldn't take much to bring them behind him. But now Charles has heard you've been telling the cottagers their children have a God-given right to proper food and schooling, and he reckons you're playing into John Slade's hands."

"All I've said is that if the slaves of America can be made free, their own turn will come, and things will get better. Don't you believe that?"

"Oh, things will change – but please God, not by riots and uprisings. This fellow Slade's a firebrand, Kate. Before long, he'll have the labourers and the farmers at one another's throats – and the poorest people will be the ones to suffer most."

"Do you think I'll start a riot with carbolic soap?"

"No, I don't believe you will. That's why I'm not even going to try to keep you at home as Charles demanded."

"Well, I'm blowed! The gall of the man! I've never set out to make trouble – honestly, Adam – but I can't help saying what I think. If your precious nephew wants me to stay home all day, then he can darn well take these round the cottages for me." I dug in my pocket and pulled out my hand with a flourish. "Reading glasses!"

I was amazingly pleased with my new idea. I'd had a whole box sent down from London – dozens of pairs of spectacles with round lenses and spidery steel frames. Grandmother Rudge had planted the notion in my head one day as she sat by her fire, and with tears rolling down her cheeks told me how even the solace of her bible was denied her by the weakness of her eyes. She was sad, but not resentful. Like her rheumatism and her deafness, she'd expected poor eyesight as the portion of old age; yet it was hard to sacrifice her bible.

The remedy seemed so obvious that I sent off at once for the spectacles . . . and within the week wished profoundly I'd never thought of them at all.

2

It was only when the chiming clock in the hall struck midday that I realised I hadn't seen Adam all morning.

"He's in the library, ma'am, as far as I know," Nell informed me, passing on her way to the dining-room with a folded tablecloth over her arm. "I haven't seen him myself, mind, but I'm sure he's there."

Adam was sitting at the great, knob-legged table in the centre of the room, his back to the door, staring out of the windows towards the lawns and the whispering trees beyond. It wasn't like him to relinquish the fireside, and I assumed he'd been studying some of the ancient books which lay open before him – mean little volumes of crabbed print whose pages crackled like dead leaves as they were turned.

He didn't look round as I came into the room, and something about the slope of his shoulders and the way he sat skewed in the chair filled me at once with an unaccountable foreboding. Quickly, I crossed the floor, slipped my arms round his neck and kissed the hollow by his ear. He leaned back wearily, his head against my cheek, and for the first time I noticed that trapped under the hand which lay across one of the yellowing volumes was a pair of my steel-framed spectacles.

"You must have found something fascinating in your books, my love. I haven't seen you all morning."

"I haven't been reading." His voice was strangely flat. "I've been sitting here, thinking."

"Then come out with me for a walk. The east wind will soon blow the cobwebs away."

"Cobwebs?" He leaned away from me over the book-strewn table. "Well, God knows, I'm old enough for cobwebs."

"Adam . . ." I tried to hug him again, but he'd have none of it. "What's the matter? What stupid book has put this nonsense into your head?"

I leaned over his shoulder, but he evaded me again, furiously pushing the nearest volume towards me so that I could examine its uneven print.

"That's what I've been reading – or trying to read." He snatched up the book and angrily riffled through its pages, sending a cloud of dust-motes into the sunshine. "Except that I can't read it. Not any more. Not this one – nor the next – nor any of them, without these bloody glasses of yours! I need a crutch for my eyes, like one of your doddering cottagers, or it's just so much waste paper."

I gaped at him for a moment.

"Is that all?" I was suddenly light-headed with relief. "You're making all this fuss because you need spectacles to read small print? Oh, Adam – really! Edmund Blewitt the schoolmaster wears spectacles all the time, and he's only a little over thirty."

Adam swung round in his chair to survey me.

"Kate – Edmund Blewitt was born short-sighted. My sight is failing because I'm getting old."

He stared at me relentlessly. "I warned you this would happen. Little by little, in spite of everything, flesh and blood betrays us. Today my eyes are failing – tomorrow my hearing, perhaps – and then . . . what next? My wits? Will you come in one day and find me blank-eyed in the dark, mumbling about the past as if the dead were still with us? Will you have to tie me into a chair to stop me falling to the floor? Will you bring me pots of jam and your damned carbolic soap, and try to pretend I'm talking sense?"

He gripped me by the wrists, staring into my face. "Or will you have done as I told you, and taken to your heels long before that?"

"I won't leave you, Adam." I gazed back defiantly. "You can't force me to go."

"You must go. Don't you understand? I don't want you here, watching me fall apart."

"It won't happen like that."

"Dammit, don't parrot that nonsense at me! You don't believe it, any more than I do."

Then all at once his anger seemed to subside, and his grip on my wrists became gentler.

"It's all so much nonsense. . . . Though, Heaven knows, I wanted to believe it. For a while I really thought you could hold back time for me. You were so young – there was never any *Do you remember* . . . to weigh me down – only the here and now. But it hasn't worked, Kate. At the end of the day I'm left with nothing but my past, and I've no claim on your future."

"But none of that has ever mattered! Not until now, at any rate – not until you looked at those stupid books."

He shook his head. "It didn't happen overnight, you know. I haven't taken these books down from the shelf for months – not since the moment I found I could hardly follow the lines, and pretended I needed a stronger lamp to read by. I knew perfectly well a thousand lamps would make no difference, but it wasn't until you brought these into the house – " he dangled the spectacles by one leg " – that I made myself face the truth. My sight's failing, and I'm getting old."

He tossed the glasses with finality on to the table, where they crouched like a hideous steel insect, waiting to devour my happiness.

I leaned forward then, and kissed him with calculated slowness – dawdling over it, lingering, putting all of my love and my need of him into the pressure of my lips – and went on kissing him until at last I felt his arms fasten about me once more. For several minutes he held me there as if I were the very life he hated to lose, piece by piece, to the robber Time.

"I'd give you my eyes, if I could," I whispered as he released me. "I could see you just as clearly without them." I touched him gently on the cheek, and he caught my hand, kissing my fingertips. "Now will you come for a walk?"

"In a few moments, perhaps. Go down by the farm, and I'll catch you up."

He watched from his chair until the library door closed behind me.

Seconds later, I heard a tinkling clatter as the spectacles were hurled to destruction in the stone hearth.

3

I never saw Adam in reading glasses – not once – and I suppose the antiquarian books remained on the shelf, unread, from that day. Yet it hardly mattered; he carried great tracts of his beloved library in his head, and if his eyes had begun to betray him, his memory was as sharp as ever.

Perhaps if we'd conceived a child – an enduring part of each of us and a claim on the future – he'd have forgotten his own years in the baby's craving for life. But it never happened. I dare say we took our loving too lightly: we weren't decent, in my father's sense of the word, making love for loving's sake, without guilt and with the lamp lit. Perhaps we laughed too much, and the God who sends babies thought we'd been rewarded enough already.

One warm summer night when Adam had stayed up late over the estate accounts, I was roused long after midnight by the spatter of gravel on the window-panes and sat up with a start, reaching beside me to an empty space in the bed.

The gravel spattered once more, and I slid out from under the covers, threw a dressing-gown over my nakedness, and pattered, barefoot, to the window. Adam was waiting below on his horse, his face turned up towards me, mischief in his eyes, and the pale shape of his shirt just visible in the warm of the night.

"Your last riding lesson," he called softly. "Come down."

"Give me a moment to dress, then."

"No – come down just as you are."

"I'm almost naked!"

"That doesn't matter. There's no one to see you."

"And where's my horse?" I peered out into the night.

"We'll ride double."

"But – "

"Come on, Kate. I won't wait for ever."

Still barefoot, I slipped downstairs and let myself quietly out of the house. Adam had moved away to the darkness of the lawn, horse and man hardly more than a black outline against the shadowy trees. As I crossed the grass towards him he took his left foot from the stirrup and reached down for me.

"No – your right foot. Like that – "

Even as I turned, he pulled me up to the saddle, astride but facing

285

him, held close against his body while the horse moved off towards the inky shade of the oaks. I leaned against him, relishing the warmth of his skin and the gentle motion of the animal's step between my thighs, guessing that our ride would end in the cool grass of the oak grove.

But we didn't dismount. Instead, his hand slid inside my thin muslin dressing-gown, firm and compelling, and I realised for the first time what he had in mind.

"Oh, Adam – this isn't possible. . . . Not on a horse!"

"Why not?" His voice was no more than a murmur, his lips at my ear. "The Tartars were experts at it. And I'm descended from a long line of Tartars."

"We'll fall off, surely . . ."

"We won't fall. And even if we do, you won't care. Trust me, little cat. Put your legs over mine."

In the absence of directions, the horse had halted among the oaks. After a moment or two I felt Adam slide his hands round my backside and lift me towards him, lift and penetrate me. The horse walked on, its steady amble rocking me gently, transferring itself to my very core in a slow, irresistible rhythm.

"What you said was true," he murmured into my hair. "For the things that really matter in life, you don't need spectacles. Only a good . . . English . . . saddle."

4

Violet had been right. Country life did suit me.

I loved the wholeness of those days, the sense of existing among the roots of things, where birth and life and death were no more than stops along the wheel's rim, never more than a turn apart.

The wheel rolled steadily through '67 and '68 as the months stole past, slipping almost unnoticed through our fingers while our eyes were fixed upon the greater rhythm of the seasons. Our calendar was all around us: we knew winter was approaching when the teal returned to the ponds and the flooded gravel pits, while the first days of spring brought the bleary toads creeping from under the flagstones of the garden. Summer meant the flicker of dragonflies among the red rattle in the ditches, and then the hurly-burly of harvest led into the mellow peace of autumn, when the sloes were ripe for gin and the blackberries for hedgerow preserves.

Odd events stand out in my memory from that time, but in no particular sequence, like beads from a broken string. I remember one of Adam's foals dying of eating water-hemlock in the marsh meadow,

286

when a grown horse would have known better – and Charles, Earl of Wellborough, almost causing a riot by closing up rights of way over his land to prevent poaching. . . . And in 1867 the government at last recognising the iniquities of the field-gang system, but making no more than a half-hearted attempt to remedy it.

Johnny Longstock – by then seven years old – could still legally scare birds in Farmer Drabber's fields; in another year he could be herded out in a field gang to work as long as daylight lasted, and to be kicked and cuffed if he failed to do his share. Nothing was done to provide a school place for each child, or to encourage parents to send their children every day. The new law was no more than a tiny improvement, and I still went out with my camphor liniment to ease the children's sores, and cake and preserves to raise their spirits.

But suffering wasn't confined to the cottages of the poor. In the autumn of 1868 word reached us at Hawk's Dyke that, in a careless moment, Louise Oliver had brushed one of the huge fires at the Abbey with the hem of her crinoline, and had instantly been enveloped in flames. If it hadn't been for the prompt action of the men who'd rolled her without ceremony in the Aubusson carpet, she might easily have died. As it was, her hands and body were badly burned; the pain had been considerable, and for several hours she'd been kept almost insensible with opium.

We waited helplessly while the critical nine days passed, and the doctors were at last able to pronounce her out of danger from shock. Then, a week later, a letter arrived for me, dictated by Louise but written for her by the dowager Henrietta. It had clearly been the product of a great deal of thought, and I wondered how much Henrietta had had to do with its contents.

"My dear Katherine," the letter began, "I shall not blame you, if you are offended by my writing to you after so long a silence. Yet I remember your nature as too generous to condemn a friend who sincerely regrets a fault. Do not throw down this page, I beg of you, but read my words instead.

"Through my own carelessness, for more than two weeks now I have been confined to bed in a wretched state. Yet even this existence is precious to me, since without the quick action of Charles and Mr Theodore Maynefield, I would certainly lie in the churchyard next to dear Mamma.

"And if I had perished, there would only have been one epitaph for me – that during my short life I was too foolish to know my friends from my foes.

"You never set out to injure me, Katherine, and yet I have treated you shamefully. I listened to the bad opinions of others instead of consulting my own heart, which remembered you as a true friend and consolation when poor Mamma died so suddenly.

"You had every right to expect my affection when you returned to Hawk's Dyke, but instead I thoughtlessly condemned you. Now, in my own extremity, I remember your honesty and loyalty with the humblest regret, and wish nothing more anxiously than to be your friend once more.

"Will you forgive my stupid pride, and call on me here? I am very much in need of your cheerfulness and good counsel, and though I fear you'll find me poor company these days, I beg you to come none the less.

"Your unhappy friend,
Louise.
"Postscriptum. Alice knows I have written to you."

The fire which had devoured her crinoline had tempered Louise's pride. *And not before time*, I thought – but only for a second, when I remembered my own hurt feelings, bruised by her first humiliating little note. Of course I would go to the blood-red Abbey and make my peace with Louise.

It was even a victory of sorts, since her sister the Countess was obliged to allow my disreputable presence in her house. I couldn't help wondering, as Alice led me upstairs with chill formality, behind which of the tall panelled doors the late Earl had ridden his housemaid into eternity. . . . But of course, it took a mistress to appreciate the irony of that.

"Oh, Katherine – thank you for coming!" Tears brimmed in Louise's eyes as she lay propped on lacy pillows, bandaged to the shape of a clothes-peg doll under her nightgown. "I thought you might not care to see me again, after the way I've treated you . . ." She raised her pathetic, bound hands towards me, guiding me to a chair by her bed.

"I always hoped I might meet you somewhere by chance. Riding perhaps, or driving in Alice's carriage."

She was watching my face – searching, I knew, for a reaction to her altered appearance. But Alice had already warned me of the patch of ragged flesh, like the imprint of a flat-iron, where Louise's brow and cheek had been scorched by the flames and her hair frizzled at her temple. They hadn't allowed her a mirror, and as Alice had begged, I did my best to pretend that Louise's fine, pale features were as perfect as ever.

288

"It's bad, isn't it?"

"What's bad, for any sake?"

"My face. Here, where it hurts." She gestured towards the place, the tips of her fingers pinkish-purple as newborn mice against the swollen whiteness of her bandages.

I made a great show of examining her face.

"It doesn't look so awful to me. You'll be right as rain in no time."

"That's what they all say. Dr Clement too."

"Then it's probably true, don't you think?"

"I don't know." Once more, her fingertips moved to explore the raw mark, her courage failing her at the last moment. "Oh, Katherine, I couldn't bear to be scarred! I couldn't bear to be a freak, with everyone staring and pointing at me! I know there'll be marks on my body for the rest of my life – " She picked ineffectually at her nightgown. "But at least those won't show. I couldn't bear to be ugly as well! I wish I'd died, sooner than be ugly!"

"And I thought from your letter you'd turned philosopher," I teased her quickly. "What's become of all these profound thoughts on the meaning of life? I can't believe you think women were only created to sit for handsome portraits."

She smiled at last – the old Louise, despite the frightfulness of her injuries.

"I've done a great deal of thinking, it's true. Alice reads to me sometimes, and the old Countess comes to talk about the days when she was a girl, but mostly I lie here and think. The nurses give me something to take the pain away so that I can sleep, but it doesn't always work."

"Poor Louise, you've had a rotten time of it."

"And all because of a silly dress! That's one of the things I've thought most about, you know. I nearly died – and all for an extra few yards of crinoline. Such a stupid reason to die."

"But not uncommon. The papers are full of it."

"*Fashion's slave*. . . . Do you remember? That's what Adam used to call me."

"You were very nearly fashion's victim."

"Yes." She looked down, her glance falling on her bandaged hands. Once more she held them up. "And now I'll never be fashionable again."

"What nonsense! Of course you will! I know you too well, Louise. As soon as you're on your feet again, you'll be off to your dressmaker – "

"No." She shook her ravaged head. "How can I ever wear a ball dress again? And in any case, what would be the point of it?"

"To go to a ball, I imagine."

"But look at my hands, Katherine! They were burned raw before the bandages were put on. The nurses try to keep me from seeing, when they change the dressing, but I look anyway. Even after they're healed, I'll have claws like a chicken. And there'll be scars on my body, too. What young man will want to dance with a woman like that – let alone marry her?"

She gazed up at me, imploring contradiction. "But I can live with all that, honestly I can – just as long as my face heals as it was before." Tears came into her eyes again. "I can hide my hands with gloves, but I couldn't bear to be stared at."

"Oh, I don't know. It isn't so bad," I said pointedly. "You'd be amazed how soon you get used to being stared at."

"Oh, Katherine, I'm so sorry. . . . It can't be easy for you – and I've talked of nothing but myself. Have people been very rude?"

"Some of the things they said upset me at first. But now I hardly notice. I never wanted the Rector's wife to call on us, anyway."

"Well, *I* shall call, depend upon it. I'll dash up to your door in Alice's biggest carriage, just as soon as I'm better."

"Your stepfather would like that," I reminded her softly. "He doesn't say much, but I know it would make him happy to see you."

Louise gazed at me, sudden doubt furrowing her brow. In the first flush of her enthusiasm, she'd forgotten that Hawk's Dyke was Adam's house, and that Adam was half of my life.

She opened her mouth to speak, closed it, then began again in a rush of words.

"I've often wondered. . . . That's to say . . . sometimes, in the middle of the night, when I can't sleep, I think about the two of you. . . . And about Mamma. And I wonder if she'd mind. All she wanted was for him to be happy, you know . . . and I could never understand why it should matter to her so much." Louise turned her eyes towards a miniature of her mother which stood on the mirrorless dressing-table. "Is he happy with you, Katherine?"

"I believe he is. Happier than he would be without me, at least."

"I told Alice you must love him, or you wouldn't stay at Hawk's Dyke. That's true, Katherine, isn't it? Though you don't have to answer my questions if you don't want to," she added hastily.

"I do love him, Louise – and I'm happy to answer any question you care to ask. I'm not ashamed of the life I lead."

"Mamma always said we should do what seemed right to us, provided it didn't harm anyone else," said Louise thoughtfully. "I think she would have wished you well."

"I haven't taken your mother's place, you know. I'll never be Mrs Gaunt."

"Is that why he hasn't married you? Because of Mamma?"

"Not entirely – but partly, perhaps."

Louise retreated into her own thoughts for a moment, and gradually her face became filled with despair.

"I should have liked to be married, one day."

"So you will."

"No. Not now."

I tried valiantly to lift her spirits. "What about Freddie Broadney? He was very sweet on you, I seem to remember."

"Freddie? Oh, he doesn't take any notice of me these days. I hardly spoke to him all Season – and besides, he's been involved in a fearful scandal. Breach of promise or something. Sir George is talking about buying Freddie a commission in a cavalry regiment, and making sure he's sent overseas."

"But there is someone you're fond of, isn't there, Louise?"

She nodded, and then sighed.

"How do you know when you really love someone, Katherine? I mean, love them enough to ignore what people say, and never regret it?"

"I wish I had an answer for you, my dear. But if there's one thing I've learned, it's that there are many, many different kinds of love. All I can say is that you *know* – deep inside, somehow you know."

Louise looked despairing.

"He was ordered to India with his regiment, just before my accident, so he doesn't even know about it. I'll have to write to him, Katherine – but I dread it so! How can I tell him what's happened to me?" This time the tears spilled over to course down the patchwork of her skin. "I'll lose him, I know. And I love him so much. Love changes everything, doesn't it?"

"Yes, it does."

I wished I could think of something wise to say. Poor Louise – she was genuinely heartbroken. Gone was the bubbling excitement of her passion for Freddie Broadney: this was a deeper, more wounding love altogether.

Suddenly, she stopped sniffing, and glanced up at me.

"Do you think it's possible my stepfather felt like this when Mamma died? You know him, and I never did. Did he really miss her, Katherine? I didn't believe he cared at all, but sometimes now I wonder . . ."

"Louise, I think he almost went out of his mind when your mother died. He couldn't bear to think of her dead – and to see the whole house filled with black and everyone in mourning made it a hundred times worse."

Tearfully, she considered this.

"If Robert was killed by those awful Afghans – I don't know what I'd do."

"Is that his name? Robert?"

"Captain Robert Nugent, 9th Hussars. Oh, Katherine, you should see him in his uniform – he's quite glorious! He'll be a major in no time, I'm sure, but he's so fearless, I worry for his life . . ."

"Louise . . ." I interrupted, "will you see your stepfather, if I bring him here? Please. Only for a few minutes, if you like."

"I don't know . . ." Louise sniffed doubtfully, and mopped her tears with her bandaged palms, but I was determined to persist, if only for her own sake. Somehow, I was sure Adam could say all the things I wasn't brave enough or wise enough to tell her.

"Please, Louise. If you really want us to be friends again, then you'll have to make up your quarrel with Adam. Not only because I love him, but because he's concerned about you. Let me tell him he's welcome to call."

"I don't know. . . . You'd have to stay with me while he was here. I don't want to be left alone with him."

"Whatever you like. As long as you agree to see him."

She fell silent for a moment, contemplating the miniature of her mother nearby.

"Very well. Tell him I'd like him to call."

5

"That poor child!" was Adam's immediate reaction to my account of Louise's misfortune. "Do you mean to say no one's dared to tell her she'll be marked for life by her burns? And what do they imagine she'll do when she finds out?"

"I can't bear to think. As it is, she's mortally afraid of being turned into a side-show for passers-by. But Adam – " I touched his hand in warning. "Louise isn't a child any more. She's a young woman, and she's Rachel's daughter, with a good deal of her mother's spirit in her. Please be careful what you say."

"I can't lie to her, Kate. If that's what you're asking, I'd better stay away from the Abbey."

"I'm not asking you to lie – only to remember how much you loved her mother. Will you treat her gently, Adam?"

He pulled me into his arms. "I'll do it because I love *you*, Kate. But don't leave me alone with her, please. As long as you stay in the room, there won't be any difficulty."

In the event, I left them together. I waited until the first awkwardness was over, and then I quietly left the room. There was a mending of old wounds to be done, and it was no place for me.

Only Adam and Louise and the four walls know how it was managed, but when I went back into the room I found Louise red-eyed in her stepfather's arms, and lying beside her the small silver mirror from the table by my bed. Adam must have brought it with him in his pocket.

"Louise and I have made a bargain," he informed me quietly over Louise's frizzled brow. "Louise has sworn to get better as quickly as she can, and I've promised that nothing in her life has changed. She's exactly the same person as she was before her accident, and no one will notice otherwise. That's so, isn't it, Louise?"

"Perhaps," murmured Louise indistinctly.

"It's true, Louise. Believe me."

"I want to. I want to, so much."

I would have given a great deal to understand how Adam had accomplished that miracle. Perhaps he'd been right when he said there was magic within each one of us: all I know is that he possessed an uncanny power of his own – call it spirit, or soul, or what you will – which was strong enough to move mountains for good or for ill. If anything could convince Louise that her life had not been made worthless by disfigurement, I knew it was Adam's determination that it should be so.

By the following spring, Louise was well enough to ride again, gloves and a veil hiding her most obvious scars. She'd begun to spend so much of her time at Hawk's Dyke that her doctor – not Dr Clement, but his young assistant, Dr Tower – took to calling on her when she was with us, often arriving without warning and staying to take tea with us in the parlour or on fine days in the garden.

The flat-iron burn on Louise's face had paled gradually from purple to faint mauve, ruching her fine skin like the thinnest silk.

"Paint it, if it worries you!" Adam instructed her one afternoon. "Paint it – powder it – isn't that what you young women do anyway? You'll never see it under half an inch of bismuth paste, I dare say."

"I do not paint!" exclaimed Louise hotly, glancing sideways at Dr Tower and knowing full well that she did.

293

James Tower, who knew it too, grinned at her over the tea-table, and I saw Louise smile shyly back as she reached out her scarred fingers for his cup.

Now I began to understand why Dr Tower called at Hawk's Dyke instead of visiting his patient at the Abbey, where a mere physician – let alone a physician's junior partner – ranked somewhere below the Rector but marginally above the wine merchant and the Earl's racing trainer. And even the Rector wasn't always admitted to the drawing-room.

And I liked Dr Tower. Dr Clement claimed he'd been a brilliant student, but I was amused to see he'd long since learned to hide his cleverness behind the aloof professional manner his patients expected. It was only round the tea-table at Hawk's Dyke, in our uncritical company, that the real James Tower emerged in flashes of wicked humour which soon had Louise's eyes sparkling once more.

Now that her own problems were mending, I returned to my plan of persuading Louise to mediate between Matthew and his father. To my surprise, I found her strangely reluctant to become involved.

"It's so awkward," she said, tugging at her fingers. "If I write to him, Matthew's sure to ask questions I don't know how to answer."

"What sort of questions, Louise?"

"Well . . . about Violet . . . and other things."

"Go on."

"I can't say any more, Katherine. I promised Alice. Please don't ask."

I didn't need to ask, though I couldn't see why Violet's mischief should hinder my plans. But before I could plead my case any further, Louise arrived from the Abbey one fine June day in a great lather of news.

"Have you heard?" she demanded. "Has he written about it to Adam?"

"Has *who* written, for goodness' sake? Sit down, Louise, and at least take your hat off." I patted the rattan chair on the grass next to mine.

"Has Matthew written to his father? Has anyone told you the news?"

"We'd be the last people to hear anything from Matthew! You know that, Louise, as well as anyone," I added reproachfully.

"Don't worry – he hasn't written to me, either. I only heard it from Alice, who had a letter from Violet, asking if she could visit for a while . . ." Louise waved her hands in the air to dispel the confusion. "There's been a fearful quarrel, apparently. A real battle, with Violet in hysterics and Matthew all tight-lipped and quiet, the way he goes when he's absolutely furious about something. Violet's in an awful state – though I do think it serves her right, the wicked creature. Do you remember, I said there were things I couldn't tell you because I'd made a promise to Alice? Well, now, of course, since Matthew knows, and you're as good as family . . ."

In the shade of the old walnut tree, Louise drew her chair closer to mine.

"Violet's been having an affair," she announced momentously. "Well actually, I think she's had more than one – but the most important of all is the one Matthew's found out about. And it isn't as if she's taken up with any Tom, Dick or Harry, either." She paused for effect. "Violet's been seeing the Prince of Wales! What do you think of that?" She paused triumphantly, and then pouted in disappointment. "Well, I must say, you don't seem very surprised."

"The only thing that surprises me is how long it's taken Matthew to find out."

"You *knew*? You knew what was going on, and you didn't tell me? What kind of behaviour is that between friends?"

"Adam's known for a while," I admitted. "Nothing ever happens at the Abbey without Henrietta getting to hear of it and coming to tell us at Hawk's Dyke. And I'm sure Alice must have known about this Prince of Wales business from the start. She and Violet are as thick as thieves."

"Nobody tells me anything!" wailed Louise. "It isn't fair!" Then her excitement got the better of her pique, and she added, "Just fancy – the Prince of Wales!"

"Louise, Prince Edward has had affairs with most of the good-looking women in London, it seems to me. I'd have been more surprised if he'd missed Violet off his list."

"Well, I think it's too bad of her. Poor Matthew! Alice says he's fearfully angry. He's talking about divorcing Violet if he can find witnesses to the affair, but I can't believe he'd really go through with it. A divorce in the family would be too dreadful for words."

"A divorce in which family?" Adam sauntered across from the stables in time to hear Louise's final words. "Not the Gaunts, surely! You *do* surprise me."

"Matthew will be lucky to find a lawyer to take the case," he concluded after Louise had finished her tale for the second time. "I can't imagine any comfortably established barrister being anxious to drag the Prince of Wales into the divorce court as co-respondent. It'd be the finish of his career if he did. And who's going to go into the witness box on Matthew's behalf? If he thinks the Broadneys' London servants will tell tales on their employer's daughter, he's making a grave mistake. *See nothing, hear nothing* – but above all, *say nothing*. It's the first rule of service."

"Then what will Matthew do?"

"Find evidence of another of Violet's adventures, I suppose. Or patch things up with her in some way. Don't forget George Broadney's Oliver shares. Turning a blind eye to his wife's misdeeds may be the price Matthew's expected to pay for them."

"Alice has refused to let Violet stay at the Abbey," Louise volunteered. "Violet's been her best friend for years, but as Alice says, it's quite different now that Matthew *knows*. Violet's a friend, but Matthew is family – and it would hardly be decent."

Adam gave a snort of disgust. "Oh, let's keep it decent, at all costs."

"Why don't you write to Matthew, Adam?" Eagerly, I seized the opportunity. "He might be glad of a chance to talk over his troubles."

"Then he can write to me, can't he?"

"But this could be just the time when he needs your help most. And you did say you'd made exactly the same mistakes when you were his age."

Adam shook his head grimly. "Not this one, Kate. Not this one."

6

No letter came, and Adam refused to write one of his own. I could do nothing: I had no right to interfere, and I might easily make matters worse. Besides, my own feelings were hardly clear in my mind. Sometimes, when I remembered how like Adam he was, my heart ached for Matthew's wounded pride. Yet he'd gone his own selfish way to disaster; as Violet had no doubt told him, Matthew had simply reaped what he had sown.

We heard no more news of the Olivers for the rest of the summer, and it seemed as if Matthew had thought better of divorcing his wife. After Alice's frosty rebuff, Violet Oliver kept her own counsel, and no one knew the terms of the peace which appeared to have descended on the Oliver household.

Louise had decided to stay in the country that summer, spending most of her time at Hawk's Dyke and sometimes coming with me on my rounds of the cottages. John Slade, the preacher-farmer, had opened a Primitive Methodist Sunday School in his Stainham chapel, and at last some of the children who'd never found their way to Edmund Blewitt's hard benches discovered the mysteries of simple spelling and arithmetic.

The Rector, it was said, took a dim view of all the "testifying" and speaking in tongues – dimmer even than the Earl of Wellborough, who thoroughly resented the nest of subversion in his rural peace. What, after all, was a fellow to make of a sect which allowed women to preach to its congregations, and saw poverty itself as a state of grace?

No one, however, rushed to bury poor Aaron Dann, who was found under a sallow bush one stormy night in December, black, gnarled and stone dead, his webbed toes bound in rags and every stitch of clothing sodden with rainwater.

There was no question of a grave in consecrated ground: too many people believed an old tale that he'd murdered his wife in Sourwell Fen and left his small son to perish in the marsh. Eventually, Adam had a grave dug for him not far from the grassy mound which was all that remained of his horn-windowed hut, on a hummock in the farmland which had once been an island in the ancient mere.

"Where do you think he went after the fen was drained?" I asked Adam curiously when he returned from the summary burial. "No one seems to have seen him for years."

Adam shrugged off his heavy overcoat and made for the parlour fire.

"Who knows where he lived? I suppose he dug a den for himself somewhere, old fox that he was. He ran off from the workhouse after two days of prayers and carbolic baths, and no one bothered to go after him." Adam rubbed his hands before the flames. "And yet he wasn't such a bad-looking creature when I knew him first.

"I was only a boy then, but Aaron Dann was already working with his father as an eel-fisher. The old man used to shout at us and throw sticks or clods of earth if we went near his traps, and Aaron would set off after us like a lurcher slipped from its lead. He was fast on his feet, too, in those days."

I found it odd to think of Aaron Dann as anything but an ugly, secretive old man who'd once convinced me my life lay under a curse –yet I supposed even secretive old men must have their self-respect.

"It was a miserable way to die," I conceded. "He frightened me badly in the fen that day, but I wouldn't wish such an end for anyone."

"I can't imagine Aaron Dann dying in a workhouse bed. I'm sure it's how he expected to go – in a ditch, like an animal." Adam stared thoughtfully into the fire. "Kate – " he said after a moment, "there's something I've been meaning to tell you . . . I've deposited four thousand pounds in your name in the Merchants' Bank in Lynn. You're the only person who can draw on the money now, so you can be entirely independent of me whenever you wish. Whether I live or die, that money's there for you when you need it."

Before I could speak, he raised a hand to prevent it. "No – don't tell me you wouldn't dream of touching a penny of it. As long as you know it's there, that's enough. And now, let's talk about something else."

I hated the feeling that sometimes hung in the air between us – the feeling of time running out, of an urgent need to make the most of each second which remained. Yet as the eighteen-sixties drew to a close and Adam's sixties advanced along with them, it was almost possible to believe that somehow we'd cheated the years and beaten back withering age, baffled, by our defiance.

Then every so often I'd notice a tiny change in him – a thumb curled stiffly across the palm of the hand; a movement of head and shoulders as one – nothing momentous in itself, but enough to make my heart lurch as I realised the enemy was still at our gates, laying siege to all I held dear. Adam rode as often and as far as ever, through wind and rain and blizzard – but I didn't dare protest as I might have done to a younger man. Half-life was no good to him. It must be all or nothing; it was the very thing I loved him for – how could I ask him to change?

Then one May morning in 1870 I found him in the stable yard, clinging to a stall door while he caught his breath.

"Adam – whatever's the matter?"

"Nothing." His voice was no more than a gasp.

"Are you in pain? Your face is white as a sheet."

"I'm perfectly well, dammit."

"There must be something – "

"Leave me alone," he snapped, and waving me furiously aside, walked off with an enormous effort towards the harness room.

My first thought was to urge him to call Dr Clement, but as soon as I'd considered the idea, I dismissed it. If Adam was ill, he knew it perfectly well; if he wanted to consult a doctor, he'd do it himself, and if he'd decided against it, nothing would shift him. Nevertheless, I was alarmed, and Adam's attempts to hide his pain from me over the next few weeks only made me more worried still. "Old age – " he'd gasp as the breathlessness subsided, and wave away any suggestion of calling a doctor. But I couldn't bear to watch helplessly, and one afternoon I tackled James Tower on the subject as I accompanied him to the door after tea.

"I've longed to speak to you alone, but this is the first opportunity I've had."

"Why? Is something the matter with Miss Oliver?" At once, the doctor became concerned.

"Oh, I'm not at all worried about Louise. She's in better spirits than I ever hoped to see."

"Miss Oliver's my star patient." Dr Tower beamed with satisfaction.

"I'm sure you're her favourite doctor, if that's of any interest to you."

"Do you think so?"

"I'm sure of it."

"Oh." Dr Tower looked delighted for a moment, and then frowned. "Patients as badly injured as Miss Oliver often form an attachment to their physician, you know. It has something to do with – oh, feelings of gratitude – dependency – that sort of thing."

"I'm afraid I don't agree with your diagnosis, Doctor. Not in this case, at any rate."

"Really?" He glanced hopefully at me again. "Oh, my goodness. Well, bless my soul."

"So I don't worry in the least about Louise. It's Adam who worries me."

"Mr Gaunt? He seems perfectly well."

"Most of the time he's as fit as a fiddle. But lately he's begun to take breathless turns – with pains in his chest, though of course he denies it."

"He should see Dr Clement."

"I know that, and I'm sure he knows it too. But he won't even admit the existence of a problem, so what can I do? I thought perhaps . . . if you could think of an excuse for examining him . . ."

James Tower looked at me quizzically. "Like an outbreak of Black Death in the village, do you mean?" He shook his head. "I understand your concern, Miss Summerbee, but I can't just walk up to Mr Gaunt and insist on examining him. He'd see through any excuse immediately."

"Yes, I suppose he would."

"Strictly speaking, Mr Gaunt's health is his own business. And yours, too, of course."

"Then what do you think could be wrong with him?"

"A touch of bronchitis, perhaps. It's quite common in older people. But I warn you, it's impossible to do more than guess at the cause without an examination."

At the beginning of June Adam went to London, but didn't suggest that I should go with him. Five days later he returned in a mood of such quiet satisfaction that I assumed his business – whatever it had been – had gone well. He seemed almost relieved, as if a weight had been lifted from his mind. All his recent irritability had disappeared, leaving a tranquil tenderness towards me which was almost more disturbing.

After dinner on the evening of his return we walked out into the Italian garden, where the last of the sunshine had gilded every leaf and flagstone with the completeness of a Midas. I strolled in the hollow of his arm along the shining aisles as far as the fountain, where on the molten surface a pond-skater was whetting its legs over a jewelled fly.

"I've brought you something from London, little cat." From his pocket Adam produced a tiny, leather-covered box.

"It's enough to have you back again, my dear. I don't expect presents."

"It isn't a present. To tell the truth, I don't know what it is. Settlement of a debt, maybe." He held the box out to me. "Open it, and you'll understand."

Inside the box was a ring – a union of two endless, intricately spiralling ropes of gold which looped and twisted about one another, separate but interdependent, like two twining stems from that gilded garden.

"It's meant to be a wedding ring, Kate. I thought perhaps it was time I made an honest woman of you."

"Marriage?" I stared at him, uncomprehending. "But you've always insisted that I should be free to leave – "

"I know what I said. I've changed my mind – that's all."

"But why? What's made you change your mind like this?"

The question should have been unnecessary, I knew; I should understand what had suddenly altered between us.

Adam took my left hand in his, and gently slid the ring on to my third finger.

"Let's say I've had a fit of respectability. I can't wait to see Mrs Rector Peasup drinking tea in our drawing-room."

"I don't believe that for a moment! You've never cared a bit for respectability."

"Well then, I do now. The parish would heave a sigh of relief if we became man and wife."

"But who would they gossip about afterwards?" I forced myself to smile, a poor attempt to disguise the anxiety which had suddenly numbed my mind. I didn't want anything to change: above all, I didn't want Adam to change – as he wouldn't, surely, if we left things exactly as they were. "This is such a surprise," I said lamely.

"It's quite simple. You've always insisted you'd stay here until . . . well, until I no longer need you. I've just given up arguing the point, that's all. I'm asking you to marry me, and stay with me for good."

He was as relaxed and confident as I'd ever seen him. He even pretended to be mildly affronted by my continued hesitation.

"You haven't said *yes* or *no*, Kate. Do you want me to go down on my knees?"

"I need time to think, Adam. I'm afraid everything will be different if I marry you, and we're so perfect as we are."

Suddenly I was afraid of losing him to respectability: I was afraid of becoming a gentleman's wife and having morning callers intrude on our solitude, or the Rector disturb our peaceful evenings in the garden. No matter how hard I tried, the ticking of the clock of life was growing louder in my ear, and I could hardly bear to share him with anyone, even for a moment.

"I promised Louise," I said, "that I'd never try to take her mother's place."

"That sounds very much like *no*."

"I don't know what to say. I wasn't expecting any of this."

"And at last you can imagine a day in the future when you might want to leave me."

"No – never. Married or not, I won't leave you, Adam, and I don't need a wedding ring to keep me here." I reached up to stroke the hair that curled behind his ear. "If we live here quietly enough, I really believe nothing will change, and you'll never grow old."

He smiled again – a curious little smile.

"Perhaps you're right. If fate is kind to us, I'll never grow any older."

I smiled myself, to think that the danger had passed so easily. And to seal our new understanding I slid the ring from my marriage finger, and slipped it on to the third finger of my right hand.

7

Why didn't I marry him? Impulse – foreboding – superstition: the reason contained a little of all those things, but it was mostly an instinctive belief that life at Hawk's Dyke was too precious to be put at risk by any change, however small.

There had always been a fragility about the existence I shared with Adam, the fragility of a playing-card house which could be destroyed by the addition of one more square of pasteboard. We both knew we'd never been intended for one another: our few years of happiness had been stolen from the grand scheme of life, and I was afraid that if I asked for anything more, the little we had would be snatched away. And so I said *no* to marriage, and Adam never mentioned it again.

We did have a wedding in the family, though, in that summer of 1870, when Louise married James Tower in Stainham Church, a glorious smile and not a little paint hiding the scar on her cheek. Charles and Alice gallantly graced a front pew, Alice kissing her physician brother-in-law on the cheek and heartily wishing him an exclusive practice in London before very long, and a knighthood to go with it.

As a wedding gift, Adam had bought the groom a medical practice of his own in Ely, somehow contriving to make that stubbornly independent man accept it without ill-feeling. It was already a matter of regret to Dr Tower that by the very act of marrying her, he fell heir to his wife's Oliver fortune, and might have to employ a coachman for the rest of his life. At any rate the day passed off entirely satisfactorily, and Louise departed for her new life as Mrs Tower in a flurry of rice and sentimental kisses, promising to write and to visit whenever she could.

And then . . . . And then Adam, for reasons I still couldn't fathom, hurled himself into the life of Hawk's Dyke like a man possessed. Missing him one day, I discovered him out in the harvest field, where he'd been flinging sheaves of barley on to a wagon with the youngest of the labourers. He was leaning against a tree, his face rigid with pain, staring up among the branches as if sheer effort of will could force his body to obey him.

"Adam – please—"

"I'll be all right." He could hardly gasp out the words.

"You're making yourself ill! You must send for Dr Clement."

"No. Leave me alone." He turned his head away, until I could no longer see the sweat that beaded his forehead, or the agony in his eyes.

One day, I found him trying to square up yew gateposts with an axe, of all things – and on another I asked Nell if she'd seen him, only to be told "He's down behind Old Hall steading, ma'am, cutting down a tree."

"Cutting down a tree? Are you sure?"

Nell nodded earnestly. "Sykes has just come up with the dogcart, saying he saw Mr Gaunt chopping away as if he bore the tree a grudge of some kind, and then nearly falling down with the effort of it."

I didn't wait to hear any more, but picked up my skirts and flew down to Old Hall Farm as fast as I could go. I heard the steady crack of the axe before I reached the corner of the steading – the *hack* as it bit into the timber, then a pause as it was retrieved, weighed, hefted, and flung forwards once more to bury its edge in the tree.

302

By the time I'd rounded the corner he'd stopped again, sprawling back against the field-gate, the axe dropped at his feet, a white wound on the trunk of an old beech testifying to the wild power of each blow. He looked desperately ill – his fierce grip on the top bar of the gate was all that had prevented him pitching into the dust below, yet he hadn't given up.

A few feet away, a circle of woodmen looked on with the embarrassment of men watching an unfair fight. They were the hewers of wood: Adam Gaunt was a gentleman, and their employer. That was how God had ordained it, until this madman had chosen to fly in the face of natural law.

"Adam – "

The men moved gratefully aside for me. Close to, I was appalled by the anguish in his eyes, and even more by his determination not to yield to it.

"Go back to the house." With a mighty effort, he staggered free of the gate.

"What on earth do you think you're doing?" By now I shared the woodmen's awkwardness. There was something obscene in that naked battle with failing flesh and blood. "Stop this, Adam – please!"

Resentfully, he put out a hand to the gate once more, his chest heaving, pain blazing from his eyes. "Give me the axe." He pointed to it, on the ground at his feet. If he'd bent to pick it up, he'd surely have collapsed.

"Give it to me."

"I will not! This is absolute madness."

"We're widening the road for the steam thresher." His voice was hardly more than a whisper. "This tree has to come down."

"These men will do it, I'm sure." I indicated the waiting woodmen.

"I want to do it myself." I believed him: I could see him fight down the agony in his body.

"Come back to the house." I kept my voice low – for the first time embarrassed in his company. "There's no need for this."

"You go back. I'll be there soon enough." When I didn't move, he snapped, "Don't interfere, Kate," and gestured to the nearest man to pick up the axe for him.

In my desperation, I became inspired.

"I feel . . . a little faint, all of a sudden." I swayed, and put my hand theatrically to my brow. "Take me back to the house, Adam – it must be the strain of all this."

He twisted round to stare at me – angry, yet concerned. Then he

303

glanced reluctantly at the half-killed tree. I gasped like a tragedy queen, and swayed once more, forcing him to stretch out an arm towards me.

"Come back to the house then, and lie down. You aren't – I mean there isn't – "

"A baby? No, nothing like that," I whispered. "I'm just a little sick, all of a sudden. Give me your arm, Adam. There now, I'm steadier already."

The truth of it was that he was leaning on me. Like a jailer, I dragged him back to the house, the crack of the woodmen's axes following us each step of the way.

But I couldn't watch him every minute of the day, and from time to time rumours reached me of stone slabs he'd tried to move single-handed or ditched wagons he'd helped to rescue. And still I couldn't understand it. Was he trying to prove his strength was undiminished? Was he challenging the pain in his chest to do its worst?

He wouldn't discuss the matter, insisting that my imagination had run away with me and that old age accounted for it all. Yet at other times he treated me with such gentle affection – almost like the first days of our life together – that I was completely bewildered. All I could do was to look forward to the frosts of winter, when the iron-hard ground would put an end to work on the farms for a while, and Adam's relentless contest with his own body would have to cease.

The frosts came, and for a while there was peace. Then, a fortnight after Christmas, the gravel pit beyond the highway froze solid, and children from far and near gathered to skate. Even the infants were accomplished skaters, schooled on the frozen rivers which stretched for miles across the countryside.

Adam, on his way to confer with Charles at the Abbey, decided to ride by way of the gravel pit to watch the fun.

"Don't mope while I'm gone," he said lightly, and kissed me.

I never saw him alive again.

Chapter Twenty-One

1

Many times in the days that followed I wondered why I hadn't sensed it – the moment of Adam's death. We were so close: how was it possible for one half of an organism to cease to exist without the other half being aware of it?

As it happened, I was upstairs before my mirror, scraping my hair into a knot on the very top of my head and wondering if Adam would like it that way, when Nell burst into the room, her face blanched by catastrophe.

She started to speak, pointing towards the window – but I already knew what she was trying to tell me. I didn't hear a word of it: only the roaring, rending, shrieking chaos of my world crashing to pieces about me, just as I'd realised it surely would – but not yet, oh, please, not yet . . .

Nell had fallen silent, her arm still stretched out towards the window. I went to it and looked out over a landscape of silver under a steely sky.

Somewhere between the two, an army was moving – a silent host, winding slowly up the Hawk's Dyke road, following a simple farm wagon towards our door.

I couldn't tear my eyes from the joyless march, from the hopelessness in the slumped shoulders and downturned faces. This was the end: there was nothing to be saved, nothing to be gained by haste.

Adam's horse had been tied to the tailboard of the wagon. His black retriever, Tess, trotted as near as she dared to the iron-shod wheels, confused by the unaccustomed fuss, refusing to be parted by more than a few inches from her master.

Behind the wagon streamed a silent throng of labourers and their wives and children, their number swollen at each roadside cottage. Why should the children care? And yet there must have been a hundred of them, some with their wood-and-bone skates still slung round their necks, some hatless or coatless, even on that freezing day – and every one of them walking in the wake of the wagon without a word to his neighbour, only an occasional glance towards the house where they knew I waited for my lover's return.

★

Six men carried him in on a hurdle. I remember that particularly: I went out to meet the wagon as it halted at the door, but I could see nothing – the floor of the massive vehicle was chest-high and filled with straw. I followed the hurdle – followed the soles of Adam's boots, as dark and wet as my father's had been, thinking irrationally how glad I was they'd left him his boots on such a cold day . . . and fussing over the white, lifeless hand which trailed from the side of the hurdle as they barged and staggered up the twisting spiral staircase.

"Why are his boots wet? Why? Why!"

Someone brought me brandy in the parlour, and led me to a chair while figures drifted to and fro like swimmers in a dream. Faces bobbed and floated, their mouths opening to make soothing sounds. The Earl had been sent for; Dr Clement had been sent for; the world still turned, the rain would rain and the wind would blow – there had been no suffering, I should console myself. . . . How could I console myself? Adam's boots had been wet through – I'd seen them – I wanted to know . . .

The mouths moved once more, prompting one another.

Adam had dismounted at the frozen gravel pit to speak to a man he knew, while the children buzzed to and fro on the ice, shrieking with excitement. Then the shrieking had turned to screams of fear. Some child – the Longstock boy, it was thought – had pushed through the cordon of frost-bound shrubs to a smaller, deeper pool beyond, where the ice creaked ominously underfoot and no one ever skated. All at once there was a howl of terror from beyond the shrubs; everyone ran in a body to the spot, to find a jagged black hole in the white surface, and nothing more.

Ordering the rest to stand back, Adam had inched out on his knees where the ice seemed thickest, and had succeeded in getting a grip on the boy's coat. All at once, with a great, resentful roar the surface of the pool had split and crazed like the opening of white fangs, gulping him down into the freezing water.

He hadn't drowned – they were sure of that. There had been no water in his lungs when they pulled him out, but he was dead nevertheless – killed, so it seemed, by the shock of the icy water round his heart.

Who'd have imagined such a thing? The mouths made circles of wonderment. But the Longstock boy was alive, they assured me – as if I should be prepared to trade one life for another, as Adam had done.

"Of course he didn't drown!" With brisk formality, Dr Clement accepted a brandy when he came downstairs again. "He wouldn't be dead now, if he'd followed my advice. One of the other men could easily

306

have crawled out to fetch the child, and there would have been no risk to Mr Gaunt. I'm sorry, Mrs – ah – Miss Summerbee. I realise that's hardly a comfort to you in the present circumstances."

"What do you mean, *if he'd followed your advice*? I didn't know you'd given him any advice."

"Didn't you?" The doctor frowned at me for a moment. "How singular. Didn't Mr Gaunt tell you he consulted me last spring about pain in his chest and arm?"

"He never said a word. I was sure he wasn't well, but he always told me it was nothing to worry about."

"It was *angina pectoris*, to be precise, Miss Summerbee. Attacks of severe chest pain and feelings of strangulation about the heart. Shortness of breath – slow pulse – clammy skin – usually only lasting a minute or two at a time, but a warning that the arteries of the heart are narrowed and obstructed."

"And what advice did you give him?"

"The same advice, I understand, which my colleague in London confirmed when he examined Mr Gaunt in the summer."

"He told me he had business to attend to in London."

"Indeed? I believe Dr Knopfeldt warned Mr Gaunt that his life was in danger unless he avoided excitement of any kind. No stimulants, such as the drinking of alcohol. No walking immediately after meals. No violent exercise."

"But he did all of those things!"

"And no sexual intercourse." Dr Clement stared at me severely over his half-spectacles.

"That too, I'm afraid."

"Hmph. Well then, since Mr Gaunt was an intelligent man – and since his half-brother died of the same condition – I can only assume he didn't care to prolong his life by giving up those things which – ah – gave him pleasure. In the event, I imagine the stress of sudden immersion in icy water was enough to cause his death within seconds, though from what you tell me, it could have happened at any time."

Dr Clement sipped his brandy and stared into the fire.

"A very determined man, Mr Gaunt. He really should have taken more care."

2

After Dr Clement had gone I went upstairs.

They'd laid Adam on the bed in a room we never used, filled to the ceiling by a tall, old-fashioned four-poster, its elaborate hangings now sadly faded. Someone had spread the bedcover over him as far as his chest, as if he slept in the blue shadow of the canopy; but Adam had never looked that way in sleep. His skin was as waxen and colourless as a cathedral effigy, his closed eyelids opaline; he seemed curiously diminished, as if warmth and movement had created an illusion of size, like a parlour trick whose workings were cruelly laid bare in the light of day.

Now, at last, when it was too late, I understood what had altered between us when Adam returned from London. He'd discovered how his life might end, if he made no effort to save it. And what was a final flash of agony, compared to the humiliation of palsied, dependent old age? If I wouldn't leave him, then he would contrive to leave me in his own time and in his own way. I thought of the boulders he'd moved and the wagons he'd set his shoulder to – and the tree he'd attacked in gasping pain, wondering each time if this new seizure was to be his last. And knowing each time that I would be left behind, alone.

If only he'd told me – if only he'd explained . . .

But he knew too well I'd have tried to cling to him, to trap him in the ageing body he feared – the empty, dimly lustrous white shell which was all he'd left me of himself.

Had his hair been so silver in life? Already it seemed hard to believe. A curl of it straggled across the pillow, and I fetched a tortoiseshell comb from the dressing-table to tidy it as best I could. If I'd done the same only a few hours earlier, his hand would have moved automatically to enfold mine; now those same hands lay, frigid and unfeeling, by his sides.

On impulse, I bent to kiss the pallid lips, as if I might still, by some miracle, transmit the force of my own life to him. The kiss left me chilled to my soul, as if I'd kissed an image behind glass, incapable of taking or giving.

In that profound silence, the soft knock at the bedroom door sounded like the bark of a gun. The door opened a fraction and Nell slid apologetically into the room.

"I came up half an hour ago, ma'am, but you didn't seem to hear." She gazed at me, soft-eyed and sorrowful. "Mrs Monk has come, ma'am, and she'd best get on. I dare say she won't take long, and you can come back later."

She didn't need to say any more. Mrs Monk was the washer and layer-out. She scuttled past me to her task, head down, swathed in rusty black, curtseying as she went. As she reached the bed I heard a whimper from under its wide valances, and poor black Tess crawled out to press against my knees, anxious to follow me from the room.

308

Now I knew for sure that Adam had escaped me.

"I'll go downstairs," I said.

Next morning the Earl of Wellborough arrived to take charge.

Charles had already called the previous afternoon, but beyond satisfying himself that Adam was indeed dead and there was nothing especially scandalous in the manner of his death, he'd said very little. Weeping women clearly unnerved him – particularly a young woman weeping for her dead lover, without even a wedding ring to regularise her tears.

By next morning Charles assumed, as he said himself, that I'd had a chance to "pull myself together". Alice sent her condolences, he informed me briskly, but wouldn't call, if I didn't mind. As for his mother, Henrietta . . . she'd spent the previous night toasting the dead man in champagne, and no one had seen her since.

Tut-tut, dear me, it was an unfortunate business. . .

Charles planted himself before the parlour fire, called for brandy, and seemed to be preparing himself to communicate something important.

Hey, ho. . . . Good Heavens, eleven o'clock already. . . . Still – it all went to show that one never knew what life had in store. . . . Such as death, come to think of it. And given the inconvenience of present circumstances, it was just as well one was . . . who one *was*, since the Rector was bound to jump to it, even at short notice, and do the needful over a departed Gaunt, or he, Charles, would know the reason why, forsooth.

The Earl drained his glass and poured himself another from the decanter.

Still . . . that fellow Clement seemed to think death had come bang-wallop out of the blue, and I should take comfort from that. The poor devil probably hadn't known a thing about it. . . . Like Charles's father – Henry, Adam's half-brother – who'd also died . . . suddenly. Hey, ho – *in the midst of life*, and all that . . .

Talking of which . . .

"Talking of what, Charles?" My nerves were humming like guitar-strings. I wanted desperately to be alone with my thoughts, and I was losing patience with his ridiculous twaddle. "You'll have to excuse me if I don't quite follow."

"Of course, of course. Only to be expected. Upset, and all that." The Earl took a deep draught of brandy. "I was talking about the funeral," he finished at a gallop.

"You told me yesterday I should leave it all to you."

"Quite. Quite. And so you can. Nothing lavish, you understand. Don't imagine he'd have wanted it. Not after the late Mrs Gaunt's funeral, if you remember what that was like."

"You're going to arrange something similar?"

"Good God, no!" Charles looked appalled for a moment, and then recollected himself. "That was – well – rather *plain*. I'm all for simplicity, but Adam was a Gaunt, after all, and some things just won't do for a member of the family. Simple, yes – but dignified. That's what Alice has suggested." Charles nodded approvingly. "Down in the churchyard, next to his wife. I mean, his first wife. No, dammit, I mean his wife."

"Rachel."

"Yes." Charles took a deep breath, like a man wading in a current too swift for him. I thought how much Adam would have enjoyed the scene.

"What I mean to say – " he began heavily. "What I have been asked to say to you – by the family . . ."

"By Alice."

"Well, yes – by Alice – though I'm sure Louise and Matthew would agree . . ."

My tears drying on my cheeks, I waited for what was to come.

"Alice feels. . . . It would be better for everyone concerned if you weren't present at the burial." Charles pulled out a silk handkerchief and mopped his brow.

"I see." I considered his request in silence for a moment. "Forgive me, but I understood that ladies don't often go to graveyards in England."

"Not often, no. But then, you're an American."

"Am I? I sometimes wonder what I am, these days. I was never Adam's wife, though I might have been. I'm not even his widow – though Heaven knows, I feel like one. And now you tell me I mustn't be there when they bury him, though I'd never intended it. Will Alice be there? Or Louise?"

"Absolutely not."

"Then you may tell Alice I shan't be there either. I have no wish to embarrass anyone."

"Oh . . . splendid. Sensible girl." Charles gulped his brandy, clearly relieved to be rid of his awkward duty. "Then I shan't trouble you any further. You may leave everything to me. Everything." He paused in the act of plunging to the door, apparently sensing that some remark

310

more in keeping with the occasion was required. With an effort, he returned and gripped one of my hands in his.

"A great sadness," he mumbled solemnly, breathing brandy into my face. "He was a fine man. Like my father," he added. "A fine man."

He shook his head as if the whims of fate were a mystery to him, and then, having delivered himself of all he came to say, seemed to revive. His head snapped up, his shoulders straightened, and he stared speculatively round the parlour.

"Funny old place, Hawk's Dyke," he remarked thoughtfully. "Wonder what Matthew will make of it, now his father's gone."

3

Strangely enough, it had never occurred to me that I was suddenly homeless once more. In the first hollow hours after Adam's death, my head had been filled with thoughts of the past. I'd pushed the future aside as if it had no right to exist any more, as if my life had stopped with Adam's. But of course it hadn't, and I realised now that I could only spend a few days more at Hawk's Dyke. In one disastrous instant I'd lost Adam and I'd lost my home; even in the depths of my grief I couldn't imagine that Matthew would waste a moment's sympathy on his father's displaced mistress.

Matthew arrived by the afternoon train, alone. Violet had not sent her condolences. Indeed Violet was in London, and from the brusque way in which Matthew announced the fact, I gathered he neither expected nor wished for her presence in Norfolk. He stared at me defiantly as he spoke, daring me to ask any more.

"Come into the parlour, Matthew."

"I want to see him, Kate. Now. At once."

"Of course. Nell will take you upstairs."

"I can find my own way, thank you."

"The large room overlooking the orchard, then."

Matthew whirled about and disappeared upstairs without even pausing to remove his coat. He looked older than I remembered. He'd inherited the hollows under the cheekbones which had defined the shape of Adam's face, the hawk nose of the Gaunts, and his father's strange, moody grey eyes; turning his head in the shaded light of the hallway, he was capable of making my heart lurch suddenly as if Adam had miraculously returned: yet he wasn't Adam. He wasn't half of Adam – not even a quarter of the man I'd loved.

He came down to the parlour after ten minutes, pale and oddly subdued. His coat was now over his arm. Dropping it on to a sofa, he sat down in silence beside it.

"There's brandy if you'd like it, Matthew." I indicated the decanter on the table, now only quarter-full.

Matthew glanced up at me as if he'd suddenly remembered my existence.

"I beg your pardon?"

"Brandy. If you'd like some."

"No. No thank you." He ran a hand abstractedly through his hair, and then leaned forward, clasping the hand with its fellow between his knees.

"I'm sorry if I've been a bit short with you, Kate. All this has come as rather a shock." For a moment he examined his clasped hands. "Do you know – when I heard the news, I couldn't believe it? I just couldn't believe he was dead, until I actually saw him there . . ." Matthew shook his head. "Ridiculous, really. . . . My father was only mortal, just like the rest of us. And yet, somehow, it was inconceivable to think of him dying."

"It wasn't so ridiculous. I felt exactly the same."

"Yes?" He glanced at me curiously, and then looked down at his hands again. "I think I told you how he disappeared once, long ago, and how everyone thought he was dead then. I grew up believing my father had died before I was old enough to remember him. But he came back, all the same. That time, he did."

Matthew unclasped his hands and pressed his fingertips together.

"Suddenly I was faced with an awkward stranger who'd pushed his way into our lives and seemed to think he'd a perfect right to order me around. And to my amazement, my mother took his side – the side of a complete stranger – against her own son."

"Perhaps she thought you needed a father."

"Adam Gaunt was never my father! A father is someone who's there as you grow – not an ordinary man with failings and weaknesses, but someone above all that: older, wiser, and bloody bad-tempered when it suits him, but always *there* to be looked up to. And Adam Gaunt was never there. Not until I was too old to need him in that way."

"Is that why you kept Jonas Oliver's name?"

"Jonas tried to be a father to me, at least. In his own limited, nit-squeezing way, he tried to do what he called his 'duty' by his wife's son. And when all's said and done, he left me in charge of his company – his life's work. Jonas Oliver would have died, sooner than run off and leave his duty behind."

312

Matthew paused, and I added for him, "And yet . . ."

"What do you mean, *and yet*?"

"I had a feeling there was something more."

"Oh yes – *and yet*, if you like, that man up there – " He jabbed a finger towards the ceiling. "That infuriating, obstinate, unreachable man . . . was closer to me in his own strange way than a hundred Jonases. And now he's dead. Stone dead. Gone. Vanished again, without so much as a word." Matthew kicked the brass fender beside him, finding satisfaction in its hollow clang.

"That wasn't entirely Adam's fault, Matthew. You could have written to him at any time. You could have apologised."

"Apologised? What for? For being his son? For existing at all?" Matthew glared at me. "He was the one who told me to stay away from Hawk's Dyke in future. Why didn't he write to *me*, and apologise?"

"For exactly the same reason you never wrote to him."

"Yes – well, it's too late for that now. He told me to stay away from here while Hawk's Dyke was still his, but now he's dead I presume I'm allowed to come back. Hawk's Dyke comes to me now, in any case." Matthew tilted his head defiantly. "Which gives me a perfect right, I'd say, to be here if I please."

"For goodness' sake, Matthew – " I began, controlling my temper with difficulty. "Can't you wait until he's buried? That seems very little to ask. Let the house remain Adam's until he's gone from it – and then it's yours, as you say, and you can do as you like. I'll pack my things and move out as soon as the funeral's over."

Matthew had the grace to look abashed.

"I'm not trying to drive you out. You don't have to leave until you're ready." He frowned, wrestling with an unpalatable question. "Where will you go from here? Do you have enough to live on?"

"Your father took care of that. He made sure I wouldn't starve."

Matthew nodded. "I assumed he'd make some provision for you."

"And I may well go back to America at last," I hazarded, not wishing him to see how lost and directionless I felt. "There must be something left of my old life, if I look hard enough for it."

I gazed round the mellow parlour with its stone hearth and smoke-darkened ceiling where Adam and I had sat so often together.

"What will you do with Hawk's Dyke, Matthew? Now that it's yours."

"I don't know." Matthew stretched out his legs and leaned against the back of the sofa. "I haven't decided that yet."

I'd told Charles Gaunt the truth when I said I'd never intended to be there at the churchyard, but the fact that I'd have affronted the Rector and given Stainham more cause for gossip had never entered my calculations. If I'd wanted to be there when Adam was buried, nothing and no one would have stopped me for a moment. But I didn't go, because whatever they were burying in that hole hacked from the frozen ground, it wasn't Adam.

If he was anywhere at all on that bright and sparkling morning, he was at Hawk's Dyke; and so I stayed at home, walking in our garden for what I realised would probably be the last time.

A light crust of frost still glittered on the fretwork of branches as the sun rose on its shallow winter arc. I walked slowly along the paths, recording every detail; I wanted to carry away that garden in my head, hoarding its peace to be revisited whenever I had need of it.

I found myself walking inside a fragile crystal bowl. At either side of the path, the hem of my skirt brushed miraculously rounded cushions of snowy foliage; a pattern of white footprints showed where my steps had packed the frost-flakes; even the bowl of the fountain was spread with a curd of ice, the lead spout between the dolphin's lips long since emptied of its jet.

Perhaps the garden, accustomed to the presence of two figures in its midst, suddenly realised I was alone. All around, as the sun touched them thinly with its warmth, the trees and shrubs began to shed their melted load. Sparkling drops collected on leaf-edges and down-turning twigs, growing and swelling until they spilled to the soil below like soft, sweet tears. I walked on through the sorrowing, dissolving morning, while the whole garden wept around me.

I hardly noticed the Gaunts gathering at the door of Hawk's Dyke. Carriages rumbled across the gravel in front of the house and hushed voices conferred by the drawing-room windows, but I remained apart from them in my sanctuary, no longer interested in their affairs.

I heard the click of a distant latch, and deferential footsteps advancing towards me.

"Miss Summerbee – excuse me – forgive me, please – "

"Mr Eustace . . ." I'd met Adam's lawyer only once before, and for some reason I hadn't expected to see him now. "Did you come down from London this morning?"

"I arrived yesterday, in fact. I stayed overnight in the village."

Mr Eustace's face indicated that this had involved a certain amount of hardship. "I'm sorry we meet again on such a sad occasion."

"The funeral's over?"

"It is. It was quite satisfactory."

"I'm glad."

"Miss Summerbee – " Mr Eustace gazed unhappily round the garden. "It distresses me to disturb you at such a time . . . I know you and Mr Gaunt were particularly close. It must be hard for you to come to terms with his loss."

"It is hard. It's kind of you to understand that, Mr Eustace. But then . . ." I hesitated for a second, "Adam always said you had an excellent graveside manner."

"Did he?" A glimmer of amusement lit the lawyer's eyes. "Well now, I can just imagine him saying that. And I suppose it's true. Practice, as they say, makes perfect." He took a deep breath and frowned, as if about to undertake a task he disliked, and I decided to save him the trouble of an explanation.

"If you've come to ask me when I shall be clear of Matthew Oliver's house, you can tell him I shall be gone by the day after tomorrow. I've no wish to inconvenience him."

"Well, no. . . . In fact, that wasn't my intention, Miss Summerbee. I came to ask if you'd mind coming indoors to the drawing-room. The family are anxious to begin reading the will."

"I'd rather not be there, Mr Eustace, if you don't mind. I'm sure the Gaunts will manage perfectly well without me."

"I really think you should be present, you know, if you feel strong enough. You are mentioned in the will. It does concern you."

Mr Eustace offered me his arm.

"So will you come in? Please?"

The last thing I wanted was to listen to the parcelling out of Adam's property, even if he had given the instructions himself. But it seemed I had no alternative. Leaning on his lawyer's arm, as I'd so often leaned on Adam's, I left the garden to its frosty melancholy and went indoors.

5

He'd left Hawk's Dyke to me.

All of it – all fifteen hundred acres, with its farms and cottages, its oak groves, the perch and bream in its streams, the rabbits in the spinneys, the butterflies flickering over the lawns – he'd given it all to me, every dear, wonderful inch of it.

I'd been astonished by the extent of Adam's wealth. Matthew had inherited property in London I'd known nothing about; Alice and Louise had been left money and securities which would have made them wealthy even without their own Oliver inheritance. There were other, smaller bequests to people I'd never heard of. Yet Hawk's Dyke had been closest to Adam's heart – and he'd given it to me.

I left the Gaunts to their discussions and fled to the peace of the Italian garden. My garden, now.

As I left the room, Mr Eustace touched my sleeve.

"I'm delighted for you, Miss Summerbee. Mr Gaunt was particularly determined that you should have Hawk's Dyke after his death. He instructed me to make it impossible for any of the family to challenge the bequest, and I can assure you that Hawk's Dyke is entirely yours, without any conditions attached. Completely, utterly yours."

I walked out into the garden, where the branches of the trees stood dark against the sky, and looked back towards the house which had been my home and Adam's, and would be mine still . . . in time to see the garden door open and Matthew come out.

He strode briskly towards me, his hands deep in the pockets of his black coat and his head a little bowed, like a bull preparing to charge.

He halted a few feet away and raised his eyes to mine.

"How much?"

"What do you mean, *how much?*"

"How much do you want for it? For all this – " He threw out an arm in a resentful arc.

I stared at him, hardly believing what I'd heard.

"Are you offering to buy it from me?"

"Of course."

"What on earth makes you think I'd want to sell?"

"What else can you do with it?"

"I want to go on living here. It's my home."

"It isn't your home! It was my father's home, and by rights it should be mine now."

"Your father's home, Matthew? You've changed your tune, haven't you? Two days ago, you told me you had no father. Or do you mean Jonas Oliver, perhaps?"

"This house – this land – has belonged to the Gaunts for four hundred years."

"So it has. But then, you aren't a Gaunt. Of your own free will, you chose to become an Oliver."

"You're splitting hairs. You know perfectly well what I mean."

"I can't see why Hawk's Dyke should be so important to you, all of a sudden. You hardly ever came near the place after your mother died."

"It was my father's house." Matthew's mouth set in a determined line. "I want it."

"Matthew, your father wanted me to have Hawk's Dyke, or he wouldn't have left it to me. Whatever you may have thought of him, you must admit he knew his own mind."

"Oh, certainly." A shrewd expression came into Matthew's eyes. "But are you sure you understand *why* he left it to you?"

"So that I could live here. Why else?"

"I don't believe that, Kate. And neither will you, I'm sure, when you've thought about it for a bit. Ask yourself this – why on earth should my father want to tie you to a few acres of Norfolk countryside for the rest of your life? You aren't even English."

"But I love it here."

"You say that now, but you're thinking of it as it was when my father was alive. No – it's pretty plain he only left Hawk's Dyke to you because he knew I'd move Heaven and earth to buy it back. He knew I'd pay whatever price you asked – far more than market price, if I had to. I don't resent that." Matthew waved a magnanimous hand. "My father meant to leave you well provided for. . . . But he meant me to have Hawk's Dyke."

"But Adam could have left me as much money as he wanted, surely."

"The family might have had something to say about that. We might have challenged the will. He was an old man, after all."

I stared at him for a moment, only half comprehending.

"Oh no, Matthew – that's impossible! Adam was far too straight-forward for anything so devious."

"If you believe that, you don't know my father, I fear."

"In any case, I hate all this squabbling over money. Isn't it enough that Adam's dead, without everyone picking over the remains?"

"Kate – "

"Don't call me that. My name's Katherine." Adam had called me Kate, and I hated the echo of his voice on Matthew's lips.

"Katherine, then." Matthew thrust his hands back into his pockets and stared thoughtfully at the silent fountain. "Tell me – " he demanded suddenly, "what's the present price of a turnip-cutter? Do you know? Do you know how many men are needed on Old Hall Farm for the barley harvest? Or how much a bushel of wheat fetched last market day? Can you answer any of those questions?"

"Not really."

"My father could have answered them, I promise you. For a man who spent so much time with his nose in a book, very little of what went on at Hawk's Dyke escaped him."

317

"I know that."

"But you still think you can make sensible decisions when your tenants come to you for loans, or asking to have their rents reduced for some reason or other?"

"Your father's agent will help me."

"And steal you blind, while he's at it. Katherine, for Heaven's sake – if my father had left you a riverboat, I'd say keep it, and good luck to you. But not a place like Hawk's Dyke! He never meant to turn you into a farmer. He meant you to sell Hawk's Dyke to me for some ridiculous price, and go off and live handsomely on the proceeds."

I hesitated, and my uncertainty encouraged him.

"What does the land here rent for? Twenty-two – twenty-three shillings an acre? Twenty-three for the best land, perhaps. Very well – I'll offer you twenty-three pounds for every acre he's left you. The equivalent of twenty years' rent. That's a fairer price than you'll get anywhere else. You'd leave here a very rich woman, which I'm sure is exactly what my father intended."

I tried to multiply the figure he'd mentioned, and gave up.

"I still can't believe he'd have left me Hawk's Dyke unless he meant me to live here."

"Katherine, you're upset and confused, which is perfectly natural. This is hardly the time to discuss business." Matthew assumed a solicitous smile. "I shall stay at the Abbey for the next couple of days, so there's no hurry for you to make up your mind about the price of the land. I'll come back when you've had a chance to think about it – the day after tomorrow, perhaps, at three o'clock. I'm sure we'll come to a suitable agreement then, when you realise that this is exactly what my father intended all along."

He stared at me for a moment, and then his glance slid away towards the far end of the garden.

"What have you seen?" I peered into the distance myself.

"Seen? Oh – nothing. I was just thinking how differently things might have turned out." His gaze swept back to my face, grey and penetrating like Adam's. "I never mean to argue with you, Kate – "

"Katherine."

"But somehow it always seems to happen. We've hardly met before we're fighting passionately over something or other." He paused, struck by a recollection. "Do you remember the argument we had in this very garden on the day you arrived from America? When you were so certain we were legally man and wife?"

"Do you imagine I'll ever forget it?"

"You came all that way because of me. . . . And yet you ended by living here with my father." Matthew's stare moved away to the chimney-pots. "It's strange . . . I knew for a certainty I'd lose you to him. As soon as I saw the two of you together, I knew what would happen. I even tried to warn you, if you remember."

"You didn't lose me, Matthew. I was never yours to lose."

"No . . . come to that, I don't suppose you were."

He smiled fleetingly, and then added, "Until the day after tomorrow, then. Goodbye, Katherine."

All the Gaunts had gone. Matthew was the last to leave, walking out to join Charles and Alice in their carriage, which they'd kept waiting for him. Nell and one of the maids were tidying up in the drawing-room, and behind them the slight, stooped figure of Mr Eustace lingered in a corner, gathering up the papers strewn on an album-table which had served him for a desk.

"Miss Summerbee – " Raising his head, he caught sight of me in the doorway. "I was hoping for a word with you before I left today. There are various papers which must be signed, as you'll understand, before you are legally mistress here – oh – ah – gracious me – "

I couldn't resist smiling at his confusion.

"Mistress of Hawk's Dyke, Mr Eustace, instead of the mistress of its owner?"

"In effect, Miss Summerbee. The distinction had only just occurred to me."

"Well, I may not be mistress of Hawk's Dyke for long, after all. Mr Oliver has made me a very handsome offer for the property. He seems to think his father always intended him to buy it from me."

Mr Eustace frowned. "I doubt that very much. Dear me, no – I don't think that's what Mr Gaunt had in mind at all. Though I dare say you'd be left with a great deal of money."

"Mr Oliver has made me realise I might not amount to much as a country landowner."

"Miss Summerbee, there is an envelope. . . . A letter, I believe, which Mr Gaunt instructed me to give you after his will was read and you were in legal possession of Hawk's Dyke. I have it here – " Mr Eustace fished in his bundle of papers and produced a long, cream envelope with my name on it in Adam's writing. The sight of that well-loved hand brought a lump to my throat at once.

"Perhaps you should read this before you make any decisions." Mr Eustace reached out to pat my wrist, then recalled that we were almost strangers. "Oh, goodness, please excuse me."

319

"No – I'm grateful to you, Mr Eustace. You've no idea how much I've longed for someone to do that today."

6

I walked out of the house, past the garden wall and the stables beyond, past the end of the orchard and on to where the ground began to rise behind the house. I carried Adam's letter in my hand, unopened; I'd promised myself I wouldn't read it until I'd reached that quiet place on the brow of the hill from where we'd so often looked down on the grey turtle-back of Hawk's Dyke rising tranquilly among its trees.

Pulling my coat about me I sat down on a boulder and stared at the old house until I'd almost conjured up Adam beside me once more. Then I opened his letter.

"My darling Kate,

"If you ever read these words, it can only be because I'm no longer there to say them to you, and to see you gaze at me earnestly with those great blue eyes of yours, like cornflowers turning to the sun.

"No doubt Dr Clement has told you about my heart condition and the milk-and-water existence he recommended. Forgive me, Kate, for not sharing my secret with you. You'll never know how much I longed to tell you – but I was afraid your love would make you turn me into an invalid, and I couldn't have borne that. Don't weep for me, now it's all over. My only regret is in leaving you, and causing you pain.

"By now you must know that Hawk's Dyke is yours. I give the house, the land, and the soul of the place into your keeping, and I've no doubt that you'll keep it well. I've seen you bend to touch the soft earth as if it were a live thing you felt under your hand, and lean into the east wind, smelling the wild green of the marsh. Wherever you were born, you belong here, Kate, just as I did. Let each succeeding season at Hawk's Dyke be the future we weren't able to share.

"As for me – I wandered for most of my life without knowing what lay ahead, and now I seem set to wander again. Yet if any part of me is allowed to linger like a mist-wraith in the fields of Hawk's Dyke, I promise you'll never be watched over by a gentler ghost, nor one who wishes you more happiness.

"Bless you, my darling, for being everything you are.

"With my love, always,

"Adam."

The grey rooftop of Hawk's Dyke swam before my eyes as I buried my face in my hands and wept.

7

I sent a note to the Abbey next day, asking Matthew to call.

When he arrived, I led him to the sofa in the parlour where he'd sat the day after Adam's death.

"I didn't expect to see you until tomorrow, Katherine."

"I know you didn't, but I've made up my mind about your offer to buy Hawk's Dyke, and I didn't want to keep you waiting any longer."

"I see." Matthew watched me uneasily. "You've made your decision very quickly, then. Perhaps you realised how good a price I offered you."

"It was a good price, Matthew, and I'm grateful to you for being so fair with me. However, I must tell you I've decided not to sell. Not to you, or to anyone else," I added as I saw the question flash into his mind. "No one else has even offered to buy, and I wouldn't consider it if they did."

Matthew's face had assumed the closed expression I knew so well.

"That fellow Eustace's behind this, isn't he? I saw him hanging about after the funeral, waiting to speak to you. What has he suggested? That you keep me waiting for a month or two, in the hope that I'll come back with a bigger price?"

"Mr Eustace didn't suggest anything of the sort. And it wouldn't make any difference if you did offer more – "

"Thirty pounds an acre."

"I beg your pardon?"

"I said – thirty pounds an acre. That's what I'm prepared to offer."

"That's a ridiculous price! It would take twenty-five years before you raised as much in rents."

"I'm aware of that. I told you, I want Hawk's Dyke."

"Oh, I can see that. But why, Matthew? Why do you want it so much?"

"Because it was his. Because it was my father's home and he loved it. Do you know, he used to dream about it when he went abroad – dreams so vivid he could smell the wind from the fen. He told me that once. Well, now I want it to be mine."

"He left Hawk's Dyke to me, Matthew, and he meant me to live here. I'm sure of that now."

"How can you possibly be sure? Who told you?"

"Adam told me himself. He left me a letter, explaining everything."

Matthew's face was flint-hard.

"I'll never sell Hawk's Dyke, Matthew. It's my home."

"*Your home?*" The words came out in a furious hiss. "Your reward, you mean! The reward you managed to charm out of a besotted old man!"

"Matthew!"

"I wouldn't have grudged you money, or a house in town, or anything else you'd set your heart on. But Hawk's Dyke – never! Can't you understand what this place means to me?"

"Why can't you understand what it means to me?"

"Oh, I understand that perfectly well! Hawk's Dyke means security for the rest of your life – and wealth beyond anything you can have dreamed of on that broken-down riverboat of yours."

I shook my head.

"Hawk's Dyke means *Adam* to me. That's why I want to keep it."

"And that's why I must have it."

"Matthew – are we arguing over Hawk's Dyke, or Adam himself?"

For several angry seconds we glared at one another. Then Matthew sprang violently to his feet.

"Oh, what's the use? Keep the place, if you're so determined to have it. Keep Hawk's Dyke, blast you – and I hope it makes you happy."

Turning on his heel, he marched out of the house, slamming the front door behind him.

Chapter Twenty-Two

1

After that, subtly, slowly, I became "Miss Summerbee of Hawk's Dyke", growing into my new identity as the land emerged gradually from the grip of winter. I was fortunate that my rebirth coincided with the slumbering of the land. Had I come to my inheritance in spring, the farms would have been alive with ploughing and harrowing and the drilling of grain or the squalling of newborn lambs; later in the year, hay-cutting or the grain harvest would have filled the lanes with lumbering wagons. But for that single short spell in the coldest weeks of the year work was at a standstill, and I was able to pretend that my life as the proprietor of fifteen hundred acres would go on much as it had before.

For a while I hovered between past and present, reluctant to abandon one for the other. Sitting at Adam's desk in the library, I wrote careful letters to Alice, Louise and Matthew inviting them to fetch anything of their own which still remained in the house, and mementoes of Adam too, if they wished. Matthew never replied at all, while Alice informed me coolly she'd send for her doll's house, which her daughter was now old enough to enjoy, but had no need of any keepsake of her stepfather's.

Together, Nell and I emptied the exemplary mansion, and packed Papa, Mamma and the wool-headed children into a hamper with their servants and their miniature household goods for the trip to the Abbey. With unexpected distress I watched the house itself carried on its side down the spiral stair. It wore a look of surprise on its respectable brickwork, the windows and door gaping open in astonishment at such topsy-turvy treatment; I made sure it was righted in the dogcart – knowing only too well how it felt to have one's life turned upside down in a few dreadful seconds – and watched its grey gables sway off towards the lane like a ruffled matron rescued from pickpockets.

As soon as she received my letter, Louise came herself, and stayed for three whole weeks before absence from her beloved James drew her back to Ely, scarred but supremely happy.

I could have warmed my hands at the glow of her contentment. It was a reminder of better times, as we stumped arm in arm over the frozen lawns or drove out in the landau, wrapped to our chins in rugs and shawls. Adam had given Louise what remained of her mother's jewellery on the day of her marriage, together with a silver-mounted dressing-case and other personal things; now I gave her his watch – that wonderful timepiece with its revolving constellations of stars which I'd mistakenly treasured as Matthew's. It was hard to part with even that, but I was glad I'd done so when I saw how Louise's eyes misted as I laid it in her hands. And after all – I had Hawk's Dyke.

The slam of the carriage door on Louise's visit was like the closing of a door on the past. Yet it was hard to imagine what my future would be. In three months' time I'd be twenty-six years of age – a young woman of no breeding and no reputation at all, and of small education, except for what I'd learned from Adam – but suddenly a woman of means, with tenants and servants to call me *ma'am* and treat me as if I belonged to a different world from their own.

But whose world was it to be? Not the world of Sourwell Abbey, though Henrietta continued to roll up fortnightly in her barouche to take tea with me in the parlour, plumping herself down with a sigh of satisfaction in an old wing armchair, her black satin boots thrust out towards the fire, her skirts pulled up to show stockings of startling green or Mexican blue. She brought me the gossip of the Abbey and the great houses round about, relishing every morsel of someone else's discomfort – and yet always, as she rattled on, I knew how much more she'd have enjoyed pouring it all out to Adam. That was why she came: not for me, but because old habits die hard, and just to sit in that well-remembered room was consolation of a sort.

Even the other visitor I remember particularly from that time came to me chiefly out of regard for Adam. This was Johnny Longstock, who arrived one blustery March morning, his grubby hands full of softly glowing violets and an expression of the deepest anxiety on his face. At the door he tried to give his flowers to Nell and retreat at once, but she pulled him inside and made him wait in the hall while she came to fetch me.

"I didn't mean it, miss – I mean ma'am – " he began as soon as he saw me at the turn of the stairs. "I came to tell you – " He thrust out the flowers like a gentle shield against the explosion of reproaches he expected. "I never meant to fall through the ice – I never would've gone near it, if I'd known what'd happen – I swear."

Poor child – it had been his ill-luck to give Adam the death he wanted, instead of a half-felled tree or a soulless boulder. It was unfair that he should have to bear a burden of guilt, just as I had until Adam freed me from it.

"Johnny, you weren't to blame. Mr Gaunt could have died at any time, and he would have been happy to know you were safe, at least."

"The Rector says I'm a cursed child. He says it was all my fault, and I'm a – *hinstrument of destruction*."

"Well, I don't believe you're an instrument of anything. And neither, I'm sure, would Mr Gaunt have done. You're a boy, Johnny, that's all – and boys get into mischief sometimes. It wouldn't be natural if you didn't. But I hope you're going to school regularly now."

"Yes, ma'am. Most days." Johnny's eyes slid away from mine, and I wondered precisely how many days constituted "most".

"Wait there for a moment."

Browsing among the library shelves the previous day, I'd come across a dog-eared sixpenny picture alphabet squeezed between two Latin volumes. Goodness knows whose it had been – perhaps one of the girls had brought it with her to Norfolk as a reminder of the schoolroom – but I fetched it now, and bartered it for the sweet-faced violets.

"That's for you, Johnny. You should be able to read it quite easily, if you've been attending to your lessons. Look – "*A* was an Archer, and shot at a Frog . . ." That wasn't hard, was it? And here – "*K* was a King, and governed a Mouse . . . *L* was a Lady . . .""

"She looks just like you," Johnny Longstock pronounced with conviction.

"Do you think so, Johnny? Well now . . . you never know. But take the book, and look after it. Mr Gaunt always said books were precious, and only barbarians damaged them."

His eyes round as saucers, Johnny tucked the book into the breast of his shabby coat and made off with it as if he'd stumbled on buried treasure.

I watched him run past the garden wall towards the stables and his own roundabout route home. I imagined him showing the book to his mother and to his brothers and sisters, hunched over it by the light of a candle-stub, and I wondered if he'd ever think of me, alone, with no one to share what I discovered in the pages of Adam's books.

That was when I realised that along with his house, Adam had bequeathed me his loneliness. I might be mistress of Hawk's Dyke, but elsewhere I was as out of place as a minnow in a cornfield. Walled up in my rambling home I woke alone, took my meals alone, and for exercise walked alone in the garden. In the evenings I read alone by the parlour fire until my eyelids began to feel heavy, then went upstairs to an empty bed and from habit lay down on one side only, alone.

With no one to turn to, the land itself became my companion and my solace. As the spring of 1871 brought the earth alive once more, I'd climb to the top of the rising ground behind the house, and on a clear day survey a good part of the countryside that was mine. I learned the names of the fields that were my children: Hall Barn Close – the Twelve-acre Pasture – East of the Orchard – the Mill Eight-acre – each one with its individual face and character, whether dressed up in stiff fringes of young barley or furrowed in homely corduroy.

I'd even inherited Adam's habit of fitful sleep, sometimes climbing to my vantage point before dawn and settling myself on the cool ground, my back to a boulder, to watch my land wake, little by little, and stretch itself to a new day. At that hour, the great white owl that roosted in the rafters of the Old Hall steading was still softly about his business, and sometimes a cat would slide, colourless, from the long grass to inspect me resentfully for a moment before stalking on his way.

Four . . . five . . . six . . . I lingered, half dreaming, while the church clock of Stainham divided the clear air into tidy segments with its chime. Often I remained at my post until the clatter of shod hooves from the Old Hall yard proclaimed that the first team was being led to the fields – and sometimes later still, until the distant clang of the school bell in Edmund Blewitt's hand sent me scuttling back to my solitary breakfast.

Day by day, I watched over what had been placed in my charge. When drought parched the land, I thirsted with it; when the April dust-storms blew seedlings and soil together into the ditches, I mourned their loss like a mother bereft. I planted herbs in a bed on the far side of the kitchen yard, and hovered over them: rosemary and parsley, they say, grow better if they're planted by a woman.

It was no more than Adam had asked of me years before, when he first brought me back to Hawk's Dyke – *Dream . . . create . . . cherish. . . . Isn't that what women do?* Yet now I worked from instinct, my understanding growing with the passing days. I no longer regretted the little deaths which came with winter, but filled my dreams with the first resurrected shoots of spring. Birth – death – rebirth: no matter what, the wheel would continue to turn. Adam might have died, but the land he'd given me renewed itself magically each year with exactly the same headlong, voracious relish for life I'd loved in him. I'd lost Adam, but Hawk's Dyke was mine to tend and cherish in his place.

And when the blue morning mists rose above the black ploughland of the old fens, I wondered if Adam's spirit hovered near to see whether I had remained true to his trust.

Shortly after Hawk's Dyke became mine, the elderly man who'd lived at Old Hall Farm and combined the duties of land agent and farm manager announced that he was now too old to begin life under a new employer, and that while he'd stay long enough to "see me on my feet", he'd retire as soon as someone could be found to replace him. This was a blow: the agent knew every cottage and every tree on Hawk's Dyke; he'd known the fathers of the present generation of children as boys, and understood their habits and their weaknesses like a stern uncle.

As long as I dared, I put off advertising for his replacement and set about learning from him about leases and tenancy agreements, the keeping of accounts, the division of the land into pasture and arable, the intricacies of feed and fertiliser, of muck and mole-catchers, and of the system of lodes and dykes which drained the fields. I went up to the bank at Lynn, enquired into the state of my funds and bought a town dress in impeccable black to wear in the landau to market. And to my dismay, the more I learned, the more I realised I didn't know and would probably never discover.

The agent was anxious to leave, and I still hadn't found a successor. Part of the problem was that Hawk's Dyke was a small estate in landholding terms. Adam had made his home there because it suited him, living off a large income from city rents and securities and ruling over Hawk's Dyke like a benevolent despot to whom profit was of secondary importance. His way wouldn't do for me: Hawk's Dyke was all I had – and, not for the first time, I remembered the enormous price Matthew had offered for it.

But the clever, well-trained young men who talked knowledgeably about the chemistry of the soil and white crop rotation expected 10,000 acres or more to practise their theories, and four hundred pounds per annum as a salary. My advertisement only brought broken-down military men to my door, with handkerchiefs in their sleeves and faces glowing from a lifetime of port they were now too hard-up to afford – or letters from articled clerks who'd failed their exams, or gamekeepers turned out of their posts for selling their masters' birds – and one, even, from a city butler who imagined he might enjoy a spell of country air, and assured me he was "well used to ruling persons below him".

I was soon almost in despair. And then, one evening, when I was frowning over *Diseases of Root Crops* in the parlour, Nell put her head round the door to interrupt me.

"A fellow come to see you, ma'am. About the job as agent, so it seems."

"What sort of time is this to come calling?"

"I told him that, ma'am. 'Best come back tomorrow,' I said, but he wouldn't take no for an answer."

"Oh, very well." No doubt here was yet another dismissed under-gardener looking for a comfortable berth. "Show him into the library, and I'll look him over."

"His name's William Dann," remarked Nell as she disappeared.

William Dann was dark and solidly built, perhaps five years older than I was, broad-shouldered and broad-browed, with a clear, challenging black eye and brass buttons on his moleskin waistcoat. He'd worked for several years as assistant to the agent of a large estate in Lincolnshire whose owner never visited it, but promotion was hard for him; his father had been neither a gentleman nor a farmer, and though he knew his trade well, he'd learned it in the furrows of another man's fields.

I liked the look of him at once, though there was something . . . something strange and unfathomable in those black, black eyes which unsettled me, like a sudden stirring in the depths of a quiet pool.

"I've turned men out for defaulting on the rent, though I didn't relish it," he informed me forthrightly. "I can tell you the weight of a bullock by the look of him to the nearest stone, I can thatch a stack as tight as you like, and write as plain a hand as the next man." He lifted one of his own square, capable hands to demonstrate the point.

"Do you understand the use of steam? We have reapers here, but we bring in a thresher from a contractor a few miles away."

"In Lincolnshire, we ploughed with a double-engined steam set which cost more than two thousand guineas. Though I'd not expect it on a place this size," he added hastily, seeing my mouth ajar.

"I fear the Hawk's Dyke farms are a poor shadow of what you're used to, Mr Dann."

"But I'd be my own man here, Miss Summerbee." The black eyes flashed defiantly. "I'm an ale man, not a sherry-drinker, you understand, and good places aren't so easy to find for a fellow like me. Besides, I was born in these parts, though I was raised elsewhere." Diffidently, he turned the brim of his felt wideawake between his fingers. "My father died over Stainham way about a year ago. He was an eel-fisher for most of his life."

"And his name was – "

"Aaron Dann. He was an old man, at the end. Ran away from the workhouse to die in a ditch, so I heard."

"Your father was Aaron Dann?"

Now I understood that dark, elusive gleam in the depths of William Dann's black eyes. No matter how little he'd known of the eel-man who'd crept like an animal through the marshes of Sourwell Fen, they were father and son – just as Adam and Matthew were father and son – and inescapably the wild magic had been passed on.

I'd never forgotten the blind panic of that day in the fen, however often I'd laughed at my fears with Adam. Even now it was enough to make me determined to send William Dann away empty-handed; I was rehearsing an excuse in my mind when he spoke again.

"Did you know my father, ma'am?"

"He used to bring fish and eels to the house. Mr Gaunt remembered him as a young man."

"Ah, well – that would be some time before he married my mother and built his hut in the fen. He was nigh on fifty years of age by then."

"In Stainham they say he murdered his wife and son."

"Not he! My mother was too quick for him, the old devil." William Dann snorted with contempt. "Which isn't to say he mightn't have done it one day, when he was far gone in drink. I don't drink much, myself," he added solemnly. "Alcohol steals your wits, and puts the devil in your mouth."

To hear this from the son of the demon of the fen! I was thankful he couldn't see the empty wine glass I'd left in the parlour. But already he'd passed on to the rest of his tale.

"My mother ran off one night with me in her arms, and never came back. She went to her married sister in Lincoln, and that's where I was raised."

"Didn't your father ever try to find you?"

"He was pleased to be rid of us, I shouldn't wonder. He wasn't a man to care what people thought of him."

"And now you want to come back and work for me."

For a moment he studied the worn rug at his feet. Then he raised his head and considered me a little, sideways, as if wondering how I'd receive what he had to say.

"It's a strange thing – " He stopped, and turned his hat-brim once more. "It's a strange thing, but though I wasn't raised on this land, I feel for it almost as if it was mine. Not mine to own, you understand – but mine as if it was family, like a wife and children, or people you've grown up with. *Familiar*, maybe. Riding over here, I couldn't rid myself of the notion, somehow. I felt . . . as if I was part of it all, like a tree-root or an old boulder in the ditch." He shrugged, embarrassed. "Sounds a bit mad, I dare say."

"No," I admitted. "I can understand how you felt."

"You can?"

"Perfectly." I understood, all right: how often had I stood at the top of the rise behind the house, and sensed the heartbeat of the land? It was the very quality I'd feared so much in the eel-fisher – that closeness to the essence of the living world – the gift, which Sam Duck had once claimed for me, of laying a hand on the earth, to feel it turning.

"I've only a few acres here, compared with what you're used to, but you'd live rent-free at Old Hall Farm, with as much milk and butter and firewood as you need. Do you think you'd make a good agent for Hawk's Dyke, William Dann?"

"I can only do my best, ma'am." William Dann gave the matter some thought. "But when all's said and done, I reckon my best would be good enough."

He'd almost reached the door when another question occurred to me.

"Tell me – though I'm afraid you'll think me rude. . . Do you, by any chance, have webbed feet?"

"Me, ma'am?" William Dann looked properly scandalised. "Not at all, ma'am, to be sure. What an odd thing to want to know."

3

William Dann was as hard a worker as he'd promised to be. Though my tenants might complain that whenever a man turned round he'd find the agent standing somewhere near, they couldn't accuse him of shirking his duties. Spending five or six hours a day on horseback, within weeks he'd made the acquaintance of most of the people on the five farms within our boundaries, the labourers and team-men, the yardmen and dairywomen along with the farmers and their families. He'd found out which cottagers raised pigs and which fences should receive attention before the rest; and in some mysterious way he'd discovered which of our labourers weren't above a little poaching on neighbouring Abbey lands, among the Earl's treasured pheasants.

From the very first day, he guarded the well-being of my land with a fierce devotion. In spite of his upbringing, he took a far sterner line than I did when John Slade went off to Leamington to confer with his brother Methodists and their friends, and came back with news of a National Agricultural Labourers' Union which every farm worker in the Stainham area was expected to join.

All they wanted was a few shillings more each week, for a couple of hours' less work. But by and large, the farmers in our part of the country were well organised; they banded together to turn union members out of their jobs, refusing to re-employ them, and since the spread of steam machinery meant fewer workers were needed in any case, wages were kept low. Many of the younger people gave up the struggle and drifted to the cities in the hope of making a living, or left the country altogether for new homes in Australia, New Zealand, or even Brazil.

By the end of 1874 the gentry in our part of the world were confident enough to ignore the rumblings of the agricultural unions in favour of a new topic of conversation. For a few dramatic weeks, at least, the whole of west Norfolk buzzed with the scandal surrounding Matthew Oliver's divorce.

4

Like Adam, I'd never imagined for a moment that Matthew would really rid himself publicly of his wife. Oh, everyone knew of couples who'd parted for one reason or another, or who shared the same house while living entirely separate lives – but to make a parade of the fact, to drag out the sordid details of a bankrupt marriage for the world to gape at . . . that was recklessness of a high order. Desertion, adultery – or in the case of a wife divorcing her husband, cruelty added to adultery – were supposed to be endured in dignified silence for the sake of the family ideal. Whatever measures were taken to mend matters, the arrangement was made behind closed doors, and the marriage remained outwardly intact. Now, to the horror of all his acquaintants, Matthew Oliver seemed determined to throw decency to the winds.

There was no mention in the proceedings of the Prince of Wales, despite the fact that he'd already made an appearance in the divorce court – not as co-respondent, but as a witness when Sir Charles Mordaunt attempted to divorce his wife. Though not named in the Mordaunt divorce petition, the fact that the Prince had frequently called on Lady Harriet Mordaunt and had written her letters was made much of by the Press, and for weeks afterwards he was hissed by an indignant crowd whenever he appeared in public.

"Matthew's hunting smaller game this time," Henrietta informed me sagely on her fortnightly visit. "I don't say he ever forgave Violet for that business with the Prince of Wales, mind you, but Charles talked him into hushing it up for the sake of appearances."

"And for the sake of his father-in-law's Oliver shares."

"Oh, assuredly." Henrietta stirred her tea with vigour. "And I dare say if Violet had been a sensible girl and behaved properly after that, things would never have come to such a pass."

"I thought Violet understood her position to a nicety."

"She can't have imagined Matthew would ever divorce her – she probably thought her father's Oliver shares were her insurance. Yet Matthew has his pride, just as his father had. He won't put up with being made to look a fool."

"But the Press will tear him apart!"

"Oh, they'll fall on the story like wolves! Mr and Mrs Matthew Oliver in the divorce court, for Heaven's sake – not to mention the Broadneys, though of course they've no choice in the matter. Charles says Sir George was apoplectic with rage when he heard the news."

"How does Charles know all about it?"

"Lawyer-talk, I should think." Henrietta made gossip signs with her fingers. "Apparently Matthew's found some slippery QC called Fuller to steer the whole thing through for him. A cousin on his mother's side, I believe. I tell you – " Henrietta leaned significantly towards me, "it's going to be a dirty business, Katherine. I only hope Matthew doesn't end up wishing he'd never started it. Mud sticks, you know," she added solemnly. "Mud sticks."

"But if the Prince of Wales isn't to be co-respondent, then who is?"

"Oh, my dear – " Henrietta reached out to lay a skinny hand on my arm. "That remains to be seen! But I believe there's a great deal of choice."

Reynolds' News reported the case from beginning to end, leaving out only those details which, it explained loftily, were "unfit for publication".

The gallery was jammed for the entire ten days of the case; newspaper reporters jostled, elbow to elbow, to record the names of the prominent men with whom Mrs Oliver was said to have had affairs – a Count Gregoriev from the Russian embassy, the Honourable Valerian Oxted, the seventeen-year-old Viscount Rockall . . . and a riding-master called Rio, unrecorded in the pages of the *Alamanach de Gotha*.

"A riding-master!" snorted Henrietta. "Let's hope he was handsome, at least."

Señor Rio turned out to be handsome enough to charge four guineas a lesson for his riding tuition – a fact which drew titters and ribald suggestions from the public gallery when it was revealed. Violet Oliver had made the fatal mistake of dismissing a maid for borrowing her pearl powder and her hat-pins. Now the girl appeared in the witness box to explain in graphic detail what she'd seen through the enormous keyholes of the Broadney mansion in Eaton Square.

Harold Fuller, QC, steered her expertly through her evidence.

Yes, Mrs Oliver was an accomplished horsewoman who could not be said to need riding lessons; no, she hadn't been dressed for equestrian exercise when Señor Rio called at Eaton Square, and in any case, what kind of horse was stabled in a lady's boudoir?

The girl had loitered, and listened, and finally peered through the vacant keyhole of the door which communicated with Mrs Oliver's bedroom.

"And from where you stood, could you see the *chaise-longue*?"

The maid looked blank for a moment, and then brightened.

"He didn't 'ave to chase 'er, sir. She seemed perfectly willin' to me, just as soon as the door was shut."

Mrs Oliver's counsel did his best to discredit the maid's evidence, to show that she'd lied to get revenge for her dismissal. But she stuck to her tale – and when Viscount Rockall's tutor told of afternoons he'd spent alone in the Broadney morning-room waiting for his charge to come downstairs, and when a cab driver was discovered to testify that "Mrs O" and "that Russian cove" had held a regular and energetic tryst in the back of his vehicle while it rolled aimlessly round Hyde Park, Violet's denials were pointless. The public gallery had judged and condemned her long before the petition for divorce was granted.

And through it all, the newspapers reported, Mr Matthew Oliver had sat grim-faced behind his lawyers and barristers, his eyes fixed on the royal arms above the bench, not a flicker of emotion crossing his face while the whole farcical business unfolded and his private life was held up to the hooting of the gallery.

"What the papers didn't know, of course," observed Henrietta casually a few days later, "is that George Broadney had Matthew followed by detectives as soon as he learned about the divorce action. He was planning a counter-suit, you see, if he could only find evidence that Matthew was seeing some other woman."

"How do you know that?"

"Charles heard." Henrietta tapped the side of her nose meaningfully. "Charles gets all the news whenever he sits in the House. His father did exactly the same. As far as I can see, their Lordships do nothing but gossip over their claret."

"But there wasn't a counter-suit."

"No. Because George Broadney's snoopers came back empty-handed. Matthew was apparently leading a blameless life. Pure as the driven snow."

"Perhaps he was too clever for them."

"Perhaps." Henrietta pursed her lips and studied me across the tea-table. "But they're a strange lot, the Gaunts – and Matthew's a Gaunt, whatever he calls himself. They can be saints or libertines as the mood takes them, but never moderate. There's no middle way with the Gaunts – it's got to be all or nothing. Though I'm sure you don't need me to tell you that."

Henrietta was right – I didn't need to be told. I understood that once Matthew had decided to finish his life with Violet, no discreet separation could ever have satisfied him. There had to be a complete severing of their ways, and if blood flowed, then so be it.

I returned to the newspaper description of his glacial manner in court. No artist's engraving could have done justice to that stony, closed-up expression of his – nor the fierce anger that it hid. He might pretend to be impassive, but only blind, all-consuming rage could have forced Matthew to make his betrayal public in such a squalid fashion.

I wondered what Adam would have done in the same circumstances: vanished abroad, perhaps – left his wife to her own devices and gone on his elusive way. But Matthew had stood his ground. After all, he had the Oliver Steam Navigation Company to consider, the great shipping line he loved more than any woman on God's earth. Whatever happened, Matthew still had Oliver's.

And I had Hawk's Dyke.

Chapter Twenty-Three

1

It was after the summer of 1874 that I began to notice a change in the view from my look-out post on the hill. I'd become accustomed to a chequerboard of colour stretching in every direction – in spring, a pattern of green pasture and black-brown ploughland which became a subtle weave of deep and paler green as the crops sprouted, and finally of green and gold at harvest time. Now I began to see more green pasture and less grain, and when at the start of 1875 my tenants gathered to pay their rents, each man had his own tale of low prices and hard times to tell me over the ceremonial glass of sherry which marked the end of our business together.

I always took a private room for the occasion at the "Victory" inn at Stainham crossroads, and the ritual of rent day was as time-hallowed as the British coronation. William Dann noted down each transaction in his ledger, I listened solemnly to each tenant's account of the year which had passed, and at three o'clock we all sat down to a dinner of boiled fish, roast beef, mince pies and cheese, washed down with large quantities of beer and port. Like a good landlord, I made a brief speech bewailing the state of British agriculture, called for a toast to the Queen, and departed at a decent hour to leave the farmers to their feast.

This year, however, I thought I'd sensed more than the customary note of gloom in the conversations over the sherry.

"What did you make of it?" I asked William Dann next day as we stood in the huge, cathedral-like barn of Old Hall Farm. "I know farmers are bound to complain about the size of their rents as a matter of course, but are things really as bad as they say?"

"Grain prices are falling, certainly." William Dann stared round the mottled clay walls of the near-empty building, his black eyes flashing resentfully. "It's men like your friend Mr Oliver who are spoiling our market. He must be making a tidy fortune, shipping cheap grain from North America and cheap wool from Australia and New Zealand. But it's taken ten shillings a quarter off the price our farmers can get for their wheat."

He ran a hand reflectively over the wooden flank of a grain dresser, as if it pained him to see the labours of its shutters and riddles go to waste.

"I can remember when there'd be three threshing floors in a barn like this, and maybe a dozen men at work. And now . . ."

He'd no need to finish. Nowadays a mechanical thresher was towed into the yard outside, linked up by rattling and slapping belts to a great steam-engine, and put to work swallowing sheaves and local men's jobs along with them. And still the imported free-trade grain defeated us.

At the end of that year, the Holloway family who'd been tenants of Mill Farm for almost a century gave formal notice that they wouldn't be renewing their lease. The eldest son had taken his sheep-rearing skills to New Zealand, the younger boy was at veterinary college, their daughters had married elsewhere, and liver-fluke had attacked their flock, knocking the heart out of the old couple themselves.

There was no rush of applicants for the lease of Mill Farm; after a fruitless few months William Dann took it in hand himself, and we set out to make from it whatever profit we could.

I'm sure the village expected more of me, "the American woman" who'd inherited the Hawk's Dyke land. They'd looked to me for scandal and high drama, and instead I lived alone in perfect propriety, settling further into spiky spinsterhood with every passing year.

It wasn't a state I'd sought for myself. But it had been my fate to love a man whose life did not run parallel with my own, and I'd learned to be grateful for the years we'd shared, instead of resenting the decades I'd spend without him. And besides – five years with Adam had been worth a lifetime with any of the ruddy-faced farmers who, I occasionally heard, speculated among themselves as to their chances of acquiring an American wife and fifteen hundred acres of land. By all accounts, the lady herself was already well broken to the plough, but from the look of her a furrow or two still remained to be enjoyed by the man bold enough to take her in hand.

I withdrew into myself, ignoring broad hints and heavy-handed compliments, and rejecting invitations to dine. Even at my very loneliest my flesh crawled at the thought of one of these men invading Hawk's Dyke. If I couldn't have Adam, I'd have no one. I needed only my home and my memories. I had Hawk's Dyke for a consort, and the wind which daily fluttered the leaves of the oaks to bring me the chatter of my far-flung family.

The cottage children I'd known when I first came to Norfolk were mostly adults themselves now. I'd notice a bent back in a field, and realise with a start that hardly a year since, that same back had been bent over a map of the world or a school slate. Becky Rudge – still as thin as a willow wand – was walking out with the farrier's son, and

Johnny Longstock, now seventeen, was assistant team-man on an Abbey farm, riding one of his huge charges out to the fields each day with a cheerful nonchalance that drew the eyes of every maid in the dairy.

Miss Summerbee of Hawk's Dyke was in danger of becoming an institution in the neighbourhood. In April 1877 I was thirty-two years of age – almost an "old trout" to the small boys who milled round the wheels of my landau on market days, just out of range of Sykes's long whip. I dare say I looked older: my face was thinner than before, and if my hair was as obstinately auburn as ever, it sometimes seemed to me as I put on my hat before my bedroom mirror that an indrawn, guarded expression had crept into my blue eyes.

Every market day the village would inspect me, sitting alone in my carriage, bolt upright in a narrow tie-back skirt and jacket and a plush Rubens hat, sparingly trimmed with ribbon. Louise, who occasionally came to stay at Hawk's Dyke with her three fair-haired infants and their nurse, always teased me about the plainness of my clothes.

"I can't imagine what's come over you, Katherine! Good Heavens, you don't possess a single tea-gown! If you don't take care, you'll become positively dowdy, cooped up here in the country."

"And who do I have to dress up for? No, my dear, my days of excitement are over now. I'm quite content to dwindle my life away here, dreaming about the past and turning as yellow as a dried-up leaf until no one can remember how ancient I really am. *Miss Summerbee of Hawk's Dyke* – that's my future, depend on it."

2

One person at least had different plans for me. Returning to the landau one market day in May after inspecting a new chaff-cutter with William Dann, I was surprised to find a bunch of creamy-yellow primroses lying on the opposite seat.

My first thought was that one of the cottage children had picked them for me – the flowers were simply bound with a piece of tough grass, their leaves wadded round the pinkish, hairy stems as if the gift had been the sudden impulse of a sunny morning.

"Aren't they pretty?" I held up the flowers for William Dann's inspection. "Did you happen to see who left them?"

"Not I, ma'am. Too much of a crowd hereabouts."

A few paces away I noticed Schoolmaster Blewitt staring so intently through his gold-rimmed spectacles at a litter of pigs that I wondered if he planned to enrol them in his academy.

337

"I imagine these came from one of your pupils, Mr Blewitt," I called out to him. "Will you take this sixpenny piece, and give it to whoever gathered them for me? I must say, it isn't like the children to run off without waiting in the hope of some reward!"

Edmund Blewitt smiled a little diffidently and clasped his hands behind his back.

"As a matter of fact, Miss Summerbee . . . *It was I.*"

"What was you, Mr Blewitt?"

"It was I who left the flowers for you, not one of the children. I'm gratified to hear that you like them."

"Oh, I like them very much indeed!"

"Excellent. *Primula vulgaris*, Miss Summerbee. I understand it's the favourite flower of Lord Beaconsfield – Mr Disraeli, the politician."

"I didn't know you took an interest in politics, Mr Blewitt."

He gave me a sharp look, and then observed, "There are many things you don't know about me, Miss Summerbee."

He was right: I was puzzled as to why Edmund Blewitt should have taken it into his head to present me with flowers. All I knew of him was that while he was a good and conscientious teacher, his position as Stainham schoolmaster was all he had in the world. The Rector was his absolute master; dismissed from his post, the schoolmaster would be no one at all, tossed back into the human flotsam from which he'd rescued himself years before by his own painful efforts. I was amused to find him trying to pose as a man of mystery.

"I seem to remember a time, Mr Blewitt, when you felt you knew more than you cared to about *me*."

"Ah." Edmund Blewitt's chin lifted a fraction, making the light flash from his spectacles. "That was a long time ago, Miss Summerbee. And one must judge as one finds, after all." He rocked for a moment on the balls of his feet. "May I – may I be so bold as to ask for a few minutes' conversation with you?"

"I imagine so, Mr Blewitt. Would right now suit you?"

"Perfectly, Miss Summerbee."

More puzzled than ever, I watched the schoolmaster clamber into my carriage and take the seat opposite me, where he perched on the very edge of the morocco cushion, one hand squarely on each knee like a man about to make a momentous announcement.

"Ahem."

"Yes, Mr Blewitt?"

"You look well, Miss Summerbee."

"Thank you. My health is usually excellent."

338

"Oh, I didn't mean *well* in respect of *well-being*. I used the word in a wider sense. You are in every way a handsome lady."

"Am I, Mr Blewitt?" I was utterly taken aback. "It's most kind of you to say so."

"It was merely a statement of fact, Miss Summerbee. Generally speaking, I have observed that possession of a carriage and pair tends to flatter the female appearance – and an open C-spring landau especially so."

Edmund Blewitt pushed his spectacles up the bridge of his nose and gazed about him as if pleased by the view from the mildly elevated vantage point of the landau. Then he fixed his little hedgehog eyes upon me once more.

"Your tenants speak most highly of you, Miss Summerbee, and the labourers, too. Your charity has become quite a by-word in the district."

"I don't look on it as charity, Mr Blewitt. I simply do what I can for others."

"I am favourably impressed, nevertheless. There was a time, Miss Summerbee, when I didn't expect to admire anything you might do. Yet I find myself almost . . . moved. Which is why I have been able to satisfy the delicacy of my conscience regarding this approach to you today."

"The primroses," I hazarded.

"No – not the primroses." Edmund Blewitt's nose twitched with irritation, and his spectacles slipped back to their customary position. "The primroses were merely a . . . prologue, if you like, to the proposition I am about to lay before you. I understand that flowers are required on these occasions."

He cleared his throat. "In weighing up the pros and cons of this matter – "

"Which matter, Mr Blewitt?"

"I am coming to that. One step at a time, please." The schoolmaster paused to make sure of my entire attention. "In weighing up the matter, I reminded myself that you were not a woman blessed by an education –for which, of course, I do not hold you to blame in any way – "

"I'm glad to hear it."

"No, no – circumstances conspire against the best of us, Miss Summerbee. Circumstances conspire." Edmund Blewitt cleared his throat once more. "*Remember, Blewitt*, I said to myself then, *how easy it is for a simple, unlettered girl to have her head turned by a gentleman of comfortable means, and to fall into the path of sin.*"

"Mr Blewitt!"

The schoolmaster held up a white hand to silence my indignant protest, quite transported by the flood of his own oratory.

"I pride myself I'm not in the habit of making pretty speeches to ladies. I speak as a plain man, Miss Summerbee, and I must tell you that after considerable heart-searching I have come to the conclusion that you are not by nature a wicked creature. Your past mistakes were the product of an affectionate but uneducated mind, and it would be morally wrong of me to let a healthy woman such as yourself go to waste, as it were, because of a single irregularity."

Beads of perspiration broke out on Edmund Blewitt's brow, and he gripped his knees more tightly.

"In short, I am prepared to raise you to an honest position in the eyes of the world. I shall make you Mrs Blewitt – even though I should have to resign my teaching post in consequence. I couldn't risk the innocence of the children, you understand . . ." He paused, and ran the tip of his tongue over his lips. "But never mind – I will do it: I will sacrifice my future, and make do with life as a country gentleman at Hawk's Dyke."

The schoolmaster turned to gaze greedily round the market-place – at William Dann, selling lambs on my behalf a few yards away – at my elegant landau – and finally at me. I saw him rub his damp palms.

"You sanctimonious buffoon!"

"I beg your pardon?" Edmund Blewitt's mouth formed a perfect pink "O", and I realised that he'd genuinely considered his offer an act of the greatest charity.

"You mealy-mouthed little worm! *Raise* me, would you? Make me Mrs Blewitt, and call it a *sacrifice*! Dammit, I wouldn't marry you if you were the last man on earth!" I shouted at him, and remembering one of my father's favourite insults, added "Egg-sucker!"

Edmund Blewitt rose to his feet with as much dignity as he could muster, clutching hastily at the side of the carriage as the springs swayed beneath him.

"I have never – " he began.

"Get out! Get out of my carriage before I throw you out myself!"

Muttering darkly, the schoolmaster wrestled with the door-catch, and as the door swung open, found himself slung like a hammock between its far corner and the high sill of the landau. Somehow, he scrambled to the ground, but by now I, too, was on my feet.

"And take your blasted primroses with you!"

I hurled the flowers at him with all the pent-up outrage in my soul, and the bunch exploded on his shoulder, sprinkling him with a litter of leaves and blossoms.

"Get out of my sight!" I shrieked, my foot already on the iron step.

With a look of alarm, Edmund Blewitt spun about and set off at a trot down the main street of Stainham. Outside the baker's shop his injured dignity began to return, inspiring him to stop and look round.

"Guttersnipe!" he yelled.

It was impossible to run in that tied-back skirt, or I'd have had him for sure. In spite of that, I hitched my hem up to my calves and set off in pursuit, hobbling furiously after him as fast as my pinioned knees would allow. My last sight of the schoolmaster was of his portly, black-clad back disappearing, poker straight, among the market-day crowds while his legs whirled a frantic sprint below.

3

At least I'd given the village something new to gossip about for a week or so before talk returned to the ever-falling price of grain and the consequent shrinking of farm profits. Whatever the truth of the matter, much of the blame for the farmers' troubles was laid at Matthew Oliver's door: Matthew was the shipowner our farmers knew best, so it followed that it must be the cheap Russian and American grain shipped in Oliver vessels which was forcing them into bankruptcy. For the second year running, I was forced to reduce rents at Hawk's Dyke, while the cost of repairs remained as high as ever. With no income from railway shares or coal-mines to make up my losses, I, too, began to look nervously towards the future.

Matthew, on the other hand, never seemed to doubt what the future would bring him. From Louise's letters I'd learned that the ink was hardly dry on his divorce papers before he'd hurled himself into the business of his shipping line with more determination than ever. No matter what the world might say of him – that he'd pursued his wife with ungentlemanly malice, and would now be plain *Mr* Oliver to the end of his days – Matthew answered any criticism by increasing the power and tonnage of his fleet of ships.

Business poured into the Oliver offices in Shanghai and Calcutta; the Oliver house-flag was a familiar sight in Hong Kong and Yokohama, in Madras and Colombo, in Singapore and Surabaya. But however far his ships might sail towards the east, it was the western route across the North Atlantic which remained Matthew's obsession. Since the end of the Civil War, trade between Britain and the United States had boomed. Merchants and millionaires expected a safe, fast and luxurious

341

service between the two countries, and the shipping lines' battle for the North Atlantic trade became a matter of glory as much as of profit, to be fought out in bigger, faster and even more magnificent vessels.

It was a battle Matthew intended to win. By the spring of 1878, the first of two gigantic additions to the Oliver fleet was well advanced in the builders' yard – the *Aldebaran*, to be followed by her sister the *Arcturus*, named in the tradition of Oliver's greatest ships, after stars whose names began with an *A*.

Already, an Oliver passenger vessel left Liverpool for New York every week, meeting her opposite number in mid-Atlantic and arriving after a ten-day passage at the other side. The two new sisters were designed to make the crossing at an average of twenty knots, taking little more than seven days for the trip. Once the *Aldebaran* was in service, Grand Saloon passengers would be able to spend that week in the lavish luxury of a first-class hotel, lazing in an armchair before an open marble fireplace or under the glittering chandeliers of the dining-room without ever being aware they were at sea at all.

And somewhere out of sight of the saloon grandees, the *Aldebaran* would have steerage accommodation – narrow, six-berth cabins on a lower deck where for a mere four pounds passengers prepared to bring their own bedding, eating utensils and water-can were promised the same fast voyage to the United States.

I'd long since lost interest in steerage passages to New York, but as the *Aldebaran*'s maiden voyage drew nearer, the weather took a hand in adding other, unexpected names to her passenger list.

4

How many years had passed since the warm rain of the lower Mississippi had trickled over my skin? East Anglian rain was an altogether different affair – sometimes no more than drizzle, sometimes a stinging, wind-borne assault which drenched skin and hair within minutes – but it was always cold.

For five solid months in the spring of 1878 it rained incessantly. Out in the winter-bare fields the deluge spattered on the ploughed earth, turning the furrows into brooks and the brooks into rivers with no outlet to the sea. The land became a sponge. The marsh meadows were transformed into lakes in no time at all; to walk the ploughland was to sink to the ankles in clogging mud, and even the pasture squelched and buckled beneath the boot-soles. Bedraggled sheep clustered under the trees, their feet rotten with damp. Cows slithered about in thigh-boots of mud. And still it rained, a relentless torrent which poured out of a sky like an inverted silver bowl, while the farmers watched, grim and desperate, at the gates of their unsown fields.

And as if that wasn't enough tribulation for us to bear, one day in miserable, rainy May the little river which trickled harmlessly under a bridge on the Wellborough road just short of the Stainham crossroads suddenly outgrew its modest channel, and overnight developed the temper of a tyrant. Scorning its old route under the bridge, it tore down the ancient bank of soil which had cradled its meanders, swept out across the corner of a meadow, and poured into the gully of Goosefeather Drove to maroon the Longstocks' cottage along with two others.

"The highway's under water for a good fifty yards," William Dann warned me when I insisted on going to see what could be done for the stricken cottagers.

"We'll wade if we have to, then. We can't just leave the poor creatures to fend for themselves."

"Those aren't Hawk's Dyke people, you know. Goosefeather Drove's on Abbey land."

"And how much do you reckon the Earl will do for them? Not a thing, if I know that agent of his. Albert Longstock was one of Slade's union men, and I doubt if the Earl will have forgotten that. So tell them to saddle my horse, and we'll ride over and see what's to be done."

The marooned cottages were a depressing sight. The two which were visible from the highway stood knee-deep in water, their doors thrown wide open as if the inhabitants had long since given up any attempt to keep out the flood. In one dwelling a young woman paddled across her flooded floor, her skirts looped above her shins, while her husband, with their youngest child in his arms, struggled towards the farm cart which held the few belongings they'd managed to save.

Leaving William Dann to ask where the refugees were bound, I rode on down the lane towards the Longstocks' cottage, the mare fussing and slithering over hidden stones under her hooves. Here the water was deeper, lapping at the lower window-sills; tree branches and the remains of the midden had been sucked in, a wooden stool and a child's doll sucked out.

As my horse splashed towards the cottage, I noticed that on a nearby patch of higher ground which the swollen river had turned into an island, a few pathetic sticks of furniture had already been stacked high and dry above the flood. John and his younger brother were wading to and fro, thigh-deep through what had once been a potato patch, while old Grandfather Longstock sat among untidy piles of bedding on a wooden chest, surveying the wreck through sorrowful eyes.

"Where's your mother, John?"

"Up there, scraping together what she can." He halted for a moment amid the whirling water, and pointed to a tiny casement in the thatch.

"Is everyone safe?"

"Safe enough – though my grandfer' was sleeping in the kitchen, and the river had him wet through before he knew what was up. Still – " He waved a grim hand towards his sodden home. "It's cured the weeds in the potatoes, at least."

While the Longstocks and their neighbours went off to roost in corners of nearby barns, men set about filling and carting sacks of clay to mend the embankment the river had torn down. After a few days, the water level had subsided in Goosefeather Drove, leaving six inches of stinking mud on the floors of the houses, tide-marks like tea stains on the inside walls, and despair in the hearts of everyone who saw the wreckage.

The Earl's agent wouldn't rebuild – not for a union family like the Longstocks – but sent men for two days to shovel mud. After that, since the rain had let up at last, the men departed to catch up with long-delayed farm work.

Reluctantly, the Longstocks began to re-establish their home. I gave them a mattress and some blankets to replace those they'd lost, and Henrietta sent cutlery from the servants' hall, quite forgetting it was marked, like all the rest, *Stolen from Sourwell Abbey*.

At last the family moved back into their cottage, but sadly, conscious that things had changed. After years in their house they'd been uprooted overnight, sent floating from home like their kitchen table, swilled away from their little patch of Goosefeather Drove: and suddenly the family took a hard and unsparing look at their future on the land.

What lay ahead for John and his younger brothers and sisters? Their best prospect was a lifetime of labouring and domestic service which would leave them no better off than their parents, in spite of the skills they'd learned. For the first time the Longstocks faced the unthinkable: perhaps the answer was to break with the past altogether and make a new life for themselves in a country where earls and their pheasants were not the hereditary masters of the people. Round a tallow candle at their water-bleached table, the family brooded on their future, and decided to emigrate to America.

I was surprised by their choice of new home.

"Why don't you go to Australia or New Zealand? They say there's still land there for the taking, while a great many people have gone to the United States since the end of the war."

"Ah, but you told us every man was equal in America, ma'am. Black, white, yellow – every man jack of 'em."

"The Constitution says so, certainly."

"Well then, that's good enough for us. All we ask is the same chance as the next fellow."

The Longstocks were firmly set on America. The long sea voyage to Australia terrified them, its institutions sounded too British, and they'd heard tales of convict settlements and lawless robbers terrorising the country people. And besides, wasn't Mr Oliver building a fine new ship, the *Aldebaran*, precisely to take people like themselves to New York? Now, Mr Oliver knew what was what. Money stuck to his fingers, whichever country he went to, and America had been good to him. Surely the *Aldebaran* was an omen of good fortune, if anything was.

It took the Longstocks almost a year to scrape together enough to pay for the journey, even with every member of the family earning what he could. But somehow, by borrowing, selling, and saving everything they had – and, if the truth were told, helped more than a little by me – they managed to gather up enough to pay for four steerage passages for John, his parents and his brother, and two half-fares for the younger pair. Grandfather Longstock refused to go with them. When his fingers grew too rheumatic to split hazel broaches for the thatchers – well, the workhouse wasn't such a bad place, so he'd heard. America was a young folks' country, with no use for old men like himself.

At last, in April 1879, amid tears and well-wishing the Longstocks gathered up their modest belongings and left for Liverpool in time for the maiden voyage of the *Aldebaran*.

For the next three weeks I devoured every newspaper report on the new Oliver flagship. Mr Oliver planned to send off his new vessel with a blaze of celebration; there were to be speeches by everyone remotely concerned with it, brass bands on the quayside, and a great dinner in a Liverpool hotel the night before the vessel sailed. Captain Travis of the *Antares*, I learned, had been given command of her: Mr Oliver himself, it was announced, would sail in her to New York. Lords This and That were among the passengers; opera stars were aboard, and more financiers than you could shake a cash-box at.

It seemed there had been almost indecent competition for the best staterooms. *Aldebaran* was one of the wonders of the age, and the whole of fashionable England wanted to stroll ashore in New York, casually letting drop the fact that this was how they had travelled.

And the new ship was so safe! Why, one would hardly know one was

345

at sea at all. In a mere seven days one would walk the pavements of Broadway, as if crossing the Atlantic was no more hazardous than hailing an omnibus – supposing one had ever considered travelling by omnibus, of course.

Aldebaran sailed on the morning of the 8th of May, as I sat in my parlour contemplating yet another fall in rents in the New Year and reflecting that my land was worth only two-thirds of what Adam had entrusted to me. Not for the first time, I wondered if I'd justified his blind faith. Perhaps I, too, should have sold out to someone more suited to the task, and sailed off to a new life in America.

On May 17th the British newspapers broke the news which had been telegraphed across the sea. The mighty *Aldebaran* had collided at night in the Western Atlantic with the steamer *Neustadt* and was believed to have sunk like a pot, taking a great number of her passengers with her.

Chapter Twenty-Four

1

Matthew Oliver was not among the dead. That was established almost at once. Lords This and That had perished gallantly after putting their ladies into a ship's boat; every officer aboard had gone down with his vessel, along with most of the passengers on the steerage decks in the ship's bowels. But Mr Oliver, the moving spirit behind the treacherous *Aldebaran*, had seen to it that his own life was safe. *Devil take the hindmost* – Matthew Oliver had saved his skin.

In everyone's mind, Matthew became the villain of the piece. More than a thousand people had been drowned on an Oliver vessel, and the public, led by the popular press, demanded a scapegoat. Captain Travis of the *Aldebaran* had died with his ship, and there was no satisfaction to be had from reviling a dead man; but Matthew Oliver had committed the crime of staying alive, and the newspapers turned on him with the full venom of the smugly righteous.

It didn't matter that the *Neustadt*, which had sunk within minutes, was believed to have run into the *Aldebaran*'s bow. A thousand people who'd trusted the Oliver ship to be the fastest, grandest, safest thing afloat were now at the bottom of the ocean, while Matthew Oliver, the man who'd created and owned the hell-ship, had sneaked off to enjoy his grisly profits. If the *Aldebaran*'s commander had had the decency to go down with his vessel, surely the ship's owner should have met death heroically on the bridge at his side?

For several days, the *Aldebaran* affair took up column after column in the newspapers. In vain, company spokesmen pointed out that the *Aldebaran*'s owners had never claimed it to be unsinkable – the boast had been made by the newspapers themselves. Accidents at sea, they added, were hardly rare: if the ship's crew hadn't acted with speed and bravery, even more lives might have been lost.

But the Press brushed their protests aside. Mr Oliver, they reminded the people of Britain, had been involved in a squalid divorce a few years earlier, when he'd ruthlessly exposed his wife's affair with her riding-master in open court. Small wonder that such a man had fled to a coward's place in a ship's boat, leaving women and children behind to drown.

347

Chanting crowds collected in front of the dolphin-handled doors of the Oliver offices in Liverpool until police were sent to remove them. Under cover of darkness, someone broke into the guarded grounds of the Oliver mansion and threw stones through several windows. The word "Coward" was daubed in yellow paint on the surrounding wall, and prominent businessmen took out advertisements in the newspapers offering sympathy to the bereaved and hinting that Matthew Oliver's behaviour was beneath contempt.

And when at last the story began to slip from the newspaper leader columns, Sir George Broadney gave it new life by suggesting his daughter Violet had only been driven to take her string of lovers by her husband's brutishness. The newspapers leaped delightedly on this new twist to the tale. If Violet Oliver hadn't already left for Venice with the twenty-one-year-old son of an Italian count, she'd have found herself as much of a heroine as Miss Florence Nightingale.

Every day, I studied the published lists of those who'd survived. One by one, the saloon passengers were declared either safe or drowned, but no one bothered to do the same for the nameless mass in the steerage accommodation. Their crowded, four-pound berths had been low in the bow of the ship, in the very place ripped open by the collision. All that was certain was that a few people had struggled up to the open deck and had managed to save themselves. For the rest. . . . Survivors told of hearing banging and frantic shrieks from the steerage dormitories as the vessel's bow sank lower in the water – followed by nothing but dreadful silence.

I waited desperately for word of the Longstocks. I couldn't believe all their valiant efforts to raise the price of a passage had only led them to death in a cold sea. I wrote for information to the Oliver offices in Liverpool, and a clerk replied in the weary tones of a man who'd written countless identical letters, that a handful of steerage passengers were believed to have been landed in New York, but no one had thought of taking their names or of asking where they were bound. I rode over to call on Grandfather Longstock in Goosefeather Drove, and by the light of his kitchen fire we assured one another that John and his family were sure to have been among that little group who had survived.

In June, a Board of Trade inquiry into the disaster reported that the *Neustadt* had been entirely to blame for steering directly across the *Aldebaran*'s path – but no one took any notice. Matthew Oliver had the effrontery to be alive while a thousand people had been drowned aboard his so-called "unsinkable" vessel. That, as far as the public were concerned, made the disaster Matthew Oliver's fault.

348

Yet the newspapers' relentless hounding of the *Aldebaran*'s owner was frustrated by the fact that no one had set eyes on him since he'd been hauled, concussed, from one of the ship's boats by the crew of the *City of Bristol*, which had rescued most of the survivors. There were rumours that Matthew Oliver had returned to England – that he was in London – that he'd changed his name and grown a beard – that he'd blown his brains out with a pistol and the shipping line had paid to have his remains buried secretly at sea.

And then, one drenching evening in what promised to be a ruinously wet Norfolk summer, Nell bustled through the hall at Hawk's Dyke to answer a knock at our door. She returned to the parlour with her hands clasped over her stomach and a grim expression on her face.

"It's Mr Oliver," she announced flatly. "He's come back."

2

Matthew came warily into the room like an animal sensing a trap. He was lean and hollow-eyed, and I was sure that with a single careless movement I could have sent him crashing away into the rainy night.

As it was, the shoulders of his overcoat shone with wet, and he carried a sodden wide-brimmed hat in his hand.

"Nell will take your coat."

"I won't stay. I was just curious to see if the place had changed."

"Nevertheless, you're dripping on the rug."

Matthew shot me a defiant look, but gave up his coat all the same. Nell swept out, banging the door behind her.

"Why don't you sit down?"

"I told you, I'm not staying."

Like a man determined to go his own way, Matthew prowled to the window and stared out for a moment over the rain-swept lawn, vivid green against the dull grey of the evening. Then he turned back into the room.

"You don't seem surprised to see me."

"I'm not surprised – though I can't tell you why."

"There aren't many doors open to me at the moment."

He gazed out of the window once more, the leaden evening light deepening the bitter lines at either side of his mouth where the closed-up expression had left its mark. Yet I had only to shut my eyes to see Adam watching storm clouds roll over the crest of the oaks from that same deep-silled window, as self-contained and enigmatic as Matthew was at that moment. Adam, too, had claimed the right to go his own way. And suddenly I began to resent Matthew standing there, in the place which had been Adam's – not because of the *Aldebaran* and what had happened aboard her, but because his presence threatened my dreams. Effortlessly – cruelly – he reminded me how little of Adam I'd been able to call my own.

"They've stabled my horse, I see."

"So I should think, on a night like this."

"I had the devil of a ride out here, thanks to that cat-shanked brute. He belongs to the "Victory" in Stainham."

"You're staying there?"

"I've taken a room for the night. I don't stay anywhere long."

Matthew tore his eyes away from the mesmerising downpour, and considered me thoughtfully from his post at the window.

"Were you afraid I'd want to stay here at Hawk's Dyke?"

"I wouldn't refuse you a roof over your head. You can still have Alice's room, if you need it."

"*Alice's room?*" Matthew seemed amused. "I don't imagine Alice has slept here for nearly twenty years. Is that doll's house of hers still upstairs?"

"Not any longer. She had it taken over to the Abbey after your father died."

"Nothing else has changed, then. This parlour is just as I remember it."

He was doing it again – forcing me to look with my eyes at all those things I saw only in my memory. He stood there in obstinate silence with his hands in his pockets, staring round the room, making me uncomfortably aware of the faded silk upholstery of the old sofa, the brandy browns of the once-brilliant rugs on the floor, the smoke-yellowed ceiling . . . everything I'd been afraid to change by so much as a detail lest the spell of the past slip away.

"Why have you come back here, Matthew? Now, when everyone's looking for you."

There was a moment's silence.

"I used to hunt once, you know. There was a sort of mad excitement in charging over the landscape with the hounds streaming out ahead." Matthew glanced out of the window once more. "I didn't realise how damnable it must have been for the fox."

"Are you running away, then?"

"No." He didn't seem to resent the suggestion. "I've just been wandering around, thinking. Asking myself questions, mainly."

"Do you expect to find your answers here?"

"Some of them, perhaps."

350

He came back towards the hearth and threw himself down in the old wing chair.

"I wish my father was still alive." He looked up, and saw sheer disbelief in my face. "We never agreed about anything, and yet . . . I don't believe he'd have turned his back on me. He'd have listened, at least."

"You won't find him here, Matthew. You've left it too late for that."

"Perhaps."

Deep in my heart, I felt the old challenge. And I refused to share Adam with him. The memories were mine – blurred by time, but mine alone – and now Matthew had come with Adam's face and Adam's voice, a usurper in a beloved mask. . . . And had made the past vivid, even as he stole it from me.

"You can't hide yourself here, you know. They'll find you in a day or two."

His grey eyes swept calmly back to my face.

"I dare say they will. But as I told you, I'm not running away."

"The newspapers seem to think you've good reason to run."

If he noticed the sharpness in my voice, he ignored it.

"George Broadney came to see me one night with a loaded pistol. He marched into the house without a word, and as soon as we were alone he took the gun out of his coat pocket and laid it on the table."

"If he didn't shoot you after the divorce, I can't see why he'd do it over this."

"The pistol was for me. He told me I was a worthless coward, and if I cared a damn for Oliver's I should do 'the decent thing' and blow my brains out with it. And then he left."

"You'd never do anything so stupid."

"As I said, I've no intention of running away." Matthew gave a bitter smile. "I threw the gun through a glass cabinet, and went to bed."

"I'm pleased to hear it."

"No, you aren't. You're no happier to see me than the rest of them." He studied me carefully for a moment. "This might amuse you."

From an inner pocket he took a folded wad of paper and held it out to me. The newsprint was thick and coarse – a twopenny street ballad of the kind still sold to celebrate the hangings of notorious murderers or to lampoon rival politicians. Two columns of smudged verses filled a sheet headed *The Tragic Wrecking of the Good Ship Aldebaran, and the Mortal Cowardice of her Owner, as printed by Taylor of Brick Lane, Spitalfields.*

Disconcerted, I ran my eye down the verses. They were no more than doggerel, mostly a lurid account of the tragedy drawn from the lively imagination of the poet. Then I came to the two final stanzas:

The noble Captain kept his bridge,
The Mate, he too was drown'd:
But Mr O——, he found a boat,
And sneaked off, safe and sound.

Let others die: he'd saved his life,
That yellow, craven b——d!
Small wonder that his pretty wife
Preferred her riding master!

I handed back the paper in silence, and watched Matthew fold it carefully and restore it to his pocket.

"Why on earth do you carry it around with you?"

"What good would it do to throw it away? Would it stop people talking?"

"I don't suppose so."

He was watching me again, resting his cheek on the fingers of one hand just as Adam had done.

"What if I told you it wasn't true?"

"That the ship didn't sink after all? That you didn't get into a boat?"

"Oh, I went off in a boat, all right. It's how I came to be there that matters." He paused. "Well, Kate?"

"I prefer *Katherine*, if you don't mind."

"As you please, then! We'll talk about something else. How will your farmers pay their rents after another few weeks of this rain, Miss Summerbee? I fancy it will make something of a hole in your income for the year. There now, that's an excellent subject for conversation."

"All right, Matthew – why were you in the boat?"

I heard him take a breath.

"Because someone else decided my life was worth saving. That's why."

"In all that confusion? Surely the poor wretches were too busy trying to save their own lives."

"Not Captain Travis." Matthew regarded me steadily. "Travis had made up his mind he was a dead man as soon as the ship started to sink – and he was the calmest human being I've ever seen. There was a boat stuck in the falls on the port quarter – people were pitching into it from all sides, jumping out from the deck – and Travis went down to take charge. You'd have thought he was organising a pleasure cruise, not getting ready to drown." Matthew's voice was grim. "Travis was a good man. I thought I'd done the right thing by giving him the *Aldebaran*."

The name struck a chord in my memory.

"Wasn't it Captain Travis's son you saved from the dock in Liverpool? I saw the story in the newspapers."

"The papers made too much of it. I just happened to be first in the water." Matthew made a slight gesture with one hand. "But now, in return, Travis has condemned me to this misery."

"How's that?" I couldn't keep the suspicion out of my voice.

"As soon as the falls were free, Travis ordered me into the boat."

"And you did as he said?"

"Of course not! There were women and children waiting on deck for the next boat to be launched. Do you really think I'd have left them, Kate?"

"Katherine," I corrected him automatically.

"Oh, for God's sake! Answer the question!"

"I found it hard to believe, certainly. I remember you taking down Pa's flag on the *Bellflower*, when Farragut's men were watching from their warships. You weren't afraid then."

"I was scared to death that day, if you want the truth – far more afraid than I was on the *Aldebaran*. But while the ship was sinking, I didn't have time to think of myself. I was too taken up with trying to get other people clear."

"But you didn't die, all the same."

"Travis ordered me into the boat a second time, and I told him not to be so damned stupid. I remember him saying something about *owing me a life* – his son's, I suppose. Then he gave the order to lower the boat, and just as I was leaning over the side to make sure it would clear the lower deck, he grabbed me by the shoulder and hit me as hard as he could on the jaw. My head swam, my legs gave way – and next thing I knew, he'd pitched me over the side into the boat as it swung down into the water. I remember crashing down on the gunwale and someone hauling me aboard before I lost my grip. I was pretty concussed."

"I see. Well, it's a good tale, I must admit. Who else have you told it to?"

"It isn't a tale. It's the truth." He stared at me. "Katherine – I have a thousand deaths on my conscience as it is. The newspapers were right; it was *my ship*, and I haven't tried to escape the responsibility for that." He was still staring, trying to convince me of his sincerity. "A child died – a boy of about five or six – right next to me in the boat. His mother was cradling him in her arms, hugging him, calling his name, but he didn't seem to hear. No one even tried to do anything for him – all they could think of was trying to get clear of the steamer. I'd have done anything possible to save that child, but I was completely, utterly helpless. I could send seventy-odd ships sailing off round the world, but I couldn't prevent one boy's death." At last he let his eyes slide from my face. "I don't tell lies about moments like that."

"Who else knows about all this?"

"I haven't told anyone else. What's the use, when I can't prove what I say?"

"Do you mean to say nobody saw Captain Travis throw you over the side? You were surrounded by crowds of people, but not a single soul saw it happen?"

"It was over in seconds, and most people didn't give a thought to anyone but themselves at that moment. Travis could have sworn to the truth of it, but Travis is dead."

"I see."

"Will you stop saying *I see* like that?" He stared at me coldly. "You don't believe a word I've said, do you?"

"I'm not sure, Matthew. I never know what to believe, with you. You've told me lies before, when it suited you."

"This is different."

"I don't see why it should be."

"What do I have to gain by lying to you? It doesn't make a blind bit of difference whether you believe my story or not. You can't help me."

"Yes, you're quite right – it doesn't matter what I think. In fact, it doesn't really matter what anyone thinks of you at the moment, because after a while the fuss will die down, and people will forget. You'll build more ships, the company will make bigger profits, and you'll be the investors' hero again in a year or two."

Matthew shook his head.

"No," he said quietly. "Oliver's will build ships and make their profits, but I won't have anything to do with it. Not if George Broadney has his way."

"Why not?"

"My ex-father-in-law has just about convinced the directors I'm a thorough embarrassment to the company, and the sooner they get rid of me the better it'll be for all concerned. They'd like to buy me out altogether, but they'll settle for voting me off the board."

"Can they do it? Can they take Oliver's away from you like that?"

"If they all join with George Broadney to vote against me – yes, I expect they could do it."

"That would be condemning you without a hearing!"

"That's true." Matthew smiled fleetingly. "At least you gave me a hearing first."

"I haven't condemned you." I saw his eyebrows lift in disbelief. "I haven't made up my mind yet."

"It sounded to me as if you had. And if you don't believe me, why should the Oliver's directors be any different?"

He rose to his feet as if restlessness were driving him on his way once more.

"The worst of it is that in their place I dare say I'd do exactly the same. If it was true – if I was the coward everyone seems to think – I'd say I deserved to lose my ships and twenty years of work. Yet although I know that isn't so, I'm going to lose the company anyway, simply because I can't prove my story. I'll spend the rest of my life branded a coward, and there's nothing I can do to prevent it."

Matthew stared round the parlour once more, as if salvation lay hidden somewhere in its shabby furnishings. "What would my father have said, Kate? Resign like a gentleman, and try to forget it all – or fight them to the end? That's the only question that matters any more."

3

The house seemed oddly empty after Matthew had gone, as if my own life was no longer vigorous enough to fill it. In the silence of its rooms I brooded on the tale Matthew had told me of Captain Travis and the debt which had been repaid. *A life for a life* – that's what I'd read in Ma's bible all those years before, except that I'd taken it to mean a life ended, not a life spared in return for a rescued son.

To be honest, I wanted very much to believe Matthew was lying, because then I wouldn't have to feel sorry for him. I was determined to feel nothing for him but dislike – and the way he drove a coach and horses through my most cherished memories whenever he set foot in my house left me shaking with outrage.

I had a perfect right to my staid, simple, undramatic existence. I troubled no one; I paid my own way in the world. And if Miss Summerbee of Hawk's Dyke was known as a stubborn, strong-minded woman with no close friends except her house cats, deferring to no one's opinion except that of her agent and the dowager Countess of Wellborough – what of it? Let the rest of humanity and Matthew Oliver get on with their own concerns: I wanted nothing to do with any of them.

Within a day or two of Matthew's visit, I'd convinced myself he'd told me a pack of lies in order to win my sympathy. I sent Sykes to The

"Victory" to enquire – unofficially – whether Mr Oliver was still there, but it seemed Mr Oliver had only stayed one night before leaving as suddenly as he'd come. I counted myself well rid of him, and went back to poring anxiously over the estate accounts with William Dann.

Two weeks later, Matthew reappeared. This time he'd sent down a horse of his own instead of hiring an inn-yard nag, and spent most of his time, it was said, riding over the countryside between Wellborough and Hawk's Dyke with the air of a man obsessed by his own problems. Rumours spread that Mr Oliver had gone half-way insane, unhinged by the knowledge that every man's hand was against him.

Insane or not, Matthew must certainly have been wet through for most of his visit. I can hardly remember a single dry day during that summer of 1879. If the previous year's wet spring had been a misfortune for the farmers, at least they'd managed to scrape together a late harvest of sorts. This year looked like being an outright catastrophe. Once more the fields were flooded, but this time with no promise of sunshine to dry out the soil. The grain was sparse and spindly, easily beaten flat by the downpour, and even the root crops struggled in the waterlogged ground, reaching with crumpled yellow leaves to a sun which never shone.

It was impossible to stay indoors while the plague lay upon us; if fire and hail had rained upon the land, I would still have been bound to go out and share it. Almost every day I set off on my mare to look over the destruction for myself, well wrapped in a waterproof ulster, a broad-brimmed beaver hat pulled low over my face. And on all sides I read the same sad story. There was hardly a field where the crop stood upright enough for the sail-reaper to cut it; now the stems were matting where they lay, thatching the rot which devoured them from below.

The rain continued to fall: and every time I went out, I rode over the Hawk's Dyke land in all directions without finding a single thing to cheer me.

It was on one of these excursions that I met Matthew Oliver again. He didn't recognise me at first, with the collar of my ulster pulled up round my ears to channel the drops spilling from my hat-brim. Then a second glance as he rode past told him the identity of the horsewoman waiting by the field gate, and he halted alongside me.

"It looks bad."

"It's dreadful." I couldn't tear my eyes from the devastated grain, from the trampled, mustard-yellow landscape which should have been a sea of glowing corn. I shook my head, and plumes of water flew from my hat.

"I can't even see how scythes will cut that field. And look – the wheat's beginning to sprout, in any case." I pointed to where tiny pale shoots had begun to worm their way from the sodden ears nearest to the gate. "If we could have cut it and stacked it – even damp – it might have dried out enough to be threshed. You can do that with wheat, though not with oats, because they heat too much. But it's too late now. This crop's lost."

"How the dickens do you know all that?"

"This is my home." I stretched out a hand to it. "I know every field on Hawk's Dyke. They're like . . . my children, almost. I know exactly how they smell when they're newly ploughed – sweet – rich, like a cake just out of the oven. And I can tell when they're sick – like now, when that sour smell bites at the back of your throat, or patches of earth are rank with weeds."

I glanced across, to be sure he understood. "Most days I go up to that ridge behind the house, and wait for the land to smile at me, and grow fat and sleek – and when there's something wrong, I know it. I can't tell you how I know, but I do."

For a moment, Matthew was silent, his hands crossed on the pommel of his saddle, the reins loose between his fingers.

"I could never comprehend why my father left Hawk's Dyke to you, Kate. You didn't belong here. You were a river-brat who couldn't tell a plough from a paddle-wheel. And yet – now – I'm beginning to see the sense of it. My father cared more for Hawk's Dyke than for anything else in the world. I think you were his legacy to the land, not the other way round."

This was such a startling admission I simply sat there in the rain, gaping at him like a fool.

"If we're going to sit here, come over where it's drier." Matthew turned his horse under the dripping shelter of a giant chestnut nearby, and I followed automatically.

"You've never liked living in the country, Matthew. Why do you keep coming back here now?"

"Perhaps I'm waiting for one of your fields to smile at me, too. I must say, it would be pleasant if something did."

"It isn't like you to give up without a fight. That shipping line is your whole life – why aren't you in Liverpool, looking after your business?"

"In the Oliver office?" Matthew gave a short, bitter laugh. "The longer I stay away from the office the better, as far as the Oliver's people are concerned. Can you imagine what it's like when there isn't a soul in the place who can look you in the eye? Whenever I walk into the counting house there's complete silence – even that confounded typewriting machine stops knock-knocking away. No, they've made it quite plain in their own subtle way they'd prefer me a thousand miles distant. Not one of them has shaken my hand and said he was happy I'd survived the collision."

Matthew took off his hat and slapped the rainwater from it against his thigh. "Do you wonder I've left them to carry on without me?"

To my surprise, I heard my own voice blurt out, "I was pleased to hear you hadn't drowned."

"Well, thank you, Kate." Matthew's tone was sarcastic. "That's handsome of you."

"What do you expect me to say, for goodness' sake?"

"Oh, I don't know! But I'd like to hear you say you believe my story – that if it hadn't been for Travis's sense of obligation I'd be at the bottom of the Atlantic by now, and a dead hero instead of a live villain." He stared at me directly. "Well? Can you say it?"

"I don't know what to believe."

"So now you think I'm a liar, as well as a coward."

"I know you can bend words to suit yourself, Matthew! Though I've never thought you a coward, it's true. A coward would never have gone through with that awful divorce."

"Hah." Matthew flicked his rains crossly. "So you say."

"I read about you sitting in court, day after day, listening to all the things people said about you . . ."

"I didn't listen. I just sat there until it was all over, and then I went home." Matthew contemplated the waterlogged field beyond the canopy of the chestnut, his lips pressed together in a hard line. Then he looked down at his hands.

"This is quite different. This time they're going to take Oliver's away from me. It would have been better if I'd died on the ship after all."

"You say that now – but the hurt will go in time."

"Would you have sold Hawk's Dyke, if I'd offered you enough?" he asked suddenly.

"I'd never have sold it, no matter how much you offered." I glanced out through the curtain of rain, beaded with great drops from the edge of the chestnut's leafy umbrella. "I still wouldn't sell, in spite of all this."

"And if someone took it from you? If someone stole it?"

"I wouldn't let them! I'd fight! I'd never let it go."

"Exactly." Matthew regarded me thoughtfully for a moment, and then gathered up his reins. "You'd fight – because Hawk's Dyke is all

358

you have. Your children, you said. Like a family. You're fortunate, then," he concluded flatly, urging his horse out from the shelter of the tree into the rainy lane. "It looks as if I shall lose my ships, whatever I do."

Kicking the horse into a canter, he disappeared rapidly into the deluge.

4

Next day, for the first time, I hesitated to go out on my rounds of the farms in case I met Matthew again. Yet if I hadn't been so anxious to avoid his brooding presence I might well have been in Stainham or calling on a tenant when the letter arrived, addressed in painful pothook and chicken-track letters to *Miss Summerbee of Hawk's Dyke, near Stainham St Agnes, Norfolk, England*. It wasn't until I'd torn open the cheap envelope and glanced at the foot of the page inside that I saw the name *John Longstock*.

By sheer chance, it seemed, the Longstocks had survived the sinking of the *Aldebaran*. If it hadn't been for young Helen, constantly sick since the Mersey Bar, Mrs Longstock and her two daughters wouldn't have been on deck at that time of night, seeking fresh air instead of the closeness of the steerage berths. If it hadn't been for the impudent Londoner who'd waylaid Mrs Longstock earlier in the day, her husband wouldn't have insisted on accompanying his women on deck. And if it hadn't been for Mr Longstock's habit of punching first and asking questions later, his sons wouldn't have felt obliged to chase after him up the steep companionway, bringing the entire family out on deck just as the *Neustadt*'s bow drew fatally near to the *Aldebaran*'s side.

They'd felt a shock run through the vessel, and had run aft – uphill, John Longstock reported in amazement. More people had appeared on deck than had ever been seen at the Valentine's Fair at Lynn, running to and fro like headless chickens – and squawking like them, too. Somehow the Longstocks had managed to keep together, but they'd found it hard to struggle towards any of the boats rapidly filling at the ship's side. The habits of a lifetime kept them from pushing forward through the gentry until John himself made a path for his mother and sisters by main force, and saw his family safely installed in a boat before climbing in himself.

Yet still there had been delays. The "hooks" from which the boat was suspended – like a hay-fork point-down, said John – had somehow jammed, leaving the boat swaying unevenly in mid-air and all the people in it frantic with fear. Then the ship's captain had come to the rail, shouting orders and finally snatching a great hammer from one of his men to hack at the blockage. Mr Oliver had arrived – John had pointed him out to his sisters as an omen of salvation – and sure enough, in a moment or two the boat began to sink slowly towards the water.

Glancing up, John had seen Mr Oliver and the Captain arguing at the rail – and then, wonder of wonders, the Captain had landed a colossal blow on his employer's jaw, and as he slumped across the rail, had pushed him over the side. Fortunately, added John, Mr Oliver had fallen half-way into the boat, handy enough to be pulled in by the nearest passengers; otherwise he might easily have slipped into the water and drowned.

"Nell – tell Sykes to go into Stainham at once, and see if Mr Oliver's still at the "Victory". If he is, ask him to come straight away to Hawk's Dyke. And mind – if Sykes stops for a second along the way, I shall certainly get to hear about it."

It was clear that John Longstock had no inkling of the storm which had burst about Matthew's head in the British Press. The Longstocks had been landed in New York by the *City of Bristol* and taken to a charity hostel, where they'd been fed and given beds. Originally, John added, they'd intended to go west of the city to look for farm work, but it remained to be seen what would happen to them now. At least they were alive, for which God should be thanked. He hoped I didn't mind his writing to me, but Grandfather Longstock had never learned to read more than his own name, and the family trusted I'd call on the old man and set his mind at rest.

They were grateful, said John, for all my past kindnesses. Still in his pocket, he added, was the illustrated alphabet I'd given him from the library at Hawk's Dyke – one of the few things they'd managed to salvage from the *Aldebaran*.

O was an Owner, I thought . . . or an Oliver. The Longstocks might have salvaged more than they dreamed.

Chapter Twenty-Five

1

"Well?"

Matthew flourished John Longstock's letter under my nose with a vigour I hadn't seen since he'd returned to Norfolk.

"Well? What do you have to say about this?"

He dropped the crabbed page on to the parlour table and continued more calmly, "If you're going to say you're sorry you didn't believe me – don't bother."

"I wasn't going to say anything of the sort. I've no reason to trust anything you tell me, Matthew Oliver, and you know perfectly well why that should be so."

"Women!" Matthew threw up his hands in exasperation. "Always dragging up the past! Always throwing it in a man's face!" He confronted me squarely across the table. "Are you ever going to forget that business in New Orleans?"

"No."

"Well, at least we know where we stand! You're an unforgiving bitch, Kate, do you know that?"

"*Katherine.*" I leaned forward, meeting his glare. "And if I'm such a viper, I might as well throw that letter into the kitchen fire, and let you find your own way out of the mess."

"You wouldn't dare." Hastily, Matthew snatched up the precious page, folded it, and made as if to thrust it into his pocket.

I reached out and whisked it from his fingers.

"I'll thank you to remember that letter is my property, and if I want to burn it, I shall."

"Don't, Kate. I mean Katherine."

"*Please* don't."

"Please don't, then!"

I held out the letter between finger and thumb.

"I simply wanted to hear you say it." And as Matthew snatched the folded paper, I added, "That's a modest price, it seems to me, for something that might just save your reputation."

"Oh, so you believe my story now?"

"I believe John Longstock's story, at any rate."

Matthew shook his head, defeated. "What the devil did my father see in you, Kate? You're the stubbornest woman I've ever met! Here you are, handing me the means of proving my innocence, and you still won't give way an inch." He indicated the tiny measurement with his fingers. "Not one single inch."

"I don't trust you, Matthew, that's why – not when everything's going the way you want. The only time you're even half-way human is when your back's to the wall, and you need my help. But I've learned my lesson, don't worry. I'll help you out this time because I reckon you've been unfairly treated, but I know better than to expect any gratitude."

"Charmingly put." Matthew came round the table and took me by the elbow. "And now – just tell them to bring your carriage to the door, and we'll be off."

"We? And where are *we* supposed to be off to, may I ask?"

"To the Abbey, of course. The landlord of the "Victory" told me George Broadney's been at the Abbey for three weeks now, advising Charles on the management of his blasted birds. I don't want to miss a chance of tackling the old devil in front of witnesses."

"You don't need any help from me, then. Go and fight your own battles."

"But I do need you! You'll have to explain who these Longstock people are, and why they should be writing letters to you."

"They lived in an Abbey cottage, not one of mine. The Earl should know who they are."

"If they were pheasants, I dare say he would. Come on, Kate!"

"Oh, very well – but you'll have to wait while I change. We'll ride over to the Abbey by way of Goosefeather Drove, and give old Mr Longstock the good news. Or I'll burn the letter, Matthew!" I added, seeing him about to protest.

"By Heaven, you know how to get what you want!"

"Of course I do, Matthew. I learned that from you."

2

It was still raining, of course, and by the time Matthew and I reached the swathe of fine gravel before the door of Sourwell Abbey our coats and hats were almost wet through. But Matthew was in no mood for delay. The footman in the tiled hallway had no sooner offered to see if His Lordship was at home than he found himself brushed aside as Matthew took the great staircase at a charge, a trail of water showing where his dripping overcoat had passed. With a whimper of alarm the footman chased after him, and I followed behind as fast as the skirts of my riding habit would allow, the ranks of long-dead Gaunts watching grimly from their frames as the bizarre pursuit clattered past.

The Earl of Wellborough, true to the habits of a lifetime, was exactly where Matthew had expected him to be at that hour on a day of torrential rain – in the saloon, drinking sherry and eating madeira cake with his wife, his mother, and their guest.

Charles wheeled round in astonishment as Matthew blasted open the double doors and strode across the floor.

"Oho!" Crumbs of madeira cake flew like yellow snowflakes. "Wicked Cousin Matthew! This is a surprise."

"Good day, Charles. Good day, Alice . . . Countess . . ."

"Matthew. . . . How pleasant . . ." murmured Henrietta vaguely. "And Katherine, too."

"I see your manners haven't improved." Alice, rigid as an icicle in the shimmering grey-green currently known as "moonbeam", regarded us coldly from under her lace morning-cap. "Edward will take your coats."

The footman, still gasping from his sprint upstairs, leaped forward, smoothed his powdered head, and grasped the shoulders of my ulster from behind.

"I wouldn't encourage them to stay, if I were you, Charles." Sherry glass in hand, Sir George Broadney stepped into the open space before the elaborate fireplace. Obliquely, the huge overmantel mirror transformed his head and one ear into a squat, pink jug.

"In fact," he added, "I'm dashed if I'd put up with a blackguard like that coming bursting into my home, dragging – well, dragging that woman with him – "

"Be careful, Broadney." Matthew's voice was as thin as a knife-blade. "You aren't my father-in-law any longer."

"I wish to blazes I never had been!"

"I say – steady on, George." The Earl stopped brushing cake crumbs from his lapels and flapped a hand in mild protest. "Ladies present, and all that. Edward, didn't you hear Her Ladyship tell you to take those wet coats downstairs?"

The footman, who'd fallen back in confusion, laid hands once more on my ulster.

"No need for that." Matthew waved the footman away like a persistent fly. "I beg your pardon, Charles, but it's your friend Sir George I came to see – though I'll need you all as witnesses."

"Oh?" George Broadney's pink snout lifted in suspicion. "Witnesses now, hey? I must say, I wondered when you'd come up with one of your devious little schemes. You've been a great deal too quiet lately – but then, you've had plenty to be quiet about." Brusquely, he took the folded sheet which Matthew held out to him, and shook it open. "What's this supposed to be?"

"It's a letter sent to Miss Summerbee by people called Longstock, who survived the sinking of the *Aldebaran*. John Longstock mentions seeing me pushed against my will into one of the ship's boats."

"Longstock?" George Broadney frowned. "Do we know the fellow?"

"The Longstocks lived in a cottage in Goosefeather Drove." I saw the Earl turn at the sound of my voice.

"That's Abbey land."

"Indeed it is. The Longstocks' cottage was flooded last year, and because no one saw fit to repair it they decided they could do better for themselves in America."

"I sent them spoons," Henrietta remarked in a sepulchral voice, adjusting the silk rose at her shoulder.

"What on earth for, Mother?" Charles swung round to stare at her.

"And forks."

"How in the world did you come to know about these people?"

"I hope they didn't lose everything when the ship sank." Henrietta's eyes grew round with alarm.

"They almost lost their lives, by all accounts."

"Katherine, my dear!" Henrietta looked amazed. "How very thoughtless of them, when you'd done so much to help!"

"So this Longstock fellow is a friend of yours?" George Broadney's small, shiny eyes swept over me.

"I regard him as a friend, yes."

"I thought you might." Dismissively, the baronet folded the paper again, and held it out curtly towards me.

"What exactly do you mean by that?"

"Yes – what do you mean, George?" The Earl frowned in perplexity. "I must say, I find this whole business very hard to follow, what with forks and spoons and lifeboats and so forth." He took the paper from his friend and unfolded it again. "Let's have a look at this blessed thing."

"Don't bother with it, Charles. The letter's worthless. It's a patent forgery – a fraud – a put-up job. Oliver and this woman – "

"*Miss Summerbee*, or this *lady* – " Matthew interrupted sharply.

"These two have got together to cook up some cock-and-bull story

364

about the sinking of the *Aldebaran*, and they've either paid this Longstock fellow to write it out in a letter, or got some friend in America to fake it for them. Dash it – the Summerbee woman's American herself! No doubt she has all manner of crooked and obliging relatives over there."

"You're wetting the Bokhara, Matthew. It's too bad of you," Alice observed plaintively from the sofa. "I do think you might have left your coat downstairs."

"Confound the carpet!" Matthew suddenly burst out. "I tell you, that letter explains exactly how I came to be saved from the *Aldebaran*. Captain Travis refused to let me drown because he thought he owed me his son's life. And because I wouldn't go, he hit me – and then pushed me into the boat as it went down into the water. Otherwise I'd never have left the ship."

"The old Earl's dogs used to make pools like that." Henrietta's voice sliced through the conversation like a ship's whistle. "I used to cut circles out of the carpet where they'd been. Dirty things," she added disgustedly.

"For Heaven's sake be quiet, Mother! This is important, and it's complicated enough without you butting in. Now – " The Earl turned ponderously to Matthew. "You say this letter proves you didn't leave the *Aldebaran* of your own free will."

"Of course it does."

"It damn well doesn't!"

"I was coming to you next, George," said the Earl heavily. "Turn and turn about, you know. Now – *you* maintain the letter's a fake, and these Longstock people don't exist at all."

"They certainly do exist," Henrietta put in. "I sent them spoons."

"Well, then, they must have been paid to write this nonsense! Oliver here has had plenty of time to fix it all up." George Broadney's jug head bobbed vigorously. "Anyone can see the letter's a fake. He can't bear to lose control of his shipping line, and that's why he's done it."

"You're calling me a liar, Broadney." Matthew's voice was ominously soft, and the Earl stepped quickly between the two men.

"Now, let's not say something we'll be sorry for later. There are better ways of settling this."

"Such as?" Matthew demanded.

"Well . . . I'm sure there must be."

"That letter – " Matthew stabbed his finger towards it. "That letter is an eyewitness account of what went on aboard the *Aldebaran* on the night of the collision. What more proof can you want, for Heaven's sake?"

365

"I'll tell you what I want." Sir George Broadney's eyes glittered unpleasantly. "I want this Longstock fellow in England, where I can see him and speak to him. Give me ten minutes with your precious farm boy, and I'll soon knock his nonsense out of him. I haven't been a magistrate for thirty years without knowing how to send a ruffian off with a flea in his ear."

"But the whole family's in America!" I objected hotly.

"I thought you'd say that." The baronet turned to regard himself smugly in the mirror. "Your sort always have an answer."

At my side, I suddenly heard Matthew's voice.

"If you want the man Longstock here, then I'll bring him back."

"Matthew, that's impossible!"

Matthew ignored me completely.

"If you want him here in England to testify to what he saw, then so be it. I'll find him and bring him back to Liverpool, and he can tell his story in front of you and the other Oliver directors."

In the mirror, I saw George Broadney smile. He turned slowly back to face Matthew, his head a little to one side, one fat thumb thrust through the buttons of his waistcoat.

"Today's the 9th of July," he declared. "On the 7th of August, I've asked for a meeting of the Oliver's directors to decide what's to be done about you. Not that there's anything to decide, of course. We're all agreed that the sooner Oliver's is rid of you, the better, and if you haven't had the decency to resign by then, we'll force you to do it."

George Broadney's pink snout twitched in triumph. "There isn't one person working for Oliver's who isn't ashamed to be associated with you. You're a clever devil, Matthew Oliver, but you aren't clever enough to talk your way out of this."

He removed his thumb from his waistcoat buttons and stroked his chin. "By my reckoning you have twenty-nine days' grace. Do whatever you please with it. Run off across the Atlantic if you must, but this time – " George Broadney thrust his face into Matthew's. "This time you can drown properly, for all I care."

"I'll be at that meeting on the seventh, don't worry." Matthew returned the baronet's glare with cool loathing. "And John Longstock will be there with me. And when you've heard him out, I'm going to force you to apologise, Broadney. I'll make you crawl – in public, where everyone can see."

As the saloon doors closed behind us, I heard Henrietta's voice raised conversationally.

"He's getting more like his father every day, don't you think?"

3

"What if John won't come back with you?" I demanded as we descended the massive staircase. "He's a free man – you can't force him to leave his family and come back to England, simply to answer a lot of offensive questions."

"I won't need to force him." Matthew seemed quite confident.

"I don't even think he'd do it if you offered him money."

"Not for me – no, I don't think he would. But I suspect he'd come back if you asked him."

"Oh no, Matthew – " At the foot of the stairs, I stopped dead. "You can forget that idea right away. The Longstocks are my friends, for goodness' sake! I can't possibly ask them to come back here after all they've gone through. It wouldn't be fair."

"And what about being fair to me?" Matthew turned to survey me bleakly. "Kate, this man Longstock is the only hope I have of clearing my name. I'll arrange for him to travel in a first-class cabin on the *Alcyon*, with every luxury he can think of, and I'll send him back the same way when he's told his story. I'll bring his whole family across, if that's what he wants. Is that fair enough for you?"

"Even supposing we could find him, why should he want to risk another crossing, after what happened to the *Aldebaran*?"

"He'll risk it if you ask him." Matthew followed me out of the door to where two grooms stood glumly in the rain, holding our horses. He seemed amazed at my reluctance to do as he wanted.

"For goodness' sake, Kate, there's more than just Oliver's at stake, you know. I'm fighting for myself – for my self-respect, or what's left of it. You and I know I didn't run from the *Aldebaran* – but that's no use unless the whole world knows it. Do you want to see me called a coward for the rest of my days? Would you let a swine like George Broadney take Oliver's away from me?"

Matthew paused in the act of mounting his horse, staring at me, willing me to understand.

"Just promise me you'll help me find John Longstock, and persuade him to come back with us to Liverpool."

"I can't, Matthew. I can't possibly leave Hawk's Dyke."

4

It was ludicrous, when you came to think about it. I'd carried the prospect of returning to America in my head for so long – hoarding it like a cure-all, finding reassurance in its very existence – and now, with hardly more than a word, Matthew had exposed it for the myth it had always been.

I could no sooner leave ravaged, beleaguered Hawk's Dyke than I could turn my back on a child of my own in distress. My rain-beaten fields cried out to me, and I ached to take their suffering upon myself, and set them free.

Hawk's Dyke needed me: even Matthew had admitted that. I was part of the place, I belonged to it – *Miss Summerbee of Hawk's Dyke*. Wasn't it my whole reason for living? My consort? My lover?

"I can't leave Hawk's Dyke, Matthew. Not while I'm needed here."

Not ever was what I meant.

We'd hardly reached the Wellborough road when a flying figure intercepted us – William Dann, riding flat out through the downpour, a look of grim concern on his face.

"The bank of the big drain at Sourwell Fen's given way," he yelled through the rain, wheeling his horse to a stamping halt beside us. "They've sent over from Mill Farm to say the land's bright already in the nine-acre pasture, and at the rate the water's pouring in, there'll be two feet of it by evening and more tomorrow."

"Can't the steam-pump clear it?" I yelled back.

"The pump broke down two days ago, and the engineers still have it in pieces."

"Can you mend the drain while the field's flooded?"

"We'll try, at any rate." William Dann wiped rainwater from his eyes with a brush of his sleeve. "The bank's down in two places, east of the Mill Spinney. I'm on my way there now to see what can be done."

We followed him, Matthew and I. I knew what to expect when William Dann described the land as "bright" – there was no more graphic word for the shimmering, glistening wetness which lay on the surface of the soil as it hung between farmland and mere.

The possibility of a flood had increased with the passing years as the peat floor of the old fen dried out, shrinking down to expose and weaken the banks of the drains which had stolen its moisture. Now, filled to bursting by the endless torrent, those clay walls had ruptured – a "crevasse" we'd have called it on the Mississippi levee – and had allowed the water to surge back over the land.

At the edge of the marsh, the steam-pump could only raise its cold brick chimney in silent reproof, helpless as Canute to halt the tide.

By the time we reached Mill Spinney the ground was more than bright. A shallow lake had already formed where a day before there had been pasture, the surface of the water pitted by the constant downpour. Beyond its margins, land which had yielded ten coombs of oats to the acre not two years earlier was turning back into a marsh, as if the fen had always reserved the right to revert one day to its own wild nature.

From out of the weeping sky, brown, fish-backed ruffs had arrived to pick among the shallows. Even as we watched, dunlins and ringed plovers skimmed over the hedgerows to investigate the sudden bounty of the flood, and in the distance, no more than a scratch in the leaden sky, I thought I caught a glimpse of a hunting harrier, the blue hawk restored at last to his fiefdom.

"I'll get some men down here right away with sandbags and shoring. The drain's as good as empty now, so we should have the banks mended before long." William Dunn inspected the damage with an unholy relish.

"How long?"

"Oh – a week or so, maybe."

"And how long before the pump can clear the land again?"

"Another week – perhaps two. Don't worry, it isn't near as bad as it looks." William Dann turned to grin at me, shin-deep in the flood, and for a moment I had a vision of his black-visaged father, rising from the water like a monster from the marsh. If anyone should understand the mysteries of the fen, it was William Dann.

"As I say, it's no great problem." He paused to gaze round the watery waste. "This is the kind of thing you pay me to fix."

He splashed off cheerfully down the drain bank, searching for damage. The land was the land, flooded or dry: but there William and his father parted company. There was no good side to a flood in William Dann's book. It was an affront to his notions of progressive farming to see drowned fields and fences knee deep in tea-coloured water, and I knew he wouldn't rest until the breached drains were decently whole once more.

After he'd gone, Matthew and I stood in silence, contemplating the lake which had so magically reappeared.

Do you see? I wanted to say. *Do you see how much it needs me?*

But more than that, I wanted Adam there to see his beloved fen restored, if only for a few fleeting days; and in my mind's eye, I began to recreate him at the edge of the flood, wild as the marsh itself with his gun and his black retriever . . . I reached into my memory for his image as I'd done a thousand times before – only to find I could no longer lay my hand on it. It was as if the soft glow of his lamp in my soul had been quenched by the brightness of a dawn. Matthew's presence had somehow extinguished the past, just as I'd feared it would. Nothing remained of Adam but a name; and no one answered that name when I called it in my heart.

William Dann returned, tramping the water under his feet as if it had no right to be there.

"You go off home, Miss Summerbee. I'll see to all this, don't worry. It won't be the first time a bit of farmland's found itself drowned for a while in these parts, and I don't imagine it'll be the last. We're living in hard times, right enough, but there's always a change. Nothing lasts."

He rubbed his hands with satisfaction, finally crushing the magic of it all between his palms.

"Could you manage without me for a month or so, William?"

"Why bless you, yes." William Dann's black eyes gleamed, and for the first time I realised how much he'd relish the chance to take sole charge of the place, to hold Hawk's Dyke between his own two hands and be master of its moods. I began to feel as slight and as irrelevant as one of the insects hovering over the rim of the marsh. Adam had left me: was Hawk's Dyke about to turn from me too?

"You'll come to America, then?" Matthew's head had snapped up as if an electric charge had run through him.

I shrugged, and spread my hands in defeat. There seemed to be nothing more to say.

Chapter Twenty-Six

1

We had twenty-nine days.

To be more precise, Matthew had twenty-nine days, since I refused to involve myself in his problems. I had grave misgivings about going to America at all, to explain his difficulties to the Longstocks. Why should they be expected to help Matthew Oliver? What had he ever done for them except import the cheap grain and wool which had forced them to leave the home of their ancestors for another country and almost drown themselves in the process?

I told Matthew flatly that I wanted no part in persuading John Longstock to come back to England, even temporarily. I'd vouch for Matthew's account of his troubles, but then I'd make it plain I'd think no less of John for wanting to stay with his family: the decision was his alone. Matthew grumbled when I told him my terms, but he'd no option but to accept them. That's when I realised that with Adam gone I must be the one person in his life he couldn't buy, or sell, or bribe, or threaten, or cajole – and I realised, too, how much he resented it.

And yet somehow I found myself travelling to Liverpool as he'd asked to board a ship for New York.

I hated the noisy, hard-hearted city after the peace of Hawk's Dyke, but it seemed as if my land had no need of me after all – not of me, particularly, the way a lover listens for one single step and one voice out of a thousand. That discovery had been the hardest loss of all.

I looked round the city of Liverpool, and wondered how I'd like New York.

Privately, in my hotel room, I calculated how long our crossing might take. Twenty-nine days should see us comfortably from Liverpool to New York and back – but there was the Longstock family to be found between sailings, even supposing they were still in the city and hadn't disappeared into the farming country beyond the Appalachians.

But Matthew had refused to consider the possibility of failure. The *Alcyon* was due to leave in two days' time, taking eight and a half days for the crossing, and he'd already telegraphed the company's New York office to start off a search for the family. Yet when he called at my Liverpool hotel that first afternoon, I could tell by his manner as he waited for me in the lobby that he could barely contain his anger. He stalked over to meet me at the foot of the stairs.

"Come into the writing-room. We have to talk."

"What's the matter? What's happened now?"

Matthew steered me to a corner of the writing-room and brusquely pulled two chairs together.

"We can't sail on the *Alcyon* after all. Every cabin's taken, so they tell me – though I don't believe it for a moment. The plain truth is that I'm being refused a passage on my own vessel."

"An Oliver ship? And they won't allow Matthew Oliver aboard?"

"In effect."

"Then why don't you send for the passenger list, and confront them with it?"

"Because I doubt if it would do any good."

"Do you mean to say you'd let a bunch of booking clerks keep you off your own ship?"

"This has nothing to do with booking clerks. I imagine the ship's master has refused to carry me."

"But you're chairman of the company! Can't you dismiss him, and find another captain?"

Matthew snorted. "I wish I could! But every master in the fleet would resign if I tried it. I dare say it would all be resolved in time, but we only have twenty-nine days. Twenty-eight, after today."

"Then we can't go." I tried to keep the relief out of my voice.

"Nonsense. We'll sail with another line."

"White Star?"

"I've tried White Star. The *Bombastic*'s next out of Liverpool, so I went down to their offices straight away." Matthew twisted his hat-brim between his fingers. "But it seems the *Bombastic* has no room for us either." Angrily, he tossed the hat on to a nearby writing-desk. "At least Cunard were quite blunt about it. Mr Oliver would not be accommodated on any of their ships."

"What are you going to do, then? Call yourself Smith or Wilson?"

"I'll see them damned before I do that!" Matthew's eyes suddenly blazed with long-suppressed fury. "I won't have it said I lied my way aboard like a criminal. I won't do it, Kate."

"Then what will you do?"

"I haven't tried *Northern & Equatorial*. They sail into Boston, but at least it's on the other side of the Atlantic. I'm on my way to their offices now."

"Then wait here while I fetch my hat. I'm coming with you."

372

★

The Northern & Equatorial offices were small compared with the brass-bound splendour of the Oliver headquarters. Mention of the Oliver name was enough to have us swiftly conveyed to the proprietor's private room, where an interview with one of his masters had just ended. As luck would have it, we all met face to face in the anteroom doorway.

"Captain Ecklund – " Northern & Equatorial's proprietor looked a little disturbed. "I suppose you know Mr Matthew Oliver?"

"I know *of* Mr Oliver." Glaring, the Captain resumed his cap. "Good day to you, Mr Arbuthnott."

"Captain – "

"Well, sir?" The Captain paused heavily in the doorway and glanced back towards his employer.

"I believe Mr Oliver would like to sail with you to Boston."

"Then you may inform Mr Oliver he'll never sail aboard any vessel *I* command – and be damned to him for a gutless craven!"

With a final scowl in our direction, the Captain tramped out.

Matthew descended the stairs in a frigid silence which continued while he paused to put on his hat as we left the building. I was more shaken than I'd have liked to admit, and embarrassed to have witnessed the scene. It was the first time I'd encountered the loathing Matthew had aroused among the community of the sea.

"Someone's bound to take us," I ventured at last.

"What's that?" He stared at me, frowning, and I realised he was so accustomed to such insults that he'd already put the incident behind him.

"I don't know how you can bear to have people speak to you like that."

"Most of the time they don't speak to me at all."

"Don't you care?"

"Not any more. I go my own way, and let them say what they please."

As he spoke the words, I heard Adam's voice again – Adam, who retreated further from me with every day passed in Matthew's company. Matthew's peace of mind was costing me dear.

"I've been working on a solution to our transport problem," he announced.

"Oh yes?"

"I should have thought of it earlier. We'll take *Harvester* to New York. She's chartered for Cowes next month, so she must be coaled up and pretty nearly provisioned. Another day should see her ready, and at least her master's in no position to argue moralities."

"I didn't know you still had *Harvester*. Is it safe to sail to New York in a little yacht?"

"*Harvester*'s hardly a little yacht! She'd sail all the way round the world, if necessary. She isn't as fast as the *Alcyon*, but that doesn't matter – we'll be able to leave a day sooner to make up for it. Yes – " he added to himself, "*Harvester*'s the answer."

"What about this man who's chartered her for his yachting trip? Won't he be upset?"

I was snatching at straws. To travel aboard a 5,000-ton passenger ship among hundreds of other people was one thing – but to be confined for days aboard a steam-yacht with Matthew Oliver was quite another.

"The charterer? To hell with the charterer!" Matthew waved an impatient hand. "Let him sue me, if he's so upset. He can dine out for weeks on the story of what the villain Oliver has done to him. In any case, by the time he finds out he's lost his yacht for Cowes we'll be half-way across the Atlantic, doing a good fifteen knots."

"But if your yacht takes more than nine days to cross the Atlantic, that hardly leaves us a week to find the Longstocks. You'll never be back in time for the Oliver's meeting."

"We'll be back, depend on it. If I have to swim across, towing *Harvester* in my teeth, we'll be back in time."

I was becoming more uneasy by the minute.

"This isn't what we agreed, Matthew. You'll have to go on your own."

"But you promised to come! There's no point in my going at all if you aren't there to speak to these Longstock people. You gave me your word, Kate!"

"That yacht of yours. . . . It isn't what I expected."

"*Harvester* isn't what anyone expects, I assure you. Wait until you see her."

"But there'll only be the two of us . . ."

"Oh, for Heaven's sake!" Matthew stared at me in disbelief. "It's rather late to be concerned for your reputation, isn't it? Or is it my reputation you're worried about?"

"I don't give a damn about my reputation – or yours, for that matter. But you know as well as I do that shutting the two of us up in a poky little yacht for days on end is as bad as putting a couple of fighting cocks under a pail. I've no desire for your company, and I don't imagine you'd enjoy mine. You can go on your own to New York, seeing you've such a mind to."

I turned my back on him and began to walk firmly away.

"Oh no, you don't!" With a lunge, Matthew gripped my arm and set off without ceremony towards my hotel. "You're coming with me, and that's an end to it. If we can't manage to ignore one another on a two-hundred-foot yacht, then the whole of England's not big enough for us. We needn't set eyes on one another from Cape Clear to the Hudson. Is that good enough for you?"

"Let go of my arm this instant! People are looking at us."

"To hell with them! I'm not letting you out of my sight until I see you safely aboard *Harvester*. Not what you expected? I'm damn sure she isn't!"

2

It was quite true: in my wildest imagination, I'd never expected anything like Matthew Oliver's yacht.

From a distance she resembled one of the graceful tea clippers which had once raced home each year from the China Sea with their fragrant cargo. Her bows were just as hollow, and her stern like the daintiest tea-saucer ever seen – but at closer range, a businesslike funnel became visible half-way along her gleaming white length.

Yet even tied up to her Liverpool wharf, *Harvester* hovered upon the water, riding her own ghostly reflection over the endless ripples of the dock. All that was missing, I thought enviously, was Violet Oliver in one of her favourite pastel dresses, leaning languidly on the polished brass rail.

I remembered reading that Violet had supervised every detail of the fitting out herself, down to the choosing of the inkstands and deckchairs – and as I followed the steward to the stateroom allotted to me, I had the strange sensation of strolling through the mind of another woman, passing from one splendid, empty saloon to the next, searching for a single sign of humanity in that cool perfection.

Traditional dark oak and mahogany were not to Violet's taste. *Harvester*'s saloons were airy with white paint and maple panelling; parchment-pale Bidjar or Aubusson carpets cushioned our steps; the furniture was all tulipwood and bird's-eye maple, florid with ormolu and marquetry, the chairs gilt and silk-striped. There was even a white marble fireplace in the main saloon surrounded by ormolu lions and a huge overmantel mirror – but without even a trace of ash to indicate that a fire had ever burned in it.

Violet had filled her yacht like a jewel box. Where, I wondered, did alabaster clocks hide when *Harvester* put to sea? What happened to five-foot Chinese vases or ponderous jardinières, bronze nymphs or precious Meissen dessert services?

On that first night aboard I was relieved to find *Harvester*'s master waiting with Matthew in the saloon before dinner. Not that he had a great deal to say, unless the conversation turned to passage times or the peculiarities of rigging. Still, his presence avoided the animosity which would surely set in when Matthew and I took our meals alone; and I began to dread the following day, when we'd be far out at sea, beyond the possibility of retreat.

In a fit of respectability I'd brought along Daisy, the parlourmaid from Hawk's Dyke who also looked after my clothes, as maid and female companion. But there was little companionship to be found in her. From the day we left Norfolk Daisy had expected to feel seasick at any moment, and even as I changed for dinner in my stateroom that first evening, she was picking over her symptoms. Hawk's Dyke had been dull, goodness knows – said Daisy – but you didn't feel queasy in Stainham High Road, and that was a fact.

In spite of Daisy's misgivings I slept well. Perhaps the gentle motion of the yacht against her wharf murmured a lullaby of the old days at river landings; or perhaps I was simply exhausted by the tensions of the day. I didn't even wake when some time during the night we made our way softly out into the Mersey and headed for the open sea. I woke next morning to find *Harvester* thoroughly roused, and her long sea-stride and the steady beat of her steam heart already counting off the miles to New York.

In the echoing saloons of the yacht, the clocks and vases and figurines had vanished into store as if by magic, and there was no sign of Matthew. Mr Oliver had breakfasted in his stateroom, I was told when I enquired. Abashed, I returned to mine, and breakfast arrived on an immaculate silver tray a quarter of an hour later.

For the rest of the morning I explored the yacht without ever catching a glimpse of Matthew. In fact, considering the crew numbered almost thirty souls when all the stewards, cooks and engineers were included, the vessel seemed amazingly deserted.

Matthew, I knew, had a stateroom and a study behind one of the panelled doors near my own, but there was nothing at all to indicate which it might be. Once, I caught a glimpse of his valet hurrying down the carpeted passage towards the crew's accommodation with one of his master's coats over his arm, but that was all. When I returned to my own cabin I found that it, too, had been mysteriously tidied and the bed made during the time I'd been away.

The silence of the vessel was so complete that I jumped when a sharp rap sounded on my cabin door. It was the yacht's senior steward, presenting Mr Oliver's compliments and a message.

"Mr Oliver will be taking his meals in his stateroom until we reach New York. Might I ask when you'd prefer luncheon to be served – and if you'll take it in the dining saloon, or here in your stateroom?"

"Oh, in the dining saloon, I think."

All at once I decided I couldn't stand another minute of my own company. "And I'd be obliged if you'd ask Miss Daisy Bunch to step along here right away. Miss Bunch and I will take luncheon together."

It seemed that Daisy had made a miraculous recovery. While I'd been wandering through the vessel, disconcertingly alone, my maid had found plenty of company below decks, where she'd eaten a hearty breakfast with the yacht's officers. Overnight, she'd developed a taste for yachting undreamed of among the fields of Hawk's Dyke. Suddenly a private yacht was the *only* way for ladies and gentlemen to travel: she reeled off the names of the principal British yachts and their owners, of the yards on *Harvester*'s foremast, of the hatches and scuttles – until I realised that mealtimes below decks were to be devoted to coaching Daisy in the language of the sea.

All through lunch we sat at either side of the long dining table, suddenly with nothing in common. Hawk's Dyke was quite forgotten, as far as Daisy was concerned, in the excitement of the present. And I, who had no present to speak of, picked at my boiled fowl in its béchamel sauce, and wondered why on earth I'd ever agreed to come.

3

I took dinner in my stateroom, leaving Daisy to her lessons in seamanship with a spinsterly warning about sailors being sailors, and the dangers of invitations to inspect out-of-the-way parts of the yacht.

After dinner, having nothing better to do I went for a stroll on deck in the fading light, and for the first time on that silent ship heard the sound of human laughter drift up from an open porthole near the bow.

There was no longer any land to be seen. *Harvester* had become a temporary continent, moving like a pale ghost over the grey Atlantic swell; lulled by the endless rise and fall of the vessel's stern, I leaned against the wire shrouds of the mizzen mast, only to find them as cold and impersonal as the rest of Violet's perfect yacht.

And on the deck of that lavish ocean-going mansion, I began to think wistfully of the old *Bellflower*, the rickety, stern-wheeled, floating shed on which I'd spent my childhood. We'd managed to exist pretty well without Persian carpets or sofa tables; never mind an overmantel mirror, we hadn't even possessed a decent looking-glass. But at least the *Bellflower* had had life about her – my father cursing and muttering over his cargo receipts, Sam crooning softly to his piston-rods or Luke chasing some particularly desirable lump of driftwood along the boat's guard with a cargo hook, whooping in the excitement of the hunt. But *Harvester* had no voice at all, unless it was the bland, impersonal murmur of her engine.

Behind me, I heard steps approaching along the deck – halting – and then drawing nearer.

"Good evening, Katherine." Matthew's tone was coldly formal, as if we were only very distantly acquainted. For a moment I wondered if he was going to shake my hand.

"I hope you're enjoying your stroll." He halted beside me and let his gaze roam round the empty deck. "Are the stewards looking after you well enough? You've only to ask, if there's anything you want."

"Thank you. I have everything I need. Your yacht is very comfortable."

"Good." Matthew continued his examination of the deserted deck. "I realise you're only aboard *Harvester* for my sake, and I'd like to make the trip as pleasant for you as possible."

"Is the yacht always as quiet as this?"

"Do you find her particularly quiet? I know Violet hated to hear the crew clumping about overhead. We never set the sails because of it."

"I've hardly seen a soul all day."

This time he gave me a swift glance.

"Wasn't that exactly what you wanted? You made it quite plain that you don't relish my company, and at least if I keep to my own quarters you'll have the run of the ship."

"It isn't necessary to shut yourself up in your cabin."

"It's no sacrifice, I assure you. I have letters to write, and other things to keep me occupied. As a matter of fact, if I'd known you were on deck this evening, I'd have kept out of your way." He looked round once more, and took his hand from the rail. "I've trespassed on your privacy as it is."

"You don't have to leave. It's a pleasant evening, and surely there's room on this deck for more than one."

I watched him consider the situation, and then make a slight bow of acquiescence.

"As you please. I'll stay for another five minutes. As you say, it's a fine evening."

After a moment's awkward silence I felt obliged to find some innocuous remark to continue the conversation.

"I often walk in the garden at home, at this time of day. There's

378

something about the quality of the light. . . . Or perhaps it's the way the wind seems to drop in the evenings . . ."

I became aware of Matthew watching me intently.

"You must have been lonely after my father died."

"I had Hawk's Dyke," I said quickly. "I had my memories." He was still watching me, and I added resentfully, "Why should I need anyone else's company? I can manage by myself."

"Of course." Matthew considered this in silence. "Though I expected you to have married by now. An unattached lady with fifteen hundred acres of your own. . . . But as you say, you obviously manage too well alone to need a husband."

"Oh, I've had proposals, I assure you." This was stretching the truth, but I was annoyed by the suggestion that I was too much of an old maid to catch a suitor. "As a matter of fact," I declared rashly, "one of the gentlemen who proposed was an educated man, with a respectable position in the district."

"Indeed?" Matthew's eyes lit up with suspicion. "And who was this paragon, if I may be allowed to ask?"

For the first time, I hesitated.

"Mr Edmund Blewitt, the schoolmaster."

"What? That whey-faced ninny!" Matthew hooted in disbelief. "I can't believe you'd look twice at Edmund Blewitt after living with my father."

"I refused him, as you see," I said stiffly.

"How that fool had the effrontery – "

"I told you, I sent him packing."

"The very idea of letting that creeping, boot-licking lackey of the Rector's get his greedy paws on Hawk's Dyke – "

"If it comes to that," I snapped out suddenly, "I notice you haven't remarried *since your divorce*."

The acid in my voice brought him up short. The scornful expression fled from his face, and he turned away to examine some object far out across the darkening sea.

"When you've once put your hand in a flame and been burned for it," he remarked at last, "you're a fool to make the mistake a second time."

"A third time, to be exact."

Matthew drummed his fingers irritably on *Harvester*'s rail.

"Two – three – whatever you want to call it. The result's the same. There won't be another Mrs Oliver."

"You're very certain of that."

"I am certain."

"Yet you told me once – most insistently, as I remember – that a man in your position needed a wife." I couldn't resist goading him further, still smarting from his gibes about Edmund Blewitt. "What was it you said? Oh yes, you needed a gracious hostess who could entertain sultans and presidents in the proper manner, and generally add lustre to your name – weren't those your requirements?" When he didn't answer I added, "And of course, Violet did all those things so well."

"Enough!" Matthew snapped savagely. "You've made your point. And since I don't seem able to find a wife I can trust, in future I'll just have to do without. Because, like you, I can manage on my own." He swung round to face me. "The world is full of accommodating women, and not all of them expect to become wives. But of course, you'd understand that – wouldn't you, Kate?"

"I don't regret anything I've done. Not a single thing. And you're ill placed to sneer at Edmund Blewitt, it seems to me. At least in his own ridiculous way he cares about the children he teaches. He does some good in the world! What do you do, except scramble around, piling up money and trying to keep hold of your tinpot empire? You don't care for a living soul except yourself. *Love*, Matthew! Have you ever heard of it? If you'd managed to spare a little love for your wife, she might not have turned to other men for attention."

Now Matthew's eyes were alive with outrage.

"How dare you! Even if you had the remotest understanding of my marriage – how dare you pass judgement on me!"

"Because it's true! You deliberately married a woman you didn't love – then you managed to hate her for taking up with someone else." Recklessly, I plunged on. "If you never give anything, Matthew, you'll never get anything back. You were even jealous of the happiness I found with Adam, though you couldn't wait to be rid of me yourself – "

"*You?*" Matthew was white with anger. "If you believe I've ever lost a moment's sleep over you, then you're even madder than I thought. You're a bitter, dried-up woman, Kate Summerbee – living in the past. All you've got in the world is your precious land, and you sit on it like a spider, scaring everyone off, terrified someone will steal a yard of it away from you. I haven't finished – "

But I'd already turned on my heel and marched away – *clack, clack, clack* across the deck and down the companionway, straight on without a pause until I'd reached my stateroom, banged inside and slammed the door. I knew if I'd stayed near Matthew a second longer, I'd surely have struck him.

About half an hour later, I heard footsteps in the passage followed by a soft knock at my door.

"Who is it?"

"Me."

"Matthew?"

"Yes."

"Go away."

"I want to talk to you."

"Go away, I said."

"I've come to apologise, Kate." There was a short silence. "Are you going to open this door and listen to me?"

After a moment's consideration I opened the door, to find Matthew leaning on the jamb, examining the carpet at his feet. He raised his eyes as the door swung wide.

"Thank you. I wasn't sure you'd want to see me again."

"I don't want to see you."

"In that case I'll say my piece, and go. I simply wanted to tell you I'm sorry for what I said about you half an hour ago. I was angry, but anger's no excuse for cruelty."

I hesitated for a second, torn between pride and truth. In the end, truth narrowly triumphed.

"I said some pretty horrible things, too. I just got back what I gave out, I guess."

Matthew glanced at me curiously.

"I've never heard you apologise for anything before, Kate."

"Nor you."

We stared at each other, sharing an awkward intimacy.

"There was something else I wanted you to know." Still leaning against the doorpost, Matthew returned to his study of the carpet. "I don't suppose it'll make any difference to your opinion of me, but you might as well hear it."

"Go on."

"When I divorced Violet, it wasn't for what you imagine. Oh, I know the official grounds were adultery, but I could have forgiven her for that – I even understood why she did it, in a way. You were right – I didn't give Violet much of my attention, when all's said and done, and she was used to being admired and made a fuss of."

Matthew glanced up at me, as if he wanted to be sure I believed him.

"But there was something else I couldn't forgive, something that was never mentioned in court. Shortly after we were married, Violet told me she'd discovered she couldn't have children. She made a huge scene over it, weeping like a tragedy queen. But it wasn't the truth. All the time, she was doing things to make sure she didn't become pregnant." Matthew smoothed a tuft of carpet with the toe of his boot. "Violet cheated me, Kate, right from the start. She knew I wanted children, and she cheated me."

I knew he was telling the truth; if I needed proof, there was the conversation I'd had with Violet in the lane near the gravel pit, when she'd gloated over the deception.

"Children need love and attention too, you know. When would you have had time for them?"

"I'd have made time." To my surprise there was passion in his voice. "I wanted a child of my own. Can't you understand that, Kate? Children give their love without putting a price on it. I'd never have hurt a child the way my father hurt me. I'd have been there when I was needed." He gave up the struggle to explain, and added simply, "A child is something to work for, and plan for."

"You need another wife, it seems to me."

"No. That's one thing I don't need."

"Some day in the future you'll feel differently."

"No. I'm quite sure of it, Kate. Now and for ever. For goodness' sake, haven't you just finished telling me you don't need a husband?"

"But it's different in your case – "

He raised a warning hand.

"Here we go, arguing again as usual. And the truth is that we're both too set in our ways to change." He smiled fleetingly – and for a moment the years fell away from him, leaving a face I'd once glimpsed for a few precious seconds, asleep and unguarded in the shadows of the *Bellflower*'s cabin before Pa burst in on our awakening.

The smile disappeared, taking the secret Matthew along with it.

"If we're thrown together, we only end up fighting," he said flatly. "Which is why it's better if I keep to my own quarters until we reach New York. I've told the stewards to give you the freedom of the vessel. Don't hesitate to ask for anything you want." He half turned, about to leave. "I hope all this unpleasantness doesn't spoil your sleep. Goodnight, Kate."

I watched him walk away, the familiar hollow desolation rushing in to enfold me once more.

Chapter Twenty-Seven

1

I saw Matthew another three or four times before we reached New York, but that was all. He kept strictly to his own suite aboard *Harvester*, and when I say that I saw him, I mean that I caught sight of him and little more. On those odd occasions when we did encounter one another he was politely distant, greeting me as formally as a maiden aunt and exchanging a casual remark about the weather or the state of the sea before vanishing again to his own domain.

For the rest of the nine and a half days it took us to cross the Atlantic I sat alone in one of *Harvester*'s saloons or rested in my cabin. The discovery of well-filled bookshelves near the main companionway saved me from hours of brooding over my own forlornness, but without banishing the solitude itself. If I wandered the decks in search of sunlight and sea air, I'd inevitably come upon Daisy Bunch spooning in a corner with one of the handsome young officers. They'd spring apart as I approached, sly and pink and rather ruffled, and I'd scold Daisy for it later, feeling sanctimonious and spinsterish.

A bitter, dried-up woman, Matthew had called me. Yet I was only thirty-four years old: countless women went on bearing children into their forties, if fate saw fit to fill their wombs.

I peered at myself in the mirror over the marble fireplace, and a woman I didn't recognise stared bleakly back, her blue eyes hard with suspicion. I took a step backwards, amazed as if I'd encountered a stranger in a window. Had I willed myself into this new flesh? Had something withered in me when Adam died, taking so long over its own decay that I'd never noticed its loss?

The woman in the mirror began to look concerned. I saw her smile – nervously – as if she'd forgotten which muscles drew up the corners of her mouth.

I found myself pitying her: she wasn't old, and she was passably pretty when she smiled. Her hair might be quite glorious if she bothered to arrange it instead of scraping it back from her brow and imprisoning it with combs.

I raised my hand to my own hair, and saw the mirror-woman copy the movement. I took out one of my tortoiseshell combs, and then another, and the woman matched them both. We shook our heads, and hair flew; already the mirror image looked better. Colour bloomed in her cheeks, her eyes shone, and her lips parted a little with the excitement of discovery.

I, too, was exhilarated, happy to be there to watch her find herself – for there was no one else to see. She was all alone in her great golden frame – as completely alone as I was.

I turned away from her into the saloon, quickly wound up my hair again, and stabbed it with the combs.

2

Matthew appeared again, austerely businesslike in black twill, black silk hat in hand, as we sailed through the Narrows into New York harbour on the eleventh day of our twenty-nine. Mysteriously, *Harvester*'s saloons had filled up once more with Violet's clocks and statuary, and when the manager of the Oliver's New York office presented himself half an hour after we'd docked, I watched him stare round, whistling under his breath at that stunning example of European decadence.

I almost burst out laughing. Here was a countryman of mine, to be sure, turning up his strait-laced republican nose at the lushness of Violet Oliver's yacht. I could imagine him later that evening, telling his wife about the "regular floating bordello" which had steamed into the East River. Why, it was no wonder Matthew Oliver had got himself into a mess of hot water! Maybe it was true, what everyone was saying about him running like a rat from the sinking *Aldebaran*. One thing was certain – if the feller thought he could do business with honest American males from a fancy art museum like that yacht, then he, Joe Manager, was a Dutchman.

Yet Matthew wasted no time in getting down to the business which had brought him to New York, only to find the local office almost as hostile as the Liverpool headquarters. They'd made a show of following his instructions – he was still chairman of the line for the time being – but the manager had disappointingly little to report.

There had certainly been Longstocks aboard the *Aldebaran*: the steerage passenger list mentioned the name, though the exact number in the family had been noted, scratched out, noted again and finally smudged beyond recognition. Later, the *City of Bristol*'s Third Officer had attempted a rough head count of those picked up from the *Aldebaran*'s boats, and the name *Longstrake* on the grimy sheet he'd turned in was thought to refer to the Longstocks. It was known that the

German Society, the Catholic Church and the Italian St Raphael's Society had all carried off their own people from the penniless group on the dockside; but where the displaced English yeomanry had found shelter, nobody seemed to know.

"A family of six can't just vanish into thin air!" Matthew's uplifted hands indicated the completeness of the Longstocks' disappearance.

"This is New York, sir. Thousands of men, women and children pour into this city every week – many of them on your ships." The manager looked aggrieved. "Some of them pass through, some of them stay. A good half of them couldn't write their names if their lives depended on it. I tell you, as soon as we got your telegraph message we made enquiries all over – but I reckon these Longstock people are going to be harder to get hold of than fog."

"It's vital that we find them. Don't the immigration authorities keep some kind of record?"

"Ordinarily, they register anyone passing through the Castle Garden depot, and send the charity cases and the maniacs over to Ward's Island. But you have to remember, these folks didn't come in by the regular route. They were landed on the dockside as survivors from a shipping accident."

"Then some charitable organisation may have taken charge of them."

"Could be, I guess."

"Well then, the next step's obvious! Send round all the almshouses and charity hospitals until you find them."

"That's a tall order, Mr Oliver. This is a big city, and growing every day." The manager glanced up in time to catch the murderous glint in Matthew's eye. "But I'll get on to it right away, Mr Oliver. Yes, sir, I can see it's important that we find these folks for you. I'll put a couple of my clerks on the case as soon as I get into the office tomorrow. Right away, sir. Right away."

Four days passed – four more precious days of our twenty-nine. Matthew had calculated, in consultation with Captain Willard, that *Harvester* must leave New York for Liverpool on Monday, July 28th if at all possible, or the 29th at the very latest, if he was to attend the vital meeting of the Oliver directors. Even then, Captain Willard warned him, bad weather or engine trouble in mid-ocean could easily put an end to his plans.

By Thursday 24th, the tension of the search was beginning to leave its mark on us both. A dozen times a day I told myself it didn't matter to me in the least if Matthew Oliver lost control of his company and spent the rest of his life branded a coward; yet the more silent and withdrawn he became, the more I suffered on his behalf, longing for even a small piece of good fortune to ease that impenetrable torment. *Harvester*'s two apprentices almost wore out their boots running to the Oliver office to ask for news; each time they returned I saw hope kindle in Matthew's eyes, only to be snuffed out like a candle when he learned they'd nothing to report.

One by one, the almshouses and hospitals were checked and scratched from the list. Grim-faced, Matthew ordered enquiries to be made at every railroad and steamboat depot in case a ticket-seller remembered the passing of a family answering the Longstocks' description. When none did, we seized on it as evidence that the Longstocks were still in New York – knowing perfectly well in our hearts that the chance of any clerk remembering six pale faces out of hundreds of thousands was impossibly remote.

Unable to wait, inactive, aboard *Harvester*, Matthew took to wandering the streets himself, visiting one police station after another in the vague hope that a Longstock might have been locked up for some misdemeanour.

"They're decent, law-abiding people, Matthew!" I protested.

"And I have four days left to find them. After that – " He spread his hands. "Nothing."

Advertisements were placed in all the newspapers, resulting in half a dozen loafers of various nationalities arriving at the Oliver offices, all claiming to be a long-lost Longstock. One Bohemian didn't even speak English, and brought a friend to interpret for him.

By Thursday, Matthew had hired three private detective agencies to hunt for the Longstocks in different parts of the city. On Friday, consumed with impatience and mounting desperation, he engaged another, a villainous-looking crew housed in a tenement cellar on the lower East Side. By this time it was beginning to seem as if the only people in New York not searching for the Longstocks were the family themselves; yet still the searchers returned empty-handed.

On Saturday evening – with only one day left before our Monday departure date – Matthew suddenly appeared in the dining saloon for dinner. He'd only just returned from the searingly hot pavements of the city, and was still wearing the dusty coat and trousers of his long march.

"I haven't changed. I hope you don't mind."

"Not at all. I'll be glad of some company, for once."

He glanced at me – wondering, I suppose, if I'd meant the remark as a criticism – then, reassured, sat down at the opposite side of the table.

"I didn't feel like eating alone tonight, somehow."

"Still no progress?"

"Nothing at all." Matthew turned a table-knife over and over on the cloth in front of him. "One of the Oliver clerks thought he'd found them in a shanty out at Dutch Hill, but it turned out to be people called Longbaugh." He picked up the knife and drummed its point on the table. "I suppose it's possible they're in Chicago by now – or St Louis – or any of a thousand little townships scattered all over the country."

"I don't think so. John definitely said in his letter that they couldn't afford to travel west, and that they were stuck in New York. And anyway, I can't believe I've spent days getting blistered feet on the streets of this city just to hear that the Longstocks are sitting in a railroad car in Wisconsin."

Matthew looked up in surprise. "I didn't expect you to join in the search."

"I had to do something. Daisy and I have toured most of the streets between here and Broadway, looking at everyone we pass. I have to keep Daisy out of mischief somehow," I added quickly, afraid Matthew was about to thank me for my efforts. "She's becoming too fond of ship's officers for her own good."

"Ah." Matthew turned his attention back to the cutlery at his place. "I see. But thank you for trying, all the same."

"It passed the time."

"I imagine it did."

An awkward silence descended over the table until a steward arrived with a dish of whitebait served in a warmed damask napkin. After several minutes I realised that Matthew had eaten nothing at all; he'd simply marshalled the crisp little fish into ranks on his plate like the endlessly staring crowds in the city streets. All at once he glanced up and caught me watching him.

"I don't have much appetite, I'm afraid."

"You ought to eat something."

"Why?" He stared at me curiously. "Why do people always say that?"

"To keep your strength up, I suppose. We still have a day left to search for the Longstocks."

"One more day – and then we sail for England again." The knife drummed on the table once more. "You must be anxious to get back to Hawk's Dyke."

Guiltily, I realised I hadn't given a thought to Hawk's Dyke for almost a week.

"I wonder if it's still raining in England."

"Bound to be." Matthew pushed his plate away. "Kate – I know it's none of my business, but can you manage financially if farming goes on as badly as this?"

"I'll manage somehow. There's some money in the bank which your father gave me in case anything ever happened to him. I've never touched a penny of it, but this year I may have to."

"Promise me something, Kate. If you ever have to borrow money, come to me before asking the bank for a loan."

"You want to lend me money?"

"I'll give you better terms than any bank."

"Why?" I stared at him suspiciously.

"No reason – except that I don't want you to have to give up Hawk's Dyke."

"*You* want *me* to go on living at Hawk's Dyke?"

"I know how much it means to you. It's hard to lose something you've built your whole life around."

Hawk's Dyke – and the shipping line: what we'd each wanted most in the world.

"You haven't lost Oliver's yet," I reminded him.

"Maybe not. But there isn't much time left."

"Matthew. . . . What will you do if we don't find the Longstocks, and George Broadney forces you to resign?"

"I haven't the faintest idea. I might travel, I suppose. There are still parts of the world I haven't seen. Or I could buy a country estate, and spend my time playing backgammon and slaughtering pheasants like Charles."

"I didn't know you played backgammon," I said, startled.

"I took it up quite recently – just for something to do. I never had time before."

"Adam taught me . . ." I stopped, disconcerted by the coincidence. The door opened noiselessly, and two stewards advanced on the table, one to remove the remains of the whitebait, the other bringing a cold chicken masked in velvety *chaudfroid* and elaborately decorated with patterns of coloured aspic. Matthew waited until the stewards had left, then indicated the extravagant dish.

"Last time, it was catfish. Do you remember?"

"Catfish?"

"The last time we had dinner like this. On the *Bellflower*, that night in New Orleans. You skinned a catfish and fried it for dinner, and then your father went ashore, leaving us with half a million dollars in Confederate gold and the Federal warships not twenty miles down-river."

He pushed the platter of *chaudfroid* towards me, and leaned back in his chair.

"It was just as impossible then – waiting for someone else to decide my future."

"You were so angry with Pa . . . I didn't dare say a word, in case it set you off. I remember you stamping across the deck in a temper . . . I don't suppose I'd even hear you on these carpets," I added as an afterthought.

"And this time there's no levee, and no fire-raisers – and no Federal ships, and no burning cotton."

"And no dancing among the fires."

"No."

A profound silence fell between us, swallowing up the other differences between that single, sensual night of madness and the one that stretched ahead.

"It isn't at all the same, really." Agitation sharpened my tone. "Everything's changed so much. You – me – circumstances . . ."

"You're right, of course. It was just . . . an odd feeling. Something called it all up again – perhaps because I needed your help then, too."

"I haven't forgotten how you repaid me for that help," I said meanly, rebuilding my defences.

I'd expected him to look away – to seem disconcerted, at least – but he didn't. He continued to regard me thoughtfully from the other side of the table.

"Why are you here, then, Kate? If I treated you so badly in the past, why on earth did you agree to come to New York with me?"

"*Katherine.* I wish you'd call me by my proper name."

"Nonsense. You're a Kate, if ever I saw one. You're just about the most thoroughgoing Kate I can imagine. I wouldn't want to know you as Katherine. And you haven't answered my question."

"Why did I come here with you? I came because you didn't give me any choice in the matter – you almost dragged me aboard your wretched yacht."

"Kate, Kate – nobody can force you to do something you don't want to do. I know that better than anyone. So I'll ask you again: why are you here?"

"Because I believe you've been unfairly treated, I suppose."

"As unfairly as I treated you?"

"Maybe – and now you know what it feels like."

"But you came here with me, in spite of the pain I caused you."

I hated the way he was looking at me, as if I should have an answer for him that would give some significance to the ruins of his life.

"I came here because it's what Adam would have wanted me to do. He cared about you, Matthew, more than he'd ever admit, and that's why I'm here – because I loved Adam, and for no other reason. And now, if you don't mind, I'm tired and I'd like to go to bed. Goodnight."

If he said anything more, I didn't hear it. In another instant the doors of the dining saloon had closed behind me.

3

Next day, the private detectives from the lower East Side cellar discovered the Longstocks.

As luck would have it, they were living less than a mile from our East River berth. They'd found shelter in the rear of a crumbling frame house sandwiched between two tenement dwellings which had themselves been erected behind a busy warehouse. The alley which connected the Longstocks' home with the street was no more than a black tunnel alongside the bulging warehouse wall. When Matthew and I first negotiated it at the heels of one of the genial brigands from the agency, it was almost impossible to avoid the filthy pools and heaps of refuse underfoot. A mongrel scuttled out of our path, dragging a strip of bloody entrail; clouds of insects buzzed in the sunless heat; somewhere overhead raucous, quarrelling voices echoed from wall to wall, swelling as they descended like the chorus of a Greek tragedy.

"This is a dreadful place." A pigeon flew up from the stained paving on ragged wings, and I thought of the flocks which swooped through the clear air of Hawk's Dyke. "Poor John. Poor Mrs Longstock, to come to this."

They thought at first we'd come to dun for rent. The door opened barely an inch in response to my knock, and Mrs Longstock's eyes peered out. They were red-rimmed, I noticed, as if she'd been weeping.

"Miss Summerbee? Is it you?"

"It is, Mrs Longstock. Don't worry – I've come to help."

"Mercy on us!" Still holding the door, the woman turned back into the room. I heard her cry, "John! Mollie! It's Miss Summerbee! Can you believe it?" and another voice calling upon her to open the door for any sake and let the visitor come in.

They only had one room – which was two rooms fewer than their

390

cottage in Goosefeather Drove; I guessed that if their water supply came from a pump in the yard through which we'd passed, it was no more healthy than their old well, and that for this princely accommodation their landlord must be demanding five or six times the rent they'd paid in Norfolk.

Apart from a rickety table, a few stools and two old iron bedsteads, there were almost no furnishings. One window stood open in the hope of catching a breeze, but admitted nothing except the fragrance of rotting vegetables in the yard beyond.

Mrs Longstock wiped her hands despairingly on her skirt.

"It isn't what we'd have wished, ma'am. But after the bother on the ship, and all – "

Her son John had risen from his seat at the table, and came to put an arm round his mother's shoulders.

"You've no idea how hard we've looked for you, John. We've had men hunting all over New York – "

I saw John Longstock's gaze travel to a point behind me, where Matthew, having sent away the detective who'd guided us to the house, had turned back into the room.

"It's Mr Oliver, isn't it?"

"Yes," said Matthew quietly.

"Well, I'm blowed. Last time I saw you was when that ship of yours went down. Went to the bottom like an anvil, she did."

For an awful moment I thought John was about to accuse Matthew of having caused the disaster which had cost his family everything they owned in the world. Then he came forward, his right hand extended.

"We were both in one of the *Aldebaran*'s boats, sir, though you weren't in any fit state to notice me. I'm pleased to see you safe and sound again."

"And you, too." Matthew shook him by the hand, while I wondered guiltily if John's greeting would have been quite so warm if he'd known of the errand that had brought us.

I looked round for the rest of the family. Mollie, the elder girl, stood by one of the iron bedsteads, stroking the sleeping head of her sister Helen, but there was no sign of the others.

"Alfie and my father'll be back later." John interpreted my glance. "They're rag-picking down by the wharves. Alfie's pretty quick at it, but Father reckons it's no better than begging, and he don't like it. I've been luckier – I got work straight off with a contractor putting up houses near 42nd Street, carrying bricks and shifting rocks. This being

Sunday, I thought I'd do a turn with the other two, but Helen's been sick, and I called back to see how she was getting along."

"She didn't take well to the crossing," Mrs Longstock explained anxiously. "She was sick the whole way, and she hasn't been well since. I thought she had a little more colour yesterday, but she was bad again this morning."

I went over to inspect the child in the iron bed, and realised she wasn't asleep as I'd thought. Her eyes were open, but glazed and dim; her face was flushed, and there was a slick of dampness on her upper lip.

"How old is Helen, Mrs Longstock?"

"She's seven, ma'am. I lost three, you see, between Mollie an' her."

"Has she been taken ill like this before?"

"Not at home, ma'am. Not at all. She was always a healthy little thing. It must be the heat," she added hopefully.

"Let me see." Matthew crossed the room to stand beside me. Detecting movement, the hot little face in the bed turned in our direction, eyelashes spiky with tears, light brown curls plastered to the luminous brow like the petals of a rain-blighted rose. Gently, Matthew reached out to touch a swollen cheek. "The child's fevered, surely, Kate."

"Only a little." Mrs Longstock rushed to Helen's defence. "She's no trouble, really."

"But this is hardly a healthy place for a sick child. She should be somewhere there's light and air."

"You shan't take my baby away from me!" Mrs Longstock darted across the room, and pushed herself between us and the bed. "I'll never see the poor mite again, if you take her away to one of those hospitals."

"I wouldn't dream of taking a child from her mother." Matthew frowned over the misunderstanding. "I was going to offer to move your whole family out of here to somewhere better. If you'd care to move, that is."

"We can't afford better than this, Mr Oliver." John Longstock had remained near the table. "The city rents are higher than we expected, and we're trying to save a few cents each day so we can move west."

"John Longstock – " Matthew paused, choosing his words carefully. "I'll be perfectly honest with you. Miss Summerbee has come here as a friend of your family, because I asked her to. I've come particularly to speak to you. To ask a favour of you, in fact."

"Of me, sir?"

"A considerable favour."

"You'd best tell me what you want, then."

"You've no idea what I'm talking about?"

"None at all, sir. I wish I had."

Matthew smiled. "You don't read newspapers."

"I don't read much at all." John Longstock glanced sheepishly in my direction. "That is – I can read if I put my mind to it, but I'm not often in the mood. And newspapers cost money."

"True – otherwise you might have seen a good deal about me lately, in the British Press at least. The newspapers have been telling their readers I deliberately deserted the *Aldebaran* on the night of the collision – saved my own life by jumping into a boat and leaving women and children behind to drown. That isn't something people find easy to forgive – not in the owner of the vessel concerned."

"But you didn't jump, sir! I saw Captain Travis throw you over the side! It was lucky you landed in the boat at all."

"Captain Travis was determined to save my life, even though I'd refused to leave the ship. It was only when I read the letter you sent to Miss Summerbee that I realised one person aboard, at least, knew the truth of what happened that night. But unless someone comes forward publicly to support my story, it's only my word against the whole of the British Press."

"But plenty of people saw what happened! I wasn't the only one, by a long chalk."

"Then why hasn't anyone spoken up yet?" I burst out. "Don't they care that a man's been unfairly accused?"

"Ah, but you see, most of the people on deck by then were steerage passengers, same as in the boat. They saw what happened, but how were they to know you were Mr Oliver who owned the whole ship? You were just another nob from the saloon as far as they were concerned – someone who'd fallen into a panic, and been roughly dealt with by the Captain. I'd never have known you myself, if I hadn't been used to seeing you riding about near the Abbey. And now, of course – " John Longstock shrugged. "Most folks that had friends to lend them the fare have left the city and gone elsewhere. We'd have gone west, too, if we'd had the money."

"So you see, John, your sworn testimony could prove to the people who matter most to me – to the other directors of my company – that I've done nothing to be ashamed of. If I can't prove that in the near future – well, it'll cost me my reputation, and the company I've spent my whole working life building up."

"So much?" John Longstock stared in astonishment. "Just on my word?"

"On your word alone."

"Then John must write out all that he saw, and sign it," said Mrs Longstock immediately. "You can bring a lawyer here to see the story's written out properly, and to witness it and make it legal. We may not have much in the world, but we can still see you get justice."

"I'm afraid I need more than a written deposition, Mrs Longstock." Matthew paused for a second. "I need your son to come back to England with me, and testify before the directors of my company at a meeting in Liverpool."

I saw Mrs Longstock's eyes widen in alarm, and flick round to meet her son's.

"Oh, no, John, not back to England!" she whispered. "Not away across the sea when I need you so badly – with your father being so down, an' all . . ."

"Hush, Mother, don't concern yourself. I won't leave you, Mr Oliver will have to make do with a paper, as you said."

Matthew laid his hat on the table.

"I know it's a great deal to ask. Your family are in difficulties, and your sister's sick. But that's why I offered to move you all into decent lodgings – at my expense. I promise you, your family will be well taken care of while you're in England. You'd travel to Liverpool with me in my yacht, and return in a first-class stateroom on an Oliver steamship. You could be back in New York in a little over three weeks. And after that I'll pay for you all to travel anywhere you want in the United States – in comfort."

I watched John Longstock digest this offer in silence. At his side, his mother watched too.

"And what if I don't agree to come with you and testify? Will you leave us in this room, where we are now? Is that to be the price of my word?"

"John!" exclaimed his mother, shocked. "Don't speak to the gentleman like that!"

"I'll say my piece, Mother, and if Mr Oliver's offended, well then, I'm sorry for it, since I didn't intend any harm. But we're in America now, where one man's as good as another, and I mean to take care of my family. What d'you say, Mr Oliver? Will you move us out of here, or not?"

I turned to look at Matthew.

"I don't put a price on justice," he said quietly. "I'll find you decent lodgings and pay for your travel whether or not you come back to England with me. There are no conditions attached."

"Well then, that's generous of you, sir. Do you hear that, Mother? Mr Oliver's going to find us somewhere better to live."

"Oh, sir – " Mrs Longstock tried to take hold of Matthew's hand. "Bless you, sir. You're a good man, just as your father was. And maybe John shall go to England for you in a bit, when Helen's better, and my husband's in proper work."

"I'm afraid it's more urgent than that, Mrs Longstock. If my yacht doesn't leave New York tomorrow I shall miss the meeting in Liverpool. And after that, it's too late. Even if John came to England in a few months' time, I doubt if it would do any good."

"You're leaving tomorrow?" John stared at him, startled.

"Tomorrow." Only the tiny movement of a muscle at Matthew's jaw betrayed the gravity of the moment. "You'll have to sail with us then if you're to come at all."

John Longstock looked round the single squalid room, and his glance rested for a moment on the sick child in the bed.

"I don't know . . . it's all a bit sudden. What do you say, Miss Summerbee? You've been a good friend to our family in the past. What do you think I ought to do?"

"No one can tell you what to do, John." I glanced up for a second, and my eyes met Matthew's. "If Mr Oliver says he'll help you whether you come to England with us or not, then I believe he'll keep his word. He's in a great deal of trouble over this *Aldebaran* business, it's true, but that's his affair, and not yours. You must do as you think is right."

This time when I glanced towards Matthew he gave a slight nod.

John Longstock rubbed the back of his neck with a work-reddened hand.

"I'd need to talk it over with the family first, and maybe see them settled into the new place before I made up my mind."

"Very well." All at once, Matthew seemed to have come to a decision of his own. "We'll wait another day in New York. We'll sail on Tuesday instead."

"Matthew – can you risk another day's delay?"

"We'll cut it fine, I dare say, but we should still be able to make Liverpool in time."

Matthew retrieved his hat from the table, and glanced towards John Longstock and his mother.

"You know how important this business is to me. I won't say any more now, but if I may, I'll come back at the same time tomorrow to hear what you've decided. In the meantime, I'll have the Oliver people here find clean, comfortable lodgings for you in a healthier part of the city."

Mrs Longstock followed us to the door with her eyes, her lips moving silently all the time; but whether she was calling down a curse or a blessing upon our heads I couldn't decide.

4

Goodness knows what arguments raged over the Longstocks' meagre supper that night, or how the great decision was made. I couldn't have helped them at all, though my heart ached for their predicament; I knew only too well how small and vulnerable they must feel on the threshold of that foreign land.

Somehow, the matter was resolved. When Matthew and I returned to the ramshackle frame house the following morning John Longstock was waiting for us, his mind made up.

"I'll come with you, Mr Oliver, if you still want me to. My father and I don't exactly agree on the matter, but I'm mindful I've a debt to pay to your family, and it's been owing a long time." John Longstock glanced briefly at me. "I haven't forgotten that Mr Gaunt died trying to help me, Miss Summerbee, though you were good enough not to remind me of it."

After that, there was only the change of lodgings to be arranged. Matthew had taken rooms for the family in a German boarding house near Rivington Street, where the laundered sheets and scrubbed floors were a paradise compared with their present quarters. We took John to inspect the place, introduced him to the bustling *Frau* in charge, and in front of them both repeated the terms of the arrangement – that bills should go to the Oliver office for however long the Longstocks wished to stay.

"We'll go west as soon as John gets back," his father insisted. "We're farming people, Mr Oliver. John ought to be working with horses, not carrying stones like a dumb beast."

"And it's so hot in these yards," Mrs Longstock added. "I'm sure half of Helen's trouble is being in this airless place."

She looked back over her shoulder towards the bed where the child lay, tossing in a restless sleep.

"We'll move to Rivington Street this afternoon, and then you'll see a change. She'll start to mend as soon as we're out of here, definitely."

At last *Harvester* began to come alive in anticipation of setting sail next morning. Late into the night, lying sleepless in my brass-railed bed, I heard the sound of footsteps and whispered conversations as last-minute supplies were brought aboard and the ship made ready for departure.

396

At half-past six in the morning, Matthew and I waited on deck for John Longstock to arrive, unable to settle to anything else until we saw our passenger aboard and our mooring lines thrown from their bollards.

Ten minutes later, a familiar stocky figure swung down the quayside towards us, a ridiculously small paper parcel of belongings under his arm. At the landward end of the gangway he hesitated, glanced back the way he'd come, looked over the yacht apparently without seeing her, hesitated again, and then with a great sigh walked slowly aboard.

"John – what's the matter? You haven't changed your mind, I hope."

"No." He shook his head. "No, I gave my word, and I'll stick to it."

"Then what's wrong?" I almost shook him in my impatience. "Doesn't your mother like the boarding house after all?"

"I think she'll like it well enough – when she gets there."

"But you were all supposed to move in yesterday evening! Where did you spend the night?"

"At the old place." He glanced up and saw my incomprehension. "Helen took a bad turn last night, and my mother thought it best not to move her."

"What did you say?" Matthew joined us in time to hear the last few words. "Is your sister no better?"

"Worse. A lot worse. She doesn't seem to know where she is any more. She keeps calling for her friends at home in Goosefeather Drove. Mother's in a fair old state about her."

Matthew stared at him. "What did the doctor have to say?"

"We haven't called a doctor."

"But for goodness' sake, you must! What's your mother thinking of?"

"Doctors cost money, Mr Oliver," John Longstock reminded him soberly. "More money than we have, at least, and my father don't hold with debt."

"Even when his daughter's life is at stake?" Matthew held up a hand. "No, I understand." He fished out his watch and consulted its Roman dial. "Captain Willard! I'm going ashore for an hour or so. I'll expect you to be ready to sail as soon as I get back."

Captain Willard frowned at us from the wheelhouse doorway.

"As long as you understand it's another hour off our crossing time, Mr Oliver. I can't work miracles, you know. Not even on *Harvester*."

"I'll take full responsibility, Captain." Matthew glanced at me defiantly. "Well, Kate? What would you do in my place?"

"I'd fetch a doctor, Matthew. And Matthew – " I laid a hand on his arm. "Thank you."

We left the quayside in separate cabs – John and I to go back to the ramshackle house in its East Side yard, Matthew to find a doctor. Goodness knows how he did it, but in less than half an hour he came marching through the stinking pools of the warehouse alley, followed reluctantly by one of the most eminent medical men in the city.

In another five minutes the doctor had made his diagnosis. Helen had pneumonia – there was no doubt of it, and her condition was critical. The child's lungs were already seriously congested, her temperature 104 degrees. The crisis could not be far away: only then could anyone tell whether she would live or die.

Mrs Longstock and Mollie boiled kettles for steam until the cramped room – already full of summer heat – began to resemble the crater of a volcano. The doctor had left opium; Helen's brother and her father were dispatched for the makings of the linseed poultices he'd ordered.

John said nothing, but his eyes spoke volumes whenever he looked in our direction.

Through the steam I saw Matthew, his back squarely against the peeling wall, watching the scene with an expression of philosophical calm. I went over and leaned against the wall next to him.

"What time is it?"

"We've been here more than an hour already."

"How much longer can we afford to wait?"

He turned his head and surveyed me wearily for a moment, before his gaze was drawn back to the small, fevered figure in the iron bedstead whose racked breathing filled the room.

"Kate . . . how can we possibly leave?"

Chapter Twenty-Eight

1

At noon, one of *Harvester*'s apprentices arrived to see what had become of us, and was sent back with the same instructions as before – *be ready to sail whenever we return.*

"Go back with him, Kate. There's no need for you to wait here."

"There may be something I can do. Mrs Longstock's almost exhausted."

"Her husband's here. And John."

"And you." It occurred to me that Matthew suddenly looked old and worn compared with the hopeful hours of the morning. "You should still try to be at that meeting in Liverpool, Matthew, even alone. If you aren't there, George Broadney will call it an admission of guilt. He'll say you've effectively resigned by default."

When he didn't react, I tried again.

"Go back to *Harvester*. If you leave right away, you might still be in time. Tell them about John Longstock – show them the letter, and promise them John will come to Liverpool himself in a couple of weeks to answer their questions. I can stay here in New York in case the Longstocks need help."

Slowly – firmly – Matthew shook his head.

"More than a thousand people were drowned on the *Aldebaran*, Kate – families like this one, all lost. I've never forgotten the face of that young boy in the boat. . . . To watch a child die, and not to be able to prevent it . . ." He lifted his hands helplessly. "*Aldebaran* was my ship."

"But the collision wasn't your fault. Those people died because the *Neustadt* failed to keep a look-out."

"Maybe so. But suppose there's something I can do for Helen?" He gestured towards the bed. "Suppose there's something she needs, and no one to get it for her?"

"She needs nursing, Matthew. That's all. Her mother's love is all that can help her now."

"No – you're wrong, Kate. Do you know what brought the doctor down to this part of town, away from his fashionable Washington Square patients? Money – that's all. I offered him such a large fee, he pocketed his scruples along with it. He'll be back again in an hour or two, because he knows I'm good for a few hundred dollars more."

He smiled bleakly. "You should be pleased, Kate. Didn't you tell me to *give*, if I wanted to get anything back?"

"I didn't mean money – you know that."

"Even the rich have their uses."

I was grateful to him, but not in the way he imagined. The word *money* had brought me to my senses just in time, just as I was beginning to think that perhaps he'd changed, and there was more to Matthew Oliver after all than a cold, heartless opportunist with a cash-box for a mind. Always, we came back to the same theme – *money*, the cure-all – money which could buy him a clear conscience, just as he'd once tried to pay me off with his father's watch. In spite of my better judgement, I'd begun to feel compassion for him: now Matthew himself had supplied the remedy for that.

I went quickly over to the table where Mollie was pouring beef tea from a heavy iron kettle, swilling its contents dangerously near her little fingers. Busy there, I could ignore the sight of that same Matthew Oliver watching over the struggles of another sick child while his shipping line, the mainstay and purpose of his life, slipped slowly from his grasp.

2

Matthew's high-priced doctor came again in late afternoon, pronounced the patient unchanged and prescribed vapour of chloroform to ease the pain of her breathing. Exhaustion was the chief danger, he said. If the crisis was too long delayed, the child might have no strength left to meet it.

After he'd gone, Mrs Longstock suddenly swayed and slumped down in a chair, her own energy spent. Mollie and I laid her on the second bed, where she consented to rest providing I took over her watch and promised to call her if there was the least change in Helen's condition.

I settled down by the bed, and prepared to wait.

After half an hour I heard a knock at the door followed by muttered conversation; suddenly – bizarrely – the splintered, makeshift table in the middle of the room began to fill up with the most exquisite food. At one end a great pink lobster flourished his claws over a bed of watercress; at the other a capon lay stuffed fat with oysters, while the table between them was spread with dishes of delicately fried sweetbreads, of game pie, of lemon custards – even a towering Charlotte

Russe which the heat of the evening had already begun to dissolve among its Savoy biscuits and the ice in which it had been packed.

"Where on earth did all this come from?" I whispered to Matthew.

"Delmonico's."

"Oh, Matthew, bread and cheese and some ham would have been enough, I'm sure. No one has the heart to eat."

"I can't do much right in your eyes, Kate, can I?"

He sounded so hurt that I began to regret my scolding. How else could he think of helping, poor creature, except by spending his wealth?

We waited – and gradually, the shadows gathered round us in that shambles of a room, softening its squalor, spreading a merciful veil over the neglected feast on the table. The stains on the wall began to assume familiar shapes: circling birds . . . hazy willows . . . all the fanciful landscapes of half-sleep. I didn't even notice the smell from the yard any more, or the frenzied scratching and pattering which began with the falling of darkness.

Mrs Longstock dozed on the second bed with Mollie beside her; her husband snored in the corner in which he'd spent the day, while John and Alfie carried on a murmured conversation by the door. Brittle as crystal in the lamplit bed, the sick child coughed as if each new, painful breath might break her, rolling her head restlessly from side to side in an attempt to escape from her fever.

I've no idea for how long I sat on a stool beside her, cooling the hot little brow with cloths wrung out in ice-water from the ruined Charlotte Russe. I can't even remember being aware of Matthew coming to sit on the floor nearby, his back to the wall and his hands clasped round his knees.

"You'll ruin your clothes, you know, sitting down there."

"It doesn't matter." He moved a hand in dismissal. "How is she now?"

"Much the same, I think. Sometimes her eyelids flutter open, and she seems about to speak. Then she slips away again, and I can't reach her."

"You should have had a child, Kate." From his post on the floor, Matthew studied me gravely. "You look . . . softer, somehow, sitting there. No hard edges. No brick walls."

"Yes, well, unfortunately we don't always get what we want in this world," I said, more sharply than I'd intended. "Though that never seems to have been a problem for you."

I realised Matthew was still watching me in silence.

"Not until now, at least," I added more gently.

"There was a time when I was sure of what I wanted, it's true. Now – Heaven knows what's the matter with me." He leaned his head against the flaking paint of the wall. "Looking back, I suppose things started to change long before the accident to the *Aldebaran*, but so gradually I never noticed. It was going back to Hawk's Dyke again – sitting in the parlour – walking across the lawns. . . . That's what made me realise. I suddenly began to see everything differently."

A leaden chill gathered round my heart. Hawk's Dyke: no wonder he'd offered to lend me money – urged me to put myself in debt to him.

"You still want Hawk's Dyke, don't you?" I hissed at him furiously. "That's what was behind all the talk of a loan – I wondered why you'd suddenly become so generous. You came to Norfolk, saw how it was with us, and thought you'd found a way of getting your hands on Hawk's Dyke once and for all. You've always believed it should have been yours after Adam died."

He didn't deny it. For several minutes he said nothing at all, absently stripping the leaves from a piece of watercress which had fallen from the table.

"I'd give a great deal – " he reflected at last, "if it could only be as simple as that. I wish I could say *yes – give me back what's rightfully mine*, and know I'd be satisfied. But no . . . it isn't the land or the house. . . . It's something more complicated than that – something Hawk's Dyke stands for, if I could only work out what it is." He thought for a moment, and then shook his head again. "No – you can keep your precious fields, Kate – they're quite safe from me."

In the bed, Helen stirred and moaned, her face glistening with a rush of moisture. Great drops gathered on her cheeks and rolled into her hair; she threw out her arms, groping for something invisible; her eyes flew open, her breathing quickened, her lips parted and she cried out – *Ma*, or *Mam*, I couldn't be sure.

Matthew was on his feet at once, bending over the bed. "What's happening to her?"

"Wake Mrs Longstock, quickly. Her heart's beating like a steam-hammer."

But Mrs Longstock was already at my shoulder, roused by her daughter's cry. Reaching out as if neither Matthew nor I existed at all, she caught up the child in her arms, enfolding the wild limbs, murmuring anxious words, holding her daughter tightly against her.

Tears came into my eyes, but I brushed them away before Matthew could see. I recognised that fierce, exclusive embrace: I'd tried to clutch

402

Hawk's Dyke to my breast just as passionately, only to find I couldn't fill my arms and my heart with timeless earth. Only the fragile and the finite can be loved in that way.

Matthew had already sent John for the doctor.

"I don't care if he's asleep. Tell him Matthew Oliver wants him here right away, and he can send his bill to me later."

By the time the doctor arrived, Helen lay still and pale on the bed – profoundly asleep with her hand in her mother's, serenely unaware of the turmoil which had raged around her.

3

Harvester sailed later that morning with John Longstock aboard. The crisis past, in the mysterious way of children Helen had begun to rally almost as soon as she wakened, her sole concern the alphabet book her brother had saved from the sinking steamship.

"I told the doctor to send his overblown bills to the Oliver office."

Matthew stood beside me at the yacht's rail, bleakly watching the grey walls of the Castle Garden rotunda fall astern of us with the rest of Manhattan. "The office can take care of the Longstocks for the time being. I assume I'm still chairman until the seventh."

"And even after that, perhaps. There are still eight days left of your twenty-nine – eight and a half, since the directors' meeting isn't until the afternoon of the seventh. You never know – the meeting may have been postponed for some reason, or *Harvester* might even reach Liverpool in time."

"You're dreaming, Kate. And you're nearly dead on your feet from exhaustion, though I'm sure you'd never admit it. Go below and get some rest. There's precious little else we can do now."

When I woke again it was late afternoon and we'd left land far behind. I dressed and went on deck, to find *Harvester* steaming manfully into a lively sea and Matthew standing at the rail by the main shrouds, sombrely watching the rise and fall of the yacht's elegant bow.

"How are we doing?" Clinging to the rail, I made my way forward towards him.

"Oh – thirteen knots or so." Matthew tore his attention away from the mesmeric sight of wave after wave dashing itself under *Harvester*'s forefoot. "A pretty respectable speed for a fifteen-year-old yacht. At this sort of pace, we'll probably make Liverpool on Friday the eighth, or Saturday, perhaps."

"No earlier?" I was profoundly disappointed, and puzzled by his air of casual indifference. "Don't you care?"

He gazed at me for a moment, and then shrugged.

"It seems to matter less every day."

My eye travelled up, overhead, to where the stays and shrouds of the mainmast met at the trestle-trees; beyond them the topmast soared dizzyingly upwards, the Oliver house-flag at its truck. All of a sudden, it occurred to me that the mast was bare – naked of anything but its rigging.

"Don't you ever set the sails on this thing?"

"I don't ever remember using them."

"Well, why not set them now? Wouldn't it give us some extra speed?"

"Half a knot, maybe a little more. But still not enough, Kate – even supposing this wind keeps up." He gave a brief smile. "Thank you for bothering, at least."

A grey-green wave burst over the bowsprit, exploding into feathers of spray, and as Matthew glanced towards it I studied him uncomprehendingly. This was a totally unknown Matthew Oliver – numbed, aimless, indifferent to the future he'd once reached for with such ruthless resolve.

All of a sudden, I caught myself pitying him – and almost shook him in my resentment. The Matthew Oliver I remembered from the *Bellflower* would have fought, and lied, and schemed to the bitter end, no matter how many people were hurt in the process. I'd never known him admit defeat in his entire life.

I took a deep breath, and sallied forth to find the enemy.

"Well, you've changed, I must say!"

Slowly, Matthew turned his head and regarded me in cold silence.

"You've changed, all right!" I repeated belligerently. "I always reckoned you were a rat, Matthew, but I never figured you for a quitter."

"Go away, Kate. I'm not in the mood for an argument."

"No? So George Broadney's got you whipped, after all, has he?"

Matthew turned away, ignoring me.

"You admit it? You're going to let that fat baronet steal your company without even putting up a fight?"

"I've no way of stopping him."

"I can't believe this! I can't believe I'm looking at the same man who refused to give up his blasted gold bars when half the Yankee fleet was firing on him. Oh, you've changed, all right, Matthew Oliver. Between them, Violet and her father have knocked all the stuffing out of you."

All of a sudden, Matthew seemed to come alive.

404

"Go on, Kate! Don't stop. Surely you can do better than that! The best time to kick a man is when he's down, don't forget."

"Oh, I haven't finished by a long way!" With a lift of my heart, I saw the resentful, angry glint in Matthew's eye, and I knew that if George Broadney's name had roused him, there was another which would make him even madder.

"I told you once you weren't half the man your father was – and I was right, wasn't I? This – " I pointed to the naked masts above us. "This proves it. No fight! No nerve! Adam would have sailed this yacht up Water Street, sooner than let George Broadney trample on his pride."

"You bitch! Leave my father out of this!"

"Why should I? I was his mistress for five years – or had you forgotten?"

"Kate – " There was pure steel in Matthew's voice. "Don't push me too far. Not now."

I leaned forward until I was staring into his face.

"Can you imagine your father moping like a little boy who's lost his sailboat? Can you?" I put on a petulant expression. "Boo-hoo, the nasty man's taken my ships! I don't want to play any more . . ."

"Dammit, Kate, hold your tongue! I won't listen to any more of this."

Matthew swung round to leave, and I clutched his arm.

"It's just as well you call yourself *Oliver*. You're not fit to call yourself a Gaunt."

He spun back towards me, and my heart soared to see his face set in the stony, unforgiving mask I knew of old.

"Very well! We'll set the bloody sails, if it means so much to you! And after that you can go to the devil, for all I care."

It was no more, I suspected, than Captain Willard had itched to do all along. As soon as Matthew had given the word, he sent *Harvester*'s men speeding about their work with an efficiency which suggested they were more experienced in sail-handling than Matthew realised. Within minutes, the headsails, the main and the mizzen were free of their gaskets, and the long gaffs were swaying up the masts, the halyards squealing in their blocks as the sails quickened, filling with the first press of the breeze. With a clatter of hoops, the foresail flew up its mast and was sheeted home.

"Topsails, sir?" *Harvester*'s mate shouted back towards the wheelhouse.

"All sail, Mr Jones!"

An hour later, *Harvester* heeled to the sea under every stitch of sail she would carry. Roused by the din, John Longstock emerged on the canting deck, clutched the fife-rail for support, and gazed about in surprise; I saw Daisy's head pop out of the deckhouse door for a moment, her eyes wide with amazement. This – this was yachting, indeed.

"Almost fourteen knots, by the log," Captain Willard announced with satisfaction, shading his eyes with his hand and peering aloft. "Never had gaff topsails on her before. Ticklish devils to set. Still, everything helps, I dare say." He strutted back to the wheelhouse, fighting hard to suppress a grin.

The excitement of the chase shivered through the vessel like an electric charge, affecting everyone aboard. I wanted to share the moment – to release the surging joy of that winged flight through the water.

I looked round, but Matthew had vanished.

4

He was nowhere to be seen in the wheelhouse or the deck saloon; concerned, I went below. The main saloon was as deserted as the rest, only the gentle swish of its curtains testifying to *Harvester*'s new sprightliness over the waves.

By now I was certain Matthew had withdrawn to his own quarters to brood over his troubles, but the blank row of doors in the carpeted passage gave no clue as to where I should knock.

This was no time to be cautious. Beginning with the nearest door, I worked my way down the row, banging loudly on each set of panels as I came to it. After a moment or two of this racket, the fourth door flew open, and Matthew stood thunderously on the threshold.

"What the hell do you think you're doing?"

"Fourteen knots, Matthew! We're doing fourteen knots, or very nearly. You should see Captain Willard – he's tickled to death, though he'd burst before he showed it."

"Fourteen knots isn't enough." Matthew made as if to shut the door, but I jammed my foot in the opening.

"You can't be sure of that."

"I'm certain of it. We won't make Liverpool in time. Now, stop barging about like a fishwife and let me shut this door."

"How do you know we won't be there in time? Suppose the wind gets up even more – "

"It's just as likely to go round to the east and blow in our faces. Be sensible, Kate. And take your foot out of the doorway."

"Well, I think we're going to be in Liverpool by noon on Thursday. I can feel it inside me."

"Rubbish! If you feel anything at all, it's probably seasickness. Now, will you let me shut this door, confound you? Can't I have any privacy aboard my own yacht?"

"At least hear what Captain Willard has to say." With white knuckles, I struggled to prevent Matthew from prising my fingers from the door jamb.

"Go away, Kate!"

"I won't! Not until you speak to the Captain."

"All right – " Matthew glowered at me from the doorway. "All right, I'll make a bargain with you. If Willard says there's no chance of *Harvester* getting to Liverpool in time, will you promise to leave me alone until we dock? To get out of my sight – anywhere you like – and leave me in peace?"

"Oh, I promise, I promise – if that's what it takes to pull you out of this terrible mood."

At the end of the passage, a steward appeared with a bottle of brandy on a silver tray. As the man reached his door, Matthew deftly commandeered the bottle.

"Mr Oliver's compliments to Captain Willard, and I'd be obliged if he'd step down to the saloon for a few moments." The man turned to go, and Matthew shot me a warning glare. "Remember – we have a bargain, Kate. Once Willard has convinced you we don't stand a chance of making Liverpool on Thursday, I'm going to come back here, slam the door and open this bottle – and there won't be a blind thing you can do about it."

So certain was Matthew of the rightness of his case that he left his coat in his cabin, and followed me in shirt-sleeves to the saloon.

"We're making fourteen knots – or very nearly," Captain Willard confirmed when the question was put to him.

"Good – but not good enough. Is that correct?" Matthew stood, legs astride, before the marble fireplace in the main saloon, swaying a little with the movement of the vessel.

"If I could get another half-knot out of her, sir . . . then we'd have a chance, I'd say."

"But the fact remains, at full steam and with every sail set, fourteen knots is our limit."

"We've even set a spare staysail as a ring-tail on the mizzen to try to push her on a little. The mate's shirt'll be next."

"Fourteen knots, Captain Willard. Am I right?"

407

"I fear so, Mr Oliver. I can't see us improving on that – and as you say, it isn't quite enough to make Liverpool by noon on Thursday. If I'd had time to alter her trim before we left the Mersey a couple of weeks ago. . . . But you would go at once."

"What's wrong with her trim?" Matthew eyed the Captain suspiciously.

"I've always felt she was a mite down by the stern. Not enough to matter in the ordinary way, but when you push her to the limit, it can make half a knot of difference." Captain Willard pursed his lips. "I was going to move a few tons of ballast out of her before we left for Cowes, but when you changed your plans we just had to go as we were."

"Why didn't you do it in New York?"

"You told me to stand by to sail at any moment, sir. I couldn't start opening her up at that stage."

"And it's too late now, I suppose?"

"Impossible at sea, sir."

"Well, then – " Matthew turned to me. "There's your answer. We'll miss the meeting, whatever we do. Thank you for your patience, Captain Willard. Miss Summerbee was convinced we still had a chance."

"I'm sorry, sir. We sailed half a day too late."

"Couldn't be helped, Captain. At least it was in a good cause."

After the Captain had left, Matthew turned to me again.

"Well? Are you satisfied now? Have I put up enough of a fight to earn some peace and quiet?"

"You can't just crawl off into a corner and get drunk."

"Why not, for Heaven's sake? This is my yacht, and I'll do what I like."

"Drinking doesn't help." I thought of my father and his anaesthetic binges. "Things only look worse when you sober up."

"I'll be the judge of that." Matthew headed for the door.

"Then at least bring the bottle along here, and we can both get drunk together! It's bad for your health to drink alone," I added mutinously.

Matthew halted half-way to the door and came back across the saloon towards me. "You really are an extraordinary creature."

"No, I'm not. I just don't want you to be miserable all on your own."

"I thought you didn't drink."

"I've learned."

He ran a hand through his hair. "Kate Summerbee – you are the most contrary female I've ever met."

"I'm not contrary!" I shouted at him.

"There you go again!" Suddenly, he reached out, deftly whipped the tortoiseshell combs from my hair and hurled them through the open porthole.

"That's better. If you're going to bawl at me like a river-brat, you might as well look like one." He took a step backwards to admire his handiwork, and nodded. "That's just what you looked like on that first morning aboard the *Bellflower*, when you came out on deck with your hair like a rat's nest – "

With a howl of fury I snatched the watch and chain from his waistcoat pocket, and flung those, too, through the porthole.

"Confound you, Kate – that was a gold watch!"

All of a sudden, I saw him hesitate.

"A gold watch . . ." he repeated slowly. His hand travelled to his empty waistcoat pocket, and his eyes to the open porthole. When he turned back to me, there was a strange expression on his face – a new determination, certainly, but a bitter, vengeful determination I couldn't understand.

"Yes . . . that's what we'll do!"

"What will we do, for goodness' sake?"

"*Harvester*. We'll take some ballast out of her."

"What on earth are you talking about, Matthew?" I was close enough to snatch at the lapels of his white drill waistcoat.

"I've thought of a way to take some weight off our stern. To get rid of some dead weight we don't need – exactly what Willard was talking about."

And gripping my upturned face between his two hands, he kissed me hard on the lips.

"Dammit, what was that for?" I was breathless, and thoroughly alarmed.

"This marble column – " Matthew strode over to a squat black marble plinth from which a classical bust had been removed for seagoing safety. "How heavy do you suppose this is? Four hundredweight? Five?"

He ran a hand almost lovingly over the inky flank of the pillar.

"And what about that fireplace?" He jabbed a forefinger towards it. "There's half a ton in that, if there's an ounce. Yet a man with a crowbar could have it in pieces in five minutes."

I followed his glance to the open porthole, and then stared at him again. There was a dangerous gleam in his eye now – a wild, crazy light which made me almost afraid.

"You aren't serious! You wouldn't really throw Violet's fireplace over the side?"

"Why not? Who ever heard of a marble fireplace on a boat? It's a nonsense – a toy! It's better at the bottom of the sea."

"Matthew – you haven't been drinking already, have you?"

"Drinking?" Matthew's eyes were alive with grim purpose. "Not a drop. I've never been more sober in my life."

He spun round and marched towards the companionway leading to the open deck, while I scuttled at his heels, hampered by my tight skirt. As we passed through the dining saloon, he waved a hand at the mirror-bright table flanked by its double row of chairs. "Those can go, for a start. There's hundredweights of lead in them to keep them steady in a seaway. And the table, too."

"But it's worth a fortune!"

Almost at the foot of the companionway, Matthew swung round.

"Not to me. It's worth precisely nothing to me, Kate. Not any more."

5

I still couldn't believe he meant to do it – not until a procession of seamen appeared on deck, labouring under the burden of the dismembered white fireplace, and solemnly tipped each piece over the vessel's rail. It took four men to manhandle the black marble pillar up the companionway stair and to roll it to the edge of the deck, where a section of rail had been taken out. There was hardly a splash as the column tumbled down into the sea.

Then Matthew himself appeared, his arms wrapped round one of the lead-weighted chairs from the dining saloon; behind him came John Longstock and ten members of the crew, loaded like a line of ants. One by one, the great carved chairs were dropped into the Atlantic, watched tearfully at a small distance by the dining-room steward.

The man hid his eyes as the table followed, in several disconnected pieces which floated astern like highly polished rafts, rearing up on the waves to look back in astonishment at the vessel which had so summarily discarded them.

"What's the matter, Kate? Can't you bear the sight of it?" Matthew reappeared at my side lugging a bronze nymph, one smooth brown arm curled sensuously over his shoulder. "You wanted me to fight, didn't you? Don't tell me you've no stomach for the battle!"

"I can't believe you're doing this."

"I should have done it a long time ago."

With a splash, the nymph plunged into the sea, and Matthew straightened up again. "Come on, Kate – you're the cause of all this, so don't tell me you're squeamish. The sooner it's done, the sooner we put on some extra speed. That's what you want, isn't it?" He grabbed my hand, and pulled me after him along the deck. "You'll enjoy it! You've never approved of my money, after all."

He'd thrown open the store where the cream of Violet's extravagance lay cocooned in its purpose-built boxes.

"Here – " An alabaster clock had emerged from the doorway in disembodied hands; Matthew took it and thrust it brusquely into my arms. "Go on, throw that away, since you despise my wealth so much. Drop it over the side."

"But this clock can't possibly make any difference to our speed! It only weighs a few pounds at the most."

"I don't want it! Can't you understand? I don't want to see it again." Roughly, Matthew turned me by the shoulders and gave me a push. "Get rid of it."

By now, a continuous line of men jammed the companionway – climbing up, laden with furniture, or returning empty-handed for more. Clutching the clock, I stumbled up to the deck in the wake of an exquisite walnut bureau and pursued by the great gilt overmantel mirror from the saloon. No one seemed to question the rationality of it all: Matthew's orders were justification enough. At the rail, I took a deep breath and opened my arms. Instantly the creamy clock dropped plumb into the water, flashed green as jade, and whirled out of sight.

The clock had hardly disappeared when the giant gilt mirror flew out horizontally over the sea to join it. Craning over the rail, I caught a final glimpse of my shocked mirror-self, her eyes as round as pennies, before the mirror dragged her down.

Her hair had been loose again, that poor, bewildered mirror-woman. I stood at the rail, mourning her passing, strands of hair blowing into my eyes to remind me that Matthew had thrown away my combs, too.

River-brat. I left the rail, and went below once more.

6

Down in the hollow caverns which were *Harvester*'s saloons, a demon of destruction had been unleashed. Nothing was safe from Matthew's scouring fury – not the ship portraits on the walls, not the blue-john jars, not the bronze statue of winged Fame from the lobby. Like an avenging spirit he stalked through the yacht, banishing any object which caught his eye, hurling fire-dogs after epergnes and console tables after jardinières, wrenching down elaborate lamps, ridding himself of all their glittering grandeur as if taking personal vengeance on each and every one of them.

Long after the heaviest objects had gone – long after Captain Willard was satisfied that the yacht's propeller turned where it should in the water, and suggested a halt – Matthew raged on with his mission. The crew filed back to their normal duties, but Matthew never paused, charged with diabolical energy and a driving need to sweep every precious object from his sight.

Fourteen and a half knots! came a call from the patent log, yet Matthew was deaf to it, consumed by a passion to eradicate every shred of that treacherous magnificence. No one dared go near him. I saw the mate murmur something to Captain Willard, and the Captain shrug and shake his head. Mania? Brainstorm? What insanity inspired a man to destroy the rewards of more than twenty years' obsessive labour?

I found him in the bare-walled dining saloon, braced against the movement of the ship, an expression of furious concentration on his face. It was only when I came nearer that I realised he was hurling Meissen plates one by one through the porthole by the light of a single lamp.

"Fourteen and a half knots, Matthew! It's enough!" I clutched his arm. "Do you hear me? Captain Willard says if the wind holds, we might even reach Liverpool in time."

"Take these – " He shook me off, swept up a pile of plates from the floor, and pushed them at me. "Out with them."

The plates nestled in my arms, the gilding on their delicately fluted rims glinting softly in the lamplight.

"Oh, Matthew . . . I can't. They're too beautiful to destroy."

Without a word, he snatched back the pile of dishes and began to fling them in twos and threes into the ocean.

"Stop all this, Matthew – please."

"No!" The savagery of the destruction increased. "I'll stop when all this wretched, useless, contemptible *trash* has gone – and not before."

"But why must you destroy it all? I don't understand – not any more!"

"No?" Another plate spun out towards the sea. "Well, then, you're fortunate. It makes perfect sense to me."

"If you'd definitely lost the company – if George Broadney had won beyond any doubt – " I was forced to move aside as Matthew reached for an oval serving dish, smashed it in two, and hurled it after the rest. "But we may still reach Liverpool in time! There's hope for us, Matthew!"

412

"Is there?" For a moment he rested his hands on the brass sill, and stared out at the dark, greedy sea which showed no trace of the fortune it had so recently swallowed.

"I don't care about getting to Liverpool in time for the meeting." His voice was so low I could hardly hear the words.

"You don't care?"

"Not any more. Even if I do manage to hold on to the company . . . what then?" He swung round to stare at me. "At last I've finally screwed up enough courage to ask myself that question. Even if I do keep control of the company, and the ships, and all the rest – what do I have? What do I, Matthew Oliver, *have* of my own? House after house filled with expensive toys – that's all." Furiously, he snatched up a silver sugar caster and flung it into the water. "God in Heaven, even the Longstocks – back there, in that miserable hovel of a house, with rats scratching at the walls and a pump full of piss-water – they have more in this world than I'll ever have. At least they have each other!"

I'd managed to forget the pain I'd felt as I watched Mrs Longstock cradling her child in her arms, murmuring over the flower-like face turned up to her own; now I felt it again, in all its hollow agony.

"How dare you say you don't have enough!" I cried bitterly, raising my voice to drown out the howl that welled inside me. "Whatever you had, you always wanted more!"

"Then you'll be pleased to know it's brought me nothing but wretchedness!"

With an oath he hurled the second sugar caster after its fellow, and looked hungrily round the near-empty room.

"I don't enjoy seeing you miserable, Matthew."

He gave no sign of having heard me. He was already half-way to the door leading aft from the dining saloon, like a wolf in search of new prey. The ship rolled as he reached the end of the room, and I saw him pause and grip the doorpost to steady himself before disappearing into the corridor beyond.

"I never wished this for you! Matthew – wait!"

I ran after him through the door, only to stumble against the wall of the passageway, which was rearing and falling disconcertingly with the vessel's movement. Ahead of me, Matthew reached his stateroom door, wrenched it open and plunged inside; cannoning along the passage, I tumbled through the doorway after him. The yacht rolled again, banging the door shut behind me.

There was no question of opening a porthole here; we were on the lee side of the vessel, where the ports were washed continually by the sea, blotting out what fading sky remained. Thwarted, Matthew glared round while the lamp swung crazily over our heads, swirling the silk-hung cabin in its circling saucer of shadow.

"Stop all this – please!"

He was holding the foot of the mahogany bedstead for support, and I skidded over to the opposite post, clutching the polished knob between my hands.

"What possible good can this do?"

"Don't lecture me, blast you! *Miss Summerbee of Hawk's Dyke*," he mimicked cruelly, "the woman whose life is so satisfying, she doesn't need anything more. How fortunate you are! You don't need a single thing to make your life complete – not even another human being."

"I didn't say that!"

"Oh yes, you did."

"Well, then – " I hesitated for a fraction of a second. "I didn't mean it. Not the way it sounded."

"Then how did you mean it?"

Hopelessly confused, I threw my hands in the air, almost lost my balance, and clutched the bedpost once more.

"I don't know. Perhaps I didn't mean it at all."

"*I can manage alone*. That's what you said." He was staring at me accusingly. "Or didn't you mean that either? Was it a lie, Kate? Were you lying to me?"

"I'm not a liar! You're the one who can't tell the truth to save himself!"

"I'm telling you the truth now! Listen to me, Kate – *I don't want the bloody company back!* Do you hear? I don't want it."

"Not much, you don't." Releasing a hand, I made a poor attempt to snap my fingers in his face. "All right, then – if you don't want the company, and you don't want any of this, what *do* you want, for Heaven's sake?"

The vessel rolled once more, and Matthew made a grab for the mahogany footboard. Hand over hand, he began to work his way along it towards me.

"Isn't it about time you made up your mind, Matthew?" I shouted at him, clinging desperately to the bedpost. "What in the world *do* you want?"

All of a sudden he let go of the mahogany rail, lunged at me, and swept me up in his arms. Together, we crashed into the wall and ricocheted off it on to the bed.

"I want you, Kate. And you want me."

"No I don't!" As the ship rolled, I struggled in his arms. "You're crazy! I wouldn't want anything to do with you if – " From a distance I suddenly heard myself – proud, pathetic and ridiculous. "Oh, that isn't true! Yes, I do – I do."

His hands were in my hair, his lips on mine, straining to make me understand something beyond any words he possessed. Gasping, dizzy, drunk on desire, we fell back and he began to kiss my throat, pulling open my bodice to slide down to where my breasts spilled from the top of my corset.

The yacht heeled again, and we rolled across the bed, over and over, entwined and oblivious. All at once *Harvester* slid into the trough of a wave and we fell in a heap to the floor, both of us tangled in the flounces of my skirt, one of my breasts gloriously unfettered and cupped in Matthew's hand, a curl of my hair caught on his shirt-button.

"Oh, gracious Heavens – oh, Matthew – "

"Damn this bloody corset! How can you breathe in it?"

"Wait, I'll unhook it – "

"It's done – "

"Wait – "

"Shut up, Kate. I can manage – "

"You'll never find – ohhh . . . do that again . . ."

"Don't talk – " And his mouth on mine once more, and somehow in all the welter of washing silk, and flounced muslin, and tumbled hair, and lost buttons and missing shoes, and warm, yielding, yearning flesh – the rhythm I'd discovered on that night of fire aboard the *Bellflower*, the rhythm of life, and love, and creation, and cherishing, and all the other things that have to do with woman – and man, too, in that moment.

"Don't talk, Kate, just love me – "

And goodness knows, I did – there on the floor by the mahogany bedstead, as the sea flung us up and sucked us down, caressing the shell of the emptied saloons, tossing us tenderly, stroking and licking, running liquid fire where the light of the ship's lamp touched it, spilling itself, the source of all life, over us where we lay together.

And after a while the great tide of Matthew's bitterness diminished and he lay like a silent sea. In the hollow of his arm, I fought back tears: it had all been too much and too little, at one and the same time.

In all honesty, Matthew still exerted a power over me capable of breaking down every defence: but it was a power of the flesh, not of the heart. In triumph or despair he remained Matthew Oliver, and the river-brat couldn't allow herself to forget it. The lonely, bewildered mirror-woman must be lonely still.

415

With a shudder which ran along the whole length of the vessel *Harvester* took a great wave on her shoulder, and Matthew's weight carried us painfully against the foot of the bed.

"This is nonsense, Kate! I'll tell Willard to take in sail."

"Then you'll miss the meeting in Liverpool."

"To Hell with the meeting!" Matthew drew me into his arms. "I told you, I'm sick to death of all the scheming and struggling to hold on to the company. I've no heart for it any more." He took a deep breath, and let it out in a long, peaceful sigh. "Perhaps that's what's been eating away at me all along, except that I'd never admit it. Maybe this is what I wanted all the time. Stay with me, Kate – and George Broadney can take the company and the ships, and the counting house, and do what he likes with them. It's high time Oliver's had someone else in charge of it."

"No." I made an attempt to push myself free.

"What do you mean – no?"

"If Captain Willard thinks he can make Liverpool in time for the meeting – then you must let him try."

Beyond the confines of the cabin, *Harvester* hesitated on the crest of a wave, trembled, and then slid crazily into the trough, throwing me into Matthew's arms once more.

"I want you to have Oliver's back." Firmly, I pushed myself away again.

"That's loyal of you, Kate, but – "

"It has nothing to do with loyalty."

"Then why?"

"I want you to have Oliver's back . . . because as soon as we reach Liverpool I'm going straight back to Hawk's Dyke, and I don't intend to see you again as long as I live."

At his side, I sat up, and began to retrieve my scattered clothing.

"You'd be lost without Oliver's, Matthew, and there's no point in trying to deceive yourself. For more than twenty years, every thought in your head, every breath you've taken, has been for the company, and I don't believe you'll ever change. Once you have Oliver's back, you won't need me or anyone else in your life. You'll be perfectly content – and so will I, providing we're at opposite sides of the country."

"No!" Matthew caught hold of my wrist as I tried to button my bodice. "That isn't true! You can't just run off back to Hawk's Dyke as if none of this has happened! You can't, Kate!"

I turned to look at him directly.

416

"Why shouldn't I run off as if nothing has happened, Matthew?" I paused for the length of a heartbeat. "You did."

7

I wouldn't let him slow *Harvester*'s crazy dash through the sea by so much as a second. In any case, I don't believe that Captain Willard, presented with such a challenge to his seamanship, would have consented to slacken our speed for a moment. He intended to reach the Mersey by the afternoon of the seventh and that was that. With her wings spread and trailing smoke like a triumphal pennant, *Harvester* bounded over the spume-flecked miles to our journey's end.

Even the Heavens smiled upon us; day and night, the wind blew hard on our backs, never once going round to a troublesome quarter. No doubt Sam Duck would have said the storm and water *loas* owed us their favour, sated as they were with ormolu and tulipwood and Meissen plates.

We took our meals in the devastated dining saloon, perched on cane chairs from the deck round a plank trestle disguised with spotless damask. What John Longstock thought of it all, I never discovered; having made up his mind to return to England, he seemed to take the whole experience in his dogged stride, as if he saw nothing at all strange in a gentleman's hurling dining chairs from his yacht in a torment of despair. The irony of it was that the Longstocks' belongings, too, had disappeared into the sea – except that they'd had no choice in the matter. But if John despised us for our excesses, he was too polite to show it.

There were hardly two matching plates on our table any more, except for the thick white china borrowed from the stewards' mess – but with *Harvester* rolling like a clipper ship in a monsoon no plate stayed in its place for long, and our meals were haphazard affairs of spilled soup and vegetables which leaped like cannon-balls from their dishes.

But I continued to say "Never!" whenever Matthew seemed about to abandon the race. And he, poor devil, apparently still believing I could save him from some lonely misery of his own if only I cared to, let me have my way.

We made love again – over and over again – and sometimes in the greedy heights of ecstasy I could almost believe we had been reborn untouched by the years which had run like an angry river between us. The river was aflame once more, and I was too fascinated by the fire to draw back.

It was reckless of me, but it was a calculated recklessness. What is any

417

ocean passage but a sea-dream, after all – time briefly unhinged between coast and sober coast? When the clocks ticked again and the calendar pages turned on their way, then, in the sane world of Mondays and Thursdays, I'd knot up my hair, and knot up my indulgent body too. Liverpool lay ahead like a chaperon waiting on the quayside to enforce a parting; secure in the future, I didn't even try to resist the irresistible present.

8

It was after Cape Clear that time resumed its mastery of our lives, and we began to count off the hours to the Mersey. By the time we made the mouth of the river at two o'clock on the afternoon of the seventh, the fever of the race had infected everyone aboard from the Captain to the galley-boy, and some of Matthew's old combativeness had returned.

On his express order we flew without pause past the waiting pilot-boat, refusing to heave to and ignoring the outraged howls in our wake. Captain Willard was instructed to put us ashore as near to Water Street as he could, and if a steamer or a ferry found itself discommoded, then its master could address his complaints to Mr Matthew Oliver next morning.

I don't imagine the clerks in the Oliver's office had seen their chairman in a round peaked cap and pilot-cloth coat before; the door-keeper certainly hadn't, and had opened his mouth to demand our business before snapping suddenly to attention.

I'd refused to be part of it all, intending to leave quietly for a hotel with Daisy and our luggage, but Matthew would have none of that. Snatching my hand, he pulled me bodily ashore, and with John Longstock pounding behind us, ran with me towards the line of waiting cabs.

"You want me to have the company back, don't you? Then you can damn well see it through."

He led us at the same relentless pace to the first floor of the Oliver building, through the general office where the clerks lifted curious heads like cows in a field, and down the long brown corridor to the room set aside for directors' meetings. The directors must have heard us coming, clattering over the linoleum; but nine startled faces swung towards us as the doors crashed wide – nine faces which immediately registered embarrassment, annoyance, dismay . . . and triumph. Sir George Broadney, at the distant head of the table, could hardly conceal his delight. He positively glowed with the joy of conspiracy. I found myself loathing him even more than before.

We were too late, he declared: they'd discussed the matter – not that there had been much to discuss – and had voted in the proper manner – unanimously, as it happened. Matthew was no longer chairman or managing director; and if, added Sir George on his own behalf, the craven blackguard had an ounce of decency in his entire body, he'd resign his directorship *tout de suite* and save the shareholders the task of kicking him out. Furthermore – Sir George Broadney drew a deep, triumphal breath – he, Sir George, would like to know what Matthew Oliver meant by bursting like a damned Hun into a directors' meeting, dragging a pair of his ruffianly friends behind him.

"Now hold on, George – " came a voice from half-way down the table. "There's no need for unpleasantness."

Matthew pushed John Longstock forward.

"You must hear what this man has to say. You owe me that, at least."

"There's no *must* about it, Oliver," growled the baronet. "You aren't cock of the walk here now. Not any more."

I saw Matthew hesitate. I could read, quite clearly, the thought in his mind, the impulse to turn on his heel and march away from that room – from Oliver's, from his ships, from his life's work. For an instant our eyes met . . . and Matthew turned back to the directors' table.

"This man – " He indicated John Longstock, standing four-square at his side, turning his hat-brim over and over in his hands. "This man and his family were passengers on the *Aldebaran*. We escaped from the ship in the same lifeboat, though I didn't know it until he wrote to Miss Summerbee from New York, to tell her he was safe."

By his side, John Longstock nodded in solemn agreement.

"In the letter, he explained how he'd seen me pushed over the *Aldebaran*'s rail by Captain Travis – against my will, and half-conscious from a blow on the jaw. This man – " Matthew held out a hand, "has come all the way from New York to tell you in person what he saw. I ask you to give him a hearing – no more than that."

"I warned you, gentlemen." George Broadney tossed down his pen and leaned back in his chair. "I told you we could be in for theatricals before the day was out. Frankly, Oliver – " his drawl rose in pitch, "I get as much play-acting as I want at the Theatre Royal. The plots are generally more convincing there, too."

A murmur of nervous amusement ran round the table.

"It has all been a most unfortunate business." A white-bearded man nearby waved an apologetic hand. "I'd hoped we might dispose of it with some dignity, but this is squalid – squalid."

"Are you going to deny me a hearing?"

"Dash it all, Oliver," exclaimed a dark man on George Broadney's left, "you've had more than two months to come up with this tale! And you've had the whole way from New York to coach this fellow in his part!"

"Now, see here – " Frowning like a thundercloud, John Longstock stepped forward.

"That's perfectly true," remarked another director with his back to us. "The last thing Oliver's needs now is a public row over who-says-what." He twisted round in his chair to face us. "No one's denying you've done a great deal for the company in the past, Matthew – but since the loss of the *Aldebaran* all that has changed. People have no confidence in a shipping line with a . . . with you at its head. That's all there is to it, and the sooner you accept that, the better. It's too late to come up with excuses. The facts of the matter are too widely known."

"What facts?" Matthew demanded hotly. He pointed at George Broadney. "His facts?"

"You're wasting your time, Oliver." At the far end of the table, the baronet made a great show of weariness. "No one's going to listen."

"And why not, I'd like to know?"

Nine astonished pairs of eyes – eleven, if you count Matthew's and John Longstock's – swung round towards me as I stepped forward. I dare say I presented a pretty strange picture, with my hair dishevelled and my face flushed from running and from sheer indignation at their obstinacy. Why, I'd gone all the way to New York – twice sailed the Atlantic – simply so that Matthew Oliver could get back the shipping line which was the love of his life and which he had a perfect right to – and now this pack of self-important, soft-handed robbers were trying to say we'd come too late!

"Let me tell you—" I began . . . dimly, distantly aware of a note of fear in my voice – fear of what would happen if Matthew didn't get his company back and returned to brooding over what might have been, and what still might be, if he could only talk me round.

"Let me tell you, I've never come across such a bunch of narrow-minded, stubborn . . . egg-sucking bigots in my life!"

"Egg-sucking?" repeated the white-bearded man in amazement.

"I'm ashamed of every one of you, turning your self-righteous backs on the truth whenever it gets a little inconvenient! You reckon if you get rid of Matthew Oliver, then the whole *Aldebaran* business can be swept under the carpet and forgotten, and you can go on making your profits as if nothing has happened. Oh, I know what's in your minds, don't you worry!" I raked the table with a glare, challenging them to meet my eye.

420

"Because if Matthew Oliver's story is true and he can prove he didn't run from the *Aldebaran* like a coward, then you're all morally obliged to stand behind him and fight to clear his name – and you haven't the stomach for that. That's really why you don't want to listen. Heaven sakes – " I leaned over the table towards them, "if there's cowardice here, then it doesn't take a clever man to see where it begins!"

"My dear lady – " A director in front of me tried to interrupt, but I wouldn't let him.

"And another thing! John Longstock here–" Poor John was saucer-eyed with amazement at my audacity. "I can tell you, gentlemen, I've had dealings with some of the biggest darn liars in the western world, and John Longstock isn't one of them. Matthew Oliver – well now, I won't say I'd trust him not to bend the truth when it suited him – nor the rest of you, when there was money to be made from it – but not John. I've known him since he was six years old, and anyone in the neighbourhood of Stainham village will tell you he's as honest as the day is long. If he says he saw a man pushed into a lifeboat, then the man was pushed, you can be sure of that.

"And now John's come all the way here at no gain to himself, purely out of respect for the truth. It remains to be seen whether you honourable gentlemen have half his darned grit! Good day to you all."

The head clerk found a chair for me in a corner of the general office, and a glass of tepid water to go with it. I sat down to wait . . . and waited . . . until the head clerk began to study his watch and dart anxious glances at me out of the side of his eye.

Loftily, I ignored him. Someone must be saying something in that room at the end of the corridor – and if John Longstock hadn't emerged yet, there was an even chance it might be him.

At long last I saw the doors opened a little way, briefly releasing a murmur of voices. Matthew came out and shut the doors carefully behind him; I saw him turn and lean against them for a moment before advancing down the corridor and looking round for me in the general office.

Anxiously, I rose to my feet and attracted his attention.

"Well – it's all settled." Matthew halted before me and thrust his hands into his pockets.

"Settled?"

"They listened after all – and asked questions about everything from the collision to the colour of the stokers' shirts. But John stuck to his tale, and in the end they believed him. It was patently obvious he was telling the truth."

"And – "

"And. . . . It's been decided the company will pay for John Longstock's statement to be printed in *The Times*, with a few lines to say that Oliver's are satisfied his version of events is true and verifiable."

"And?"

"They're going to stand behind their story, whatever the consequences."

"And what about you, for goodness' sake?"

"I'm still chairman of Oliver's."

"Well, by all the saints – you took a long time to tell me that!"

For a moment I almost threw my arms round his neck in sheer relief. Then I saw him studying me with those grey eyes of his, and realised that was exactly what he'd hoped for.

"That was a pretty fine speech you made, Kate." He stared at me bleakly. "And all to get rid of me."

"I don't need to make a spectacle of myself to get rid of you, Matthew."

His answer was lost when the double doors at the far end of the corridor suddenly swung open, and the Oliver directors emerged in a body, John Longstock and the white-bearded man deep in conversation at their head. Another moment, and they'd spilled into the general office.

"Matthew – " The white-bearded director held out his hand to be shaken. "I'm delighted for you, truly I am. I always found it hard to believe what the newspapers said about you."

This was followed by a general murmur of agreement, and a queue of sincere smiles and outstretched hands.

"Voting a man out of office is all very well," continued the white beard after Matthew had coolly received the universal congratulations. "But calling a gentleman a liar before his business associates is quite unpardonable. While I realise there's always going to be bad blood between you for – ah – various reasons . . . I've made it clear to George Broadney that an unreserved apology is called for, if he wants to remain a director of this company." He glanced round. "George? Where the devil have you got to now?"

The rank of sombre coats divided to allow George Broadney to swagger through it with the exaggerated, stiff-legged stride of a small boy called to account for some prank. His hands were thrust deep in his pockets, his chin stuck out aggressively, and his shoulders remained defiantly squared.

"It seems you were telling the truth after all, Oliver," he conceded grudgingly. "That was lucky, wasn't it?"

"I don't call that an apology," objected the white-bearded man. "You should withdraw the word *coward*, at the very least. Go on, George."

"Very well – I withdraw it," muttered the baronet sulkily.

"Unreservedly."

"All right – unreservedly."

"Gracious of you, Sir George." Matthew regarded George Broadney with undisguised contempt. "But before you go – " for the baronet had already turned away, "you owe Miss Summerbee an apology, too. You were appallingly rude to her a few weeks ago in front of Lord Wellborough and his family, simply because she tried to help me."

Slowly, George Broadney turned himself about, favoured me with a look of profound distaste, and followed it with a short little bow, just a hair's breadth this side of condescension, judged to a nicety by a dozen generations of arrogance.

"*Deeply* regretted, I'm sure."

All around us the office was closing down for the night, the clerks clumping shut their enormous ledgers, impaling piles of bills on steel spikes, and hopping down from the stools on which they'd spent the day. A buzz of conversation rose into the dusty gaslight; arms were stretched and shoulders flexed; pens were retrieved from behind ears; papers were shuffled into drawers; chair-legs howled across the linoleum floor as the clerks made a decorous stampede for the door.

Matthew seemed oblivious to the rush to leave. Drawn by curiosity, I watched from the doorway of his own spacious office as he wandered round it in silence, gazing at his enormous desk and the chair behind it, caressing them lightly as if there'd been a moment when he'd feared never to see them again. I watched his long fingers trail slowly over the great world globe which stood next to the desk, uncomfortably aware of the electrifying touch of those same fingers on my skin. India . . . China . . . the Pacific Ocean . . . Matthew spun the globe, tracing a path . . . to America – where he stopped it with the pressure of a fingertip on the Mississippi River.

"You're pleased for me, then, Kate."

"Of course I am. This is your life, here in this room."

Thoughtfully, Matthew spun the globe again.

"Until now, maybe."

"It won't be any different in future."

"It will – because I've made it different." Matthew spun the globe, whirling the countries of the world into a blur of blue and gold. "I told the directors today that I'm prepared to stay on as chairman of Oliver's, but I'll resign as managing director as soon as we find the right person to take on the day-to-day company business." He stared at me over the spinning planet, a man who'd deliberately set his world on its ear.

"You don't mean that, Matthew. You'll have changed your mind by tomorrow morning."

"No." Matthew halted the globe by gripping it decisively with both hands. "This isn't a sudden decision. I've been thinking about it for days – lying beside you, sometimes."

I shook my head. "But what will you do instead?"

"Live a little, perhaps." He looked up again, and met my gaze directly. "Marry me, Kate. That's how much I need you."

Startled, I made a lame joke of his proposal.

"You'd take your father's mistress for a wife? Heaven sakes – what a scandal that would be!"

"It's no more than everyone expects from the dreadful Gaunts." Matthew looked defiant. "But I don't give a damn what they say. The divorce taught me how little it matters."

Uncomfortably, I heard Adam's voice echo once more in Matthew's.

"It would never work, Matthew. You'd be living in your father's shadow."

He hesitated, but only for a moment. "I could bear that. The years with my father are part of you – though I can't pretend it's been easy to accept the fact. But Adam Gaunt is dead, Kate, and I'm alive. Alive – look! Leave the past to mourn itself, and say you'll marry me – "

"No."

He stared at me, puzzled. "Just because of my father?"

"No. Because of you." The tension which had carried me through the long day had begun to ebb away, leaving profound weariness behind it. Why did Matthew always make me feel I was being needlessly cruel? Why couldn't I do as he'd once done – enjoy blind, unfeeling pleasure, and then forget? I felt guilty, and longed to escape to my undemanding existence at Hawk's Dyke.

"You don't love me, Matthew. That's enough reason not to marry."

Matthew spread his arms, helpless to disagree.

"I don't know what you want from me, Kate. All I know is that I need you as badly as if you were part of myself. I need to hear your voice – to listen to you laugh, to see you smile, to hold you in my arms. . . . Isn't that love? Isn't that enough for you?"

"Needing isn't enough."

"It was, for my father." Suddenly, Matthew's eyes blazed. "I asked

424

you once why you loved him, and you told me it was because he needed you. Well then, I need you!"

"But I trusted your father! I'd have gone through fire and water for him."

"And you don't trust me."

"I'm sorry, Matthew, but you must understand why that should be."

"That's Miss Summerbee of Hawk's Dyke speaking again. The old Kate was never afraid to take risks."

"We all change, Matthew."

"Exactly! We change. You – me – all of us." He spread his hands across the surface of the globe, sliding them disconcertingly over the polished continents. "I'm not the man you remember, Kate. Not any more. I believe we can start again from the beginning, both of us – and if you find you loathe the man I've become, then so be it."

I couldn't bear to watch those mesmeric hands. Another moment, and I'd say something disastrous.

"I'm tired, Matthew. I can't argue with you any more."

"Where are you going?"

"To the Adelphi. I told Daisy to take rooms for us there."

"You can't hide yourself in a hotel, Kate!"

"I don't imagine they'll turn us away."

"You know what I mean." Matthew devoured me with his eyes. "And after the Adelphi – where then?"

"Home. Hawk's Dyke. Where I belong."

"It's no good, Kate." Matthew shook his head. "I don't believe you can simply run off to Norfolk and forget me. It can't be as easy as that. Dammit, I won't let it be easy for you! I'll visit you – " He stopped suddenly. "May I visit you?"

"Hawk's Dyke was your father's house. I've no right to keep you away."

"Then I'll come to Norfolk as soon as everything's settled here. I won't let you forget me, Kate. You say there's nothing between us, but that isn't true – there's a good deal of heartache, certainly, but there are good things, too. I don't believe you can put them out of your mind, any more than I can. I'm sure of it – whatever you say now, one day you will marry me."

I didn't wait to hear any more. I turned on my heel and left the room.

"Sooner or later you'll marry me, Kate!" he called after me along the brown-painted corridor.

I'd almost reached the far door of the general office when I heard his voice again.

"You will marry me, Kate!"
His confident shout echoed round the rows of empty desks.
"All over again. . . ."